KISS OF DEATH

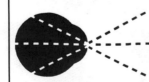

KISS OF DEATH

MERYL SAWYER

WHEELER PUBLISHING

An imprint of Thomson Gale, a part of The Thomson Corporation

THOMSON

GALE

Detroit • New York • San Francisco • New Haven, Conn. • Waterville, Maine • London

THOMSON
GALE

4/0 7

LIBRARY OF CONGRESS CATALOGING-IN-PUBLICATION DATA

Sawyer, Meryl.
   Kiss of death / by Meryl Sawyer.
     p. cm.
   ISBN-13: 978-1-59722-482-6 (hardcover : alk. paper)
   ISBN-10: 1-59722-482-0 (hardcover : alk. paper)
   1. Iraq War, 2003 — Veterans — Fiction. 2. Uncles — Fiction. 3. San Diego (Calif.) — Fiction. 4. Show dogs — Fiction. 5. Large type books. I. Title.
PS3569.A866K58 2007
813'.54—dc22   2007000429

Published in 2007 by arrangement with Harlequin Books S.A.

Printed in the United States of America on permanent paper
10 9 8 7 6 5 4 3 2 1

The best way to love anything
is as if it might be lost.
— G. K. Chesterton

This book is dedicated to my "girls":
Debbie
Marcy
Susan
And our mascot, Redd

PROLOGUE

Adam Hunter, you're dead.

Adam knew he was at death's door and his gut cramped. In less than a split second he realized his life was over.

Finished.

The other guys hadn't sensed the danger, didn't know death was a heartbeat away. Adam watched — his breath suspended in his lungs — unable to utter a word.

His body didn't seem to belong to him. It was almost as if he were seeing a film, as if this must be happening to someone else — not him. He wasn't meant to die — not now, not here.

Some distant part of his mind still functioned, warning him. Blood coursed through his veins and reality arced through him like a jolt of electricity, spurring him to action. Move! Run! But there wasn't any time to run — nowhere to run — no place to hide.

A garbled sound clawed its way out of his

throat. *Duck!* In an instant his world exploded in all-consuming pain and the bleak darkness of hell.

Shreds of bloody images dissolved into the present. His uncle's chauffeur was driving Adam to Calvin Hunter's Greek villa. Adam was still too engulfed in a tide of memories to notice much as the limousine sped along the narrow road. The panicky, trapped feeling returned and surged through his body with vivid reality, then subsided as he realized the danger had passed. By some strange miracle, Adam had survived.

He'd cheated death.

The others had not been so lucky. A half ton of steel surrounding them and seven pounds of reinforced Kevlar per man hadn't protected them.

Adam hadn't managed a good night's sleep since escaping death. He thought if he could go home, he would be able to finally get some rest. Adam longed to put his head down on his own pillow and stretch out on his own bed — safe at last.

Home.

What a concept. He didn't have a home. All his so-called worldly possessions were in a storage unit, gathering dust.

He was still alive and traipsing around in

paradise. He was a long way from the hell-hole in Iraq where he'd come within inches of dying. Thanks to an inexplicable twist of fate, Adam had now arrived at his uncle's villa in the Greek Isles. His uncle had sent his private jet to Turkey, where Adam was supposed to be recuperating at the U.S. Air Force base.

Calvin Hunter greeted him with a smile some might have mistaken for the real deal. "Adam, how was the flight?"

Adam shrugged dismissively. He realized it was a rhetorical question. Hell, Calvin knew the flight to Siros Island on his jet had been spectacular. His uncle would expect Adam to be impressed, but once you've looked death in the eye, it's hard to be impressed. Damn near impossible.

"How are you feeling? Are you okay now?" his uncle asked, touching his arm in a way that was meant to show concern. Adam doubted his uncle was worried about him. If anything, Calvin seemed a bit nervous. He kept looking around as if he was expecting someone.

"Never better." This was a bald-faced lie, but Adam didn't know his uncle well enough to discuss how he was feeling. Maybe if Tyler were here, Adam could tell his best friend how he really felt, but Tyler

9

was halfway around the world in California.

"Nice place," Adam said because he felt it was expected. *Nice* was an understatement — like saying Versailles was "nice." The villa must contain as much loot as Versailles, too. Security guards manned the front gate and ringed the perimeter of the walled estate. The limo that had brought him here had been armor-plated and had bulletproof glass. The man riding up front with the driver had been armed.

His uncle gazed at him for a moment with shrewd eyes. Adam tried to gauge what the older man was thinking, but didn't really give a rat's ass.

"Let me show you —" Calvin gestured with a strong hand that sported a pinkie ring with a large canary-yellow diamond "— your suite."

Adam looked down a hallway he could have driven a Hummer through with room to spare. The villa on Siros was over the top, just like the Citation jet. His uncle had always been larger than life and an enigma.

He trudged behind his uncle, still wondering why Calvin had sent for him now. His uncle had always distanced himself from their small family. Even though Calvin Hunter's primary residence was in San Diego, he hadn't bothered to return when

10

his half brother had died four years earlier. Adam had handled his father's funeral arrangements alone. Of course his father's friends had offered to help, but there had been no other relatives at his side. He was still pissed with his uncle. Calvin had sent a floral arrangement and a condolence telegram. That was it.

He supposed that cheating death had somehow gotten his uncle's attention. That must be why he'd stepped back into Adam's life and sent the jet to pick him up.

Calvin Hunter was in his early fifties but looked a decade younger. He retained a military stride from his years in the navy as an arms specialist in naval intelligence. The hell of it was, Calvin Hunter was a dead ringer for Adam's father. Adam hadn't been able to feel much since "the incident" last month but now — seeing his uncle — memories of Adam's father resurfaced. And he hated Calvin for resurrecting the past with all its sadness.

"This is it," his uncle said as he gestured toward the open door of a suite with a sweeping view of the harbor.

Without a hint of enthusiasm, Adam muttered, "That's a killer view."

Calvin studied him with cool blue eyes, as if he were an egg about to crack. "Why don't you change into fresh clothes and join me on the terrace for a drink?" Without waiting for a response, Calvin pivoted in place, then walked away.

Adam sauntered through the room and tossed his well-worn duffel on the brocade bedspread. Fresh clothes? Yeah, right.

He crossed the marble-tiled room again and went out onto the balcony. The majestic sweep of ocean and rolling hills beyond captured his attention. The timelessness of Greece and its long history awed Adam. He was the center of his own world, but being here reminded him that the earth was bigger than one man.

Others had died needless, bloody deaths. And countless men had cheated violent ends to their lives. He wasn't unique. In the long history of this planet, Adam was merely another man who had been granted a second chance. He should be grateful, but somehow, the shock hadn't worn off yet.

Adam stood silently and gazed at the boats bobbing at anchor and the crescent-shaped stretch of cafés lining the quay until he lost track of time. The sharp, frantic barks of a dog sent him back into the suite, which consisted of a sitting area that opened through a vaulted archway into the huge bedroom where Adam had carelessly tossed his duffel.

He rummaged through his things and found a pair of jeans and a *Coldplay Rules* T-shirt. Neither were what his mother — God rest her soul — would have called clean, but he didn't possess anything better. One of the guys in his unit must have thrown a few things in a duffel as he was being Medevaced to one of the field hospitals set up in Iraq.

He scrounged around and came up with his dop kit. If his clothes weren't pristine, at least he could shave. He wandered into the bathroom and spotted the claw-foot bathtub with a handheld shower.

"When was the last time you showered?" he said out loud. His mind was playing tricks again. He couldn't remember, but he must have bathed in Turkey.

The words echoed in the high-ceilinged room. He shucked his jeans and shirt, then peeled off his shorts. They dropped to the floor beside the tub.

He turned on the taps but didn't wait for warm water before stepping into the tub. It had been over two years since his last real hot shower. The field units had cold showers, which the guys actually liked since the desert was hotter than hell. A fine spray misted over his still-bruised body. Unexpectedly, needles of scalding water pummeled his skin. He stared at the showerhead for a moment before the thought — hot water — registered. He adjusted the taps.

Using the bar of soap from the wall-mounted wire rack and a washcloth, he scrubbed his entire body twice. The shampoo on the rack smelled like peaches, but he used it anyway. His fingers told him how long his hair had gotten without him quite realizing it. He'd been overdue for another military buzz cut when he'd almost died. After that, no one bothered with his hair.

He dried himself, then found his comb in the dop kit and slicked his hair back behind his ears. It hung down to the nape of his neck. He found a throwaway razor in his kit, but there wasn't any shaving cream. He used the bar of soap to lather up.

Adam caught his reflection in the gold-rimmed mirror. Beneath brown brows a shade darker than his hair, Calvin Hunter's emotionless blue eyes stared back at him. Well, shit, what did he expect? He and his father, as well as Calvin, had all inherited Grandpa Hunter's eyes. But his father's and grandfather's blue eyes had sparkled with life and good humor. He'd had those eyes once, too.

Dressed in the black T-shirt and jeans, he

wandered down the hall in search of the terrace. The villa was obviously old but immaculately maintained. Potted palms with ivy cascading from their bases were dramatically placed among what had to be authentic antiques. He spotted armed men moving about — not quite out of sight. More guards?

"Thees way, meester," called a small man who must be one of the servants. He pointed to a double set of French doors that were opened onto a terrace overlooking the magnificent harbor. The setting sun bled into the night and washed the sea with a peaceful amber glow that reminded Adam of his childhood years in California.

His uncle, attired in white slacks and a navy sports jacket, rose from a round garden table. He looked over his shoulder at the house, and Adam saw the curtains move, then caught a man's profile. One of the guards must be watching to make certain Adam didn't harm his uncle or something. Weird. Friggin' weird.

In his uncle's arms was a small dog that had no fur on his body except for tufts of hair on his paws and tail. His head had some hair, and long hanks of fur sprouted from his ears. The poor mutt was a genetic disaster.

"Feeling better?" his uncle asked in a deep baritone that matched his military bearing.

"Ask me after I've had a drink."

Uncle Calvin gestured to a chair facing the view. "Have a seat. What would you like?"

His automatic response would have been "beer," but he stopped himself. "Got a good pinot noir?"

"Of course." His uncle turned to the servant and said something in Greek. The little man scuttled away.

Calvin proudly explained the goofy-looking canine was an international show champion. Not only had the dog taken Westminster "by storm," the pampered mutt had won the Frankfurt International.

Adam decided his father would have hooted at how taken Calvin acted with a dog. When Calvin had retired from the navy, Adam's father had expected him to spend time in San Diego, golfing and hanging out at the officers' club. Instead, Calvin had gone into dog shows with baffling enthusiasm.

Who'da thunk? Calvin had taken to the show circuit. He became a judge and had flown around the country to dog shows. Soon he'd gained quite a reputation and had become an international judge, sought by dog shows worldwide.

Was the freaky little dog worth a lot of money? Was that the reason for the guards? Nah, he decided. There was too much security around to be guarding one small dog. Something else had to be going on.

The servant arrived with a glass of pinot noir. Adam took a sip. He couldn't remember the last time he'd relaxed with a glass of wine.

"You're probably wondering why I brought you here."

"Didn't give it much thought."

Two beats of silence. When his uncle spoke there was a slight tremor in his voice that vanished after the first few words. "Adam, what was it like to be in the crosshairs of death?"

"I don't want to talk about it."

His uncle gazed into the distance for a moment. "I need to know —"

"What in hell for?" Adam realized he'd shouted. "Sorry. It's hard for me to talk about. My good buddies died — yet I was lucky enough to live. It's not cocktail conversation."

His uncle's gaze softened. "I didn't mean for you to think I was taking this lightly. I know it must have been . . . more horrible than I could possibly imagine."

Adam almost said: *Got that right.* He stopped himself in time. He wasn't firing on all cylinders here, but he could tell his uncle was anxious about something. "It was unreal. It happened so fast. I hardly had time to think."

"Yet you escaped serious injury."

"Lucky me. I can't explain it. By some miracle, I survived."

Calvin studied him for a moment, then spoke. "I think someone is going to try to kill me."

Adam wasn't certain he'd understood his uncle. He'd been pretty screwed up since the explosion. He didn't respond for a moment as he let the idea settle in his brain. Who would want to kill a man who showed dogs? He thought about the guards and the armor-plated limo. Obviously, his uncle was more than just a little concerned.

"Who? Why?"

"Telling you would only put your life in danger." He fed the dog sitting in his lap a bit of cheese from the platter of appetizers on the table. "As my only living relative, if anything happens to me . . . I'm asking you to investigate."

The words detonated on impact. Adam jumped to his feet, sloshing the wine over his hand. "You're serious, aren't you?"

His uncle slowly nodded. "I wouldn't ask this of you if I didn't believe there's a real __"

"You've got to tell me more. I can't help __"

"Too much is at stake. I won't put you in danger. You've suffered enough."

Adam decided not to press his uncle right now. He'd always been an insular man. Calvin would tell him when he was ready. "If anything happens, I won't give up until I learn the truth. You have my word on that."

CHAPTER ONE

"This is my least favorite stop," Miranda told Whitney with a sigh. The cousins pulled up to a mansion overlooking the Pacific on Old La Jolla Farms Road. They hopped out of the Grand Cherokee and unloaded Whitney's Golden retriever from the back. Lexi at their heels, they walked up to a dazzling limestone estate with statuesque palms accenting the motor court in front of the home.

"Don't you have enough dogs to service without a problem one?" Whitney asked.

"Brandy's a love. It's his owner who's the pill. Trish Bowrather owns a swank gallery on Prospect Street in downtown La Jolla. She insisted on meeting you before she'll allow you to take care of Brandy. My other clients know you're my cousin and trust my judgment. Unless you screw up big-time, they'll keep you."

Miranda rang the bell and a few moments

later, a patrician looking blonde in her mid-forties greeted them with a withering expression.

"Your dog's only pet quality," she told Whitney before Miranda could open her mouth to introduce them.

Without looking down, Trish dropped a long-nailed hand to the shiny head of a Golden retriever the color of warm cognac. "Brandy could have been a champion, but I just didn't have the time."

Whitney tried for a smile that didn't quite work. She knew many show dogs had professional handlers. If Trish Bowrather had really wanted to show her Golden, she could have hired a pro.

Ever bubbly, Miranda exclaimed in her cheeriest voice, "This is my cousin, Whitney Marshall. She'll be taking over my route."

"Come in. Let's discuss Brandy's schedule."

At the mention of his name, Brandy swished his tail through the air. Lexi wagged her tail in response. Fortunately, Lexi was a lady. She made no move to sniff Brandy the way most dogs would have. Whitney had no doubt Trish wouldn't tolerate a dog who "misbehaved."

With a stiff nod, Trish showed them inside. Whitney decided the home reflected the woman. Sleek, impressive, cold.

"Just a second," Trish said. "I hope your dog is on flea medication."

"Absolutely," Miranda assured the woman before Whitney could. "Lexi's on the Program."

Whitney gave her dog a pill on the first day of every month. It protected Lexi against fleas and ticks for thirty days.

"Good." Trish studied Whitney for a moment. "Do you intend to bring your dog —"

"Her name's Lexi. I find dogs walk better and enjoy themselves more if they have a companion."

Trish considered this information, then nodded thoughtfully. They followed her inside to a living room with a floating stairway that led to the second level. A sweeping expanse of glass showcased a mesmerizing view of the ocean. Through the doors that opened onto the deck, Whitney could smell the briny scent of the sea and hear the thunderous crash of the surf on the rocks just beyond the house. The water shimmered in the midday sun, but in the distance a band of dark, ominous clouds sulked along the horizon.

In the center of the living-room ceiling, a mammoth chandelier of glass orbs tinkled in the breeze drifting in from the ocean. They sat on a pearl-gray leather sofa with accent pillows of dark charcoal in a nubby material that was scratchy to the touch. Perfectly behaved, the dogs settled at their feet. Automatically, Whitney reached down and stroked Lexi's smooth head.

"I understand you're divorced," Trish said, as if Whitney had a contagious disease.

"Yes. It was final two months ago."

Trish offered her a thin-lipped smile. "Trust me. You're better off without the bastard. I dumped mine seventeen years ago."

Whitney nodded and wished her heart was as hard as Trish's seemed to be. The serrated blade of pain went through her despite her best efforts to brace herself. Would she ever recover from Ryan's betrayal?

"I hope you took the jerk to the cleaners," Trish continued.

Actually, all Whitney had to show for nine years of marriage was an aging SUV and Lexi. Ryan had given up the Grand Cherokee easily but he'd fought hard to keep their house and a worthless piece of property out in the boonies.

"Whitney plans to open a dog spa in a year or so, when she's saved enough money," Miranda said. It was obvious to Whitney that her cousin wanted to steer the conversation away from Whitney's divorce. She knew how touchy Whitney was when it came to Ryan Fordham.

"Really?" Trish was clearly astonished. "There are already several in the area. Competition will be stiff."

"Mine will be different," Whitney replied. Why did Miranda have to mention it? She wasn't positive just what she was going to do. She'd worked for a software firm until a month ago, when they'd outsourced her job to India. With so many changes hitting her all at once, Whitney wasn't certain exactly what plans to make. She'd mentioned the spa as a *possibility* — not a sure thing.

"She's going to be using organic products to groom animals and feature holistic treatments like acupuncture," Miranda volunteered in her upbeat voice.

"I see," Trish replied with an undertone of indifference.

"Whitney's great with animals," Miranda said, filling the awkward silence.

"You're living locally?" Trish asked Whitney.

"I've moved into Miranda's place in Torrey Pines. She won't be needing it now that —"

"I'm getting married," Miranda interrupted, every syllable charged with excitement.

"Really?" Trish cocked one eyebrow. "You never mentioned being engaged."

"We've been together a long time. We just decided to make it official."

"This is what I have for Brandy's schedule." Whitney wanted to move the topic to a more professional level. There was something in Trish Bowrather's expression that said she disapproved of Miranda's plans. What business was it of hers? Clearly, she'd had a miserable experience, but that didn't mean Miranda couldn't have a successful marriage.

Whitney went through a list of activities that Miranda had given her, which included a walk each morning, a weekly visit to the Dog Spaw for grooming and a massage, a biweekly trip to the Bark Park where he could "socialize" with other dogs, a standing appointment each month with the vet for a checkup whether Brandy was ill or not and a monthly appointment with a canine dentist.

No question about it. Brandy was a gold mine. Miranda charged per visit and tacked on a mileage fee. It would be like taking care of three dogs. From what she could see, Brandy wouldn't give her any problems.

"That is correct," Trish said when she'd finished going over the schedule. "Just remember to check his paws when you pick him up at the Dog Spaw. Sometimes they forget to lacquer his claws. We want Brandy to look his best." She petted the dog's head. "Don't we, boy?"

The dog thumped his tail. It seemed obvious that no matter how snippy Trish Bowrather was, she genuinely cared about her dog. And she'd been through a divorce. Whitney wouldn't go so far as to say she liked her, but Trish wasn't as bad as she'd first thought.

"Brandy has standing appointments. They don't mind if you're a few minutes late, but for his morning walk, I need you here at nine sharp. He must be back by nine-thirty. I take Brandy to the gallery with me. We open at ten."

"I understand. I won't be late," Whitney assured her.

"If you are, I'll find someone else."

Trish gave her a few more instructions before walking them to the front door. "Tomorrow, promptly at nine," Trish again reminded Whitney as they left.

Miranda waited until they were in Whitney's SUV before saying, "See what I mean? The woman's a bitch, but Brandy is a love and Trish pays on the minute."

"I think I can handle it." Whitney thought for a moment. "Did you see all that expensive art and stuff? It makes me nervous to have a key and the code for her alarm system."

Miranda patted her arm reassuringly. "That's why I'm bonded. The insurer has transferred the policy to your name. Since I started Marshall's Pet Concierge, I've only had one problem. A woman's ring was missing after I'd spent the weekend at her home dogsitting."

Whitney groaned inwardly. Picking up animals at so many expensive homes when the owners were gone made her wary. Her cousin's company — now hers — was insured, but still . . .

"My insurance company paid the woman for her missing emerald ring," Miranda said. "Know what happened then?"

Whitney regretted not knowing the story. She wished they'd been closer after Miranda had unexpectedly come to live with her family, but their personalities had been too different. Then Whitney had married Ryan. He hadn't cared for Miranda. Whitney had been stupid enough to allow her husband to drive her away from her only living relative.

"She found the ring?"

"No," Miranda replied with the smile Whitney remembered fondly from childhood, when she'd thought her older cousin hung the moon and envied the string of broken hearts that trailed behind Miranda like a comet. "A year later she reported another robbery. She claimed some expensive paintings had been stolen from her home. The insurance company became suspicious, and their investigator proved she'd never purchased them. During the investigation, he discovered she'd never owned an emerald ring, either."

Whitney shuddered. "Wow. Did your insurer get the money back?"

Miranda waved her hand. "Are you kidding? She'd long since spent it, but my rates had gone up because I had a claim against me. They refunded my overpayments and reduced my rate back to where it had been."

"We live in a litigious society. People love to sue and file insurance claims." Whitney thought a minute. "What about Jasper's house? Is that covered?"

Not only was Whitney taking over her cousin's pet concierge business, she had moved into Miranda's tiny caretaker's cottage behind a mansion in Torrey Pines, an upscale suburb just north of San Diego. Her cousin had been receiving free rent in exchange for taking care of a small dog and watching the main house. The owner had died, but his dog was still there. The executor had agreed to pay for the animal's care until a relative came for the dog later this month.

"You're covered by their home owner's insurance. Why are you so worried?"

"I wander around a lot in that big old house because I can never find Jasper and he doesn't come when I call."

"Forget calling for him," Miranda advised. "Look for him in the dog run on the side yard or under the coffee table in the living room."

"Yesterday I bumped into a credenza, searching for him. I nearly knocked over some antique that's probably worth more than I'll make in a year."

"Don't worry about it. Jasper will get used to you. He hid from me in the beginning. He's lonely and confused. He's probably waiting for his master to come home."

How sad, Whitney thought. She remembered the first days after she and Ryan had split up. She'd wandered around their tomb of a house, waiting for the door to open and her husband to return.

It had been frighteningly lonely. She could only imagine how a poor animal must feel.

He wouldn't understand that his owner had died and was never going to walk him, play with him or pet him again.

"You might try bringing Jasper to the cottage to stay at night," Miranda said. "I didn't because I was over at Rick's so much, and he doesn't like dogs."

Never trust a man who doesn't like dogs, Whitney thought. She wanted to warn Miranda about Rick, but considering the mess she'd made of her marriage, how could she criticize?

"All set to leave?" Whitney asked when they'd completed their pet rounds and had returned to the cottage Whitney was taking over from Miranda. They'd brought Da Vinci, a Chihuahua, with them to stay while the dog's owners were in Las Vegas. The little dog was accustomed to being carried everywhere. Whitney had him in one arm and a tote with his food and toys in her free hand.

The wind had kicked up and voluminous clouds with leaden underbellies hovered overhead. Rain had been predicted for several days, but the fronts had blown over, leaving the ground dry during a drought that could lead to another drastic fire season.

"I have a few more things to store in the garage, then everything else will be at Rick's. Our flight to Fiji isn't until ten." Miranda's laugh sounded a little giddy. "When I come back, I'll be Mrs. Broderick Babcock."

Whitney mustered a smile. She wished she were comfortable cautioning her cousin about this man. She'd never met the attorney, but his reputation as a legal shark was well known. They were keeping the wedding a secret so his clients wouldn't panic because he wasn't ten minutes away.

The whole situation seemed a little odd to Whitney, but she told herself that this was another man — like Ryan — who put his career first. And like her ex-husband, the man Miranda was so anxious to marry didn't seem to care to meet Miranda's closest relative.

It was after dark by the time Whitney helped Miranda move the last of her things into the single-car garage behind the cottage. It was small and narrow compared to modern garages. The estate had been built in the 1920s when caretakers were lucky to have a car. Miranda's older-model Volvo was parked in the carport, which had been constructed sometime after the small garage had been built. It was time to send her cousin off, but Whitney needed to find the words to express her feelings first.

"Thanks for all you've done. I really appreciate it. I don't know what —"

"Don't be silly. You would have done the same for me." Miranda hugged her tight and held on for so long that it embarrassed Whitney a bit. She hadn't realized how much Miranda cared about her. Finally Miranda released her and opened the door to her car.

"I still want to repay you the money you spent on Mom."

"I told you before. I don't need it. Besides," Miranda added with a smile that seemed a bit melancholy, "I owed it to your mother. She took me in when no one else would. It's the least I can do." Miranda kissed Whitney's cheek and hugged her again. "Take care."

"Be happy," she called to the trail of exhaust Miranda's car left in the moist air that held the promise of rain. For some reason the silence sent a chill through her. It was probably just the oncoming storm, but a vague sense of dread kept her from moving.

You're just upset about all the changes in your life, she told herself. No, it was more than her husband's betrayal and the loss of her job that bothered Whitney. Despite the way Miranda made light of the situation, there was a lot unsaid and unsettled between them. And it was Whitney's fault.

She slowly returned to the small cottage with Lexi and Da Vinci. Boxes of her things were piled everywhere. Even though she'd spent several nights here, Whitney had unpacked only what was absolutely necessary.

The cottage consisted of a small sitting room with a kitchenette off to one side and a tiny bedroom with a bath. It wasn't much compared to the large home she'd shared with Ryan but she didn't mind. She changed out of her clothes and into a filmy Victoria's Secret nightie. She preferred their cotton nightshirts and had several. She couldn't remember where she'd packed them, so she'd put on the sexy nightgown Ryan had given her last Valentine's Day. When she found her nightshirts, she'd throw the darn thing away.

The telephone rang, startling Whitney. It must be a client needing a dog walked or something. She wended her way through the stacks of boxes just as the answering machine clicked on.

"Whitney?"

It couldn't be Ryan's voice, could it? She

must be imagining this, the way she'd dreamed he'd come back to her — begging forgiveness. Saying he still loved her. In her dream, she would let him dangle before reluctantly agreeing to give him a second chance. Then she would wake up and realize nothing had changed. Her husband had left her for another woman.

"Are you there? Pick up."

She'd once loved the man behind the voice too, too well. Her throat became as taut as a bowstring, making it difficult to swallow. *Never give up so much of your heart — ever again.*

"Listen, babe. I need to talk to you." The last voice she ever wanted to hear continued to come through the small black box. "It's *really* important. Call me. You know the number."

His demanding tone irritated Whitney. Whatever was "really" important probably wouldn't mean anything to her. No doubt it was something trivial, like Ryan's lost college yearbook. He'd accused her of taking it, then he'd found it but hadn't bothered to call. She'd rummaged through dozens of boxes for nothing. Whatever he wanted this time could wait until morning.

CHAPTER TWO

Adam jerked upright in bed, his hand reaching for a gun that wasn't there. Another explosion rocked the room.

Run. Take cover.

Heart battering his ribs like a fighter's punches, he lurched to his feet, then remembered where he was. Home. Well, not home exactly but close enough for government work. He had just returned to the United States and was staying in his uncle's house. His life wasn't in danger. A thunderstorm had blown in — that's all.

He groped in the darkness for the lamp he remembered seeing on the nightstand. He turned the switch. Nothing. Aw, hell. The power must be out.

Adam stood there, recalling his promise to his uncle. Should Calvin Hunter die, Adam would thoroughly investigate the circumstances, though his uncle had refused to give him any details. Now, just over two months later, Uncle Calvin was dead. The coroner's report stated a massive coronary was the cause of death.

Someone will try to kill me.

His uncle's words echoed through his head. Since being notified of his death, Adam had wondered if uncle Calvin had really died of natural causes. Heart problems did run in the family. Adam's father and grandfather had both died of heart attacks.

A jagged blast of lightning lanced through the bedroom, revealing the small dog cowering under the covers beside him. The rain pelted the windows — fast, loud and explosive — like machine gunfire. A sharp sense of danger racked his body. He sucked in a stabilizing breath and tried to get his bearings.

What was that?

It sounded like breaking glass downstairs. Was his imagination running wild? Since nearly being killed, Adam hadn't been able to conquer this jumpy feeling. Trauma — mental and physical — did crazy things to your head. He could come undone in a heartbeat, he realized.

Had he gone over some unseen edge?

Adam fumbled in the dark until he found the jeans he'd slung over the foot of the bed and scrambled into them. He strained to catch another sound, but all he heard was the rat-a-tat of the rain pummeling the roof. Something like a cat's whisker brushed the back of his neck. He felt the top of his bare spine, but nothing was there.

The house had been broken into once already during his uncle's funeral. According to the police, all that had been taken had been his uncle's computer. The theft had fueled Adam's suspicions. The house was full of valuables. Why had a laptop computer been taken while other things had been left behind? It was possible something had scared off the burglar, and now he had returned.

Adam plunged into the darkness with a bone-chilling dread that must be a form of post traumatic stress. This was nothing. He'd been through worse and had lived to see another day.

Don't go down there! Are you nuts?

Adam refused to listen to the voice in his head. Some unseen force propelled him forward. He groped his way in the dark, tiptoeing along the corridor and venturing down the sweeping staircase to the first floor. If a burglar had broken in, he intended to surprise him. This time he would be ready. He wouldn't be trapped again.

Adam halted at the bottom of the stairs

and squinted into the darkness. He'd been so jet-lagged when he'd arrived that he'd hardly noticed the layout of the lower floor. He'd headed directly upstairs and settled into one of what appeared to be several guest bedrooms. He seemed to recall a large living room with a dining room opening through an archway off to one side.

Breath suspended in his lungs, he listened to the shadows. He thought he heard something. Or maybe it was nothing. The storm was just unleashing its full fury, making it difficult to tell. He opened his mouth to call "who's there," but the words stalled in his throat. The muscles in his neck quivered. What was he thinking? Only an idiot would give away his position.

Although the area was as dark as a dungeon, he detected movement — little more than a darker shape in a pitch-black room. The burglar must have broken one of the small panes on the French doors to get into the house. He thought he saw a shadow shift and heard what might have been a muffled thump.

Adam flattened himself against the wall, anticipating being exposed by another flash of lightning. He watched the intruder, but it was impossible to tell much. Shapes were discernible only by varying degrees of darkness. The short man seemed to be wearing a raincoat and some type of cap.

The intruder had something that glinted in his hand, probably a flashlight. No. The guy would have a flashlight turned on. He must be armed with a gun or a knife. Knowing he himself was unarmed, it took Adam only a split second to decide what to do.

Legs pumping like pistons, he charged across the room and leveled the guy with a flying tackle. Thrown off balance by the powerful thrust of Adam's body weight, they went down in a bone-crushing jumble of limbs. With a whoosh, the air shot out of the prick's lungs. Thunk! The weapon hit the tile floor. He scrambled to grab the man's arms, intending to pull them behind his back and haul him to his feet. The wiry little guy contorted like a pretzel and emitted a pitiful-sounding wail, but Adam kept him pinned down.

Still trying to control the man's arms and get them behind his back, Adam's hands encountered something surprisingly soft. His fingers dug in, clutching a soft mound of flesh beneath sheer fabric.

What in hell?

His breath lurched painfully and his heart stutter-stepped. A female. No way! The two years he'd spent without a woman in his life must have backfired on him. He really *was* losing it.

Adam reached up and yanked a wet knit cap off the intruder's head. Out spilled a tangle of blond hair, bringing with it a whiff of spring-fresh shampoo. The scent distracted him for a second. The body shifted beneath him, soft — undeniably feminine. Aw, crap.

Couldn't be.

He double-checked, his fingers finding smooth skin beneath the open front of her raincoat. His thumb accidentally plunged into the hollow between her breasts. Man oh man, was she built. Not centerfold breasts, but tantalizing just the same.

The feminine smell. The soft skin. His brain reminded him that she was a thief, but his body didn't give a damn. After months upon months of seeing women covered from head to toe or clad in baggy military uniforms, his one-track mind excluded everything except the erotic signals her body was sending.

A flicker of lightning in the distance illuminated the room for a split second. He had the fleeting impression of blazing green eyes. Her mane of wild blond hair tumbling alluringly across the floor. An open raincoat revealed half-exposed bare breasts. Heat spiraled through him, pooling in his groin.

He had to steel himself to keep from running his hands all over her. She twisted beneath him, arching her hips, struggling to free herself. His body tingled from the erotic sensation. In a heartbeat the iron bulge of his sex jutted against her.

"Help! Help!" She ripped out a screech that lashed through him like a razor-sharp blade. Reality returned. This was a thief, not a woman to be seduced. What *was* he thinking? Women could be every bit as dangerous as men — a lesson he'd learned the hard way. But what were the odds of encountering two deadly women within a few months?

She shrieked again. He jerked his hands off her breasts but kept her pinned to the floor with his body. She might be a woman, wearing a weird outfit, but she'd broken into the house.

"Lemme go!"

She bucked violently and rammed her head into his chest while she unleashed a frenzy of beating fists and kicking legs in a futile attempt to dislodge him. He held fast, trying to decide how to handle this situation. Women usually didn't break into places on their own. A man must be lurking somewhere nearby. She cut loose with another scream that could have been heard on the far side of hell.

"Shut up!"

She clawed his face and speared at his eyes, but he ducked in the nick of time. Her fingers caught the base of his neck, raking down the tender flesh.

"Cut it out!" His nose was just inches from hers, and he had the impression of an oval face and a trembling lower lip.

"Get off me!"

She thrashed and tried to knee him in the groin but he held her down. He needed to tie her up with something while he called the police. She grabbed a fistful of his hair and yanked. "Lemme go!"

With one hand, Adam twisted her wrist and broke her hold. "Don't make me hurt you."

She bit his arm, sinking her teeth into his flesh, but he didn't relent. "I've got you outweighed by a hundred pounds," he told her from between clenched teeth. She wasn't very big, but she was a hellcat. "This is a fight you can't win."

She bit his arm again, clamping down for all she was worth. Pain shot up to his shoulder and he bent double, certain she'd drawn blood. Her teeth were still attached to his arm. With both hands he grabbed her neck to frighten her and make her let go. Suddenly her body went slack.

He hadn't choked her too hard — had he? The bile rose up in his throat. He hadn't meant to hurt her — just stop the vicious biting. He released the woman and jumped up, disgusted with himself.

She shot to her feet and torpedoed away. The little faker wasn't escaping from him. He rushed after her, caught her in two long strides and grabbed her by the shoulders, then locked his arms around her. For a moment they moved together like dancers. She kicked backward, slamming her heel into his shin and shrieking like a demon. Undoubtedly she was attempting to alert her companion and get his help. He must be outside, where the storm masked the ruckus.

"Goddammit," Adam roared. He hauled her backward, accidentally stumbling into the sofa and losing his balance. They landed on the cushions, but this time she was on top, still braying like a pissed-off mule.

"Don't you dare hurt me."

"I'm not going to hurt you." He pushed her off him. They were side by side, breathing like marathon runners. It took him a second to tell her, "Just shut up and stay put while I call the cops."

44

"*You're* calling the police?"

"Hey, I don't care if you are a woman. You broke into this house —"

"No, I didn't." Darkness obscured her face but he felt her long hair whipping across his nose as she turned on him. "You're the one who shouldn't be here."

"What?" Adam was dead certain she was going to scream again. He put his hand over her mouth and anchored her sexy bod in place with the weight of his leg. "Listen. I'm Adam Hunter. I inherited this house from my uncle. I have every right to be here. Who the hell are you?"

He felt her soft lips moving beneath his palm. He slowly lifted his hand. And waited for another bone-rattling shriek.

"I'm Whitney Marshall. I live in the caretaker's cottage. I just came in to get Jasper."

Jasper, the butt-ugly show dog he'd first seen at his uncle's villa in Siros. The little mutt who'd crawled in bed with him the moment Adam had turned down the covers. Could she be telling the truth? Was she taking care of the dog? "I heard breaking glass."

Two beats of silence. "I know. I knocked over something with my umbrella while I was looking for Jasper so I could feed him."

"You weren't calling Jasper."

"It doesn't do any good. Jasper won't come. He usually hides under the coffee table."

"What about the weapon in your hand?"

"Weapon?" Hostile silence, then, "That was my umbrella."

Umbrella? Shit. He lifted his leg off her, reluctantly admitting, "I guess I made a mistake."

"Do you always act like a raving lunatic when you make a mistake?"

She attempted to climb over him, and his sex-starved body again kicked into overdrive. She was caught up in the raincoat and what little she was wearing beneath. Her soft, full breasts brushed his bare chest. She jerked back and he expected her to hit him . . . or bite him again. She scuttled sideways and crashed to the floor, then scrambled to her feet and charged off into the darkness.

Adam slowly rose, scalp prickling, arm throbbing, blood trickling down from the base of his neck onto his chest. He could still smell her perfume and feel her sexy body beneath his. Of all the freaking luck.

CHAPTER THREE

Sweating and panting, her heart thundering painfully against her ribs, Whitney raced out into the downpour. She managed to reach the cottage, slam the door shut behind her and quickly lock it. She could still feel the brute's weight crushing her, his huge hands locking around her neck in a death grip. She'd never been forced to physically defend herself until tonight.

Squeezing her eyes shut and leaning back against the door, she willed her body to stop shaking. She hadn't been able to get a good look at the creep, but even now she could see his fiendish eyes glittering as if he were on some controlled substance. His features had been obscured by the darkness but she had the impression of white teeth the size of tombstones.

Just when she thought her life was turning around this had to happen. She'd counted on living here, but with that monster in the main house, it would be impossible. She could understand him mistaking her for a burglar — after all, the house had been hit during Calvin Hunter's funeral — but the creep's marauding hands . . . inexcusable.

The big goon probably had a felony record for sexual assault. She heaved a sigh, attempting to catch her breath, and assured herself the man was nothing more than a letch. Still, how could she live here with him so close? She would never get a good night's sleep.

Where could she go? Her bank account was down to less than a hundred dollars. Her only alternative was to hang in there until Miranda returned, then borrow money from her cousin to rent another place.

Whitney gingerly touched the throbbing lump forming on the back of her head from when he'd knocked her down on the hard tile. The bump was so tender that her eyes watered. The salty tang of his blood was still on her lips from biting him. She'd been dead certain he intended to rape and kill her. So what if she'd drawn blood?

"Serves the creep right," she muttered out loud.

Lexi and Da Vinci were hovering at her feet, tails swishing in the darkness. She slipped out of the lightweight raincoat and let it drop to the floor. All she had on beneath was the sheer nightie. When she'd thrown on her raincoat to get Jasper, she'd never dreamed she would run into anyone.

"Okay, okay, out of the way," she told the dogs, her voice shaky.

She bumped into a box and stubbed her toe on the way to the chair beside the sofa, which was loaded with clothes and things she'd heaped there while unpacking. She dropped into the welcoming cushions, feeling slightly nauseous. A panicky feeling returned in a wave of fear that surged upward from the depths of her queasy stomach.

The electric power returned with a blinding flash and the cottage lit up. Not being alone in the dark calmed Whitney a little. She checked the locks on the front and back doors. She was safe.

Briiing-briiing. The telephone rang, and Whitney tensed. She let the machine Miranda had left behind pick up the message.

"It's me again." Ryan's disembodied voice filtered across the room. "Call me no matter how late you get in. It's really important."

Naturally, Ryan presumed she would do as he told her. Let him rot in hell along with the beauty queen. They'd married two days after his divorce from Whitney became final. She removed the receiver from the hook. If he called back, he wouldn't wake her. Let the jerk wait.

Whitney sent the dogs out the back door to do their business before going to bed. Clouds tumbled across the moon as the wind herded them inland. The rain had slackened to a mist, but it dripped off the trees and bushes, plopping onto the small used brick patio behind the cottage.

Whitney wiped off Lexi's paws with one of Miranda's old towels. "Good girl. Ready for bed?"

Lexi scampered off for her doggie bed at the foot of Whitney's bed. Da Vinci was still sniffing around and trying to decide which bush to bless by lifting his leg on it. She allowed him to take his time, remembering Miranda's warning. They're called *Chiweewees for a good reason.* Da Vinci was evidently prone to boo-boos and often left suspicious stains on the rug. She waited until the Chihuahua finally selected a spot and hoisted one little leg. She dried him off, then put him on the floor.

Whitney knew she'd locked the front door, but she double-checked anyway. Peering through the small panes of glass, she saw the light upstairs in the main house was still shining. Just knowing the pervert was there creeped her out.

Now the rain had stopped, leaving a somnolent dripping from the eaves. The storm had passed, thunder only a distant rumble, lightning a flicker to the east. A lone coyote howled. Its bleak call struck her as overwhelmingly lonely.

Something about the emptiness of the night disturbed her, which was silly. She wasn't alone. Granted, the place was a good distance from the next house, but this was suburbia, for God's sake. She flicked off the porch light, unable to shake the feeling her world was no longer familiar. Or friendly.

She went into the bathroom to get ready for bed. As she brushed her teeth, she thought about Ryan's call. What could he possibly want? They hadn't spoken in months. Rather than hire expensive attorneys to split what little they had, she'd agreed to arbitration. She'd allowed him to keep the house with the huge mortgage.

Whitney had taken the Grand Cherokee. Although the SUV wasn't new, it was paid for, and she needed transportation. They'd had little else except a full service of china and a worthless piece of property that Ryan — who didn't have a head for business —

had insisted they purchase as an investment. The land turned out to have toxic waste in the soil and couldn't be sold without going through an expensive decontamination process. She'd quitclaimed the land to Ryan along with the house in order to keep Lexi.

And to get Ryan Fordham out of her life forever.

Whitney awoke the next morning with Da Vinci licking her face and wagging his tail. The spoiled little dog had slept on the bed with her.

"No," she groaned, looking at the alarm and realizing she'd failed to set it properly. She'd overslept. "You have to go out, don't you?" At the sound of her voice Lexi popped up from her bed and shook her head. The movement made her ears flap, Lexi's signal that she had to relieve herself.

"Let's hit it." Whitney shrugged into a robe and escorted them to the back door. The small fenced patio and patch of grass were still wet from the rain. When they'd finished, she quickly fed them, showered and threw on some clothes. She did *not* want to be late to Trish Bowrather's on the first day.

She walked to the carport attached to the single-car garage that was so crammed full of Miranda's stuff, there wasn't room for the SUV. Whitney glanced up at the main house. All the curtains were drawn. If she didn't know better, she would think no one was home. The jerk must still be asleep.

She loaded the dogs and was backing out when she realized a car had pulled in behind her, blocking her exit. She didn't know anyone who drove a silver Porsche. It might be Adam Hunter, she thought, then wondered why he would be using the back driveway when a four-car garage was located on the other side of the house. Of course, after last night, there was no telling what that maniac might pull. But a man in a suit stepped out of the sleek sports car.

Ryan.

In a heartbeat, her world shifted and became out of focus. Just the slightest patina of sweat sheened her forehead. She could have blamed it on the bright morning sun and the humidity in the air from the storm, but she knew better. How could he have this effect on her? Hadn't the pain of his betrayal made her a stronger person?

Lexi immediately stuck her head out the window and barked a happy greeting. *Why me?* Whitney asked herself as she slid out of the SUV. Whatever Ryan wanted had to be really important for him to drive out to Torrey Pines from San Diego when patients would be waiting in his office at nine.

"You didn't call me back." Ryan sounded genuinely shocked, but then, he always was when he didn't get his way.

"What do you want?"

His mouth quirked into a smile, but she knew him too well. He was merely flashing his chemically whitened teeth. The man could turn on the charm like a searchlight, when it suited him.

Tall and imposing, with surfer blond hair and a golden tan, Dr. Ryan Fordham made women's hearts pound just by walking into a room. He was a shade shy of pretty, Whitney told herself, something mean curdling inside her. A tide of heartbreak rushed in, sweeping away rational thought.

"There's a little problem." He reached into the open window of the Jeep and stroked Lexi's head. The little turncoat couldn't wag her tail fast enough.

"What's the matter?" She battled the urge to tell him to get his hand off her dog. Although Lexi adored Whitney, the retriever had always been very fond of Ryan. Why not? He'd never had a cross word for the dog.

He stopped petting Lexi and turned to Whitney. "I'm joining a new practice. I need to sign a lease for an office building and finance some equipment. The credit check showed your name is still on the house and the property in Temecula."

"I thought the settlement agreement handled the transfer of title on both places. The judge accepted the documents."

Ryan studied the tips of his highly buffed shoes. "Apparently the judge was in a hurry and didn't notice it wasn't notarized. So it couldn't be recorded. I have the papers in the car. All you have to do is sign in front of a notary. I'll take them right to the county recorder's office to be legally registered."

Whitney was amazed that Ryan could get *any* credit. He was up to his ears in debt with a huge mortgage. He also had the lease on the office he'd used before switching from general surgery to the more lucrative field of cosmetic surgery. On top of everything was an astronomical malpractice premium that had to be paid quarterly. He walked over to the Porsche and she added expensive car leases to the list of her ex-husband's debts. No telling what Ashley — his girlfriend, now wife — was driving.

Ryan returned with a bound sheaf of papers in his hand. He flipped it open in front of her to a page with a red Post-it flagging a space for her signature. "All you have to do is sign here." He zipped to another page. "And here." He paged to the end of the document. "And here. But you must do it in front of a notary."

A warning bell sounded in a distant part of her brain. Why were there so many pages? The original document from the arbitrator had been much smaller, hadn't it?

"Come with me now," Ryan continued in his smoothest voice. "There's a notary at American Title who'll take care of everything. They open at nine."

"I can't today. I'm already running late. Besides, I want an attorney to look over everything before I sign."

"What?" Ryan slapped the side of the Jeep with the document. "Why let a lawyer pad his bill by reading something you've already agreed to? Besides, you don't have the money for a lawyer."

Whitney realized she was dealing not with the charming Ryan Fordham but the imperious Ryan Fordham. Once she'd thought this persona was authoritative. Now he merely sounded arrogant. She manufactured a smile and bluffed. "Miranda is marrying Broderick Babcock. He'll read the papers for nothing."

That stopped him. Ryan stared at her slack-jawed. Broderick Babcock was a legend in San Diego, in the state. He'd successfully defended several high-profile clients that most people believed were guilty and didn't have a prayer of avoiding prison.

"Why bother Babcock?" Ryan asked, his voice smooth again. "This isn't any big deal."

"I still want him to review the document. But it'll have to wait. He took Miranda to Fiji for a two-week honeymoon."

"What?" The word exploded out of Ryan. "Wait two weeks? No fucking way! You come with me right now. We'll be at American Title when they open."

He was shouting now, the way he occasionally did when things didn't go his way. Ryan had a hair-trigger temper that rarely surfaced. Between his charm, good looks and assertive attitude, people usually gave in to him. Whitney always had — but not anymore.

"I'm not signing anything until Rick has read and approved the document." She said this as if she knew the attorney, even though she'd never met the man. "Now move your car. I'm late for work."

Ryan grabbed her by the shoulders and shook her hard. "You bitch. You're doing this to get back at me for falling in love with Ashley."

She told herself this wasn't true. It was only prudent to have an attorney read what appeared to be a complicated document — a different document than she'd originally signed. But she had to admit Ryan had put her through hell. His betrayal had been acute, devastating. She'd sacrificed her dream of becoming a veterinarian to put Ryan through medical school. Now she was penniless and forced to start over.

"Let go of me." She tried to wrench away, but he only tightened his grip and began to shake her with even more force.

"I want you out of my life forever. This has to be settled today."

"Leave me alone," she snapped as she struggled to control the quaver in her voice. A bolt of fear shot up her spine. She'd seen Ryan upset many times, but never like this. Something else was wrong besides the improper transfer of property.

"Come with me now or else —"

"Don't threaten me. Let me go this instant."

Ryan shook her so hard that her head snapped back, wrenching her neck and shoulders. Pain lanced down her neck into her upper arm.

"You heard the lady. Let her go." The order sounded like the crack of a whip.

Ryan instantly released her, and they both whirled around to see who was speaking. A tall, powerfully built man stood in the trellised opening of the bridal wreath hedge that separated the main house from the caretaker's cottage. He must be Adam Hunter. The air whooshed out of Whitney's lungs as if the brute had tackled her again.

Head cocked slightly to one side, Adam Hunter gazed directly at Whitney. His arresting eyes were marine blue. If he was on something — the way she'd thought last night — it was an overload of testosterone. His eyes weren't fiendish at all; they were alert, predator's eyes. There was nothing more exciting to a natural-born hunter than vulnerable prey. Last night, clad in little more than a nylon raincoat, she'd been an easy mark.

In the utter darkness, she'd assumed him ugly. He was far from it, but she wouldn't call him handsome, either. He was attractive in an edgy, masculine way that said he was world-weary but aching to throw a punch if given any excuse. She imagined him clobbering Ryan and smiled inwardly.

Adam was dressed in well-worn navy Dockers and a gray polo shirt, but she had the impression he played the hand life dealt him. He would be at home in a boardroom, wearing Armani or dressed as a hit man in black, brandishing a gun fitted with a silencer. She would bet her life that the hit-man mode would be his choice.

His straight nose was slightly long, his square jaw was stubbled with hair the same shade as the black mop that was long overdue for a haircut. He had a well-toned body that she doubted came from hours at a gym. Somehow she couldn't see him on a treadmill or pumping iron beside a bunch of other guys.

"Look," Ryan began in his most placating tone. "My wife —"

"Ex-wife," she corrected, then didn't know what else to say. How could she expect the guy who'd manhandled her to be much help? The endless moment stopped when she managed to say, "He's trying to force me to sign papers that I want my attorney to review first."

Adam's take-no-prisoners glare said this was more than he needed — or wanted — to know. He shifted his weight from one foot to another, but his stance remained just as defiant.

"She's just being stubborn." Ryan gave Adam a man-to-man look.

"You were *way* too rough with the lady," Adam replied in a tone that could have frozen vodka. "Leave — now."

Ryan opened his mouth, set to argue, thought better of it and stomped off to his car. His wimpy exit showed Ryan for what he was — a pretty boy who relied on charm. When that failed he turned into a bully. With a screech of tires, the Porsche shot out of the driveway.

Whitney turned, but Adam Hunter had vanished as stealthily as he'd appeared.

CHAPTER FOUR

Trish Bowrather was backing her midnight-blue Jaguar out of her garage when Whitney arrived. Brandy was in the passenger seat, his head out the window. Trish slammed on the brakes and rolled down her window, yelling, "You're late."

Whitney jumped out of the Jeep and ran over. "I'm sorry. My ex-husband showed up unexpectedly. He wouldn't let me out of the driveway until a neighbor helped get rid of him."

She hated bringing up personal issues, but she had no idea what else to say. She'd never had Miranda's aptitude for shading the truth.

Trish's eyes became distracted for a second, as if she was recalling something from long, long ago. "I thought your divorce was final."

"It is. He claims there was some mix-up in the paperwork involving the property settlement. I think I should have an attorney look over these new documents before I sign."

"Absolutely!" Trish stepped out of the car, dressed in a chic black suit accented with sterling-silver jewelry. "You need a lawyer to check. It sounds highly unusual."

"That's what I thought."

Trish studied her a moment, an understanding expression softening her features. "Was he physical with you?"

Whitney realized she must still appear shaken from the incident. "Well . . . a little, I guess. Ryan didn't hit me or anything but he grabbed my shoulders —"

"File a police report. Then get a restraining order," Trish shot back, conviction underscoring every word. "That'll keep that bastard away from you."

Whitney managed a weak nod. She didn't want to antagonize Ryan any more than she already had. There probably wasn't a valid reason not to sign the documents, but a little voice kept insisting she consult an attorney.

Trish put her hand on Whitney's arm. "Look. Take Brandy for his walk. Stop by the Daily Grind for a latte. Relax a little bit, then drop Brandy off at the gallery. There's a police station nearby. File a report. If the jerk threatens you again, get a restraining order."

An unconvincing "Good idea" was the best Whitney could muster.

"Here, Brandy," Trish called, and the dog scrambled out of the open driver's door, his leash in his mouth.

"Take your time," Trish advised as she walked back to the Jag. "Calm down. Don't let that creep ruin your day."

"Don't worry. I won't," Whitney said to appease her.

Whitney watched Trish speed away. She couldn't help being shocked at the change in the woman since yesterday. Evidently, Trish had suffered through a very rough divorce. She understood how unreasonable ex-husbands could be.

Get a restraining order?

She reluctantly admitted to herself that Trish had struck a nervous chord. Today Whitney had seen a side of Ryan that he hadn't revealed in nine years of marriage. Ryan had been cold and verbally abusive at times, but he'd never been rough with her.

Was he cracking up?

Surely not. Ryan was just stressed out, she assured herself as she hooked Brandy to his leash and opened the door for Lexi. Her ex's switch to cosmetic surgery had meant leaving his old partners and finding a new practice. Cosmetic surgeons needed to maintain a certain image. Sophisticated offices and the latest in equipment attracted the kind of clientele who gladly parted with stratospheric sums of money in order to appear more youthful. That consumed cash at a rapid rate.

Most people believed doctors made boodles of money, but that was no longer as true as it once had been. Malpractice insurance and the cost of equipment had eroded doctors' earning power. Ryan had compounded his problems by making several bad investments, like the property with the toxic chemicals in the soil.

Well, he'd gotten what he deserved, she assured herself. During the last year of their marriage, Ryan had behaved unforgivably. Always moody and temperamental, he'd become more so. She'd asked him dozens and dozens of times if she could do anything to help. He'd denied anything was wrong, claiming it was just the pressure of his first year in practice. His long hours became longer and more erratic, his fuse shorter. Still, Whitney hadn't suspected anything until she'd discovered the receipt from La Valencia, an expensive hotel in La Jolla.

He could have leveled with her and said

he'd fallen for another woman, but he hadn't. Even when she confronted him, Ryan continued to deny it until she'd told him that she'd called the hotel and found out he'd registered with his "wife." When she'd had him dead to rights, Ryan had walked out the door "to find himself."

She was halfway down the street, with Brandy and Lexi on their leashes and Da Vinci snuggled into his custom-built sling harnessed to her chest, when her cell phone rang. She switched the leashes to one hand and grabbed the phone clipped to her waist.

"I hope you've had time to come to your senses."

She was tempted to hang up on Ryan, but that wouldn't deliver the message she really wanted to send. She'd had all she was ever going to take from this man.

"Well, Ryan," she replied in the sweetest tone she could manage. "You were unforgivably physical with me and I have a witness. I'm filing a police report and if you come near me again, I'll get a restraining order. You may recall that I have a friend who works for the *Tribune.* I'll make sure this appears in the paper. Should do worlds of good for your business, don't you think?"

There was nothing but dead air on the other end of the phone. No doubt Ryan was in shock. She'd never talked back to him like this when they'd been married. He'd presumed she was going to do just what he wanted.

"You wouldn't." He didn't sound as sure of himself as he usually did.

"I mean every word," she bluffed. "Just mail me what you want signed. As soon as Rick and Miranda return, I'll have him look over the documents. If he approves, I will, and I'll get them back to you immediately."

He grunted something that might have been "okay" and hung up. Whitney knew he was pissed. She told herself she was being prudent to wait until a lawyer could look over the papers, but a small part of her conceded she wanted to make things difficult for Ryan. What he'd done still hurt more than she cared to admit and she deserved a bit of revenge.

She'd first bumped into Ryan Fordham while rushing to a class at UCLA. He appeared to be another surfer being forced by his parents to study, but the opposite proved to be true. Ryan was brilliant — a fact not lost on the man — and he was attending college on an academic scholarship, studying premed.

He didn't have time or money to date but he carved out a place for Whitney. Before she knew it, she'd moved in with him. When she'd been accepted to UC Davis to study veterinary medicine, she'd been faced with a choice. It was much harder to get into vet school than medical school. Still, she'd allowed Ryan to persuade her to put her plans on hold until he received his medical degree.

They'd married just after graduation. Ryan's mother and Miranda, Whitney's only living relative, accompanied them to the Santa Monica courthouse, where they were wed. For reasons Whitney still didn't understand, Ryan hadn't liked Miranda.

True, her cousin could be a bit of a wild child at times, but who could blame her? Miranda had been orphaned at fifteen when her parents died in a car crash. She'd appeared at their door with a social worker the day before the funeral. While the older woman met with Whitney's mother, a single parent, Whitney had consoled Miranda.

"I don't have anywhere to go," her cousin had whispered, tears in her eyes.

Now it was Whitney who had nowhere to go — thanks to Ryan Fordham. She honestly didn't know what she would have done without Miranda. Her cousin had taken her in without asking any questions.

Ryan could rot in hell until she had someone look over the papers. It wasn't much, but she had to admit it gave her satisfaction to see him squirm.

Ashley Fordham heard the opening bars of "Proud Mary" and knew she had a call on her cell phone. Whenever she heard the song, she fondly remembered her father. She could see him smiling, his slight overbite making him appear happier than he really was.

"Just a minute," she told Preston Block, her personal trainer. "I'm expecting a call from Ryan." She yanked her phone off the waistband of her yoga pants.

"It's me, babe." Ryan sounded discouraged.

"Did Whitney sign?"

A long beat of silence. "No. She wants to show the papers to an attorney."

"Why? She signed them after arbitration."

"Whitney's just being difficult to get back at me," Ryan said wearily.

Ashley caught Preston's eye and smiled even though she wanted to scream. Why couldn't Ryan have convinced the bitch to sign? How hard could it be?

Ashley tried for a teary voice. "We'll lose the house."

She had her heart set on a spectacular home with a dock for a yacht in Coronado

Keys, just south of Ryan's offices in down-town San Diego. In order to buy it, they needed to sell the monstrosity of a house Ryan and Whitney had owned.

"It's not just the house," Ryan replied, his voice charged with anger. "It's . . . every-thing."

Ashley used an encouraging tone. "You'll think of something. You always do."

He told her he loved her and they hung up. She loved him, too, and had from the first day she'd met him. She knew Ryan was under a lot of pressure right now. The expense of buying in to a new practice. Skyrocketing malpractice insurance. The house she wanted. She would do anything to help him.

Preston was still watching her, and she hoped her frustration and anger didn't show on her face. No sense in getting frown lines over this. Too much was at stake. If Ryan couldn't handle his ex, she would. Ryan didn't have to know a thing. Like many men she'd encountered since childhood, Ryan needed to believe he was in charge.

"A problem?" Preston asked.

Ashley had been working out with Pres-ton at Dr. Jox Fitness Center for the last three years. He had the hots for her. She could see it in his eyes as he put her through

70

the workout he'd custom designed for her.

Ashley had known she was beautiful since her mother had entered her at age five in the Little Miss Idaho contest and she'd won. But years of countless contests hadn't led to a first in the Miss USA or Miss America pageants. Worse, she hadn't received the lucrative modeling contract that her mother expected. A ruptured appendix that she didn't seek treatment for until it was too late unexpectedly cut her mother's life short, leaving Ashley alone in San Diego to prepare for the Miss San Diego contest.

Ashley had decided she was sick of beauty pageants — something she'd never had the courage to tell her mother. At twenty-four, she was getting too old to compete. She had to find a job, but she just had a high-school diploma and no marketable skills except her looks.

She'd landed a position as a receptionist with a group of cosmetic surgeons. It didn't take her long to see how much money the doctors made from nips and tucks. She allowed one of the doctors to enhance her naturally pouty lips with a touch of Restalyne and had a chemical peel that made her flawless skin look perfect even without a bit of makeup.

When she could claim she'd been "enhanced" by the cosmetic group, she moved up the food chain from the entry-level receptionist's position to "spokeswoman" for the group. She met with patients in "preliminary sessions" to show what could be achieved with their services. Ashley was living proof of how skilled the surgeons were.

Prospective clients assumed her breasts were silicone and her naturally high cheekbones a result of implants. Liposuction must account for her trim tummy and slim thighs. Ashley merely smiled and never mentioned Mother Nature's gifts. Instead, she encouraged the women — and a growing number of men — to use the doctors' services.

She was good — invaluable really — a natural-born salesperson who could persuade anyone to go under the knife without them realizing they'd been conned. After years of automatically turning on the charm in her quest for a beauty title, this was a no-brainer. Within a year her salary quadrupled based upon the number of patients who mentioned her when they signed up for cosmetic "enhancements."

Kah-ching!

Ashley knew what she wanted — a husband with a successful cosmetic surgery practice. Then she could give up the parading around and convincing ugly women that surgery could improve them. She didn't want to pitch plastic surgery all her life. She wanted her own home; she'd been on the road since childhood. She planned to take courses in interior design and decorate her own home herself. Eventually she might open a design studio, but she wasn't sure she wanted the headaches owning a business might bring.

Ryan Fordham had appeared at the cosmetic group — an answer to her prayers. She'd been contemplating starting an affair with an older member of the group who had a wife who could haunt a house and charge by the room. But Ryan had immediately changed her mind. He could have had his pick of beautiful women, but he was genuinely interested in her.

They'd gone for coffee — to discuss a "spokesperson's role" in promoting a cosmetic surgeon's practice. After their short conversation, for reasons Ashley could never explain, she was totally in love with Ryan Fordham. She'd never been in love before, but now she knew how her mother had felt when she'd met Ashley's father. Ashley thanked her lucky stars that Ryan was a doctor, not an electrician. If he had been, Ashley still would have loved him just the way Ashley's mother had loved her father. Even after her father left them, her mother never looked at another man.

She'd known when Ryan first gazed at her that he was interested. Men were so transparent. They tried to hide what they were thinking, but she could always detect their lust. It was a skill her mother had taught her before she was eight. Judges, even those evaluating little girls, had that telltale glaze in their eyes. You smiled, batted your lashes, twitched your fanny and played them to your advantage.

The more time she spent with Ryan, the more she loved him. He was driven to be successful, which was second only to his valiant attempts to make her happy. She'd assured him she was happy; he was the man of her dreams. Still, Ashley wanted more — for him and for herself.

If he had any drawbacks, Ryan was weak with his ex-wife. Ashley understood. It was guilt — plain and simple. The woman had sacrificed to put him through medical school. Whitney had played the martyr to the hilt, exiting the marriage, asking for nothing except a beat-up SUV and a dog. Ashley had to be careful not to appear conniving while handling this for Ryan.

"I do have a bit of a problem," she confessed to Preston. Even though he wanted her just like countless other men had over the years, she needed Preston as a friend. The problem with being so beautiful was that other women were jealous. Preston was her only friend and sleeping with him would ruin their relationship. More important, she would never cheat on Ryan. Still, she realized she could use sex to manipulate Preston.

"Enough for today," she told him. "Let's hit the juice bar."

Dr. Jox had a pricey juice bar that served fresh squeezed juices and made healthy smoothies. Ashley ordered pomegranate juice because its antioxidant properties would keep her skin flawless, while Preston asked for a wheatgrass smoothie. She signed the tab for both drinks and they went outside to one of the small tables under the canopy of a towering ficus tree.

"What's the problem, Ashley?"

She told him part of the story and kept the emphasis on the ex-wife who was so jealous that she was refusing to sign papers she'd already signed once. She laid it on thick about never having had a home and always being on the road. Just when she'd found her dream home, the conniving ex was determined to ruin everything.

"There might be a way," Preston said when she'd finished with tears studding her long eyelashes. "What does the ex value the most?"

Ashley hadn't a clue. Whitney was an attractive blonde with innocent green eyes, but she was nowhere near Ashley's league. They'd never met, but Ashley had seen photographs of Whitney in an album she'd found in the trash.

Then it hit her. The mutt. Ryan's ex had demanded the dog. "She's crazy about her Golden retriever."

"That's the key," Preston assured her with a confident smile. "Use the dog as leverage."

CHAPTER FIVE

Adam sat across the desk from Jerold "Jerry" Tobin, his uncle's attorney and executor of Calvin Hunter's estate. The portly, balding lawyer leaned back in his swivel chair, steepled his fingers across his chest and shook his head.

"I'm afraid Calvin's left us with a mess. Probate could take a year at least — maybe longer."

How convenient. Tobin would rack up a huge bill. Judging by the pictures lining the wall, the lawyer spent countless hours on the golf course. What better way to pay for expensive greens fees than a complicated probate?

"There may not be a lot left for you to inherit," the lawyer told him. "It's hard to tell at this point just what Calvin had and what he owes. I've brought in a forensic accountant to go over your uncle's files."

"Is there any problem with me staying in

the house?"

"No. We're paying the woman in the caretaker's cottage to look after the place and take care of the dog. I forget her name —"

"Whitney Marshall." Adam wasn't about to forget her name — or the way she'd felt beneath him last night when he'd mistaken her for a burglar. Honest to God. What *had* he been thinking? He'd pawed her like some horny teenager in the back of a car.

This morning, when her ex-husband had been shaking her, Whitney had seemed vulnerable — nothing like the spitfire who'd kicked and bitten him. What kind of a prick got rough like that? It was none of his business, he reminded himself. But his mind kept drifting to her all morning.

"I could terminate the woman —"

"No. Don't do that." He didn't want to add to Whitney's problems. It appeared that she had enough to deal with right now. Besides, he owed her big-time for the way he'd behaved last night. "I'll just be there until I can find a place of my own."

"All right. We'll leave the arrangement as is."

"Did my uncle have any business partners?" Adam asked. He didn't add that one of them might have wanted Calvin

Hunter dead.

"No. Not that I knew about." The lawyer studied him a moment, a calculating gleam in his eyes. "I don't suppose there's any reason why you can't see your uncle's file. You're going to inherit all his assets and liabilities."

"Liabilities?"

"I just warned you about Calvin's finances," the attorney reminded him. "Since your uncle held several properties in joint tenancy with you —"

"Wait a minute. What are you talking about? I don't own anything with my uncle."

Tobin leaned back in his chair and stared wordlessly at him for a moment. "Didn't your father or uncle tell you?"

"Tell me what?"

"When you were a minor, your uncle signed over half the house in Torrey Pines as well as two buildings in San Diego to you. They're held in rather complicated corporations. Your father came to this office when I prepared the documents and signed them for you since you were underage."

"He never told me a thing."

For a moment Adam was shocked, then he realized what his father had been thinking. He hadn't wanted Adam to rely on someone else's money. He'd always pointed out how rich kids got into trouble and never made anything of themselves.

Uncle Calvin had tried to pay for his education when Adam had transferred from the University of San Diego to the John Jay College of Criminal Justice in New York City. Adam had refused the offer. It wasn't just his pride; his uncle hadn't been around much. He barely knew the man.

Now that he thought about it, Calvin Hunter had been proud of Adam in his own way. He'd flown to New York from God-only-knew-where in Europe when Adam graduated at the top of his class at John Jay. He'd taken them out to dinner at some swank restaurant in Manhattan. Then, as usual, Calvin Hunter had flown out of their lives.

It had been another five years before he'd heard from Calvin again. When Adam was promoted to detective, Uncle Calvin called to congratulate him. His swift promotion had been the result of hard work, but the degree from one of the most prestigious criminal justice colleges hadn't hurt. Uncle Calvin had reminded him of this fact when he'd called. It was almost as if going to John Jay had been his uncle's idea.

"I can't say for sure how bad things are until the forensic accountant conducts an audit, but you may be responsible for any outstanding debts against the property you owned jointly with your uncle."

Great. Just what he needed — more bills. Being deployed overseas didn't stop car payments or the bills he'd inherited from his father. "What about the villa on Siros and the Citation?"

"Both were leased and your uncle was behind in the payments. Same with his house here. When he died, I brought the house payments up to date. It's a valuable asset. I didn't want to risk foreclosure."

"I was under the impression my uncle was wealthy." Adam didn't really know or care about his uncle's money, but his father had always said Calvin had made numerous investments, and they'd brought him a lot of money.

"That's what I thought, too. I worked with your uncle for years. He had a great many valuable assets." The attorney spread his pudgy hands wide, palms up. "This . . . cash flow problem seems to be a recent development."

"What did he do with all his money?"

"Hard to say. We'll know more when the accountant goes over everything." The attorney shuffled through some papers on his desk before adding, "Do you know anyone that your uncle would have given three thousand dollars in cash on the fifth of every month?"

"No. I have no idea." Adam thought a moment. "Maybe he used the cash himself."

"I don't think so. He withdrew cash periodically from ATMs during the month, and he charged a lot to his American Express card. This monthly withdrawal has been going on for over a year."

"There are plenty of people — gardeners, pool cleaners, car-detailing services — who want cash so they don't have to report it to the government."

"True, but I've accounted for those employees. I'm thinking he was giving out a lump sum each month . . . for some reason."

Adam shifted in his chair. "Are you thinking blackmail?"

"No, no, no," the attorney responded just a bit too quickly. "I'm sure there's a reasonable explanation. The forensic accountant may turn up the answer."

Adam's next stop was the coroner's office. He knew the assistant coroner, Samantha Waterson, from his time on the San Diego police force. The woman didn't miss much. She handled most of the autopsies for the coroner even though he signed all the death certificates.

"Hey, Adam. It's great to see you," Samantha greeted him. The redhead had a smile that dominated her face and almost made you overlook the spray of freckles across her nose and the smallish brown eyes magnified by round tortoiseshell glasses. "How long's it been?"

"Over two years." He'd last seen Samantha at his farewell party the night before he shipped out.

"So how was Iraq?"

He shrugged. No sense depressing people with the truth. His National Guard unit had been sent over for what was supposed to be two years. Their stay was extended for another eight months. Even after he'd nearly been killed, Adam had been stuck at a desk job until his tour was over.

"I stopped in to discuss the autopsy you did on my uncle."

"I received your message from Iraq about Calvin Hunter. I made sure I performed the autopsy myself."

"The cause of death is listed as a massive coronary."

"That's right. His heart was in really bad shape. Don't worry, though. He didn't suffer. He died instantly."

"Is there a medication or a poison or

something that could cause such a heart attack?"

"Is that why your e-mail requested a full toxicology report?"

He decided to level with Samantha. When he'd been on the force, she'd always helped him. Aw, hell. She'd autopsied his cases first whenever he'd asked. "I saw my uncle in Greece about two months ago. He was worried that someone might kill him."

"Wow! Why?"

"He refused to say. He thought I'd be in danger if I knew too much. Then seven weeks later he keels over of a heart attack. It makes me suspicious."

The more he thought about his uncle's warning, the more sense it made. In his own way Calvin Hunter had cared about him. Maybe as he aged, he missed having children and had tried to make up for it by giving Adam part of his holdings. And warning him about the danger.

Samantha swiveled in her chair and studied the plaques and awards lining her office wall for a moment. "I assume you read the police report."

"I did." He didn't add that a buddy on the force had faxed him the info while he was still in Iraq.

Samantha nodded thoughtfully. "An unidentified female phoned 911 and said your uncle was having a heart attack. Paramedics arrived within minutes but no one was around. They assumed someone had been passing by."

Adam took a deep breath. "My uncle was dead."

"The 911 record says the call came from your uncle's telephone."

Adam nodded, wondering who the mysterious woman could have been. "Someone was in the house with him — then disappeared. He keeled over in his office upstairs. It's impossible for a passerby to see into that room. The whole place is set too far back from the street for someone to merely be passing by and notice anything."

"Your uncle definitely died of a massive coronary," Samantha assured him. "But was it induced or natural? From what I could tell, it appeared to be natural. It'll take four to six weeks to get the tox screens back, so I won't be positive until then. They went out two weeks ago, so it'll be at least another two weeks before I have anything to tell you."

He knew toxicology reports were processed at the Fulmer Center in Santa Barbara. They performed toxicology reports for most of Southern California's municipalities except Los Angeles, which was large enough to have its own lab.

Adam thanked her and left, his mind on his uncle. Calvin Hunter hadn't outwardly shown how much he'd cared — at least not in a way a growing boy would notice — but his uncle had tried to help. Now it was his turn.

He had no intention of sitting on his ass and waiting. His gut instinct said Calvin Hunter had been murdered — just as his uncle had feared. Adam had given his word he would investigate. Nothing was stopping him. He planned to see just what his uncle had been involved in financially. That might lead him to the killer.

"This is your office," Tyler Foley told Adam.

"Great view," Adam responded, still in shock. Just before he'd left for Iraq, he and Tyler had barely scraped together enough money for a rat hole of an office in a run-down warehouse that had been converted to a warren of bleak little cubes.

Tyler grinned, the same ingratiating smile that had assured him the "good cop" role when he'd worked homicide with Adam. "I guess you didn't believe my e-mails. I told you HiTech Security was going gangbusters."

"I received your messages." Adam could have said the e-mails had been the highlight of his existence, but one thing he'd already learned was that people didn't have a clue about how bad things were in Iraq. Death or boredom were constant companions, depending on where you were at any given moment. A message from home was heaven-sent. Tyler's brief accounts of the progress of their fledgling company had sent his spirits soaring. It propelled him out of the hellish confines of the present into the limit-less possibilities of the future.

"Why don't I review our accounts' files so that I get up to speed," suggested Adam.

A beat of silence, then Tyler said, "I'll have Sherry teach you how to access the accounts on the computer."

Adam glanced down at the chrome-and-glass desk that was pushed up against the window of his new office. A large flat-screen monitor dominated the space. Beside it was a keyboard and a telephone with buttons for several extensions.

"You've gone paperless?" he asked Tyler.

"Just about. It's the wave of the future. Everything's on a disc these days. You'll learn —"

"Not a problem," he assured Tyler. "I had a lot of downtime in Baghdad. One of the guys was a computer guru in his real life. He taught me a lot."

Tyler cracked a laugh that might have sounded a bit forced; Adam wasn't sure. "You're probably ahead of me. Sherry handles everything. She knows where all the bodies are buried around here."

Tyler left Adam to "make himself at home" in his new office. Adam sat at the desk and gazed out at the Pacific. The water was calm now and appeared to be a glistening sheet of stainless steel. He felt like a third wheel. Obviously, Tyler had done exceedingly well without him.

Where did he fit in now?

Did he fit in at all? Anywhere?

Well, he might be able to help grow the business even more. A receptionist, two women in the office. They could hire more people and expand, once they decided which direction to go in.

When Adam and Tyler had both tired of detective work that was usually drug-related, they'd decided to launch their own private-investigation company. They'd set up shop, seeing corporate security as an emerging field.

Then Adam's unit had been called to duty. Obviously, the company had taken off in another direction. Adam had been able to tell a little about this from Tyler's e-mails.

Adam surfed through the account files for the better part of an hour. The company seemed to be very successful. The receivables were up to date, showing how financially healthy the company was, but it wasn't involved in corporate security, the way they'd intended when they'd formed HiTech.

Adam rose and walked out of his office, heading down the hall to Tyler's office.

"Mr. Foley's with a client," called Sherry.

"Please let Tyler know I need to speak with him."

Adam nodded to the brunette and returned to his office. He had the vague impression she didn't approve of him. Who could blame her? His hair was in desperate need of a cut and his clothes were barely passable. He'd spent the earlier part of the morning, after his encounter with Whitney's ex, sorting through the stuff he'd hastily put into a storage unit before shipping out. Most of it had mildewed during this overseas deployment and wasn't even fit for Goodwill.

When it came right down to it, nothing much was left of his previous life. He needed to start over — with a fresh attitude. After all, by some miracle, his life had been spared. He should make the most of this second chance. As soon as he spoke with Tyler about the company's direction, Adam was going shopping.

With nothing better to do, he Googled the articles written about his uncle's death. The few lines recounting Calvin Hunter's career in the navy were eclipsed by his win at the Frankfurt International Dog Show with Jasper. Not one of the articles mentioned a 911 call made from Calvin's home by a woman who'd fled the scene before help arrived.

That mystery followed by a robbery during which the thieves had ignored priceless antiques, but had stolen his uncle's computer and discs, disturbed Adam. What could be on his uncle's computer? Expense reports, no doubt. His uncle must have claimed judging shows was his business and probably wrote off many questionable expenses, like a Citation and a villa in the Greek Isles.

Calvin Hunter had been in financial trouble, according to his attorney. Adam needed to find out just what caused the problem and the extent of the difficulty. If his uncle had been murdered as Adam suspected, the trail might begin with his finances. From his work as a homicide detective, Adam knew most murders were crimes of passion or the result of disputes over money. Judging from what Adam had seen of his uncle's home, no woman had been sharing it with him. The money trail was the place to start.

Adam stood in his office, his fists rammed into the back pockets of his well-worn Dockers, staring out at the sea in the distance. He was just as glad his uncle hadn't left him a lot of money — just buildings with debts. When all was said and done, he wanted to know he'd built his own business. It was all about pride, he decided.

His father had been the same way. Matthew Hunter had been a building contractor. When he'd unexpectedly keeled over from a heart attack, the small savings Adam had accumulated had gone toward finishing his father's last job. It hadn't been enough, and Adam had been forced to take out a loan to complete the project and protect his father's good name.

Adam's thoughts strayed from memories of his father to Whitney Marshall. He'd been dating a woman when he'd left for Iraq. He'd told Holly that it was over before he went, and she'd quickly replaced him. He'd thought returning might trigger old feelings, but it hadn't. Instead he kept seeing Whitney's deep green eyes and tousled blond hair. He pushed brain Pause and rewound his thoughts to last night. He could feel Whitney beneath him. So soft. So sexy.

So . . . right.

Whitney was gorgeous, and he'd wanted to tell her so, but thought better of it. How could any man in his right mind be so attracted to someone he'd thought was a burglar? Of course, Adam might not be in his right mind. He'd been changed in ways he was still discovering.

"Hey, Adam." Tyler interrupted his thoughts. "You wanted to see me."

Adam slowly turned away from the view and tried for a smile. "Yeah, I was looking over the accounts. Seems like we're into private guard services big-time."

"Look, you've been out of touch. There's been an explosion of gated communities around here. Providing gate ambassadors —"

"Ambassadors?"

"It's a fancy term everyone uses for guards. No one wants to say guards. That implies crime. So everyone goes with ambassadors." Tyler chuckled. "It's a no-brainer, and it's our bread and butter."

Adam detected more than a hint of defensiveness in his friend's tone. He hadn't intended to make him anxious. "You've really built the business while I was gone." Adam didn't remind Tyler that most of the money to start HiTech had been his. Tyler had put up very little cash, but he had done all the work when Adam's unit was sent to Iraq. "I just thought we'd agreed to go into corporate security."

"I know, but that's a tough nut to crack." His tone was accommodating, more like the Tyler that Adam had known before leaving. "Corporate security takes a lot of computer geeks and expensive equipment. I don't think we should head in that direction yet."

"I'm not second-guessing you," Adam assured him. "I'm just getting a feel for what's happening. You've done a helluva job."

Tyler rewarded him with one of his trademark smiles, but Adam couldn't help wondering what his friend was thinking. Adam knew he'd changed a lot in the last two and a half years. Apparently, Tyler was different as well. Were they going to be close friends again? Would they be able to work together?

Hell, he hoped so. During his time overseas, Tyler had been like a lifeline. He'd e-mailed Adam at least once a week. True, most of his messages had been about the company — very little personal stuff — but they'd meant a lot to Adam. Without many relatives and not having many close friends, Adam had counted on Tyler's moral support.

"Look . . ." Tyler shuffled over to the window, looked out at the view for a moment, then continued, "About Holly. We didn't mean . . . for anything to happen. It just did."

"No problem," Adam replied, and he meant it. Okay, maybe some small part of him had wanted Holly to wait and give their relationship a chance. But almost three years was a long time, especially since he'd given her the big kiss-off just before he'd left. Hell, most of the married guys in Iraq had problems making their marriages work long-distance. He'd been right to end the relationship when he had.

"You'll hook up with someone new," Tyler assured him. "You always were the one the women went after."

Adam couldn't help thinking about Whitney. He knew damn well she wouldn't agree with Tyler. He'd frightened the wits out of her. Worse, she had an ex who was still in the picture.

Aw, hell. No one had ever accused him of being sensible. Something about Whitney sent his brain into a tailspin. He found her really sexy. And he'd spent so much time without a woman that he needed sex in the worst way — yet something inside him was desperate for so much more than a quickie.

What did he want? Seeing death so often — so close — made him value life. He wanted a family, and that meant kids . . . and a wife. He needed a woman, someone special to share things with, someone to discuss important things with — someone special. He kept thinking about Whitney. She might not be that person, but it wouldn't hurt to investigate.

He smiled inwardly. Hell, he was good at investigating.

CHAPTER SIX

Ryan Fordham stared out at the bay just beyond Peohe's restaurant. A Coast Guard cutter slogged its way out to sea while yachts whizzed by, their sails amber in the light of the setting sun. Beside him, Ashley chatted about the house she longed to possess. He didn't have the heart to tell her that he'd already contacted the broker and had withdrawn their bid. What choice did he have? Until Whitney signed the documents and he had full control of their property, he was precariously low on funds.

Almost totally broke, he grudgingly admitted to himself.

What money he had managed to raise must go into his new practice and toward paying off Domenic Coriz. Just the thought of the big Native American sent a bead of sweat crawling like a centipede down the back of his neck.

Why can't you stop gambling? he asked

himself for the hundredth time.

You can, responded the logical part of his brain, the way it had countless times during the last three years. Over and over, he'd told himself he would never step into a casino again. Each time he broke his promise.

Gambling was an addiction, he reminded himself, and it was just as powerful as being hooked on cocaine or alcohol. Maybe more so. Winning gave him a high that he couldn't achieve even with the hottest, kinkiest sex. Losing was a total downer, but the high's promise was enough to lure him back to the tables again and again.

"What?" he asked, realizing Ashley had said something. "My mind wandered."

Ashley studied him for a moment, then repeated, "I said I picked up papers to file for my resale license. I need to put down the name of my business. I can't decide between Ashley's Interiors or Ashley's Designs."

" 'Designs,' " he said emphatically. " 'Interiors' limits you to decorating. With 'designs' you can branch off into other things, like art or clothing. With your talent, you can do almost anything."

Ashley rewarded him with her winning smile. It was accompanied by an adorable mischievous glint that fired her blue eyes. That captivating expression had instantly won his heart the minute he'd introduced himself to her on his first visit to the cosmetic surgery group he'd later joined. Until he'd met Ashley, Ryan hadn't believed in love at first sight. Now he was convinced.

Ryan had thought he'd loved Whitney, but he'd been mistaken. What he'd felt for his ex-wife had been a certain fondness magnified by sexual attraction. But it was so much . . . less than the heartfelt emotion Ashley evoked.

"You're right," Ashley told him. "Ashley's Designs it is. I'm going to start with a small office in the house."

"Good." He didn't mention that he didn't have the capital to bankroll even the most modest business. Damn Whitney. The bitch had already agreed to the settlement. Why did she have to pick now — of all times — to become uncharacteristically stubborn?

"Dr. Fordham?" Their waiter interrupted his thoughts. "A man in the bar needs to see you."

"Have him join us," Ashley responded.

"Don't bother." Ryan stood, a little unnerved. Who knew they were here? It had been a spur-of-the-moment decision to enjoy the sunset over the bay. "We don't want our romantic dinner interrupted. Do we?"

Without waiting for an answer, Ryan followed the waiter, his apprehensive feeling intensifying. Had someone been following him? Was that how he knew they were here?

What now? His new partners were pressing him to line up financing for his portion of the long-term lease on the state-of-the-art cosmetic surgery facility. He was several payments behind on his first and second mortgage and on the home equity line of credit he'd taken out when real estate skyrocketed last year. Home sales had since flattened, yet bills kept marching across his desk with frightening regularity. But nothing could beat the pressure he was getting from Coriz.

The waiter led him into the bar area. It was jammed with twenty-something Gen-Xers trying to hook up. Ryan spotted a lone man in the far corner. He looked like a guy from the wrestling channel attempting to pass for normal in street clothes.

One of Coriz's men. Christ! They *had* been following him. The goon stepped forward as Ryan shouldered his way toward him, and the waiter melded into the crowd.

"Fordham."

The single word was low, gruff and

wouldn't be noticed by the people standing around like cigars jammed into a box. Still, the menacing tone cut right through Ryan like one of the lasers he used on his patients.

He forced himself to employ his most arrogant voice. "Do I know you?"

"Naw." The creep shrugged and emphasized powerful shoulders beneath his Tommy Bahama shirt. "I'm one of Dom's guys."

Dom. Only Domenic Coriz's closest associates called him "Dom."

"Dom wants a progress report. Did your ex sign the papers?"

"Not yet, but she will," Ryan assured him, though he had his doubts about how soon he could expect to see signed documents.

"Dom don't want no fuckin' lawyers involved."

For a second Ryan's knees wobbled. How could they know Whitney planned to consult Broderick Babcock? They must be eavesdropping on him with some sophisticated device as well as following him. Those cocksuckers!

Ryan drew himself up to take full advantage of his height. Dom's man might be muscle-bound but Ryan had a good six inches on him at least. "You tell Dom that I'll take care of my ex."

The goon studied Ryan with dark eyes as if he were inspecting some alien species, then his lips curled into a smirk. "Remember this is time . . . s-sensitive."

The way he'd stumbled over the word told Ryan the man had never used it before. Dom must have told him what to say. Not that "time sensitive" had appeared to be in the Native American's vocabulary either. He'd probably heard the term from his fish-faced attorney.

"I'm well aware of the time factor involved."

Dom's man edged forward and for an instant Ryan thought he didn't understand what *factor* meant. Quick as a snake, a meat hook of a hand whipped out and grabbed Ryan by the balls. One deft twist of the man's wrist and Ryan had to bite the inside of his cheek to control a scream of unimaginable pain. Despite his efforts, a choked grunt escaped his lips. No one in the noisy bar noticed.

The man released Ryan's gonads, saying, "Dom always gets what he wants."

Without waiting for a reply, the cocky prick muscled his way through the crowd and vanished. Ryan didn't need the threat spelled out. *Deliver or you're dead.*

It took several minutes for the pain in his

groin to ease enough to move. Both hands in front of him to protect his balls, Ryan wended his way out of the crush of kids hustling each other. He walked haltingly, each step bringing another stab of pain. He stopped and stood at the edge of the crowd for a moment, waiting until the ache subsided. He didn't want to hobble back to the table and face Ashley's questions.

He'd managed to keep his gambling a secret from Whitney. She'd thought his late night forays had been to the hospital. It had worked during his two residencies, but that excuse no longer held water. Cosmetic surgeons didn't go to the hospital at night unless there was an emergency. And having worked for a group of cosmetic surgeons, Ashley would know this.

He couldn't fool her. Just as well, he decided. He'd sworn off gambling. Still, the pull was there. A sense of inevitability seeped through him like a powerful narcotic. If only he could score big — the way he had in the past — his problems would be solved.

Remember. Dom always gets what he wants. Ryan knew he had no choice but to deliver.

It was already dark when Whitney returned to the cottage. After her confrontation with

Ryan, she'd been playing catch-up all day. In addition to Da Vinci, Whitney now had Maddie, a fluffy white bichon frise, while her owner traveled to a gala in New York City.

She hoisted Da Vinci out of the carrier strapped to her back. "You're spoiled silly. I'm going to have a bad back from carrying you around all day."

Da Vinci scampered after Maddie, intent on chasing her and not caring one bit about Whitney's aching back. Oh, well. Being a pet concierge brought in the money she needed, but who promised it would be easy?

Lexi licked her hand and Whitney took time to pet her retriever. The dog seemed eerily in tune with her. When Whitney had been despondent over Ryan's betrayal, Lexi had never left her side. Whitney could see what a help Lexi was going to be in her new venture. She had a calming effect on other dogs because she obeyed and didn't get excited over little things like unexpected noises or other pets.

A sharp knock on the front door stopped Whitney halfway to the kitchen to prepare two special diets and scoop a bowl of kibble for Lexi. Da Vinci went into a frenzy of sharp yips and Maddie joined in, dancing a jig on her hind legs.

"No. Bad," she scolded them. "Quiet."

It must be Ryan, she decided. The man just never knew when to give up. Once she'd thought it was an admirable quality. Now she'd been exposed to the dark side of his behavior. Trish might be right about needing a restraining order. Her anger at Ryan put steel in her spine, and she swung open the front door, saying, "Get out of here or I'll call the police."

The dark figure was backlit by the dim porch light. All she could make out for a moment was a tall, broad-shouldered silhouette. Too tall, too big for Ryan.

"I hope I'm not interrupting your dinner, Whitney."

She instantly recognized Adam Hunter's voice. He unnerved her in a way no other man ever had, but then, she'd never been attacked before. She reminded herself that he'd helped her this morning. Stay calm; the guy wasn't all bad. "No, I just came home."

He took a step forward, and the light from inside the cottage washed over him. Their brief encounter this morning hadn't prepared her for this clean-shaven man with a fresh haircut. Now he was dressed in crisp tan slacks and a light blue polo shirt that emphasized his dark hair.

His crystalline blue eyes lacked warmth or spark. They seemed vacant, almost haunted. And they bore into her with unwavering intensity. She suddenly remembered Adam had lost his uncle. The death must have upset him the way her mother's death had stricken Whitney.

She took a deep breath and forced a smile. "Thanks for helping me this morning."

"Your ex-husband seemed . . . unreasonably angry."

"He'll get over it."

He gazed at her for a moment in his direct way, and she knew he saw through the lie. Ryan held a grudge like an ayatollah, but she didn't give a hoot. Let him stew.

"I went to see the executor of my uncle's estate. It still isn't settled, but I'm going to stay here until I find an apartment. We want you to continue taking care of Jasper." He snapped his fingers and Jasper appeared out of the shadows. The Chinese crested gazed up at Adam as if he'd hung the moon.

Oh, well. The little dog was an international champion who'd made countless transatlantic flights. Obviously, the altitude had addled what brains the champ had once possessed. Jasper didn't come when she called his name, but he responded to a snap of Adam's fingers.

"What about the relatives who are supposed to take Jasper?"

"That's me. I'm the only relative Uncle Calvin had."

Whitney tried for a sympathetic smile, but it was difficult after last night. She again reminded herself of the incident with Ryan. Adam Hunter wasn't as bad as she'd first believed, but a gentleman would apologize.

"You'll be taking Jasper with you when you find an apartment."

"It depends." He studied the dog at his side for a moment. Jasper had no hair on his body except for his head and feet. Brown and white fur sprouted from his paws and shot out from his ears like a patch of crabgrass. Whitney had always considered the nearly hairless dogs to be a little goofy. Jasper had done nothing to change her mind.

"Depends," she prompted.

"Some apartments don't allow pets," Adam replied, a hollow tone in his voice.

There were plenty that did, she thought. Obviously, Adam didn't care enough about his uncle to give the orphaned dog a good home. It took him down another notch in her estimation.

"Jasper's a champion. Maybe I can locate

a breeder who would like to show him or use him as a stud."

"He's due to be bred in a few days. That breeder might want Jasper, but I promised my uncle that I would look after his dog."

This did *not* make sense. How did he plan to take care of the dog if he rented an apartment that didn't accept pets?

"I'll feed Jasper in the morning," he told Whitney, oblivious to her concern. "If you could walk him once during the day, it'll help. Most nights I won't be home until late. Give me your number and I'll let you know if I'm not going to make it home in time to feed him dinner."

Whitney walked over to the small nook that Miranda had set up as her office and took a business card out of the box that she'd had printed at Speedy Press. She turned to give it to Adam and discovered he'd moved into the center of the room without making a sound. The dogs were hovering around his feet, sniffing.

"This has my cell number and the number here. Try the cell first. I'm usually out taking care of animals."

"Right." He reached into the cluster of dogs and plucked out Jasper. He headed for the door, the little pill of a dog tucked under one arm, then stopped. "I'm sorry about last night. I overreacted."

She couldn't help herself. "Do you always try to rape intruders?"

"Rape?" He snorted. "Is that what you thought?"

"Pardon me if I'm wrong, but when a man tackles me, then has his hands all over my body . . . well, rape does come to mind."

"I don't usually find naked women prowling around in the dark in my house."

"I wasn't naked. I had on my jammies."

"Jammies? Well, call me a dog, but my idea of jammies and yours are worlds apart. You were nearly nude."

"Stop it! I'm tired of people blaming me—" The astonished look on his face stopped her short. She knew she hadn't meant "people." Ryan had been the one she had in mind. He'd always managed to find a way to make anything that went wrong seem like her fault. She expelled an exasperated breath. "Okay, it was a Victoria's Secret nightgown."

They stared at each other for a moment like gunslingers waiting to draw. Whitney reminded herself that she needed a place to live until Miranda returned. *The man might have made an honest mistake. Smile. Show that you can forgive and forget.*

At Whitney's attempt at a smile, he said,

"The house was robbed right after my uncle died. I thought you were a burglar."

"Did they get much?" Whitney had been in the house several times before Miranda left and hadn't noticed any signs of a robbery.

"They cut the burglar alarm wires and took my uncle's computer but left a lot of valuable antiques. When I heard you downstairs, I assumed they'd returned."

"I understand," she said, trying to convince herself that she did. *Remember, he's not Ryan. Adam did help you this morning.*

"I didn't mean to paw you. I was . . . trying to confirm you were a woman. Most robbers are men."

She nodded slowly, not mentioning the erection evident during "his pawing to confirm" maneuvers.

"Anyway, you're perfectly capable of defending yourself," he told her with the suggestion of a smile.

"I am?"

He cocked his head to one side and pointed to the livid red scratch at the base of his neck. It had been hidden by the collar of his shirt. He then showed her the large bandage on his forearm. "You bit me and drew blood."

She stared at the flesh-colored bandage,

clearly remembering the metallic taste of blood. The edges around the bandage were purplish-blue. Evidently a deep bruise surrounded the bite. "You had me outweighed. All I could do was bite."

"And scream," he added with an attempt at a chuckle. "I'm sure the devil heard you all the way down in hell."

She wasn't about to apologize for defending herself, but the adorable way he had of tilting his head slightly while he was talking muted her anger. The whole incident had been a mistake. Not taking it too seriously or making more out of it than necessary seemed to be the best course.

Whitney looked up into his blue eyes — about to say something — then forgot what it was. An electrical current arced between them, and her breathing became uneven. She had the disturbing feeling that Adam was about to kiss her. For a moment, she was almost dizzy with anticipation.

"When my uncle had the fatal heart attack, a woman called 911. Was that you?"

Her brain scrambled to get a grip on the question. All she could think about was what it would be like to be held in his powerful arms. "Me? No. I wasn't living here. My cousin, Miranda Marshall, had this cottage until two days ago."

"Did she mention calling the paramedics?"

Whitney shook her head, still trying to keep her emotions from showing. "No. Miranda told me about it, but she wasn't home. She stayed with her boyfriend at night. They're off in Fiji now on a honeymoon."

He reached out and lightly touched her cheek with one finger. Their eyes held and she forced herself to remain steady even though a swarm of butterflies was fluttering through her tummy.

"Sorry about last night. Friends?"

She mustered the strength to nod, but it was difficult. Heat seemed to suffuse her entire body.

He left without another word. For a long moment she stood there, then remembered to lock the door.

CHAPTER SEVEN

Tyler guided Holly out of Croce's. Even though it was half past two and the club had announced the last call over thirty minutes ago, people were still hanging around. The club was dedicated to the memory of the creator of "Bad, Bad Leroy Brown," Jim Croce. It was located in one of the renovated Victorian-style commercial buildings in the historic Gaslamp Quarter. There were hundreds of clubs, restaurants and galleries in the area. Croce's had been among the first to open in the seventies when the city began pumping life back into the decaying area. It was still one of the most popular clubs.

"Adam came into the office today," Tyler said as they walked back to his condo along streets lit by authentic gas lamps.

"Really?" Holly responded, in a tone he couldn't quite read. "How is he?"

Someone who didn't know Holly might

not realize she had been crazy about Adam Hunter. Tyler had always assumed he was Adam's best friend, but Adam hadn't confided his reason for splitting with Holly.

Tyler had waited two agonizingly long months after Adam had left for Iraq before asking Holly out. He'd taken it slow and easy, giving her plenty of space to get over Adam. Tyler's strategy had worked. Holly was practically living with him now. She kept a small walk-up on Coronado Island near her boutique, but she spent most nights at the condo Tyler had purchased in the Marina District that bordered the Gaslamp Quarter.

"Adam seems okay physically, but he's . . . different."

"Different?"

Now Holly sounded interested. He glanced at her, but the wavering shadows from the gas lamps and her long brown hair concealed her face. Maybe it was just his imagination. Anyone would be concerned about a friend who'd nearly been killed.

"Adam's quieter. Doesn't joke anymore." Tyler thought about the way Adam had behaved during lunch. "He's pretty intense."

"Are you going to be able to work with him?" she asked.

Now her concern seemed to be for him,

and Tyler kept his smile to himself. "Good question. Adam's still hot to go into corporate security."

Holly didn't comment. They walked in silence to the end of the block, where the historical area merged with the Marina District. Here eye-catching skyscrapers and luxurious condos captured the view of the bay. The area had a number of hotels, but it was also the trendy place to live downtown.

Tyler had sunk all the money he'd made from HiTech Security into his new place. After years on the police force, when he'd been barely able to make his monthly rent payment, it felt awesome to have a brand-new home overlooking the harbor. He'd let Holly decorate it, and she'd done an amazing job.

It was sleek and modern, furnished in stainless steel and beige leather several shades darker than the walls. It was masculine yet had enough touches of softness for a woman to be comfortable. After all, he planned to live here once he and Holly were married. Later, when they had children, he supposed they would buy a home in the suburbs. Their kids would need space to play. By then HiTech would be going great guns — even more stable and successful than it already was — and he would be able to afford anyplace Holly wanted.

"Did you explain to Adam that it's too expensive to go into corporate security?" Holly asked.

"Yeah. We talked about it." Their discussion over lunch had been strained. Tyler wasn't sure if it was the direction the company had taken or Adam himself that had made their conversation tense. "Adam's going to check into it and see exactly what it'll take."

"Then he'll realize, the way you did, that HiTech will be more profitable providing guard services."

"Probably," Tyler said, although he didn't necessarily agree. "Adam's pretty hung up about his uncle's death."

"I didn't think they were close."

Adam must have told her, Tyler decided, the back of his neck tightening. "They weren't really close, but —"

"Adam feels responsible. That's the kind of guy he is."

"I guess."

Like most women, Holly had a lot of emotional insight. Adam had probably cut off his relationship with her in case he was killed in Iraq. Holly must have figured this out. When he'd been with Adam today, Tyler had glossed over his relationship with

Holly. A year and a half ago, he'd e-mailed Adam that he was seeing Holly. He'd never mentioned her again even though he e-mailed Adam on a weekly basis. Today, he might have made a mistake by not letting Adam know how much Holly meant to him. He wondered if Adam would contact her.

The phone on his hip vibrated, and he stopped. At this hour it could only be the watch commander at his guard service. "Yeah?"

"It's Butch. We've got a no-show at Ocean Heights and the backup isn't answering his phone."

"Christ!" Ocean Heights was a ritzy sub-development and one of his most lucrative accounts. Their board insisted on a twenty-four-hour guard at their gate. After midnight residents could have used a remote control to open the gate, the way residents in many other gated communities did — but no, Ocean Heights needed a "gate ambassador" all night long.

Weeknights it was easy to have college kids man the gate because they liked to study when things were slow, but on the weekend, they suddenly became "ill." Problem was he didn't have enough backups. If someone didn't show, he was in trouble.

He was forced to tell Butch, "I'll take it."

He flipped the phone shut and turned to Holly. "I've gotta go, babe. One of the guards didn't come in, and we can't leave the gate at Ocean Heights uncovered."

"Can't you hire more backup guys?"

She sounded a little peeved. He couldn't blame her. This was the third Saturday night that he'd skipped out on her. "It's hard to find guys willing to be on standby all weekend, not knowing if they're going to get called."

"What if you paid them to wait around?"

Sometimes Holly was *way* too insightful. To make more money, Tyler kept guys on standby, but didn't pay them unless they worked. "I may have to do that or go to a sub-par list."

"What's that?"

"Hire guys who can't pass a background check." If a man had an arrest record for even a minor crime like petty theft or a DUI, he couldn't pass the check. Gated communities were suspicious of anyone with any type of a criminal record. "Wait at my place until I get off."

Holly shook her head. "I'm going home. The boutique's big sale starts tomorrow."

"Okay." He'd be dead tired anyway. The shift wouldn't be over until seven. He'd need to crash for a few hours, then head into the office. "I'll call you tomorrow afternoon and see how the sale is going."

She was silent while he walked her to her Passat. Sometimes it was hard to tell what Holly was thinking. She wasn't as open with him as his previous girlfriends. The slight air of mystery added to her appeal.

She drove off, and he stood there for a moment, thinking. He hadn't asked Holly to marry him, but they discussed the future as if they intended to spend it together. Now Tyler had the vague feeling that he knew too little about Holly's actual plans.

He drove to Ocean Heights and called Butch on his cell phone. Butch was a beefy Irishman who would develop a Sumo stomach if he didn't spend his days in the gym.

"I'm sick of this shit," Tyler told him.

"I hear you, man."

"Know of any guys who might be a little shaky on a background check but are actually okay to work standby for us? I'll pay them to be on call."

Butch said he would check at his gym. Tyler hung up and drove around the bend to the mammoth wrought-iron gate at the entrance to Ocean Heights. Beyond the guard kiosk that would have been home to several families in a third world country were brand-new Tuscan-style mansions built on lots the size of a cocktail napkin. The guard on duty was pissed because he'd had to work over an hour beyond his shift.

Tyler settled in, put his feet up and wished he had thought to pick up a magazine. Nothing was more boring than the graveyard shift. His cell phone buzzed. "What the hell," he said out loud. It was almost three-thirty in the morning. He checked the caller ID. Oh, fuck! His father.

Quinten Foley had been a commander in the navy. They'd lived all over the world until his father retired. His father had prodded Tyler to enlist, but Tyler joined the police force instead. He was a major disappointment to his father. Quinten Foley never mentioned it, but Tyler couldn't shake the feeling.

He hadn't heard from the old man in months. A call now must mean bad news — his father only checked in a few times a year and never in the middle of the night. This wouldn't be about his family. Tyler was an only child. His mother had committed suicide when Tyler was in high school. There wasn't anyone else except distant relatives somewhere in New England.

Tyler forced himself to keep his voice upbeat. "You're back in town."

"No. I'm on the Gulfstream, heading in."

His father worked as a consultant for weapons manufacturers and helped smaller countries decide what to buy, then expedited those purchases. He often supplied soldiers of fortune with the latest weaponry. His clients had to be extremely wealthy to afford his services. He never failed to let Tyler know he was in a limo or on a fancy jet. It was just another way of reminding Tyler that his own father was out of his league.

"Did I wake you?"

"Nah. Holly and I were out late hitting the clubs." No way was he going to confess to his father he was sitting on his ass in a guard shack.

"Meet me for breakfast at eight at the Outpost." It wasn't a request. It was an order to appear at a trendy restaurant frequented by retired naval officers on their way to the golf course.

"What's going on?"

"We need to discuss something."

Tyler knew that was all he was going to get out of his father until they were face-to-face. Years of working in naval intelligence and weapons had made him frickin' paranoid about what he said over a cell phone. Tyler seriously doubted any spies were monitoring his father's calls but the old man always acted as if his every word, every move was being scrutinized by "foreign operatives."

Tyler hung up and stared out into the darkness. Quinten Foley was rarely interested in his opinion. Could his father want to talk about his will? The old man was in his early fifties, an appropriate time to consider discussing his future with his only child.

Tyler convinced the morning-shift guard to come in an hour early so he could get home, shower and shave before meeting his father. His old man treated him with a little more respect now that he'd been able to purchase a condo.

His father probably wanted to discuss his wishes should he become ill as well as his finances. Tyler couldn't bank a smile. Quinten Foley seemed immortal, but, of course, no one was. Tyler had no idea how much his father was worth. It didn't matter. He'd suffered enough to deserve every penny he'd inherit.

He drove into the lot of the Shelter Island restaurant. As usual there were several rows of late-model American cars. Buying American had been an unwritten rule for the naval officers of his father's generation. Tyler parked his Beamer next to his father's black

Hummer — not an H2 or H3 model but the original Hummer the military had used.

The Outpost was some decorator's attempt at a hunting lodge. Animal skins were nailed to the log walls in the entry, where a hostess in a safari outfit seated people. One wall of the huge room was a fieldstone fireplace bracketed by tree trunks twenty feet tall. Opposite it a soaring glass wall faced the bay. In the distance the Naval Air Station on Coronado Island glistened in the too-bright morning sun.

This was a great vantage point for the retirees to watch the Navy SEALs train while they ate. His father was already seated at the prime booth by the window. When Quinten gave you a time, he arrived at least ten minutes early himself.

"How was your trip?" Tyler asked as he slid into the booth opposite his father.

"Same old, same old."

Tall and erect, Quinten Foley had a military bearing that was impossible to miss even in golf clothes. His square jaw told the world he was accustomed to his orders being obeyed. His slate-blue eyes could level a man at fifty paces. His full head of black hair had turned silver, but it only added to his commanding presence.

"I ordered huevos rancheros for you. I

know how much you like them."

Tyler didn't even attempt a smile. He'd been an eggs Benedict man — until Holly reformed him. He'd never cared for huevos rancheros.

"I have to be on the course at eight-thirty." His father smiled. "Hope all my traveling hasn't screwed up my handicap."

Tyler nodded as if he gave a shit.

"I hear Calvin Hunter died while I was away."

Adam's uncle and his father had both been navy commanders. Calvin had skippered a nuclear sub before moving to some top-secret naval intelligence position on land. The men had been golfing buddies when they both were in San Diego at the same time.

"He died of a heart attack."

"Too bad. Wish I could have returned for the funeral, but I was in Zimbabwe negotiating a deal for a client."

"Adam couldn't get back either," Tyler commented as their waitress poured him a cup of coffee. "He just returned. His uncle left him everything, including a mountain of debt."

His father's ice-blue eyes narrowed. "Calvin didn't have any debt to speak of. He made a lot of money."

"Showing dogs?"

A beat of silence. "No, in real estate."

Tyler thought a moment. "Maybe. They're just sorting through the estate. Adam doesn't know much. He wasn't close to his uncle. In fact, he was blown away that he left him everything."

"Everything?" His father actually looked stunned. The only other time Tyler could remember seeing that expression was when his father had come home to find the MPs, and his wife dead. Tyler had been huddled in the corner with the chaplain, but his father never saw him.

The waitress arrived with a heaping plate of huevos rancheros for Tyler and put scrambled eggs, tomatoes instead of potatoes, in front of his father. To the side was a single slice of toast. The old man wouldn't butter it.

"I was wondering if you could do something for me."

"Sure." Tyler ran his fork through the gooey mess and waited for the "if I should become ill" bit.

"I was in Istanbul last year and ran into Calvin. My laptop was on the fritz. Damn things aren't reliable. I stored some info on Calvin's machine. Now that he's gone, I need to retrieve that file. Could you ask

Adam to let me into Calvin's office? I'd call him myself but I only met him the one time."

How well Tyler remembered that day. They'd graduated from the police academy together. Adam's father was there — so, so proud. He'd been with Adam's uncle Calvin, who'd also been very proud of Adam. Quinten Foley had grudgingly attended, then left before the group went to celebrate at a nearby Mexican restaurant.

"No need to bother Adam," Tyler said, recalling his conversation at lunch with Adam yesterday. "Right after Calvin Hunter died, thieves broke into the house. All they took was his computer and some discs."

"You're lying."

Tyler slammed down his fork, anger building in his gut. His father had insulted him many times over the years but he'd never called him a liar. He shot back, "Why would I lie about a robbery?"

Quinten Foley flinched at Tyler's unexpected outburst. He'd never raised his voice to his father. "Sorry, son. I just can't believe . . ."

"As an ex–police officer, I can tell you that robberies after a death are quite common, especially if the newspapers give the time of the funeral. Criminals know everyone will

125

be at the cemetery and not at the house."

"I see," his father replied, his tone preoccupied.

"The thieves left behind lots of valuable antiques and other things. That means they were after stuff they could sell quickly for drug money. Newer model computers can be sold in minutes on the street."

All the color leached from his father's face. His voice faltered. "R-really?"

"Swear to God." He could have added "hope to die," but he didn't allow himself the pleasure. Until last night he hadn't thought about his father's death. But one day — in the not too distant future — his father would die. Then, like Adam, Tyler would inherit a bundle.

CHAPTER EIGHT

Whitney walked into Trish Bowrather's Ravissant Gallery, Lexi at her side. This morning when she'd picked up Brandy for his walk, Trish had invited Whitney to stop by after her morning rounds to have coffee with her. Trish wanted to chat, and Whitney had a feeling she knew what was on the older woman's mind.

Ryan Fordham.

Whitney hadn't heard from her ex last night. She'd been half expecting another call, but it hadn't come. While she'd been out, FedEx had delivered an express envelope. In it she found the papers Ryan wanted her to sign but no note from him. She read the document; it seemed to be a longer, more legalese version of what she'd signed after arbitration, but she couldn't find the original document. It was probably in one of the boxes she'd yet to unpack.

"Hi," Trish called to Whitney, her hand over the mouthpiece of the telephone. She gestured toward a black lacquer chest that had to be an expensive Chinese antique. On top was a coffee machine and porcelain cups. Cream, sugar and artificial sweetener were beside the coffeemaker.

Whitney unhooked Lexi from her leash. The retriever bounced over to join Brandy, who was perched on a bronze silk harem pillow. It served as his dog bed while matching the studied elegance and sophistication of the gallery. She helped herself to a cup of coffee and added a splash of milk.

The gallery was a commercial version of Trish's own home. Whitney wondered if the same architect had designed both. The matte-white walls displayed enormous abstract oils. One drew Whitney nearer. Whitney shuddered, but couldn't help walking closer and closer.

"Thought provoking, don't you think?" Trish asked.

Whitney practiced her smile. The mammoth painting was mesmerizing. The oil canvas could have doubled as a wall in her small cottage. It was streaked with globs of red and neon-green paint. Off to one side was a large cobalt blue eye that seemed to follow Whitney as she moved. "Who's the artist?"

"Vladimir. He has some long, unpro-nounceable Russian last name, so he just goes by Vladimir. He's one of the most suc-cessful artists in the area."

The eye gave Whitney the willies, but she didn't mention it. This morning when she was loading the dogs in the SUV, she'd looked up to the second-floor window of the main house. For a moment she'd thought the curtains had shifted. Now she imagined Adam Hunter, his intense blue eyes becoming one, staring down at her from behind a razor-wide gap in the drapes. Just like the haunting eye in the painting.

"Aren't you exhausted?" Trish said. "How many dogs have you walked this morning?"

"Eleven. Three were only short walks before drop-offs at their groomers." She fol-lowed Trish across the white marble floor to a sitting area with a black leather sofa and two matching chairs. She lowered herself into one chair, careful not to spill her cof-fee.

Trish sat on the sofa and crossed long legs clad in beige linen slacks. "Have you heard anything more from your ex-husband?"

Whitney shook her head. "No, but he Fed-Exed the papers to me. I don't see any reason I shouldn't sign —"

"Not without having a lawyer examine them."

"Right." Whitney had planned to contact an attorney, but she found Trish's attitude a little overbearing. "Miranda just married a lawyer. I think his firm might check my papers and —" She stopped herself before saying that she planned to ask to be billed later. Trish must have guessed she didn't have much money, but Whitney's pride kept her from letting the woman know just how broke she was.

Trish put down her cup of coffee on the Lucite cube-style coffee table next to the sofa. "Miranda married a local attorney?"

Whitney hesitated a moment, remembering the well-known lawyer didn't want his clients to know he was away on his honeymoon. "It's very hush-hush."

Trish's brow creased into a frown. Whitney didn't see any reason for not telling her. Miranda would be returning soon and would have a splashy reception. Then the whole town would know.

"Miranda married Broderick Babcock."

Trish blinked hard as if trying to clear her vision. "You're kidding."

Whitney shifted in her seat, more than a little uncomfortable discussing Miranda's business. If her cousin had wanted Trish to know, Miranda had had plenty of opportunities to tell her. She shouldn't have told, but something had urged her to confide in Trish.

"Promise me you won't mention this to anyone. Rick doesn't want his clients to know he's out of town."

"I won't say a thing."

Whitney waited for Trish to comment, but the older woman studied Whitney as if she were a painting by a child that had suddenly appeared on a wall in her gallery. Finally, Trish said, "I wanted to talk to you about your ex-husband. Did you file a police report?"

"No. I don't think that's necessary. I'm sure when I sign the papers, I won't ever hear from him again."

"Good. I thought it over and did some surfing on the Net. You know, to check the latest."

Whitney nodded, but she couldn't imagine why the woman was taking such an interest in her. Didn't Trish have a life?

"When I told you to file for a restraining order . . ." Trish let the unfinished sentence hang in a heavy silence. "Well, I was back in the past, when I was living in New York City. I was recalling my own problems."

Trish stood, absentmindedly shook the

creases out of her linen pants, walked across the gallery and stared out the window at the passing traffic. Whitney silently cursed herself for wondering about Trish's motives. She'd guessed correctly. The woman related to her because of something that she had experienced.

Two beats of silence, then Trish turned, saying, "I had an abusive husband."

"I'm sorry." The trite words came out before she could think of something better to say. "What happened?"

Trish returned to her seat, and for a moment Whitney thought she wasn't going to answer. When Trish did respond, every word grew softer until she was almost whispering. "About a year after we were married, Carter slapped me during an argument. Of course, he was upset with himself immediately. He apologized all over the place and claimed to love me more than life itself."

Whitney had heard similar stories in interviews she'd seen on television, but this was different. She knew this abused woman personally. She couldn't help thinking about Ryan. This didn't fit the profile of their relationship at all. Now that she thought back, Ryan had been verbally abusive toward the end of their second year of marriage. But he'd never raised a hand to her until yesterday. He didn't need to; Ryan could devastate her with his sarcastic remarks.

"A few months went by, and we had another fight. This time Carter shoved me into a wall. I had a bruise that ran the length of my back and four broken ribs."

"Oh my God! What did you do?"

"Left him." There was a pensive shimmer in the shadow of Trish's eyes. "I wanted to go home to my parents, but I had too much pride. You see, they hadn't wanted me to marry Carter, but I'd insisted."

Whitney wished her mother were still alive. She would love to know how her mom would feel about Whitney's divorce, but she'd died. The only person she had in this world was Miranda.

Again, she found herself wishing her cousin were here. They could talk — as adults — in a way they'd never been able to discuss things when they'd been in high school. Back then, they were too different — or so it had seemed. Now, Whitney wondered if Miranda's reckless attitude had been her way of dealing with the unexpected death of her parents.

"That's when the stalking began." A short, mirthless laugh followed, taking Whitney by surprise. "Of course, Carter didn't see it as stalking. He kept insisting he was checking on me."

Whitney couldn't imagine Ryan "checking on her." He had another woman in his life. Why would he bother?

"Carter scared off several men who tried to date me and got me fired from a job in a gallery. That's when I finally went to the police," Trish added sourly. "They were reluctant to even take a report."

"How terrible."

"Back then, less was known about stalking and abusive husbands." Trish was silent for a moment; the only sound came from the cars going by on Prospect Street. "Weeks went by and I didn't hear from Carter. I thought the police had told him about the report, and it made him stay away. Wrong. He was still spying on me, but he was getting sneakier. I didn't see him until a man — just an acquaintance — drove me home from work. He walked me to my door. Carter leaped out of the bushes and beat the guy senseless with a baseball bat."

Whitney shuddered at the image of a bloody, battered man sprawled across the cold concrete.

"Then Carter rounded on me. The only thing that saved me was a neighbor who'd heard the commotion and called the police. My jaw was broken as well as my arm."

"My God. What happened to your friend?"

"He survived, but he had to spend months in the hospital and needed three reconstructive surgeries." Trish sank deeper into the sofa with a ragged sigh. "My father sent him money to pay his bills."

"You went home to your parents?"

"Of course, wouldn't you? At that point, I just wanted to get away from Carter before he killed me."

For a moment, Whitney remembered the night she'd thrown her things into the SUV and driven away from the home Ryan had insisted on buying. It had been the day she'd been served with divorce papers, and she'd realized all hope of salvaging her marriage had vanished. She'd spent the night with Lexi in a cheap motel. It would have been nice to chuck her pride and return to loving parents. Instead, she'd found a house-sitting job in the newspaper.

"At least you got away from him."

Trish rested her head against the back of the sofa and gazed up at the stainless-steel ceiling fan silently spinning overhead, just barely stirring the air in the gallery. "Carter followed me to Miami."

"Y-you're kidding," Whitney stammered

in bewilderment. "Wasn't he jailed for assault?"

"The man couldn't identify Carter. The first blow with the baseball bat hit him from behind. The guy didn't see who struck him, and neither did my neighbor who called the cops. Carter ran off when he heard the sirens coming up the street. It was my word against his. The prosecutor was a man. He believed Carter's story that I was a rejected wife out to blame her husband for a mugging. Even the police report I'd filed earlier didn't sway him."

"I can't believe it. What a nightmare."

Trish's gaze met Whitney's. "About a month after I returned home, I drove out of my parents' home in Coral Gables. There was Carter, standing on the sidewalk, staring at our house."

"I'll bet you freaked."

"Of course. I had no way of defending myself. My jaw was wired shut and my arm was in a cast." The recollection seemed to weigh on her, choking the life out of her voice. "Besides, I was stunned that Carter would leave the law firm where he was on track to become a partner to chase me. It made no sense; that's when I knew he was unbalanced. I told my father and he finally convinced the police to issue a restraining order."

"That helped, right?"

"My father wouldn't take any chances. He sent me to Italy until the divorce was final."

Trish stopped there, but Whitney felt there was more to the story. She stood up and went over to the sofa and sat next to Trish. She looked into the older woman's eyes. "That wasn't the end, was it?"

"No. I came home and found Carter had moved to Miami and had taken a job with another law firm," she responded in a low, tormented voice. "He made no attempt to contact me for over six months. I thought, 'Okay, so he lives here. It's a big city. Forget him. Go on with life.'

"Then one evening when my parents were out, I came into the living room and there was Carter aiming a gun at me. He said if he couldn't have me — no one would."

Whitney put her hand on Trish's trembling knee and gave her a reassuring squeeze. "What did you do?"

Stains of scarlet appeared on Trish's cheeks. "Nothing. I froze. All I could think was that I was alone in a huge house with a maniac. I honestly thought I was dead."

"What happened?"

Trish clicked her fingers twice and Brandy bounded over. She threaded her long nails through the soft fur on his ears. "My father's boxer raced into the room, snarling and barking like crazy. It distracted Carter just long enough for me to run out of the house."

"This sounds like a nightmare that just wouldn't end."

Trish nodded. "Exactly. The police came, but Carter was long gone. When they interviewed him, he had an alibi."

"No way."

"He found some guy that was willing to swear they'd spent the evening playing Texas Hold 'Em."

"What did you do?"

"I moved away. With my father's help, I changed my name and got a new start here." A tense silence enveloped the gallery. Trish stopped petting Brandy and the dog settled at her feet. "It worked. Carter's remarried and doesn't bother me anymore."

"You never married again?"

"No. Why put myself through all that? I'm happy, successful. If I need an escort, there are plenty of men available."

The man had ruined Trish's life and left her bitter, distrustful. How sad. Trish had suffered and continued to suffer. Whitney wondered if there was any way to help.

"I didn't mean to make this all about me."

Trish paused, but her melancholy eyes prolonged the moment. "I rarely discuss my past, so please keep what I've said to yourself."

"I will," Whitney quickly assured her.

"I only told you so that you would realize I understand what you're going through."

Whitney wanted to protest that her situation was nothing like what Trish had experienced, but the woman had shared so many deeply personal things that she didn't want to discount those confidences.

"I put the past behind me until you came along, Whitney. I instantly knew I had to help you, and I'm afraid I may have given you bad advice."

"What do you mean?"

"Sometimes a restraining order can be a death warrant. You've heard about women who are killed by their husbands or boyfriends *after* they've obtained a restraining order."

"I've seen it a lot on television. I can't understand why —"

"They say — shrinks say — when the man realizes he's lost power over the woman, he goes nuts. The restraining order represents a higher power. My divorce showed Carter a higher power had taken over, and he couldn't accept it."

"Makes sense." Whitney hadn't given much thought to spousal abuse until the incident yesterday morning. She still doubted Ryan would resort to real physical violence.

Trish leaned closer. "Don't file a police report unless you have bruises they can photograph or a broken bone. Then —"

"I'm sure Ryan would never —"

"Never say never. This is the worst-case scenario. Here's what you do. Keep a journal." Trish rose and walked over to her desk. She took a leather folder the size of a paperback book out of the second drawer and handed it to Whitney. "Write down the time, date and place of each encounter. If there's a witness like there was yesterday, put down the complete name, address and any other contact information."

Whitney thought about Adam Hunter. How much of the argument had he seen and heard? Would he help her if necessary? Granted, she was attracted to Adam — but after hearing Trish's story about an abusive man, Whitney should keep in mind how physical Adam had become on the night they'd met.

CHAPTER NINE

Adam relaxed in the dark living room of his uncle's home, his feet up on a leather ottoman that didn't appear to ever have been used. Now that he thought about it, the whole house seemed more like a model home than a place where anyone had actually lived. The only room here with a "lived-in" look was his uncle's office.

When he'd come in, he hadn't bothered to turn on a single lamp. The only light bled in from the nightscaping outside that artistically illuminated the plants and trees. There was no movement in the house other than the slight whoosh of his own breath and the barely audible hum of the refrigerator in the kitchen nearby.

The night had become his friend, a lesson he'd learned in Iraq. Their enemies avoided darkness, preferring to strike during the light of day. Darkness soothed, took the sharp edge off Iraq's blistering sun. The night welcomed him in a way that daylight did not. Night posed less threats, offered more possibilities.

Allowed him to think.

Daylight hurled distractions at him. In the dark, Adam could concentrate. He mentally reviewed the events of the day. He'd visited the forensic accountant who had been assigned his uncle's case. Adam had been expecting an older man in a staid office. Instead, a punk kid who lived and worked out of a loft in the Marina District had been hired to review his uncle's financial records. Despite Max Deaver's tattoos and gelled hair that shot up like a rooster's comb, Adam liked the accountant and could tell he knew his business.

Deaver had just gotten started on the case, but already described Calvin Hunter's finances as an elaborate shell game. According to Deaver, his uncle had switched his funds back and forth between various Swiss and offshore accounts to other secret accounts. Why? Deaver claimed it was too early to tell exactly what his uncle had hoped to accomplish with these maneuvers.

Click. The faint sound made Adam jerk upright. A key in the back door's lock. Whitney. He stood up and quickly switched on the lamp next to his chair. The amber light revealed Jasper huddling under the nearby coffee table.

"Jasper," Whitney called softly. "Here boy. Are you in there?"

Adam scooped up Jasper and headed toward the kitchen. "He's here. I've got him."

He rounded the corner and found Whitney standing by the oven, wearing shorts that emphasized her tanned, trim legs and a T-shirt that hugged her breasts in a way he found damn sexy. Her cheeks were pink and her mane of blond hair was tousled. Her SUV hadn't been in the carport when he'd arrived home a short time ago. He'd bet she was still out, rushing around, taking care of a pack of dogs.

He could have called to say he would feed Jasper, but he hadn't. His mind refused to turn off. He kept thinking about Whitney all day. He wanted an excuse to see her.

"I didn't realize you were here," Whitney said a little anxiously, as if she was still afraid of him. "Has Jasper eaten?"

Hearing his name, the Chinese crested licked Adam's hand and gazed up at him. *Swell. Get used to it.* For reasons Adam couldn't fathom, the little dog had a thing for him.

"No. I just got in. I haven't fed him. Why

don't you go ahead since you're here? I'm not exactly sure how much to give him. Show me."

"Okay." She opened the walk-in pantry, where a large bag of kibble was kept. Adam noticed there wasn't much else on the shelves. Another sign of a house not really being used. "I didn't have time to walk him. I thought I would take him out after he ate."

"Good idea." He watched her scoop kibble into a silver bowl with Jasper's name engraved on it. She bent over, giving him the opportunity to check out the provocative curve of her cute butt.

"Have you noticed the red bump behind Jasper's ear?" Adam asked, just to keep the conversation going.

"No. Where is it?" She put down the bowl and Adam set the dog on the floor beside it.

Their gazes collided. He resisted the urge to reach out and touch her soft skin. *Take it slow and easy. Let her get to know you.*

He almost laughed at himself. When he'd left San Diego for duty in Iraq, he'd been a hard-charger. He would have come on hot and heavy if he'd been attracted to a woman. So much had changed. *Not really,* he thought. The world was pretty much the same. He was different.

He had more insight now than he'd had

back then. He could sense Whitney's vulnerability. She'd been through a miserable divorce. She wasn't ready for a man to come on too fast.

Jasper sniffed the kibble but showed no signs of being hungry. Unlike the lovable mutts that Adam had been raised with, Jasper didn't seem to care much about food. He spent most of his time sleeping or hiding. He was so shy that it was difficult to imagine the dog prancing around a show ring. But what did he know? The only dog show he'd ever seen had been on television and he hadn't watched the entire program.

Adam reached down and held Jasper by his collar. On the right side beneath the little dog's ear was a red bump half the size of a dime. "See this?"

Whitney leaned over and her luxuriant hair tumbled forward. He caught a whiff of the rain-fresh scent he remembered from when he'd tackled her. His pulse kicked up a notch. *Uh-oh.* He did his damnedest to keep his eyes — and mind — on the dog.

Whitney inspected the raised weltlike bump carefully, then leaned back against the counter. "It looks like something irritated him a little. You know, since Chinese cresteds are almost hairless, they are susceptible to skin irritations that don't bother most dogs. I think we should keep an eye on the bump. If it doesn't get better, we may want to take him to the vet."

"Right. Let's watch it."

She gazed at him steadily without — she hoped — giving away her inner turmoil. She hadn't expected him to be at home in the dark house. *Be careful,* warned an inner voice. *Don't alienate him. Just get away from here.* He'd explained why he'd mistaken her for a burglar, but she still couldn't bring herself to trust him. Maybe it was instinct; maybe it was hearing Trish's story.

"How are your cuts?"

"Not a problem. How's your head?"

She offered him a tentative smile. "I have a little bump. No big deal."

Jasper finally deigned to munch a few bites of kibble. While he was eating, Whitney tried to think of something to say. "Looks like that's all he's going to eat right now. You should see Lexi. She wolfs down everything in two seconds. She's in the backyard now with three other dogs just waiting for dinner."

Adam reached into the pantry and pulled Jasper's leash off its hook. "Jasper's spoiled. Let's walk him."

Say no, Whitney told herself. *Don't be*

*alone with this man any longer than neces-
sary.*

"Let me show you the route Miranda recommends," she heard herself say. "You can let the dogs off the leash and they can run. It goes along the bluff. When it's light you can see the ocean."

Adam followed her, noting that Whitney had taken a small flashlight out of her pocket. She stuffed blue plastic "poop" bags into the back pocket of her shorts.

"There's enough moonlight tonight to see the trail, but I keep the flashlight on and aimed at the ground so the dogs will come right back to me. Canines have an incredible sense of smell, but cats see much better at night."

The footpath started — or ended — at the edge of his uncle's rose garden, depending on how you viewed the trail. Neighbors had obviously hiked along it enough so that the trail was well worn. He wondered if this might have been the way the robbers had come. If so, it could account for why so little had been taken. There was only so much you could carry along this winding path and still get away in a hurry.

The trail was wide enough for two people, and Adam walked beside Whitney. "Have you seen many people up here?"

"A few, but remember, I haven't been here long." Whitney looked up at him, but it was too dark to tell much about her expression. "Miranda showed me the trail and we took Lexi along it for quite a distance. We stopped at the tennis court that you can see from the bottom of the hill. I think the trail goes another mile or so, but I'm not sure. We didn't walk very far. Why?"

"Remember I told you that a woman called 911 the night my uncle died. I don't think she saw or heard him from the street. They might have been walking on the trail."

Whitney remembered Adam asking if Miranda had called the authorities. She stopped and shined her flashlight on the path. "You can see it's well used. Someone might have been out for a walk and heard your uncle call for help or something. Have the police checked on it?"

After a slight pause, Adam told her, "I went to see the investigating officer today. I knew him. Not well, but I knew him from back when I'd been on the police force."

"Really?" She couldn't hide her surprise. "You're a policeman?"

"I was a detective. I worked homicide."

"Interesting" was all she could think to say. How wrong she'd been. She'd mentally categorized him as a hit man or worse.

Something menacing about him still bothered her, but Whitney didn't have time to analyze it.

"The investigating officer didn't think it was unusual that the woman who called 911 disappeared. Apparently, it happens all the time. People just don't want to get involved. Since there were no signs of foul play, they didn't pursue it."

Something in his tone told Whitney that he was suspicious, or maybe just bitter. "Your uncle died of a heart attack?"

"That's what it appears to be. The coroner is running a few more tests. Then we should know for sure."

He seemed preoccupied, but Whitney ventured another question. "You're no longer on the police force?"

He walked a few steps in silence, then said, "No. Too many homicides were drug deals gone sour. I got sick of them. Half the time witnesses were too frightened to talk. When we could nail a suspect, he was back on the street in no time thanks to a screwed-up system and slick lawyers. I started a private security firm with a friend. Then my National Guard unit was called for duty in Iraq."

Iraq. How horrible. Images she'd seen on newscasts and what she'd read of the horrors flashed through her mind. Small wonder the man was so edgy. No telling what Adam had been through.

"What was it like?"

"You don't want to know." The way he said it, Whitney could tell this was a closed subject. He bent down and let Jasper off the leash. The little dog bolted into the darkness beyond the path.

"Are you sure you should let Jasper loose? He doesn't come when I call. I let Lexi off all the time, but she always minds me. Jasper's another story. I won't risk having him disappear by letting him off the leash when I'm walking him."

Adam stopped, his gaze on Jasper's ghost of a shadow disappearing into the brush. "He comes when I call."

"It must be a male-bonding thing."

Adam chuckled, a deep, masculine sound. "When is Miranda returning from her honeymoon? Maybe she knows the names of some of the neighbors who use this trail. I'd like to ask if one of them called the authorities the night my uncle died."

"In about twelve days, I think. She said two weeks but didn't leave me an exact time or date."

"Where's she staying? I could call her. Two weeks is a long time to wait."

"I don't know." Her revelation was greeted by silence. In the darkness she couldn't read his expression to guess what he might be thinking. "My cousin and I aren't really all that close," she felt compelled to explain. "I married and lived out of state until last year when my ex came back to open his practice. He didn't get along that well with Miranda. We didn't see much of her."

That was an exaggeration, Whitney admitted to herself. She'd called her cousin to let her know she was back in town, but hadn't invited Miranda over or gone to see her. She'd behaved shamefully. She could blame it on Ryan, but in truth, it was her own fault that Miranda no longer had been part of her life.

"Like my uncle," Adam replied, his voice low. "I knew him but I had almost nothing to do with him until recently. Then suddenly he's gone."

She heard a heartfelt note of regret in his voice that mirrored her own feelings. She wouldn't have believed she had anything in common with the man who'd tackled her, but she was wrong. They both realized they'd missed an opportunity to develop a close relationship with a relative. She might have a second chance with Miranda, but Adam never would with his uncle.

"I regret not seeing more of my cousin. I should have made the effort. When I left my husband, Miranda took me in immediately. But now, I think she'll be busy with her own life. I doubt I'll see much of her."

"You never know," Adam replied, but he didn't sound convincing.

They walked a short distance in silence. Whitney couldn't see Jasper but she could hear him ferreting around in the underbrush.

"You know to be careful that coyotes don't get Jasper," she told him. "It's a big problem in these hills."

"You're right. I'll take better care of him. I always had large dogs that coyotes wouldn't bother." He whistled for Jasper and the little dog scampered out from the brush.

"Speaking of dogs. I'd better go feed mine." She turned to head back toward the house.

"Why don't you feed them, then come up to the house? I'm ordering a pizza from Mama Gina's. The works. Everything on it, if that's okay."

Say no, cried an inner voice. *What's the harm,* she decided with her next breath. Adam had been a policeman and he'd served in Iraq. Just because they'd gotten off to a bad start didn't mean they couldn't be friends.

"Mama Gina's makes the best pizza. The works is great. I'm easy. I even like anchovies," she finally said.

"So do I."

It was too dark to see his face, but she could hear the smile in his voice.

CHAPTER TEN

Adam had phoned in the pizza order and was opening a bottle of Chianti he'd found in the sparsely stocked pantry when he heard Whitney calling to him.

"Adam! Adam! Have you seen Lexi?" She rushed through the door, a frantic look in her eyes.

"No. She wasn't in the yard?"

Whitney shook her head. "No. The gate was ajar. I'm sure I shut it, but she may have nudged open the latch."

"Are the other dogs there?"

"Yes. Just Lexi's gone. She may have come looking for me. We've only been here a few days. She really isn't used to the area."

"Let's turn on all the lights in the yard. She's probably sniffing around out there." He flipped the switches on the panel next to the door. Light flooded the back and side yards of his uncle's home.

"I don't see her," Whitney said as she

stepped outside. "Here, Lexi. Here, girl."

Adam followed Whitney into the backyard, but the Golden retriever wasn't in the pool area, and there was no sign of her in the well-manicured bushes.

"I don't think she could get into the dog run along the side of the house," Adam told her. "It's only accessible from the dog door off the kitchen. That's how Jasper comes and goes, but let's check."

There was no sign of Lexi in the dog run. Whitney kept calling and calling but the retriever didn't respond. Adam had a bad feeling about this. Lexi was a female, small for her breed. If she'd followed them out onto the trail, a pack of coyotes could have taken her down.

"I saw a Mag flashlight in one of the kitchen drawers. I'll get it, then let's check out the trail."

"Good idea," Whitney answered, a quaver in her voice. "She may have followed my scent in that direction."

It took Adam a few minutes to locate the flashlight and determine the battery was still working. He ran out of the house. Whitney was standing at the edge of the trail, calling for Lexi. The hollow tone of her voice told him that she didn't expect her dog to come.

"No sign of Lexi?"

"No. I'm just kicking myself for not double-checking the gate."

They hurried onto the trail. The wide beam of the Mag light illuminated the path and the brush alongside it. Ground squirrels skittered away from the bright light, but there wasn't any indication Whitney's dog was out here.

"Could she have gone the other way toward the street?" he asked.

"I guess, but I don't know why she would. I walk her along the trail or around my clients' homes. We haven't used the street."

Adam understood. This section of Torrey Pines was hilly and didn't have sidewalks. Cars traveled faster than they should. It would be dangerous to walk along the road. That's why whoever had called 911 for his uncle must have been walking along the trail or had driven up to the house in a car. They heard his uncle cry out for help . . . or something. They'd gone upstairs to the study, found the body sprawled across the floor and called 911.

That was one scenario. But if his uncle had been murdered, the killer could have been in the house. The first responders on the scene found the front door unlocked. That didn't sound like Uncle Calvin, but Adam didn't know him well enough to be positive. This was a safe, affluent area. The neighbors might not have been concerned about safety, but Calvin must have been, considering what he'd told Adam in Greece. Could Calvin have been expecting someone and left the front door unlocked for that person? It could have been a fatal mistake.

"Why don't I drive you through the neighborhood?" he asked. "Flash the light into the bushes and call to Lexi."

They searched the area for over an hour but couldn't find a trace of the dog. They drove back to his uncle's house in silence.

"Now what?" he asked. "Animal control doesn't pick up strays at night."

Whitney's lower lip trembled as she spoke. "Lexi's chipped so if she is picked up by animal control, they'll wand her and call the chip center. All the chip shows is an ID number. The center has my updated info. They'll call me right away."

"Let's leave on the yard lights and your porch lights. That way if she's out there somewhere, she can find her way back."

"I will," Whitney replied, her voice barely above a whisper.

"I don't suppose you want any pizza." He'd given Mama Gina's his credit card. He was sure they'd left the pizza while he and Whitney were out. "It's probably cold, but we could zap —"

"Thanks, but I'm going to keep looking for Lexi. Miranda didn't mention any dognapping problems around here, but L.A.'s had a lot of trouble. I've dropped off many dogs at groomers'. They're usually the first to know if there's a snatch-and-run scam operating in the area. Owners put up reward signs at groomers' on the off chance whoever took the dog will bring them in for a bath."

"You mean thieves snatch dogs, then ransom them?"

"Sometimes, but there are rings that grab dogs and pass them to someone else who takes them out of the immediate area. That person often gives the dog to yet another person. The animal is sold quickly for less than market value."

"It wouldn't have papers."

"Not necessarily," she reflected with bitterness. "A computer can generate a document that looks amazingly like an AKC certificate. People don't ask questions because they're glad to get the dog at a bargain price."

Adam was amazed. "I thought people just wanted puppies."

"No. The thieves have great stories about owners who've been transferred or died or something to explain why they're selling a full-grown dog. This appeals to people who want to bypass the house training ordeal. The new owners get a pet that's housebroken and well trained."

"They must be selling them over the Internet."

"Exactly, but from what I understand, they post a picture of a dog that belongs to someone in the ring. Even if I surf the Web, I won't necessarily see Lexi's picture. People who respond to the ad are told to bring cash and meet the seller at a public place like the parking lot of a fast-food restaurant, where the exchange takes place."

Adam could understand why Whitney sounded so discouraged. If dognappers had stolen Lexi, the retriever would be long gone by morning. "I guess thieves remove a dog's collar, but what about Lexi's microchip? Won't that tell who she really belongs to?"

"Yes, if a vet has a reason to check the chip in her neck. It's routinely scanned by animal control, but that means a dog has to be picked up first. It happens, but people are usually careful with purebreds, so animal control doesn't have any reason to check them." She lowered her head and studied her hands, clutched together in her lap. "A chip's easy to remove. I could do it with a long needle, but they don't usually bother."

Adam had to admit finding Whitney's dog didn't sound promising. If a pack of coyotes hadn't dragged off the retriever, thieves must have taken her. A thought occurred to him. "Why didn't they take any of the other dogs? Didn't you say they were smaller? Wouldn't they be easier to handle?"

"True, but certain breeds are more in demand. Golden retrievers, pugs and Labs rank right up there. It's also possible they had an order for a female retriever. From what I've been told, thieves target dogs they know they can sell instantly."

"You mean Chinese cresteds aren't at the top of the list?"

Whitney attempted a laugh. "Most people wouldn't recognize one. Until Kate Hudson starred in *How to Lose a Guy in Ten Days,* Chinese cresteds weren't on the radar screen."

"Hey! My uncle told me the same crested won the ugliest dog in the world contest two years in a row."

"That dog was pitiful. Most Chinese cresteds look more like Jasper."

That wasn't saying much, in Adam's opinion. It was hard to believe people actually bred dogs to look like Jasper. It was even more difficult to understand how shy little Jasper had become an international champion. Go figure. Still, he had to admit he was developing a soft spot for Jasper. It was hard not to like a dog who adored you.

"Do you think it's possible your ex took Lexi? He seemed really angry with you."

"I can't see Ryan taking her and leaving the gate ajar. The other dogs could have run off, and I would be in serious trouble." The words weren't out of her mouth one second before she gasped.

Ryan stared at his computer screen. He'd made a list of the bills he owed and ranked them by order of importance. The bank was already sending late notices on his home loan. He was behind on the second mortgage and home equity loan as well. He didn't have any hope of paying off his debts if his new partners realized his financial plight and dropped him from the new cosmetic surgery group.

Talk about hell on earth.

Maybe if he took what little cash he had, he could play the slots and parlay it into enough to hit the tables. With luck, he could run it into real money. Perhaps he could win enough to make all or part of the house payment.

Those problems paled when compared with the threat from Domenic Coriz. Being in debt was one thing; being dead was another. It wasn't an idle threat. The Indian tribes in San Diego County earned megabucks from their casinos. The operation had spawned a rough element that used mob tactics ruthlessly. They would kill Ryan without a second thought and dump his body on the rez where no one would ever find it.

Whitney had to sign those papers — immediately. He desperately needed a debt-consolidation loan. The interest rate would be stratospheric but it would just be temporary. When the cosmetic surgery group was up and running, he would pay off all his loans.

In the distance, the doorbell chimed. He glanced at his Rolex. Nearly eleven o'clock. Who would be at his door so late? *Domenic or his goon* flashed into his mind. They might hassle him at home. Sweat peppered the skin just under the hair on his forehead.

He heard Ashley answer the front door and voices drifted across the large living room to the back of the house, where he'd converted a rear bedroom into an office. It sounded like a woman.

"I don't know what you're talking about," he heard Ashley protest in a frantic voice.

"You have my dog! I know you do. Don't deny it." He recognized Whitney's voice. "How could you steal my dog right out of her yard? Isn't it enough that you have my husband, my house?"

Oh, shit! Just what he didn't need. Whitney going postal on Ashley. The deeper rumble of a male voice sent him dashing through the living room where Ashley had been rearranging furniture again.

"We need to check the house and the yard," a stern male voice boomed through the large entry.

Ryan rushed into the foyer. "What's going on?"

He slammed to a stop, stunned to see Whitney and that jerk who'd ordered him off Whitney's driveway standing in the entry. Ashley was flushed and her lower lip was trembling. He raced to her side and put a protective arm around her.

"Lexi's missing!" Whitney pointed at him. "You took her, didn't you?"

"What? You've hit a new low."

"No, I haven't," she yelled in a strident voice he hadn't heard once during their marriage. "You stole Lexi to get back at me."

"I wouldn't take Lexi. You know that."

"I didn't think you'd hurt me, either," Whitney shrieked. "No telling what you'll do next."

Out of the corner of his eye, Ryan saw Ashley gaze up at him, a questioning look in her eyes. Shit! Why did she have to frighten Ashley? He'd momentarily lost his temper — that's all.

"I didn't hurt you. I just needed you to see reason and sign the papers."

"I want my dog back. You got this damn house and the furniture. All I asked for was Lexi. I want her back — now."

"I don't have her." He glanced at the powerfully built man with Whitney. He was frowning at Ryan like he wanted to deck him. "I swear I don't have the dog."

"Since this is legally still half Whitney's house, she has the right to look around and see if you have Lexi." The man spoke in a low, level voice, but his commanding presence reminded Ryan of Domenic Coriz.

"I don't appreciate your barging in here and scaring my wife," Ryan told Adam, but Adam could see the wimpy doctor was shaken. "I didn't take Lexi. Why would I?"

Adam had been on homicide long enough and had interrogated enough lowlifes to realize Ryan Fordham was telling the truth. They weren't going to find the dog here.

"You took Lexi to get back at me for not signing the papers," Whitney insisted.

"Oh, for Christ's sake." Ryan ground out the words. "I'm not that childish. If you acted your age and signed the document you'd already agreed to, we could go our separate ways."

Adam didn't know exactly what was in the document or why Whitney had refused to sign it, but Fordham made Whitney sound peevish. Adam fought the impulse to turn and leave. He never became involved in family feuds — particularly divorces. Tempers flared and emotions ran deep. He didn't want to be in the middle of this.

"Look around." Ashley waved a manicured hand sporting a diamond the size of a golf ball. "You won't find her."

Adam nudged Whitney. "See if Lexi's here. I'll wait for you."

Whitney dashed to the right, heading toward the kitchen. From where Adam was standing he could see the wavering blue-white light reflected on the windows. Evidently there was a pool beyond the house, and Whitney had mentioned a dog run where Lexi once had a doghouse.

"What happened?" Ryan Fordham curtly asked him. Again, Adam had the distinct impression the doctor hadn't a clue about

Lexi's whereabouts.

Adam told the doctor and his bombshell wife who he was and explained what had happened to Lexi. Fordham tried to frown but his brows barely moved. Must be injecting himself with Botox, Adam decided. It figured; cosmetic surgeons, even ones as young as Fordham, couldn't afford telltale wrinkles.

"That's strange. Lexi never wanders," Fordham told him in a puzzled tone. "We've had her since she was a puppy. Nearly five years. She never once ran off."

"Maybe the dog's confused," Ashley suggested in a breathy voice. "She thinks this is her home. She isn't used to her new place yet."

Fordham gave the sexy blonde an affectionate squeeze. "Good thinking, sweetheart. It's also possible thieves snatched Lexi and sold her to a test lab. There are several in the area. Golden retrievers are easy marks. They're trusting and anxious to please. Experimenter's favorites."

"Oh, no," Ashley moaned. It seemed a little put on, but who was Adam to say. "How terrible."

"I'll make some calls first thing in the morning," Ryan offered. "If she's at a local lab, I'll be able to track her down."

"Good idea," Adam said, and he meant it. He was positive Ryan Fordham was telling the truth. It would be so easy if Whitney's ex had taken the dog, but it was more likely the retriever would vanish into thin air. Whitney might never know what had happened to her pet.

"It would help if you could convince Whitney to sign those papers. She agreed to the settlement already, but the judge screwed up. He didn't notice the document hadn't been properly recorded." Ryan gave his wife a one-armed hug. "Then we can go our separate ways in peace."

Adam found himself nodding. He hadn't known her long, but he wanted Whitney to feel free, to want to start over. These papers — and the dog — seemed to be her last link to her ex. Was she playing it for all it was worth? he suddenly wondered. Could Whitney have the dog stashed somewhere, using this as an excuse to get back at her husband or something?

Why had he become involved? He was thinking with his dick. After nearly three years without sex, he'd gone bonkers over the first attractive woman to cross his path. Granted, Whitney was sexy as hell — and interesting — but he didn't need to be involved in a domestic dispute like this.

"Look, Doc," he replied, aware he'd made "Doc" sound like a four-letter word. "This isn't any of my business. Take it up with Whitney."

CHAPTER ELEVEN

Whitney stumbled into the cottage. Da Vinci and Maddie greeted her with high-pitched yips. They ran in happy, excited circles around her feet. It was all she could do not to shout: Which one of you opened the gate? Who let Lexi out?

She collapsed onto the small well-worn sofa, admitting that it must have been Lexi who'd used her nose or paw to spring the latch on the gate. The other dogs were too little to reach the lever. Lexi had never done anything like that — ever. She'd never shown the slightest tendency to wander. But there was always a first time. Blaming the other dogs, yelling at them wouldn't bring Lexi back.

"Please, God," she whispered, "I'll do anything."

Then she remembered what her mother had always said. *You can't make deals with the universe. God has more important things to do.*

Still she prayed, because that was all she could do. Hot tears slowly seeped from her eyes and drizzled down her cheeks. Lexi's collar had a tag with her name and this phone number clearly engraved on it. Whitney had always taken precautions not to lose Lexi. When she'd first left the home she'd shared with Ryan to house-sit, she'd immediately gotten Lexi a new tag and called the chip center to update the information. She'd switched the tag for another one the first day she'd moved in with Miranda. She'd contacted the chip center again with the current information.

"It's too soon to give up hope," she told Da Vinci, who'd hopped up beside her and was trying his best to lick the tears dribbling off her chin.

A paralyzing depression gripped her. *How do we sense things before we know them?* she asked herself. When she'd left Adam to feed the dogs, something had alerted her. A sense of dread like a slow-moving fog had engulfed her on the stone path from the main house to the cottage.

The minute she'd opened the front door she'd . . . known. She'd raced to the back door to the small yard where she'd left the dogs. The gate was ajar. Lexi had vanished.

She'd rushed around like a crazy woman. Searching and calling. Searching and calling. Yet in her heart of hearts, she'd known she wouldn't find Lexi.

Even when she'd had the hissy fit at Ryan's, she'd known deep down that it was a vain hope. When he didn't get his way, Ryan did little vindictive things like "accidentally" throwing out cherished photographs of her mother. But she didn't believe he'd taken Lexi.

Another wave of tears brimmed in her eyes and streamed down her cheeks. What had her last words to Lexi been? "Go on, now. Do your business."

She tried not to think of what she'd read on the Golden retriever rescue Web site. Almost three-quarters of lost Goldens were never returned to their owners — despite having identification on them. They were intelligent, loving dogs. People who found them tended to keep them.

"Lexi belongs to me," she whispered to herself.

She remembered every day and every training session. Lexi had been so easy, caught on so fast. Still, Whitney had been the one — never Ryan — to put in the necessary time.

Why would a dog that was so well trained

run away? It didn't make sense. She had to admit Ashley might have been correct. Lexi could have been confused by leaving the home where she'd been raised to move first to a house-sitting place and then here. She must have released the latch to go search for Whitney.

Because Lexi had simply vanished, Whitney realized she would always wonder about her dog. Was Lexi locked up somewhere, alone and afraid? Was she in pain? Did she need a vet?

And some part of Whitney would always hope that one day she would open the door and miracle of miracles — Lexi would be there. Sitting, of course. Waiting to be petted.

Whitney realized she would wonder and worry for years. Even when Lexi's natural lifespan was over, Whitney would continue to agonize over her loss. She would still know that no matter who'd kept Lexi, the Golden was hers. And no one else's.

"She's a nut case," Ashley said just after Adam and Whitney left.

Her voice was still shaky. How many overly emotional women could he handle in an hour? Ryan eased his arm away from his wife's shoulders.

"Whitney's crazy about that dog. Always has been."

It shocked Ryan to realize Whitney cared more about Lexi than she had about him. He hadn't known it until just now. Seeing how distraught and unreasonable Whitney was convinced him. Even when he'd walked out on her, Whitney hadn't been this upset.

"Let's get to bed," Ryan told Ashley. There wasn't anything he could do in the office tonight. Getting laid would take his mind off his problems for a few minutes.

On their way to the master suite, Ryan heard his cell phone ringing in the distance. It was still in the office, where he'd left it beside the computer. Who would be calling him at this time of night?

"A wrong number," Ashley suggested.

"Probably. I'll check and turn it off."

He hurried back to his office and grabbed the cell phone off the stack of bills on his desk, dreading answering it.

"Fordham," the man said before Ryan could utter a word.

"Yes." He tried to project confidence even though his balls ached at the sound of the voice.

"Dom wants to meet you tomorrow. He has a plan."

Ryan listened to the instructions, then

hung up. He sank into his chair. He ran his tongue over his lips, but his mouth had gone bone dry.

A plan?

He wanted no part of any plan Domenic Coriz concocted. How was he going to get out of this mess? Now he knew why people committed suicide. If you had no way out, death might be your only choice.

You're stronger than that, he reminded himself. He'd grown up the youngest child in a working-class family. The youngest was supposed to be the baby, but it hadn't worked that way in his family. Youngest meant his older siblings raised him. They'd teased him mercilessly or ignored him. He'd never known what to expect, so he'd struck out on his own. He'd worked hard to put himself through college and medical school. True, he'd married Whitney and she'd been responsible for his medical education, but he had struggled to get ahead. And he'd made it. This was a temporary setback — nothing more.

Mentally reviewing his limited options, he meandered back to the master suite, taking time to turn off the backyard lights that Whitney had thrown on during her desperate search for Lexi.

"Are you really going to call the testing

labs tomorrow?" Ashley asked when he wandered into their bedroom.

She was in bed, propped up against an armada of pillows and dressed in his favorite sheer black negligee that half exposed her perfect breasts. He'd performed more than his fair share of boob jobs and appreciated the real thing more than most men.

"Yes. I'll call around." He kept talking as he went into his large walk-in closet off the bedroom. He raised his voice so she could still hear him. "Lexi's my dog, too. I don't want anyone experimenting on her."

Ashley waited a second before responding, "Of course not."

For an extended moment, he stood there, one leg out of his trousers, the other still covered by the fabric. An unsettled feeling caused his shoulders to twitch. Something about Ashley's reaction to Lexi's disappearance bothered him.

He finished undressing and tossed his dirty clothes in the hamper he kept next to six long rows of shoes. Some, like his black patent leather tuxedo shoes, he rarely wore, but seeing them all lined up and polished made him smile. He had a shoe fixation for some reason, and he knew it. A shrink might ask if he'd lacked shoes as a kid or been forced to wear hand-me-downs. No. His family hadn't had much money, but he'd always had his own sneakers and church shoes.

Still, he never failed to notice people's shoes when he met them. Ashley had been wearing strappy high-heeled sandals when he'd seen her for the first time. Tonight, Adam Hunter had on new black Pumas. As usual, Whitney was wearing ratty cross-trainers she'd bought on sale. Dom Coriz's man had been wearing steel-toed boots most often seen on construction jobs.

He left his Nikes in their spot on the shoe rack and walked naked into the bedroom. Ashley was still sitting upright, her blond hair cascading over her shoulders. The thought niggling at the back of his mind resurfaced.

"Ashley, do you know anything about Lexi's disappearance?"

"Of course not," she replied a bit too quickly.

He stopped at the foot of the bed and asked himself how he knew she was lying. Nothing about the innocent expression on her face gave her away. Still, little red flags had been popping up since he joined her at the front door. Her tone of voice. Her flushed face.

"Don't lie to me."

The anger and frustration he harbored over his gambling losses and Dom's threats underscored each syllable. Ashley clutched the silk top sheet as if she expected him to backhand her. He held his temper and stared at the woman he loved. "Is there something you want to tell me?" he finally asked when the silence had lengthened.

Ashley blinked back tears with two sweeps of her long lashes. It was the first time he'd seen her cry. Ashley was his wife, the woman he loved in a way that he'd never loved anyone on this earth. At another time, tears might have moved him. Tonight his mind was numb from all the jackals after a piece of his hide.

"A — a friend swiped her dog," Ashley confessed.

"Aw, shit! Why?"

Ashley scrambled out from under the covers, dashed to his side and pressed her centerfold body against his. "We thought that if the dog went missing overnight, Whitney would be motivated to sign the documents."

"What? Of all the harebrained ideas! How was she supposed to link the dog to the papers?"

"In the morning my friend is going to call Whitney and tell her what to do if she wants her dog back."

Christ! Ashley *was* legally blond. "What if Whitney calls the police? They'll come after me."

A bitter-sounding laugh slipped out from between her pouty lips. "It would be her word against yours — and she wouldn't stand a chance of getting Lexi back. My friend will make that crystal clear."

Ryan had to admit the scheme might have worked, but it also would have told Whitney how desperate he was.

He backed away from Ashley. "Call your friend. Get Lexi back to Whitney. Have her say she found the dog wandering. Do *not* let her say or do anything that would make Whitney suspect we were involved. Understand?"

He stomped into his closet and grabbed a pair of slacks off a hanger. Ashley followed him in and stood at the door. She didn't say a word but he could feel her watching him as he dressed.

Finally she asked, "Why are you getting dressed again?"

He shoved his bare feet into a pair of navy Topsiders he didn't remember ever wearing. "I need to get out of here and think. When I come back, I expect you'll have taken care of the problem."

"I will," she whispered. "Don't worry."

Ryan rushed out of the bedroom. He wasn't concerned. Ashley would do as she was told and her girlfriend would return Lexi. This gave him the excuse he needed to drive to the casino and see if Lady Luck would smile on him.

Ashley waited until she heard Ryan's Porsche roar out of the garage before she called Preston Block.

"Sorry it's so late," she apologized.

"Not a problem." Preston didn't bother to ask who it was. They spoke every day and instantly recognized each other's voices.

"Ryan's ex stomped in here tonight," she told him. "Whitney thought we had her dog."

"So? She couldn't have found a thing. The dog's right here beside me."

"Ryan's so smart. He figured out I was behind Lexi's disappearance. He went ballistic. He insisted I have —" Ashley paused "— my girlfriend bring back the dog right away."

Preston chuckled. "Your girlfriend? That's a joke."

"I didn't tell him about you. He's really upset and I didn't want to make him any angrier."

Preston didn't respond. Ashley knew he

had a thing for her, but she tried her best to ignore it. She needed a friend, not another man with the hots for her.

"Do something for me." She hated the pleading tone in her voice, but what could she do? "Get that dog back right away."

"Tonight?"

"Yes. Please. Do it for me."

Ashley hung up, then turned off the light, but she couldn't sleep. She kept listening for the sound of Ryan's car. He was so jumpy and angry lately that she didn't know what to do. Something was bothering him. She tried to tell herself that it was the pressure of putting together a new practice, but now she wondered if that was all it was.

Ashley had to pull her hand away from the telephone. She was sorely tempted to try to reach her father. He lived in Bakersfield, not far north. Like Ryan, he was a man who worked for a living and owned his own business. He must know about stress. He might have some idea of how to handle Ryan.

But it had been years since she'd spoken to her father. He'd said he would always love her, but he'd left them. She was too proud to go sniveling to him. She could handle the situation.

■ ■ ■ ■

The telephone on Adam's uncle's desk rang, startling him and waking up Jasper, who'd been asleep at his feet. A quick glance at his watch told him it was nearly three-thirty in the morning. Who would be calling at this hour? The caller ID screen read: Marshall.

Whitney.

What did she want? After her futile search for Lexi, they had driven home in silence. There was no need for words. Her eyes reflected a deep, inconsolable grief. It was impossible to gaze into those green eyes and not be touched.

As attracted as he was to Whitney, Adam refused to be drawn into this any more than he already had been. He'd convinced himself he possessed the good sense to realize Whitney was still emotionally attached to her ex-husband.

Adam did not want any more trouble. He'd spent the last hour sorting through his uncle's papers. He needed to keep his focus on investigating Calvin Hunter's death. Let Whitney attend to her own problems.

He was half tempted to let the machine pick up the call but he'd told Whitney to phone him immediately if anything happened. From the cottage she could see that his lights were on and would know he was still up.

"What's happening?" he asked as Jasper leaped up onto his lap.

"Good news," she cried, the sound of tears in her voice. "A jogger found Lexi."

"At this hour?"

"Yes. He's bringing her home right away."

"That's great. I'll be right down —"

"Don't bother. You've done enough." There was a slight pause. "I'm sorry for imposing on you. Thanks so much for all your help. Good night."

She hung up before Adam could respond. He stared at the receiver for a moment, relieved but still bothered by the late-night reappearance of the retriever. His police training made him question the situation even more. Kicking himself for not minding his own business, Adam trudged out of the house and down the path to the cottage that had once belonged to a full-time gardener. Jasper scampered along beside him.

Whitney must have heard his footsteps on the wooden porch. She flung open the door before he could knock. Her happy smile evaporated as soon as she saw who it was.

"Oh, I was hoping it was the guy who

found Lexi."

Adam stepped inside with Jasper underfoot. He nearly stumbled over the little dog who'd become his constant companion. "I didn't want you meeting some strange man so late at night. There are all kinds of people around. It's good to be cautious."

The crunch of tires on the gravel driveway made Whitney charge by him. Adam followed a few steps behind her. A tall guy in a blue T-shirt and khaki pants got out of a Camry that had seen better days. He had sun-streaked blond hair and a bronze body. His biceps said he could snap a man's neck like a toothpick.

"Lexi!" Whitney raced toward the car as the man opened the back door and a Golden retriever jumped out.

The dog tugged on the leash and whirled in a circle, barking. Whitney dropped to her knees, arms outstretched, and the dog lathered her with kisses. Tears of happiness streamed down her face.

The guy flexed his powerful shoulders, his version of a shrug, and grinned at Adam. "I guess it's her dog, all right."

"Looks like." Adam stepped off the porch, still a little suspicious. He tried for his good-old-boy tone, the one he'd once used to put potential criminals at ease when questioning them. "Where'd you find her?"

"Down on Memorial Drive. I was out for a run and noticed her in the bushes."

"A little late to be running, isn't it?"

The buffed-out guy smiled, revealing California-white teeth. "I was helping out a buddy at Boomerang's, bouncing kids with phony IDs."

Adam remembered the place from his days on the police force. It was a punk hangout that had been busted numerous times for serving liquor to minors. As much drug dealing went on in the joint as it did over the border in Tijuana.

"I was kinda keyed up, so I went for a run on my way home. Spotted the dog, then she started following me. I checked her tags, then called the number."

Whitney wouldn't let go of the retriever. Her tears had stopped but her voice was still shaky. "Thanks so much. I've been out of my mind worried." She unhooked the leash attached to Lexi's collar. "I'm Whitney Fo— Marshall."

"Preston Block."

"Adam Hunter," he said. "I'm Whitney's friend. I live right there." He gestured toward the house on the rise behind them. For reasons he didn't have time to analyze, he wanted this guy to know he lived nearby.

Block pointed at Jasper. "Is that eyesore a dog?"

It took Adam a second to realize the jerk had insulted Jasper. He stepped forward, ready to cut loose with a smart comeback. He had to admit Jasper wasn't winning any beauty awards, but the little dog belonged to him now.

Whitney came to Jasper's defense. "Jasper's a Chinese crested. He happens to be the international champion."

Don't say he's worth a fortune, Adam silently cautioned. *We don't want another dog to disappear.*

"Really?" Block responded with a smile. "Coulda fooled me."

Adam battled the urge to whack him. Who was he to criticize Jasper?

"Let me give you a reward for returning my dog," Whitney offered, standing up. "You have no idea how grateful I am."

Good move, Adam thought. Block must have recognized the address on the tag as one of the more upscale neighborhoods and expected some money. That had to be the reason he was so anxious to return the dog in the middle of the night.

Block shook his head. "Nah. I don't want a reward. I'm just glad I could help. I know if my dog wandered off, I'd be outta my friggin' head."

There you go. What a sweetheart of a guy.

"What kind of dog do you have?" Whitney asked.

"I don't have one right now. I'm in an apartment, but I grew up with German shepherds. I'm getting one as soon as I can."

"German shepherds are great," Whitney said, stroking her own dog's head. "I'd better feed Lexi. She missed dinner."

"I'm outta here," Block said.

"Goodbye. Thanks again. I'm really grateful."

From the other side of the car, Adam watched as Whitney gave Block a grateful hug and thanked him yet again for returning her dog. Lexi followed Whitney up the steps toward the door of the cottage.

Adam kept his voice low, asking, "Do you always keep a leash in your car?"

Block had his body half in the door of his car — a tight wedge, considering his size. "Nah." He held up the leash. "I picked this up along with a Red Bull at the Stop 'N Go on Harborside. I thought I might have to walk her around for a while. There's an old biddy in our complex. Goes ballistic if she even sees a dog visiting."

"Gotcha. Some folks aren't dog friendly." Adam turned toward the cottage, Jasper at his feet. Whitney had already taken Lexi inside. "Thanks again for your help."

"No problem," the man said through the open window.

Adam watched Block back down the driveway. He had returned Lexi on a cheap nylon leash, the kind a minimart would sell, but something nagged at Adam. He wasn't sure what was bothering him. The guy seemed to be telling the truth. Adam noticed the Camry had a California plate and memorized the number.

CHAPTER TWELVE

Whitney was so intently watching Lexi eat that she didn't realize Adam had come back into the cottage until she heard a soft sound behind her. She turned away from Lexi and smiled at him. "That gate needs a lock. Obviously, Lexi can figure out how to open it."

"I think a combination padlock would be easiest." He paused. "We have a storeroom at the office with all kinds of locks and security devices. I'll bring one home to-night."

"Thanks. I appreciate all you've done." She ruffled her hand through her hair, remembering how she'd flung accusations like hot coals. "Wow! I really overreacted. Much as I hate to admit it, I owe Ryan an apology. I'll call him first thing in the morn-ing."

"Why don't you have an attorney look over those papers? If he says it's okay, sign them. You need to move forward."

"You're right," she assured him. "I'm ready to start over. I really am."

He studied her for a moment, then moved closer. "Are you?"

Electricity arced between them, so strong she could practically feel its heat. Her breath caught, then rushed out ragged and fast. His intense blue eyes dilated as he gazed at her and waited for a response.

"Absolutely." The word fell from her lips as a soft plea. "I want to get on with my life."

She wasn't sure how Adam felt, but she knew she wanted him. After that first scary encounter, she'd been afraid of him, but her impression had changed. He was an attractive man, but more than that, he was a kind person. She couldn't imagine Ryan running around in the middle of the night searching for a lost dog owned by a woman he hardly knew.

"Come here." There was a huskiness to his voice that spiked her pulse. When Adam reached for her, Whitney eased into his arms with a sigh that floated through the air.

He crushed his mouth to hers, muttering something that sounded like a low growl. Her lips instantly parted and she squeezed her eyes shut. She folded her arms around his neck and pressed her body to his as his tongue swirled into her mouth — hot, greedy. Her breasts molded against the hard planes of his chest and her nipples immediately began to throb. He tasted every bit as masculine and erotic as she'd imagined he would.

The warmth of his powerful body sent a heady sense of anticipation through her. What would it be like to make love to him? she wondered as he continued to kiss her. During the last year with Ryan, their lovemaking had been sporadic. She'd sensed his indifference and tried everything she could think of to please him. It had been so stressful that she couldn't remember what it was like to be desired. With a thrill, she realized this man wanted her as much as she wanted him.

Forget Ryan! He's so-o-o over.

Adam's hands wove through her hair, changing the angle of her head so he could kiss her more deeply. The feel of his fingers on her scalp sent languid heat radiating through the lower reaches of her body. Her toes curled. His tongue kept tangling with hers until she was nearly mindless with the need to have him inside her.

His hands left her hair and caressed the taut muscles of her back. Too many long, lonely nights seemed like something that had happened to a stranger. For an instant she wondered about Adam's past, about the haunted look in his eyes. But those thoughts vanished as his hands roved lower and squeezed her bottom, then pushed her flush against his erection. Senses reeling, she arched her back and moved invitingly against the turgid heat of his arousal.

He edged one hand between their bodies and captured her breast. The nipple was already a tight nubbin, but the heat of his hand made it ache with a need more intense than anything she'd ever experienced. She longed to feel his mouth on her breast, her nipple between his lips.

His thumb swept back and forth across her nipple, teasing the sensitive bead through the sheer fabric of her T-shirt. A primal moan rumbled from deep in her throat. She honestly couldn't get enough of him.

A chirping sound made her pull back. "W-what?"

Adam gave a snort of disgust. "My cell phone. I'm on call, but I don't know what could be going on at this hour." He yanked the tiny phone off his belt. "Hunter."

Whitney turned, noticed Lexi had finished eating and was standing at the back door.

The retriever always went to the bathroom right after she ate. She let the dog out and stood watching her. The gate was closed, but she refused to take any chances.

She put a hand to her moist lips. Her heart was still pounding, her knees still jittery. What had she been thinking? She was acting like some wanton woman who'd been on a deserted island for the last year. Granted, few of her peers would fault her, but she had her own standards. Whitney had never been one to throw herself at a man. She heard Adam come up behind her and looked over her shoulder.

"I've gotta go. An emergency at one of our guard posts. Could you take care of Jasper?"

"Of course," she replied, resisting the urge to ask when she'd see him again.

He bent down and brushed a soft kiss across her lips. "I'll come back with the lock."

After he left, Whitney trudged into the bedroom, so exhausted she could hardly think. Jasper and Lexi followed her. They found Maddie and Da Vinci asleep on Whitney's bed. Creatures of habit, they'd put themselves to bed earlier in the evening. Surprisingly, the sound of a car and Lexi's return hadn't disturbed them. Common sense told her to take them outside — especially Da Vinci, who was prone to "slips," but she was too tired.

She nudged them aside so she could have a place on the queen-size bed, reminding herself that over forty percent of dog owners slept with their pets. She wasn't so strange. Jasper sprang onto the bed and joined the two other small dogs. She scooted sideways to make room for Lexi. She patted the mattress. Lexi stood there a moment, perplexed. She usually slept in her cushy dog bed on the floor. A second thump on the covers, and Lexi sprang up beside Whitney, then settled in.

Whitney stroked the soft fur on the retriever's head, her heart stutter-stepping when she thought how close she'd come to losing Lexi. Something hummed inside her chest. She wasn't sure if it was a cry of relief or despair. A post she'd read on Muttsblog .com sprang to mind.

When did Fido become Fred? The online question had been followed by a very thoughtful post about how the Fido of the fifties — a house pet — had become Fred — a bona fide member of the family. As society changed, the blogger claimed, pets assumed a new role. Dogs began to fill the emotional gaps in people's lives as the world became increasingly disconnected.

When Whitney met fellow walkers — dog owners often walked at the same time along the same route — they referred to her not by name but as "Lexi's mom." This implied her retriever had the status of a child. Few of those dog owners in the neighborhood where she'd lived with Ryan knew her name.

A soft snuffling sound told her Lexi was asleep but Whitney kept petting her. It was true, she conceded to herself. Lexi filled so many voids in her life. From the time they'd bought Lexi almost five years ago, the dog had begun to move into the place that Ryan had once occupied. It was the beginning of the end of their relationship. Looking back, she realized Ryan had begun to withdraw shortly before he brought home the puppy.

Without family or many friends, there was an empty space in Whitney's heart that she hadn't realized existed until now, when Lexi moved into it. She had been on the brink of utter despair when Lexi vanished. The depth of Whitney's vulnerability had been even worse than when Ryan had left her. She'd almost lost it — in front of Ryan and the bimbo he'd married. In front of Adam.

"You need a life," she whispered into the darkness.

Adam's face appeared on the screen in

her mind. She could almost feel his lips against hers. If his phone hadn't disturbed them . . . well, they would have bounced Maddie and Da Vinci onto the floor.

She considered the situation for a minute, stopped stroking Lexi and rolled onto her other side. A person without friends or family shouldn't leap like a fool into . . . into what? A one-night stand? No, not with Adam. A new relationship should be entered into with more caution. After all, she'd already proven how poorly she chose men.

She needed family and friends. When Miranda returned, Whitney planned to make up for all the time they'd lost, but her cousin might be so absorbed in her marriage that she wouldn't need Whitney. All she could do was make the effort and see what happened.

As for friends, Trish Bowrather was the only person with whom she'd had much contact. She was friendly in a dominating sort of way. Still, they had a divorce and Golden retrievers in common.

In her mind's eye, Whitney saw Trish's impressive home and exclusive gallery. The woman might seem to have it all, but Whitney suspected Trish was lonely.

Whitney said out loud, "Tomorrow is the first day of the rest of your life." True, it was a trite saying, but it fit her situation. She refused to live a "disconnected" life with only a dog to care about her.

Adam asked himself why in hell he was in a guardhouse at the gated development of Ocean Heights. For some reason the guard had simply up and left without even calling the command post. A resident had returned and found the post deserted. Somehow he'd futzed with the computer until he'd contacted HiTech. Butch had attempted to contact Tyler at home and on his cell, but couldn't get a response. In desperation, he'd called Adam.

What Adam knew about running a guard post came down to opening the gate for residents, guests and service people. Over the phone, Butch had been able to walk him through the procedures. It was a little after four o'clock in the morning. He didn't expect much traffic until seven, when the next guard came on duty. If HiTech was making so much money, the least they could do was have a backup guard on call. Tomorrow, he'd take up this and a lot more with Tyler. If backup had been available, Adam would be snuggled in bed with Whitney.

Okay, *snuggled* might not have been it. Hot, sweaty sex was what sprang to mind.

He could almost feel her beneath him, feel himself driving into her soft, sweet body.

He wanted a woman; he needed a woman — in the worst way. *Not just any woman,* he realized. Nearly dying had changed his outlook on life.

Once he'd believed he had years and years ahead of him to find a woman, have a family. His father's death — at a relatively early age — had been the harbinger of things to come. But he hadn't heeded the warning: Life is too short. It had taken his own near-death experience for him to appreciate just how fragile life was. Uncle Calvin's death sealed his impression.

"Get your mind off sex," he muttered under his breath. As it was he was going to have blue balls for a week. He'd left Whitney's with an erection like an iron pike. He didn't need to sit at a guard post with another one.

He called Butch at the command post. "I need our pin number for Total Track."

"Anything going on?" Butch asked with a note of curiosity in his voice.

"Nah. I'm bored. I want to check out a guy I met."

Butch gave Adam the series of numbers and letters that would allow him to access the database of the private company used by many security firms and some of the smaller police departments. Total Track kept information from the DMV, utility companies, cable television services, as well as credit card reporting services. The system was used to determine an individual's current address, place of work, credit status and a lot of other supposedly confidential information.

Total Track was very expensive but worth it to security companies trying to locate people. Before Adam had been forced to leave for Iraq, HiTech had been poised to go into the security business. But now it seemed to be nothing more than a guard service. He wondered why they were still paying for Total Track.

Once he was in the system, Adam typed, "Preston Block." In the next breath up popped the standard information.

Address: 1297 Thurston Place Unit 4B
Place of Employment: Dr. Jox Fitness Center
Automobile: 1992 Camry (blue)
License: HWZ943

Adam scanned the guy's credit history. One credit card. Block made the minimum payment on time each month and carried a balance that was roughly half his limit. Typical. Most people in America carried a hefty balance and paid the minimum each month.

His Bank of America checking account showed a balance of just under five hundred dollars. Block didn't have a savings account. No surprise there. America had turned into a nation of debtors, not savers.

He scrolled down the screen. Holy shit! Preston Block had a sealed juvenile record. For what? In rare cases, a sealed juvenile record concealed a serious crime like rape or murder. Odds were against it. More likely Block had been convicted of petty theft or joyriding in a "borrowed" car.

He rocked back in the chair and stared at the screen. Block seemed to be a regular working stiff. Nothing unusual except he'd been jogging and came upon a lost Golden retriever.

So what was bothering Adam?

He logged out of Total Track and Googled "Preston Block." The guy had a Web site. Interesting. Adam clicked on the Web site. Up came a picture of Block, appearing even more buff than he had tonight. He'd oiled his muscles like weight lifters did so the guy looked very impressive on the screen.

Block advertised his services as a personal trainer. "I'll come to you or you come to me!"

What a guy. Adam clicked through a series of photographs showing Block working with clients at Dr. Jox Fitness Center. Most of Block's clients seemed to be women who were so toned and pretty that it was hard to believe they needed a trainer. But that was only his opinion.

Adam got tired of looking at all the babes that Block made his living training. It was just making him think about Whitney's sexy bod. He returned to the Ocean Heights screen and forced himself not to think about Whitney.

Like a chop to the back of his neck, it hit him. Now he knew what bothered him about Preston Block's story. Okay, okay, what freak went jogging at nearly three-thirty in the morning? That had been the first clue.

But it wasn't just that. There was a chink in Block's story. Adam had spent enough time on the streets of greater San Diego as a homicide detective to remember many of the businesses — particularly on the main thoroughfares.

There wasn't any Stop 'N Go on Harborside. Why would Block lie about where he bought the leash?

CHAPTER THIRTEEN

Whitney checked her reflection in the towering plate-glass doors of the high-rise in the Marina District where Broderick Babcock had his offices. Her pale pink twinset and navy slacks didn't seem businesslike enough to visit a criminal defense attorney. Well, it was the best she could do.

Whitney had walked only the dogs that absolutely needed to be taken out before rushing downtown. She'd called Ryan to apologize and tell him Lexi had been found but he'd already left. She'd nearly choked on her apology to Ashley, but she'd managed to spit it out. Ashley had been "totally thrilled" to hear Lexi had been returned. Whitney told her to contact Ryan immediately. She didn't want her ex wasting his time calling test labs, searching for Lexi.

As she swung open the tall glass door and walked into the immense marble-floored lobby, she admitted to herself that a sense of relief had replaced the animosity she'd felt toward Ryan and his new wife. She wanted the divorce behind her. Last night, while she'd been in bed with the dogs, she'd realized how much she needed to begin all over. She told herself not to see Adam Hunter as part of this new life. *Put him out of your mind,* she kept thinking. But in the next minute, swear to God, his image would pop up unbidden.

She checked the directory on the wall and found Broderick Babcock's office was in the penthouse. Silently rehearsing what she would say to the attorney, Whitney rode the elevator to the lawyer's offices. Another glass door led into a large waiting room decorated with minimalistic furniture in muted shades of cocoa. It was empty except for an older woman behind a desk.

Whitney entered and the woman with blue-tinged hair and a gray suit looked up with a smile. "May I help you?"

"I'm Whitney Marshall." She expected "Marshall" to ring a bell. Apparently, it did not. The woman waited for her to continue. "I have a divorce agreement I'd like an attorney to look over." She stopped right in front of the desk.

"We're a criminal law firm," the woman

responded pleasantly. "I can recommend —"

"I would really like to see someone here," Whitney replied. "You see, since my cousin — who's like my sister — is on her honeymoon with Mr. Babcock, I thought . . ."

"Your cousin?"

"They're honeymooning. You know, in Fiji." Was it possible the attorney hadn't told his office staff? The woman seemed perplexed, but she was smiling. The wedding was supposed to be a secret from his clients. She'd assumed his staff had been told, but she might have blown it by coming here and spilling the beans.

"Married?" the woman asked as if she'd never heard the word.

"Yes. I just thought maybe another attorney in the firm could take a quick look." She waggled the document she had brought with her.

"What did you say your name was?"

"Whitney. Whitney Marshall. My cousin is Miranda Marshall, now Miranda Babcock."

"I see." She rose, saying, "Wait here. Someone will be right with you."

The woman disappeared behind double doors that must lead into the inner offices. Whitney took a deep breath and gazed out the window at the amazing view of San Diego Harbor. Looking at an aircraft carrier slowly moving toward the navy yard, she again rehearsed what she would tell the attorney. She needed to inquire about making payments on his fee. That was the important part; she had almost no money.

The door opened and the receptionist said, "Right this way."

Whitney followed her down a long corridor. She glimpsed several people diligently working at desks in various offices. At the end of the hall she saw a large office and beyond it the gleaming blue waters of the harbor. It had to belong to a senior partner, she decided. Her simple settlement agreement wasn't worth bothering someone so important. Why couldn't one of the other attorneys look at the document?

Before Whitney could suggest this, the receptionist stepped into the office and announced, "Whitney Marshall, sir."

From behind a glass desk the size of a pool table rose a tall man with black hair burnished at the temples with gray. His dark brown eyes warned her that he missed nothing in his field of vision. They also said he was a man who didn't know the meaning of the word *compromise.* What had she gotten herself into?

"Thanks, Karen," he said to the receptionist with a smile.

Whitney relaxed a little as the older
woman closed the door. Men who were kind
to their staff were kind in general. Right?

He extended his hand across the desk.
"Broderick Babcock."

A whooshing sound like a shrill wind
swept through her head. Whitney's lips
parted and she croaked out the words
"Whitney Marshall." She managed to ex-
tend her hand, but it felt limp in his.

"Sit, sit." He waved her to a chair in front
of his desk.

She dropped into the seat, inhaling
sharply, struggling to comprehend what
she'd just heard. How could this be Broderick Babcock? What was going on?

His bold gaze assessed her with searching
gravity, then he allowed himself to smile.
"People have tried lots of tricks to get in to
see me when they know I'm not taking any
cases because I'm overbooked, but this
beats all. That's why I told Karen I'd see
you. I wanted to look eye to eye at the
person who'd concoct such a story."

Beam me up, Scottie, was all she could
think. Obviously, Miranda had played a
trick on her or something. "I didn't concoct
a story," she responded in a weak but high-

205

pitched voice, sounding like Minnie Mouse's timid sister. "I actually thought . . . Never mind." She stood with as much dignity as she could muster. "My cousin must have played a practical joke on me. Obviously, I made a mistake. I'm sorry to have taken up your time."

"Sit down and tell me about it." He pointed to the stacks of papers littering his glass desk. "I need a good laugh."

Whitney had no trouble seeing how the attorney swayed juries. His words were spoken in a persuasive voice that permitted no argument. She dropped back into the chair. "My cousin convinced me that she was going on a honeymoon to Fiji. I hadn't seen Miranda much until very recently so I hadn't met the man she was supposedly marrying — Rick Babcock."

"That was her first mistake. I use Broderick professionally because big fancy names impress people, especially juries. But my friends call me Rod."

For the first time, it struck Whitney that Miranda might never have met the attorney. Strangers might think Broderick would be shortened to Rick, but his friends knew to call him Rod.

"Go on," he prompted.

"Miranda was very convincing. She moved

everything out of her place and let me have it. You see, I'm going through a divorce. Ah, actually, I am divorced, but . . ."

"Either you are or you aren't. It's like being pregnant. You're pregnant or you're not." He said this in a joking tone that forced Whitney to smile, but she felt more like strangling someone — Miranda.

"I thought I was divorced." She held up the document she'd been clutching in her left hand. "I signed an arbitration agreement months ago, then my ex reappeared. He claims it isn't legal because it needs to be signed in front of a notary."

"That's correct."

"I'm a little —" she started to say *suspicious,* then amended it to "uneasy because the document seems longer than the original. That's why I decided to have an attorney review the papers. I came here because I fell for Miranda's prank."

He shook his head slowly, saying, "Arbitration. What a laugh. Arbitrators are usually law students who couldn't pass the bar. People think they're saving money. Most end up at an attorney like you."

She smiled weakly. "I'm sorry to have bothered you. I'll find another lawyer to review these papers."

"It's not a bother," he quickly assured her.

"Leave the agreement with me. I'll have someone review it and get right back to you."

She hesitated. "I came here because I believed Miranda's story. I thought I could work out a payment plan because we were, you know . . . related."

He chuckled again, and she couldn't help smiling at him. She would bet he had most juries in the palm of his hand.

"I won't charge you. This probably isn't any big deal. Just leave the papers." He reached across the desk, and she handed him the document. It was slightly curled from her death grip. "I'm interested in your cousin and why she made up such a wild story. Tell me about her."

Whitney wasn't sure where to begin. Miranda's deception had been so unexpected. She hadn't had time to think.

"Miranda Marshall. Do I know her?"

"Maybe. She's my age, thirty-two going on thirty-three. We're first cousins and look a lot alike. Blond hair. Green eyes. We're the same size."

"I've never seen you before. Trust me, I have a good memory for faces."

She believed him. Broderick Babcock probably kept an entire law library in his head.

"Where does your cousin work?"

"She owns — owned — Marshall's Pet Concierge. That's a dog-walking and pet sitting service. Mostly dogs and a few cats."

He leaned back in his chair and frowned. "I don't have a dog. I can't imagine where we crossed paths."

"Maybe she just made it up. You're very well known. It —"

"It's still odd. I hope she didn't spread this all around town. I'm divorced —"

"I'm sure she didn't," Whitney quickly told him. "Miranda warned me not to tell anyone. She claimed you wanted to keep it secret so your clients wouldn't know you were out of town."

"Does your cousin have a history of mental problems?"

"No, of course not," Whitney assured him. But she realized how little she actually knew about Miranda.

Ryan came out of Le Bistro, a fine sheen of sweat coating his entire body. Domenic Coriz had him by the balls and the prick knew it. There wasn't any way out of this mess except to let Coriz have his way.

He sat in his Porsche and checked the messages on his cell phone. He'd had it on vibrate and knew several calls had come in while he'd been with the Native American. Ashley had left three messages. Walter Nance, the head of the group of cosmetic surgeons he was joining, had called.

Shit!

What was he going to tell Walter? He didn't have his share of the money for the new building. He had little chance of getting it for a while.

Last night, Lady Luck had spit in his eye. He'd left Ashley for the casino in hopes of accumulating enough money on the slot machines to have a run at the craps table. He'd bottomed out.

Ryan pressed speed dial and Ashley answered on the second ring. "What's up, babe?"

"Lexi's back with Whitney. She called to tell us and apologized for being so hysterical last night."

"I hope you were nice, considering . . ."

"Of course. I was very pleasant. She insisted I call you. She didn't want you contacting a bunch of testing labs when Lexi was already home."

"I appreciate that. Listen, sweetie. I've gotta go. I have a meeting with Walter."

He pressed End and heaved a sigh. Under normal circumstances, he would have ridden Ashley hard for having her girlfriend swipe Lexi, but he was nearly at the point where he was going to have to confess how broke they were.

Busted!

He couldn't imagine how Ashley would handle it if he confessed he had a gambling habit of this magnitude. She'd tried to be nonchalant but Ashley hadn't been able to conceal from him how happy she'd been to quit her job at the cosmetic surgery center. Money had been tight her entire life. She was counting on him to support her in a lifestyle that suited someone as beautiful as Ashley.

He stared beyond the steering wheel at the wall of the restaurant. He was positive Ashley loved him. But his financial situation and his status as a doctor meant a lot to her. She deserved the best and he was going to give it to her. No matter what it took.

It was after lunch before Preston Block appeared at the gym. According to the punk manning the reception desk, Block had spent the morning visiting clients at home.

"Block," Adam called as the buff guy slammed his car door shut.

He turned around and looked across the lot to see who had called his name. Block tried for a smile, but it didn't take a rocket scientist to realize the guy wasn't thrilled to see him. "Hey! How's the dog?"

Adam walked close enough to look into Block's eyes. "Lexi's home where she belongs."

Block switched the backpack he was carrying from one hand to the other. "I really don't want a reward. I —"

"I didn't come about a reward. I want to know the truth. You weren't jogging when you found Lexi, were you?"

"Of course I was."

"Bullshit. There isn't a Stop 'N Go on Harborside. You didn't buy the leash there. Why did you steal the dog?"

"Man, you've lost it. I found her, just like I said I did."

Adam glared at Preston Block and let his words hang like a noose in the air. Lies were like cockroaches. If you spotted one, others were nearby. A minute dragged by before Adam said, "I checked with Jake Conavey at Boomerang's. You didn't help out there last night."

If Block was surprised that Adam had contacted the owner of the punk bar, it didn't show in his face. He shrugged as if to say: So?

Adam was tempted to ram his fist down the cocky jerk's throat. Instead, he told him,

"Before my unit was called up for duty in Iraq, I was a detective with the San Diego P.D."

That got Block's attention. His nostrils flared ever so slightly, a visceral sign of his anxiety. Adam didn't add that he was no longer affiliated with law enforcement. He allowed Block to assume he'd be going back to work on the police force.

"Now, this can go one of two ways," Adam said in a casual voice. "You can tell me the truth or you can expect a lot of nosing into your personal life. I'm sure you don't want to be looking in your rearview mirror every time you get in your car. I'm sure you don't want to smoke a joint and wonder if you're going to be busted. I'm sure you don't want to be late to your clients because you've been pulled over for something."

"That's harassment. I'll report you."

"You've got a sealed juvenile record. Maybe your clients wouldn't like you so much if they received copies of that report." Adam was bluffing with this. It was nearly impossible to access a sealed juvenile record.

"Oh, shit!" Block glanced toward the entrance to the gym as if he expected someone to come out and help him. He inhaled deeply, his nostrils flaring out even more this time. "I didn't mean any harm. I brought the dog back, didn't I?"

"Why did you take her?" Adam ground out the words.

Block ran his shovel-like hands through his hair. "It was my plan — all mine. It seemed like a good idea at the time. She didn't have anything to do with it."

"She? You mean Ashley Fordham?" Seeing the pretty women featured on Block's Web site had made Adam wonder about Ryan's new wife, but Dr. Jox was so far from where they lived that he hadn't been sure about the connection.

"Yeah. Look, man . . . Ashley wanted this new house. She was really upset. She's been on the road her whole life. One apartment after another; one city after another."

"A tragedy, sure, but what does this have to do with the dog?"

"I've been working with Ashley for three years, since she moved here to try out for Miss San Diego. We've become close friends. I was the only one at the funeral when her mother died. We celebrated together when the doc gave her that killer ring."

Adam just bet Preston Block was overcome with joy at Ashley's engagement. Any jerk could see the guy was bonkers over the bombshell Fordham had married. "Okay, pard, I get the picture. What does your friendship with Ashley have to do with the Golden retriever?"

"I thought we could use it as leverage to persuade the stubborn broad to sign some papers. Then the doc's credit history would be clear, and they could buy a new house. Ashley told me the ex had already agreed to this settlement, but she refused to sign it now."

Adam kicked himself for not figuring this out on his own. He'd run off Fordham while he'd been physically attempting to force Whitney to sign. "What made you return the dog in the middle of the night? Doesn't sound like part of the plan."

His gaze lowered, as did his voice. "The doc figured out Ashley was responsible for the dog's disappearance —"

"Fordham didn't know anything about it?"

"Christ, no. He went ballistic when he discovered what she'd done. He insisted Ashley have her girlfriend return the dog."

"Girlfriend? He doesn't know about you?"

"Nah, he wouldn't understand our friendship." His expression clouded. "Look, the dog's back. No harm, no foul. Right? Don't tell anyone what really happened. It'll only hurt Ashley's marriage."

"I think Whitney deserves to know

the truth."

"What's the point?" Block shot back. "She should do what's right. Sign the agreement and move on. I'll bet you anything, Whitney won't believe her ex wasn't involved. She'll use it to stir things up even more. Ashley deserves a chance."

Adam wondered if Block didn't have a point. Whitney was seeing an attorney this morning. She expected him to okay the agreement, and then she'd sign it and return it to her ex-husband. What good could it possibly do for her to know Ashley's personal trainer had deliberately taken Lexi? She probably would think Ryan was involved.

All right, all right. *He* wanted Whitney to move on with her life. If he were honest with himself, he would admit that he wanted her to make a clean break now. He believed Preston was telling the truth. Whitney's ex hadn't taken Lexi. Whitney had her dog back. She didn't need to know all the details.

Leave well enough alone, he told himself.

CHAPTER FOURTEEN

"I can't imagine why Miranda would say she was going to marry Rod Babcock. What do you think?"

Whitney was sitting in Trish Bowrather's gallery and eating a salad. She'd come here directly after leaving the attorney's office. She'd walked Brandy again while Trish ordered lunch. Lexi and the other dogs were safely locked inside the cottage.

While she'd exercised Brandy, Whitney kept asking herself: Why? Why? Was Miranda in some kind of trouble? Could she be running from an abusive boyfriend? Debtors?

Whitney ruled out creditors. There hadn't been any dunning phone calls or collection agents hovering around. True, they could still appear, but Whitney doubted it.

What was so wrong that Miranda couldn't share it with Whitney? She'd poured her heart out to Miranda and told her the details of Ryan's betrayal. Miranda had never mentioned any problems and seemed really happy about her upcoming "wedding."

Of course, Whitney now knew why Miranda had never introduced her "fiancé" and why she wanted to keep the honeymoon secret. If Whitney hadn't been prompted by her encounter with Ryan and Lexi's disappearance, she never would have gone to see Broderick Babcock. She wouldn't have missed Miranda for at least another two weeks. Had Miranda been buying time?

Trish toyed with the romaine leaves in her chicken Caesar salad for a moment before replying, "I can't even begin to guess why your cousin would make up such a bizarre story then disappear. You're sure she took *all* her clothes?"

"Yes. I helped her pack them. She put books and office stuff and — I don't know — junk in the garage." She thought a moment. "She took her laptop computer, too."

"If she took all her clothes and her computer, she planned to relocate somewhere. She left in her car, right?"

"Yes." Whitney remembered her cousin driving off at dusk in her Volvo.

"Miranda must have car payments and credit card bills. I think there are ways of checking on the Internet but I'm not sure how."

Whitney nodded slowly. She thought Adam would know how to track down her cousin. How could she impose on him yet again?

"Don't make Miranda's problems your problems," Trish cautioned.

"You'd think she would have told me something."

"Not necessarily. You said you two hadn't been close in some time. Maybe she didn't want to involve you."

"Anything's possible," Whitney admitted. She remembered how she'd felt in bed last night with the dogs. There wasn't much in her life except Lexi. She'd counted on reconnecting with Miranda, but now that seemed impossible.

"What's Rod Babcock like?" Trish asked, unexpectedly changing the subject.

"He's older. Mid-forties." As she said it, Whitney realized this was about Trish's age and hoped she hadn't insulted her. When Rod and Trish each smiled, little fanlike lines appeared at the corners of their eyes. She rushed on. "Attractive. Really smart. It was nice of him to agree to check over that document for me."

"It's been my experience that men — especially lawyers — don't do anything without expecting something in return."

Trish's horrendous experience with her ex-husband had clearly made her distrustful of all men. Perhaps that was why she'd never remarried. It certainly wasn't her looks; Trish was strikingly attractive.

Trish rose, went over to her desk and returned with several envelopes. "Here are some invitations to my next exhibition this Friday evening. You were admiring Vladimir's work. Come meet him at the opening."

"Great," Whitney said. The Russian artist who used just one name had painted the malevolent eye she'd once associated with Adam. The enormous eye was watching her even now.

Trish handed her the envelopes. "Bring a friend, and give one to Rod Babcock. I'd like to meet him. I'm sure he can afford Vladimir's work."

"I'll try," Whitney replied. "I'm not sure I'll see Rod again. Someone on his staff —"

"You'll see him. Mark my words."

It was late afternoon when Tyler returned to the office. Sherry had told Adam that his partner had been out on "reviews" with several homeowner associations.

"Yo, Adam." Tyler stuck his head in

Adam's office door. "You wanted to see me?"

Adam looked up from the computer analysis of security equipment that he'd been reviewing. "Come in and shut the door."

"Uh-oh. Sounds serious." Tyler closed the door, then sat in the chair beside Adam's desk. "What's up?"

"The guard at Ocean Heights walked off his post last night. I —"

"I know. Sorry about that. Doesn't happen often."

"Shouldn't we have guards on call?"

Tyler smiled sheepishly. "It's hard on that shift, but I think I've got it worked out."

"Good." Adam didn't ask any more questions. The guard business was Tyler's baby. He'd developed it and worked with the accounts. "You were right about corporate security. We would need a lot more capital."

"It might be possible later," Tyler replied, but he didn't sound all that interested.

"I have another idea. We could go for it right now."

"Okay, shoot."

"Protecting buildings and offices has become a huge business since 9/11, right? I'm not talking about security personnel. I'm referring to security barrier systems like concrete barricades."

"Gotcha. We've had people call to see if we have things like that in stock." Tyler nodded slowly. "We might be able to move in that direction."

"I've located a company up north that makes swinging security arms like the ones we already have at guard kiosks and parking garages. Instead of being the lightweight type we use now, these are reinforced steel. They can stop a five-ton truck going seventy miles an hour. No one can just barrel in and blow up a building."

"That's really impressive." Tyler thought a moment. "If the arms are so much heavier, the motor that lifts them will have to be more powerful. It would mean changing our existing motors and buying new ones. I'm not sure homeowner associations —"

"I was thinking of businesses and the military installations around here, not gated communities."

"Doesn't the military have their own contractors?"

"Yes, but a lot of them have been diverted to Iraq. There's a serious shortage here," Adam replied. "I think we should start with bollards."

"What are they?"

"Knee-high cement posts that prevent cars or trucks from driving too close to buildings. There's a new type that can be temporarily removed if someone needs to access the building to move in or out or install large pieces of furniture or equipment."

"Okay. I know what you mean now."

"I'm going to start right away by getting us certified and arranging for security clearances. Could we use your father for a reference?"

Tyler cleared his throat, then replied, "I'm sure he'll agree. We actually had breakfast together, and he mentioned your uncle. I guess they met in Istanbul sometime last year. My father put some of his business info on your uncle's computer because his wasn't working. He'd like to retrieve it, but I told him the computer had been stolen. Any chance there's a backup disc somewhere?"

"I doubt it. I've been checking all the software the burglars left behind. There isn't much. What they did leave seems to be just discs for software installed on the computer like QuickBooks and Excel."

"Could you keep looking?"

Tyler sounded a little anxious. Adam knew his friend's relationship with his father wasn't very good. Obviously Quinten Foley must be upset about the theft and pressuring his son. "Sure. I should finish going through his office tonight —" he thought about Whitney "— or tomorrow. I'll let you know."

"Great. I'll —"

The buzzer on Adam's phone interrupted them. He picked up the receiver.

"There's a Max Deaver here to see you," Sherry told him. "He says it's important."

"Thanks. Send him in." Adam hung up. "I've got to talk to this guy. Let's touch base tomorrow."

Tyler nodded and left without another word. The forensic accountant hired by the attorney handling Calvin Hunter's estate entered Adam's office as soon as Tyler left.

"Hope you don't mind me dropping by. I have a client in the Halstrom Building next door."

"Not at all." Adam waved Deaver to the seat Tyler had just vacated. "What's up?"

Deaver sat down, his expression grave. "I'm still chasing your uncle's offshore accounts all over the place. It's a first-rate shell game. Best I've seen since I've been in the business. He might have had a pro help him."

"Really?"

"It's very likely. Most guys who show dogs wouldn't —"

"Remember, my uncle was in military

intelligence before he retired. He might have learned these maneuvers in the service."

"It's possible." Deaver shifted in the chair. "That's not what's bothering me. Yesterday, twenty-five thousand dollars was withdrawn from one of his offshore accounts in the Cayman Islands that I did manage to locate."

"How could that happen? I thought you needed the account number and a password."

"You're right. That's exactly what's necessary. Someone knows about this account. Whoever it is has his special password, too." Deaver leaned forward slightly and his tone became even more serious. "As far as I can tell, that Cayman account is the end point of the shell game. It was harder than hell to find. Your uncle deliberately shifted all his money around and around so that it would be nearly impossible to discover where it was."

"Yet someone has found it."

Adam stared out his window at the ocean in the distance. The late-afternoon light reflected off of it like a mile-long mirror. "I can't find any of his account numbers. They don't seem to be listed on anything in the house. Of course, it was burglarized. The account numbers and passwords might be on his stolen computer."

"Could be, but it wouldn't be a very smart move for a man in the intelligence field. People tend to write down passwords and hide them. With an estate this large and complicated, the access numbers might be in code or something."

"Whoever withdrew the money knew exactly where it was."

"That's the only explanation, and if they were testing, as I suspect, they now realize the password is correct."

"Is there anything I can do to stop that person from withdrawing any more money?"

"You could contact the bank. As heir to his estate, they might put a hold on the account, but it's unlikely. Secret accounts often have partners who wish to remain anonymous. Banking establishments honor those relationships."

Adam thought for a moment. "It seems to me that I read somewhere that secret partners in Swiss accounts are often terrorist groups."

"Exactly. Legitimate organizations or individuals deposit money in Swiss accounts, then funds are withdrawn by God-only-knows-who. That's why the Swiss have come under such scrutiny. Going into this, I doubted your uncle's money would be in

Switzerland. Too many prying eyes. He moved his cash from there to several other banks in the Maldives and Panama. They aren't as closely watched by the Feds looking for the sources of terrorists' funds."

Adam thanked Deaver for his time and the forensic accountant left. Uncle Calvin had been a very secretive man. Adam couldn't imagine him trusting anyone with such important information. The code *must* have been on his stolen computer. The thief or thieves had been after the code. It certainly explained why nothing else had been taken from the house.

Adam decided to talk to Quinten Foley. He might know something that would help. If not, whoever had the code could drain his uncle's remaining assets. Then Adam would be left with his uncle's bills and little money to pay them. He would run out of money in no time.

CHAPTER FIFTEEN

Whitney checked her cell phone, then put it back in her pocket. She told Adam, "I've never tried call forwarding before."

"Trust me. It works. I use it all the time."

They were on Adam's patio watching the sun set. Adam had phoned on his way home from work. He'd bought steaks to grill and ingredients for a salad.

"A prospective client called earlier to make sure I was going to be home this evening to discuss taking care of her dog. This will be the first client that I've gotten on my own."

Adam finished lighting the grill and turned back to her. "What kind of dog?"

"A poodle. I think the owner is a foreigner. She said Fiona was a *poo-dell.*"

"Large or small?" Adam poured them each a glass of pinot noir.

"I didn't ask. I assume small because you see so many of them, but it could be a standard poodle. She must have gotten my name from a client, but she didn't say who."

"Did you see an attorney?"

Adam's tone sounded a little guarded. She wondered if he might be reluctant to pressure her. "Yes. Broderick Babcock is looking over the papers."

"You saw Babcock himself? What about the honeymoon?"

She sighed. "There wasn't one. Miranda made it all up."

His eyes flared in disbelief, then narrowed while Whitney explained exactly what had happened at the attorney's office.

"Babcock didn't even know your cousin?"

Whitney shook her head. "I guess Miranda read about him or saw him on television. He's a local celebrity."

"Yeah, probably," he replied, but he didn't sound convinced.

"I wonder where she's gone," Whitney said. "Maybe something happened to her. Miranda might be in danger —"

"When people disappear like that they're usually running from something or someone."

"I don't have a clue what was happening with her. I've only been here a few days. When I arrived, needing a place to stay, Miranda asked if I wanted to take over her business. She claimed to be leaving to get married."

"What about her other relatives? She might be with them."

"No. I'm her only relative except for some really distant cousins. Her parents were killed in an auto accident. If my mother hadn't taken Miranda in, she would have gone into foster care."

Adam touched her shoulder. His hand felt warm and reassuring. "It's damn hard to disappear without a trace. I suspect your cousin will be easy to track down." He stood up. "While the grill's heating, let's go upstairs to the office. I'll get on my computer and see what I can find out."

Whitney followed him up the wide curved stairway. Jasper scampered along beside him. She kept Lexi, Maddie and Da Vinci with her on leashes. After last night, she wasn't taking any chances. She had to wait at the top of each step for the smaller dogs to scramble up beside Lexi.

Inside the wood-paneled office, Adam went to a laptop computer that was already open on the desk with a screensaver of crashing waves on it. Jasper hopped up onto his lap. Whitney settled into a chair next to the desk and the dogs clustered around her feet.

"At work we use Total Track. It's a service that collects personal information like credit card activity, bank accounts, court records and DMV registrations. Let's see what it has on Miranda Marshall. Does she have a middle name?"

"Leighton." Whitney spelled the family name Miranda's mother had given her cousin. "Isn't a lot of this information private?"

"It's supposed to be, but in this computer age, there's virtually nothing that's totally confidential. The Total Track guys got into the business by going to courthouses every day and recording info that was public record. Court records like DUIs and even prison sentences aren't entered into a computer every day. Understaffing is common and it can be weeks before they input the info. Total Track immediately chases down those reports and sells their service. It's expensive but it became a hit right away. A lot of smaller police departments use them because they don't have the manpower to keep up with all the information that's out there."

"I see." Whitney wondered what info they had on her.

"Okay. Here's your cousin's screen." He glanced over at her. "She has two credit cards and they're paid off. No activity on either one in three weeks." He touched another key, then frowned at the screen.

"What is it?"

"She closed her Wells Fargo checking account a week ago and withdrew the three-hundred-and-twenty-seven dollar balance. Her car's paid for and her other two credit card accounts at Nordstrom's and Macy's have been closed."

"So all Miranda has is a little cash and two credit cards."

"Looks like that's it. But she hasn't used the cards. Existing anywhere for a period of time on less than three hundred dollars is difficult."

"She might have had more cash with her." Whitney tried to recall exactly what Miranda had told her. "Some of her clients paid in cash. She told me to offer new clients a discount for cash."

"If you receive cash," he said, "and don't report it, you keep those earnings off the IRS radar screen, but it's illegal."

"I know, but it means she might have more cash with her than it appears." Whitney replied with a shake of her head. Her cousin had always been one to play the angles. "The question is, where is Miranda? And why did she just disappear?"

"From what you've told me, I suspect she had this planned for some time. She knows enough not to use her credit cards."

"I think anyone would know that. Just watch television. The second someone goes missing, police look to see if their credit cards have been used."

"True. Probably the best way to track her is to focus on the car. You'd be surprised how many fugitives get parking tickets or are pulled over for a missing taillight or some minor violation. It goes into the system and bingo — we know where they are."

"If nothing happens, we may never find her."

Adam shook his head. "Possibly, but I doubt it. It's harder to disappear than you'd think." He tapped a few keys on the computer. "I'm checking the Highway Patrol database. They gather all the information from local authorities for Homeland Security. Since 9/11, law enforcement has become very interested in all sorts of vehicles that could be used by terrorists especially since San Diego sits on the border." He let out a low whistle. "I'll be damned. A hit!"

She jumped up and looked over his shoulder at the screen. She saw a license-plate number followed by: Location — metered parking at Lindbergh Field.

"Miranda's car is in the airport lot. She left it at a meter that's expired. Does she have friends she might have flown to visit?"

She slowly shook her head. "Friends? I don't know. Since she's lived here from the time she was fifteen, you would think all her friends would be local."

Adam picked up the telephone and dialed a number. "Gus?" he said after waiting several rings. "It's Adam Hunter."

She watched him while he listened to something Gus was saying. Then he said, "I need a favor. Could you check security lists at Lindbergh and see if a Miranda Leighton Marshall boarded a plane? If you find her name, let me know where she went."

Adam's voice was a low rumble that Whitney found very intriguing. Despite the seriousness of the situation, she couldn't help remembering last night. She wanted to be in his arms again, but she reminded herself not to rush things. Slow down. Her life was complicated enough with Miranda missing.

Adam listened a moment, then said, "Nah. I haven't lost a girlfriend." He winked at her and she couldn't help smiling back. "Miranda's family is worried about her. I told them I would check." He listened again. "Thanks, Gus." Adam gave him his telephone number then hung up.

"You think she left the country?" Whitney asked.

"That's a possibility, since she doesn't seem to have friends or relatives she could visit." He logged off his computer, put Jasper on the floor and stood up. "If she bought a ticket, she had to show ID or her passport. It'll be in the records. Gus will find it. He's SDPD's point man with Homeland Security."

"I can't imagine where she'd go," Whitney said, bewildered.

Adam slipped his arm around her shoulders and guided her out of the room. "The grill's ready. Those steaks are waiting. There's nothing we can do until Gus checks and calls back."

She maneuvered to avoid tripping over the three dogs on leashes hovering at her feet. "How long do you think that will be?"

"Gus said he has time tonight. He checks info that comes in from the border crossing with Mexico. It's a slow night because it's raining south of Tijuana."

Whitney stayed in the kitchen to assemble the salad. It didn't take much work. Adam had bought bagged lettuce, a tomato and a cucumber. He'd also bought blue cheese dressing. Not a fat-free choice but she guessed after his time in Iraq, he wasn't counting calories.

She thought about the way he kept looking at her while he'd been on the computer and talking to his friend. When she'd first met Adam, he'd been so . . . so stoic. It was almost as if he wouldn't allow anything to touch him. He didn't want to be bothered to think or feel. Now he seemed to be coming back to life by degrees.

Had something happened to him?

She suddenly wanted to know everything about him. Her emotions had been chafed raw by her experience with Ryan. She hadn't asked enough questions. She'd fallen for him and believed love could make up for the quirks in Ryan's personality.

Ryan had been great in bed but he'd always been emotionally unavailable. She smiled to herself as she sliced the cucumber. "Emotionally unavailable" was a term she'd heard on some self-help talk show. The minute she'd heard it, Whitney knew it fit her husband.

He never shared his thoughts or feelings. Other than saying he was exhausted after his shift at the hospital or when he'd been studying, Ryan hadn't expressed much about himself. She didn't bother to wonder if he was different with Ashley.

Ryan Fordham didn't matter to her any longer.

It was a relief to have him out of her life, she decided. As soon as Rod Babcock gave her the okay, she was signing those papers and closing that unhappy chapter of her life. She smiled inwardly and splashed a little dressing on the salad.

She brought the dogs outside and tethered them to the gatepost. That way they'd be nearby while they ate.

"I don't think you have to keep them tied up," Adam said from the grill, where he was tending the steaks. "We can keep our eyes on them."

She headed back into the kitchen for the salad. Over her shoulder, she replied, "I'm too nervous to take any chances."

Whitney returned with the salad and the plates. She set their places and served the salad. It was going to be a typical "guy" meal. A huge steak and a side of salad. She'd bet Adam wouldn't have bothered with the salad at all if she hadn't been there.

He brought over the sizzling steaks. The smell made her stomach growl and had all the dogs standing at attention, their tails wagging. "Medium rare, I think. Cut into yours and see if it's okay before I turn off the grill."

She tested her steak. It was a little rare, but she said, "Perfect. Let's eat."

Adam sat down and immediately cut into his steak and took a bite. She could almost hear him sigh with satisfaction.

"I guess the food in Iraq wasn't too good."

"Got that right." He took a sip of the pinot noir. "They try, but feeding hundreds of soldiers isn't easy. There's nothing like home cooking."

"Was your mother a good cook?"

He shook his head. "My mother died when I was about seven. She had breast cancer back when there wasn't much they could do. All I remember her making for me was cereal. After she passed away, my dad did his best, but home cooking was mostly macaroni and cheese or microwave dinners. What about your mother? Did she like to cook?"

"Yes," Whitney replied with a smile. "We cooked on the weekends. You see, Mom was a single parent. My father walked out on us when I was less than a year old."

"Do you ever hear from him?"

"No. Never."

"Have you tried to contact him?"

"No. I figure if he didn't care about us then, he won't now."

Adam was silent for a moment and they ate without talking for a few minutes. Finally he asked, "What about Miranda?"

Whitney hesitated. She didn't want to admit that she'd ignored her only relative for so long. "I went off to UCLA but Miranda didn't have the grades to get into the UC system. She went to San Diego Community College. I came back the first two years for Thanksgiving, Christmas and spring break. We saw each other then."

Whitney gazed into the distance for a moment. "You know, the older we became, the more alike we looked. People assumed we were sisters. They expected us to be as close as sisters, but we weren't."

"Did Miranda have friends or boyfriends that you met?"

"No. She had her own apartment. It was a small place near Mission Bay. I was really envious because I had to live in the dorm, where you couldn't think or study."

"How was she able to afford it?"

"Her parents had life insurance. Miranda received half a million dollars when she was eighteen."

Adam whistled. "That's a lot of money at that age."

"Mom wanted to handle it for her, but Miranda insisted she could do it."

Adam chewed his steak and gazed at her thoughtfully. "She doesn't seem to have any of it left."

Whitney shifted uncomfortably in her chair. "When my mother became ill with cancer, there were things the insurance didn't cover. Miranda took care of it. I tried to pay her back but she wouldn't let me. She insisted Mom deserved every cent for taking her in when no one else would." With a pang of guilt, she added, "That's why I have to help her now. If I'd spent more time with her when we moved here, she might not have disappeared without telling me what was wrong."

"How long have you been back?"

"A little over a year. I called Miranda right away. We said we'd get together but we never did. I tried — once. I invited her to dinner but she already had plans. I never called her again, and she didn't call me."

He cut up his last bit of steak into little pieces. Obviously, Jasper was in for a treat. "Wasn't that strange?"

"Not really. Miranda and Ryan didn't get along." The admission brought back so many memories — all of them troubling. "I guess Miranda saw things in Ryan that I didn't. I should have asked her — paid more attention to what she was thinking."

CHAPTER SIXTEEN

Tyler leaned back, his feet propped up on the rail, and gazed out at the harbor lights from the balcony of his condo while he sipped his beer. A cat's paw of a breeze brought the briny scent of the ocean across his face. God, he loved this place.

He turned his head and intently watched Holly. She'd seemed preoccupied all evening. He wished she would be a little more open about what she was thinking.

"Should we eat, then hit one of the clubs?" he asked in case she was bored. The great thing about living here was being close to the best restaurants and a hot club scene.

She shook her head and sent her silky brown hair fluttering across her bare shoulders. "No. Let's catch a bite, come back and watch a movie."

"What do you feel like eating?"

"How about Wok 'N Roll?"

"Sounds great," he agreed, even though

the Thai café with its aquarium walls and trendy sushi bar wasn't his favorite.

Holly stood up and pulled down the skirt of her dress with a smile that made eating Thai food worth it. "I'm going to grab my pashmina. I'm a little chilly in this dress."

While she went into the bedroom to get her shawl from the closet she used when she was here, Tyler closed the sliding glass door to the balcony. The cell phone on his hip jingled and he pulled it off his belt. It had better not be Butch at the command post. He didn't want to tell Holly that he had to fill in for a no-show again.

He'd told Butch to hire a few guys with minor violations on their background checks. He'd also authorized Sherry to pay them to stay on call during the graveyard shift. As he checked the caller ID, he saw "blocked" and knew it wasn't the command center.

"Did you talk to Adam about that backup disc?"

As usual, his father was all business. No inquiries about how he was or how things were going. No question about whether he was interrupting anything.

"I spoke with Adam." Tyler kept his tone low. He didn't want Holly to overhear him. Maybe it was just his imagination, but he wasn't as comfortable with her as he had been before Adam's return. He half expected her to say they were through. They'd been together for over two years. He had no reason to think she would leave but the idea kept popping into his mind. "He says the burglars took most everything, but he'll look —"

"I'm going to call him and tell him that I'm coming over to help search. Do you have his number? There's no listing for Calvin Hunter. Knowing Calvin, he must have had an unlisted telephone."

Holly walked out of the bedroom, a bright pink shawl draped over one arm. She'd put on fresh lipstick and sprayed on the perfume he'd given her for her birthday.

"I have his cell number back at my place," he fibbed. "I'm on my way to dinner with Holly. I'll call you with the number later."

"Later? I'd planned on going over there tonight."

Christ almighty. This missing info must be really important. Quinten Foley usually spent his evenings at the officers' club with his cronies when he was in town.

"I doubt he's home." Tyler deliberately did not use Adam's name. Holly was standing next to him now, waiting to leave for a late dinner. "He has a girlfriend." This was a stretch. Adam had mentioned a woman who was living in the cottage behind his uncle's house. Something in the way Adam had said it had made Tyler wonder.

"All right. Call me with his number as soon as you get home." A faint click followed by a burst of static told Tyler that his father had hung up.

"Who's that?" Holly asked.

"My father. He's in town for a while." He hadn't mentioned his breakfast meeting with his father. Holly's parents lived north of San Diego in Newport Beach. They frequently invited Tyler and Holly for dinner or barbecues on the deck of their home on Linda Isle. Tyler was embarrassed at the way his father blew into town but never considered entertaining them, even though Tyler had made it clear he was serious about Holly.

"Who has a girlfriend?"

They were in the hall now and Tyler was locking the condo door. He considered lying, but not telling his father the truth was one thing. The bastard deserved it. Holly meant too much to him. Besides, it might be better if she thought Adam was seeing someone else.

"Adam."

The word detonated on impact. Tyler

could see it in the spark of light that suddenly fired Holly's brown eyes. "Really? He just got back."

"You know Adam. He's a fast worker."

Holly didn't respond until they were in the elevator on their way to the street level. "Why don't we get together with Adam and his new girl? Let's have them for dinner. I'll make lasagna. He loves it."

"Okay," Tyler replied without any enthusiasm. The last thing he wanted was to have Adam around Holly.

Ryan sat at the kitchen table and watched Ashley rinse off their dinner dishes before putting them in the dishwasher. It was after nine, a little late to be eating, but Ryan had been with Walter Nance discussing new equipment for the cosmetic surgery facility they'd be opening soon. He'd sidestepped the money question, but Ryan wondered how much longer this would work.

"My mother made Swedish meatballs whenever we had a place with a kitchen," Ashley told him. "That's where I learned how to cook them."

The meatballs made of hamburger rolled around in his belly like golf balls. "We're going to need to eat home more," he told her. "For a little while."

Ashley looked over at him with wide blue eyes. "Okay. Whitney left several cookbooks in the cabinet over there. I'll try some new recipes. Mother didn't teach me much. We ate fast food mostly."

Ryan smiled and noticed Ashley didn't question his reason for eating at home, which made it more difficult to segue into a financial discussion. "We're a little tight for money until Whitney signs those papers."

She closed the dishwasher and started it. "I was thinking. Maybe we should sell this house and rent until we can afford to buy a place like the one we loved in Coronado."

He tried to keep his expression neutral. This was *exactly* what he'd been on the verge of proposing. Not that selling this place would net them much money after the loans were paid off, but at least he wouldn't have those huge payments clobbering him each month.

"You don't like this house much, do you?" he asked.

She sat down on his lap and stroked the back of his neck. "It's okay, but I'd rather take the pressure off you while you're getting the new practice up and running."

"Then I'll buy any place you want." Ryan kissed Ashley and cradled her in his arms for a few minutes. "I'll call a Realtor tomorrow —"

"I'll do it. You're too busy."

He met her gaze dead-on and saw how much she loved him and wanted to help. "I need to cut a deal. I don't want to pay some dufus Realtor full commission. Once I've settled —"

"I'll take care of it. My mother and I had to make lots of deals for clothes and things so I could compete."

"Okay," he said slowly. She'd been a great saleswoman for the cosmetic surgery firm when he'd met her. That meant selling but in a way that clients never realized they'd been "sold" anything. She might be able to handle this.

Ryan let Ashley lead him off toward the bedroom. He was exhausted. He'd been at the casino until dawn. He'd intended to tell her about his gambling when he mentioned selling this house. Now wasn't the time. If Lady Luck smiled on him, Ryan's life would be back on track.

"Did your girlfriend have any trouble getting Lexi back to Whitney?" Ryan was in his closet now, undressing. For a moment he thought Ashley didn't hear him. She'd gone into her own closet opposite his.

"No. Whitney thinks the dog wandered off."

Ryan didn't give a shit what his ex thought. He wanted their marriage to evaporate as if it had never existed.

"I don't think the new client is going to call."

It was nearly eleven-thirty. Adam and Whitney had been watching *Nuts for Mutts* on Animal Planet and talking since dinner. *Companion Carnivores* was on next. As attracted as he was to Whitney, Adam didn't think he could sit through another program about dogs.

"It's late for her to call, but she'll probably phone tomorrow."

Whitney nodded. She seemed distracted. She was probably still worrying about her cousin. He had to admit disappearing after concocting such an elaborate story ranked right up there with the bizarre. He'd been in law enforcement since he'd graduated from college and he'd never encountered a disappearance as strange as this.

It wasn't as if Miranda had left suddenly. You heard about those cases all the time. A woman goes out for milk and vanishes. This wasn't one of those incidents. Miranda had planned her disappearance probably for some time.

Why?

As if on cue, his cell phone rang. Gus was finally getting back to him. "Find anything out?"

"Yeah. Miranda Marshall didn't get on any plane."

"She didn't board a plane," he repeated for Whitney's benefit. "But her car's at the airport."

"There's two, maybe three explanations," Gus told him. "She could have left the car there to make someone think she took a flight. It's possible she has ID showing another name, and she used it to board a plane."

"That's two possibilities. What's the third?"

A beat of silence. "Any chance there's another set of car keys around?"

The light dawned and Adam covered the phone. "Is there another set of keys to your cousin's car around the cottage?"

Whitney sat up straighter. "I think so. There are several sets of keys in the kitchen drawer. I'm pretty sure one of them is for her Volvo. Why?"

He didn't answer her. Instead, he told Gus, "We have keys. Thanks for your help. I —"

"Just a minute. There's something else."

It had been several years since Adam had

worked with Gus, but he recognized the concern in his friend's voice. "What is it?"

"After I ran Marshall's name through the system and came up with zilch, I asked around the department."

Adam listened to what his friend had discovered about Whitney's cousin, made a mental note of several details, thanked him for his trouble, then hung up.

"What's going on?"

He regarded her with a speculative gaze, not knowing how to put this exactly. "Gus thinks I should check the trunk of Miranda's car. He gave me its location." He leaned a little closer to her. "You see, it's fairly common for homicide victims to be found in the trunks of their own cars."

She stared at him wordlessly for a moment. "Why do you think someone killed her?"

"It's just a possibility. Her name didn't come up on an ID check for flights. If she was in some kind of trouble, she could have been killed."

"Ohmygod," she whispered in a choked voice. "Why didn't she tell me? I would have done anything to help her."

Adam put his arm around her shoulders and drew Whitney to him. "Don't jump to conclusions. This is merely police procedure. We're eliminating things."

She pulled out of his embrace and jumped to her feet. "Let's check it out. I'll look for the keys right now."

"Okay," he agreed even though it was late. "There's one other thing."

Whitney must have picked up on the troubled note in his voice. "What? Tell me!"

"Guys on the vice squad told Gus that they knew your cousin. Miranda had never been arrested, but they'd seen her several times when they went out to Saffron Blue. It's a nightclub."

Whitney frowned, puzzled. "She never mentioned waitressing there."

"She wasn't waiting tables. Miranda worked as a stripper."

CHAPTER SEVENTEEN

Whitney stood next to Adam and gazed at the trunk of Miranda's Volvo.

"I don't smell anything," Adam said, his voice almost a whisper.

They'd driven to San Diego's Lindbergh Field in Adam's Rava. It hadn't been difficult to find the metered parking space where her cousin had parked her car. They'd pulled up behind the vehicle and had gotten out, leaving all the dogs in the SUV.

"Smell?"

"A dead body —"

"Okay. I get it." Her stomach did a slow backflip as she imagined Miranda crammed into the trunk. *Please, God, don't let Miranda be in there,* she silently prayed. Whitney's neck muscles quivered as she watched Adam insert the key she'd found in the kitchen drawer of the cottage into the trunk.

The lid flew open.

Whitney braced herself and peered inside.

"It's empty." *Thank you, God.* Miranda must be alive somewhere, she decided.

Adam asked, "Feel better?"

Whitney managed a nod and leaned toward him slightly. She suddenly felt light-headed. Relief or fear? Both. She was relieved that Miranda wasn't in the trunk of the car, but after finding out her cousin had worked as a stripper, Whitney's anxiety had increased. Had Miranda's job gotten her into so much trouble that she'd lied to her only living relative and fled?

Suddenly, Whitney recalled the way Miranda had acted the night she'd left. Miranda had hugged her fiercely . . . almost as if she had been saying goodbye forever. Something about Miranda's "wedding" story had bothered Whitney from the beginning. At the time, she'd attributed her misgivings to a boyfriend who didn't want to meet his fiancée's only relative. Now she wondered if she hadn't been picking up subtle clues that her cousin was lying.

"Are you okay?" Adam asked.

For an instant she wavered, her blue eyes flickering with uncertainty. Then she drew herself together and nodded. "I'm fine. Just worried about Miranda, is all."

He slipped his arm around her and brought her close. A little lurch skittered from her heart downward until she felt it in her toes. She was tempted to rest her head against his shoulder but didn't. *Be strong,* she told herself. *You've been through a lot. Don't get involved with another man so quickly.*

He placed a comforting hand on the back of her neck. Her body flushed with hot awareness. Despite all the problems she'd had with Ryan, despite common sense telling her to slow down, despite everything — she wanted Adam Hunter. It was as simple as that.

His mouth met hers, warm, sweet, and her lips parted. One large hand wove through the hair at the back of her neck while the other hand found its way to the lowest reaches of her back and urged her closer and closer until her whole body was flush against his.

Push him away, she ordered her body, but she was powerless to resist temptation. He teased her lips apart with the tip of his tongue. She returned the kiss, her tongue greeting his. The contact sent a bolt of pure pleasure through her entire body and her pulse went haywire, throbbing in intimate, sensitive places.

She ran her hands over the strong muscles of his back and shoulders, enjoying the sensation. The woodsy scent of his shaving cream filled her lungs as she clung to him. She knew better than to keep kissing him, but she didn't have the willpower to stop.

How long had it been since she'd kissed a man with so much passion? She honestly couldn't remember the last time. *Don't think about Ryan,* she warned herself. *Live in the moment.*

At the sound of an engine, they reluctantly pulled apart. A security officer drove around the corner in a patrol car. Whitney stepped out of Adam's embrace, a little embarrassed.

"Something wrong?" the man asked.

The airport had closed for the night. Lindbergh Field was located near residential neighborhoods and flights were terminated before midnight to control noise. At this hour the parking lots were deserted. Whitney had no doubt they appeared to be very suspicious.

"No. We're just checking for Whitney's cell phone." He put his hand on her shoulder. "It isn't here. She must have left it somewhere else."

"I see," the man responded, but his tone said he had his doubts.

Whitney and Adam got into the SUV. Opening the door awakened the dogs. Lexi spotted the security patrolman. The retriever decided she was a watchdog. Lexi's barking incited the others, and a second later they joined in.

"No. Bad." The stern tone of Whitney's voice was enough to silence Lexi, but the others kept barking.

Adam turned around. "No!"

The dogs stopped barking. Jasper meekly lay down. Whitney doubted Adam had ever raised his voice to the little dog before this. He started the car and drove away slowly. The security car followed them until they arrived at the pay booth.

Whitney waited until they were on the freeway before suggesting, "Why don't we go to Saffron Blue? Maybe the other girls or the manager knows something about Miranda."

"No. The girls will be so busy right now that they won't take time to spit on you. Most people don't realize it, but strippers earn nothing but tips."

"Really? I had no idea. I assumed . . ." She'd never given strippers much thought until she discovered what Miranda had been doing. The screen in her mind played a sleazy bar filled with smoke and lecherous men. Cheap-looking women with teased hair and bobbling silicone breasts flaunted their bodies on a stage beneath a blaring spotlight.

"Forget your assumptions. This is an upscale club with a hundred-dollar cover charge. The police receive calls to Saffron Blue occasionally. Usually it's a fight in the parking lot. Jared Cabral doesn't put up with troublemakers. His bouncers kick them out at the first sign of trouble."

"Jared Cabral owns Saffron Blue?"

Adam turned off La Jolla Parkway onto Torrey Pines Road. "Yes. Cabral owns eight clubs — last I heard. Southern California, Arizona and Vegas. All cater to upscale clientele. Gambling's legal in his Vegas clubs. The others have illegal high-stakes games going most nights in a private room."

"Illegal gambling and fights. I suppose there are drugs around, too."

"Undoubtedly, but Cabral keeps illegal activities outside so he won't be busted."

A shudder passed through her. "I can't imagine why Miranda would be working there. She had plenty of money from the insurance policy."

"Don't be too sure. If it was in a bank or a brokerage house in the U.S., the money would have shown up on the Total Track report."

She moistened her dry lips and tried to

think clearly. How could she have lost touch with Miranda like this?

"It's been, what? Almost fourteen years since Miranda received the money?" Adam didn't wait for a response. "She could have spent it on school, rent, vacations, jewelry, clothes and stuff."

"I don't think so. Miranda was working part-time to pay the rent when she was attending junior college. That's what she told me when she paid some of Mom's medical bills. She acted as if she still had most of the money." Whitney thought a moment. "What she gave Mom was less than five thousand dollars."

"Miranda certainly didn't spend it on a fancy car. That Volvo was new in the late eighties."

"She didn't buy a lot of clothes, either. I helped her pack. She had a few nice things, but nothing extravagant."

"Do you know how long she lived in my uncle's cottage?"

"About two years. We talked at Christmas and birthdays so I knew when she moved from her little apartment in Mission Bay. The cottage came rent-free if she took care of Jasper when your uncle was away." Whitney was silent for a moment, thinking. "You know, Miranda was always the frugal type.

It wasn't like her to have squandered the insurance money."

Sirens behind them interrupted their conversation. Adam pulled to the curb, and the dogs who'd fallen asleep jumped up to see the fire engines whiz by.

After the last fire trucks passed, Adam asked, "Was Miranda the type to work as a stripper?"

"No way." Whitney released an audible sigh. "I guess I didn't know her as well as I thought. Anything's possible. She could have spent the insurance money."

Adam drove away from the curb. "Tomorrow I'll go to see Cabral. He may be able to shed light on Miranda's disappearance."

They rode toward their street in silence. Ahead, Whitney saw an orange glow above the trees, lighting the dark sky.

"Looks like there's a house on fire." Adam sounded concerned.

Whitney knew fire was a real danger in San Diego. In the last several years, fires that started in the brush-filled hillsides had rampaged out of control and destroyed many homes. It was early summer and the hills were still green. It seemed to be too soon for a brush fire, but anything was possible.

Adam braked suddenly as they rounded

the corner. Fire engines and police cars blocked their way, red and blue lights flashing. Smoke filled the air and made it difficult to see exactly what was on fire. It was too close to be the hills. If it wasn't their place, it had to be a home nearby.

A police officer held up his hand to stop them. Adam rolled down the window. Warm smoke billowed into the car.

"Do you live on this street, sir?"

"Yes. We're at number 265."

"The small house behind yours is burning. Do you know if anyone was in there?"

Was? Her heart slammed against her rib cage in painful thuds. Suddenly it became difficult to breathe, and she could barely think. Thank heavens, they'd taken the dogs with them. Things could be replaced, she reminded herself, living beings could not.

"No one's in the cottage." Adam cocked his head toward Whitney. "She lives there alone."

"Park your car," the officer told him.

"I can't believe this," Whitney cried. "Thank God I have the dogs with me."

They parked, jumped out of the car and followed the officer up the street. Murky, acrid-smelling smoke curdled the air. Firefighters in neon-yellow suits blocked her line of vision. She couldn't see up the driveway to the small cottage. Adam's hand was on her arm, and he guided her forward.

"Hunter," called a man in slacks and a sports jacket. Apparently he was with the police and knew Adam.

"What's going on?"

The man in a sports jacket and a polo shirt walked up to them. "This is your place?"

"Yes," Adam replied. "Why are you here?"

Whitney registered the subtle change in Adam's voice. His expression was different, too. What was there about this man that disturbed him?

"Neighbors reported the blast."

"Blast?" Whitney choked out the word, her mind reeling at the scene before her.

"Who are you?" he asked.

"Wh—Whitney Marshall. I live in the cottage."

"I'm Dudley Romberg with homicide." He studied her for a moment, then asked, "Do you know anyone who would want to kill you?"

"No. Of course not," she managed to say, her stomach roiling.

"Someone threw a pipe bomb through the bedroom window. It caused the fire."

"Ohmygod! Why would they do that?" She caught Adam's eye. In a heartbeat the answer hit her. *Miranda.* The bomb had been intended for her cousin. This news, coupled with the earlier revelation that Miranda had been a stripper, crippled Whitney's ability to think clearly.

"What makes you say it was a pipe bomb?" Adam asked.

"The broken window. The first fire unit to respond called Reserve Officer Wells. He's with the Naval Explosive Ordnance Disposal Center at Miramar Air Station. He's right over there."

"Let's talk to him," Adam said to her.

Adam guided her up to a tall, gaunt man with pewter-gray hair in a military brush cut. He had his back to them, watching the fire. The flames weren't as high as they had been when they'd driven up, but the cottage was still burning.

"Officer Wells," Adam said, and the man turned to them. His face was ruddy from the heat of the fire. "I'm Adam Hunter. This is my home. I understand that you think a pipe bomb caused the fire."

"There'll have to be a post-blast investigation to confirm my analysis. The first responders took Polaroids of the scene." He handed three pictures to Adam.

Whitney looked over Adam's shoulder at them. When the photos had been taken, the fire was burning at the rear of the cottage. The front, now a smoldering ruin, hadn't been burning. The black-and-white photo clearly showed the shattered window.

"See —" Wells pointed to the picture "— no glass on the outside." He motioned for Adam to look at the next photograph. "Notice the mailbox?"

Whitney saw that the mailbox at the path leading up to the cottage was buckled in two.

"Pipe bombs are simple to make," explained Wells. "Instructions are all over the Internet. You just need a length of pipe, blasting powder, a power source — usually a nine-volt battery — and end caps for the pipe. The end caps fly off when the bomb detonates. They shoot out like they'd been fired from a rifle. A cap hit the mailbox. One of the firefighters was alert enough to spot it and notice there wasn't any glass on the ground the way there would have been if heat from the fire inside had caused the window to explode."

Dudley Romberg walked up to them again. The detective asked her, "Where were you when the fire started?"

"At the airport," she said.

He shook his head slowly. "Lucky you. If you'd been in the house, you'd be dead.

Seems the pipe bomb was full of shrapnel. If the explosion didn't get you, flying shrapnel would have."

"Like the bombs in Iraq that kill so many people."

"Exactly." Adam's expression was more than grim.

"Don't go anywhere," Romberg said. "I'm going to need to talk to you."

He walked away. Adam waited a moment, then said, "Now we know why Miranda hightailed it out of town. She was mixed up in some serious shit. Someone wanted her dead."

"I can't imagine why." Fear sent hot blood pumping through her veins. "At least the dogs were with us. No life was lost. That's what really matters, isn't it?"

He slid his arm around her shoulders. "You bet. That's what matters, but we need to find out what's going on before anything else happens. Don't tell Romberg that Miranda was working at Saffron Blue."

"Why not?"

"I want to talk to Jared Cabral first."

"Won't Romberg know? All your friend had to do was ask around the station."

"True, but Romberg's a few beans shy of a full burrito. Around the station they call him Dudley 'the dud' Romberg. It'll take him a while to ask if the beat cops know your cousin. Meanwhile, I'll get first crack at Cabral."

Chapter Eighteen

Whitney gazed at Adam from the armchair where she was sitting. He was walking Romberg to the door of his uncle's home. The detective had interviewed Whitney, asking her questions about Miranda. Since Whitney had lived in the cottage less than a week, the investigation was focused on Miranda. Whitney had not brought up Saffron Blue. She felt a little guilty about not disclosing this information, but Adam had helped her so much already and she trusted him.

She leaned down to give Lexi's head a quick pat. The cloying smell of smoke and the commotion of firefighters had spooked the dogs, especially Da Vinci. The Chihuahua was huddled against Jasper on the sofa with Maddie nearby. At least they were all safe.

Lexi's disappearance had prompted Whitney to keep all the dogs at her side. If she hadn't, they would have been in the cottage and died in the fire. She couldn't imagine a worse fate for a helpless animal than to be trapped in an inferno.

What about Miranda? she asked herself. Whoever had thrown the pipe bomb hadn't cared what kind of horrible death she suffered. *How could Miranda have gotten herself involved in something that would result in this?*

Adam closed the front door behind the detective and walked back into the living room.

"I'm sorry about the fire," she told him.

"Don't blame yourself. It's your cousin's fault — not yours." He dropped down onto the sofa where he'd been sitting when Detective Romberg had questioned her. The motion caused Da Vinci to leap up on his short legs and look around anxiously. Seeing nothing troubling, he lay down again and snuggled up against Jasper.

"I would never have guessed Miranda was in this much trouble." Whitney twisted the hem of her shorts between her fingers. She'd been doing it since she'd sat down. She told herself to stop.

"I want you to be very careful," he told her. "You look a lot like your cousin, right? They could come after you by mistake."

She nodded. "When do you plan to visit

Saffron Blue? I'll need to reschedule some of my walks to go with you."

Adam shook his head. "I'm going alone. Cabral isn't the easiest man to talk to. Cops make him antsy because he's sure they're looking for an excuse to bust him, which is true. He won't open up in front of a woman."

Whitney started to protest then the reality of her situation hit her. "I don't have anything but the clothes I'm wearing. I guess I'll have to go shopping first thing in the morning. Luckily all my client info was in my BlackBerry, and I always keep it in my purse." Another wave of reality crashed over her. "My Jeep —"

"The fire started in the bedroom where the pipe bomb was thrown, then leaped backward toward the carport and garage before the wind kicked up and sent it toward the front of the house. If the fire didn't destroy your SUV, then it suffered a lot of smoke and water damage. We'll know more in the morning when it's light enough to see."

She stared at him and blinked, her mind suddenly becoming focused. She'd been thinking about Miranda and who might want to kill her. She hadn't given much thought to her own plight. She had no place to live. No car.

Nothing.

Suddenly, the spacious living room seemed too tiny. The walls were closing in on her. She tried to breathe but her lungs refused to take in air. Throbbing started in her temples, then exploded through her head.

Her anxiety must have been reflected on her face. Adam rose to his feet and came up to her. Without a word, he pulled her into his arms. She tried to draw back but his arms tightened around her. After a moment, he took her face in one hand. One finger gently brushed her cheek. His other hand skimmed soothingly over her back.

"Don't worry about anything." He rested his cheek against the top of her head. "We'll work it out. I'll help you."

Adam seemed so strong, so supportive, and she felt so lost. She permitted herself to savor the moment, the comfort he offered.

But as tempting as it was to nestle in his arms and let him take over, Whitney asked, "Why? You hardly know me."

"I know all I need to know. When you saw your place was on fire, you weren't concerned about yourself. You cared more about the dogs."

Whitney didn't know what to say. She had

always loved animals. When she'd seen the flames, her first thought had been relief. The dogs were safe. She didn't know how she could have faced their owners and told them their pets had been burned alive.

"You can stay here as long as you want," he told her. "The maid's quarters are off the kitchen. You'll have room for the dogs there and a lot of privacy."

She almost told him she couldn't stay here, then asked herself where she could possibly go. Who could she turn to? Not Ryan. Trish Bowrather was a possibility, but their friendship — if she could call it that — was new, untried. She wouldn't feel comfortable asking Trish for help.

"Thank you," she whispered, her voice choked.

He brought her over to the sofa and pulled her down beside him. "Escaping death does something to you," he told her. "It alters the way you see the world."

He was right, of course, but until he said it Whitney hadn't quite come to grips with her own close call. The bombing had been a devastating shock. All she could concentrate on was Miranda and the dogs. It was just now sinking in. She'd narrowly missed being killed by whoever was determined to murder her cousin.

If she hadn't come here for a barbecue, she would have been in the cottage, asleep in the bedroom where the pipe bomb had been thrown. She would have died. In a delayed reaction, her composure started to crack.

"Why didn't Miranda warn me?"

"She probably didn't realize what she was involved in would have such deadly consequences." His arm was around her, his tone comforting. A minute passed while she tried to calm herself. In the aftermath of her divorce, Whitney's emotions were unstable. Knowing her only relative had betrayed her made something inside Whitney shatter into a million jagged pieces.

There was no way to sugarcoat this, she decided. "Miranda must have known. No matter how happy she seemed, she vanished without a trace for a reason. She should have warned me."

Mind-numbing disbelief brought the sting of hot tears to her eyes. The tight rein she'd kept on her emotions collapsed. She refused to cry, but her body began to tremble so hard that she had to clutch her bare knees with both hands to keep the shaking under control.

"Try not to be upset," Adam said. "Things will get better. Time will help. I know." He squeezed her shoulders, but she didn't feel any better. "I know what you're going through."

"How could you? I don't mean to be ungrateful, but I just lost everything I have on this earth. Not that things matter, but I almost died."

Adam didn't reply. She fought back the tears, then took a minute to let her painful breathing return to something near normal. "I'm sorry. I didn't mean to sound ungrateful. I don't know what I'd do without you."

He studied her a moment. His expression darkened with an unreadable emotion that revealed something she couldn't decipher. He'd shared almost nothing about himself and had shown little emotion. She had no idea what was going on in his mind.

"We have a lot more in common than you might think. My uncle was the last of my family. At least you have your cousin."

At this point Whitney couldn't honestly say that was a good thing. Family protected each other, didn't they? Miranda should have said something, done something so Whitney could protect herself.

"I had a brush with death that was even closer than yours."

His tone brought her up short. She'd never seen him this intense . . . this serious.

She waited for him to continue but he didn't.

"You did?" she prompted. "When?"

She gazed into his eyes, but he didn't respond. His shuttered expression warned her that he might not want to talk about this.

Finally, he cleared his throat and spoke. "I was in Iraq with my National Guard unit. I'd known the guys for years. We were weekend warriors who never expected we'd find ourselves in a battle zone."

There was so much emotion in his words that she understood the Adam Hunter she'd known up to this point had been little more than an impression. From the moment he'd attacked her, Whitney had *assumed* things based solely upon her own conclusions — not facts. Adam had a power and depth to him that she hadn't realized existed.

"Our unit was in charge of the security checkpoints between Baghdad and the airport. It's five miles of hell. Every terrorist and every political faction wants to control the road or shut it down. I worked with Ed and Mike most of the time. We searched vehicles and checked identification at the first security post beyond the airport. After having our tours extended because we had special expertise, we were just ten days from

273

coming home when we drove up to the Green Zone that morning."

"That's the safe area around U.S. head-quarters, right?"

"Supposedly. We were in an armored vehicle, just the three of us, at the entry checkpoint. A woman came up with a baby in her arms. You could see the kid was sick. Its face was red and it was bawling. She held out the baby to us —"

Whitney waited for him to continue. She was almost afraid to hear what he was going to say.

He averted his eyes and directed his gaze across the living room to the landscape painting on the wall. "It happened all the time," he finally began, his voice pitched low. "Innocent civilians — kids and even babies — were injured in terrorist attacks. Their medical facilities sucked so they often came to us for help. Mike waved her off and just as he did I had this . . . feeling."

She waited in stricken silence, half knowing what he was going to tell her.

He turned back to her. "I knew. I don't know how, but in that instant I realized she was going to kill us."

Whitney tried to imagine how horrible that must have been, but couldn't. Until tonight her only experience with death had been her mother's battle with cancer. She had been warned. Death had been expected.

"I knew we were as good as dead. There was no way to get out of the vehicle in time. Hell, I didn't even have the chance to open my mouth and warn my buddies."

Anguish colored every syllable he uttered. She suddenly felt ashamed of herself. Her brush with death had been nothing compared to his.

"I still can't believe it. That mother had a bomb concealed under her clothes. She knew it was going to kill her and her baby."

Whitney couldn't imagine it either. How could any mother take the life of her own child?

"She detonated the bomb just as I yelled, 'Duck.' An explosion of light, a bang like nothing I'd ever heard, then the world went as black as hell itself."

Whitney didn't know what to say. Obviously, he'd survived. Had either of his friends?

"I woke up a week later in a field hospital. I had a massive concussion. I wasn't allowed to lift my head for another week. It hurt like a sonofabitch. There was a helluva ringing in my ears. The nurses had to shout for me to hear them." He shrugged dismissively. "My friends weren't so lucky. They were blown to bits."

The naked emotion in his voice told her how deeply he felt the loss. Nothing she could say would bring his friends back or make this situation easier. After a few seconds, she managed to whisper, "That must have been horrible."

"Not as horrible for me as it was for their families. You see, Mike had a pregnant wife. Ed had a wife and three kids."

She tried to imagine what their families must be going through but couldn't. True, she'd lost her mother, but there hadn't been young children involved. Her mother's cancer had slowly eaten her alive over the course of two miserable years. There'd been enough time to brace herself for the inevitable.

"I'm sorry I whined. My experience wasn't anything — not nearly —"

"Death is death. Like I said, knowing you almost died is a mind-altering experience."

"Yes, but you were wounded. You physically felt it."

"Small difference."

She waited a moment before telling him, "When Mom died I learned something very important. There are things in life that money can replace. Then there are the things in life that no amount of money can replace. I would have given all I had or ever hope to have to save my mother. But it didn't matter. She died anyway."

"I'm sorry, sweetheart." He reached over and took her hand.

"I'm sure you learned the same lesson. Money isn't everything. When I saw the fire, my first thought was the dogs hadn't died. It wasn't until a bit later that I realized someone wanted Miranda dead."

They sat in silence for a few minutes. Talking had calmed Whitney a little and made her realize others had been through much worse. Not just Adam, she decided, but thousands upon thousands of people she didn't know. Around the world others had faced death and had survived. She knew Adam was suffering from survivor's guilt, but she couldn't think of anything to say or do to ease his pain.

Adam rose to his feet and she let him help her up. "Let's find some bed linens and get you settled in the maid's quarters."

She followed him up the stairs to the linen closet in the hall. She noticed how neatly stacked the sheets and towels were. Military training, she decided, and wondered what his uncle had been like.

"How about one of my T-shirts to sleep in?" he asked.

It seemed a little personal but she had no choice. She was going to have to wear these clothes until she could buy new things. "Thanks."

She waited in the hall while he went into a bedroom. A cold nose on the back of her leg told her Lexi had followed her upstairs. The others were right behind her and Whitney couldn't help smiling.

Adam returned and handed her a blue T-shirt. "Get some sleep."

"Thanks, I'll . . ." Her voice trailed off as their fingers touched. She took a reflexive half step back.

What was wrong with her? She'd kissed this man — really kissed him. Why did this feel so much more intimate? Because she was alone with him in a big isolated house, she decided. Not only were they alone, she was going to be sleeping in a shirt he'd worn dozens of times. The fabric felt soft in her hand and she imagined it against his skin. Unexpectedly, her heart was racing.

His eyes gleamed at her, the pupils dilating as he spoke. "I wish I had something better, but —"

"No, no. It's fine, really." An anticipatory shiver tiptoed up her spine. She could feel the air between them almost sizzle. Heat unfurled deep inside her body, her heart now thudding against her rib cage.

He reached out with one hand and touched her cheek. It was a simple gesture, but his fingertips were warm and slightly callused — and unbelievably erotic. It was all she could do not to throw the T-shirt to the floor and fling herself into his powerful arms.

"Adam." His name came from between her lips in a whisper filled with longing.

He gazed down at her, his eyes dark, restless with the same desire she felt. Their bodies were just inches apart. She could feel the warmth seeping from his rock-hard body to hers. It wouldn't take much, she realized. All she would have to do was make a forward move.

She took a deep breath, intending to part her lips for a kiss. A trace of smoke lingered in the air and its smell reminded her of what had happened tonight. She awkwardly took a side step.

Adam got the message, saying, "The keys to the Rava are on the kitchen counter. You take it —"

"I couldn't. I —"

"It's okay. I'll drive my uncle's car. You have to work, don't you?"

She nodded. Right now she needed money and taking care of the dogs was her best way of making it. "Thanks."

"You can help me out by taking Jasper to the breeder. He's supposed to be there tomorrow morning. I'll put the address and phone number by the keys."

She turned to go. "Call me as soon as you talk to Jared Cabral. I want to know what he has to say about Miranda."

CHAPTER NINETEEN

Ashley tried to concentrate on doing one more leg lift, but her mind wasn't on the workout. She told Preston, "Let's grab some juice and talk."

He shrugged, lifting impressive shoulders. "Okay."

He followed her into Dr. Jox's juice bar. She ordered her usual pomegranate juice and he asked for a Redline.

"What's that?"

"A new drink. Like Red Bull but with a bigger kick."

Red Bull made Ashley jittery but a major jolt of caffeine didn't seem to bother Preston. They took their drinks and went outside. Ashley hadn't had a chance to discuss the fiasco with the dog. The workout stations were too close to each other to risk someone overhearing their conversation.

She sat at the table under the tree with the shady canopy. "I'm sorry about the other night. Ryan somehow figured out I was involved."

"You told me that when you phoned me to return the mutt." His clipped tone told Ashley he was angry with her.

"You're upset with me. I'm sorry." Ashley didn't want him to hold this against her. She needed a friend now more than ever.

Preston chugged his Redline. "Don't blame yourself. It was my idea. I just didn't count on cops getting involved."

"Cops? What are you talking about?"

"Adam Hunter's a cop. He was here first thing yesterday morning."

Ashley listened while Preston explained about Adam's visit. "He agreed not to tell Whitney that you were behind her dog's disappearance. This way she won't blame your husband."

"Why didn't you call me?" Yesterday had been one of the two days each week that Ashley didn't train with Preston. When she'd been competing, she worked out for hours every day. Since her mother's death, Ashley allowed herself time to do things she enjoyed.

"I tried your cell but kept getting voice mail. I didn't want to leave a message in case . . ."

His words hung between them. She knew

he intended to say: in case Ryan picked up her messages. She couldn't help being touched by the way Preston always tried to help her.

"Do you think Adam Hunter will keep his word?" She didn't want Ryan to find out her "girlfriend" was really a man. He had nothing to worry about, but Ryan was overly protective of her.

"I thought so. Then I saw the news this morning. I expect the police will be knocking on both our doors."

"What?" She stared at him slack-jawed, certain she'd misunderstood him.

"Didn't you catch the morning news?"

"No. I usually have the TV on while I'm dressing, but not today." When she'd awakened, Ryan had left already. It had been too early for him to go to the office where he was still practicing until the new clinic opened. She wasn't sure where he'd gone, but having him out of the house had given her the opportunity to look through the things on his desk.

In the bottom drawer she'd found a manila folder with DOMENIC CORIZ written across the top. Inside were names and telephone numbers. She couldn't decide what they meant.

Then Ashley had dressed and hadn't been

able to find her ring. She thought she'd put it on top of her jewelry box last night, but it wasn't there. She might have left it on the windowsill when she'd prepared dinner. She'd been so nervous about cooking her mother's meatballs that she couldn't remember. She'd left the house without being able to locate the ring. She was going home to hunt through the trash.

"Someone firebombed the cottage where Ryan's ex lives."

It took a second for what he'd said to register. "How terrible! Was anyone hurt?"

"The reporter said no one was home even though it was late at night."

"Whitney was probably with Adam."

"What makes you say that?"

How could she explain women's intuition to a man? They didn't seem to have hunches the same way women did. "Trust me. Women know these things. When they came to the house, I could tell Adam has the hots for her."

"Whatever." Preston tinkered with his Redline can for a moment before tossing it all the way across the patio and into the trash can. "We can expect the police to contact both of us."

"Why? We had nothing to do with it."

"They'll question Whitney. She'll tell them

about her divorce and Lexi's disappearance. The police will chase down all the leads."

"You're probably right," she replied. "What are we going to say?"

"Tell the truth. They'll find out anyway. I told Hunter. He's bound to —"

Ashley's cell phone erupted with the opening bars of "Proud Mary." She rummaged in her gym bag for a moment before locating it, thinking again about her father. Was he happy? Did he ever think about her?

"Hello?"

"Ashley? This is Whitney Marshall. Is Ryan there?"

It took her a second to remember she'd used call forwarding. Whitney thought she'd reached their house. "No. He's at his office."

Whitney didn't respond for a moment. "I called there, but he's not expected in today."

"Oh, yes, I forgot." Her quick comeback was a total lie. Why wasn't Ryan in the office? Could he be with Domenic Coriz?

"Would you give him a message for me? We had a fire here last night. The police questioned me. I had to tell them I'm finalizing a property settlement after a divorce. They may come to talk to Ryan. Tell him it's routine." Whitney paused before adding, "I'm not trying to make any more trouble."

"How's Lexi?" Ashley had been so shocked when Preston had told her about the bombing that she'd forgotten about the dog.

"She's fine. She was with me."

"Good, good." Ashley couldn't stop herself from asking, "Did the fire do much damage?"

"Yes. The cottage is completely destroyed."

"I'm sorry," Ashley said and she meant it. She couldn't imagine losing everything. Misplacing her wedding ring was no big deal compared to this. "Do you have someplace to stay?" The second she asked, Ashley regretted prying and quickly added, "In case Ryan wants to reach you?"

"I'm staying in the maid's quarters at the main house until I can make other arrangements. Have him call my cell if he needs me."

Ashley assured Whitney that she would tell Ryan, then snapped her cell phone shut. Preston was studying her, and Ashley explained why Whitney had called.

"We'll hear from the police for sure. There aren't many pipe bombings around here. The cops will be all over this one."

Preston sounded worried. She'd never seen him brood like this. He'd always been upbeat. It suddenly struck her that although she often told him about her problems, she'd rarely asked about his. "Is something wrong?"

"Not really. I just don't like cops messing in my business."

She sensed it was more than that. "What else has you upset? Talk to me. Maybe I can help."

He rocked back on the legs of his chair. "I was in some trouble when I was a kid. I took a neighbor's car for a joyride. I was arrested, and I've hated the police ever since."

Ashley had a feeling it was more than that. Men. Weren't they a trip?

Adam waited in Saffron Blue's parking lot. The so-called gentlemen's club opened at noon seven days a week and had for almost fifty years. Jared Cabral had made his money the old-fashioned way — he'd inherited it. His father, Simon Cabral, had started the strip club back in the fifties when bare breasts and naked women were taboo.

The wily old guy had managed to keep his club going even though he'd been busted at least once a month during those first years. A workaholic who didn't seem to have a life, Simon Cabral made money hand over fist and invested it in more clubs. No one knew he had a family until he dropped dead of a heart attack just after his fiftieth birthday.

Enter Jared Cabral. He'd been eighteen when his father died. The kid had no experience with nightclubs, let alone strip clubs and their special problems. Never mind. The apple certainly didn't fall too far from the tree. Jared stepped in and stepped up.

The kid took a year or so to acquaint himself with his inheritance. The dark, dank clubs that reeked of stale cigarette smoke and featured strippers well past their prime required major changes. He got rid of the "topless" signs and flashing neon lights. He remodeled the clubs, giving them a hip look, which included wallpapering the restrooms with Trojan Magnum XL wrappers. He also brought in younger "exotic dancers" who exuded a carnal energy that mesmerized men. The clubs boomed and you could almost hear the old man applauding from the grave.

The changes brought in a new, younger clientele who were willing to spend more money for call liquor and trendy drinks like Pimp Juice. They were also heavy tippers that kept the exotic dancers thrilled with their take home money. No doubt drugs thrived around Cabral's clubs, but all the drug deals seemed to be conducted in the parking lot. The police had never been able to implicate Jared Cabral.

Saffron Blue was known for its back room, where it was rumored a high-stakes poker game went on every night. Acting on tips, the police raided the room a few times and found the players were betting toothpicks. Adam didn't think it was worth the effort. There was enough crime in San Diego without trying to trap men gambling illegally, especially with all the legal gambling going on in the Indian casinos in the area.

From a homicide case he'd investigated years ago, Adam knew Jared Cabral arrived shortly after the club opened and stayed until it closed. According to his calculations, Cabral should be arriving shortly. Adam leaned back in the silver Lexus that had belonged to his uncle. He'd taken it from the garage even though it was part of the estate and still in probate.

His mind strayed to last night. Whitney came damn near being killed because of her cousin. Adam suspected the answer could be found here. Miranda had to have run through the insurance money and needed the cash stripping generated. She'd met someone or had seen something and become a liability.

Adam didn't want Whitney to suffer for her cousin's mistakes. She'd been through enough, he decided. A devastating divorce. Then the airhead second wife comes up with a crazy scheme to snatch the dog Whitney was crazy about.

A twinge of guilt hit him. He really should have told Whitney who had been responsible for Lexi's disappearance. Then he assured himself that Whitney had too much on her mind to bother her with one more thing. Anyway, it was in the past, and it was the least of her problems.

He remembered the way Whitney had acted last night. She'd willingly come into his arms and allowed him to comfort her. His entire body had been tense with the urge to take her to his bed, but he knew better. She'd been too shell-shocked by the fire to know what she was doing.

Did he know what *he* was doing?

Adam had to be honest with himself. He wasn't positive about anything the way he'd been before Iraq. He'd told himself to steer clear of Whitney until he was sure she was no longer entangled with her ex. Aw, hell. That was going to be damn near impossible with her living in the maid's quarters.

How did he plan to go to bed when she was sleeping so close? Last night, he'd lain awake, imagining her naked. Her warm body and soft breasts were in his favorite T-shirt.

He sucked in air between clenched teeth. *Admit it, buddy. You're in real trouble here. How can you live in the same house and not touch her?*

He ached to turn back the clock to last night. He would have hotfooted it down to the maid's room. Peeling his well-worn T-shirt off Whitney would have revealed creamy smooth skin and full breasts. Just the thought of her naked bod sent heat through his groin.

He could almost feel Whitney pressing against him. Her warm body molding itself to his. Almost. He stopped himself. He needed to be in detective mode right now. What was the first thing drilled into raw police recruits? Detach emotionally.

Cabral whirled into the nearly empty lot in a lipstick-red Ferrari with vanity plates that read: CABRAL1. He parked in a reserved space near the entrance, then opened the door of the sports car and unwound himself from behind the wheel. Adam had to look twice to make sure the guy was Jared Cabral.

Since Adam had last seen Cabral, the man had changed his hair. He was now wearing it in a spiked mullet that added four inches to his tall, lean frame. Gone were the jeans and polo shirt that Adam remembered, replaced by camouflage pants and jacket. The number wasn't a damn thing like what they'd worn in Iraq. This outfit was some idiot designer's idea of desert chic.

Adam gave Cabral time to walk inside and across the lounge area to his office at the rear of the club. It was too early for the bouncer to be guarding the entrance. Adam entered and paused for a moment to allow his eyes time to adjust. It was dark inside Saffron Blue, but it wasn't the kind of oppressive darkness Adam once associated with strip clubs. Saffron Blue was upscale all the way.

The leather banquettes surrounding the U-shaped bar were a shade lighter than the indigo-blue walls. Off to the sides of the room were alcoves with sofas and comfy chairs. Down lighting and lamps no bigger than his thumb cast a mellow glow across the room and reflected off the chrome trimming the bar and chair legs.

A waitress in a leopard-print thong and a matching something that might pass for a bra bounced up to him. Her boobs didn't look like original equipment, but hey, who was he to criticize?

"What can I get you, hon?"

"Nothing. I'm here to see Jared."

A mouth coated with lipstick applied with a painter's brush formed an O. "Who shall I —"

"Don't bother. I know my way to his office." Adam took off across the club and noticed a surprising number of men were there despite the early hour. An exotic dancer was strutting up and down the top of the bar, jiggling her melon-sized boobs and smiling as if she'd just won the lottery.

The door to Cabral's office was open. Adam paused, seeing Cabral seated inside, and knocked on the door.

"Wazzup?" Cabral asked. "Hunter. Adam Hunter, right?"

Adam nodded as he walked in. Cabral didn't look the least bit wary or even surprised. *Give the guy credit,* he thought. It had been over three years since he'd questioned Cabral about a man who'd visited his club and was later shot to death outside his home. Thousands of men had passed through Cabral's clubs during that time.

Adam stopped in front of Cabral's desk. "Good memory, Cabral. How are things going?"

"Can't complain." He gestured toward a tall bottle of liquor on his desk. "Trying to decide if my bars should stock 10 Cane Rum. It's made from the first press of virgin sugarcane from Trinidad."

"I never got the virgin bit. Virgin olive oil. Extra virgin olive oil. Now virgin sugarcane."

Cabral's laugh broke free as if it had been chained down for years. "That's what I liked about you. A sense of humor. Last I heard you were in Iraq and nearly bit the big weenie."

Again, Adam was surprised, but he shouldn't have been. With his wide blue eyes and ready smile, Jared Cabral seemed innocent. Far from it. He was a savvy businessman who played all the angles.

"Sit, sit." Cabral gestured to the chair in front of his desk. "I didn't mean to make a joke out of it. One of my buddies from high school bought it when an I.E.D. blew up the truck he was in."

Adam sat in the chair. He didn't want to discuss death, not after last night. "How's business?"

"Couldn't be better. We have our own Web site. We're CampTempTation on MySpace and other sites. Brings in more new customers than my father ever could have imagined. It's the Internet age, but nothing can replace real tits and ass."

Adam let him rattle on about New Age beverages and promotional opportunities on the information superhighway. Cabral liked to talk but he never really told you squat about himself.

"What brings you here?" Cabral asked when he'd finished with the lecture on how the Web had changed his clubs.

"A woman who used to . . . dance here is missing."

"What's it to you? Last I heard, you'd left the force."

"That's true. I'm in private security now. This is a personal matter."

Cabral steepled his fingers and gazed at Adam. "I don't get involved with the dancers. They're not employees. They just try out for spots in the Saturday-night show."

Adam nodded. Cabral was clever and managed to evade taxes as well as employment issues by letting women "try out" for places in his Saturday-night revue. The tips they could earn brought out more women than Cabral could use. Certain dancers kept "trying out" night after night.

"I don't even know most of their names. They use stage names like Candy Rapper and Sin Cerely."

"Do you remember Miranda Marshall?"

Cabral's face was totally expressionless. If

he'd been playing poker, Cabral could have been holding a winning or losing hand and no one could have guessed which. He finally said, "Describe her."

Whitney had told him that Miranda looked a lot like her, so Adam rattled off a quick description.

"Could be half the cuties out there on any given evening."

Cabral sounded convincing, but Adam wasn't sure he believed him. "Last night someone tried to kill Miranda. They fire-bombed her place."

Cabral frowned. "No shit."

"Look, I didn't tell the investigating officer that Miranda worked here." Adam made it sound as if he actually knew the woman. "Level with me. Tell me what you know about her. I'll chase down the leads myself without involving the police."

Cabral stared at him a minute as if making up his mind, then said, "She called herself Kat Nippe. Her shtick — they all have a shtick — was the little-girl bit. She would prance out dressed like a kid going to school in a convent. That gave her a lot of clothes to take off."

"Do you have any idea if she ran into someone around here who would want to kill her?"

The telephone on Cabral's desk rang and he picked it up. "Cabral."

Adam waited while the club owner listened.

"Fuck no!" Cabral stared at the picture on the wall next to his desk. It was a black-and-white photograph of his father outside the original Saffron Blue. "What don't you understand? The fuck or the no?" He slammed down the telephone and smiled at Adam.

Adam tried to return his smile but he was pretty sure he just twisted his lips. The outburst had reminded Adam of what he'd learned three years ago. Jared Cabral was a man no one in their right mind would want to cross.

"If Miranda has an enemy," Cabral said, as if the argument on the telephone had never occurred, "I sure as hell don't know about it. She was a pro all the way when she worked here."

"Has she been hanging out with anyone lately?"

Cabral's eyes narrowed as he stared at Adam. "Just how well do you know Miranda Marshall?"

Something in Cabral's tone told Adam to level with him or Cabral would stop talking. "I've never met the woman. My girlfriend is her cousin. Whitney was living in Miranda's place. She almost died last night when someone tried to kill Miranda with a fire-bomb loaded with shrapnel."

Cabral shook his head. "Wish I could help, but I don't know a damn thing. Miranda hasn't worked at Saffron Blue in a year and a half."

CHAPTER TWENTY

Whitney held Jasper as she watched Kris Simpson bring out the teaser bitch. Jasper squirmed in her arms, anxious to be put down. Whitney didn't have much experience breeding dogs. When she'd been in high school, she'd worked part-time at a kennel. She'd seen two breeding sessions between the owner's Wheaten terrier bitch and a male who'd been brought in by his owner. No teaser bitch had been required.

"Ever seen an A.I.?" asked Kris.

Whitney shook her head. She supposed that if she'd thought about it, she would have realized champion dogs, like many champion racehorses, wouldn't be allowed to breed on their own. The risk of injury was too great. The sperm was collected, then the bitch was artificially inseminated.

"Mandy is in heat and so is my crested, Princess Arianna. She was best in her class at Westminster last year." Kris held up a small device that looked like a large syringe with a balloon-like sack on one end. "The teaser bitch gets the male excited, then I collect the sperm."

"You'll inseminate Princess Arianna yourself?"

"Yes. I'll freeze the leftover sperm for use on my other bitches when they come into season. That's why I paid so much money." She patted Jasper on the head. "I'll get three, maybe four litters out of this guy."

Whitney had no idea what this woman had spent for Jasper's services. Considering Jasper was an international champion, his offspring would be worth a lot. "Will we get the pick of the litter?"

Kris glared at Whitney. "Didn't you read the contract? I'll keep all of the puppies."

"I didn't see the contract," Whitney muttered. "I just help Mr. Hunter with Jasper."

Things must work differently when breeding champions, she decided. The owner of the male usually had pick of the litter.

"Put Jasper down and let him get a good sniff before I bag him."

She set Jasper on the concrete floor. He looked up at her and whimpered. "Go on now," she said encouragingly. Jasper pawed her shins, begging to be picked up again. Physically, he showed no sign of being interested in the teaser bitch.

Kris tapped her on the shoulder. "Let's leave them alone. We can watch it on the television in my office. I can get back out here before he ejaculates."

Whitney used her leg to scoot Jasper aside. She hurried out of the enclosure. Jasper scratched at the gate and yipped as if his paw had been caught in a trap.

Kris led Whitney down a short corridor to an office. The walls were lined with framed pictures of Chinese crested dogs and the ribbons they'd won. The photographs and ribbons were encased in Lucite boxes. A black satin ribbon was draped over one box and Whitney assumed that dog had died.

Kris sat behind a glass-top desk and carefully put down the collection device. Whitney took the chair opposite her. The breeder picked up the remote control and flicked on the wall-mounted flat-screen television. Jasper's plaintive yips filled the room. The TV showed the little dog still pawing the gate while the teaser bitch kept circling behind him.

Kris frowned. "That's what comes from holding a dog too much. I told Cal not to coddle his crested, but he wouldn't listen. He took him everywhere with him."

Whitney didn't interrupt to tell her that

Miranda had cared for Jasper some of the time. She must have been partly responsible for spoiling him.

"Now look, the dog can't concentrate on his business."

The cell phone clipped to Whitney's shorts vibrated. Caller ID told her it was Adam. "I have a call I need to take."

"Go ahead. I'll monitor the dogs."

Whitney could hear Jasper's yelps still coming from the television as she walked outside into a blast of radiant sunshine. "What's happening?"

"I'm just leaving Saffron Blue. Jared Cabral says Miranda hasn't worked there in about eighteen months."

"What?" Whitney stared out at the white picket fence that encircled the sprawling ranch house where the breeder lived with what appeared to be at least two dozen Chinese crested dogs.

She gazed up and down the road, mindful of Adam's warning to keep her eye out for anyone suspicious. Nothing unusual was in sight.

"I was surprised, too. I assumed she'd been working there recently, but she hasn't. Cabral didn't seem to know much. I told him about the firebombing. He couldn't think of anyone or anything your cousin had been involved in that would make someone want to kill her."

"Saffron Blue's a dead end."

"Looks that way," he agreed. "We could try going through the stuff she stored in the garage."

This morning they'd inspected the charred remains of her Jeep. The garage attached to the carport had been partially burned. The contents of the garage had appeared to be a soggy mess.

"I guess we could, but I doubt she left anything important behind."

There was a burst of static and Whitney thought Adam had driven into a dead zone, but then she heard him say, "It's our only option. The police will go through her phone records and credit card charges. They may come up with something."

"I hope so." She was still jittery after last night. Not knowing what was going on or why her cousin hadn't warned her was making Whitney even more nervous.

"Are you okay?" he asked.

"I've been careful. I'm not being followed. No one suspicious is around."

"How's Jasper doing?"

"He doesn't seem to be all that interested in mating."

"He could be a gaynine."

"What?" Whitney wasn't sure she'd heard him correctly.

"You know, a gay dog. Maybe he prefers boy dogs."

"Be serious."

"I am. Who's to say homosexuality is strictly a human phenomenon?" He chuckled and she thought about the things he'd told her last night. He was opening up, revealing a sense of humor.

"I think Jasper is just nervous," she explained. "And I don't think the nodule you noticed behind Jasper's ear is any better. Shouldn't I take him to his vet?"

"Yes. There's a file on Jasper in the office. I'm sure it has his vet's —"

"I have the number. Miranda has the telephone number for the vet of every dog she walked. Emergency numbers of the owners, too. She was very thorough. I have it all in my BlackBerry."

A burst of static followed. "My phone's cutting out. See you later, sweetheart."

Whitney said goodbye and snapped her phone shut. *Sweetheart?* Adam was full of surprises. The way he'd kissed her — well, nothing had felt so *right* in a long, long time. After her ordeal with Ryan, she hadn't expected any man to interest her. Just the thought of her ex-husband sent up red flags.

304

She cautioned herself to take time before becoming involved again. Make better, more responsible decisions about men.

She slowly walked back into the office, her mind on Miranda. Maybe she would never see her cousin again. It was possible she would never know who wanted to kill Miranda. Whitney needed to stay out of harm's way until the police came up with some answers.

Last night she hadn't been able to sleep. Adam was right. Nearly dying made her look at life differently. After her divorce, she'd become a fugitive from life by deciding to take over her cousin's business.

Whitney was realizing more and more that what she really wanted to do was become a veterinarian. She'd put her dream on hold to send Ryan to medical school. She'd passed up her chance. After all this time, she would need to take a few refresher courses in biology and anatomy before she reapplied.

She could do it, Whitney assured herself. She would have to go to school at night and scrounge to make ends meet, but she could do it. With hard work, she would be ready to take the entrance tests next spring.

If she was accepted — it was a really big *if* — she would have to leave the area. The nearest veterinary school was at University of California at Davis in the northern part of the state. It would mean leaving Adam behind.

Don't go there, she warned herself.

Her relationship with Adam was too new to factor him into her future. She had to chart her own course. She'd learned the hard way that setting your dreams aside for a man was a huge mistake.

As soon as Adam finished talking to Whitney, his cell phone rang. It was Tyler.

"Where are you, Adam?"

He heard the tense note in Tyler's voice and knew he was upset. "I was taking care of a little business. What's going on?"

"My father's been trying to reach you. Didn't you get his messages?"

"No. I've been really busy."

"Too busy to pick up voicemail?" Tyler's tone was hostile now. Anything to do with his old man made Tyler edgy, to say the least.

"I guess you didn't see the news." Adam went on to explain about the bombing and subsequent fire.

"Holy shit! You'll be tied up with insurance claims from here to eternity."

Leave it to Tyler to think about the financial ramifications of the fire. Adam hadn't even taken time to report it to the attorney. No doubt this would impact the probate.

"My father's on the way over to your place. He thinks there's a disc with a copy of the info somewhere in your uncle's house."

Missing financial records and now a missing disc. Things were not adding up. Adam was now more sure than ever that his uncle had been murdered.

"Adam, are you there? Can you hear me?"

"I'm here. I was on my way to the office but I can go home again."

"I'd appreciate it." There was no mistaking the relief in Tyler's voice. "Father's going postal over this missing disc."

Adam almost told him that Quinten Foley could drop dead. Searching the house was a waste of time. Adam had already gone over every inch. Then he recalled all the e-mails Tyler had sent him when he'd been in Iraq. He'd kept in touch, tried to lift Adam's spirits. Most of all, he'd worked hard and protected Adam's investment in the security company.

It wouldn't kill him to indulge Quinten Foley. He was the kind of guy who wouldn't take Adam's word about not finding the disc. He would have to see for himself.

Adam tried to imagine what it must have been like for Tyler to grow up with such a demanding father — and couldn't.

When they'd first met as cadets at the police academy, Adam had learned he and Tyler had a lot in common. Both had lost their mothers at a young age. He'd assumed Tyler had a great dad like Adam's own father. Then he'd met the man.

From then on, Adam had befriended Tyler. It wasn't hard. Tyler was easygoing — the opposite of his father. They'd become closer as they moved through the ranks and became homicide detectives. They both had become disillusioned with detective work at the same time. It was only natural that the two friends go into business together.

Adam assured Tyler that he'd go through all the discs with Quinten Foley. He'd rather be tarred and feathered, but there you go. Some things you did for friends — like it or not. Adam hung up and drove back to Torrey Pines.

A hulking black Hummer was parked in his driveway. Adam pulled in behind Tyler's father. Quinten Foley jumped out of the Hummer. Splotches of red mottled his face, and Adam knew the jerk would attempt to ream him a new one for not returning his messages.

"Don't you pick up your messages?" Foley bellowed at him the instant Adam opened the car door.

"Fuck off."

That got him. Foley stopped dead in his tracks. Adam was certain no one dared to curse Foley. The older man frowned and the red blotches deepened in color.

"I've been trying to reach you since late last night," Foley said as if nothing had happened, but his tone was conciliatory.

Adam headed up the walk to the front door and Foley fell in step with him. "We had some trouble here. My cell was shut off."

"What kind of trouble?"

"A pipe bombing."

"Christ! Why?"

Adam was at the front door now. He stopped, the key in his hand. "Apparently the woman who was living in the cottage behind the house got into some trouble."

"I see," Foley replied as if he had his doubts. "Did Tyler tell you what I wanted?"

Adam unlocked the front door and held it open for Tyler's father. "Yes. Something about information on my uncle's computer." Adam headed up the stairs toward the office. "It was stolen along with some other computer stuff during my uncle's funeral."

"Yes, Tyler told me. I think Calvin made a copy of the file."

Adam reached the office and flicked on the light. "What makes you think he'd copy your file?"

A beat of silence. "It's the way we were trained. You know, military stuff."

Yeah, right. Something else was going on, and it might be the link to his uncle's death. Adam dropped into the chair behind the desk and turned on his computer. "I've run the discs the burglars didn't take. What are you looking for *exactly?*"

Foley pulled up a chair beside the desk. "It would be lists of names with numbers."

Bank account numbers? Adam silently wondered. "I didn't find anything like that."

Foley craned his neck to glance around the office at the bookshelves. "It could be hidden somewhere. Mind if I check?"

Foley hadn't bothered to ask any questions about the fire or express concern. His attitude already had Adam pissed. "Yeah, I do mind. I've been through everything in this room. Nothing's hidden in any of the books or —"

"Did you check discs that seem to be something else like PhotoShop or Quick-

Books?"

"Believe me, I read every disc."

"Why?"

There you go. Quinten Foley was an arrogant SOB but he hadn't been made with a finger. "Some of my uncle's financial records are missing. I checked to see if he'd hidden them for some reason."

Foley studied him for a moment. "Look, I'm going to level with you. No one knows about this — not even Tyler."

Well, hell. This wasn't exactly news. Tyler's father didn't tell him squat.

"Your uncle was working with me on a weapons deal."

I'll be a son of a bitch! Adam had never suspected his uncle might be involved in something that was, if not illegal, damn close to it. When Uncle Calvin told Adam he was afraid, the older man hadn't mentioned this.

Why would he sell arms? Money, of course. There were countries and groups of people all over the world who would pay vast sums to get the latest equipment. But he never thought his uncle would be involved with them.

How well did you know him? Adam asked himself. Not well. The man blew in and out of his life. Adam had assumed his uncle

311

shared the same principles that Adam's father had instilled in him. Evidently, this was a serious misconception.

An arms deal gone sour could mean a bunch of pissed-off men who would stop at nothing. Maybe that was why his uncle had been so afraid someone planned to kill him.

"You see, there are times when our government doesn't want it to be known that they are supplying other governments with arms," Quinten continued. "They conduct business through a third party."

"That would be you and my uncle."

"Exactly. Information concerning a recent deal was on your uncle's computer. I can't tell you more — it's classified top secret. But I can tell you there are people who would stop at nothing to get the information."

"Would they kill Uncle Calvin?"

"No. Why would they?"

"A little over two months ago, I visited my uncle at his villa on Siros. He was worried about being killed. He wouldn't tell me who was after him or what it was about. He wanted to protect me."

Foley gazed at Adam with a stricken expression. "He didn't send me any message or try to warn me."

"Would you have warned him?"

Quinten Foley didn't respond. He didn't need to; Adam knew the answer. This was a man who didn't love his own son. How could anyone expect him to protect a business partner?

CHAPTER TWENTY-ONE

Whitney hung up and walked down the breeder's driveway to check on the dogs. She'd left Lexi along with Maddie and Da Vinci in the back of Adam's Rava. They were far enough inland that the breeze from the ocean didn't keep the air as cool as it was in the La Jolla area. If Jasper didn't perform soon she would ask Kris if the dogs could be put in one of the dog runs.

Whitney stuck her head inside the window. "Are you guys okay?"

Lexi responded by licking her chin and Maddie hopped up and down, but Da Vinci merely opened one eye and gazed at her for a second before going back to sleep.

"I'll hurry," she promised, then walked back up the driveway toward the office. Her cell phone rang again. Rod Babcock's secretary was on the line.

"Mr. Babcock is in La Jolla for a deposition. He has a noon reservation at Starz and would like you to join him. He needs to talk to you."

"Okay," she reluctantly agreed and hung up. She had rushed into Wal-Mart on the way out here. She'd bought a few changes of clothes and some toiletry items, but she didn't have anything nice enough to wear to a trendy restaurant. What she had on would have to do.

Whitney walked back into the office and found Kris had left. The television showed the breeder in the pen with the two dogs. Apparently Jasper had finally become interested in the teaser bitch while Whitney had been outside.

She watched Jasper attempt to mount the female. She kept bucking off Jasper again and again. He finally managed to corner the female and climb up on her. Jasper was going at it when Kris knelt down, grabbed him, and quickly covered his penis with the collection device. The breeder began milking Jasper and Whitney turned away.

She couldn't watch. Instead she checked her voicemail. One was a client canceling a walk and the other was Trish Bowrather.

"Call me right away. I'm *so* worried about you."

Evidently Trish had seen news of the fire on the morning television broadcasts. There

315

was no mistaking the concern in her voice. Whitney couldn't help being touched. Other than Adam, she didn't have anyone who cared about her.

"From the looks of it, you don't have a place to stay, or clothes . . . or anything. Why didn't you come in and tell me about it when you walked Brandy this morning?"

Whitney had been in a hurry when she'd taken Brandy for his walk. Trish must have been in the shower when Whitney came by for the retriever. She'd walked him then left. She'd needed to squeeze in another dog and a trip to Wal-Mart before driving out here to deliver Jasper. Whitney called Trish at the gallery but her voicemail picked up.

"Trish, it's Whitney. I'm okay. I'll tell you all about it this afternoon. I'm meeting Broderick Babcock for lunch at Starz. Afterward, I'll drop by the gallery."

By the time Whitney retrieved a very dejected Jasper and drove south, she barely had time to park the car in an underground garage, so the dogs wouldn't get too hot, and still make it to the restaurant in time. She rushed up to Starz, her hair flying behind her like a banner. Broderick Babcock was waiting at a table in the rear.

The lawyer rose and extended his hand. *He's dressed for a* GQ *photo shoot,* Whitney thought, *and I'm a walking advertisement for the homeless.*

"Are you all right?" he asked, his brows knit. "I heard about the pipe bombing and fire on the radio while I was driving here."

"I'm fine." She lowered herself into the chair opposite his.

The waitress bounced over and took her order for iced tea. Rod must have arrived early. He already had a glass of white wine and had buttered a roll from the basket on the table.

"I wasn't home when it happened," explained Whitney. She thought she sounded a little breathless and told herself to calm down. Rod was adept at reading people. She didn't want him to know how frightened she was. He was doing her a favor by reviewing the document. She didn't need to drag him into her personal affairs. "Apparently someone has a grudge against Miranda. She lived in the cottage until a few days ago. I guess they didn't know she'd moved out."

Rod studied her a moment. "Did you find out where she is?"

Whitney shook her head and let the waitress deposit a tall glass of iced tea with a wedge of lemon in front of her before continuing. "We found her car at the airport. She must have taken a flight some-where."

The attorney nodded thoughtfully. Whitney didn't tell him that Miranda's ID hadn't shown up on security checks. She didn't want him asking how she'd obtained the information.

"You needed to see me?" she asked.

"Yes. I want to clear up a few details. Let's order first. I'm starving. I had to be out here early for a deposition and missed breakfast."

Whitney picked up the menu beside her napkin and quickly selected an ahi tuna salad. She wondered why the attorney couldn't have cleared up a few details over the phone. Rod signaled and the waitress came over. They both ordered salads.

"I had my investigator go over the titles to both properties. Did you realize your former husband has taken out a second mortgage as well as a home equity line of credit?"

"No, I didn't," she replied slowly. "But I'm not surprised. We were tight for money when we split. He's starting a new practice. That requires a big financial commitment."

The lawyer didn't respond. He looked at her with an expression that said he expected her to continue.

"I'm not responsible for these loans, am I? We are divorced, right?"

He gave her an encouraging smile. "We double-checked the court records. You are divorced. It's not uncommon for couples to divorce then settle property matters later."

"Will I be responsible for loans he took out after —"

"What counts is the day the divorce papers were filed. Subsequent loans are his problem."

Whitney smiled to herself. Ryan had never been good at managing money. Let him sweat this one out with his Miss America wannabe.

"Did you realize your ex had a gambling problem?"

She bit back a startled gasp. "No," she managed to say after a moment. "I had no idea. Are you sure?"

"My sources — always reliable — tell me he's into the casinos for half a mil."

"Half a million dollars." The second the words were out she knew she'd raised her voice. She added in a lower tone, "I don't believe it."

"I've represented the tribes on several matters. They're as computerized and businesslike as Vegas. If they say Ryan Fordham owes half a mil, he owes the money."

"I see," Whitney said, the light slowly dawning. How many times had Ryan gone out in the evening? He'd claimed to be checking on patients. Now she knew the truth. When he hadn't been cheating on her, the skank had been gambling.

"I guess I'm not responsible for his gambling debts, if they were incurred after we filed. Right?"

"Correct, but it explains why he's so anxious to settle the property dispute. I doubt if he can scare up another cent."

Whitney couldn't feel sorry for her ex. She'd walked away from the marriage without much more than her maiden name. She'd lost her job, but Ryan hadn't cared how she survived. She'd taken a house-sitting job, then she'd been forced to turn to Miranda.

"You said the property near Temecula has Environmental Protection Agency restrictions on it."

"Yes. Ryan insisted we buy the land because development is moving in that direction and it would be valuable one day. When we were finalizing our divorce, he discovered the property had been a landfill. It can't be sold without an expensive cleanup and decontamination."

"Our preliminary check didn't reveal any EPA restrictions, but I'm told that isn't too unusual. A lot of those reports are given to county agencies that don't have the man-power to disseminate the information to all appropriate agencies. Often the EPA reports don't turn up until a transaction is in es-crow."

"Ryan went to a Realtor and found out about the problems."

"Realtors often know —"

"Whitney," Trish Bowrather called from a few feet away.

"This is my friend," Whitney managed to tell Rod, even though she was surprised to see Trish. "I left a message that I would be here. She has an art gallery nearby."

Trish stopped beside Whitney. Today the gallery owner was dressed in coffee-colored linen with gleaming black onyx accessories. "I heard about the fire and I was so upset."

"I'm okay. I was out with the dogs. They were safe. That's all that matters."

"That's why I trust my Brandy to her," Trish told Rod as she turned and offered him her hand. "I'm Trish Bowrather."

"Rod Babcock," the attorney replied, ris-ing. "Join us. We've just ordered."

Trish shook her head. "I didn't mean to interrupt. I just wanted to see for myself that Whitney was okay."

Whitney had the impression that the lawyer was intrigued by Trish. "You're not interrupting. I think we're finished with business."

"Yes." Rod pulled out a chair for Trish while telling Whitney, "I'll need to check a few more things before I'll allow you to sign the papers."

Whitney hid her disappointment. She wanted to put the past where it belonged — behind her.

"Do you have a place to stay?" Trish asked as soon as she was seated.

"In the maid's quarters at the main house." Whitney knew she didn't blush, but she hoped her face didn't give away how she felt about Adam.

"Sounds small," Trish said. "I have a client who's going to be in the south of France for at least six months. He's looking for someone to take care of his place."

"Thanks," Whitney replied with as much enthusiasm as she could muster. Adam cared about her, and Whitney liked knowing he was close by. She didn't want to move, but it might be for the best.

Rod waved over their server and Trish quickly ordered a salad. "I hope you're still coming to my opening Friday night."

Whitney nodded without enthusiasm. She'd forgotten all about the showing of the Russian's works.

Trish turned to Rod. "I own the Ravissant Gallery on Prospect Street. I'm showing Vladimir's works Friday night. He's the hottest artist on the local scene. Why don't you come?"

"Well, I . . ." Rod hesitated. Whitney had the distinct impression he was charmed by Trish but wanted to be persuaded.

"It'll be a lot of fun. Liquid Cowboy is catering the food." Trish produced an invitation from the elegant black bag she'd deposited beside her chair.

"How can I refuse?" Rod asked with a smile.

He was too sharp an attorney not to be able to slither out of this if he'd wanted, Whitney decided. She wondered if Trish had really dropped by to check on her or if she'd come because she knew it was an opportunity to meet a wealthy prospective client.

CHAPTER
TWENTY-TWO

It was late afternoon before Whitney could get an appointment with Jasper's vet. Dr. Robinson specialized in small breeds like Chinese cresteds.

The little guy squirmed as the vet ran her forefinger over the bump. "This is right where we implanted his ID chip. According to the records that was almost three years ago when Throckmorton —"

"He answers to Jasper. His ridiculous AKC name is Sir Throckmorton VonJasperhoven." Whitney realized the vet was about her age. She would be working with animals, too, if she hadn't set aside her aspirations for Ryan's career.

The vet consulted her chart. "Jasper was chipped at eight weeks. That was right after Mr. Hunter purchased him. I didn't insert the chip, but I'm sure our records are correct."

"It's odd that it would be infected now,

isn't it?"

Dr. Robinson shook her head. "It isn't infected. It's just irritated."

"Do you think they rechipped him for some reason? He was flown internationally a lot. He recently won best in show at the Frankfurt International Dog Show."

"I'm not familiar with international regulations. It's possible he received a new chip, but I think it's more likely that this is a skin irritation typical of Chinese crested dogs."

Whitney nodded, thinking she'd over-reacted by bringing in Jasper. "This breed is prone to skin problems, right?"

"You're right."

"Aren't many of them on special diets because of allergies?"

"Yes." The vet consulted the chart.

"Jasper's on a lamb-based kibble diet," Whitney told her. "No herring meal or fish by-products, which might cause allergies."

The vet studied her for a moment. "It's good to hear you know all this since you're taking care of dogs. Most people don't realize a number of dogs are allergic to fish by-products."

"They're in most commercial dog foods."

"Absolutely." She smiled at Whitney.

"Chinese cresteds sunburn easily because they're not covered with fur like other dogs.

I keep Jasper out of direct sunlight."

"You're doing all the right things," the vet responded. "You're a much better caretaker than most pet owners I meet."

"Thanks. I try."

The vet patted Jasper's head. "I'll give you some ointment to put on the lesion. If the redness doesn't go away, bring him back in a week."

"You know, I almost went to veterinary school," Whitney blurted out. "I was accepted at Davis —"

"Really? It's tough to get in there. Why didn't you go?"

"I was sidetracked. But I was thinking of reapplying next fall. I'd need to take a few courses first to brush up."

The vet touched Whitney's arm. "Do it. You seem to love working with animals. It's a great career."

"I'll go online as soon as I can and find out what classes I need," Whitney replied.

Dr. Robinson studied her a moment. "Next month one of our techs is leaving. You could take the job and see if you like working in a clinic before you go back to school."

"I'd love to, I really would, but I don't have any experience."

"You won't need any. Our head tech will

train you."

She couldn't believe her luck. "When do I start?"

It was two hours later when Whitney finally left. She'd met the head tech and had been given a tour of the facility. Her life was moving in a new direction, she decided. If the house-sitting job Trish mentioned worked out, Whitney would have a rent-free place to stay. And a fresh start on a new career. She kissed the tip of Jasper's nose, then put him in the back of the SUV with the other dogs. It was funny, she mused. A little thing like a bump on a dog's neck could change the direction of her life.

Adam put the shopping bags filled with women's clothes on the floor in the maid's room. Someone had left the bags on the front porch. The television coverage had gotten them a lot of attention. Evidently, one of Whitney's friends had seen a newscast about the fire and brought over the clothes.

He heard the telephone ring upstairs in his uncle's office. After the second ring the fax machine kicked in. He hoped it was copies of Miranda Marshall's telephone records and credit card purchases. He'd leaned on a detective he used to work with to sneak him the records when Dudley Romberg wasn't around. He had no history with "The Dud" and couldn't ask him to bend the rules.

He raced upstairs and scanned the cover sheet the machine spit out. Miranda's records were coming through. He sat at the desk and waited. He'd systematically put the office back together as Quinten Foley checked all the software discs Calvin Hunter had stored in the wall rack. Then Foley had gone through every book on the shelves lining the walls to see if the disc had been hidden in one of them. He'd even checked behind the pictures on the wall.

Nothing.

Adam could have told Quinten Foley that he wouldn't find a damn thing. But Foley needed to see for himself.

Adam gazed at the framed awards and photographs on the walls. Most were service commendations. Three were of Uncle Calvin fishing. Several years back, Calvin Hunter had won Bisbee's Black and Blue Marlin Fishing Tournament. The photo showed a sunburned but smiling man proudly standing beside a marlin twice his height.

Deep-sea fishing and dog shows had been his uncle's passions. Interesting. You wouldn't think the two would appeal to the same person. While he couldn't see his uncle being so involved in those two different pursuits, Adam could believe his uncle was involved in some black ops deal with Quinten Foley. Uncle Calvin had spent his career in the naval intelligence division. He knew secrets and had access to things others didn't.

This knowledge would be very lucrative on the black market. Adam stared at another picture of Uncle Calvin on a fishing boat. Radiant sunshine, crystal blue water, a smiling Calvin Hunter standing on the swim step and wearing a baseball cap. The photo was so sharp that Adam could almost read the printing on the hat.

The third photo was of his uncle on the sundeck of a home somewhere. He was holding a platter with a large cooked fish. By the smile on his uncle's face, Adam decided this was one of his uncle's catches.

From what Adam knew about weapons deals, Foley and his uncle were brokers. They were middlemen who arranged the transactions and cut a huge profit out of each deal. They didn't handle weapons themselves. But money, contracts, lists of weapons and God-only-knew-what-else had to be exchanged.

The fax machine stopped churning out

papers, and Adam left the window. Noises came from downstairs. Whitney was home.

His pulse kicked into high gear. He'd been looking forward to seeing Whitney since this morning when he'd discovered she'd left early. He stuck his head out the door, calling, "Whitney, please come up here."

Scampering, scratching sounds came from the stairway. Jasper was on his way upstairs to find him. The dog bounded up the last few stairs, spotted Adam and sprinted toward him. Adam hunkered down and Jasper took a flying leap into his arms and began licking his face.

"Hey, dude, how was your first hookup?"

"He rose to the occasion — finally," Whitney said as she reached the top of the stairs, the other dogs at her heels.

Adam stood up, Jasper in his arms. He wanted to pull Whitney flush against his chest, then drag her across the hall into his bedroom. He was reasonably sure the killer had been after Miranda, but you never knew. He warned himself that becoming distracted could cost Whitney her life.

"Did you spot anyone following you?" he asked. "Or notice anything suspicious."

"Nope, and I was careful."

"That's good. Don't let down your guard."

"The vet says the bump on Jasper's neck

isn't infected. It just needs ointment put on it twice a day."

"Great." Adam held out the little guy to check. Jasper was still furiously licking but getting nothing but air. He was a goofy dog, yet Adam couldn't help being drawn to him. He remembered how Uncle Calvin had cradled the dog in his arms when they'd been in Greece. The dog craved affection.

"I have Miranda's phone records as well as her charge card bills. The police are going over them, but I thought we should take a look."

"How did you get them?"

"That's confidential. Don't mention to anyone that you've seen them. I don't want to get my source into trouble."

"Of course." She sat in the chair on the other side of his desk, Lexi and the two little dogs plopped down at her feet.

"Women are better at shopping than men. Go over the credit card bills and see if anything jumps out at you." He handed her a pencil and a pad. "Write down the purchase and date of anything suspicious so I can take a look."

Adam settled into the chair that had once belonged to his uncle. Jasper immediately hopped up into his lap. "Didn't Miranda put the utilities into your name?"

"No. We discussed it but decided to wait. I would have to come up with deposits. I didn't have the money. I had new business cards made up, and Miranda notified all her clients that I would be taking over. She gave them my cell phone number but her home number is still the one listed on the cards."

"I'm looking at her phone records for the last month. She made very few calls from home. I don't see any duplicates among them."

"You're thinking she would call a friend more than once, right?" When Adam nodded, she asked, "What about calls from her cell?"

"It takes longer to get cellular records than regular telephone records. We won't have those for a few days."

They worked in silence for almost an hour. By that time Jasper was snoozing on Adam's lap and the sun was dropping low.

"I'm not finding much on her charge accounts," Whitney told him. "Gasoline mostly, and a few department store charges. Nothing expensive. She paid the entire balance every month."

"I'm not finding anything either." Adam gently picked up Jasper and put him on the floor. "Let's see what she stored out in the garage before it gets dark. The fire destroyed the electrical wiring so we need to take advantage of what daylight is left. We can come back to this later."

Whitney rose and stretched provocatively. He longed to reach out and pull her into his arms, then kiss the sensitive spot he'd discovered at the nape of her neck. Don't start anything, he cautioned himself.

He reached out and brushed two fingers up the gentle rise of her cheek. He needed so much . . . *more* than this fleeting touch. But he refused to allow himself the pleasure. There was too much to do, too much danger.

His cell phone rang and he glanced down to where it was clipped to his belt. Max Deaver was calling. He hadn't mentioned the accountant or the missing money to Whitney.

"Why don't you get started?" he asked. "I need to take this call."

Whitney nodded as he pulled the telephone off his belt. She was walking out the door, the dogs at her heels, when he answered.

"Any luck in tracking down those cash withdrawals your uncle made every month?" Deaver immediately asked.

"No. It doesn't make sense." Adam had decided the money had been given to someone in the weapons deal. Cash payments kept that person's name off any records, but he wasn't comfortable sharing this theory.

"Are you sitting down?" Deaver asked.

"No. Should I be?"

The forensic accountant chuckled but couldn't manage to sound amused. "Your uncle's account in the Caymans. There's been more activity."

Now Adam was sitting down. He'd plopped into the office chair the second he'd heard "Caymans." If his uncle's accounts were drained, Adam would be on the hook for anything owed against properties he owned jointly with his uncle.

"Someone wire transferred seventy-five thousand dollars into the account."

"No shit."

"No shit. Seems bizarre, man. Totally bizarre."

"Where did the money come from?"

"A numbered account in the Bahamas."

"Why would they put money into a dead man's account?"

There was a moment of silence on the other end of the line, then, "I thought you might have some idea by now."

"Not really," Adam replied. He thought about what Quinten Foley had told him. It was possible the group purchasing weapons didn't realize Calvin Hunter had died and was still paying him.

"I'm going to keep working on this. We need to have a list of the assets for the probate, although I don't know what any attorney can do with numbered account information that he could obtain only by hacking into systems."

"I guess he'll have to leave it out unless I can find the code so I can withdraw the money."

"Someone else might beat you to it."

That was becoming more of a possibility by the minute.

"You know the old saying," Deaver said, irony in his tone. "Dead men tell no tales."

CHAPTER
TWENTY-THREE

Whitney tethered the three dogs to what was left of the back gate post in the small yard behind the cottage. The lingering smell of smoke and the sooty debris in the yard was a stark reminder of last night's fire. Nearby was the carport where she'd parked her SUV. Damaged by the fire, the structure's flimsy roof had collapsed onto what was left of her Jeep.

The firefighters had chopped holes in the garage walls and broken through the locked side door to fight the fire that had quickly spread from the cottage. Peering in, Whitney saw charred, water-soaked boxes. She wasn't looking forward to going through the sodden mess.

What choice did she have? She wasn't sure she could put into words the feelings she had about her cousin. Miranda wasn't going to miraculously reappear. They would have to find her, and it wasn't going to be easy.

With a quick glance to make sure the dogs were secure, Whitney edged her way into the old garage. Huge holes had been hacked in the roof and light streamed into the darkness. All she found as she rummaged through the things strewn across the floor was clothing. She sorted through the stuff to see if any of it could be salvaged — or provide a clue.

Several minutes later a scuttling noise made her jump. She stared into the corner where the sunlight didn't penetrate. In the dark shadows something moved. She released a pent-up breath of air. Rats or mice.

She needed to lighten up and soothe her raw nerves. Whoever was after Miranda was long gone. They weren't lurking in the shadows or following her every move as she walked dogs or went to the breeder's. Adam was merely being cautious.

"Find anything?"

Even though she immediately recognized Adam's voice, Whitney flinched.

"Hey." He slid his arm around her shoulders and lowered his head until his brow touched hers so gently that something caught inside her chest. "I didn't mean to startle you."

"It's okay," she replied as she pulled away.

"I'm just a little spooked. That's all." She waved her hand at the mess on the floor. "I've checked out this stuff."

Adam pointed to several cardboard boxes. They'd been hosed down but still held their shape. "Have you checked those?"

"I looked in them. Nothing but books. I didn't see any reason to go through them."

Adam walked over to the boxes. "Things that seem to be unrelated often provide important clues or links to other evidence."

Whitney supposed he was right. Adam had been a detective. No telling where he'd found clues. Later, when the timing was better, she planned to ask him about his career. Right now she needed to concentrate on finding her cousin.

"These seem to be cookbooks mostly," commented Adam.

"They're definitely something you would leave behind if you were on the run."

"Right." Adam studied the flyleaf of a book. "This one's *The Internet For Dummies*. Do you know a Crystal Burkhart?"

"No. I don't." Whitney walked over to him and peered over his shoulder. An address label was attached to the book's flyleaf. "Textbooks are really expensive. Miranda could have bought it used at the campus store."

"I doubt it's used. Most used bookstores put a stamp inside the book. She must have borrowed this one and neglected to return it."

"It happens," she replied, her mind on her own books. She'd left most of them with Ryan but the few she treasured had been with her. They'd inspected the cottage first thing this morning. The contents had been completely destroyed. The books she'd saved from her mother's collection were gone forever.

"Look at this." Adam showed her another book. It also had Crystal Burkhart's address label in it. He pulled his cell phone off his belt. "Let's see if information has a phone number for Crystal Burkhart."

While Adam talked to the information operator, Whitney made her way over to the back wall where a number of boxes were stacked. They'd been doused with water but hadn't been disturbed. Evidently the flames hadn't burned the rear few feet of the garage. The first box she opened was filled with office supplies. Miranda had left supplies in the nook for Whitney to use. These things must have come from her previous apartment and she hadn't had room for them in the cottage.

"Thanks." Adam snapped his phone shut

and looked at Whitney, shaking his head. "There are thirty-two Burkharts in the metropolitan San Diego area. Nothing for a Crystal Burkhart or C. Burkhart."

"We could try going over to the address on the label."

"Right. Let's have dinner, then drive over there. If that doesn't work, we can call every Burkhart listed and see if they're related to Crystal."

They worked in silence for a few minutes. Adam finished with the boxes of books and joined her. "Finding anything?"

"Not really." She showed him the box she was working on now. "There are photographs in this one. It looks like Miranda just tossed them in. You know how people end up with dozens of photos. Most of the time you never look at them again."

He moved nearer. "True, but let's take a close look. Photos tell you where a person has been. Ever heard of ComStat?"

"No. It sounds like a computer program. What is it?"

"Hey . . ." He touched her arm. It was just a fleeting brush of his hand but she felt it everywhere. "You're smart. It is a computer program that analyzes crime statistics. It can tell you where in a city a certain crime is most likely to occur, right down to the time of day."

"Most people can figure that out by reading the newspaper."

He chuckled. "There's some truth in that, but ComStat goes further than simple stats. It can tell you a lot about victims and perps. Most people have what we call a Com-Z. That's a geographic comfort zone. Killers don't strike far from home — usually."

Whitney thought about the person who'd tried to kill Miranda last night. She'd believed someone from far away had been after her cousin, but now she realized the killer probably lived in the area.

"People who go missing usually return to someplace where they've already been. It's rare to find them in a totally new location."

"Then Miranda's in the state," Whitney replied. "My cousin only left California once. A boyfriend took her to Hawaii."

"Once that you know about. Isn't it possible Miranda went other places during the years you were apart?"

"Anything's possible," she admitted.

They went through the photographs one at a time. They put certain photos that Adam felt needed a closer look in better light in a pile to take up to the house.

"You know," Whitney said, unable to check the excitement in her voice, "this might be something." She showed him a series of photographs with dates in the lower right corner. "These shots were taken last December on the eleventh."

Adam took them from her and studied them closely. "She's sunning herself at the beach. Not surprising."

"I don't think she was anywhere around here. I might be wrong but I believe it rained that week. I remember because Lexi's birthday is December seventh — Pearl Harbor day. I was house-sitting at the time. I'd planned to take her to the Bark Park but we couldn't go out for days because of the rain."

"Really? All we have to do is check the National Weather Service Web site. It'll tell us for sure." He pointed to something in the background of one photograph. "See that?"

Whitney squinted. "An umbrella, right?"

"Yeah, but I'm wondering if it's the kind we'd see around here. There's a magnifying glass up in my uncle's office. Let's take a closer look."

They set those aside and inspected the rest of the photographs. "Those pictures seem to be the only ones with the date on them," Adam said. "That makes me think they were taken with someone else's camera and given to Miranda."

"I saw her pack a camera. It wasn't a new digital model." She closed her eyes and tried to see Miranda sticking the small camera into the side of a bag. She didn't recall anything more about the camera and opened her eyes.

"Look at this." Adam showed her another photograph. A beautiful dark-haired girl was tilting a large cake toward the camera. Rows of lighted candles lined the top. Garish blue icing proclaimed: *Happy Birthday, Crystal.*

"Ohmygod." Whitney gazed up into Adam's eyes. "We're going to *have* to talk to Crystal Burkhart."

Ryan carefully placed Ashley's ring just under the bottom rim of the chest of drawers built into her enormous closet. She usually put her ring on top of it, near a photograph of them taken on their honeymoon. Last night, she'd left it in the kitchen. He'd noticed the ring when he'd been watching her rinse off dishes.

Right then a germ of an idea had begun to form. The huge ring had cost him a bloody fortune. He'd willingly spent it, not just because he loved Ashley, but because back then he'd been winning big-time. He'd wanted the ring to be really large so Ashley could flaunt it.

He knew if he took the ring and had the diamond replaced by a cubic zirconia, he could raise a lot of money. He'd been right. The jeweler grumbled but gave him a nice check. True, it wasn't nearly as much as Ryan had paid, but he knew better than to expect to receive what he'd spent. Jewels were like cars — the minute they left the shop, their price dropped.

Ryan had taken the money and had gone straight to the casino. It was the middle of the day and only blue-hairs and the pros were playing. He'd won and won and won. Shit! Nothing could have stopped him except his love for Ashley. He left — in the middle of a winning streak — to pick up the ring refitted with the CZ.

He knew Ashley would have tried to put on the ring after she'd dressed. Hiding it under the bottom edge of the dresser as if it had fallen was the only plausible way to return the ring without arousing Ashley's suspicious. He faced the CZ away from the light and dug the ring into the carpet a little bit.

He heard a noise and bolted out of her closet and flew into his. He yanked off his tie and unbuttoned his shirt so quickly that he almost ripped off the buttons.

"Ryan, what are you doing home?" Ashley called.

"I'm not allowed in my own home?" he joked as she appeared in the door of his closet. She still had on her workout clothes and looked rumpled, which was unusual.

"Of course." She kissed his cheek. "I'm just surprised to see you. I thought you were in the office."

"Not today. I was looking into something for Aesthetic Improvements. That's the name we've chosen for the new group." He noticed her brow crimp into a frown. She might have called Walter Nance, trying to locate him. "I didn't mention it to anyone, but there's a guy in Newport Beach who's developed a cream to apply after laser treatments to prevent ghosting."

"Really?" Ashley perked up.

She knew better than anyone that some laser treatments resulted in pink skin that took days to return to normal. When it did, the lasering often left a line of demarcation called "ghosting." A light application of makeup concealed the ghosting, but some women resented having to use makeup, especially when working out or participating in athletic activities.

Ryan "feathered" his lasering to make the line less noticeable and blend it in, but it was still there. If anyone found a way to prevent "ghosting" it would be priceless.

"Does it work?"

"I'm iffy," he responded. "I would want to test it on a few patients first. But the guy wants a fortune for a three-ounce tube. I don't know if we want to ask our patients to buy it."

"But if it's so good I'm sure —"

"Let's not worry about it." He put his slacks in the wall-mounted ValetMaster to press the creases back into them. He usually sent his suits to the cleaners after he wore them once, but he needed to cut back expenses. "Let's go out to dinner. How about Pomodoro?"

"I thought —"

"You're right. We're saving money. Let's go to Sea Catch and buy some swordfish to grill." He'd said this impulsively. After the mess she'd served last night for dinner, who could blame him for wanting to eat out? But she was right; they did need to economize. He couldn't tell her about the money he'd won. He had it in his pocket. Tomorrow, he would pay down the loans on the house. The loans reminded him that she'd promised to contact a broker. "Did the broker agree to a reduced listing fee on the house?"

"I didn't have a chance. You see . . ." She hesitated, tears glittering like diamonds in her blue eyes. "I misplaced my ring. I've been looking for it all day."

Ryan had known she was going to tell him about the ring. He snapped back, "You lost it at the gym?"

Ashley slowly shook her head. "No, I tried to work out to get my mind off things, but I kept thinking about the ring."

"I saw it on the counter last night when you were cleaning up." He tried to sound helpful yet slightly aggravated, the way he normally would.

"I guess I must have picked it up, but I don't remember. You know how you do things automatically." She sucked in a sharp breath, then slowly released it. "I looked everywhere — even in the trash. It was picked up today. I went to the garbage collection center but they said finding anything as small as a ring would be next to impossible."

He couldn't stand to see Ashley in pain. He tossed her a lifeline. "Let's take a really good look, starting in the kitchen. Your ring could have fallen on the floor and rolled off where you can't see it."

"I looked," she protested.

"Let me get into my jeans and we'll both

check again."

Of course, nothing turned up in the kitchen, but Ryan had them down on their hands and knees, peering under everything. He insisted on opening every drawer in case the ring had fallen in and gone unnoticed. From the kitchen, they went into the dining room and living room, crawling around and inspecting every inch of the house.

"It wouldn't be in my office," he said when they finished checking the entry hall.

"No," she assured him. "I never go in there."

He had cautioned her several times about his office. He'd told her that he had documents on his computer and research information on new surgical techniques that he didn't want disturbed. Whitney would have questioned him, but Ashley left his office alone.

"Let's try the master bedroom. You're in there most often."

Of course, a search around and under the bed yielded nothing. They removed the covers and shook out the spread and shams and every shitty toss pillow the decorator had insisted "made" the room. Nothing.

"The bathroom's next," he told her. "Or should we look in your closet? Isn't that where you keep it?"

"Yes, but I've already looked in the closet. It isn't there."

"Come on. Let's take another look. Two sets of eyes are better than one."

They went into the closet, and he started checking under the hanging clothes. He wanted Ashley to be the one to find the ring. *Come on, come on,* he kept thinking. His knees were killing him.

"Oh, gosh!" screamed Ashley. "Here it is!"

Ryan jumped up. "Are you sure? Where?"

Ashley held up the ring. Tears sprang into her eyes, making her look just like a little girl. He hated making her cry, but what choice did he have?

"It was under the dresser. I must have knocked it off." Ashley slipped it back on her finger and gazed down lovingly at the diamond. "I'm sure I checked under there. How could I have missed it?"

Ryan put his arm reassuringly around her and kissed her cheek. "The light changes during the day. You just didn't see it."

"I guess," she replied doubtfully.

"It doesn't matter. You have it now. Just be more careful. When you're cooking, take it off in here first."

He heard his cell phone ringing in his closet just steps away. "I've got to get that. It could be the office."

When he picked up the phone, Ryan didn't recognize the number on the caller ID. It was Domenic Coriz. His bowels loosened and he swore his balls actually ached. He walked out of the closet and down the hall before answering. The last thing he wanted was Ashley overhearing him.

"Heard you won some money."

Unfuckingbelievable! Where did Dom get his information? Ryan had purposely gone to a casino owned by another Indian tribe. "A bit," Ryan conceded. "I need to make a house payment or I'll be out on the street."

"My heart bleeds. Now listen up, shit-head."

He listened, his knees nearly buckling. "All right. I'll do what I can."

Money.

All his troubles came down to cold hard cash. Ryan put his hand on his back pocket. He had nearly ten thousand dollars. Once it would have sounded like a lot, but now he knew it wouldn't go far. All it could do was buy him a little time with the bank.

Or he could turn it into *real* money at the craps table.

He told himself to resist the urge to gamble. What had a few dollars gotten him? He needed megabucks. Plotting his next move was much more important. Taking your enemy by surprise was the key to victory. He was pretty sure someone famous had said this, but he couldn't remember who. It was the thought that counted. Do the unexpected. Take your enemy by surprise.

CHAPTER TWENTY-FOUR

"What did they say?" Adam asked Whitney.

After finishing dinner, Adam had gone upstairs and checked an Internet reverse directory for the address they'd seen on Crystal Burkhart's books. A man's name had been listed at that location. He'd asked Whitney to call because people were more likely to volunteer information to a woman than a strange man.

"Crystal Burkhart still lives there. Guess where she works?"

"Saffron Blue."

"Exactly. She'd just left for the club." Whitney thought a moment. "I wonder if Crystal met Miranda there."

Adam had his doubts. "It's more likely that the two met at college, considering the books we found. College girls often strip to earn money. People don't realize it, but most strippers are college girls or young housewives who need cash."

"Really? I had no idea."

Adam checked his watch. "It's early yet. The big tippers don't come in until after ten. Let's go out and talk with Crystal."

"Right," Whitney immediately agreed. "I'll lock the dogs inside my bedroom. That way I won't worry about them."

Followed by all the dogs, she trotted off in the direction of the maid's room. He mentally kicked himself for making her obsessive about the dogs' safety. He should have told her that Ashley had taken —

"Where did all those bags of clothes come from?" Whitney asked as she rushed back into the kitchen.

Adam had forgotten all about the shopping bags he'd put on her bed. "They were at the front door when I came home. A friend must have left them for you."

"I can't imagine who." She headed toward the back door and he followed. "I didn't get much of a chance to look at them, but the things on top were my size."

He led her to his uncle's Lexus. "Didn't you have friends where you used to work who might have brought by the clothes?"

"No, not really. I hardly knew anyone because I worked on a computer in my own space at a cube farm. I spent the day inputting sales data. I was the last to go when the entire department was outsourced to India. I haven't spoken to anyone there in months." She thought a moment. "I guess it could have been Trish, but I don't think so. I saw her at lunch. She would have mentioned it."

They drove toward Saffron Blue in silence. He'd considered going to the club alone, then decided having a woman would make it easier to get backstage and have a little talk with Crystal Burkhart. Besides, Whitney had a vested interest in this. She had every right to come along.

Over dinner, Whitney had told him about the house-sitting job that Trish Bowrather was trying to line up for her. He hated the thought of her moving out, but he didn't have the right to tell her what to do.

"Is something bothering you?" he asked when he realized she seemed to be staring out the window into the dark.

"I'm just thinking. I was offered a new job today. I'd like to take it, but I can't just give up Miranda's business. Clients are counting on me."

A warning bell sounded. "What job?"

He listened while she told him about the vet tech position. "Will you make more money than you do now?"

"No, and I'll have to work longer hours."

He was missing something here. "Then why would you be interested?"

Whitney angled herself sideways so she was facing him. An intense expression charged with excitement lit up her face. "I'd planned to attend veterinary school before I met Ryan. I'd been accepted at UC Davis."

Adam knew the University of California at Davis had a top-notch veterinary school. Being accepted to such a prestigious program was quite an honor.

"Instead of going, I married Ryan and helped put him through medical school. I'd like to give it another shot. If I take night classes I can reapply and I may have a chance of being accepted. Working with a veterinarian will give me practical experience."

"If they give you a good recommendation, that would help."

"It won't hurt. I have to give it a try. I don't want to wake up one day and find myself saying *I wish* . . . I want to know I gave it my best."

He had to admire her courage and sense of purpose. His life had once had direction and purpose, too, but that was before his stint in Iraq. He'd wanted to go into corporate security. Now he'd lost his moorings. He wasn't sure what he wanted to do. But sure as hell, sitting on his ass, guarding rich people's homes wasn't what he had in mind.

"What was being a detective like?" Whitney asked.

"Nothing like what I imagined. Nothing." He turned onto the highway. "You're probably smart to work at a vet's. I wish I'd had the opportunity to get a close-up view of detective work before I committed myself."

"You didn't like it."

"I enjoyed helping people, but too much time goes into paperwork and homicides linked to drug deals."

She didn't comment, but then, what could she say? The average person had no idea what went on behind the scenes at the police station.

Whitney finally spoke. "My mother used to say that as long as there was a demand, drugs would be a problem."

"I couldn't agree more, but drug use is rampant in our society. It brings in big money and that corrupts even the most well-meaning people."

"Didn't you work on any interesting murder cases?"

"Not really. Most homicides are easy to solve. The perp is usually someone the victim knows. Killers rarely strike victims at random."

"There's a reason behind every crime, I guess," Whitney said. "Like the firebomb. Someone didn't just drive down the street and pick out the cottage because it was cute. Someone deliberately went there to kill Miranda."

"True, and this case is more challenging than most of those I worked while I was still on the force."

What also made this more interesting was Whitney. He'd never been personally involved before. In one way it bothered him, because being too close meant you might miss an important clue. But in another way, it gave him a sense of control. He doubted Dudley "The Dud" Romberg had interviewed Jared Cabral yet. Hell, for all he knew, Romberg hadn't discovered Miranda had worked at Saffron Blue.

He realized Whitey had stopped talking and was gazing out the window again. "What do you plan to do with your business?"

She slowly turned to face him. "I know there are other pet concierges in the area. I'm going to ask at Dog Diva tomorrow. That's the groomer. Dan's the best in the area, and he really cares about his dogs. If he recommends someone, I'll interview them and see."

"Sounds like a good plan. What about Lexi?"

"They said I could bring her to work. She'll be a calming influence on the dogs, the way she is on walks. Many animals are terrified of the vet. Dr. Robinson brings in her Lab and there's a parrot in the waiting room to help the pets chill. I think Lexi will like it."

Adam had no doubt the dog would be fine, but he didn't care for this new turn of events. Long hours. Living far away from him. He wondered how much he would see of Whitney. Not nearly enough.

He knew he was falling for her. Hell, he might even be in love with her. It had all happened so quickly that he hadn't had time to evaluate the situation. Maybe he didn't need time. Hadn't his brush with death taught him anything? Life could end in a heartbeat. Couldn't you fall in love just as fast?

Still, it was best not to plunge headlong into anything. There was stress and pressure and even danger all around. *Give this relationship time and space,* he told himself.

They pulled into Saffron Blue's half-full parking lot. A hulking guy in a neon-yellow shirt guarded the entrance. Later there would be a line and the bouncer would keep order until there was space inside the club for the men waiting.

"Does the club really need a bouncer that mean-looking?" Whitney asked.

"If guys are thinking about fighting, the bouncer intimidates them. Staff wear bright yellow because it's easy to spot in the dark. But that's not why he's at the door." He parked at the far end of the lot to be near the back of the building. "When strip joints first opened, law enforcement was under big-time pressure to shut them down. An easy way is to enforce fire regulations that limit the number of people in the club. The bouncer keeps count — on a clicker or, if he's good like Cabral's bouncers, in his head."

"Clever idea. The bouncer serves a dual purpose."

"Right. Give the credit to Jared Cabral's father. He was the first club owner in SoCal to use a bouncer to regulate the count." He put the car in Park and swiveled in his seat to face Whitney. "We're going around to the backstage entrance. With luck, Crystal Burkhart isn't performing yet. If she is, we'll have to wait until she takes a break."

They went around back where there were several doors. Adam led her up to the center one with a card-key slot above the knob. He rapped on the door.

"Yeah?" A burly guy in a bright yellow T-shirt stuck his head out the door.

"We need to see Crystal Burkhart," Adam told him.

"Go in the front and pay." He started to slam the door, but Adam held on to the knob.

"I'm her cousin," Whitney piped up, surprising Adam. "There's been a death in the family." The guy hesitated. "I really need to speak to her. It'll just take a few minutes."

He glared at Whitney but his stare crumpled when tears jumped into her eyes. Damn, she was good.

"Aah, okay. But make it quick. The rapper's bangin' the shoe —" he checked his watch "— in fifteen."

He led them down a brightly lit hall that smelled of burgers on the grill. Adam figured the vents from the kitchen leaked a bit. To his right were a series of doors. Each had a name slot on it. By simply writing a name on a piece of paper and sliding it into the holder, the name could be changed by each dancer.

"Bangin' the shoe?" Whitney whispered.

"The bar is horseshoe-shaped. They bang — dance — on it."

The guy halted in front of a door and

knocked, calling, "Yo, Candy, your cousin's here."

Adam read the plate on the door: Candy Rapper. Instead of being hand-written, this one had been engraved on a brass nameplate. Evidently, she'd worked here long enough to have a permanent nameplate inscribed for herself. Someone down the long hall yelled at the guy who'd let them in, and he hustled away from them.

The door swung open. "Cousin? What —" The woman's bright pink mouth gaped open when she spotted them. "Who in hell —"

"Please, we need to talk to you," Whitney said. "Are you Crystal Burkhart?"

The woman nodded and her eyes narrowed. She was dressed in baggy jeans big enough to house five women at once and a huge shirt underneath a XXXL denim vest. Obviously, her shtick was to pretend to be a street rapper. Layers of oversize, ugly gangsta clothing concealed a stripper's hot bod.

"I'm Miranda Marshall's cousin."

"So? That supposed to mean something?"

Crystal sounded tough but Adam decided it was just an act.

"You're her friend, aren't you?" Whitney asked.

The woman's lips curved into a smart-ass

smirk. "No."

"This is important," Adam told her. "May we come in and speak with you for a moment?" He thought she was about to refuse, so he pushed on the door and stepped into the brightly lit dressing room.

The room wasn't much bigger than a phone booth. In the center was a dressing table with a mirror illuminated by dozens of small bulbs. Makeup was scattered across the small table and Crystal's street clothes were slung over the back of a small folding chair in front of the mirror.

Crystal put a finger up to her lips to silence them. She grabbed a pack of cigarettes then headed out the door. Adam and Whitney followed the stripper as she rushed down the hall. He expected her to stop outside the stage door, but she streaked to the back wall behind three blue Dumpsters.

"You're a cop," Crystal declared emphatically.

"Not for over two years," Adam responded. "This is a personal matter. I won't bring in the police unless I have no other choice."

Crystal cupped her hand to shield the match while she lit her cigarette. "I can always spot a cop."

"He's a friend who's helping me," Whitney said. "Something's happened to my cousin. Miranda's vanished."

"Really? Do tell."

Adam asked, "When was the last time you saw Miranda?"

Crystal sucked in a puff of smoke, then slowly blew it out in a thin ribbon that drifted away in the soft breeze. It was dark behind the Dumpsters, the only illumination coming from the security lights at the back of the building. The stripper was overly made up, with stage makeup, and in the dim light she appeared clownish.

"I haven't seen Miranda in —" she hitched one shoulder "— at least a year and a half."

"Do you know if she had other friends or a boyfriend?" asked Whitney.

"What's it to you?"

Adam almost interrupted but decided to let Whitney handle this. People responded to her more easily than they did to him. "Last night someone threw a pipe bomb into Miranda's house. She isn't living there any longer. I'm staying there with the dogs. Luckily, I was out —"

"I saw it on TV. Were the dogs killed?"

"No," Whitney assured her. "They were with us or they would have been burned alive."

Crystal considered this information and a

cold smile played across her pink-pink lips. "Miranda started dogsitting because of me. I earned money for college by walking dogs. It's cash, it's easy, it leaves no paper trail for the IRS."

"When did you two turn to stripping?" Adam asked.

"Back when we were in college, a girl in my econ class told me about Saffron Blue." She waved her arm in an arc and the tip of the cigarette in her hand glowed brighter. "The rest — as they say — is history."

"You told Miranda about it?" Whitney asked.

Crystal inhaled another stream of smoke. "We came out here together for the first interview. Neither of us knew what to expect."

The feistiness seemed to have gone out of her, replaced by a tone that was almost melancholy. Adam wondered about her life. What would keep someone stripping in front of lecherous men night after night? The money, sure, but this woman had a lot going for her. She must have other options.

"They looked us over and gave us an opportunity to 'try out.' Little did we know that 'trying out' was the same as dancing. You get tips and you fork over a 'tryout' fee to the house each night."

"Why did Miranda quit?" Whitney asked.

"Damned if I know." Crystal threw down her cigarette and ground it out with the heel of her hightop sneaker. "We used to be best buds — then . . . she went jiggy on me."

Jiggy was a doper's term, but he doubted Whitney knew it. He asked, "Was Miranda using?"

"No, but she was edgy, like she was on ice."

Ice. Methamphetamine. Use of the drug had exploded during the last few years. "How did you know for sure Miranda wasn't using?"

"I was around her too much. I would have known." She shrugged dismissively as if to say: Who cares? "She up and quit. I haven't seen her since. It's been sixteen, eighteen months. Something like that."

"What about boyfriends?" asked Whitney.

"When we were first at college, she went out with a guy. Lasted a year, then he transferred to some school in Texas. She dated but nothing serious. Then we started stripping." Crystal squared her shoulders and looked directly at Adam. "Would you want your girl working here?"

An image of Whitney strutting across the stage flitted through his mind. Before he could stop himself, he said, "Hell, no."

"Men are like that," she told Whitney. "Work here, make money and get out — if you want to have a boyfriend and a real life."

Crystal wasn't nearly as tough as she'd initially tried to make them think. She'd been friends with Miranda, and Whitney's cousin had hurt her feelings. If they handled her right, the stripper would tell them what she knew.

"Please, help us," pleaded Whitney in a soft voice. "Someone tried to kill Miranda and nearly killed innocent people and animals. Have you any idea if Miranda was in any sort of trouble or anything?"

Crystal shook her head. "No, but like I said, I haven't seen her in a long time."

Adam asked, "Could she have met someone here that might have gotten her into trouble? Who were her friends here?"

"This isn't the kind of place you come to make friends. We knew each other before working here or we might not have done more than say hello."

"What about the men who come here?"

"Jared follows standard strip club rules. Men can't touch you. There's no going into back rooms or anything like what you see on TV."

"Can't they buy you a drink?"

"Sure. But no one wants to take the time.

You earn more in tips by stripping than by sitting around with one guy."

Adam tried another tack. "Were you surprised when Miranda quit?"

"Everyone was, especially Jared. You see, Miranda was good on the computer and she put Saffron Blue online. She was more than just another exotic dancer." Crystal lowered her voice and leaned toward them as if someone might be eavesdropping from inside the Dumpster. "She worked the back room. Megatips. Trust me. Megatips."

"I take it Jared runs a high stakes poker game back there."

Crystal jumped around hip-hop style as if the ground was in flames. "You didn't hear it from me."

"Why?" Whitney wanted to know. "There are a lot of casinos around here."

"True, but high rollers who know each other like to play together," Adam responded. "They don't want to be forced to mix with strangers. Between hands they talk business, as if they were on the golf course."

"You got it. Games go on weeknights," Crystal added. "Nothing on the weekend. The guys who play here are out socializing on Saturday and Sunday."

"Did Miranda mention meeting any of those men?" Whitney asked before he could.

Crystal hesitated, shook her head, then admitted, "I'm not supposed to know anything about it. You have no idea how bonkers Jared is about security. Why do you think I brought you back here?"

Adam had been wondering. Most smokers would have stood just outside the stage door.

"The dressing rooms are bugged. There are security cameras everywhere. They can't see us back here. We're out of range of the cameras at the back exit."

Adam wondered why Crystal had taken the trouble to find out the security cameras' range but didn't ask. He figured he might be pushing their luck.

"We won't mention a thing about this to Cabral," Adam assured her. "Do you know the names of any of the men who gambled here when Miranda was still working?"

Crystal rattled off a list of names, and it included many of the heavyweight leaders in town. A thought struck him. "Did Broderick Babcock gamble here?"

"Oh, yeah. He's here a lot."

"What about Ryan Fordham, a doctor," Whitney surprised him by asking.

"I don't recognize the name. What did he look like?"

Whitney described her ex and Adam

waited, watching her. Why would Ryan be out here? Sure, doctors made money, but he wasn't in the same league as the other high rollers.

"I'm not certain, but he sounds like one of the regulars. But I haven't seen him around in months. Come to think of it, Broderick Babcock hasn't been here either."

With those words Crystal Burkhart stomped off toward the stage door. They watched her go in silence.

"Your ex is a gambler?" Adam asked when Crystal disappeared inside the building.

"Yes. I just found out. Rod Babcock told me at lunch." She sounded despondent. He put his arm around her and pulled her close. "Funny, my attorney didn't mention that he's also a big-time gambler."

Adam's brain scrambled to connect the dots. Gambling. Ryan Fordham. Rod Babcock. Saffron Blue. Somehow they were all connected.

"Miranda quit just about a year and a half ago," Whitney said. "Right around the time Crystal says Broderick stopped coming here. He claims not to know my cousin, but I think there might be a connection."

"You're right. We need to ask him what he knows."

CHAPTER
TWENTY-FIVE

Whitney waited until they had driven away from Saffron Blue before adding, "In retrospect, I should have had some idea, but I didn't. When Ryan went out in the evening, I believed he'd gone to the hospital."

"At some point you must have wondered. What made you suspicious?"

She considered his question for a long moment. "I'm not sure exactly. It was just a vague feeling I had that something was wrong." She hesitated again, uncertain how much of her personal life to reveal. She hadn't even told Miranda much except the barest details. Somehow she felt Adam would understand. Or maybe she just needed to talk to him, to feel closer.

Doing her best to keep her voice steady, she continued, "To be honest, a lot had been wrong in our marriage for some time, but I'd chalked it up to the stress of a pressure-packed residency followed by the difficulties of setting up a new practice. Then I began to have the feeling it was something . . . more. I was taking his suits to the cleaners and discovered a hotel receipt. Then I knew. I thought it was just another woman, which would have been bad enough. Now I know he was also gambling and I never knew it."

"Babcock told you today at lunch?"

She picked up something in his tone that she couldn't quite interpret. "Yes, Rod was in La Jolla taking a deposition. He asked me to meet him for lunch. His firm had begun to review my property agreement. He doesn't want me to sign until he has the details about the toxic-waste report."

They were on the freeway now, heading back toward the house. Adam was staring straight ahead and didn't respond for a long moment. "Babcock could easily have discussed this with you over the phone."

For a second, her heart forgot its rhythm. He couldn't be jealous, could he?

"I think it's more likely Babcock wanted to see you again. To learn if you'd found out anything more about Miranda."

She was a tiny bit disappointed, she confessed to herself. Adam wasn't jealous. He was merely being a detective and analyzing the situation critically. "Well . . . he did ask if I'd discovered where Miranda went. I told him about her Volvo being in the airport, but I didn't tell him how we knew."

"He didn't ask?"

"No. Do you think that's unusual?"

"I'm not sure what to make of the whole situation. Babcock claimed not to know your cousin, right? And you didn't look familiar to him even though you closely resemble Miranda."

"That's right. He really seemed to be telling the truth. If he wasn't, he sure fooled me." But Ryan had deceived her, too, and she knew him a lot more intimately. How could she be certain the lawyer had been telling the truth? Something stirred deep in her brain, but she couldn't quite bring it to the surface.

"Maybe I ought to talk to Babcock."

She recalled the attorney's parting words to Trish Bowrather. "Tomorrow night, Rod will be at a reception Trish is throwing for one of her artists. I promised to be there. You could come with me. We might catch him off guard that way."

He grinned at her and winked. "Good idea."

They rode in silence for a few minutes, then Adam asked, "Did that woman who phoned to interview you about taking care of her dog ever call again?"

With all the excitement, Whitney had forgotten all about it. "No. I never heard from her, and she didn't leave any message on voice mail."

"I'll bet she's linked to whoever tried to kill your cousin. They wanted to be sure she was home."

The second he said it, Whitney realized Adam was right. "Of course. The call came to Miranda's telephone. It was the first time I've ever used call forwarding to my cell. Now that I think about it, the woman sounded funny. It wasn't just her accent — calling the dog a poo-dell. It might have been a man disguising his voice."

Adam turned onto Torrey Pines Road. "I keep going back to motive. It's the detective training."

"You told me crimes of passion and money were behind most murders."

"True, but at John Jay we learned to analyze carefully. Crimes of passion usually involve a weapon that's handy — a knife, or more likely, a gun."

"It calls for premeditation to construct a pipe bomb. It may be relatively easy to make but it takes planning. It's not something a rejected lover usually does. They like to make it more personal. Look you in the eye so you know who's killed you."

Her stomach flopped. As much as she'd come to despise Ryan, Whitney couldn't imagine killing him. She couldn't envision hurting anyone or anything.

"The more I think about this, the more I'm inclined to believe Miranda knew something, and someone wanted to silence her forever."

Again something niggled at the back of Whitney's brain. Then she realized what was troubling her. "You know, Miranda had keys to a lot of homes. She went in when the owners weren't there to feed or walk their dogs. She told me about an incident when she'd been accused of stealing a woman's ring." Whitney explained the insurance fraud scheme that had finally been uncovered, clearing Miranda's name.

"It's possible Miranda saw something or came across something," Adam said.

"I was around her for several days. She didn't seem jumpy or nervous. She didn't act like anyone was after her."

"Yet she was preparing to vanish. What could Miranda have seen or found that would make her run but wouldn't panic her into leaving instantly?"

Whitney slapped her thigh with the open palm of her hand. "I've got it! The owners weren't due back for some time. When they returned, they would discover . . . whatever. That gave her a chance to leave without rushing."

"Possibly, but if she stumbled on something illegal or life threatening, why didn't she go to the police?"

Whitney hesitated a moment, not wanting to verbalize her suspicions. "She stole something from one of the homes and knew they'd discover it when they returned. Otherwise, why wouldn't *they* go to the police? Why try to kill her instead?"

Adam considered this for a moment. "Because whatever she found was illegal. That's the only reason I can think of that would account for everyone dodging the police. Most likely it was drugs."

"I doubt it. What would Miranda do with a load of drugs? Don't you have to have a network —"

"Could have been drug money. If you report a theft of a lot of cash, you'd better have a good explanation for where you got it."

"That must be it," Whitney told him. "Miranda stole someone's cache of drug money. It doesn't have anything to do with the strip club."

Adam turned up their street. "I'm not

sure. There's a missing link somewhere. Miranda goes to work at Saffron Blue because she needs money. Then she quits just when she's making the really big tips in the back room and continues to walk dogs. A year and a half later, she skips."

"I can't explain it entirely, but the list of her customers is in my BlackBerry."

"The list she gave you, right? Miranda is one smart cookie. If she stole something, she probably deleted that particular client. What we need is her cell phone records. She must have called those people to make arrangements to care for their pet."

"Shouldn't we tell Detective Romberg what we know? He'll have more manpower to chase down leads."

He slowly nodded. "As much as I hate to rely on The Dud, we need help."

They pulled into the driveway of Calvin's home. They'd left the house and yard lights on. In the shadows, Whitney could make out the charred skeleton of the cottage.

When they stepped inside the back door, Adam punched in the alarm code. He checked the panel on the security system to make certain no one had entered, then reset the alarm.

"Should we take a closer look at the photos of Miranda at the beach?" Whitney asked as they got out of the car.

"Let's go for a swim first. It's a perfect night for it."

"Unless there's a swimsuit in those bags of clothes, I don't have anything to wear."

"I won't mind if you don't wear a stitch," Adam teased. "Or you could strip down to your undies. Won't that work?"

"I guess," she replied, attempting to keep the excitement out of her voice.

Adam unlocked the door. "Meet you in the pool. I'm going to call Romberg first."

Whitney knew better than to tempt fate by getting out of her clothes to take a swim in her underwear. But she decided to do it anyway. All the dogs were huddled inside the door to the maid's room. She nudged them aside, except for Jasper. As if launched from a cannon, the little dog bolted out of the room. No doubt he was streaking upstairs to find Adam.

Still puzzled by who'd left her the clothes, Whitney dumped the contents on the bed. Some items still had their price tags. She found shorts, capris, assorted tops and a few dresses. No swimsuit.

She changed into the black bra and thong she'd purchased at Wal-Mart. It wasn't any more revealing than a bikini — if she were in Rio. Covering up with a bathrobe she found among the clothes in the bag, Whitney grabbed a towel and left the room. Da Vinci, Maddie and Lexi followed her outside.

Adam hadn't come down to the pool yet so she took the opportunity to quickly get out of the robe and submerge herself. She released a pleasure-filled sigh as the warm water welcomed her. She looked down and decided the wavering water obscured the view of the demibra. If she kept her back away from Adam, the thong would just appear to be skimpy panties.

"That was fast," Adam called as he walked outside in swim trunks. "You found a bathing suit?"

"No. I couldn't get that lucky. I'm in my underwear."

"Want me to turn off the pool light?"

"Good idea." The light at the bottom of the pool went on automatically each evening, but it wasn't necessary for swimming.

He switched off the pool and yard lights, saying, "I spoke with Romberg. He contacted everyone on the client list. No one reported anything missing. He did the usual background check. Never can tell what you'll turn up that will lead to an arrest. Nothing much surfaced. A DUI. A guy behind on child support. A few unpaid parking tickets."

"Did Detective Romberg like our theory about drug money?"

Adam walked down the steps at the shallow end of the pool. Jasper parked himself next to the other dogs at the edge of the water. "Yeah. He'll look into it. The guy's under a lot of pressure to solve this. Pipe bombs are rare. Just say the word *bomb* and everyone thinks terrorists."

"Miranda couldn't have come across a terrorist plot, could she?"

Adam moved through the water and stopped a foot from her. "What do you say to letting the police handle it tonight? Tomorrow we can check and see what they found."

"Okay," she whispered.

The small waves his body generated lapped seductively against her skin. Above them a crescent moon gilded the water with beads of sparkling light. The moonlight played across the hard contours of his bare chest. There was something mesmerizing about his looks. His eyes were intense, but not that much different than other blue-eyed hunks. His lower lip was full, yet determined. She'd seen other lips that had been almost as intriguing. His angular face emphasized a strong jaw that sported a slight cleft in his chin. She'd studied other men's facial structure and found them equally as masculine. What set Adam Hunter apart, she realized, was her reaction to him.

Yes, other women found him attractive. She'd noticed them sneaking second looks, but she was captivated by him in a way she hadn't been drawn to another man. Not even Ryan. True, she had been taken with her ex-husband, but this was completely different, and it frightened her. Those feelings were too complex to analyze with him standing so close. She sucked in a breath that seemed to vibrate through her entire body.

Adam's eyes scanned her alluring figure. The caressing moonlight played across her soft skin and accentuated the sheer black bra lifting her full breasts. Her slim body nipped in at the waist where a thin band of black held up a small triangle of black satin. He'd seen bikinis that revealed more. None of the women wearing them had been this hot.

This sexy.

He extended his arms. "Come here."

She edged closer and her eyes glinted in the moonlight. The irises were wide and banded by a slim hoop of silver. He studied her mouth with its irresistibly full lower lip. He could feel her mouth against his, had been imagining it all day. Reliving those potent kisses.

Primitive desire coursed through him, hot and powerful. In a heartbeat he was dealing with a world-class hard-on. He reached out to pull her into his arms. She halted, a mischievous smile playing across her lips. She pivoted, jackknifed and dove away. With a few swift strokes and flutter kicks, she was across the pool.

Out of reach.

He was about to go after her when Whitney flipped over and backstroked toward him. The sexy bra lifted her breasts upward and emphasized the flatness of her tummy. The swatch of black silk between her thighs shimmered in the dim light.

Yeah, oh, yeah.

He was in real trouble here. *'S okay.* He'd been through hell and survived. He intended to live each day, each moment to the fullest. Right now every fiber of his being screamed for this woman.

CHAPTER TWENTY-SIX

Whitney stopped near Adam and tossed her wet hair away from her face, flinging a shower of tiny water droplets into the warm night air. With her hair slicked back, the rise of her cheekbones was more prominent. Her expressive eyes seemed larger and exceptionally blue. He reached out and touched the soft curve of her shoulder.

The magnetic pull of desire surged through him, dismaying Adam. The throb in his swim trunks kicked up, his pulse accelerating. Hopefully, the darkness and the water concealed his erection. He forced himself to gaze up at the whirlpool of stars overhead.

Don't rush this, Adam.

"Come here," he repeated, a slight rasp to his voice.

Her matchless eyes surveyed him with mock suspicion. "Why? You aren't thinking about kissing me, are you?"

"It might have crossed my mind." He looked over his shoulder. "But the dogs are watching."

The dogs were standing at the edge of the pool and gazing at them expectantly, as if they would be receiving a doggie treat any second.

He chuckled and took her hand, pulling her close. "I think we should give them a show."

"You could butterfly across the pool. I'm sure they would love every second."

"Sweetheart, butterflying wasn't what I had in mind."

"Oh, what did you have in mind?" she questioned, all sass.

His eyes dropped to her bra straps and followed them down to the lush fullness of her breasts, bobbing slightly in the water. Her pert nipples were taut beneath the wet fabric. And incredibly erotic.

"You know what I have in mind."

He ran his fingers through the silky strands of wet hair pushed back from her face. The eyes staring up at him were charged with emotion. He knew she wanted him, could feel it, but he didn't expect her to admit a thing. Wounds from the past were still too fresh, and even though they were joking around, he knew she was unsure of herself.

Whitney turned her head to kiss the inside of his wrist. Her lips were as soft as the balmy air and just as tender. He drew her closer. She tilted her head upward to invite him to kiss her.

His mouth met hers and he reveled in the taste of her lips. He traced the moist interior, his tongue mating with hers. The water was warm but her body, flush against his, was hot. Its heat enthralled him, coiling around his thighs and sending a carnal charge through his lower body. Her nipples were thrust against his bare torso. An urge too powerful to deny filled him, the urge to mark every inch of her sexy bod with his mouth. Taste every inch. He didn't believe he could ever get enough of touching her, kissing her.

Don't rush it, he reminded himself.

His hands coasted over her back, slowly roaming lower and lower until he reached the gentle curve of her bottom. He eased his hand right, then left as he continued to kiss her. She was wearing a thong, a strand of butt floss forming the rear portion of her panties.

Works for me.

He used both hands to press her against his aching erection. With a startled gasp, she pulled back and stared up at him with wide, glistening eyes. Her lower lip trembled just slightly.

"I'm crazy about you," he heard himself confess.

"Adam, I —"

He had the feeling he wasn't going to like what she planned to say so he cut her off with another kiss. She didn't pull away — hardly — instead she wound her legs around his. Blood throbbed through his veins and breathing evenly became impossible.

Whitney moved against his jutting erection. His pulse skyrocketed; he groaned deep in his throat. He was tempted to take her standing up — right here in the water. But he knew better than to succumb to instant gratification.

When was the last time he'd desired a woman this much? He honestly couldn't remember and didn't have the willpower to give it more than a passing thought. She was special, and he'd known it from their first strange meeting on the floor of his uncle's living room.

Whitney shuddered, her fingers digging into his shoulders. He wedged one hand between their bodies and captured a breast. Some of its fullness escaped his fingers, but he savored the tightly spiraled nipple tickling the center of his palm. He pulled back a little so he could stroke the taut nubbin with his thumb.

"You were saying?" he managed to ask.

She gazed up at him with a dazed expression, her eyes smoldering with desire. "Saying?"

"I think we're waaay past talking, don't you?"

Her response was a moan of pleasure that made something catch inside him. *Do this right,* he warned himself. He allowed the moment to lengthen. The slow undulation of the water around them lulled him. Accompanying it, the sultry embrace of the night.

This was a special time, a special moment. Whatever the future held — he'd learned not to think about it — they would never be the same. He wanted them to be closer and . . . And? He didn't have the inclination to go beyond that thought. For now this moment, this woman were all he needed from the world.

One of her hands dropped from his shoulders and wiggled its way between them. In a heartbeat, her hand was under the waistband of his swim trunks, nudging through the springy hair and coiling around him. *I'll be a sonofabitch,* he thought. He was close to losing it.

Already.

Aw, hell. What did he expect? He'd spent nearly three years in hell without a woman. Why wouldn't he go off when he was with someone so special?

"Hey, watch it," he warned, the words coming from deep in his throat.

Her hand clutched him tighter, then moved back and forth. A debilitating heat invaded every pore of his body. Christ almighty. What she could do to him without half trying. The sensation was so arousing he couldn't keep from moaning out loud.

"I need you," she half whispered, half moaned into his ear.

Adam lifted her into his arms, her head nestling between his head and shoulders. He plowed through the pool to the steps. The dogs jumped to their feet, tails wagging. He emerged and water cascaded off them. He walked toward one of the cushy chaise lounges nearby. Water sluiced off them now in small streams.

He lowered Whitney to the chaise. The dogs circled his feet and he nearly stumbled. "Sit! Stay!" He didn't spare the time to check to see if they all obeyed.

He carefully angled himself across her body to spare her the full impact of his weight. Stretched out, the full length of his body against hers, Adam didn't move for a second. He permitted himself a moment to enjoy the exquisite sensation of her warm, soft skin against his. In the dim light, her pupils were dilated and her long lashes dewy with water.

Sexy as hell.

The fragrant scent of her shampoo wafted up from her damp hair. One bra strap had slipped off her shoulder, and he pulled it down. With the black silk strap came the sheer fabric that almost concealed her full breast. Exposed to the soft moonlight, her skin took on a pearly sheen. He lowered his head and gently kissed her soft skin.

Whitney's hands found his butt and urged him closer and closer as she moved provocatively beneath him. "Yes, oh, yes."

He bit back the impulse to rip off the flimsy thong and bury himself to the hilt inside her sexy body. "Hold on," he told her, his voice rough with pent-up desire. "Let's make this special."

She ran the tip of her tongue across the skin along the curve of his neck, promising delights he could only imagine — if his brain could focus. A bolt of primitive heat lanced his groin. He'd told her to hold on, but it was all he could do to keep himself in check.

He lifted his head from the one breast he'd already exposed. He found the hook in the center of the bra and unfastened it. "Nothing like a front-loader."

Whitney might have tried to laugh. He couldn't be sure as he gazed down on her breasts, bared to the starlit sky. With a flick of his wrist, he tossed the garment over his shoulder. He was vaguely aware of the dogs scuffling for the bra as if it were some chew toy.

She arched under him, and the searing pressure of her body against his erection nearly sent him over the top. Every muscle in his body taut with need, he forced himself to concentrate on the breast he'd just uncovered. His lips circled the erect nipple, and he sucked hard, drawing it deep into his mouth.

"You're really good at this." She emitted a breathless sigh, her nails digging into his bare buttocks.

"I'm out of practice."

"Could have fooled me."

When had she shoved down his swim trunks? He managed to find the strength to stand up. His butt was half-exposed while the front of his suit looked like a tepee. He yanked down his trunks and kicked them aside. Then he bent over and eased off the barely-there thong Whitney was still wearing.

For a moment, he stood there admiring her. Her glorious body fairly glowed in the light of the most amazing moon he'd ever seen. A lover's moon.

Adam lowered himself to the chaise and settled over her, his throbbing erection finding the apex between her thighs. With a deep growl, he nuzzled her with the hot tip of his shaft. He slowly parted the moist folds and eased inside her by degrees. She was small, a tight fit, but he found the stamina to hold back until her body gradually accepted his.

She raked her nails across his bare back, murmuring, "Hurry, hurry."

With one swift movement, he surged forward and buried himself inside her hot, welcoming body. She responded instantly, moving up and down with each of his thrusts. Hips pounding, he hammered against her.

He heard a groan rumble from his chest as white-hot heat speared through him. His mind-shattering climax ripped through his skull, then shot down his spine. Trembling, he managed to hold it together and keep on moving for another few minutes until he felt her inner body tremble with release.

She cried, "You're the best!"

He mustered the strength to mutter, "Not the best, but close enough for government work."

He collapsed on his forearms to keep the brunt of his weight off her. Huffing like a racehorse, sheathed with moisture, he struggled to get his breath while his heart slowed.

She stroked the damp hair at the base of his neck and whispered, "Be serious. I'm crazy about you, too."

Ashley was waiting for Preston in Dr. Jox's parking lot when the personal trainer drove his Camry into a space as far from the building as possible. She knew his theory. People didn't take advantage of everyday exercise opportunities. Use the stairs, not the elevator. Walk fast, not slow. Park as far as possible from your destination.

"Hey, you're early," Preston called as he eased his large body out of his car, his backpack slung over one powerful shoulder.

Ashley had the top down on her metallic-blue Mercedes convertible. She'd been sitting in the parking lot for over twenty minutes, thinking. "Let's go for a ride. I don't feel like working out."

Preston stood beside her car, a puzzled

expression on his face. He dropped the backpack onto the small shelf behind the passenger side of her two-seater. "All right, but I need to watch the time. Arnold Wilcott has the slot after you. He's never late."

Preston climbed in and was fastening his seat belt when Ashley backed out and laid rubber on the asphalt. "Slow down unless you want a ticket."

Ashley didn't trust her voice enough to reply. She wanted to scream, to hit something, break something. But she hadn't a clue what would do any good. She hated losing control. It was like walking down the runway again, being in a beauty pageant and letting the judges decide your fate. When her mother died, Ashley had thought that life was behind her. Wrong.

"Upset about something?" Preston asked.

"Yeah, a little." She did her best not to sound as angry as she felt, but the weight of this was crushing her spirit.

"Wanna talk?"

She pulled into a parking space with a view of the harbor and turned off the engine. "I'm sorry. I'm always dumping my problems on you."

Preston shoved his sunglasses to the top of his head. "I don't mind."

Ashley could see Preston meant it. Sometimes she thought he cared more about her than Ryan did. Of course, Ryan had monumental problems while Preston led a stress-free life as a personal trainer.

She held up her hand. "Remember my ring?"

"You found it. Awesome! Be more care —"

"I never lost it. After I left you yesterday, I searched everywhere. I even went to the garbage collection agency that services our neighborhood. Nothing."

Preston's eyes narrowed, and she wondered if he guessed what she was going to tell him. Had she been a fool? Did other people see through Ryan?

"Know what happened to it?" she asked.

He waited for her to continue. When she didn't, he prompted, "What?"

"Guess. Tell me what you think."

He studied her a moment, and she saw the unwavering compassion in his eyes. "You found it . . . I don't know . . . somewhere you'd forgotten you'd put it. Like a different drawer or something."

Ashley shook her head, sending her hair across her shoulders in waves she could see out of the corner of her eye.

Preston shot her a questioning look. "Your husband found it and put it somewhere and forgot to tell you."

"You're closer now."

He leaned toward her. "Why are we playing games?"

Ashley stared at him a moment and asked herself the same question. This was no joking matter. Preston was her best — her only — friend. Why not come out and tell him?

He touched her shoulder in a tender way that nearly brought tears to her eyes. "Tell me what happened."

"Ryan took the ring," she said, bitterness echoing in every word. "He sold the diamond — without telling me — and had a fake stone put in its place." She waved her hand under his nose.

"Is that so bad, if he really needs money?"

"I wouldn't mind — had he told me. But the bastard had me on my hands and knees double-checking the entire house for the 'lost' ring. Then it magically appeared under my dresser."

Ashley released a pent-up, exhausted sigh. "I couldn't sleep all night. I kept thinking about how thoroughly I'd searched the closet. The ring hadn't been there. Ryan conveniently found it when my back was turned."

"I get the picture."

"I started thinking about the unpaid bills

and things I'd found in his office and I was sure he'd sold my diamond."

"Doesn't he have any other way to raise money?"

"No. He's taken loans out on everything."

Preston rolled his eyes heavenward. "But you were going to buy a new house."

"He said he planned to roll over the equity in the house and use it plus a piece of land to buy the property. After sifting through his records, I doubt the bank would have gone for it. I think Ryan was just humoring me."

Preston picked up her hand and studied the ring. "Are you sure this isn't the real deal? It looks great to me."

"This morning, I went to a pawnshop to see what I could get for it. I didn't want to pawn it but I thought that would be the fastest way to verify what I suspected."

"That's smart."

"They wouldn't give me a dime because it's a fake," she cried. "Why didn't Ryan just tell me?"

"He didn't think you would understand, and he was embarrassed."

"I know money's tight right now with the new practice and everything, but why couldn't he discuss it with me? That's what a relationship is all about."

Preston nodded his agreement. "Maybe he had a bad experience in his first marriage. That's why he doesn't feel comfortable talking over problems with you."

"Possibly. It's hard to know. He never mentions Whitney unless it's absolutely necessary."

"Why don't you just come out and ask Ryan about the ring?"

She hesitated, reluctant to confess the truth. "I'm afraid."

"Afraid of what? He won't hit you or anything, will he?"

"No, no. Of course not," she assured him, but in the back of her mind she remembered what Whitney had said the other night. Ryan did have an explosive temper. Apparently, he'd done something to Whitney.

"Okay, so, like, talk to him."

"I'm afraid of ruining our relationship. We never fight or argue. At least, we didn't until I took the dog. Then Ryan went postal on me."

Preston was silent for a moment before telling her, "The way I see it, if you don't talk to him, the relationship is ruined anyway."

There was more than a kernel of truth in what he said. Ashley hadn't been in a long-term relationship until now. She couldn't remember her parents talking about anything except her competing in endless beauty pageants. No wonder her father had walked out. As a teenager, she hadn't understood it, but now, she was an adult. A marriage couldn't be healthy without two-way communication.

Too late, she realized she should have called her father when her mother had suddenly died. Bakersfield was only a couple of hours north of here. He easily could have driven down. She hadn't called because she'd assumed he didn't care. Now she saw the situation from a different perspective. She knew her parents loved each other, but her mother had been obsessed with Ashley winning a beauty title. Her father had understood what a pipe dream it was and how little Ashley would gain from the title should she win.

She considered talking to Ryan tonight, but they were going out with Walter Nance and his wife. Ryan was determined to impress the head surgeon in his new practice. He'd told her to look spectacular. If things went well, Ryan might be in the mood to have a serious discussion afterward. She stopped herself. Why did so much of their life together have to depend on his moods?

"If only I could help Ryan in some way. You know, offer up a solution to the money problems when we talk."

"The solution is getting that woman — Whitney — out of your lives."

Preston was right, and she knew it. Ashley felt for Whitney. She'd lost Ryan, nearly lost her dog, then a fire destroyed everything. But that was no excuse for ruining Ashley's life.

On the spot, Ashley made a decision she hoped she wouldn't regret. Ryan had enough on his mind. She could take care of this on her own.

CHAPTER
TWENTY-SEVEN

Adam parked his car in the visitors' section of the lot behind the coroner's office. He looked around to see if anyone had followed him. When he'd left the house this morning, he'd carefully surveyed the street to see if any strange vehicles were parked close to the house.

Nothing.

Not that he expected anyone to be tailing him, but he couldn't stop worrying about Whitney. There wasn't any reason for concern, he assured himself. Whoever had thrown the pipe bomb had been after Miranda. Still, Whitney was constantly in his thoughts.

Since the night of the pipe bombing, he'd been worried someone might mistake Whitney for her cousin. He was even more troubled now, but he didn't know why. Okay, maybe he did. Making love to her had triggered a very masculine instinct. Protectiveness. When you cared about a woman, you wanted to protect her.

Whitney had come to mean a lot to him in a short period of time. Once he would have questioned this, but after facing death — and surviving — he knew how quickly life could change. Falling for a woman this soon no longer surprised him.

He walked into the building and down the stairs to the level where Samantha Waterson had her office. He'd received a text message this morning that the assistant coroner wanted to see him.

"Hey," Samantha greeted him when he appeared at her office door.

"Hey, yourself." Adam walked in with a smile for the redhead. "I received your message."

She waved him into the chair next to her desk. "I received the advanced tox report on your uncle. Nothing out of the ordinary."

Adam stared blankly at her for a moment. He couldn't believe this. He'd been so sure a toxicology screen would turn up something. "Nothing?"

"Nope. Traces of ibuprofen. That's all. Aspirin or Tylenol turns up in ninety-eight percent of all tox screens. It's the most common drug in America."

Adam recalled Quinten Foley's visit. They

were dealing with sophisticated people who would stop at nothing to get what they wanted. He didn't know of any reason they would want to kill his uncle, but then, he didn't have all of the facts.

"Is there anything that wouldn't show up on a tox screen?" he asked.

"Sure. Lots of things. Rohypnol, for starters."

"The date-rape drug?"

"Yes. It's out of your system in twenty-four hours. If a victim isn't tested immediately, it's almost impossible to prove in court that a defendant slipped a woman the drug."

"How would Rohypnol figure in my uncle's death?"

"Victims go into a blackout state and don't remember anything. He could have been given the drug, then forced to exercise so vigorously that his heart gave out."

"I'm not sure . . . someone would have to have known heart trouble ran in the family. Even if they did, there's no guarantee it would work." He shook his head. "Anything else?"

"There are lots of designer drugs around. Remember the steroid substitutes invented to get around baseball's steroid ban?" she asked, and he nodded. "Like those designer steroids, there are a number of drugs that can elude toxicology panels. The one that comes to mind in this case is curare."

"That stuff that Indians in the Amazon used on their arrow tips?"

"Exactly. It's sold under a variety of names by drug companies. It's most commonly administered when a doctor is operating on someone's lungs. The drug causes paralysis so the lungs don't move during the operation. If your uncle was given an overdose, all his internal organs would have shut down. The process could have mimicked a heart attack."

Calvin Hunter had been involved in dangerous arms transactions. Considering those deals, the men wouldn't have wanted to find themselves involved in an investigation. They would have used something untraceable.

"I guess this is a dead end," he said with heartfelt regret in his voice.

"There's one other possibility," Samantha told him.

He refused to get his hopes up. "What's that?"

"Dr. Alfonse Taggart at Stanford is working on new tests specifically designed to detect drugs that current tox panels don't show. In this case, I would send him slides of the liver. Curare in any form impacts the liver. I didn't notice any inflammation and it didn't come up on the tox panel either, but maybe Dr. Taggart can find something. It's a long shot."

"Thanks. I owe you," he told her.

It was nearly noon by the time Whitney arrived back at the house. She punched in the alarm code and entered the home followed by the dogs. During her rounds, she'd stopped in at Dog Diva. Daniel, the owner, had given her the names of two women who also worked as pet concierges in the area.

She'd spoken with one of them. Lyleen Foster sounded promising. She lived nearby and had an excellent reputation. She could take on several dogs, but not all of them. It was going to be necessary to split up Miranda's clients.

"Okay, guys, settle down," she told Lexi and Da Vinci. Maddie's owner, Debbie Sutton, had picked her up. Whitney was down to three dogs. Jasper came scampering into the kitchen at the sound of her voice. She assumed he'd been in his favorite hiding spot under the coffee table.

She went back into the maid's room and took a closer look at the clothes someone had left for her. Was there anything she could wear to Vladimir's exhibition tonight?

"You're queen of the clueless," she said under her breath. She had no idea what anyone wore to an opening. If she couldn't find something, she would have to spend money she didn't have on a dress.

Sorting through the clothing, she relived last night. Lord have mercy. Not only was Adam a hunk, he was an exceptional lover. She cautioned herself to keep this physical and not allow herself to fall for him.

She found a raspberry-colored sundress of sheer gauze. The fabric was held up on one shoulder by a lime-green butterfly while the other shoulder was bare. She smoothed out the dress and inspected it more closely. It wasn't very dressy, but it would work, she decided.

She tried to imagine what Adam would think. She'd tried so hard to be pretty for Ryan. He always found fault. She knew Adam wouldn't be hypercritical. He'd like whatever she wore. Still, she was determined to look her best.

Whitney hoped Trish's friend wouldn't need a house-sitter. She would just as soon live here with Adam. *That might not be such a good idea,* she reflected. Would she be able to study with him around? Wouldn't she just be jumping into another relationship too soon?

Well, she silently conceded, she *was* in a relationship. She never had casual sex. What had happened last night meant a commitment — to her. But after living with Ryan and having a marriage end in heartbreak, she wasn't sure she should be sharing a house with Adam. A little distance was probably a very good idea.

Becoming a vet would mean giving up a lot, and it would test a relationship. She'd buzzed by the animal hospital on her way home to see if they could suggest another person to help take over her cousin's business. They had a few suggestions. And while Whitney was there, she'd been drafted to help with a Jackahuahua.

The combination Jack Russell terrier and Chihuahua had been crossbred to create a unique dog. So-called "designer" dogs had become popular. Breeders mated two different types of purebreds like Labrador retrievers and poodles to create a Labradoodle. Golden retrievers had also been crossed with poodles to have Goldendoodle puppies. The positive characteristics of the Labs and Goldens combined with the fur of poodles appealed to people who were allergic to dogs but wanted a family-friendly pet that was easy to train. Jackahuahuas were new to her, and Whitney wasn't sure why they'd been crossbred.

The Jackahuahua had severely impacted anal glands. She'd nearly been bitten before they'd been able to bring the pet some relief, but she hadn't minded. Just being in the clinic and seeing the variety of things she'd need to learn excited her, even the gross procedures like expressing anal glands. The road wouldn't be easy, but becoming a vet was the career for her. She'd languished too long in a cube farm inputting data when she should have been doing something she loved.

"Don't set aside your dream because of a man," she said out loud. If Trish's friend needed a house-sitter, Whitney intended to take the job.

She was ironing the raspberry dress when she remembered the photos of Miranda taken last December. She and Adam had gone up to his bedroom immediately after they left the pool. They'd spent the night making love. Neither of them had given a second thought to the pictures.

She finished the dress and hung it in the maid's room. The photos were still on the kitchen counter and she took them up to the office, the dogs at her heels. She located the magnifying glass in the top drawer of what had once been Calvin Hunter's desk. She examined the photos closely, taking care to check the umbrella that Adam had noticed in the background.

It was a *talapa*-style umbrella made of dried palm fronds. Across the top, letters were stitched in blue. The words were a little grainy but she made out "Corona." The popular Mexican beer. Could the picture have been snapped in Mexico?

That would account for the dazzling sun in December when it had been raining here. Had it rained on that day? Adam had planned to consult the weather service Web site.

She spun around in the office chair and turned on Adam's computer. A quick check of the site confirmed what Whitney had remembered. It had been raining as far south as Ensenada, Mexico, which was an hour's drive beyond San Diego.

So Miranda hadn't gone there, even though it would have been an easy drive. But she could have caught a cheap flight to Cabo San Lucas at the tip of the Baja California peninsula. It hadn't been raining that far south. Or Miranda could have been in any number of places in Mexico. There were lots of inexpensive flights out of San Diego to destinations on the sun-drenched beaches in Mexico. Acapulco and Puerto Vallarta were among the most popular but other places were possibilities.

"Does it matter?" she wondered out loud. The other dogs were snoozing nearby, but at the sound of her voice, Lexi cocked her head. Whitney took the time to give her a loving pat.

Where Miranda had been last December could be very important. If Adam's theory was correct, Miranda might have returned to this sunny spot. But why hadn't her name appeared on the passport check? She gazed at the smiling picture of her cousin.

What had Miranda been thinking?

She studied the photo for several minutes. There was more writing on the *talapa*. The magnifying glass showed a smaller word after Corona. It looked like "de." No. There was another letter. An L. The second word was "del."

Maybe it wasn't the name of a beer after all. She'd taken three years of Spanish in high school. Corona meant crown. That accounted for the crown logo on each Corona beer bottle.

The third word was blurred. Evidently, the breeze had ruffled the dried fronds and they had concealed part of the letters. The magnifying glass had a small circular insert that magnified a bit more. She positioned it over the third word. "Mar," she finally decided.

Corona del Mar. Crown of the sea.

Okay, Crown of the Sea. Was it a resort or a restaurant? No, probably not a restaurant, she decided. The *talapa* was shading a beach chair. There wasn't any sign of food.

She went onto the computer again. Expedia didn't have any listing for a resort in Mexico called Corona del Mar. She tried Google and had over seventy hits. One was a beach in Southern California. Another was a swim suit manufacturer.

She diligently checked each one to see if there was any possible link. She was on fifty-three when she discovered Corona del Mar, an upscale development on the Mexican Riviera south of Cancún. The "villas" were in a tropical reserve called Mayakoba and started at a million dollars.

Miranda couldn't have been there. She didn't have that kind of money.

Whitney thought about it for a second as she leaned down to pet Lexi again. "Doesn't work," she told Lexi. "Does it, girl? Not unless Miranda did come across a bundle of drug money."

Adam stood beside Whitney, a glass of

champagne in his hand. He'd gotten home late, and he'd forgotten all about the opening. They'd rushed to make it to the gallery. Luck had been with them and they'd found a parking space down the street. They hadn't needed to waste time waiting for the parking valets who had been hired for the evening and were stationed in front of the gallery.

"That's Rod Babcock over there," Whitney told him in a low voice. "Next to the tall blonde. She's Trish Bowrather, owner of the gallery."

"Let's see if we can edge our way close enough to talk to them. Make it seem casual," he told her. "We want to catch Babcock off guard."

Adam had never been to a gallery opening. He'd expected a lot of dressed-up folks, but not this many. Either the Russian was a huge draw or the gallery owner had an impressive list of clients who were willing to turn out for free champagne and appetizers.

He put his hand on the back of Whitney's waist to guide her forward. He wasn't letting her out of his sight. When she'd waltzed out of the maid's room in a pink number that clung to her sexy bod like wet silk, he'd wanted to drag her upstairs and throw her on his bed.

"Dynamite," he'd told her. And he'd meant it.

Every guy in the place was gawking at her. Well, okay, not every guy. The gallery was so damn packed that only those close to them could see Whitney. Those men couldn't get enough. Sure as hell, he wasn't leaving her alone with some sleazebag lawyer.

"That must be Vladimir," Whitney said to him over her shoulder.

Adam assumed she meant the little guy with the grizzled goatee and wisps of white hair arranged on his bullet-shaped head in the comb-over from hell. His name had conjured up an image of a young, fit guy, but obviously Adam's imagination had taken flight in the wrong direction.

"I leave here five, all but six years," Vladimir was saying as they shouldered their way up to the attorney and the blonde.

Adam decided the Russian had been living here almost six years. His English was iffy, but who was Adam to judge. If he were living in Russia, he seriously doubted he could speak their language any better after five years.

"Whitney, there you are," exclaimed Trish Bowrather. The gallery owner's eyes surveyed Adam for a moment, then she smiled

411

at the attorney.

Broderick Babcock was dressed in a black mock turtleneck and a beige linen sports jacket that hadn't come off the rack. His chocolate-brown trousers had creases sharper than most knife blades. He appeared fit with black hair burnished with gray at the temples. Adam had to admit that Babcock might have walked straight out of central casting to fill the role of a high-profile attorney.

"Whitney adores your work," Trish told the Russian. "Don't you, Whitney?"

"Very impressive." Whitney sounded convincing, but on the way over she'd confided in Adam that she found Vladimir's immense canvases strange.

"You look great," Babcock commented, his eyes assessing Whitney in a way that made Adam want to punch out his lights.

Whitney introduced Adam to the attorney, and the guy blessed him with a brief glance. He couldn't keep his eyes off Whitney. Trish kept smiling, but her lips were crimped. Adam would bet his life the gallery owner wanted Babcock all to herself.

"Trish! Trish!" called an old battle-ax with garlands of pearls around her neck.

"Come on." Trish grabbed Vladimir by the arm. "Geraldine Devore already owns two of your paintings. She's dying to meet you."

Adam eyed Babcock while the lawyer and Whitney watched Trish tow Vladimir through the crowd. They were both smiling, on the verge of laughing. Babcock's eyes shifted left and checked out Whitney's cleavage.

"Let's go outside and get some air," Adam told Whitney.

The attorney took the bait. "Good idea."

It took the trio a few minutes to maneuver their way through the crowd. Along the way beach bunnies dressed as cowgirls offered them a variety of appetizers from Liquid Cowboy, the caterer. Adam noticed the opening was in full swing. Bored husbands quaffing martinis. Women checking out each other's jewelry. A few people looking at the art.

Prospect Avenue was on the bluff above the ocean. Outside the gallery a balmy breeze drifted in from the Pacific, bringing with it the briny scent of the ocean. There were a few guests on the sidewalk but it wasn't too crowded for a private conversation.

Whitney gave him an opening. "Rod's helping with my property settlement. I went to him because of Miranda."

Adam looked directly in the attorney's

413

eyes. "They look a lot alike, don't they?"

"So I'm told." Babcock took a swig of scotch. "I never met the woman."

"Really?" Adam did his best to sound surprised. "Jared Cabral told me you were a regular at Saffron Blue."

Babcock's expression didn't change, but his eyes might have narrowed just slightly. "Jared didn't tell you anything. It's easier to persuade a dead man to talk."

True. So true. Adam had blown it intentionally to gauge Babcock's reaction. "Okay. Cabral didn't tell me. Let's just say someone mentioned you were a regular at Saffron Blue."

"That's right. I was — past tense. I haven't been to the club in ages." Babcock turned to Whitney. "What's this got to do with your cousin?"

"You must have known Miranda. She worked there. You know, in the back room."

Babcock's expression never faltered. He casually sipped his scotch, then said, "You never mentioned that. You claimed your cousin walked dogs."

"She did. Miranda also danced at Saffron Blue. I didn't find out until after I went to your office."

"You could have told me at lunch."

Whitney gave him an apologetic smile. "It

414

slipped my mind with the fire and everything, then Trish joined us. I forgot. Sorry."

"I went to Saffron Blue on occasion." Babcock didn't seem fazed. Adam gave the
lawyer credit. The guy was damn good.
"You said your cousin looks a lot like you. I
don't remember —"

"Does the name Kat Nippe sound familiar?" asked Adam.

Babcock stared at Whitney. "Of course,
now I see the resemblance. But Kat had jet-
black hair. I never thought of her as a
blonde."

Whitney turned to Adam. "She must have
been wearing a wig."

"When was the last time you were out
there?" Adam asked.

"It's been a year and twenty-three days,"
Babcock said matter-of-factly.

"How can you be so sure?" Adam wanted
to know.

"I realized I was gambling too much. I
mentioned it to a doctor friend while we
were golfing. He told me a number of
patients who took a certain medication to
treat Parkinson's became chronic gamblers,
even though they'd never had the problem
before. He suggested I see a doctor at the
Mayo Clinic who's been treating gambling
addiction in Parkinson's patients. The treat-

ment blocks the same part of the brain the Parkinson's medication affects. I tried it, and the pills work. That's why I know how long it's been. I don't gamble any longer."

"That was the last time you saw Miranda . . . Kat?" Whitney asked.

"Yes. I used to tip her quite a bit, when I won. It's considered good luck to tip the back-room hostess." He finished off the dregs of his scotch. "Come to think of it, Kat wasn't around the last few months I was there. She quit or something."

Adam waited for Whitney to ask if Babcock had encountered Ryan Fordham in the back room. Just then a blue Bentley pulled to the curb, and the parking valet hustled to open the passenger door. Right on its bumper was a metallic-silver Porsche. Out of the sports car stepped a knockout blonde in a black sheath that fit like a tattoo.

CHAPTER
TWENTY-EIGHT

Whitney noticed Adam gazing over her shoulder, preoccupied by something. She didn't want to be rude and turn around to look. There were answers she needed from the lawyer that were more important. "Did you happen to meet Ryan Fordham while you were gambling in the back room?"

"Your ex?" Rod asked. "No. I would have recognized his name on the documents you gave me and mentioned it. Besides, the reason we play in a private room is to play with guys we know."

"I understand. I just wondered if he gambled there." Out of the corner of her eye, she noticed Adam was still watching something behind her. She wished he was paying better attention. She believed Rod was telling the truth, but she'd been fooled in the past.

"He could have started after I stopped gambling."

"Possibly." It didn't really matter, she decided. It appeared that Miranda had quit even before Rod Babcock stopped gambling. Her cousin wouldn't have run into Ryan.

"You see," Rod added, "gambling can be an addiction. Once you've quit, you can't go back. I haven't had much contact with those guys. Oh, I run into a few of them here and there. But for the most part I avoid gamblers. I was in danger of gambling away everything. Luckily, I got out on the downward slide but before I hit the skids."

Whitney wondered about Ryan. He'd been obsessed with making money in the last year or so. At the time she believed he considered financial rewards to be his due after years of schooling. Now she understood gambling had motivated him. Was he near rock bottom? Was that why he'd been so threatening the other day?

Desperation did unbelievable things to people. Could Ryan — *Stop!* This man was no longer her problem. Ashley was welcome to deal with Ryan's gambling addiction.

"Walt, hey! Long time no see." Rod waved to a man behind Whitney.

"Rod, what are you doing here? I didn't know you were interested in art."

Whitney turned to the tall, slender man who'd come up beside them. He was shaking hands with the attorney when Whitney recognized an achingly familiar voice. The deep baritone she'd heard a thousand times was just behind her. She stared down at the bubbles floating to the top of her champagne glass, her stomach in an uncontrolled free fall.

Couldn't be.

Whitney edged closer to Adam as the hot flush of anger crept up her neck. She could feel Adam's hand on the back of her waist as Rod introduced them to Walter Nance and Emily, his wife. Whitney had never met the surgeon who'd convinced Ryan to join his practice, but she instantly recognized the name.

Ryan moved into their tight circle, his gorgeous wife on his arm. Whitney had only seen Ashley twice before this. Once she'd been in the car when they'd emerged from arbitration. The second time had been when Whitney had charged into the house demanding Lexi's return. She'd been so concerned about her dog that she'd barely noticed much about the woman Ryan had dumped her for.

Tonight, there was no ignoring the former beauty queen clad in a black silk sheath by some famous designer. The glamorous creature had an aura of poise and self-confidence that was exuded in every beautiful line of her face. A considerable amount of artfully applied makeup enhanced vivid blue eyes and made her lips appear soft and full. Whitney hadn't bothered with anything except lipstick. After the fire, she'd been left with nothing. She'd bought necessities but not makeup. It wouldn't have helped anyway.

Ryan spotted Whitney and blinked as if he'd seen a ghost. He usually wielded his charm as if it should be a controlled substance. Now he was smiling again, but Whitney knew him well enough to detect the fury simmering beneath the surface. Obviously, he didn't want to run into her any more than she wanted to see him.

"This is Ryan and Ashley Fordham," Walt told them.

"Meet Whitney Marshall and Adam Hunter," Rod replied as if he'd never heard of Ryan.

"Great dress," Walt told Whitney.

A strange, hollow feeling invaded Whitney's body, but before she could even smile a little at the compliment, Ryan told the group, "It should be a great dress. I bought it for Ashley."

Heaven forbid, Whitney thought, panic curdling her blood. Shock thrummed against her ribs. She had the insane urge to leap at Ashley and scratch her eyes out. The next second she wanted to run screaming into the night.

"R-really," stuttered Walt.

"Whitney is my ex-wife," explained Ryan with a chuckle that must have sounded false to everyone. They nervously looked around or sipped their drinks. "Her home burned down. Ashley tossed her a castoff. Right, honey?"

Save me, save me. Whitney prayed for deliverance, but nothing doing. How could she possibly be standing here in the beauty queen's dress? Wasn't there any justice in the world? Of all the people on the planet, Whitney would never have expected Ashley to give her clothes. What kind of karma did she have anyway? How could she run into Ryan and his stunningly beautiful new wife — and be wearing a dress the woman no longer wanted?

Her blue eyes wide, Ashley gazed at Whitney. "I wanted to help. It must be terrible having nothing. I —"

"Not as terrible as dying," Whitney cut her off. She deeply resented the woman's sanctimonious tone.

"We're late for dinner." Adam nudged Whitney. "Good to see everyone."

Whitney mustered the strength to mumble goodbye to Rod. She couldn't look at Ashley.

"Are you okay?" Adam asked as he hustled her down the sidewalk to his car.

"Never better." Tears burned the back of her eyes. She was thankful it was too dark for Adam to see.

He quickly unlocked the door and opened it for her. She scrambled inside as fast as she could, conscious of the noise from the gallery behind her. In despair, she slumped against the seat. Adam got in and turned to her.

"Oh, babe, what can I say?"

She told herself not to cry. Tears couldn't help anything. What had her mother always said? *Count your blessings.* The man next to her popped into her mind first. Then Lexi and the dogs whose lives had been spared because they'd been with her during the fire.

The fire.

Like a flashbulb going off in her brain, the fire flared on the screen in her mind. Lives could have been lost. But they'd all escaped the inferno. Now, *that* was a true blessing.

Pressure kept building in her chest and suddenly she heard herself giggling. It sounded a bit forced, maybe a little hysterical. She checked the burbling laughter. *Get a grip,* she told herself.

"What's so funny?" Adam demanded.

"Nothing. Nothing at all. Silly me. I could be dead right now. Just a charred crisp. Why let a stupid dress upset me?"

Adam cupped her chin in his warm hand. "Because the woman responsible for so much of the pain in your life owned the dress. Ashley should have left a note or something."

"True, but I'm going to be understanding. She wanted to help. Why I don't know, but she did. Maybe she felt sorry for me because Lexi had disappeared and she knew the dog was all I had."

Adam didn't respond for a moment. He dropped his hand and drew back. In the dark shadows of the car, she couldn't tell what he was thinking.

"Thanks for getting me out of there," she said softly. "It's not the worst thing that's ever happened to me. I'm sure one day, I'll look back and laugh, but tonight I wanted to run and hide."

He slid his arm around her shoulders and pulled her close. The look in his eyes was so galvanizing that it sent a tremor through her. The warm touch of his lips was a delicious sensation. She returned his kiss with reckless abandon.

He drew back a fraction of an inch and whispered in her ear, "That might have been Ashley's dress, but it was made for you. Let's not waste it. I'm taking you to dinner at Chive. We're celebrating."

"Celebrating what?"

His lips brushed her temple as he spoke. "Celebrating us."

Ashley was captivated by the enormous canvases and liked the little man who'd painted them even though he couldn't keep his eyes off her breasts. But Ryan was being a first-class jerk. Oh, he was chipper to everyone else but beneath the facade lurked a lethal coolness directed at Ashley.

So what if she'd given Whitney some clothes she no longer used? Ashley had stolen the most important thing in Whitney's life — Ryan. She felt sorry for the woman and embarrassed about her own behavior. True, Whitney seemed to have hooked up with that hunk Adam, but as gorgeous as he was, Adam Hunter couldn't be compared to a successful cosmetic surgeon.

Finally, Walter Nance decided it was time to leave. They had to wait in the valet parking line for their car. Emily kept prattling on and on about the new home they were building and how one of Vladimir's paintings was "so made for their living room." Ashley tried to listen politely but her mind was on what Ryan was going to say when they were alone.

"Ashley's not feeling well," Ryan told Walter Nance as the valet pulled up with the surgeon's Bentley. "We're going to pass on dinner."

"Are you okay?" Emily asked. "You didn't say anything."

"I — I'll be all right." Ashley glanced over her shoulder. Ryan couldn't have timed this announcement any better. There were too many people hovering in line behind him, anxious to get their cars, to discuss her health. The Nances hopped into their car, saying goodbye.

Ashley waited in silence. Ryan's Porsche was right behind the Bentley. They got in and Ryan drove off without tipping the valet. Ashley waited. She hadn't done anything *so* wrong. Why cancel their dinner plans?

"I bought that dress for you," Ryan finally said several tense minutes later. "I picked it out at a boutique with one-of-a-kind outfits. The butterfly pin cost extra."

"I'm sorry," she said. "I didn't know. I'd worn it and thought . . ." She didn't say how much she disliked the dress. She wouldn't have worn it at all if Ryan hadn't given it to her. She preferred black. It was a sophisticated color — a blonde's best color.

She could have added the dress wasn't chic enough for an evening like this, but didn't. She knew Whitney had nothing else to wear. And the raspberry-colored dress did look fabulous on her.

"I wonder why Whitney was there," Ashley said.

Ryan slapped his open palm so hard against the dashboard that she flinched. "Who gives a shit? That's not the point."

Ashley didn't ask what the point was. She was afraid to say another word. Ryan was moody at times, but he'd never been this angry with her. She recalled what Whitney had said when she'd come to the house looking for Lexi. Ryan wouldn't get physical, would he?

"That stinking bitch is holding my property for ransom, costing me an unfucking-believable fortune — and you give her the special dress I bought for you." Ryan was shouting now, and he gunned the engine. Like a rocket, the Porsche streaked down the freeway toward the home that always reminded her of Whitney.

"You don't get it, do you?" Ryan was yelling even louder now. "Whitney's the problem, yet you helped her. Do you have *any* idea how close we are to bankruptcy because of that bitch?"

Bankruptcy? Ashley had known their finances were shaky but things couldn't have degenerated this badly, could they? Like a robot she repeated, "Whitney is the problem. A big problem."

Ryan didn't say another word until he pulled into their driveway. "Get out! I'm going for a drive. I need to think."

Ashley had barely shut the car door when Ryan slammed into Reverse, then spun the car around and peeled off down the street. Ashley stood there for a second. Something told her to follow him.

She rushed into the house and grabbed her car keys off the hook by the door to the garage. She raced into the garage and jumped into her Jaguar. She flew down the street and took a hard right. She figured he would head for the freeway so he could floor the Porsche.

She sped up and caught sight of his car. Could he spot her? She doubted it. A quick look in her own rearview mirror told her how hard it was in the dark to tell what kind of car was behind her. As long as she wasn't on his bumper, Ryan wouldn't detect her presence.

He traveled north like a bullet, but she kept up with him. He slowed a bit, changed lanes, and she realized he was exiting the freeway. Maybe he was going to turn around and get back on the freeway to go home. Oh, boy. She would play hell explaining why she'd gone out.

Don't worry, Ashley told herself. She could go out if she wanted. She switched lanes and slowed down so that two cars moved in behind Ryan and her Jag. At the bottom of the ramp, he swung to the right; he wasn't getting back on the freeway to return home.

Where was he going?

For a second Ashley remembered the times Ryan had sneaked out at night to be with her. Just a tiny flare of guilt ignited deep in her chest. She'd ignored his cheating even though she knew it would be best to wait until he filed for a legal separation before dating him. She knew better, but she'd loved him so much. She hadn't been able to resist him.

The street was more brightly lit than the freeway. She was forced to drop back so Ryan wouldn't spot her. He went several blocks then turned into the Alvarda Casino.

She parked across the street and turned off her lights. Ryan got out of the car and locked it. He hurried toward the casino without even glancing in her direction.

If they were so close to bankruptcy, why was he gambling? Maybe he wasn't, she corrected herself. Casinos had wonderful food at cheap prices. Ryan had canceled dinner, but maybe he was hungry.

And needed to think.

Ashley wanted to think, too. She sat in the Jag, waiting for him to eat and come out. As much as she dreaded another fight, Ashley knew she couldn't put off talking to Ryan about their finances.

An hour dragged by seconds at a time. Ashley spent it thinking about her father.

Did he think about her? she wondered. Had someone told him about his former wife's untimely death? She doubted it. They'd moved around so much in search of an elusive beauty title that her mother had lost contact with the few friends she'd once possessed. There weren't any family members to tell her father, either.

Ashley let her head rest against the back of her seat. She kept thinking about her father and checking her watch. Had he remarried? Her mother had been beautiful; replacing her would have been difficult. But there was more to a person than looks. Surely, her father had discovered this.

Maybe he'd found someone who could

make him happy in a way that her mother never could have. No. In a way that her mother never would have bothered with. As much as Ashley resented her father's refusal to stay with them as they roamed the country, she understood his reasons.

If they'd settled down and stopped pursuing a beauty title, Ashley could have finished school in one place. She would have had friends. She smiled bitterly in the darkness. Her only friend was a guy, her personal trainer. She paid him. How pathetic was that?

When an hour and twenty minutes passed, Ashley got out of the car. She was going after Ryan. If they had to sit at some café table at a casino to talk, so be it.

She went inside but didn't see him in the coffee shop. She ignored the men who stared at her; after years of males gawking, she was accustomed to the attention. A hostess directed her to the restaurant on the second level. It was nicer up there and the place was darker compared to the brightly lit casino. She could still hear the pinging of the slot machines and the buzz of the gamblers.

Ryan wasn't in the restaurant or the adjacent lounge. From the second level she could gaze down on the gamblers below, but she didn't see Ryan. Where could he be? He wouldn't have left without his car.

Then she realized she must have crossed paths with him. He'd gone out one door while she'd been coming in another. No doubt he would be home waiting for her, more furious than ever.

She started to rush back to her Jag, then told herself to take her time. So what if he arrived home and she wasn't there? Taking a drive wasn't a crime.

Ashley went toward the spot where Ryan had parked. The distinctive silver Porsche was still there. How could she have missed him? True, it was a large casino, but she'd been able to look down at every table, every slot machine, and she hadn't see Ryan's dark blond head among the gamblers.

She walked back inside and strolled slowly through the casino. He wasn't anywhere in sight. Strange. Really strange. Then she saw a sign off to one side that advertised Texas Hold 'Em in a nearby room.

She walked around the corner and saw a small room with a lighted sign above the door. It flashed back and forth, back and forth, showing disembodied hands holding poker cards. Through the open double doors she saw a roomful of men seated at round tables. Ryan's back was to her but there was no mistaking her husband.

She started in, but a hostess dressed like a hula dancer stopped her. "Ma'am, these are thousand-dollar tables."

Ashley quickly backed away. A thousand dollars? What was Ryan thinking? No doubt he was gambling with the money he'd gotten for her ring. She slowly walked back to her car.

Whitney is the problem, she reminded herself.

CHAPTER
TWENTY-NINE

"I ate waaay too much," Whitney told Adam. "I should have skipped the chocolate soufflé."

"That's the first chocolate soufflé I've ever ordered. When I was trapped over in Iraq, I promised myself I would have one the first chance I had. I'd eaten one before and really liked it, but someone else ordered it."

She assumed he meant a woman but didn't ask. Dinner had been perfect. She'd never been to Chive. The sophisticated restaurant was in one of the Gaslamp's most historic buildings. The old Royal Pie Company had been transformed from a brick warehouse to a sleek minimalist restaurant with awesome food.

They'd enjoyed a leisurely dinner and talked about Rod Babcock. They decided the attorney couldn't help them solve Miranda's disappearance. Adam had complimented Whitney on discovering the

Corona del Mar signs on the *talapa*. He doubted Miranda was hiding out at the upscale resort but believed there was a good chance her cousin was somewhere in the Cancún area. She must have gotten into Mexico with a phony passport. Or she might have hitched a ride over the border and taken a flight from a Mexican airport.

"At times like this, I wish they had sidewalks in these hills," Whitney told him. "I'd take Lexi for a long walk. I'd feel better after all I've eaten."

"We could walk along the trail." He pulled into the driveway of his uncle's home.

"It spooks me a little. I've been jumpy since the fire. Before I wouldn't have thought twice about hiking along the trail. With a flashlight, it's not hard to see where you're going."

Except for Jasper, the dogs were waiting for them inside the back door. He came scuttling out of the living room when he heard them greeting Lexi and Da Vinci. No doubt he'd been sleeping under the coffee table again.

Adam's cell phone buzzed. "Who can it be at this hour?"

They'd talked and lingered over coffee for so long that it was nearly eleven when they'd left the restaurant. It had taken them over half an hour to get the car and drive out to Torrey Pines. Whitney thought it was time well spent. They'd fallen for each other so quickly that they needed the opportunity to get to know each other better.

Whitney let the dogs out on the side yard and watched them closely. After Lexi's disappearance, she refused to take any chances. She could hear Adam talking and realized something was going on with his business.

"I hate to say this," he told her, snapping his cell phone shut. "I have to go into the command center."

"A problem?"

"I'm not sure what's going on. Tyler insists he needs me. He took care of everything all by himself while I was overseas. I need to help —"

"Of course you do. We're fine right here."

Adam started toward the door, then hesitated. "Don't go for a walk alone. Maybe it was just my imagination, but I thought I saw someone sitting in a car just down the street. It was a little far away to be watching the house, but you never know. I'm going to take another look when I drive out. I'll call you from the car to let you know what I see, but I want you to keep the alarm set until I return."

She went over and kissed him lightly on the cheek. He hauled her into his arms and his mouth closed over hers. What she'd intended as a little parting peck suddenly became wholly carnal. One hand cupped her bottom and squeezed gently. He kept kissing her, then his body stiffened and he pulled back.

"Hey, if I'm not careful, I'll just say to hell with Tyler."

"You can't do that. He must need you or he wouldn't have called so late."

"Right." Adam brushed her moist lower lip with the pad of his thumb. "I'll be back as soon as I can."

Adam left and Whitney set the alarm and stood in the kitchen for a moment. Should she go upstairs to his room? Or should she climb into bed in the maid's room? It seemed a little presumptuous to go upstairs so she walked into the maid's room.

She caught her reflection in the mirror over the dresser. Aaargh. The dress from hell. She yanked it over her head and dropped it onto the floor. She found the bags that Ashley had used to bring her castoffs to Whitney. She was packing all of them for Goodwill when the telephone rang.

"It's me," Adam told her. "Must have been my imagination. The parked car is empty."

"Great. I'll see you later."

She hung up and finished putting the clothes in the shopping bags. Her cell phone was on the nightstand next to her bed. She hadn't taken it with her because her only purse was too big and clunky looking for the outfit. The LCD display indicated she had voice mail.

"This is Betty Spirin," the voice said when she pressed the message button. "My daughter's been in an accident. I have to go to L.A. immediately. Grey's had his dinner. I need you to walk him tonight and again first thing in the morning. I'll call you tomorrow and let you know what's happening."

The woman sounded nearly hysterical. Whitney could only imagine how frantic she must be after learning her daughter had been in an accident. Whitney had never walked this particular pet but did recall Miranda telling her about a dachshund named Grey Poupon. The dog was a regular and Miranda had given Whitney the key to his home. It was on the key chain at the bottom of her purse.

She consulted her BlackBerry and found additional information. She'd remembered correctly. The dachshund lived in a condominium complex not too far away. A quick check of her watch told her it was just after midnight. The message had been left a little before five. The poor animal needed to go out immediately.

Whitney changed into jeans and threw on a T-shirt. She knew Adam wouldn't want her to leave, but she didn't have any choice. He would be gone at least an hour and by then Grey might have an accident. She thought about calling Adam but decided to leave a note instead. With any luck she would be home before he returned.

The second Adam snapped his cell phone shut, it buzzed. "Yeah?" he said, expecting it to be Whitney. Instead it was Max Deaver. "Working a little late, aren't you?"

Max chuckled. "Banks are just opening in Zurich. Diamond traders are busy in Antwerp. London's setting the price of gold. Paris —"

"Okay. I get the picture. It's morning somewhere just like it's always five o'clock somewhere."

"True, but I'm not kidding about banks opening in Zurich. There's been another transfer of funds."

Adam groaned. "You're kidding."

"Nope, but this should make you happy.

The funds have been transferred to pay off debts against the property you and your uncle owned as joint tenants."

It took a second for Deaver's message to register. "What in hell?"

"Don't know. The money's coming from a numbered account."

"Is it one of my uncle's?"

"Not unless it's one I didn't come across when I was checking."

Adam pulled into HiTech's parking lot and stopped the car. "What do you make of this?"

"Haven't a clue, man, haven't a clue. I thought you might have some idea."

"Could it have been something my uncle set up before he died? You know, arrangements can be made with banks to transfer funds on certain dates. Hell, every credit card company in the world will be happy to zap money out of your checking account on a specified date."

"It's possible," conceded Deaver. "I just wanted to give you a heads-up."

Adam thanked him, hung up and sat in the car, thinking. He'd been stunned that his uncle had made him joint tenant of several properties. Then Calvin Hunter had saddled those properties with debt. He must have known Adam didn't have the capital to repay those loans. Before he died, Calvin had set up a payment schedule.

"What's up?" Adam asked Tyler when he walked into the command post adjacent to HiTech's offices.

Tyler was sitting beside Butch at the post's computer terminal. Red lights on the screen indicated the stations where guards were still working. Most closed at midnight while a few remained open until one-thirty.

Tyler stood up. "Let's go into my office."

Adam's sixth sense had kicked into gear the moment he'd heard Tyler's voice on the phone. He wasn't the least bit surprised to see Quinten Foley sitting in Tyler's office when they walked into the room.

"I trust I didn't take you away from anything too important," Quinten said in a general's imperious tone.

"Not unless you count my girl." It was obvious that Tyler's father didn't give a damn about Whitney. He would have walked straight out the door except for all the hard work Tyler had done while Adam had been overseas.

"I needed to talk to you tonight."

Tyler shrugged and smiled apologetically at Adam. He couldn't be angry with his friend. What would it have been like to grow up with Quinten Foley? Adam had been lucky. His dad had always been there for him. It had been over three years since his death but Adam still missed him.

Adam pulled up a chair. "You couldn't discuss this on the phone?"

"You know how my father is," Tyler told him with a touch of sarcasm. "Phones can be tapped. Anyone with the right equipment can listen in on cell calls."

"Okay, I'm here. Shoot."

Quinten Foley frowned at his son. "I need to have a private conversation with Adam."

"Fine with me. My girl's waiting for me, too." He left, shutting the door behind them.

"I had a few thoughts about the disc I'm missing."

Adam was too pissed to ask a question. How could a man treat his own son like a scumbag? Why did Tyler take it?

"Calvin may have transferred it to another format," Foley said. "That's why we couldn't find the disc."

"Such as?"

"Another type of disc, or it may even be disguised as a book. It might even be in some unusual place like the freezer."

"There was nothing in the freezer except Rocky Road ice cream. I ate it."

"It's possible it's disguised as a music CD in his car."

Under his breath, Adam cursed himself. He'd neglected to inspect the CDs in his uncle's car. When Quinten had first come looking for the disc, Adam had told him some of his uncle's financial records were missing. He didn't say he believed it was a single line of information containing a bank code. For all Foley knew, Adam was after reams of paper. He didn't trust Foley enough to tell him the truth. He hadn't confided in anyone — not even Whitney.

"Did you search the discs in the sound system around the pool?"

Aw, hell. Screwed up again. He hadn't played the music outside and didn't even know where the CD player that serviced the barbecue and pool area was located.

"I'm positive the info is somewhere in the house or car. Those are the only places it could be."

Adam thought a second. "What about the plane he leased or the villa on Siros?"

"We've checked. It's not at either location." A cold smile played across his lips. "We'd like to thoroughly search your uncle's home."

Adam's thoughts whirled inside his head like the Milky Way. Who searched the plane and villa? "It's my home, too. Check the records. We owned it jointly."

"I have. That's why I'm asking your permission to allow experts to thoroughly go over the home first thing in the morning."

"Why the rush?"

"There's info on the disc that I need now," Foley replied, but there was something about the way he said it that made Adam suspicious.

He opened his mouth to tell Foley to go to hell. On the way over here, he'd decided to take Whitney to Cancún. There was a good chance they'd find Miranda there. If not, a little vacation couldn't hurt them. He decided not to shoot himself in the foot. He'd had absolutely no luck locating the bank code he needed. Why not let the pros give it a try?

"Okay," Adam replied slowly, as if he were reluctant to go along with this. "I'll need to be present."

"I don't think that's such a good idea. I —"

"Then I won't grant access."

"All right, all right. First thing in the morning. It won't take my boys more than an hour or two — tops."

From a room down the hall, Tyler listened to every word. He'd been testing a new gadget. It was a pricey Mont Blanc pen fitted with a microphone the size of a pinhead. It transmitted everything said within a ten-foot radius to a receiver concealed in a deck of playing cards. The receiver was so powerful that it could be located anywhere within a half mile of the pen.

What was on the disc that was so important to his father? Why did Adam insist on being present? Maybe Adam wanted to make certain his father's men didn't remove anything. That didn't make sense. The pros his father would use wouldn't be common thieves. He was missing something here.

Then the pieces of the jigsaw puzzle in his brain suddenly fell into place. His father must have been in business with Calvin Hunter. He thought a moment. It could only have been weapons. His father was supposed to be a consultant, but that must have been a cover story.

Tyler couldn't help wondering if money might be hidden somewhere in Calvin Hunter's home. That would account for Adam's interest. The disc provided an excuse to search. After all, his father worked with private militias as well as foreign governments on weapons deals. So had Calvin Hunter. They could have been paid "off the books" in gold or even diamonds.

He toyed with the idea of going in and

looking himself. After all, he had been a detective. Nah, he decided. If Adam had searched the home, the disc — or whatever — wasn't easy to find.

He heard the men standing and shut off the receiver by pressing a microdot on the phony pack of cards. He sprinted out the side door and raced to his car. He was out of the lot before the men emerged from the building.

This crap with his father had made Tyler think about money. A lot of money. His father could live another twenty or even thirty years.

Granted, Tyler was making decent money, but Holly deserved the best. He smiled to himself, thinking about Adam's comment. He *did* have a woman he was interested in. Holly needed to know as soon as possible.

Tyler tried her cell number again but it immediately kicked into voice mail. He'd lied when he'd said Holly was waiting for him. They'd had an early dinner, then she'd claimed female problems were bothering her. She'd gone home. Tyler had picked up a bouquet of flowers and a box of chocolates. He'd taken them to her walkup flat in Coronado but she wasn't there.

Where the fuck could she be? Why would she lie? She couldn't possibly have another guy. No way. She spent too many nights with him.

He needed to present her with a whopper of a diamond. Once they set a date to be married, he would feel better. Not even his frustration with his father could bring him down then.

CHAPTER THIRTY

"Hey, cutie." The dachshund scurried up to Whitney, tail wagging. "Grey, right?" She dropped to her knees and held out her arms. The little dog leaped up and licked her chin.

She stood, Grey in her arms, and flipped on a few lights. "Let's see if you had an accident that I need to clean up."

"Good boy," she told the dog after she'd inspected the small, neat condo. "No accidents. Let's take you for a walk."

The dachshund lived in an upscale condominium complex not far from Scripps. If Whitney recalled correctly, Betty Spirin worked at the Scripps Institute of Oceanography. Whitney walked down a path illuminated only by low-voltage lights scattered among the plants bordering the walkway. Hadn't the moon been shining when they left the restaurant? She was positive it had, but in early summer a layer of marine clouds inched in at night, lingered, then became the morning fog that beach-goers called "June gloom."

The note she had on her BlackBerry said "back," which meant the best place to walk Grey was in the back of the complex. She headed in that direction, deciding there must be a common area behind the warren of condos. As soon as they were off the walkway Grey lifted his leg on a low-hanging bush.

"You really had to go, didn't you," she said, careful to keep her voice low. Very few lights were on in the complex at this late hour, and she didn't want to disturb the residents.

Grey finished and scratched the grass. Whitney led the dachshund toward the rear of the condominiums. The dog probably would do something more serious. She'd left her purse in the condo, so she double-checked the pockets in her shorts to make sure she had a plastic bag for a pickup.

Whitney slowed as she approached the rear of the complex. Security lights illuminated the building but five feet beyond was cloaked in deep shadows. She looked up again. Nothing but a black anvil of a sky.

Grey trotted forward. Obviously the dog had been here many times and knew his way. A sense of foreboding prickled at Whitney. Mercy, was she jumpy. She'd been nothing but raw nerves since the fire.

When she'd left the house, she'd checked for the car Adam had seen minutes earlier, but it had vanished. For some reason that bothered her when it shouldn't have. People came and went all the time. On the way over, she'd kept checking her rearview mirror. She'd spotted several cars but none of them appeared to be following her.

Near-death experiences caused anxiety, she decided. Adam had retreated into a shell after nearly being killed. He was just now emerging. It was no wonder she was upset. Someone wanted Miranda dead and that person was still out there.

"Grey, how are you, boy?" A tall man appeared out of the darkness.

Whitney nearly jumped, then managed to steady herself. It was only an elderly man walking his dog.

"Where's Betty?" he asked.

The neighbor had a Golden retriever that some people might have mistaken for Lexi. But this dog wasn't very well groomed. Tufts of fur grew out from between the toes of her paws. A definite no-no with Golden owners. The unwanted fur collected dirt that could be tracked into the house.

"Betty will be back soon," Whitney told

449

him, even though she had no clue when the woman planned to return. Miranda had cautioned her not to give out information. Pet owners didn't like anyone to know they were gone. Crime in the area wasn't a problem, but it paid to be careful.

"Good." He squinted at her. "You're not Miranda. For a moment, I thought you were."

"I'm her cousin, Whitney Marshall. I've taken over Miranda's clients."

"Really? I saw her just a week or so ago. We always talked. She didn't mention leaving."

You don't know the half of it, she wanted to scream. "It was sudden."

"Well, be careful back there." He pointed to the dark area that stretched behind them. "They're retiling the pool. Some workman accidentally severed the electric line. Can't see a dang-blamed thing."

"Thanks. I have my flashlight." Whitney pulled it from her pocket. "Good night."

He told her good-night and walked at a leisurely pace in the opposite direction, the Golden at his side. Whitney switched on her flashlight. It cast a narrow tunnel of light on the ground nearby. A row of parking places marked Guests was along the back of the building. She'd parked on the street but made note of it for future visits. She swung the flashlight around and spotted the fenced swimming pool and adjacent greenbelt.

Grey tugged on the leash. Obviously the animal had been here often enough to know where he wanted to go. The dachshund led Whitney down the asphalt drive toward the greenbelt.

Suddenly, high-beam headlights flared on, blinding her. The driver revved the engine and the car shot forward — an explosion of sound in the stillness — hurtling directly at her. Whitney had a split second to act. She lunged to the side, yanking the leash and hauling Grey with her.

Leaping from the pavement onto the soft surface threw her off balance. She skidded on the wet grass, stumbled, lurched sideways, dropped the flashlight, then looked back. There wasn't enough light to make out more than a vague hulking shape. The car's tires squealed as the driver veered hard to the left. She heard herself scream as she realized he was changing course to aim directly at her.

If she didn't run like the wind, the car would mow her over in a heartbeat. Ahead and to her right was the flat greenbelt where she would be completely vulnerable. To her left was the large pool enclosed by a wrought-iron fence.

Blood pounding in her ears, Whitney realized she was as good as road kill. On the verge of utter panic, a galaxy of options swirled through her brain in a nanosecond. There was only one way to save herself. If she could make it to the pool fence before the car hit her — she had a prayer.

Just a prayer.

Dragging the dog, she charged forward, arms pumping, legs moving faster than pistons. Grey's piercing yelps of pain filled the night air. She tried to drop the leash, assuming the dachshund would be better off on his own, but Whitney had wound the leather strap around her palm and it was taut from pulling the dog.

All she could concentrate on was reaching the fence. *Had to get there. Had to. Had to. Had to.*

At her heels, she heard the ominous rumble of the car's engine. Even though she wasn't close enough to climb the fence, she launched herself at it, realizing this was her only chance. She smashed her knee against one of the fence's wrought-iron bars. Pain shot down her leg, and she screamed. Grabbing the vertical bars with both hands, she managed to vault several feet off the ground. She hung on, scrambling upward, using her tennis shoes for traction.

She grasped the top rail with both fists even though her arms were ripping out of their sockets. Poor little Grey was dangling from the leash, his weight tearing at Whitney's arm and wrenching one shoulder downward. The dog's terrified shrieks assured her that his neck hadn't snapped. Whitney was alive but in excruciating pain and she couldn't do a thing to help the little dog. Her heart lashed against her ribs like a caged beast.

Hang on. Hang on.

The car's lights shone from behind her and illuminated a drained pool with tiles stacked around the sides. Heart pummeling, she wondered how much longer she could hold on to the fence before her muscles gave out. She ventured a glance over her shoulder.

The glaring headlights blinded her, but she could tell the car wasn't moving. With each gasping breath, energy drained from her body. Already she'd lost the feeling in her fingers. She squeezed her eyes shut and willed herself to have the strength to hang on. She knew what would happen if she fell to the ground.

"What's going on?" shouted a male voice from a short distance.

"Help!" shrieked Whitney. "Help me!"

The car careened sideways and tore off across the greenbelt with a roar and a plume of exhaust. In the darkness its taillights appeared to be two evil eyes, reminding her of the malevolent eye in Vladimir's painting. The eyes glowed in the dark and vanished in less than a few seconds.

She released the bars and crashed backward.

Adam saw the flash-flash-flash of the blue-white police car strobe lights as soon as he rounded the corner near the condominiums. He'd just walked in the door and read Whitney's note when the telephone rang. An older-sounding man told him there had been an accident, but Whitney wasn't seriously injured. The moment he learned this Adam had forgotten how furious he was with her for leaving the house.

He left his car at the first open spot he found, then stormed up to the cluster of people standing near two police cruisers and a paramedic van. Whitney was sitting on the curb, clutching a dachshund to her stomach as if holding herself together with the dog. An EMT was tending to a cut on her leg that didn't appear to be serious.

Adam elbowed aside a policeman he

didn't recognize. "What happened?"

Whitney looked up at him, her expression blank, as if he were a total stranger. She finally opened her mouth to respond but no words came out. She averted her eyes. He dropped down onto the curb beside her and gently eased his arm around her shoulders.

"Are you all right?"

She slowly nodded and met his eyes. When he'd left Whitney, she'd been vibrant, happy — now she couldn't utter a coherent sentence.

An older man with a Golden retriever on a leash told Adam, "Someone was trying to scare her. They chased her with a car. A prank."

Adam's blood boiled. He wasn't buying this explanation. He asked the policeman, "What makes you think it was a prank?"

"We've had other incidents where cars have driven over our greenbelt," the older man responded before the cop could. "Ruins the grass. When the pool's finished, we're relandscaping and putting in big boulders to keep cars from driving on the grass."

"This is our second call to this location," confirmed the uniformed policeman, who was taking notes for a report.

"Did they chase anyone else?" he asked.

"No, but they might not have had the opportunity." The policeman flipped his notebook shut. "The other incident occurred just before dawn."

"That time rap music from their car's radio awakened one of the owners who lives close by," added the elderly man. "They called the police."

The EMT stood up. "I don't think you're going to need stitches," he told Whitney. "It's just a bad scrape. You'll probably have a doozy of a bruise, though."

"Th-thanks, th-thanks . . . so . . ." Whitney's voice quivered, then trailed off.

The EMT backed away and joined his partner. The policeman said to Adam, "She's badly shaken. You'd better get her home."

"Hot milk or tea might help," advised the man with the retriever. "Or bourbon."

"I wish I could say we're going to catch this jerk," the policeman told Whitney, "but I doubt it. Without a description of the car or . . . anything."

"I'm telling you, it was too dark for anyone to see a blasted thing." The old man pointed to the dark area behind them. "I've still got twenty-twenty and I couldn't tell you what kind of car it was. I heard screeching tires, then screaming. I came running.

I'm not as fast as I used to be. All I saw was the outline of a car."

"He couldn't even tell us the color, except that it wasn't a light color," added the police officer. "Neither could she."

Adam bent close to Whitney. "Did you see anything? Was it big like an SUV or was it small?"

Her glassy eyes were wide, the pupils dilated. She hadn't been crying, but shock and a desperate need to control her emotions showed on her face. "I — It all happened so fast. M-my impression is mid-size. I don't think it was an SUV but I'm honestly not sure."

It had seemed like the right idea at the time. The paramedics didn't think she needed to go to the emergency room. He'd been anxious to get her out of there, get her home. Now, Whitney was sitting on the edge of his bed, and he wasn't so sure.

She'd insisted on bringing the dachshund with her, almost as if she was afraid to let the little dog go. She hadn't said a word on the short drive home. When he'd directed her upstairs, she obeyed in a robotlike way.

Shock.

Adam had seen it often enough in Iraq. He'd dealt with it himself after the suicide bomber killed his friends and almost took his life as well. There wasn't much he could do for her. Time and sleep helped. He'd learned that much from his own experience.

"Are you sure you're all right?" he asked. "Is something wrong with your shoulder? You seem to be favoring it."

She put down the dachshund and scooted between the sheets. Da Vinci and Jasper were already curled up on top of the bed and Grey joined them. Lexi was on the floor looking anxiously up at Whitney, mirroring what Adam was feeling.

Whitney leaned against the pillows he'd arranged for her while she'd been in the bathroom changing into his T-shirt. "I'm fine. My shoulder's a little sore because Grey was hanging from me."

"Do you feel up to telling me about it?" He didn't have any more information than what he'd learned at the scene.

She reached down to the end of the bed and stroked Grey. "You know what's amazing about dogs?" She didn't wait for him to respond. "They forgive you for anything."

Her answer seemed a little spacey and he wondered if she'd hit her head during the so-called prank.

"Even the most abused dog will lick his owner's hand — first chance the dog gets.

You'd think they would bite or run away. They don't. Dogs are so forgiving." She petted Grey's head and the little dog nosed her with his snout. "I nearly killed this dog. He doesn't even know me, but the second we hit the ground, Grey licked my face to see if I was okay."

Hit the ground? Where had she been? Adam sat down on the bed beside her. He did his best to keep anger and fear out of his voice. "Tell me what happened."

He listened carefully as she described the car that appeared suddenly from out of nowhere. He envisioned it deliberately changing course and wheeling to the right and charging directly at her. Imagining her on the fence, the dachshund hanging from her arm, made him smile despite the situation.

"Good thinking," he told her. "Fast thinking. You might have been killed otherwise."

"If that's what was happening." She edged backward until she was propped up against the pillows again. "Mr. Fisher — he's the older man with the Golden — thought it was a prank. He may have been right."

"Why do you say that? It sounds intentional to me. If not, it was dangerous as hell."

"When I looked back, the car had stopped

several feet behind me. It didn't ram the fence even though it could easily have crushed the back of my legs."

Adam had to admit that did seem a little odd. "Maybe he didn't want to damage his car."

"And maybe I overreacted. Even if it had been a prank, it was dangerous. I could have been accidentally killed. The driver needs to be found and stopped before someone gets hurt."

Adam wasn't sure what to think. His training as a detective warned him that two near misses on the same person's life wasn't just a random coincidence. "Maybe someone mistook you for Miranda," he said, thinking out loud.

"I doubt that. There's been enough publicity about the firebombing for anyone to realize Miranda isn't around."

"Criminals often seem clever, but most of them are stupid. I remember a case we had in Robbery — Homicide. There had been a series of bank robberies. The banks started booby-trapping money with vials of indelible ink that exploded when thieves removed the paper banding a stack of bills.

"We were pissed because the media found out about the trick and publicized it. Everyone and his mother knew about it. A few days later, another bank was robbed. We caught the guy because he was covered with ink. He hadn't seen the news reports."

"You think someone believes I'm Miranda?"

"It's the only thing that makes sense."

"It's possible, I guess. Mr. Fisher mistook me for Miranda at first."

Adam mulled over the facts for a few minutes but couldn't come up with a better explanation. Mistaken identity, or just a prank? "Listen, I'm going to hop in the shower. Why don't you get some sleep? We'll see what the police come up with tomorrow. They'll make plaster casts of the tire tracks in the lawn. That should tell us what type of car it was. With luck, that will help."

He leaned over and gently kissed her lips. He wanted to pull her into his arms and squeeze her tight — to reassure himself that she was all right. But she'd been through so much that he didn't want to risk hurting her.

She pulled the sheet up to her chin, and he turned out the light. He stood in the shower and let the water stream over his body. He felt helpless, the way he'd felt when he'd arrived at his uncle's villa in Siros. He hated not being in control, not being able to help Whitney.

As soon as Quinten Foley's men searched the house tomorrow, he was going to Cancún with Whitney. If Miranda wasn't working in a shop at Corona del Mar, he believed they would find her in Cancún. She had the answer to this —

"Holy shit!" he said out loud. He leaped out of the shower, wound the towel around his waist, left the bathroom and raced through the dark bedroom. He was down the hall and in his uncle's office before he saw Lexi had followed him.

"Go guard Whitney," he said, then realized Whitney was with the dog.

"What's the matter?" she asked, her eyes wide.

Adam grabbed the picture of his uncle fishing off the wall. "It just hit me. Something's written on my uncle's baseball cap." He flung open the middle drawer of the desk and found the magnifying glass.

"You think . . . ?"

He examined the script on the cap. "I'll be damned. Corona del Mar." He gazed at her, thinking out loud. "How much do you want to bet Uncle Calvin took Miranda to Cancún last December?"

"But her passport —"

"Would have been examined by customs officials but not necessarily stamped. Airports for private planes operate differently."

"Do you think they were, you know, involved?"

He slapped his forehead with the palm of his hand. "Good thing I'm not on the force anymore. They'd bust me down to writing traffic tickets. I should have considered the romance angle before now."

'I didn't think of it, either. The age difference —"

"What? Twenty years — give or take. My uncle was a good-looking guy with a lot of money. It wouldn't be the first time a woman ignored a few years when a guy was rich."

CHAPTER
THIRTY-ONE

Ryan shaved and inspected his reflection in the mirror. Where in hell was Ashley? It had been almost dawn when he'd come home. He'd expected her to be asleep but it was evident that she hadn't even touched the bed. He'd lain awake — thinking, wondering.

He was willing to admit that he had been harder on Ashley than necessary. Poor baby couldn't help it if she had a heart of gold. She hadn't wanted Whitney to suffer. Ashley had no idea how much trouble Whitney was causing him.

"Wait!" he exclaimed to his reflection. "That's it."

Last night he had told Ashley they were on the verge of bankruptcy. Ashley must think she'd caused their troubles. She loved him so much that she might be trying to singlehandedly solve their problems. She might have gone to borrow money from someone she knew.

In the middle of the night?

Ryan splashed on the aftershave lotion Ashley had given him. "She's mad at me," he again said out loud. "She spent the night with a friend."

That made sense. He probably deserved it, but she had no idea what pressure he was under. Thanks to Whitney.

Ryan walked into his closet to get dressed. He halted and spun around. How long was Ashley planning to stay with her girlfriend? He went into her closet, but he couldn't tell what she'd taken. She had too damn many clothes.

Brooding, he wandered back into the bathroom and checked the vanity area where Ashley kept her cosmetics. "Oh, shit!" What did women do with all this crap? He couldn't tell if she'd removed a thing.

It didn't matter, he decided. He had to get dressed. A hell of a day was ahead of him. Tonight, Ashley would be here waiting for him. He wouldn't make it easy, but he would forgive her.

He loved Ashley so much that it hurt sometimes. It pained him not to be able to give her everything she wanted or be the successful doctor she believed him to be when they'd met. He needed her love in a way that he'd never needed anything else.

Adam looked out the airplane window at the aquamarine water. It was so clear he could see the reefs below the surface. The ocean off California and the west coast of Mexico was deep blue. Here on Mexico's eastern shore the sea was the blue-green of the nearby Caribbean. Judging from the beaches below, Cancún enjoyed the same white sugar sand, too.

He glanced to his right and saw Whitney was still asleep. No wonder. They'd talked until almost dawn, then she'd been forced to get up and walk her clients' dogs, arrange care for her own dogs and buy some things for this trip. He'd arranged to have a security guard from HiTech go with her — just in case.

The timing couldn't have been better. While she was out, Quinten Foley's team had thoroughly searched the house.

Nothing.

They'd gone through every book, checked every CD and DVD, examined each photograph for hidden text, knocked on paneling to see if there was a secret hiding place and they'd used some special machine to inspect the stonework for loose places where the disc might have been hidden.

Nothing.

If Calvin Hunter had hidden the disc at the house, the experts hadn't had any better luck than Adam. When they'd finished with the building — interior and exterior — they'd gone over Uncle Calvin's Lexus sedan.

Nothing.

While all this had been going on, another team had searched the charred, water-soaked contents of the garage where Miranda had stored her things.

Nothing.

Adam would have bet that they were coming up empty because the disc wasn't here. He was positive Miranda had it. Now that he thought about the situation, it made perfect sense. She'd faked the robbery and made off with the computer and the disc or discs.

The information on the disc was worth a lot of money. Not for the first time, he wondered if Miranda had killed his uncle. If they'd been involved, his uncle might have confided in her. She would have had access to the house, his car, his computer.

Beside him, Whitney stretched and yawned. "Are we almost there?"

"Yes. You can see the beaches below." He

moved back so she could look out the window.

"Wow! Such white sand. It's nothing like Acapulco or Puerto Vallarta. Their beaches just have regular sand like California."

He nodded his agreement, thinking how special Whitney was. He needed to clear up this mess before something happened to her. He'd tried to piece the puzzle together but hadn't been able to make things fit. Miranda was the key.

Last night, after they'd discovered his uncle had also been to Corona del Mar, Adam went round and round in his head trying to decide how much to tell Whitney. He would have told her everything except she was still shell-shocked by the incident with the car.

In the end, he'd elected not to complicate matters by explaining his uncle's involvement with Quinten Foley in some clandestine government deal. What did he know for certain anyway? Not a damn thing, really.

He thought back to the last time he'd seen Calvin Hunter. His uncle had been worried, certain someone was going to kill him. He'd refused to reveal any details, but Adam felt his death had to be linked to the missing disc.

What other explanation could there be?

The plane had been slowly descending for some time. Now it dipped lower on final approach. The endless blue of the sea stretched out to the horizon.

"What's our first move?" Whitney asked.

He wanted to lure her to some cabana where sea breezes would cool their naked bodies while they made love. *Business first,* he reminded himself. There would be plenty of time for them later.

"Have a margarita and take a swim."

"Seriously," she replied with a laugh.

"Check into our hotel. Change clothes, then drive out to Corona del Mar for a drink. The cocktail hour should bring out residents who may have met your cousin."

"You think Miranda is out there?"

They'd discussed this last night, but Whitney had been a little groggy. "Hard to say. If she's not there, someone may recognize her picture. Cancún isn't that big. The thing to do is check Corona del Mar. Then we'll show the photos you had made around at *supermercados* and other places people who stay here long-term would shop. If she's living here, she's shopping somewhere. She can't be eating out all the time."

It was nearly ten when Ryan checked the clock mounted on the wall beside the pool.

The device gave the temperature and the time. He didn't need to check the temperature. He could tell it was still in the mid-seventies even though it was dark and the temperature had dropped the way it usually did on summer evenings.

Where in hell was Ashley?

He'd been ready to forgive her, but now he was pissed big-time. He'd come home to an empty house and a refrigerator with nothing but low-fat yogurt and cottage cheese in it. He'd gone for a swim to keep his body toned, expecting Ashley any minute. He'd been home for three freaking hours when he tried her cell. It immediately kicked into voice mail.

Ashley was in for it now. *Suggest a trial separation,* he told himself. That would upset her no end. Wouldn't it?

Ryan admitted to himself that he was no longer as sure of things as he once had been. His world had been on track. True, he'd had to make a midcourse correction and switch from general surgery to cosmetic surgery, but even then, things had gone his way.

The trouble had started with Whitney.

"Jesus H. Christ!" He cursed out loud and jumped to his feet. Would Ashley have gone to see his ex-wife? It was possible. After all, Ashley had given Whitney the dress that started this crappy argument.

He slung the towel over his bare shoulder and stomped inside. Ashley didn't have an office. What the fuck would she need one for? She used the nook area in the kitchen to keep a few things, like her checkbook and calendar.

He threw on the lights and searched the nook. Not much. Travel brochures for Hawaii. Nordstrom catalogs. An accordion folder with returned checks filed by date.

He rummaged through the stuff, searching for her telephone book. She kept phone numbers in a small leather booklet. It must be in her purse, Ryan decided. He didn't want to lower himself by calling the friend who'd helped her snatch Lexi, but if Ashley didn't show in another hour, he would.

The only friend Ashley had ever mentioned was her personal trainer. They'd been close when Ryan first met Ashley. He'd never met the woman because she lived across town and worked most of the time at a gym. Come to think of it, he didn't even know the woman's name.

What gym? He could call there and see if Ashley was around. Shit! She hadn't told him the name of the gym. Well, maybe she had and he'd forgotten it. He remembered Ashley saying she paid her friend in cash.

The woman couldn't afford to pay taxes. Unfuckingbelievable! Who could? He'd been forced to instruct his accountant to file late this year.

He searched through her returned checks, for lack of anything better to do. Manicures. Pedicures. Boutiques. Nothing extravagant, but still — it was money they hadn't had. Ashley hadn't known this, he reminded himself.

Dr. Jox. The check stopped him. The memo line indicated Ashley had purchased vitamins. That must be the name of the gym where Ashley's personal trainer worked. He got the number from Information and called. He would have put it off, but most gyms closed at ten. He needed the number tonight.

"I'm a friend of Ashley Fordham's," he told the young-sounding guy who answered the telephone. "She recommended a trainer there. I was wondering if I could get her number."

Ryan didn't want word to go around the gym that he was looking for Ashley. He wasn't sure why he gave a shit. Personal pride, he guessed. Not just every guy married a beauty queen. No sense in seeming jealous when he wasn't.

"*Her* number?" the kid parroted back.

"Yes. Ashley really likes this trainer's workouts." Ryan heard a muffled sound as if the kid had put his hand over the mouthpiece.

"Just a minute," the kid told him. "I'll let you talk to my manager."

Ryan waited, getting more irritated by the second. What was the big deal? He would have driven over there but Dr. Jox was halfway across town.

"This is Al Schneider. What can I do for ya?"

Ryan repeated his spiel. Silence. "The trainer is still working there, isn't she?"

"You're Mr. Fordham, right?"

Ryan started to deny it, then realized the guy must have his name on the caller ID screen. "Yes. Ashley recom—"

"That trainer isn't accepting new clients."

The manager hung up before Ryan could ask another question. What the fuck? He almost hit Redial, then stopped himself. Something was going on.

Why wouldn't a trainer who needed money badly enough to risk trouble with the IRS not want new clients? He thought about it for a moment. He paid all their bills. He remembered commenting to Ashley about the number of calls made from their home phone. Not that it cost much;

they had a wide-range dialing plan. But he knew he didn't make many calls.

Back in his office, Ryan pawed through the growing cluster of bills on his desk until he found last month's telephone bill. This would be the third month in a row that he'd neglected to pay it. He checked the local calls. Several were to the office he still had until the new group was up and running. Others he vaguely recognized. His service. Walter Nance.

One number came up several times. He thought he recognized it from previous bills but couldn't be sure. He'd trashed them or he would be able to check.

Ryan plopped down into his chair and booted up his computer. It was cool inside and he rearranged the damp towel over his shoulders to keep warm. It took several minutes to locate an Internet reverse directory for San Diego and look up the number. It was registered to a Preston Block with an address across town.

Block could be the trainer's father or a roommate. He studied the screen and memorized the address. He needed to speak to Ashley in person.

It took a little more than half an hour to drive to the address listed for Preston Block. It was a bunker-style two-story apartment building that wrapped around a pool with cloudy water. The place had been new in the seventies. From what Ryan could tell in the dark, that was the last time it had been painted. Exactly where he would expect a trainer subsisting hand to mouth to live.

He found the directory with Block/Swanson listed for apartment 2B. He stood there a moment to formulate the speech he'd mentally rehearsed on the way over. He didn't want to admit how much he missed Ashley. He planned to say her father had called.

Was that even possible? Now he wished he'd asked more questions. He knew Ashley had suffered through her mother's tragic death alone. Her father lived in some crummy town in the central part of the state, but he hadn't come to the funeral. Had she told her father about their marriage? He didn't remember Ashley mentioning it.

Unable to think of a better excuse, he climbed the stairs. A potted palm missing most of its fronds stood outside 2B's door. He mustered an assertive knock.

A television was playing inside, but a moment later the door swung open. A surfer built like a brick shithouse stared out at him.

"I'm looking for Ashley Fordham's

trainer."

"Preston's out. He works nights now."

He? *He?* Ashley's personal trainer was a woman. Wasn't that what she had told him? Ryan blinked and tried to recall exactly what Ashley had said. The first time she'd mentioned the trainer had been when they were in bed and he'd been admiring how perfect every inch of her body was.

I work with a trainer five days a week.

The guy's smile evaporated. "Who are you?"

"Dr. Fordham. Ashley's husband." He couldn't keep from adding, "I'm looking for her."

"She's not here."

Ryan turned and trudged away without another word. Of all the scenarios he'd envisioned, he'd never imagined Ashley — his Ashley — being involved with another man. The knowledge made him dizzy, weak.

He ambled along, his mind unable to process any thought except: Ashley had betrayed him. He'd loved her so much — too much.

He'd given her everything she wanted, hadn't he?

No, he silently corrected himself. There were things Ashley had wanted, like the house in the Coronado Keys. He'd been too strapped for money to purchase it. Ashley had spent her life on the road. She deserved a home of her own. If Whitney hadn't been such a bitch, this never would have happened.

CHAPTER
THIRTY-TWO

"It's beautiful," Whitney said. "Even more spectacular than I expected."

"Why not? The homes around here start at a cool mil."

They were sitting in the Frio-Frio — cool, cool — bar at Corona del Mar. They'd checked into their hotel in Cancún, changed clothes and had driven out here in their rented Mazda.

It was so humid, the short skirt on Whitney's sundress was plastered to her legs by the time she walked from the air-conditioned hotel to the car. Mexico's beaches were popular tourist destinations in the winter, but by this time of year, the temperature skyrocketed and visitors tapered off. Their hotel was only half-full, as was the bar at this expensive development.

"This seems too . . . too sophisticated for Miranda," she told Adam.

"That doesn't mean she isn't working

here. Tips must be great. Better than in Cancún. If she visited here last December, she could have lined up a job."

"Possibly. Should I ask our waitress?"

A woman wearing a wraparound skirt in the coral and azure tropical pattern of the resort was heading their way with double margaritas. Whitney had brought photographs of Miranda that she'd doctored on the computer at Speedy Press yesterday morning. It was the shot taken of Miranda on the beach last December. One picture showed her as a blonde while Whitney had altered the other to make her cousin have black hair.

"Give it a try. Use the blond photo first."

The waitress put down their drinks with a smile, and Whitney said, "I think my sister visited here." She showed the woman the photograph. "Does she look familiar?"

"Fam-lar?"

Whitney realized the waitress spoke some English but not enough to understand the question. "Do . . . you . . . know . . . her?" she said with deliberate slowness.

The waitress squinted at the photograph, then shook her head. Whitney was ready and whipped out the second photograph. "See . . . her?"

The woman's dark eyes studied the second

photograph. *"No se."*

The waitress left the table, and Adam said, "Miranda might not come in here. We can't expect to find her at the first place we try."

"True." She hated to think this was a wild-goose chase, but it was a definite possibility. After the terrifying incident last night, it had seemed imperative that they find Miranda as soon as possible.

Whitney was still a little disturbed from the shock of the incident, and numbness had replaced the lingering questions. She couldn't decide if someone had mistaken her for Miranda — which meant they'd followed her from home — or if it had merely been a dangerous prank. She refused to dwell on it. If she did, a wave of fear broke over her.

They sipped the slushy margaritas and gazed out at the sea. The sun had slipped into the ocean, leaving shimmering streamers of crimson and gold on the water. It was a very romantic setting, she decided.

If the stress of the situation hadn't been so intense, she could have appreciated it. She really needed things to calm down so she could evaluate her true feelings for Adam. There was no denying he was a great guy. Last night and after the fire, he'd been the one to comfort her.

Despite cautioning herself to take this slow so she'd have the time and space to truly get over Ryan and his betrayal, events hadn't permitted Whitney that luxury. She'd been pressed into an intimate relationship. There was the obvious attraction factor, but if what seemed to be developing between herself and Adam was merely chemistry, she might have dealt with it more easily. What she was feeling went deeper, meant more.

Over Adam's shoulder she noticed their waitress was talking to the bartender. They kept looking in Whitney's direction. The young bartender came out from behind the bamboo bar and headed toward their table.

Whitney kept her voice low. "Looks like our waitress told the bartender we're searching for someone."

"Buenas noches," said the dark-haired man as he came up to their table.

They told him good-evening in Spanish, then complimented him on the excellent margaritas.

"Cuervo Gold," he replied, and Whitney decided he meant the expensive tequila gave the margaritas their smooth yet distinctive flavor.

"Looking for someone?" the man asked.

"Mi hermana," Whitney told him. *My sister.* It was a fib but it sounded better if Miranda

481

was her sister.

The bartender pulled out a chair and sat down. Whitney tried to catch Adam's eye, but he was studying the younger man.

"You don't have to practice your tourist Spanish on me," he told them. "I'm Cuban. From Miami. My English is perfect. I just work here during the season. It's back to the States next week."

Whitney smiled and wondered how much to tell this guy. After the incident with the car and the fire, she wasn't in a very trusting mood these days. On the fly, she came up with a story.

"My mother is very ill." She leaned closer to the bartender as if divulging a secret. "Cancer. She and my sister haven't . . ."

Adam got the drift. "They haven't spoken in almost three years. We think she's down here but we don't know where."

"We'd like to find her and bring her home before it's too late." Whitney managed to add a touch of tears to her voice. She handed him the photo of the blond Miranda.

The bartender shrugged. "She looks like a lot of blondes whose parents have places here." He gazed at Whitney for a moment. "I can see you're sisters."

Whitney tried for a smile and pulled out

the second photograph with dark hair. "She may have dyed her hair."

His eyes shifted from the photograph to Whitney. "I don't recognize her, but not everyone comes into the bar." He stood up. "Sorry I couldn't help."

They thanked him and the bartender hustled back to his station to serve a couple who'd just arrived. Whitney took another sip of her drink.

"What's our next move?"

"Tonight, I think we should check the shops nearby on the off chance someone will recognize her. Then let's get dinner and hit the sack early. Tomorrow we should come out here and speak to the sales office. They'll have records of people who visited the resort to consider a purchase, and they may recognize Miranda."

They chatted about Lyleen Foster, the pet concierge Whitney had asked to take care of her clients while she came here. Daniel had highly recommended the woman, but Whitney didn't like giving her charges to someone she'd just met. She supposed they would be fine for a few days, but Lexi had taken off once already.

"I hope Lexi doesn't try to run away again," she told Adam.

"I'm sure she won't."

"I wish I felt as positive as you sound."

"Look, I should —"

The bartender walked up and interrupted Adam. "You know, I've been thinking. This might be nothing, but . . ."

"But what?" Adam asked.

"Let me see the picture again. The one of the chick with black hair."

Whitney produced the photograph and told herself not to get her hopes up.

The bartender squinted at the picture, then said, "She looks a little like Courtney Hampton but it's hard to tell. Courtney's hair is red and really short."

Yes! Whitney silently screamed. Miranda's hair was a sandy blond. It would be easier to conceal her roots if she kept it in one of the short, sassy cuts that were so popular.

"Courtney lives at the far end of the road. She and her husband came here last Christmas to look over the place. They purchased a villa not too long ago."

Disappointment knotted inside her. It couldn't be Miranda. She wouldn't be with a husband.

"Her husband died. A sudden heart attack." The bartender shook his head. "Not surprising. The dude was a lot older than Courtney."

■ ■ ■ ■

Whitney stood beside Adam at the door of the villa owned by the widow Courtney Hampton. It was located at the end of a cul-de-sac on a secluded cove. Apparently, the other owners had left for the season. The only lights in the area were on at this house.

Adam rang the bell and whispered in her ear, "Remember what I told you. Say as little as possible at first. Suspects often reveal much more if you just let them talk."

It was a full minute before they heard anything. Muffled footsteps came through the arched wood door.

"Who is it?"

Whitney instantly recognized Miranda's voice. She nodded enthusiastically at Adam, and he smiled.

"Miranda, it's me, Whitney."

Dead silence. For a moment, Whitney thought her cousin wasn't going to open the door. Then it swung open. The woman before them had copper hair in a spiked pixie cut, but there was no mistaking Miranda Marshall.

"Whitney, I — I a-a-ah . . ."

Whitney barged in, followed by Adam. Miranda's expression darkened with an unreadable emotion. A thousand questions pummeled Whitney's brain but she waited to see what her cousin would say.

"W-what are you doing here?" Miranda asked.

Instead of responding, Whitney looked around. The interior was furnished in Key West mode with comfy-looking woven wicker chairs and a chaise lounge-style sofa in the living area just beyond the entry. There were no paintings or anything on the walls or accessories on the end tables. The only homey touch was a hint of cinnamon in the air that must have come from the candles flickering on the coffee table.

Whitney turned back to Miranda and glared at her. And waited.

"Why are you here?" Miranda repeated. "It isn't even two weeks yet."

Whitney realized Miranda was referring to her two-week "honeymoon." Evidently, her cousin didn't think anyone would miss her for at least two weeks. "Some honeymoon."

Miranda reacted to the unbridled sarcasm in Whitney's voice by wincing just slightly. "I know you must be upset, but I can explain."

"Don't let me stop you."

"Maybe we'd better sit down," suggested Adam.

"Who are you?" asked Miranda.

"Adam Hunter."

The air emptied from Miranda's lungs in a rush. "Calvin's nephew. Of course."

She led them into a great room that faced the cove. The sun had set but there was still enough light to appreciate the fabulous view. Knowing Miranda was out here by herself, though, made it seem lonely and isolated. Whitney told herself not to feel sorry for her cousin until she knew more. Thanks to Miranda, she'd lost every possession she had — and was lucky to be alive.

Miranda took a chair while Adam and Whitney sat side by side on the sofa. Whitney let the silence lengthen.

Finally, Miranda spoke. "I didn't want to lie to you, but . . . I needed to protect you."

From what? Whitney wanted to scream, but Adam squeezed her hand to remind her to let Miranda talk.

"You see, I never expected you to appear on my doorstep, needing a place to stay. My plans were already in motion. I had to get out of town." She waved her hand, gesturing to her surroundings. "We'd planned to come here. Everything was all set. I was just taking care of the final details when you surfaced out of nowhere."

An uneasy hush followed her breathless explanation. Through the open doors that led outside, Whitney heard the soft purling of the surf on the sand.

"We?" prompted Adam.

Miranda studied Adam for a moment before saying, "Your uncle and I had been together for over two years. We planned to move here after —" she hesitated "— Cal stopped judging dog shows."

Whitney waited, expecting Miranda to say more, but the only sound in the room was the waves on the shore, bringing a trace of salt into the cinnamon-scented room. Out of the corner of her eye, Whitney glanced at Adam and saw he was studying Miranda.

Finally, Whitney couldn't stand the tension any longer. "Why would someone want you dead so badly that they would firebomb your house and nearly kill me?"

The thick lashes shadowing Miranda's cheeks flew up. "What? Someone . . ."

"You heard me. Someone firebombed the cottage. By the grace of God, I wasn't home at the time."

Miranda stared at Whitney, her face stricken with horror. "What? I can't imagine —" She jumped to her feet and rushed to the open doors that led out to the patio. Miranda faced the sea for a moment, then slowly returned to her chair. "I — I'm sorry — so sorry. I never thought it would come to this." She frowned. "So soon. I didn't expect anything to happen so soon."

"Why don't you explain it to us?" Adam asked, his voice sympathetic.

He must be playing the good cop, Whitney decided. He almost seemed like a stranger with no stake in these events. She was ready to scream at her cousin for not warning her about impending trouble.

"I-it's a long story. I don't know where to begin."

"We have all night." Adam glanced at Whitney. "Whitney nearly died. She's lost everything she has —"

"Was Lexi killed?"

Whitney shook her head. "No. The dogs were with me, but the pipe bomb thrown into the cottage caused a fire. I lost everything but what I was wearing."

"Oh my God." Miranda closed her eyes for a moment, then directed her response to Adam. "I'd been living in the cottage awhile before I really got to know your uncle. He was away judging dog shows overseas most of the time. Then we started seeing more and more of each other. We fell in love."

Whitney tried to imagine Miranda in love. Her cousin always had guys trailing after her, but she'd seemed older and more sophisticated than they were. Miranda had never been serious about any of them. Whitney could understand why an older, more worldly man would appeal to her cousin.

"Cal didn't want me to work so hard. He began giving me money."

"We know you were stripping at Saffron Blue," Adam told her.

Miranda's eyes flew in Whitney's direction. A hint of crimson seemed to flower beneath her tan. "I did some stripping," she replied apologetically.

"My uncle didn't like that. Did he?"

A flicker of a smile brightened Miranda's face. "No. Cal was old-fashioned in many ways. He insisted I quit."

"He gave you three thousand dollars in cash at the beginning of every month, right?"

How did Adam know this? Whitney wondered, an uneasy feeling creeping through her.

Miranda nodded. "Yes. It wasn't as much as I was making at Saffron Blue, but I didn't need more."

"What did you do with the insurance money you received from your parents'

490

death?" Whitney asked.

"I invested most of it in the stock market. Tech stocks were hot back then and I thought I would make a killing. At first, I did — on paper. Then I lost every penny. Luckily I'd kept some to live on, so I was able to help your mother when she needed it. That was the last of my money."

A twinge of guilt passed through Whitney. She hadn't known Miranda at all. She'd never considered her cousin to be the type who would risk money in the market, but she was wrong. It touched her that Miranda had used what little she'd had left to help Whitney's mother.

"Last year Cal brought me down here," continued Miranda. "I thought it was just a trip so he could fish." She gazed wistfully out toward the ocean for a moment. "He adored fishing. He could spend hours bobbing up and down in a fishing boat waiting for a bite. I never saw the attraction. But what did it matter? I hung out on the beach, worked on my tan and read a book until sunset when the fishing boats came in."

"Your passport doesn't show any record of a visit here," Adam said.

"Cal leased a jet. We took off from a private airport and landed on a private strip constructed especially for this development.

I had my passport with me, but no one bothered to stamp it."

Adam replied, "Private airfields are notoriously lax."

"Turns out Cal wasn't just interested in the fishing at Corona del Mar. He wanted to buy a place. He picked out this villa because of the view. He loved looking out at the ocean. You can see it from here, the kitchen and the master bedroom." She drew in a slow, deliberate breath and tears welled up in her eyes. "Too bad he didn't live to enjoy it."

Adam stared at Miranda, his gaze intense. "How did my uncle die?"

"Early in the evening, Cal complained of chest pain. He'd never had heartburn, but he claimed that's what it was." Miranda flung out her hands in simple despair. "If only I'd taken him to the hospital, but I believed him. Later, we were in the office, checking the computer for the Cancún weather report, and he gasped." She cast a pleading look at Adam, a lone tear dribbling down her cheek. "A loud gasp like nothing I've ever heard. It seemed as if Cal wanted to scream but couldn't, then he slumped over in his chair. I tried to get a pulse. Nothing. I immediately dialed 911."

"Why did you leave?" asked Adam. "No

one was around when the paramedics arrived."

"Cal always insisted we be very careful. He didn't want anyone to know we were involved." Her eyes darkened with fear. "In the days before he died, Cal said his life was in danger. I was afraid I might be killed."

"Why didn't you tell me?" Whitney cried.

CHAPTER
THIRTY-THREE

Whitney waited for Miranda to respond. "Why didn't you tell me?" she repeated.

Her cousin brushed the moisture off her cheeks with the back of her hand. "Whitney, I swear, I never thought you were in the least bit of danger."

"Why not? We look enough alike to be mistaken for each other."

Miranda huddled in her chair. "Our eyes maybe, but I don't think anyone would . . ." She turned to Adam. "Do you think we look alike?"

"Not to me. But then, I'm sitting very close to you. At a distance, you're both slim blondes with green eyes —"

"I'm two inches taller," interjected Miranda. "My face is longer."

"In the dark — all bets are off," said Adam. "Someone who didn't know you well could —"

"Why didn't you just warn me?" Frustra-

494

tion echoed in every syllable Whitney spoke.

"I didn't think it was necessary. They aren't due back until next week."

"Stop." Adam held up his hand. "Go back. Explain everything. Who are 'they'?"

Miranda was silent for a moment as if deciding just where to begin. "Cal and I fell in love. He said he wished he'd met me years ago. You see, Cal always wanted a son. Someone like you."

If this touched Adam, he didn't show it. His face remained attentive, yet strangely impassive. It reminded Whitney of the way he'd acted when they'd first met.

"Even though Cal was almost twenty years older, he wanted children. I can't tell you how excited he was when I told him I was pregnant."

"Ohmygod," cried Whitney. "You're pregnant."

Miranda lightly patted her tummy. "A little over three months along."

Whitney's eyes cut over to Adam. His detached expression hadn't changed. Was he made of stone? she wondered. The baby would be his cousin.

"If you're carrying his child, why didn't my uncle change his will?"

"He wanted you to inherit his real estate. The bulk of his money was in offshore accounts. He arranged it so all of his money would go to our child should anything happen to him."

"Something did happen to my uncle."

Unexpectedly there was a flare of biting sarcasm in Adam's voice. Miranda flinched as if he'd physically slapped her. What was Adam implying? That Miranda had something to do with his uncle's death? It was a simple heart attack, wasn't it?

"Your father . . . Cal's fa-father —" Miranda's voice faltered. "Both died at relatively young ages of heart problems. I tried to persuade him to eat better and exercise more but —"

"Did he take any medicine the night he died?"

"No. Why?"

Instead of answering, Adam asked, "Where did you eat?"

"We barbecued at home. Swordfish. It was the only fish he liked." Miranda forced a laugh. "He loved to fish but didn't like to eat it. Oh, he would prepare fish like a gourmet, but he just picked at what he'd cooked." Miranda hesitated a moment, looking out toward the cove where darkness had fallen. "I get it now. You think I killed him."

"Did you?" he shot back.

"Of course not! I loved him." Miranda gazed at Whitney. "I guess Cal reminded me of my father, but it was more than that. He was so smart, so well traveled. He was a man — nothing like those boys I used to date." She turned her attention to Adam again. "I didn't kill him. Who would want to go into hiding all alone?"

"Why *are* you hiding?" asked Whitney.

Miranda didn't respond. Whitney gazed at Adam. His stoic expression hadn't changed but she suddenly had the feeling he knew the answer. If not, he knew a lot more than he had told her. A slow burn began to creep through her.

"We came down here last December," replied Miranda. "I didn't know it at the time, but it was a test of sorts. Cal wanted to see if I liked it well enough to live here full-time.

"On New Year's Day, Cal told me he was going away — for good. You see, I'd gotten used to him disappearing overseas for weeks at a time for dog shows, but he explained this would be different. He wouldn't be returning for several years, and he wouldn't be able to contact me. In short, I might never see him again."

"Several years?"

"That's what I asked," Miranda replied in

response to Whitney's question. "Cal said it might be two, three even five years before he returned. He wanted me to come with him, but he said I needed to think it over very carefully. Would I be comfortable not coming back for such an extended period? Would I be able to exist without contacting anyone?"

Adam asked, "Didn't his request seem strange?"

"Of course. I demanded to know why, but your uncle said he'd explain the details only if I decided to go with him."

"How could you agree? Your life, everything is in San Diego," Whitney insisted.

"Really? What life? Babysitting dogs? I went to junior college, but I'm not like you. I hated it. I never found anything I really wanted to do . . . except be a mother."

Whitney understood. Miranda's family had been cruelly taken from her. She'd never gotten over it. Whitney decided she might have reacted the same way.

Miranda said to Whitney, "I knew you were back in town, but we never saw each other. I didn't have anyone or anything to keep me here. All I had was Cal. I truly loved him. I was willing to go anywhere with him."

Whitney couldn't help feeling ashamed of

herself. She should have made more of an effort to see Miranda.

"I slept on it, but first thing the following morning, I told Cal I would come with him." She was silent for a moment, gazing out at the water as if recalling every detail of that conversation. "Cal explained a little bit about his business. He told me he'd been brokering arms and weapons."

"Using the dog shows as a front," interjected Adam.

Wow, thought Whitney. *What a scheme.* She'd been correct. Adam certainly did know a whole lot more than he had told her. Poor little Jasper had merely been a cover, a reason for traveling overseas.

"Exactly. I was shocked, of course. He'd always e-mailed me pictures of Jasper's shows. Other events he merely judged, but he always sent me messages, telling me about the places he'd stayed or eaten. Looking back, I guess I should have been suspicious because he never once asked me to come with him."

Whitney tried to imagine waiting at home for weeks on end. She couldn't, then she suddenly realized it wouldn't have been much different from her life during Ryan's two residencies. He'd been at the hospital six days a week. When he came home, he just wanted to eat, then sleep. He might as well have been on another planet.

"Cal's clients had been in Africa or South America for the most part, but he brokered the deals in Europe. He always made certain his travel was related to shows. You see, he made arrangements for arms transactions but didn't actually handle anything."

"Was it illegal?" Whitney asked.

"Depends upon what he was selling," responded Adam. "Most weapons the United States allows to be sold are highly restricted. Our government doesn't like encouraging rebels or supplying guerilla armies."

Miranda shrugged. "Cal claimed if he didn't broker the deals, someone else would. He told me the trouble began when he discovered that a shipment of armaments he'd sold to a group in the Sudan ended up in the Middle East."

"He should have seen it coming," Adam commented. "Bin Laden was in East Africa before relocating to Afghanistan."

"Maybe Cal did realize what was happening," Miranda said in a tone bordering on wistful. "Maybe he didn't want to tarnish the image I had of him. Anyway, I agreed to go with him."

"You accepted this without asking more?"

Whitney couldn't help being astonished. A second later it occurred to her that she had often taken Ryan's word for things — without checking or asking questions. The revelation that Ryan had a severe gambling problem should have been something she'd sensed, but she hadn't. She'd been blissfully clueless.

"I wasn't sure I wanted to know more. Cal was leaving the business. We were going to be starting over." She hesitated for a beat. "He explained that the men he'd been dealing with would never allow him to just quit."

"Without giving them his contacts and access to his routing," Adam said.

The tension building inside Whitney kicked up another notch. She could tell none of this surprised Adam. He'd known all along, but never gave Whitney a hint. Why not? Miranda was her cousin. Didn't Whitney have a right to know?

"Exactly," Miranda said. "Cal didn't want Americans hurt with weapons he'd arranged to be sold. Adam, when you were almost killed, Cal felt responsible. Alarming amounts of weapons were surfacing in terrorists' hands.

"Not only did he want out, Cal wanted to shut down the pipeline. He told me it would be just a matter of time before the terrorists made a dirty bomb or even a nuclear weapon. He didn't want anything to do with it."

It sounded very self-serving to Whitney, but she didn't voice her opinion. She knew only too well how women in love overlooked serious flaws in their men.

"Cal went about shifting his funds around so no one could find them, and he created new identities for both of us. I didn't actually take it seriously." She threw up her hands. "I mean, I did and I didn't. I believed everything Cal had told me, but I didn't realize how serious the threat was until one night about a week before Cal died."

Miranda stopped speaking, jumped up and rushed toward the kitchen. She returned a few seconds later with a tissue in her hand. She plopped down in her chair again, saying, "I'd bought this sinfully sexy red nightie. I put it on and hid in his office closet. I wanted him to be working hard — he always blacked out everything around him when he was on the computer — then I planned to jump out and we would have sex right there on his desk."

If the situation hadn't been so serious, Whitney would have giggled. She recalled the number of times she'd tried to entice Ryan with sexy lingerie. It had worked —

temporarily — or so she'd thought.

"Cal came into the office with two men. I was stunned. He was supposed to be alone. They were talking business. I tried to be quiet, but I was hunched over, squeezed under a hanging shelf. A charley horse hit my calf. When I bent my leg a little to relieve the cramp, my foot hit something that made a scraping sound. Next thing I knew, this strange man threw open the door."

Whitney tried to imagine this but couldn't.

"I've never seen anyone look so positively evil. I thought they might shoot me on the spot. But Cal put his arm around me and explained we were about to be married — which was true. We were going to be married once we moved here. Cal told them I helped him with every deal. He insisted I had always been his silent partner."

Adam asked, "They bought it?"

"Yes. It took some convincing, but they finally accepted it. I was at his side when he arranged to give them what he called the support information."

"The routes he used. The ways he arranged for weapons to be shipped from the manufacturer to points overseas. People who helped," Adam said without hesitation. "Armaments must be carefully concealed, and you need a variety of routes. Too big a shipment is a risk because it attracts attention. If it's lost or confiscated, alternate routes become vital or the deal falls through."

"I guess." Miranda suddenly sounded tired and desperately unhappy. "It took some talking but Cal persuaded them to return in a month. He said 'we' would gather all the information and put it on a computer disc."

"That appealed to them because they could share it online with others in their group." Adam sounded so certain that Whitney became even angrier.

"That's right. They went for it because Cal demanded a million dollars for the disc."

CHAPTER
THIRTY-FOUR

"A million dollars," Whitney blurted out. "Didn't they think that was outrageous?"

"No. Uncle Calvin was selling them connections and shipping routes that it would take years to build."

"That's right," agreed Miranda. "Later Cal told me the money angle saved us. These men think Americans do everything for money."

"Did my uncle make the disc?"

"Yes. I saw him working on it. He had info hidden in different places. He assembled it —"

"Why," Whitney asked, "if he wasn't going to give it to them?"

"He planned to take the disc to a friend he knew from his days in naval intelligence. Cal didn't trust many people but he trusted this man, who was now working at the Pentagon. He was going to take him the disc then disappear forever."

"Who was his contact?" asked Adam.

"I don't remember. Cal only mentioned his name once. It was an unusual name."

"Could it have been Quinten Foley?"

"Yes. That's it!"

Whitney was surprised Adam knew the man, but then Adam knew much more than he'd chosen to disclose to her. Like a corrosive acid, anger was eating away at her. Why hadn't he given her *some* indication about the extent of this situation?

Adam quietly asked, "Did he give you the disc?"

"No." Miranda shook her head. "When Cal died, I knew I had to carry out his last wishes. He wanted you to have his property. It was mortgaged because Cal said he needed to create confusion with his accounts. He moved funds all around so no one would think he had any money left. That way they wouldn't come looking for him."

"His money is nearby," Adam said, "in the Caymans. You withdrew twenty-five thousand dollars a few days ago."

Miranda's eyebrows rose in surprise. "Yes, I did."

"You also deposited money, or was that some kind of a wire-transfer payoff for one of Uncle Calvin's deals that he completed shortly before he died?"

"I closed out a smaller account and consolidated," she replied, her words measured. "I paid off the loans on the properties you owned jointly with Cal."

"Where is the disc?" asked Adam.

"Cal told me he hid it for safekeeping. I didn't even think about it until after he died."

"It must have been stolen on the day of the funeral," Adam said. "What I can't understand is why they would want to kill you with a pipe bomb if they had the disc?"

"Because I can identify them. They contacted Cal several months ago and threatened him. This time their leader came to 'persuade' him. That's why Cal wanted to make certain we were long gone when they returned to pick up the disc. He told me they would kill us both — even if he handed over the disc."

"My uncle warned me in Siros that someone would try to kill him. That must have been right after they contacted him the first time."

"What doesn't make sense is them wanting me dead before the pick-up date next week. You see, they can't possibly have the disc."

"Why not?" Adam asked. "Wasn't it with

the computer they stole?"

Miranda tried for a laugh, then said, "No way. I stole Cal's laptop."

"You? Why?" Whitney and Adam asked almost in unison.

"I assumed the info was on his computer or on the software discs in his office. I didn't want those men to find it. I went to the funeral but didn't attend the reception at the officers' club. After all, no one knew about me . . . about us. I told the few people I met that I was Cal's renter. I came home, faked a break-in and swiped the computer."

"Smart move," Adam said, then glanced at Whitney. "Quick thinking runs in the family."

"It wasn't that smart. I've gone through all his files. It isn't there." Miranda sighed and sank lower in her chair. "If you don't believe me, you can check for yourself. The computer is in the guest bedroom."

Ryan's cell phone vibrated. He grabbed it, threw down a hundred-dollar chip on the craps table and walked away. Casinos had strict rules about cell phones. He usually shut his off completely but he didn't want to miss Ashley's call.

He flipped open his phone. He didn't recognize the number on the LCD screen.

"Just a minute," he whispered.

Ryan shouldered his way through the double set of sweeping glass doors that led from the casino to a bar wrapped around a geyser of a fountain.

"Yes?" he said, louder now.

"Ryan Fordham?"

He didn't recognize the female voice. Shit! He'd walked away from the table with a hundred on the line to take what had to be a call from a bill collector.

"Who is this?" he demanded.

"Trish Bowrather."

The rich blonde who owned the swank gallery where Walter had taken him. That's where all the fucking trouble started. He could still see Whitney standing there in the sexy dress he'd bought for Ashley.

"Ravissant Gallery, right? Great show." He made an effort to flatter her. After all, Walter highly recommended the woman's taste in art. One day, he would again have enough money to indulge Ashley's desire to have a fabulous home filled with priceless art.

"That's right. I'm glad you enjoyed the show. We're looking for Whitney. We're wondering if you have any idea where she is."

"Who's we?"

"I'm with her attorney, Rod Babcock."

Babcock. Hadn't the guy married Miranda? Wasn't that what Whitney had told him? Now that he thought about it, he hadn't seen Miranda at the gallery. If that cocksucker was looking for Whitney, it was a very bad sign. "No," he made himself say calmly. "I'm remarried —"

"Yes, I know. I said this was a long shot." She covered the phone and all he could hear was muffled voices.

"How long's she been gone?" he asked, when the voices stopped, not liking the idea that had just cropped up in his mind.

It was bad enough that Whitney's attorney wanted to speak to her. It would be total disaster if Whitney and Ashley were together. Whitney would poison Ashley's mind and no telling what would happen.

"Do you know where Whitney is?" the woman shot back in a clipped tone that warned him to be careful.

"No, not really . . . Why?"

There was another long pause and more muffled voices he couldn't understand before Trish Bowrather replied, "I'm not sure how long Whitney's been gone or where she is. She had a total stranger walk my dog this morning."

Whitney must have gone somewhere last

night. Ashley couldn't have left him to see Whitney, could she?

Ah, fuck, his life was unraveling like a cheap sweater.

Ryan snapped the cell phone shut without saying another word. Just as he slid it into his pocket, someone tapped him on the shoulder. He turned and found himself nose to nose with the shithead Dom used as a gofer.

"Dom's outside. He wants to see you."

"I've got a bet on the table." Ryan had been winning all night. When Lady Luck deserted his private life, the hussy rewarded him at the tables.

"Forgetaboutit."

The goon latched on to Ryan's arm and shoved him out the gate that led into the parking lot. Idling at the curb was Domenic Coriz's black limo. The cocky prick yanked open the rear door and shoved Ryan into the car.

It was dark inside except for the glow of the cigarette in Dom's hand. For a moment the burly Native American didn't say a word. When he spoke, his voice was low, guttural.

"Your wife called me."

The bottom dropped out of Ryan's stomach. How could Ashley know about Dom?

She must realize he had a gambling problem. She had to be furious that he'd kept the truth from her. "Sorry, I —"

"We're through fucking around. Through. Understand?"

It was all Ryan could do to keep from wetting himself. "I understand."

It was almost midnight when Miranda and Whitney left Adam in the guest bedroom set up as a home office. He'd gone through the files on his uncle's computer and was checking the software discs. So far he hadn't located the information.

Miranda and Whitney decided to stretch their legs by walking on the beach instead of leaning over Adam's shoulder while he searched. The air was almost as warm as it had been during the day, but a light breeze drifted across the water. The ebony sky was strewn with brilliant stitches of stars. A bright crescent moon cast enough light for them to see. Like a glistening ribbon, the beach wound along a cove protected from the open water by a reef. Lazy waves pushed garlands of seaweed up on the sand.

"I'm sorry . . ." Whitney didn't know where to begin. "I've been a lousy relative. We're all that's left of our family. I never should have let Ryan —"

"He hated me from the minute he set eyes on me, didn't he?"

"*Hate* might be too strong a word." She didn't want to make excuses for her skank of an ex-husband, but she doubted Ryan expended the effort to "hate" Miranda. She wasn't important enough in his life.

"I think I know why Ryan hated me," said Miranda. "He's the type who needs to possess someone. He didn't want you to have friends or interests outside him. Basically, he's insecure."

Whitney started to deny this. Ryan was a handsome man that women fawned over. He was intelligent enough to win scholarships, be accepted to a top-flight medical school and be selected for the most prominent residency programs. Why would he be insecure?

She'd read enough to know sometimes the most unlikely people were insecure. It often had to do with their childhood. Ryan had siblings, but they weren't close. In fact, they rarely spoke. Ryan claimed they'd gone their separate ways. She'd suspected his siblings were blue collar and he was ashamed of them.

"Maybe you're right," she told Miranda. "Ryan is very possessive. It doesn't matter now, does it? He's out of my life."

"I'd say you've improved things considerably."

Whitney smiled, happy to feel close to Miranda again, but uneasy about Adam. Tonight proved how little he'd confided in her, how little she actually knew about the man. She'd met him just a week ago, as hard as that was to believe. In some ways she'd grown to feel as comfortable and as close to him as she'd ever been to any man. Obviously, he hadn't felt that close to her. She was angry and terribly upset with Adam but didn't want to burden her cousin with anything else. She changed the subject.

"Speaking of improving things. How did you come up with Broderick Babcock's name?"

Miranda gave her a smug smile. "I had to think hard, believe me. I needed to get away, but I didn't want to answer any questions. Why wouldn't I introduce you to my fiancé? Why would we go off on a secret honeymoon?

"Then it came to me. An attorney. They're slick. Secretive. No one would question their plans. You didn't. I'd met Mr. Babcock when I worked at Saffron Blue. His reputation said he was the kind of guy who might insist on a secret honeymoon."

"I bought your story." Whitney went on to

explain how Ryan's sudden reappearance in her life with the property agreement led to her visiting the attorney.

"That's how I discovered you'd vanished."

"I'm sorry. I would have trusted you with my secret, but we hadn't been close. I thought —"

"Were you ever going to come back?" Whitney asked, raw emotion underscoring every word. "Were you going to tell me?"

Miranda stopped and slid one arm around Whitney's shoulders. "Of course. I was going to return and tell you everything."

"When?"

"I was going to call you — and not tell you where I was — next week. I thought the men might show up around that time. I was going to warn you, but I wasn't going to tell you enough to get you hurt." Miranda dropped her arm and gazed off across the wine-dark sea into the night. "I'm not sure when I was going to come home. Not for a year or more." She put her hand on her tummy. "I have to protect my — our — baby."

Whitney tried to see life through her cousin's eyes. The man she loved had died, ruthless killers were after her and she was pregnant. "Look, I can't change the past. But I can promise to be a better cousin."

"We should be like sisters," Miranda said, the threat of tears unexpectedly surfacing in her voice.

Whitney hugged Miranda. "You're right, we should be as close as sisters. I tried when you came to live with —"

"I know. You were so sweet. All I did was push you away. I didn't realize it at the time." She dug a bare toe into the wet sand. "I've been alone so much recently that I've had plenty of time to think. I'm sure I pulled into a shell of sorts after my parents were killed. I didn't want to risk getting close, then losing someone else. Still, I did feel close to you. Then you went off to college."

"And disappeared from your life."

"You visited when your mother was alive."

"I'm sorry," Whitney said. She meant it, but "sorry," like "love," was an overused word. But right now she couldn't think of any better way to express herself. "I'll do better. I want to be with you when the baby is born."

"No. If they haven't followed you down here already, those men are sure to find me if you keep visiting. The only way I'll be safe is if you leave me alone."

"But I don't want you to go through labor all by yourself in a strange country."

"There's an American hospital in Cancún. I'll go there. Don't worry."

"I am worried," Whitney protested. "I want to be with you. I —"

"They'll kill me if they find me." Miranda tried for a smile. "I'll come back when it's safe. Until then, the only way you can help is to leave. Don't call. Don't do anything that might lead them to me. I need you to promise me — for the baby."

CHAPTER THIRTY-FIVE

Adam sat in the crowded air terminal in Cancún. It was the off-season, but you wouldn't know it by the gaggles of tourists sporting lobster-red burns and toting bags filled with *Bye-Bye Cancún* T-shirts and other souvenirs.

"Miranda will be fine," he assured Whitney.

She was sitting beside him, her feet resting on the small overnight case he'd found in his uncle's closet and had given her for the trip. She'd been quiet, preoccupied since they'd left Miranda's villa. When he'd discovered nothing on his uncle's computer by morning, he insisted on taking the next flight home.

"I'm coming to stay with Miranda just as soon as those men are found. I don't want to put her in danger, but I don't want her to be alone when she delivers."

Adam patted the leather case that held his

uncle's laptop and computer software. "The answer's here. None of us knows how to find it but Quinten Foley will have computer experts. Foley will bag those terrorists. Then Miranda can return home."

"Let's hope so."

Adam silently reminded himself to contact Samantha Waterson tomorrow and have her stop the special toxicology test on his uncle's liver tissues. At least now he had peace of mind. Calvin Hunter had not been murdered.

"I'm surprised that those men want to kill Miranda just because she can identify them. Most terrorists seem thrilled to get their pictures on the evening news. So what if she ID'd them?"

Adam glanced around quickly. No one seemed to be paying attention to them, but he kept his voice low. "These guys obviously plan to use my uncle's contacts and shipping routes. This is a no-brainer for them — if they keep quiet and don't call attention to themselves. Miranda's a weak link."

"That makes sense. But why kill her before they get the disc with the info?"

"Good question. I assumed they had gotten it when this baby —" he patted the laptop "— disappeared. But as I was searching through the files on my uncle's computer last night, I decided he may have given them a phony disc. He just didn't tell Miranda — or maybe he died before he had the chance to explain it to her."

"Why would he do that?"

"To fool them into thinking they had the info they needed. He could have been buying additional time. When they discovered the disc was a fake, he would have disappeared."

"Maybe," Whitney replied, but she didn't sound convinced.

They sat in silence for a few minutes. Whitney seemed withdrawn to Adam. Evidently finding her cousin and learning Miranda was pregnant had a profound impact on Whitney.

"I'm going to see if I can buy a magazine." He rose, hefted the laptop over his shoulder and headed toward the small gift shop.

A few minutes later, he stepped out of the shop with a *Time* magazine tucked into the side pocket of the laptop case. He scanned the room to see if anyone was following them, but he didn't spot anybody. Whitney was talking on her cell phone when he returned and sat down beside her. Cell service down here was iffy at best. Whitney had tried to call the woman who'd taken over her dogs but hadn't been able to get through.

"Anything happening?" he asked when she shut her cell phone and dropped it into her purse. "Are Jasper and Lexi okay?"

"They're fine," Whitney replied in a tight voice.

"What's the matter?"

"Nothing. Lyleen Foster seems to be doing a great job with the dogs. I had a message from Trish. Remember the friend of hers who needed a house-sitter?"

Adam recalled Whitney mentioning it. The fine hairs on the back of his neck prickled. "What about him?"

"He's left town. Trish told him I would house-sit."

He didn't like the thought of Whitney staying anywhere but with him. He could tell himself that he wanted her around until they settled this mess with her cousin and the disc — but that wasn't the reason. He cared about her. He wanted Whitney to become part of his life.

"I'm supposed to move in as soon as I get back."

A flare of anger hit him. "You decided all this without talking to me?"

She jerked sideways to face him squarely. "You haven't bothered to consult with me."

"What are you talking about?" he asked,

although he had the sneaking suspicion he knew. He'd noticed the grim expression on her face at several points during the conversation with Miranda.

"Don't pretend you don't know! All that talk about Miranda and your uncle. Why didn't you tell me?"

He put his finger to his lips to indicate they should keep their voices low. "It didn't involve you, and I didn't want to worry you."

"I was already worried," she hissed at him, but lowered her voice. "I had the right to know but you didn't see fit to confide in me."

He couldn't deny it. There had been more going on than he'd permitted Whitney to learn. He hadn't wanted to upset her any more or he would have told her that night.

"I'm sorry," he said. "I should have told you. It won't happen again."

"Is there anything else I should know about?"

Aw hell, he cursed silently. Why had he listened to that overbuffed jock? He should have told her that Ashley had been responsible for Lexi's disappearance. "Lexi didn't wander off."

Whitney sat up straighter. "She didn't? What happened?"

"Ashley convinced her personal trainer — Preston Block, the guy who returned Lexi — to take her. They planned to hold her for ransom until —"

"Ransom? How could Ashley possibly think I had any money? Didn't Ryan tell her the truth about our divorce?"

"I assume he did. They wanted you to sign the property agreement immediately. There was a house Ashley really wanted, and your ex couldn't qualify for financing unless he could show he owned everything so he could arrange for a new loan."

"That bastard! How could he take Lexi and scare me like that?"

"Ryan had nothing to do with it. That's what Block told me, and I believe him. He claimed it was his idea. After our visit, Ryan guessed Ashley knew something and insisted she return the dog."

"Really?" She studied her hands for a moment. "I guess I underestimated Ryan." She shifted in her seat, thinking about Ashley and the clothes that had appeared after the fire. "No wonder Ashley brought me clothes. She isn't the sweet, innocent woman she pretends to be. She felt guilty for taking my dog. Why else would she have given me an expensive dress?"

Adam wasn't going there. He hadn't a

clue what went on in women's minds. "I suppose that's the reason, but who knows?"

"Her reasons don't matter. Why didn't you tell me? I don't get it."

Again Adam cursed himself. "I should have, but Block was persuasive. He said you wouldn't believe Ryan wasn't involved. You'd cause more trouble and Ashley wouldn't get her house. I liked you a lot — more than a lot. I decided you had your dog and it would be better to close the book on the past."

Adam waited a few agonizingly long minutes before switching the subject and asking, "What did you tell Trish?"

"Nothing. I could pick up my messages yet I can't seem to call out. But I intend to take the job."

"Why? If it's money —"

"It's not. I'm starting over. This is the time and the place. I'm going to become a vet. I'll need to split my time between working at the vet's and taking classes."

"You're saying there's no time for us?"

"I'm not sure there is an us. You haven't shared things with me. You should have told me about Lexi. Every time she was out of my sight, I worried. There wasn't any need. She's not going to run away because she never did in the first place."

"Would you feel this way if I'd told you about Lexi and my uncle?"

"It doesn't matter. I've learned you can't change the past, but you can do things differently so the future isn't a replay of the past. I'm not going to have much spare time. When I do, I intend to spend it with Miranda."

Adam opened his mouth to argue, then decided against it. Maybe a little distance wasn't such a bad idea. It would give them both time to think. It would also get Whitney away from the house. He was pretty sure the media coverage had made it clear that Miranda had been the object of the firebombing — and she was no longer living there. But it didn't hurt to be careful.

Whitney picked up what few clothes she had and moved to the address that Trish had left on the machine. She and Adam had exchanged less than a dozen sentences — all of them necessary — between Cancún and San Diego. He'd dropped her off at the mansion overlooking the ocean in La Jolla. He'd waited for her to find the hidden key and let herself in before leaving.

Whitney wandered around the home, telling herself that Adam had his pride. He wasn't going to beg her to stay with him.

Part of her wished things were different but another — wiser — part accepted the situation. She'd found her cousin and knew the truth about Lexi. Her life had a new direction now.

Time would tell if she and Adam had a future.

She heard the doorbell ring and knew it was Trish. She'd called her friend to say she was moving in, and Trish said she would meet her at the house to show her how everything worked.

Whitney opened the door and Trish breezed in, a happy smile lighting her face. "Where were you? I almost didn't tell Ian that you were going to take the house-sitting job. For all I knew you were gone forever."

Whitney followed her into the great room that overlooked the pool. In the distance the marine blue of the Pacific glittered in the midday sun. "Adam and I got away for a bit."

Trish arched one finely plucked eyebrow and smiled. Adam and Whitney had agreed not to reveal anything to anyone about their trip to Cancún. No one was to learn Miranda's whereabouts until this mess was straightened out.

"Sounds like fun," Trish said with a wink. Whitney half expected the older woman to warn her about treacherous men, but she didn't. "Ian Finsteter has an impressive collection of art."

Whitney had wandered through the new home and had noticed a number of paintings and fine sculptures on display. Knowing the owner of the home purchased art from Trish had told Whitney the collection was valuable.

"Ian usually has the alarm on with motion sensors. He left it off until you moved in and I gave you the code."

"What about Lexi? Won't she set off the motion sensors?"

Trish shook her head. "Not unless she moves one of the sculptures."

"Really? The motion sensors are under the pieces?" She glanced over to a postmodern sculpture of a ballerina gracefully pirouetting on one toe.

"Yes. It's state of the art. The alarm goes into a special security service that only takes extremely wealthy clients. They'll be here within three minutes if someone moves a piece of art and trips a motion sensor."

"Lexi won't touch a thing. I promise."

"Where is she?"

"With Lyleen, the woman taking over my pets. She's bringing Lexi here soon."

Trish opened the sliding glass door that

led out to the pool. "I met her. She seems . . . okay. Brandy's happy, that's all that counts."

Whitney wanted to remind her that Golden retrievers were easy to please and thought everyone was their friend. That was why Lexi had gone off with Ashley's personal trainer. But she didn't open her mouth. Why alienate Trish when she'd gone out of her way to help her?

"Isn't this fabulous?" Trish waved her arm to indicate the pool. Off to the side was a large polished black rock precariously balanced on a much smaller rock. "Don't touch *Obsidian I*. It's a priceless sculpture by Diego Rameriz, the Spanish sculptor who died recently."

"Is it protected by a motion sensor?"

"Of course." Trish led her closer until Whitney could see her own distorted reflection on the glossy-black surface of the sculpture.

"I better keep Lexi away from this."

Trish patted the rock. "She'd have to jump on it to trigger the alarm. The sensors are designed to stop thieves from stealing the art. They're not so sensitive that a maid dusting them will cause a problem. You would need to knock this off its base to activate the alarm. Lexi doesn't strike me as the type of dog to cause problems. That's what I told Ian when I explained this fabulous house-sitter came with a dog."

"Thanks. We'll both be very careful."

They went through the magnificent home and Trish showed her what needed to be taken care of and how to do it. Whitney explained why she'd decided to work for the vet even though Trish hadn't inquired, which seemed odd.

"Smart move," Trish told her when Whitney finished. "I was in my later thirties before I opened my gallery and found my calling."

Whitney could have reminded Trish that she'd had a wealthy family backing her, but she didn't. Despite having money Trish had suffered a lot.

"What are you doing for a car?" Trish asked.

"Tomorrow I'm contacting the insurance company to see what they can do."

"You're welcome to use Ravissant's minivan. I won't need it for a few days."

"That's great. I really appreciate it."

They were standing in the opulent master bedroom — all white silk with sterling accent pieces — and admiring the ocean that stretched in an endless sweep of blue toward the distant horizon. Sometimes the beauty of nature overwhelmed Whitney, making her life, her troubles seem small.

"Hear anything from Miranda?" Trish unexpectedly asked.

How could Whitney lie to a friend who'd helped her so much? She evaded by saying, "I'm hoping she'll be back soon."

"Rod's really curious why she used his name."

The second the words were out of Trish's mouth, Whitney got the picture. Trish was interested in the attorney.

"I'm sure you and I are the only ones Miranda told. Rod won't have to explain all over town."

"Rod's not worried," Trish assured her. "Just curious."

Now Whitney had the complete picture. Trish wasn't just interested in the man from afar; they must be involved. Great, she decided. Trish had let the past haunt her for too long. It was nice to know her friend had found someone to care about.

"Rod's been trying to reach you," Trish added. "I tried to help him by calling your ex —"

"You didn't!"

"I did," Trish replied defensively. "Only because Rod needs to reach you. He's desperate to talk to you."

"About what?"

"He didn't tell me. You know how lawyers are. He flew to San Francisco this morning."

"It must be about the property agreement. I'm ready to sign it and have Ryan out of my life."

This was a new start, Whitney reminded herself. As soon as she signed those papers, her life would head in a new direction.

So why wasn't she happier?

CHAPTER
THIRTY-SIX

It was late afternoon by the time Lyleen dropped off Lexi. Her dog was excited to see Whitney, but not nearly as excited as Jasper. The crested kept spinning in circles and yipping. Whitney realized she was going to miss Jasper. He had his quirks but he was a lovable dog. She would miss Adam, too, but she tamped that thought down.

The fiftyish woman had a nest of gray curls covering the crown of her head, but the rest was buzzed from ear to ear and along the back of her neck. Lyleen seemed a little intense to Whitney, but very competent. As Trish had said, the most important thing was the dogs liked her.

"I tried to reach Mr. Hunter but he's not home," the woman told her. "You said Jasper was skittish, and I knew Lexi had gotten out. Do you think I should leave such a valuable dog in the side yard?"

"No. Let him stay with me tonight. I'll

have Adam set up an appointment with you. He needs to explain Jasper's schedule and show you the dog's special hiding places, like under the coffee table."

"All right. I'll ring him again."

They said goodbye and Whitney went over to the telephone in the media room just off the entry. Jasper and Lexi were at her heels. She remembered she didn't have food for either one of them. She needed to make a quick run to the supermarket, but first she wanted to call Ryan.

"Ryan, it's me."

"Where are you?" He sounded upset.

"I'm house-sitting for a friend of Trish Bowrather's."

"Where?"

She hesitated. Adam had warned her to keep her whereabouts secret if possible. The killers after Miranda probably realized her cousin no longer lived in the cottage, but it paid to be careful. Also, after the way Ryan had shaken her to bully her into signing the papers, Whitney wasn't sure she wanted him to pay her another visit.

"Where are you?" Ryan repeated.

"Why?"

"Trish Bowrather called here looking for you." Something new entered his voice. Harder, more judgmental. "I didn't know where you were."

She wanted to tell him, *There's no reason why you should.* Then she reminded herself that she was starting over. The past was behind her forever.

There was no reason not to tell her ex where she was living. After all, they'd been married. It would take some time before people stopped contacting Ryan when they wanted to find her.

"I'll be at 211 Ocean Vista for the next few months."

"That's a pretty swank neighborhood."

Trust Ryan to recognize a prestigious address. Whitney let the comment pass. "I want to thank you for making Ashley return Lexi. I realize her disappearance wasn't your fault." She waited but Ryan didn't respond. "My attorney's in San Francisco. He'll be back tomorrow. I'll sign the papers and get out of your life."

A grinding silence greeted her words. She finally asked, "Is Ashley there?"

"Why?" he snapped.

"I wanted to tell her that she's lucky I didn't file stolen-property charges against her. Lexi's a valuable dog. If Ashley comes near —"

"She's out." He slammed down the receiver.

Whitney hung up, a little annoyed with herself for being so peevish. Ashley had returned the dog. Why threaten her? She put the dogs in the minivan Ravissant Gallery used to deliver paintings. They had so much room that they started to play in the back.

"Settle down," she called over her shoulder.

She was on her way to the market when she decided to drop by the veterinarian's office and use the computer to update Lexi's chip. She wasn't due to start working until next week but maybe if she told them she was available she could start sooner. Heaven knew she could use the money. She was going to have to charge groceries and dog food.

"We're closing in ten minutes," the woman told Whitney when she walked through the door with both dogs on leashes.

Whitney explained she was going to be the new assistant, and the receptionist looked relieved not to have two sick dogs just before they closed at six.

"I don't have a computer at home." Whitney walked behind the counter to the computer. "I need to update Lexi's chip info."

"Go ahead, but did you know it can be

done over the telephone?"

"Really?" Whitney responded as if she didn't know. She'd hoped to see one of the doctors and let them know she would like to work immediately. "Where is everyone?" Whitney casually asked as she logged onto the system and typed in the Web address for Pet Locate.

"They're at a Neuticles demo."

"What's that?" A small charge of excitement buzzed through her body. She hadn't had much sleep last night — just a short nap on Miranda's sofa and another quick nap on the plane. She was exhausted and looking forward to climbing into the white silk bed, but hearing about advances in veterinary medicine interested her.

"Testicular implants."

"No way!"

"I'm not kidding," the receptionist assured her. "Lots of people want their dogs — you know — unable to reproduce, but they don't like the look."

"Oh my gosh. It sounds painful and totally unnecessary."

The woman giggled. "I doubt if Dr. Robinson will be doing them, but she went to see what all the fuss was about."

Whitney changed Lexi's contact information to reflect the new address where Whitney was house-sitting and gave that phone number in addition to her cell. Lexi hadn't wandered off, but why take chances?

While she was at it she checked to be sure Adam had updated Jasper's information after his uncle's death. The pets were listed under the owner's name but nothing came up for Calvin Hunter. Pet Locate was the main chip database, but Whitney knew at least one other company was now providing the service.

"Isn't there another chip service?" she asked.

"Sure. PetFinders.com. It's bookmarked at the top of the screen."

Whitney quickly located the database. Calvin Hunter's name did not appear. "That's strange," she said, thinking out loud.

"Don't you remember what service you used?" asked the receptionist.

"I've updated my dog's information, but I wanted to change Jasper's." She pointed to her feet, where Jasper was wagging his tail at the sound of his name. "His owner died, so the info has to be changed. He's an international champion but I can't find his late owner's name in either chip database."

"A champion? Really?" The woman smiled at Jasper but shook her head.

"Yep. Best in show at Frankfurt."

"The breeder probably listed him. That's what usually happens."

"You're right. I'll have to check his file and get the breeder's name." Secretly she was thrilled to have another reason to talk to Adam. There was no excuse for what he'd done but something in her longed to forgive him.

"Good night," she told the receptionist. "I'll be starting next week, but if I'm needed sooner, I can come in. Would you tell —"

"Could you work for me?" The woman almost shouted the question. "My husband's company's sending him on a trip to Hawaii. I can't go unless I can find someone to work —"

"I'll do it."

"Oh, great. I owe you one. Come in tomorrow for an hour or so and I'll show you what to do." Whitney happily agreed and was halfway back to the minivan when it hit her.

The Chip.

Calvin Hunter had used dog shows as a cover for his arms deals. Could he have somehow transferred the information from a regular computer disc to a microchip? She knew the technology was there. Adam's uncle had once been in naval intelligence.

Surely he knew how to do it. That would account for the skin irritation that appeared on Jasper's neck *after* he won at Frankfurt.

She rushed back inside. "Let me use the wand for a moment."

The receptionist was turning off lights, but she cheerily replied, "Go ahead. It's in the drawer in room two. Do you know how to use it?"

"Yes." With both dogs in tow, Whitney dashed into the room and found the wand. She had no idea why they called the electronic device the size of a pack of cigarettes a wand, but everyone did. It was a simple mechanism with an on/off switch and an LCD display where the number on the chip inserted behind the pet's ear came up.

She hoisted Jasper onto the examining table. Lexi wagged her tail as if expecting to be lifted up, too. Whitney switched on the wand and brushed it across the small bump on the back of Jasper's neck.

Letters flashed across the LCD screen. A name — not a number. The chip was supposed to show a number. That number, when put into the chip center's database, should yield owner information like the pet owner's address and phone number. She stared at the screen, not quite believing what she was seeing, although she'd suspected she might discover something like this.

She switched off the wand, replaced it in the drawer. Her insides jangled with excitement. She carefully lifted Jasper off the table. *How cruel,* she thought. Chipping a dog didn't hurt the pet, but imagining Jasper needlessly being jabbed with a needle upset her.

"You're not just worth thousands," she told Jasper. "You're worth millions."

The little dog licked her nose.

Adam sat across the desk from Quinten Foley in the older man's home. It had taken Adam the better part of the afternoon to locate Foley. He'd been on the golf course with his cell phone off. He'd told Foley that he had Calvin Hunter's laptop and software discs.

Foley leaned back in his chair and studied Adam. "So, Miranda Marshall is in Cancún. She had the computer all along."

Adam didn't respond, but he gave Foley credit. He must have had them followed. "She's long gone now," Adam said to protect Miranda. "She gave me his computer. It's going to take an expert to find the information."

"You tried?"

"Yes, but I'm just your average guy. No expert. I figure it's embedded somewhere. In Iraq the guys showed me how to access porn sites. Go to a seemingly innocent site and click on some part of the picture that comes up. Bam! A screen concealed behind the picture appears. Give your password — and if you've paid your money, you're into an orgy of porn."

"Exactly. Kiddie porn is often accessed by clicking on a chicken in a barnyard scene. Chicken-hawkers love the irony." Foley leaned forward and put both elbows on his desk. "You think Cal hid information like that?"

"Must be. I can't find any sign of it. Maybe if your guys —"

"I'll see if I can locate someone to —"

Adam shoved the laptop in the case with the software programs across the desk. "Don't bother to bullshit me. We haven't got the time. I know you work at the Pentagon. CIA?"

"No," Foley replied after an emotion-charged silence. "I'm with a special unit of Homeland Security."

Adam didn't have a whole lot of faith in Homeland Security but hey, maybe it was just him. Right now, he didn't have anyone else to turn to but Foley. Adam didn't even know if the terrorists had a phony disc and would return — mad as hell — for the real one. He assumed that was what would happen — but who knew.

"Operatives are expecting to pick up the disc with the info on it next week," he informed Foley. "We're not sure if they realize my uncle is dead or not. Even if they do, they're planning to wire transfer a shit-load of money. I'm betting they'll show, expecting Miranda to deliver the disc."

"Why would they think she —"

"Miranda met them at my uncle's home. He convinced them that she was his partner."

Foley unzipped the computer case and ran his hand lovingly over the lid of the laptop. "This is a chance to catch them."

"Absolutely. But we'd better have something to give them. These aren't just couriers. They're high-ranking terrorists. I'm sure they'll have a laptop with them to scan the disc to make certain they have what they paid for."

"You're right. We're going to need Miranda here. Can you —"

A thunderous banging on the front door interrupted Foley. Adam instinctively grabbed the computer case, zipped it shut and hid it between the desk and the wall.

"I'll get rid of whoever it is. Probably Jehovah's Witnesses. They've been working the neighborhood."

Adam heard the front door open followed by the sound of Tyler's voice. "What's Adam doing here?" Tyler asked in a belligerent tone.

Quinten Foley responded, "We're discussing his uncle's estate."

The sound of footsteps meant they were coming toward the office. Adam stood up and tried for a welcoming smile. His brain kept insisting: *There's no time to waste.* "Hey, Tyler, how's it going?"

Beside his partner stood Holly. Adam hadn't seen her for nearly three years, but she was still as pretty as ever. Long shiny brown hair, sparkling amber eyes. "Holly, you're looking great."

"Hello, Adam," she replied with the warm smile he remembered so well. "It's good to see you."

"Trust me, I'm happy to be back in the States." He smiled at her but made sure he also smiled at Tyler. Adam didn't want his best friend to think he was hitting on his girl.

A troubling silence followed. Adam looked at Quinten Foley, who was now behind his desk again. The older man didn't seem inclined to say much.

"We didn't mean to interrupt," Tyler said, his voice tight. "But I have something to say to my father."

"I'll go in the other room," offered Adam. Normally, he would have left the house, but every minute counted.

"Don't bother. This isn't secret stuff." Tyler faced his father. "Holly is very upset with me. She thinks I don't love her because I don't make any effort to have my family get to know her."

Adam shifted uncomfortably. This sounded a helluva lot more personal than he'd anticipated.

"Th-that's not true," Quinten Foley awkwardly replied.

"Holly's family is one of those close-knit groups. They spend time together and expect to get to know their daughter's boyfriend." Tyler gazed at Holly, and she smiled back. Adam could see they loved each other. He couldn't help thinking about Whitney. Aw, hell. Despite the short length of time he'd known Whitney, Adam realized he loved her. But he'd royally blown it.

"I explained to Holly that we aren't close," Tyler told his father, unable to conceal his bitterness. "I hardly know you. We never see each other even when you're in town. Isn't that right?"

His father responded without a trace of regret or concern. "I'm a busy —"

"He's always been too busy for me," Tyler said to Holly. "Even after my mother killed herself, he didn't have a second to spare for his only child. I was shuttled off to military school."

"That's not fair. I —"

"It doesn't matter. I've learned to live with it. I just wanted Holly to understand our family. Not asking her to spend time with you isn't a reflection on her. It's about us." Tyler was on the verge of shouting now, but he couldn't help himself. Years of pent-up anger exploded out of him. He felt Holly's restraining hand on his arm and lowered his voice. "Holly can't expect to get to know you when I don't."

In the bruising silence that followed Tyler stared at his father. Until this morning, when he'd confronted Holly, half expecting her to tell him that she wanted to end their relationship, Tyler had believed money was keeping them apart. She'd made him realize his mistake.

The old saying about money not buying you love was true. Holly cared about him and had since they began dating — when he'd had nothing but prospects. His father could take his money and rot in hell for all he cared. The company he had started with Adam was off to an awesome start. He wanted to look back and know he'd built it on his own. He wanted Holly to understand that he was a man she could be proud of.

"I don't need you," Tyler told his father as he slipped his arm around Holly and pulled her against his side. "But I need Holly. If she'll have me —" he turned his attention to Holly "— I want to marry her."

"Oh my gosh!" cried Holly. "You want to get married?"

"Of course." What did she think their discussion this morning had been about? True, he'd asked her where she'd been, and she said she'd gone to Newport Beach to visit her parents. But he'd asked what was wrong and she'd told him that she didn't think he was serious about her because he'd never allowed her to get to know his family.

"You never mentioned marriage," Holly said softly.

"Hey! That's great." Adam slapped him on the back. "Holly's a great gal. The best, and you're the best friend a guy could have. You deserve to be happy." He smiled at Holly. "Both of you."

"Maybe we ought to go somewhere and

talk about this," Holly suggested in a high-pitched, excited voice.

"You're right. Let's get outta here." Tyler couldn't keep the excitement out of his own voice. As angry as he'd been a few minutes ago, now he was happier than he could ever remember being.

Adam watched them leave, his mind on Whitney. He was thrilled for his friend and knew things would work out. What he needed to do was tell Whitney he loved her. Admit he'd made a huge mistake by not trusting her with more information about his uncle and an even worse mistake by not telling her the truth about Lexi. Then he'd tell her how much he loved her. True, they hadn't known each other long, but he was positive about his feelings.

"Where were we?" Quinten Foley asked, as if nothing important had happened.

Foley was a tough man focused on his career. A lot like his uncle, Adam guessed. Too late, Calvin Hunter had found someone to love and had realized he wanted a life.

"You know, I had a close relationship with my father. Not a day goes by that I don't miss him."

Foley nodded, but Adam had the feeling the man was just humoring him. He wouldn't have bothered except he could see how upset Tyler was by his father's attitude. Even with Holly's love there would be a void in Tyler's life unless his father had an attitude adjustment.

"My uncle found someone to love but he died before he could enjoy life with her. My own father died at an early age." Adam watched Foley's eyes narrow slightly. The man was listening, but it was impossible to tell if Adam's words were having any impact. "I was almost killed in Iraq. Both guys beside me died, but by some miracle I lived. I know what's important in life — and it isn't money."

"I have a job, duty —"

"Is that all you're living for?"

"Of course not," Foley assured him.

"You made a lot of money off the arms sales. Money must mean —"

"I was working undercover for the government the whole time. I never made a dime beyond my salary."

Shock thrummed through Adam's brain. From what Miranda had said, Adam had gathered Foley was a government agent and one trusted by his uncle. But Adam believed Quinten Foley had made a ton of money dealing arms on the side. It was difficult to believe the man hadn't profited from selling contraband weapons.

"I did it all for my country," Foley said.

Kicking himself for assuming the worst, Adam asked, "What about Tyler?"

Foley's world-weary eyes were tempered by a face that revealed no emotion nor gave any hint of his inner thoughts. The older man seemed to consider the question for a long moment as if he had to come to grips with it. "I care about my son, sure. I loved his mother —" Foley turned away and walked to the window overlooking the swimming pool. In a very soft voice that bordered on a whisper, he added, "I didn't just love Claire. I worshipped her. When she killed herself, I couldn't bear to look at Tyler." He turned back to Adam. "He has her eyes, you know, her animated smile."

Adam felt a pang of sympathy. "My dad loved my mother. I look a lot like her, but he didn't give up on me." This was stretching the truth a bit. He did have his mother's hair but he looked more like his father. He was willing to fudge a little, if it could help his friend. "I am what I am — because he loved me."

"I never understood why Claire killed herself. She seemed a little depressed because we moved so often. I —"

"That was years ago. What about Tyler?

Would your wife want you to treat him like this?"

"She loved Tyler. Her suicide note said, 'Love him for me.' I just couldn't — still can't — be around him without thinking of her."

"Get over it. Life goes on. I'm betting Tyler and Holly get married soon and have children. Don't you want to be part of their lives?"

"Yes, but I'm not sure I know how to act. I guess I could try. Invite them to dinner or something."

"That's a start." Adam reached over and picked up the telephone. He dialed Tyler's cell number, then handed Quinten Foley the receiver.

CHAPTER
THIRTY-SEVEN

Whitney climbed the stairs to the white silk bedroom overlooking the ocean. The sun had dropped into the sea, leaving behind a faint glow of tangerine light that would quickly be consumed by darkness. She was dead tired but she didn't want to go to sleep until she'd spoken to Adam. As soon as she left the vet's, she'd tried to call him, but his cell phone's voice mail immediately picked up.

She'd swung by Calvin Hunter's home, thinking Adam might have shut off his phone and gone to bed early. He had to be even more tired than she was. He'd worked while she'd napped on Miranda's sofa.

Adam hadn't been there. She left him notes in several places so he couldn't miss the message. She'd been afraid to put in writing what she found. The notes said to call her — it was an emergency.

Whitney could have left Jasper there for

Adam, but she told him in each note that she had the dog. She doubted anyone else knew the Chinese crested was carrying such valuable information, but she wasn't taking any chances. Jasper was safer with her.

Earlier she'd deposited two soft-sided suitcases containing her clothes just outside the double walk-in closets in the master bedroom. Jasper and Lexi followed her when she inspected the closets and found one was empty. She placed her suitcases on the floor inside the empty closet, but didn't have the energy to unpack what little she had.

Whitney thought a dip in the pool might refresh her and keep her awake until Adam called. She put on the swimsuit she'd hurriedly bought to go to Cancún and had never worn. She smiled inwardly, remembering the man from Adam's security company. Adam had insisted the man should go along to guard her. He'd been more than a little embarrassed to be hanging around Skinny Dip while she tried on suits.

Now that she looked back on it, Whitney decided she was stronger than she sometimes believed. Instinct had launched her at the fence. That quick action had saved her life. She shouldn't have allowed the incident to cause an emotional meltdown. After the way she'd freaked out, no wonder Adam hadn't wanted to tell her about his uncle. She could almost forgive him.

Almost.

If only he'd revealed Ashley's part in Lexi's disappearance, Whitney might have been more forgiving. But he hadn't. It said a lot about his character, she reminded herself. It told her even more about their relationship.

"Come on, gang," she said to Jasper and Lexi. "It's chow time."

They scampered behind her as she went down the sweeping staircase. After stopping to leave the notes for Adam, she'd swung by the supermarket and charged some necessities. While the dogs ate, she unpacked the groceries and put them away.

Inside the walk-in pantry, she froze. What was that? It sounded like a thump. The nearest house was too far for her to hear anything. She listened, attempting to detect something else over the crunching sounds of the dogs eating. Her hand shook when she eased the pantry door back so she could have a better look. She peeked out and saw the dogs with their noses in the fancy dishes that she was using for their bowls. Obviously, they hadn't heard a thing.

What a sniveling display of shredded nerves

you are.

Every house had its own special sounds, she assured herself. She would just have to get used to this one. She could put on the alarm, but Adam might drop by without calling. She scribbled a note, saying she was in the pool, and taped it to the front door.

When she returned to the kitchen, the dogs had finished eating. "Come on," she told them, and they followed her out to the pool. Since the area was new to them, the dogs engaged in a sniff-fest. By the way they were hovering around the low-hanging bushes, Whitney guessed another dog had been out here recently.

"Stay away from the rock," Whitney told Lexi even though the dog wasn't anywhere near the obsidian sculpture.

It was dark now and the lights around the pool unexpectedly snapped on. Her limbs locked in place. Fortunately for Whitney, her brain was still functioning. The lights must be on an automatic timer.

Dozens of low-voltage exterior lights now artfully highlighted the plants and the house. Brighter lights on the rafters of the open-air overhang were aimed at the water. Like most pools, this one had a light at the bottom of the deep end. The rest of the yard was dark shadows.

When would she get over being so jumpy? she asked herself. A disturbing chill enveloped her. There was cause for concern. Calvin Hunter had gone to a lot of trouble to hide the information on a microchip and plant it under his dog's skin. But the people after the info didn't know Jasper had it — and couldn't possibly find her if they did.

What she was experiencing was the psychological aftershock of the fire followed by the scare with the car. *Get a grip!* Taking a deep, calming breath, she tamped down the wave of anxiety. If she didn't confront her fears, they would get the better of her.

She had a toe in the water when she remembered her cell phone was on the counter in the kitchen. Adam had the number of this house, but he might call her on the cell. She went inside and retrieved it. Returning to the pool area where the dogs were waiting, tails wagging, she again had the eerie sensation someone was watching her.

Get over it.

She put the cell phone down on a small table near the middle of the pool where she could get to it easily no matter where she was in the water. Lexi barked excitedly. Whitney whirled around and saw a big dark shadow blocking the light. A man.

The hulking shape moved and the lights trained on the pool hit her in the eyes, blinding her for a moment. He walked closer and a scream almost ripped from her throat. In the next breath, she realized it was Ryan. Whitney released a pent-up sigh of relief.

Ryan was dressed in a polo shirt, pressed jeans and a lightweight bomber-style jacket. As always he wore loafers that could have passed for new. Lexi scampered up to him, but Jasper scooted under a chaise.

"Ryan, what are you doing here?"

He looked around the dark yard. "Have you seen Ashley?"

"N-no, of course not." His question surprised her. Why on earth would he think Ashley was here?

Ryan walked closer and Whitney instinctively backed up, but not too far. She was already near the edge of the pool.

"Have you heard from her?"

She'd lived with this man long enough to recognize stress and anxiety in his overwrought voice. "No. Why would she call me?"

"To explain about the clothes."

She didn't like what she saw in his eyes. Something had happened with Ashley and he clearly blamed her.

"She's not here, and I have no idea where she is." In her toughest voice, she added, "You'd better leave now."

"I will." He ground out the words. "But your nine lives are up."

His unanticipated anger directed at her was like a slap in the face. "What do you mean?"

"You'll see."

Now there was a deadly calm about him, in spite of the lethal tone of voice. Whitney suddenly became disturbingly aware of her situation. She was standing — as good as naked — at the edge of the pool without a weapon of any kind. She didn't need a weapon, Whitney told herself. She was panicking again for no good reason. She'd been married to this man. "Ryan, what's wrong?"

His eyes narrowed, bore into her. "Get in the pool. Start swimming."

"What? You're not making sense." Was he on something? she wondered.

Unexpectedly, both his hands slammed into her shoulders and shoved her backward. She hit the pool with a startled cry and sucked a mouthful of water into her lungs. She surfaced, gagging and struggling to get her breath in spastic gasps. Treading water and coughing, she looked up at her former husband looming above her.

She'd never seen Ryan this angry, this out of control. Suddenly all the years she'd put up with his antics infuriated her. What had she been thinking? This man was nothing but a self-centered egomaniac. Evidently, the beauty queen had seen the light and left him. It must have sent him over some psychological edge into lunacy.

"Start swimming, Whitney."

She sputtered, still unable to catch her breath, her throat burning from the chlorine in the pool. Finally she managed to ask, "Why? What's going on?"

He didn't answer and that sent a fresh surge of panic through her. She tried to touch bottom with the tips of her toes, but it was too deep. She took a few quick strokes to the edge of the pool near Ryan's feet. She grasped the rim of the pool with both hands.

"What's wrong with you?" she asked.

"Nothing you can't fix."

Whitney laughed — more of a cackle really. Once she would have walked on water to "fix" any of this man's problems. "I'm not interested in fixing a damn thing."

Whitney dipped under the water and swam to the shallow end where she could walk out. She surfaced, stood up, flung her head back and swept her wet hair out of her eyes. Ryan had beaten her to the shallow end. He stood there pointing a gun fitted with a silencer at her.

It took a second to absorb what she was seeing. Where had he gotten the gun? He'd never had one when they'd been together. He didn't know how to use it, did he? Doubts clouded her thoughts. The gambling. There was a lot about this man she'd never known. Often the craziest people appeared sane, she reminded herself.

"This can go one of two ways," Ryan said with unexpected savagery. "You can swim until you're too exhausted to take another stroke . . . and drown . . . or I can shoot you."

This had to be a sick prank, didn't it? That hope flared, then died when she assessed the hatred gleaming in Ryan's eyes and noted the deadly weapon in his hand. This was no joke. "Why?" she managed to ask. "I had no idea Ashley had left me those clothes. It was just an accident that I was wearing the dress —"

"Shut up. Leave Ashley out of this." He waved the gun and the blue metal caught the light. "Start swimming or I'll shoot."

"If I'm going to die, I have a right to know the reason."

For an instant, his eyes squeezed shut, then opened. He gazed at her as if seeing her for the very first time. "My, ah . . . friends tried to get rid of you. But you weren't home when you should have been. All the pipe bomb did was start a fire."

Her lower lip trembled as his words registered. Oh my God! They'd been after her — not Miranda. Whitney hadn't quite accepted Adam's explanation that Calvin Hunter had given the terrorists a fake disc. She assumed that believing they had the real one, they'd tried to kill Miranda. Now she knew why that scenario didn't make sense. And she realized why she'd been so panicky. Her sixth sense kept warning that she was in danger.

"Why would they want to kill me? I never harmed anyone."

"No, but you can be very clever when necessary. You climbed that fence in the nick of time, didn't you?"

His attempt at a laugh raised every hair on her body. A thousand thoughts whirlpooled through her brain as she realized that she'd come close to death twice already. This time might be the end — if she didn't keep her wits and turn the tables somehow. *Don't panic, don't freeze up. Not now.*

Adam's face appeared in her mind. Suddenly, she felt silly for putting up such a fuss over things he hadn't told her. He'd believed her, taken so much on faith even though he'd just met her. If she hadn't suffered through so many lies with Ryan, she might have been more understanding. Now she might never have the chance to tell Adam she loved him.

"I'll stay out of your life, Ryan. I swear I will."

"If you'd signed the property agreement, you would have been history and none of this would have happened."

Was this about the property settlement? He must owe a lot more money than Rod Babcock had told her. "I'll sign tomorrow when my lawyer returns. He has the papers."

"No, you won't. Babcock already called me. He knows the truth." Ryan shifted the gun from one hand to the other and back. "There's no toxic landfill. There never was. That land might as well have oil underneath it."

"What do you mean?" *Stay calm,* she reminded herself. *And think.*

"It's not far from the Indians' casino. They're expanding, putting in a bigger hotel and a second casino that will dwarf every other casino in the state. With you gone, the land belongs to me."

You're a fool, she silently raged at herself. Why hadn't she changed her will? How stupid could she be? "I'll sign it over to you."

"Too late. At the end of this week, the proposal comes up for approval by the county commission. The Indians need to have all the deeds in order. Your hotshot lawyer will talk you out of signing unless I promise you a bundle of money." He pointed the gun directly at her head. "This changes everything."

"You'll never get away with it. The police will know —"

"An accidental drowning? I don't think so."

"Then I'm not swimming. You'll have to shoot me."

"Suit yourself. It'll look like a burglar killed you."

"No, it won't." The soft voice cracked out of the darkness behind Ryan.

He spun around. "Ashley, what are you doing here?"

Well, this beats all, Whitney decided in frantic amazement. The situation could *not* become weirder. She watched the two of them stare at each other. Whitney couldn't just stand in waist-deep water. Already her legs were spongy, ready to give out.

Her first instinct was to bolt, to lunge

through the water, legs splashing, arms flailing as she prayed for good luck. She'd read somewhere that even the most highly trained sharpshooter had less than a fifty-fifty chance of hitting someone who was running in an erratic zig-zag pattern. She bet guns were new to Ryan. Except at point-blank range, he probably couldn't hit her.

Ashley hadn't responded to Ryan's question. After a moment's silence, he asked, "Where have you been?"

There was a desperate note in his voice, Whitney decided, almost a pleading tone. She realized he loved this woman in a way that he'd never loved her. Not that she cared, but she might be able to exploit the situation to save herself. She edged closer to the steps out of the pool, taking care not to disturb the water and call attention to her movements.

"I went to Bakersfield to see my father." A look of pure anguish washed over Ashley's face, then vanished so quickly that Whitney wondered if she'd imagined it. "He agreed to give me every cent he had to help us get out of debt. I also personally went to Domenic Coriz, but he didn't want money. He wants the land."

"Ashley, honey, get back in your car," Ryan responded in the unemotional tone of a therapist. "I'll explain it to you later."

"Don't treat me like a child! I've been following you. I overheard you threaten Whitney. I know what you're up to."

"I just want the best for both of us." His calm tone unnerved Whitney even more. He'd gone ballistic before; now he was psycho.

"Killing an innocent woman won't end your problems. You're addicted to gambling."

Whitney sidled nearer to the steps. Ryan hadn't turned away from her, but his attention was focused on Ashley. If only she could get out of the pool.

Ryan cleared his throat, then gave Ashley a small, anxious grin. "I'll get help tomorrow. I promise I will. Just wait in the car for me. Okay?"

"No."

Ryan blinked and hesitated before saying, "Look, if you'll just wait in the car for me, I swear I won't hurt Whitney. We just need to have a little talk."

Whitney's toe bumped the first of two — or was it three? — steps out of the pool. Ryan's smile expired when Ashley didn't budge.

"Liar! I'm not letting you hurt Whitney."

Without warning, Ashley lunged for

Ryan's arm in an attempt to knock the gun out of his hand. Ohmygod! At this close range, Ryan might kill her. Not taking a second to think, Whitney hurtled out of the pool and flung herself at them as they struggled over the gun. She saw her own hand lash out in a desperate grab for the weapon.

Face contorted, Ryan fought them with manic savagery. He was taller than both of them and had them outweighed. He still had control of the gun.

Whitney pounced on him, clinging to him with both arms and legs the way a drowning person would. She had a split second to decide what to do so she bit the exposed part of his neck.

Pop!

Something sounded like a firecracker, she realized. Swirling colored stars burst behind her eyes. Then darkness obliterated the bright lights.

CHAPTER
THIRTY-EIGHT

Adam was reading the note on the front door when he heard a scream. Gathering all his strength, he charged into the door, shoulder first. It hadn't been properly closed and burst open. He crashed into the entry, off balance, and stumbled sideways. He regained his footing, then raced through the crypt-dark house. He rounded the corner into a large room. Beyond it he saw a pool area.

Another muffled shout echoed through the dark night. He charged out the open sliding glass door and saw Whitney sprawled beside the pool. He sprinted to where Ashley Fordham was standing over Ryan, a gun in her hand.

What in hell was going on here?

"I've killed him. I've killed him." Like a robot, Ashley jerkily turned to Adam and offered him the gun.

Adam tugged his shirt out of his pants.

Careful not to leave fingerprints, he used the cloth to glove his hand and grabbed the gun. He dropped it on a nearby table. Had Ashley shot both Ryan and Whitney? He yanked off his belt and grabbed Ashley, binding both her wrists.

"No. Stop," she cried. "I was trying to save Whitney. Honest."

"Yeah, right." He shoved her aside. "You expect me to believe that? You stole her dog." He had a thousand questions for her, but right now all that mattered was Whitney.

She lay crumpled on the pool deck, bleeding. In Iraq his closest friends' blood had been splattered all over him, and Adam had nearly died. That was nothing compared to the way his gut twisted at the sight of Whitney's blood.

Next to her, Ryan Fordham lay flat on his back, blood gushing from a wound in his chest. His flat, unseeing eyes told Adam the man was dead.

"Whitney, Whitney." He dropped to his knees and felt for a pulse. By some miracle she was still alive, but blood was seeping from a shot just above her waist. He prayed it hadn't hit any vital organs.

"Ryan shot her," cried Ashley. "I had to stop him before he fired again."

With trembling fingers, Adam pulled his cell phone out of his pocket and dialed 911. Somehow he managed to give them the address and order an ambulance on the double.

"Hang in there, sweetheart," he told Whitney as he examined the wound. He was afraid to move her in case it caused more bleeding. He applied pressure above the wound.

Jasper and Lexi circled the two bodies. One look told him the dogs had no clue how serious this was. "Get out of the way!" he yelled at them. Both dogs cowered. "Sit. Sit. Stay," he said in a calmer voice.

He barely heard Ashley babbling about what happened. The gambling debt. The supposedly toxic land that was so valuable. Something about her long-lost father and money.

Adam didn't give a rat's ass. All that mattered was saving Whitney. He heard the wails of an ambulance and police cars coming closer and closer.

"Hurry, hurry," he heard himself plead. He tried to think over the pulse thrumming in his temples, but there was nothing he could do except wait and pray. Her body was pathetically still, nearly lifeless, all color leached from her beautiful face.

"Aaah, aaahhh," Whitney moaned, her eyes still closed.

"I love you, Whitney," he said even though now was not the time to say it. He might never have another chance.

"A-a-ah-adam." Whitney's eyelids fluttered, then opened so slightly that he doubted she could see him.

"Shh. Don't try to talk."

"Ja-ja-jasper . . . ch-chip . . . neck." Suddenly her eyes snapped shut.

"We heard about it on television," Holly told Adam. "We came right away. We knew you'd need us."

All Adam could do was nod at Tyler and Holly. He wouldn't need anybody or anything if Whitney didn't survive.

They were sitting in the surgery waiting room. It had been more than two hours since the ambulance had sped away with Whitney. She'd been rushed immediately into surgery. A nurse had come out with one update: Whitney was still alive. The seconds had ticked by like days.

"I'm here. I'm here," announced Trish Bowrather as she rushed into the waiting room with Rod Babcock. "Is she —"

"We don't know anything yet," Tyler told them when Adam couldn't speak.

"What happened?" asked the attorney.

There was a long silence, then Adam heard himself begin to talk. "According to Ashley Fordham, Ryan tried to kill Whitney."

"Lord have mercy. I warned her," cried Trish, turning to Rod. The lawyer put his arm around her and pulled Trish close. "I warned Whitney, but she wouldn't listen."

"On TV they said Ryan Fordham had been shot and killed," Tyler told everyone. "The police have arrested Ashley Fordham."

Adam slowly nodded. "I guess Ashley killed him. There was a scuffle or something. I don't know the details."

"Whitney wasn't able to tell you anything?" asked Holly.

"No. She only rallied for a moment." He turned to Trish. "All she could think about was the dogs. She was worried about Jasper."

"Just like Whitney," Trish replied, then hesitated a moment. "She didn't mention Lexi? That's strange."

"She could barely utter a syllable," Adam told her. He lovingly recalled her last words. Jasper, chip, neck.

Holy shit!

She'd been trying to tell him something.

■ ■ ■ ■

Whitney strained to lift heavy eyelids crusted with sand. Light. She finally glimpsed a single ray of light, but she seemed to be looking at the world through gauze.

"Whitney," someone called to her from very far away.

Adam hovered over her with his arm around . . . Miranda. Whitney tried to speak but her parched tongue could barely move. A white-hot bolt of pain lanced up her side, as if someone were twisting a shard of glass.

Where was she? What had happened? She struggled to remember. She saw the bank of frightening-looking machines with tubes attached to her body.

"Can you hear me, sweetheart?" Adam asked, his hand on her shoulder.

She parted her lips to respond. In a flash the room morphed into darkness and she was scrambling out of the pool again. Ryan was going to shoot Ashley if she didn't do something — fast. In freeze-frames her brain replayed the struggle over the gun.

"A-ash . . . ley?" she managed to say through a miasma of pain and confusion.

"She's all right," Adam assured her. "She got the gun away from Ryan and shot him." There was a change in the pressure of his hand on her shoulder. "He's dead."

Ryan — dead? Her muddled brain was too traumatized to process the information. The light slowly seeped away until she was all alone in the dark again.

"Whitney . . . Whitney."

The myriad machines twisted and garbled her name. She thought she heard it again but couldn't be sure. She seemed to be floating high above the earth on clouds like feather beds. She willed her eyes to open and they reluctantly obeyed. She sensed time had passed. It could have been minutes, hours or even days.

The room was dark now, the only light glowing from the armada of machines that gurgled and beeped. In the next breath, she realized the drip-drip-drip she heard was an IV pumping life-giving fluids into her body. Woozy, she struggled to remember what had happened to her.

A face emerged from the shadows. "Hey, are you awake?"

"Adam?" She realized her left side ached so much she could barely speak. "Don't leave me."

"I won't." He brushed his lips to her

forehead. "I love you. I haven't left your side."

"You love me?" she found the strength to whisper.

"You bet I love you." He bent over and gently kissed her cheek. "I should have told you before — before I came damn close to losing you."

Those all important words — *I love you* — made her giddily happy despite the pain. The knowledge made her aware of the fracture deep in her soul. This man had touched her in a way no one else ever had. He made her accept how much she longed for love and trust.

When she'd been in the pool and realized Ryan had gone berserk, she'd fervently wished she'd told Adam how she felt. Now she had a second chance.

"I love you, too."

"You had me scared to death. I thought I was going to lose you."

She mustered the strength to give him a little smile. Memories eclipsed by drugs and pain slowly floated to the surface as the blurry watercolor softness of drugs lifted a little. "Ashley's all right? Did you tell me that or did I dream it?"

His warm hand cradled hers. "You didn't dream it. Ashley went home with her father to Bakersfield. At first, the police arrested her, thinking she'd shot both of you in some lovers' triangle."

"Oh, no. She —"

"I know, I know. She was trying to help you. The police corroborated Ashley's story very quickly. Forensics confirmed Ryan had fired the gun. After he shot you, Ashley grabbed the gun and killed him. The police know it was self-defense."

"Ryan was a very sick man. I never realized."

"Neither did Ashley."

"I . . . feel bad for her. She could have run away or something but she returned and tried to save me."

"Don't worry about her. I'm sure she'll be upset for a while but she's reunited with her father. And Preston Block cares about her — a lot. She won't be alone. I'm positive she's going to be fine."

"I hope so." Whitney tried to capture an elusive memory, but the drugs slowed her thought process. She stared at a framed travel poster of Venice on the wall. Adam offered her some water, and she took it. The thought resurfaced as she swallowed. "Ryan's friends threw the pipe bomb. The car —"

"We know. Ashley gave us Domenic

Coriz's name. He's stonewalling but one of his men admits throwing the pipe bomb and driving the car. It was all about the land you and Ryan owned."

She listened, ignoring the persistent ache in her side. Another thought exploded in her brain. How could she have forgotten? "Jasper! His chip."

"I know. You told me."

"I did?" She couldn't recall telling him about her discovery.

"Yes. You came to for just long enough to tell me before the ambulance arrived." He kissed her cheek, and she looked into those blue-blue eyes she loved so much. "I thought it might be the last thing you ever said. You've really had me worried."

"Sorry. I didn't mean to."

"You couldn't help it. You've been very sick."

"What's wrong with me?"

"The gunshot ruptured your spleen. You had massive internal bleeding that was hard to control. You've been here eight days."

"Eight days? How could I have lost track of so much time?" Another thought niggled at her brain. This one surfaced more easily. "What about those men and the disc?"

"Quinten Foley arranged to transfer the info from Jasper's chip and put enough of it on a disc to fool the terrorists."

"Miranda?" She had a muddled impression of seeing Miranda hovering over her with Adam. How many days ago had that been?

"I called Miranda while you were in surgery. She flew here immediately. She's just stepped out to get coffee. Your cousin is as brave as you are. Wearing a wire, she took the disc and met the terrorists. The wire caught enough on tape to keep them in prison for years."

"Is Miranda in trouble or anything for her part in the arms deals?"

Adam shook his head. "She cooperated fully with the authorities and has given them access to the offshore accounts. They waived any charges."

Whitney closed her eyes for a moment, trying to absorb it all.

"Get some rest," Adam told her.

She snapped open her eyes. "No way. I've been out too long. You solved the case without me."

"Be serious. If you hadn't discovered the chip, the terrorists would never have believed Miranda had the real deal."

"Then it's over, really over. I can begin a new life."

He lovingly studied her face for a moment. "Yes. It's time for act two. You're the star. I know you want to become a vet. I'm with you all the way."

"What about you? I might have to move up north."

"Don't worry about it. I love you. We'll work it out," he told her with a reassuring smile. "I've arranged to let Tyler buy me out over time. I'm not really interested in the business he's developed. I've always thought computer security is the wave of the future. After this chip thing, I'm sure I'm right."

All that truly registered in Whitney's brain was *I love you.* That was what really mattered to her. She'd taken a wrong turn, but now she was finally on the right path. "Adam, I couldn't love you more."

He squeezed her hand. "I think we should take some time for ourselves. To really get to know each other. Let's drive up North with the dogs and —"

"Oh my gosh. Is Lexi all right? How's Jasper?"

He kissed her cheek, his lips warm against her skin. "They're fine. Lexi sleeps curled around Jasper. They've taken over the bed. We're going to play hell getting any space for ourselves."

Whitney giggled, then smiled up at Adam.

"It's okay. We'll figure something out." What really counted, she knew, was that they were together.

ABOUT THE AUTHOR

Meryl Sawyer is a *New York Times* and *USA TODAY* bestselling author of twenty-four romantic-suspense novels, one historical novel and one anthology. Meryl has won a *Romantic Times BOOKreviews* Career Achievement Award for Contemporary Romantic Suspense as well as *Romantic Times BOOKreviews* award for Best New Contemporary Author. Meryl lives in Newport Beach, California, with her three golden retrievers. She loves to hear from readers and may be contacted at her Web site at www.merylsawyer.com.

The employees of Thorndike Press hope you have enjoyed this Large Print book. All our Thorndike and Wheeler Large Print titles are designed for easy reading, and all our books are made to last. Other Thorndike Press Large Print books are available at your library, through selected bookstores, or directly from us.

For information about titles, please call:
   (800) 223-1244

or visit our Web site at:
   www.gale.com/thorndike
   www.gale.com/wheeler

To share your comments, please write:
   Publisher
   Thorndike Press
   295 Kennedy Memorial Drive
   Waterville, ME 04901

Born in May 1924, David was the youngest of a Lancaster family of six. Dyslexia led to frustrated years at school, but a gifted teacher unlocked the door of learning, enabling him to pass an Air Crew Selection Board in 1942. He went on to complete a tour of thirty operations with No 49 Squadron, Bomber Command.

THE PERPETRATOR

When seven old men, survivors of a Lancaster bomber crew from World War II, book into a hotel for their annual reunion, someone has decided that they will suffer for the activities of their youth. They are to remain physically unharmed, but anguish and despair will ruin their final years. Unknown to them, their loved ones are no longer safe — the Perpetrator is making sure of that. The old men will never know the origin of the attacks. The Perpetrator does not seek overt dominance. The secret knowledge of what he has done will be satisfaction enough.

DAVID MILLETT

◆

THE
PERPETRATOR

Complete and Unabridged

ULVERSCROFT
Leicester

First published in Great Britain in 2000

First Large Print Edition
published 2007

The moral right of the author has been asserted

British Library CIP Data

Millett, David
    The perpetrator.—Large print ed.—
    Ulverscroft large print series: adventure & suspense
    1. Suspense fiction
    2. Large type books
    I. Title
    823.9'14 [F]

    ISBN 978-1-84617-937-2

Published by
F. A. Thorpe (Publishing)
Anstey, Leicestershire

Set by Words & Graphics Ltd.
Anstey, Leicestershire
Printed and bound in Great Britain by
T. J. International Ltd., Padstow, Cornwall

This book is printed on acid-free paper

The Cast

The crew	Their wives
Peter Newell	Hillary
James Daly	Betty
Jeffrey Beaumont	Zoe
Arthur Brown	Mary
Bob Greeves	Jenny
Harry White	Hester
Tom Williams	(Single)

Prologue

'SEVEN, a number not to be forgotten.'

Peter, like the others, had been puzzled. Why had the card been placed on his pillow and by whom? What was its meaning? It hadn't been scribbled on a scrap of notepaper but printed onto high quality material which prompted Peter to show it to the whole crew. The crew! To him for the moment that was what they seemed to be again. However, though the card was somewhat intriguing, it was soon dismissed as a bit of nonsense — perhaps a young employee of the hotel playing a silly game.

Lying in his bed, Harry was unable to dismiss the card and became restless. He was sure somehow the card was a threat. Of course, he admitted to himself that his character housed more suspicion than most. But his suspicions were justified more often than not. Had it not been so, he wouldn't have retired from the force as the highly successful Detective Chief Inspector Harry White.

As often was the case the obvious hadn't

been noticed — 'Seven, a number not to be forgotten.' They themselves were SEVEN. Seven old gentlemen. Former members of a Lancaster bomber crew. Yes, ex-Detective Chief Inspector Harry White was suspicious all right. He smelled a threat.

1

The old gentlemen were gathered about two tables in the cocktail bar of the Saracen's Head. One held a glass of white wine, while the remainder drank beer.

All the men were in their seventies; the year, two short of the millennium. To the onlooker the old gentlemen appeared to be a happy bunch, almost boyish at times as they laughed at a companion's remark. They had a jovial air that made them seem buoyant, as if youth was once more trying to reach into their old bodies.

The proprietor, who was doing a stint behind the bar because it was something he liked to do, thought that maybe the group was on a pensioners' outing. But somehow, even to this young man the label 'pensioner' didn't seem quite right, for he felt he would not be out of place if he were to join them.

The landlord, reaching along the bar, said, 'Will you take another whisky, Grandpa? Your glass is empty.'

'Thanks son. I'll have another Grouse, please. But you know, you're wrong in thinking you wouldn't be out of place with

1

that lot,' he said, inclining his head towards the group at the tables.

'How did you know my thoughts?' asked the grandson, surprised.

'I've been watching your expression. Besides, I've known you a long time,' he laughed.

The old man had himself been the proprietor of Saracen's before handing the reins over to his grandson. Down the years he had seen similar gatherings to the one over there — several a year in fact, different groups and yet somehow the same. In the past the groups had been of young men but as time went by they had become older, like himself, and the occasions were now rare.

If his grandson were to join the old gentlemen, he would find he had entered memories of a world of which he knew nothing — a terrible, evil world. A world of violence and unspeakable horrors, but also of love and undying loyalty brought about by fear, reliance and the bravery of others.

There wasn't one of the old men who hadn't witnessed a torn, blood-splattered body being transferred to the 'Blood Wagon' from a shattered bomber. Nor who hadn't given a helping hand while being hampered by his bulky flying kit.

The reunions, held in the county of

Lincolnshire where in decades past the air had vibrated to the roar of the mighty Merlins, were not to reminisce on the past, but to rejoice in an indestructible friendship forged by ordeal. Nevertheless, it was hard at times not to slip back to the days when they were not much more than boys. Common memories pushed to the fore of the mind simply because they were together once more. How could it be different at times like these? How could they not 'see' again the vivid flash from a Lancaster receiving a direct hit while still carrying its full bomb load? How could they not remember the intense, short-lived brilliance from its exploding glare which silhouetted a dozen other bombers against the backcloth of earth or clouds? — as though to remind the crews within they were not alone in some great void before again being quickly swallowed up by the night, the darkness now flawed by the incandescent remains of a once mighty machine with seven souls.

After a short airing, such memories were replaced by those of modern times and the proud stories about the achievements of children and grandchildren. Was it really possible that young Jeffrey was already a qualified doctor? The old bomb-aimer, himself a retired medical man, not only had a son who'd followed him in his profession but a grandson too.

Actually, old Jeff, after whom the grandson had taken his name, looked every bit the old-fashioned distinguished practitioner with his tall upright bearing and smart conservative attire. Even his white flowing moustache, always kept immaculately groomed, didn't seem out of place. The 'tash' was a legacy from his days on the squadron when, like the rest of his hair, it had been a rich dark brown. Jeff never had been inclined to remove it. 'It seemed to represent something — my old 'flying officer kite' moustache,' he'd say.

James excused himself and made for the toilet. These days he found his visits becoming much more frequent. In fact an appointment was already made for a prostate operation. He had told Jeff about it and had been reassured by him that it was a straightforward business these days, not at all the serious bloody mess it once was. All the same, he'd be glad when it was over and done with.

It was a good thing, he thought. There were no such problems when he was standing next to the Skipper in the old Lanc, doing his flight-engineering bit. It was enough not to dirty your pants at times when old Fritz was handing out the rough stuff. Even so, during a raid most of the crew made at least one visit down the fuselage to the elsan for a pee, which was often enough, when you had to try to find your dick through all the thick flying gear.

It was a bit like that now, he thought, finding his penis beneath his extended belly. The fact that he was a short man at only five feet six inches didn't seem to help. James would say it was nature that made him like a barrel, though he knew it was mostly from self-indulgence. The old engineer's healthy hair, still showing some red amongst the grey, capped a ruddy and heavily jowled face — largely the result, according to his doctor, of his well-stocked drinks cabinet. But it must be said; his wife's excellence as a 'Cordon Bleu' cook contributed more than a little to his ample proportions, not to mention her own full girth. Betty's appreciation of her own efforts in the kitchen quite equalled that of her husband's.

'Come on then, if we're going to take a stroll about the town we'd better get to our rooms for a brush up,' said Peter, the pilot of old, as he eased out of his chair. When he stood up, Arthur knocked the table and toppled a glass. Quick as a flash Bob caught it before it reached the floor.

'Nothing much wrong with your reflexes,' observed Peter.

'Good job it's empty, if it wasn't it would have been a sacrilege in the past,' laughed Mike.

Peter led his old crew to the stairs, but it was Bob who forged ahead, taking the treads two at a time like a young gazelle. He had always been fit and lithe and it seemed the aches of age had passed him by. If James was envious of Bob's agility, he didn't show it. Breathing heavily, he struggled with the top few steps.

'We have three rooms,' Peter said. 'Two doubles and one for three bods. I expect I'll be in the large room with Tom and Bob as usual.'

'Oh lord, I'll be with Arthur again. If his snoring hasn't improved I'll smother him, so help me,' James grumbled.

Everything about Arthur was loud. His cultivated voice, the enormous checked squares in the suit he wore. Even, one could imagine, his body movement gave off reverberations. He had been a front-line rugby forward at one time, a fact not contradicted by his bulk. The noisy chattering of his guns in the old days, placed in the Lancaster's mid upper turret, must have seemed friendly to Arthur, had it not been for their deadly purpose. Yes, here was a loud, conspicuous man blessed with immense generosity.

Unlike himself, Arthur's wife Mary was a slip of a woman with her weight probably not more than eight stone. A neighbour thought: 'Funny how compatibility works out sometimes. Arthur and Mary had nothing in common regarding appearance or in interest and yet they thought the world of each other.' And the neighbour reckoned she should know, having lived just down the road for years. James had first met his wife during the war on a bomber-station in Lincolnshire, where she knew Mary had been a WAAF in the accounts office. But she never knew what James had done in the war as it was something he didn't talk about. She imagined he might have been the station's sports officer.

After a wash and a short rest, for they had travelled from homes spread across the length and breadth of the United Kingdom (some having to rise at the crack of dawn), the comrades strolled into the town which was routine on these reunions. Only Bob seemed to be holding back as he kept pausing after reaching ahead a little. The others, laughing at humorous remarks or studying the contents of a shop were in no hurry at all.

Then Arthur paused to shield the small flame from the breeze while lighting up a cigarette.

'Those weeds will kill you one day,' Peter told him.

'They're taking their time about it then, I've been dragging at them for sixty years or more,' he retorted.

During the war the whole crew smoked. In the room, where the tired crews still in full flying gear were de-briefed, or interrogated, there was always a cloud of smoke drifting about. All the tables around which the returned crews sat had several packs of 'Nelson' cigarettes on them which were provided gratis. Of course, in those days the boys knew nothing about smoke-related cancer or heart troubles. Anyway, the bigger percentage of them would be killed long before the dreaded weed could do its worst.

Having stood yet again in the grounds of the derelict castle and later, looking over the parapet of the bridge at the river below, they finally made for their one-time 'local', just to see if the parrot was still in its cage. A silly homage, for all knew the parrot had long since gone but tradition dies hard amongst the old. In the days past the parrot seemed to mean something to the superstitious bomber crews when they hit the town during a 'stand down'. 'You made it back. You made it back,' the old bird squawked.

Back at the hotel they again retreated to their rooms to freshen up before the routine visit to the bar that preceded their evening meal. The drinks would flow again, though at a much more reduced pace than earlier reunions twenty or thirty years ago. It was Harry who once said, 'I never laugh so much as I do during these events.' There was general agreement with Harry's comment. In fact Tom who lived alone and who, as all were aware, suffered from depressions, had said there was a period when he had been physically unable to smile as a natural reaction. He had to consciously shape a smiling expression to his face, which of course was no smile at all.

Then came that reunion. By the time Tom arrived in the cocktail bar with two companions where they had agreed to meet, the others were waiting. The banter began at once and something let go in Tom. Straight away the best navigator the squadron had ever known was doubled up in marvellous, uncontrolled laughter. It didn't cure Tom's loneliness but his spirit was certainly lifted and his natural smile, when greeting others, had returned to stay.

The evening meal, as usual, had been excellent. The Saracen's Head never once had failed them down the years and now the old gentlemen were mellowed from the good wine as well as from advancing years. In times long past they had been a bomber crew but now they felt like one large family.

The warmth from the friendship, together with the drowsing effect of the wine, ensured that the seven veterans slept soundly. Even Arthur's snoring barely disturbed James. Only Harry had some difficulty in dropping off. He was curious about the card which Peter found lying on his pillow. It bothered him enough to prevent sleep for a while. He was reminded of the old days when, as wireless operator, his head still seemed to be full of the da-dit-da-dit-da Morse signals which disturbed his sleep. Now, though, it wasn't the noise in his head. This time it was a swimming vision before his eyes of the heavy print on a top quality card.

'SEVEN, a number not to be forgotten.'

Peter, like the others, had been puzzled. Why had the card been placed on his pillow and by whom? What was its meaning? It hadn't been scribbled on a scrap of notepaper but printed onto a high quality material which prompted Peter to show it to the whole crew. The crew! To him for now that was what they seemed to be again. However, though the card was somewhat intriguing, it was soon

10

dismissed as a bit of nonsense — perhaps a young employee of the hotel playing a silly game.

Lying in his bed, Harry was unable to dismiss the card, and became restless. He was sure that somehow the card was a threat. Of course, he admitted to himself that his character housed more suspicion than most. But his suspicions were justified more often than not. Had it not been so he wouldn't have retired from the force as the highly successful detective Chief Inspector Harry White.

As so often was the case the obvious hadn't been noticed.

'SEVEN, a number not to be forgotten.' They themselves were SEVEN. Seven old gentlemen. Yes, ex-detective Chief Inspector Harry White was suspicious all right. He smelled a threat.

2

'How did the reunion go this time, dear?' Jenny asked after Bob had settled in.

'Great. It's always a treat to be with the boys again and we still manage to have a few good laughs,' her husband replied.

'To be with the 'boys'! I think that's a laugh for a start. You're seventy-four years of age and the youngest of the group. Boys indeed,' said his wife smiling warmly.

'Well I must admit, I do feel whacked out, and I'm supposed to be the fit one. It's a long way from Dundee to Lincolnshire; nevertheless, honey, it really is worthwhile.'

'How were the 'boys' anyway? Were they all fighting fit?'

'Absolutely. Well, old James was wheezing about the place a bit, but he wasn't any worse than last year. Like I say, it was great, but it's good to be back home,' he said, kissing her on the cheek.

'Oh, Norman phoned to say he'll be round soon,' Jenny told him.

Bob said, 'That's good, I love him coming, but we're not seeing as much of our grandson as we once did, are we dear? I hope he isn't finding us too boring in our old age.'

'I'm sure it's not that, pet. Norman has only just finished at Oxford and you know how busy the last few months prior to his finals must have been for the poor boy. Anyway the times Norman does come here you can see how loving he is towards us. There's no need to worry about the loyalty of that young man, I'm sure,' said Jenny convincingly.

'Yes, you're right of course. Dorothy did us proud, producing a boy like Norman. It's a pity she wasn't able to have more children. I know Dave would have liked a larger family but he has never blamed Dorothy. Anyway, he prizes the one they have all right.'

'Dorothy, bless her, took after me in that regard, only being able to give one birth. We are a small family but a loving one, Bob, aren't we?'

'You are right there,' the old man said, giving his wife's bottom a tender pat.

'Hi, anyone at home?'

'Here's Norman now. We're here at the front,' exclaimed Bob joyfully.

The lounge door opened and the boy was hugging Jenny before she was halfway across the room, while at the same time asking his Granddad how the reunion had gone.

'Great, as always, but how are you,

Norman? Now you've finished with Oxford what are you planning to do?'

'For starters I'm going on a skiing holiday with Debbie. Next week we're off to Austria and am I looking forward to it after these past few weeks at the University!'

'You're going with your young lady, are you? I think it's high time we met this Debbie of yours,' Grandma said.

'And you shall. I am bringing her tomorrow if that's OK. I would have brought her with me today, but she'd to do some shopping for our holiday.'

'We'll look forward to meeting her. Grandma and I will need to give our approval you know,' Robert said, with a smile.

'Oh, you will, there's no danger there. Debbie's a smashing girl,' Norman said with enthusiasm.

'How long have you known her?' asked Grandma.

'More than six months. I met her at a party during the last vacs. She was also at Oxford reading English so we've been able to see quite a lot of each other fortunately.'

'Where's her home?' Grandma enquired.

'Aberdeen. Her father is an engineer with one of the oil companies. Debbie is twenty-two, five feet eight inches tall with long silky blond hair. She is slim, has a great sense of humour, and of course is very beautiful. Anything more you would like to know?' he asked, with a cheeky grin.

Grandpa said, 'I think that will do for now, but we shall see for ourselves tomorrow,' he chuckled.

★   ★   ★

'This is a nice car, darling, I'm pleased it's white because that's what I would have chosen.'

Norman said, 'Yeah, it's great, runs beautifully. It's been really cared for and with only twenty-two thousand miles on the clock, it's as good as new.'

'I think you're really lucky, I'm jolly sure my father wouldn't buy me a car just like that, he'd say I'd have to earn it,' Debbie said.

'It wasn't exactly 'just like that' darling. I wouldn't have got it if I hadn't got a first at Oxford. That was Dad's condition and fortunately I managed to pull it off. It'll be convenient parking it at the airport while we're on holiday since our return home will be on a night flight.'

'Oh darling. I am looking forward to our holiday, I'm sure it'll be magic, but I am a little apprehensive about this skiing business — I've never done any before.'

15

'You'll be OK, sweetheart, they'll look after you on the nursery slopes, I promise. It's a pity you haven't spent time at Aviemore — I used to go there at every opportunity. I suppose I'm a reasonably experienced skier really — but Debbie, you won't mind, will you, if I spend some time on the piste while you're with the beginners' group? It would be a shame for both of us not to take advantage of Austria. As for any other time, well you try just to get away from me if you can!' Norman said, reaching to squeeze Debbie's knee.

The busy airport concourse, the checking-in procedure, and seeing her luggage disappearing as it seemed to transport itself from the weighing scales, fascinated Debbie. 'Are you sure we'll see it again?' she asked, laughing.

'Yes, of course. Have you really never flown before?' Norman asked incredulously.

'No. Well yes, once, but I can't remember anything about it since I was only two. I went with Mum and Dad to stay with my Uncle Joe in America for a while. Apart from that I've never been abroad. Never wanted to, actually. I much preferred spending my holiday times painting in my own country. Scotland, with its hills, valleys, lochs and coastline is marvellous. And the light is always changing so that you never know what

16

the next day will offer you. For an artist it's quite superb.'

'It surprises me you've done so much painting when I know you're a fun girl, loving parties and social activities. I imagine painting — especially open air scenes — must be a lonely occupation,' Norman remarked.

'It's very good to be on one's own at times darling, particularly if you have paints and a brush. One's mind really gets focused when you're building a distance image onto a canvas. Anyway, sometimes I was holidaying with a painting group. That was quite good,' Debbie smiled.

As is the case with most people who are to experience their first flight, Debbie was sensing a mix of anxious anticipation and keen excitement. She was a little surprised at the amount of force which pushed her back into the seat as the jet sped down the runway. When she commented on this to Norman, he told her the more often she flew the less noticeable it would become. She told him he talked as if he was always jetting around the world. An embarrassing flush came to his face, which she thought was rather sweet, but he still thought it strange that a girl of Debbie's age, who had been to Oxford, hadn't yet travelled abroad.

Slightly startled, Debbie asked what the

thump was she had heard? Norman told her that from the large number of hours spent jetting around the world, he had learnt the thump came from the wheels as they were retracted into their bays. He had winced as he felt the power of Debbie's fist punching his upper arm.

Though the beat of her heart was steadily returning towards its normal rate, her fascination with her flight remained intense. The plane was climbing through clouds, blocking any view Debbie had hoped to see. But the glow from the wing-tip light danced as refracted light changed when the speeding wing passed through thickening or thinning cloud. Then, quite suddenly the feeble glow was swamped by powerful sunlight when the jet burst out of the cloud into the clear cold air above. Captivated, Debbie watched the sheet of cloud falling thousands of feet below. All around, the air had become crystal clear, and high above was a deep blue sky. 'Oh Norman, how beautiful,' she exclaimed.

★　★　★

Norman held Debbie close at the entrance of her room where he kissed her tenderly before she stepped back through the door. She'd left him standing in the corridor as it closed.

Lying in his bed he imagined he saw again her beautiful face and radiant blue eyes. He ached to have her slim body lying next to him and hoped ardently that before the holiday ended she would share his bed. 'It was the first day after all,' he told himself, 'and it had been a long tiring day.'

Debbie was a virgin, she had made that clear to him right from the start. At the time Norman had been a little surprised by her chastity — in these modern times! Even though he often ached for her it pleased him nonetheless. He had known a few girls — what young man hadn't? But none had really meant anything to him. Though at one time he had thought Bunny was special, after meeting Debbie he knew different. If he had to wait until they were married, so be it. But the answer was simple. They must marry soon. So after this holiday he had better start looking where he could put his excellent mathematics degree to good use.

The next morning Norman and Debbie shared the car-lift with other happy skiers. They were climbing to the piste for their first run of the day, but first he would take Debbie to meet her instructor and would remain a while until she felt comfortable in her new environment. But he was sure she would quickly feel at home with the other beginners.

As the car slowed near the restaurant, Debbie was staggered to see the 'forest' of skis 'sprouting' from the snow from where they would be retrieved when required by their owners. 'Just look at that 'crop', darling, there are dozens of them,' Debbie said, pointing.

'Hundreds,' corrected Norman.

The sun was hot on Debbie's face but she had been firmly warned of the danger of sunburn in the thinner air of the mountains, and had already taken precautions. Enjoying the warm glow, she had never felt fitter. It came as a surprise therefore when her hands plunged deep into the soft snow as she fell for the first time. Almost at once they seemed to freeze. She thought she had never felt anything so cold as those super-cooled ice crystals, or were they hot? For now her hands seemed to burn. Hastily she replaced her gloves, understanding why she had been told not to remove them.

After a breathtaking day in the hills the couple spent a boisterous evening at the hotel with a mix of nationalities. But true thrill came when, again at the door of her room, Norman heard his love whisper: 'Come in darling. I want you to stay.'

Closing the door, Debbie gently placed her hand upon Norman's cheek and said, 'You must promise we will not go all the way. I do want you, my darling, I want you badly, but I'm not changing my mind about remaining a virgin until marriage. It's important to me.'

'I promise, my darling, I promise,' Norman said tenderly.

Fascinated, he saw her undress down to her bra and panties. He watched as she sat at the dressing table brushing silky hair, and he saw in the mirror the slight pink glow the sun had put on her lovely face. 'How have I been so fortunate to win such a gem?' he wondered.

Debbie trembled slightly as she slid beneath the sheets where Norman waited, his own excitement rising on feeling the warmth of her body and again he marvelled at her beauty. He kissed her head, each eye in turn, then with a smile he kissed the tip of her small slightly tilted nose, for the tilt seemed to be just right as it suggested a little impishness.

Two pairs of lips met, eager to explore. His hand removed the bra to couple her breast but this wasn't enough. Norman removed his mouth from tender lips to find the proud nipple. Debbie sighed.

As passion heightened, their hands searched more boldly. Panties and shorts were quickly discarded, to be thrown aside and Debbie cried out at the invasion of her love by the caressing fingers of her lover.

After only a slight hesitation, she found his hard manhood and was surprised at her own pleasure from the fondling of penis and genitals. Tenderly, yet in desperation, Debbie proclaimed her true love to Norman as he felt her, with knees bent, climb onto him. Without further thought he made to enter, then, in anguish his lover rolled away, exclaiming; 'No, we mustn't — our promise!' But before full disillusion struck, Norman heard Debbie utter: 'Oh God,' prior to easing herself onto his throbbing member. At the breaching of the maidenhead she uttered a soft cry and Norman felt himself held in a vice-like grip.

A little later the lovers relaxed in a warm glow and Norman gazing at his love through tender eyes said, 'I love you, my darling.'

'And I my dear, I always will — forever.'

★ ★ ★

'Anything of interest in the paper, dear?' Jenny asked her husband as she cleared away his coffee cup.

'No, nothing of note. Both the dailies have completely different front-page headlines — I always consider that to be a good thing. If anything really dramatic or serious is happening, all the papers'll have similar

22

major headlines. Perhaps it's a bit more exciting when they do, but definitely it's not as peaceful,' Bob philosophised.

'Yes dear, you're probably right. Have you finished with the biscuits?'

'Yes thanks. Is that the phone?'

'It is. I'll answer, dear.'

'Hello,' Jenny said, brightly.

'Oh Mum, it's Dorothy, oh Mum!'

Jenny was sure she had heard a sob. Full of concern now she asked, 'What is it Dorothy, is there something wrong?'

For a moment the line was silent, then she heard her daughter's strange voice say, 'Norman is dead.'

'What?'

'It's true Mum, my dear boy is gone — Norman is dead. Oh Mum,' she sobbed.

Bob, having caught the inflection in his wife's voice, came to the phone: 'Something the matter?' he asked. Then he saw Jenny was trembling and had turned a ghastly pallor.

'It's Norman,' she said, finding the chair by the table on which the telephone stood.

'Norman? You mean our Norman? What's wrong? Let me speak to him,' he said, reaching for the instrument.

'But Dorothy says he's dead,' and Bob saw his wife had aged ten years in as many seconds.

'Dorothy, tell me what's going on?' he asked his daughter anxiously.

At the other end of the line, David took the phone from his wife who was too distressed to continue. 'Dad, it's Dave.' He sounded grave.

'Yes David, what's happening? Grandma says Norman is dead.'

'Yes Bob, it's true, my boy is dead.'

'Oh my God,' the old man exclaimed. He had worshiped his grandson. To him there was no one like Norman. 'How? What happened?' He felt feeble as nausea struck.

'No one seems to know exactly. Debbie called her mother from Austria and now Mrs Johnson has contacted us. She says her daughter was beside herself with grief and hardly knew what she was saying, but she gathered that while Debbie was on the nursery slope Norman had gone off to the piste. Shortly after there was dismay amongst the gathering as word spread about a dead man being found.'

'And it was Norman?' Bob whispered.

'Yes.'

Later, as the evening light faded on this dreadful day, Bob felt the need to communicate with someone outside the family. Maybe it was his subconscious reaching out for comfort, and where better than from his other 'family'.

Jeffrey's finger swept the side of his 'tache before reaching for the telephone. 'Hello. Dr Beaumont here,' he said.

He heard a voice quietly say, 'Jeff, it's Bob. I hope I'm not disturbing you at this hour, but I need to talk.'

'Of course you're not disturbing me. How are you, is everything OK? You don't sound your normal lively self.'

'I'm not. A terrible thing has happened. Jeff, it's my grandson Norman, he's dead.' On hearing a snivel, Jeff's heart went out to his old friend.

'That's dreadful, Bob, how on earth did this happen?'

'That's the odd thing, no one seems to know anything about it. Norman was on a skiing holiday in Austria with his girlfriend and earlier today she phoned her mother to tell the awful news but the girl was mostly incoherent. Mrs Johnson, the girl's mother, phoned my daughter.'

'It sounds to me Bob as though the girl's suffering from shock, but hasn't anyone else from Austria made contact, the police or someone?'

'Well, yes. About an hour ago the local police made contact with the police here. All they were able to say was that Norman seemed to have had an accident. It appears he was found in a forbidden area that was plainly marked with warning signs. The locality is vested with dangerous outcroppings of rocks and obviously, hitting one at speed could easily result in a disaster.'

'That's all you know? Not the cause of death, such as a blow on the head for instance?' the medic asked.

'I know nothing more Jeff, except I feel life is not worth a toss any more. That boy meant everything to me. Nothing in life has devastated me more than this.'

'Your love for Norman had always been plain to see. The whole crew's known that for years but, you know, Bob, time really does heal, though you may not think so now. Believe me, your wound will mend even if the scar remains.'

'You say time heals, but who has time at my age? Time is all but gone. Anyway, what's the point, Jeff? I don't see one anymore. Jenny and I were never blessed with the son we longed for, that's why I saw Norman as what might have been. Sorry, but I'm just not interested anymore, Jeff. I know I shouldn't talk to you like this but right now I want someone outside the family to lean on. Within the family I must be the support. I'm sure you understand.'

'Of course I understand, old chap, who of

us wouldn't?' he said with compassion, then continued. 'When the immediate aftermath of this sad business is over, why don't you and Jenny come to stay with us a few days? I know it's a fair distance to Stroud, Bob, but to be away from that environment would help to get your minds off things.'

'You're very kind, Jeff, but at the moment I am not in any mood to make a decision. Later I'll have a word with Jenny. I'll ring off now, but we'll be in touch.'

Jeff remained still a few moments after the line had gone dead. 'Poor Bob, he's been hit hard,' he thought.

★   ★   ★

Via the grapevine the news of Bob's tragedy spread out to the crew, resulting in six cards of condolence for their old rear gunner and his wife.

In phone conversations it was decided they should attend Norman's funeral. Someone suggested it might seem to the younger generation like an intrusion. But it was felt they must show their respect to their old buddy — show that they cared.

Of course, they all had real compassion for their old comrade, knowing as they did, Bob's deep affection for his grandson. But, ex-chief inspector Harry White not only had compassion, he also was concerned about the cause of death.

Why was there such a dearth of information?

Was there heavy bruising, which may have indicated a cause for death? If so, why is there no mention of the fact? Hitting a rock at a speed fast enough to kill just had to leave some evidence. Certainly with no obvious cause of death an autopsy must follow, but none had taken place. Why not?

Surely, no one would want to kill the young man? All the same, things didn't appear to be quite right to Harry. He had that feeling of old. That sixth sense.

3

Kurt von Haydn was pleased to leave the congested streets of Frankfurt behind him and to power the Mercedes along the Autobahn. Even at seventy-three years of age he dispensed with the service of the chauffeur whenever possible, though the policy of the bank stipulated he use a driver when on company business. That directive applied to all board members, not only for the most senior one.

Kurt had been in banking all his working life and had risen to the heights in a business in which his competence was so valued he had twice been persuaded to postpone his retirement. Recently however, he had felt the tiredness developing much earlier in the day. It was a physical thing rather than mental, since he was never weary. Weariness, he knew, was a product of a mind having been overloaded, but his never was. All his life he felt he could take in more information. Making decisions was not a problem for him once he had weighed the pros and cons. Because Kurt's mind was clear, never contaminated with muddy waters, it did not tire and when he laid his head on the pillow he simply switched off. But now his body, if nothing else, told him it was time he must go.

For the first time, the banker felt he could enjoy full retirement. Kurt had had a good working life, being immersed in and fascinated by the financial world, but quite suddenly, its consequence had diminished. For the first time, it seemed, he was seeing the real beauty of the Taunus' countryside as he drove through this affluent part of Germany in which Kurt's family home had been established a few kilometres from Konigstein. *Haus Falkenstein* had for generations been the abode of the von Haydns.

High on the hill, over to his left, Kurt caught a glance of the Nervenkrankenhaus. It was a forbidding place which had always left Kurt feeling wretched after his occasional visits. Happily the establishment was closed down now, wiser councils having prevailed in bringing about new ways for dealing with the mentally impaired. This had enabled his brother's boy, Hans, to live with the rest of the family at *Haus Falkenstein*.

Since returning to the family home Hans' behaviour hadn't been unreasonable, though Kurt did think his nephew had some odd mannerisms. It wasn't normal to stand like a statue for up to fifteen minutes at a time with not even an eye flickering. But Kurt was never sure during such moments if Hans was in deep concentration, or if he really was as inane as he seemed. Certainly there had been times when the boy — to Kurt all his nephews and nieces were still boys and girls — had shown the brightest of intelligence if handling a difficult problem. Then, as though right out of character, his mind would become fixed on some obtuseness that bordered on idiocy. Kurt nevertheless surmised that such power of concentration, which the boy certainly had, must be unusual with one so afflicted and might explain his statue-like trances.

Hans' general appearance and deportment in no way let down his family. The boy was tall, blond and handsome, causing female heads to turn easily in his direction, a pointless exercise as Hans' interest in the fair sex was nil. Yet he did revere the memory of his mother; indeed her death was the last straw which opened the door of the Nervenkrankenhaus.

Hans had entered the world a few years after the end of Hitler's war. He had been told many times how his mother's joy for living never returned after the death of her dear friend Hildegard who had died along with the other five members of the 'team'

31

who had shared their schooldays at the convent. The date of Hildegard's death was the 15th October 1944, which was also the fiftieth anniversary of the local tennis club's inauguration. All the convent's 'team' were members.

The committee had decided that a party was to be held in the pavilion to celebrate the club's half-century. It had started out as a good night for the girls, even though most of the men were away fighting the war. But the evening was not enjoyed by Anna, who had to leave early after complaining of feeling sick. Her loyal and loving friend Hildegard wanted to escort her home, but Anna had insisted she remained to enjoy the evening.

Later, Anna put out the lights so she could draw back the curtains and open a window before she climbed into bed. Even though it was winter, she felt the need for fresh cool air and now, as she lay there, she felt sad at having to leave her friends and wondered what had brought on her sickness. But her mood changed quickly when she heard the gunfire somewhere in the sky and she knew men were fighting for their lives up there. There wasn't any heavy ground-fire, so Anna knew she was hearing the sounds of what they called a 'dog fight'. Aeroplane against aeroplane, people would say, but she knew it was really men against men. As a child Anna had heard many stories from Gunther about fighting in the sky.

Before the war, even before she attended the convent school she sometimes played with Gunther who was nice and always kind to her. It was in the park where they'd met and played. She had been walking with her mother who had paused to talk to Gunther's nanny whom she knew slightly. The ladies had enjoyed passing the time of day so their meetings in the park became frequent.

A few years later, when Anna had reached her early teens she met Gunther again. This time he had been with friends in the *Kaffee* and had noticed her by the counter choosing a cream cake. Leaving his friends, he at once crossed over to her. Gunther's pleasure at meeting her again was so obvious Anna couldn't prevent herself from blushing, which filled her with embarrassment, but they drank a coffee together before he escorted her to her bus.

That chance meeting in the *Kaffee* had led to others and Anna found she was beginning to like Gunther von Haydn a lot. Like most of the other boys, he was in The Hitler Youth but he said he didn't like it much, though he knew most of the boys did. He told her the marching was all right and the singing was really good, but all the leaders told you the same things. And when Gunther told his father he answered that he thought it all very silly. Then, looking very stern, he told his son he mustn't tell anyone what he had said. His father sometimes did look very stern, he told Anna.

'Why have you told me? That was wrong,' Anna had rebuked.

'I know, but I won't tell anyone else. You won't tell, will you, Anna?' She had said she wouldn't.

It was about the time that Anna started at her new school when she met Hildegard and an empathy grew for the girl which brought about feelings she hadn't previously known. Their friendship quickly deepened to depths neither girl had thought possible. And Anna found she didn't want to meet Gunther anymore, even though he was a very nice and considerate boy.

He missed Anna whom he thought was such a lovely girl. But he soon found others, though there were none whom he wanted to continue seeing — not like he had with Anna. All the same, what with school and The Hitler Youth he was kept busy, leaving little time to brood.

He continued to have mixed feelings about the youth movement. Certainly, he had some good times, even exciting times, and there was a wonderful comradeship. But somehow he always sensed a bizarre bias which ran everywhere through the movement and it made him uncomfortable.

Von Haydn was a patriot, but he didn't much like what was happening in his country. He considered Hitler and his Nazi Party to be obnoxious and hated what they were doing to Germany. It was true that for some years after the end of the Great War things were very bad. No employment, starvation rife and inflation running wild. The Nazis had created work and Germany appeared to be on its feet again, but von Haydn wasn't a fool. He knew the armament factories were working hard. Due to his privileged place in the old German society he 'heard' things.

What were the armaments for? The whole of Europe was virtually disarmed, except perhaps France, but she presented no danger. Of course, no German government could be blamed for wanting the return of the Alsace, which would, given time, have surely come about through diplomacy. The new *autobahns* were excellent, there was no denying they improved communication wonderfully, but they could also be a godsend to heavy military traffic. When he considered all that was going on in Germany, von Haydn had little doubt about the real purpose of those *autobahns*.

Then there was his son, Gunther, in The Hitler Youth Movement. Von Haydn certainly didn't like that at all. He knew the boys were being brainwashed, but what could one do? These Nazis were dangerous and would tolerate no criticism. He, von Haydn, might get away with it, even the Nazis would think twice before letting the great German public witness any defaming of one of their glorious heroes, but he was less sure about his son.

Gunther was never allowed to forget for long the esteem in which his father was held. 'The son of 'The' von Haydn?' was the usual response when introduced to strangers. He even felt great himself at times from the respect he received after his affirmative reply.

But those times had gone. Von Haydn's past trepidation of the Nazi party had proved justified, and now, in 1944 Germany was reaping her 'reward'.

* * *

When Anna awakened her sickness had gone. She shivered as she closed the window and wondered how the party had been. Later she would phone Hildegard.

Anna showered, dressed and made coffee.

Although her sickness had gone, it had left her not wanting breakfast. But, at least, a second coffee would be agreeable. Maybe later she would have lunch. Putting down the empty cup she went to the telephone. Asking to speak to her friend, she was informed that Hildegard was dead.

The convent 'team' was no more. They had died along with the destruction of the tennis pavilion when it was hit by a crashing aeroplane which had fallen from the night-sky.

★ ★ ★

Von Haydn, sitting in his favourite chair, pulled the travelling rug closer to him. Even this gentleman, no favourite of the authorities, was unable to obtain fuel during the bitter winter of '44 but his heart warmed with the pleasure of spending the evening with his two boys.

It seemed a long time since he had last seen his Gunther; even so, he was very fortunate to have him at home now as U-boat captains didn't last long. Even in the days when Germany seemed to be winning the Battle of the Atlantic and they had all but starved Britain out, with Hitler within a whisker of winning the war, the British still managed to inflict fearful losses on the U-boats. But the tide had turned as the Royal Navy and the RAF got the upper hand. In 1944, the U-boats were practically a spent force. Even Admiral Dönitz had lost his command.

'God, it's good to be home, Father,' Gunther said, as he replenished their glasses with Schnapps. 'To be honest, I didn't expect to make it. Each time we reach a home port I think it's a marvel, but as the English say, I keep turning up 'like a bad penny'.'

His brother said, 'Sometimes I feel really guilty in my safe job while you are risking your life all the time. If you were killed, Gunther, I know the guilt would never leave me.'

'Well then, I mustn't be killed,' he replied, swallowing his Schnapps in one gulp.

'Whatever happens, Kurt, you need not feel guilt. It is no fault of yours that your eyes prevented you from fighting for your country. Anyway, is this a war for which Germany gets any credit? I think not,' observed the old hero.

Kurt said, 'I agree, if I had to fight I hope it'd be for a just cause and not simply to satisfy our leader's lust for power.'

'When I was on the Western Front during the Great War I never thought my poor country would come to this. If only the Munich *putsch* had failed, the Nazis might never have got off the ground,' their father said.

Kurt continued, 'I really worry about you, Gunther, and pray you'll get through this lot, because I feel so lucky myself. I have a good occupation and it makes me feel better knowing the firm I'm with is in the medical industry. The chairman told me recently the board thinks I'm the most effective accountant they've had. 'You have truly found your vocation, Kurt,' he said.'

'Gunther, I've noticed you're not wearing your Iron Cross,' von Haydn commented.

'No, Father, not when I'm at home. Other times I dare not leave it off as it would no doubt be construed as an insult to the Führer, but I'm not proud to display the 'honour'. I have seen too many men blown to pieces with their ships, and far too often I've seen men choking from the oil in their lungs. I am sure their cause is more honourable than ours.

'I and my men have been lucky so far, as most in the U-boats go down like ninepins. My crews are mostly not much more than boys; decent German boys, though many are fanatical Nazis, as a result of their Hitler Youth years. This is a dirty war, father, and the war at sea disgusts me. I can't believe it was the same for you?'

'On the Western Front, you mean? It was not. Then we were Germans first, not Nazis. Of course the trenches were dreadful, but they were crowded with ordinary decent men on both sides, all suffering the consequences of stupid governments. At times, after heavy rains and continuous shelling for days on end, their squalor was deplorable.'

'But you didn't share the horror of the trenches, Father. Your war was so different. I imagine in those days air-warfare must have been exciting.' Kurt had always been so proud of his father. Von Haydn — the great fighter ace — holder of The Iron Cross first-class, won in man-to-man combat.

★ ★ ★

Von Haydn's thoughts slipped back down the years to the field at the Western Front which had been the base of the Imperial German Jagdstaffeln 67. In his mind he clearly saw the Fokker triplanes with their bright yellow spinners at the centre of their propellers and the checkered fuselage, painted as if to attract the enemy's attention — to issue a challenge. He saw himself again clambering into the open cockpit, hampered by the great leather

40

coat which was so necessary to fend off the cold at high altitude. The pungent smell of oil seemed to enter his nostrils as he saw himself placing the flying goggles into position that covered much of his face. The triplane shook as he juggled the throttle before racing across the field to find the enemy. When the bouncing stopped, the little aeroplane had found its element, ready to soar into the sky.

Out on his right Kai edged towards his leader, Helmut, the new boy, closing in from his left. For a moment von Haydn wondered how long this fresh-faced lad would last? Maybe two or three weeks, he thought sadly — or had the appointment to meet his Maker been made for this day?

The formation headed south as they climbed, keeping east of the line and hopefully the enemy. Von Haydn knew how aggressive the British could be. If they failed to meet over the trenches they wouldn't hesitate to fly their Sopwith Camels deep into German territory looking for trouble, and oblivious, it seemed, of the prevailing head wind which they'd have to fly into on their return westward. Many a crippled fighter had crashed on the German side because of the headwind.

The base of the cumuli was at six thousand feet, their tops towering up to twelve thousand. Von Haydn, in his imagination, led the Fokkers between the clouds trying to remain undetected by enemy patrols as he turned to make his way to the front.

Today he hoped to find a British reconnaissance plane photographing the German positions. If so, if possible it must be destroyed and prevented from returning with the plates. The RE8s the British used were slow and had poor manoeuvrability, rarely managing to escape from a Fokker attack. The pilots and observers of those machines were incredibly brave in their determination to get photographs.

The German ace searched the sky continually. Hoping not to be bounced, he placed the cloud between his Fokkers and the sun whenever he could. The British have a saying — 'beware of the Hun in the sun' — But he knew the sun didn't withhold its favours from the foe.

Presently Abbeville came into view nestling far below, and the battlefields with their trenches seemed to reach out to infinity. Today was 'All quiet on the Western Front', but how quiet would be the Western sky wondered the fighter leader? Then he saw the RE8 far below, two or three kilometres behind the German lines and the German leader knew it would run for home after its camera had clicked. Reconnaissance machines didn't loaf about when their work was done.

He averted his eyes to make another thorough search of the sky. He knew that RE8 could be a decoy to induce their enemy down, so as to be bounced by their fighters diving from above. But the air below and the sky above seemed to be empty, but he'd checked the sun again. With a clenched fist to block the direct light from striking his eyes, he searched the perimeter of the gloved hand.

The leader paused to give his iris time to dilate, then, with his vision improved, he glanced across his formation to see Kai off his right wing leaning over his cockpit and pointing at the RE8 below. Von Haydn gave a curt nod before turning to Helmut on his left to indicate to him the presence of the enemy. The new man hadn't seen him and it took him a short time before he smiled an acknowledgement.

The leader decided it should be an easy blooding for the young pilot, so he would allow Helmut to make the attack. There was very little chance for the two-seater to escape even if the boy botched it, because one of the others would be sure to bring him down.

After a final glance about the sky, von Haydn pointed down, signalling Helmut to attack. With an intake of breath the boy dropped from the formation, while his leader watched his descent until the little fighter appeared to be no more than a spot when it closed in on the RE8.

When von Haydn expected his young comrade to open fire, he saw instead the machine break away from the attack. The boy hadn't moved in close enough to his quarry before shooting and by turning away he had exposed his plane's blind underbelly to the observer's gun.

Von Haydn saw Kai violently breaking from his position, throwing his Fokker into a steep dive. Surprised, von Haydn followed. Kai was a disciplined flyer and only an emergency would have caused him to break away from formation without warning his leader. Then he saw the three Camels diving very fast towards the two-seater. They had been concealed behind clouds, watching their man below. As the German Jagdstaffel followed Kai, their leader thought, 'Helmut's appointment was indeed for today.'

By the time he and his pilots were amongst the British it would be too late for Helmut. Their mad dive brought them within a kilometre when they saw the short black trail of smoke with the burning wreck of a Fokker at its base and within which sat the youthful pilot blistering in the flames, while the RE8 crossed the lines westwards under full throttle.

A Camel, from a tight right-hand turn, had got onto the tail of a Fokker and was pumping rapid short bursts of machine-gun fire into it. With a desperate movement, von Haydn slammed the stick over to the right, while at the same time pulling it back and kicking on hard right rudder. He just managed to prevent a collision and from the corner of his eye he saw Kai's Fokker grimly hanging onto a Camel's tail before loosing him from sight in the medley.

Kai's Camel went down spinning to crash in no-man's-land and the ace knew his squadron would quickly finish the remaining two, though the Camels were fighting for their lives like savage animals. He pulled out of the fray, standing off, leaving a less cluttered space for his men. After they had destroyed the Camels he would lead them back to base, his squadron having downed three enemy during the patrol; not bad!

It was only five minutes since the arrival of the three British planes, but it felt like an age to the men twisting and turning, avoiding flying bullets and trying to get a bead on their adversary. The strange thing about dog-fighting was the sudden calm which followed. One minute all hell was loose then, suddenly the sky seemed empty. Those aircraft that were not down were running for home out of ammunition. Some having been riddled were limping back, praying not to be bounced when unable to fight.

A second Camel was blazing on the ground but von Haydn didn't know which of his men would lay claim to it. More than one, most likely. The third and final Camel hugged the ground, twisting like a demented gull in an attempt to impair the aim of his pursuers. He could feel pity for the Britisher as he fought for his life, knowing there would be no escape.

Then the German ace stiffened momentarily before crashing the stick and rudder brutally to the left as English bullets smashed his instrument panel, one tearing leather from the shoulder of von Haydn's flying coat. The British pilot being harassed below suddenly felt the blast from an exploding Fokker only yards behind his tail which had fallen to the guns of an SE5. He had been counting the seconds to his death, but now his fight would continue. From nowhere it seemed, the SE5s had arrived to make the battle equal, squadron against squadron.

The SE5s had screamed in unobserved by the combating aircraft and von Haydn's own life had been spared by a whisker. He swore at his lack of diligence towards the open sky while he had been watching the medley. Now men were going to be lost because of it — his men's lives.

He threw his plane into the fray, quickly lining his guns onto an enemy harassing a Fokker but before his aim was true the British pilot had seen him and turning hard, spoilt the ace's aim as well as his own. For the moment von Haydn had lost his prey, but so had his adversary. He had saved the life of his comrade, for the moment at least. Pressed hard down in his seat from the effects of the turn, von Haydn was less than fifty metres behind the Britisher. The SE's turn was very tight but unless the ace turned his aircraft even tighter to allow for the deflection, his bullets wouldn't strike home.

Without warning an aircraft shot across the SE's nose which made its pilot quickly roll his machine out of its turn to avoid colliding. The manoeuvre had brought his machine dancing in front of the Fokker's nose and von Haydn fired. The bullets ripped into the Englishman's engine and as he twisted violently the pilot turned to look directly into the German's face, just before a mass of flames burst back to his cockpit. Von Haydn felt he had looked into the face of Helmut, then he saw his victim stand tall to give a

47

sudden wave and jump to a death less painful than burning.

He watched the start of his victim's fall to earth, but there wasn't time to follow the boy all the way if he didn't wish to join him. Down to his right, he saw one of the remaining Camels trailing smoke as it fell spinning from the sky.

An SE, having pulled out of a dive, reached in its climb for the belly of an unsuspecting Fokker and before von Haydn could intercept, the Britisher had finished his work and seeing the incoming German, appeared not to care as he continued to fly in level flight.

The man is a fool or cleverly experienced, considered the ace, but from the way he had dispatched his last victim, he decided on the latter. Anyway, the German ace never allowed himself to forget that while the French were very brave airmen, they knew when they were beaten: whereas the British were brave, but never knew when they were beaten. The German drove in hard and fast at the Britisher, expecting him to take evasive action at the last moment. 'My God, he's leaving it late,' he thought, as he was about to open fire.

Von Haydn had expected the SE5 to be thrown towards him into a tight defensive turn. Instead, the Britisher, by now having slowed down, shot the joystick to his left while applying full right rudder. Von Haydn saw his quarry suddenly dropping sideways in a vicious sideslip and saw his own bullets streaming over the right tip of the steeply tilted wing. The unexpected change in their relative speed caused his Fokker to overshoot the SE which was now below him.

Alarmed, the German turned his machine hard to his left, and at once cursed his error. It would have been far better to distance himself from his enemy by trading his superior speed for height but glancing back he saw the Britisher was already behind him, though beyond the effective range of his guns. But von Haydn, turning hard, wasn't preventing the SE from gradually closing in.

The fighter ace pushed the Fokker into a screaming dive, then brought its nose up to climb rapidly above the horizon. Glancing back, he saw the SE following him. Arcing the climb at the top, as though to continue into a full loop, the German half-rolled instead, bringing his Fokker upright and flying in the opposite direction from that of the start of the dive. The enemy, no doubt having been surprised by the half roll, would be far below continuing the loop.

Nevertheless, von Haydn flew in straight flight for only seconds before turning tight. He had to be sure his opponent was gone.

But, when he scanned behind, bullets ripped the canvas of the lower right wing and over the howl of the wind he heard the rattle of the British machine guns from only metres behind.

All the skill and experience gained from fifty-two kills was being utilised by the German ace but he was not able to shake the Englishman from his tail. It was only his great knowledge of aerial combat that prevented him receiving the 'coup de grace'. As the duel persisted, the German's whole body ached from the continual forces exerted by the tight manoeuvres and he knew that very soon his flying would become sloppy and then the Englishman would make his kill. But his enemy must also suffer fatigue and von Haydn prayed he would be the first to fail.

The first to fail, because of fatigue! This was where skill couldn't be applied and he was fighting for his life. Since the Englishman was in control and couldn't be shaken, von Haydn must attempt a change of tactics. He would hug the earth a few hundred feet below, where obstacles would force a change in fighting technique. He lost height while turning tight, for the German knew a straight dive for the earth would be suicide giving the Englishman an easy non-deflection shot.

Still turning hard to keep the required

deflection too tight for the Englishman to make his kill, von Haydn skirted his Fokker round a farm building below roof-top height which momentarily shielded him from his adversary and enabled him to suddenly reverse the Fokker's turn. The movement, taking barely two seconds, had been accomplished by the time he was back in the Englishman's view.

The Britisher followed suit at once, for not to have done would have meant the field opening up to give his enemy room to manoeuvre without the certainty of receiving a hail of bullets from his guns. But von Haydn's unexpected half-roll from left to right while he was obscured had gained him ground. His opponent, not seeing, had been unable to match in unison but could only execute it after a delay which had been enough to take him out of line.

Chancing being struck from extreme range, the ace flew level on full power before pulling firmly back on the control stick to lead into a stall turn. The machine climbed vertically until its speed faded — not even full power from the engine was sufficient to overcome the direct pull of gravity. He pushed his left foot hard and allowed the propeller's slipstream to hit the deflected rudder and cause the yaw necessary to swing the Fokker round until its nose pointed straight down at the earth.

As expected, the Englishman followed, his tenacity unshaken, but if the German was to live he must outwit this man, and this he would achieve, not by pulling out of the mad dive to be pressed into his seat from a positive 'G' pull-out as his rival would expect, but he'd escape instead by exiting the dive from pushing under. Only his straps would save him from being thrown from the cockpit during the inverted pull-out and the following inverted flight. The Englishman would see the two aircraft were flying in opposite directions, making it too late for him to re-engage.

Because of the proximity of the ground this was a desperate and highly dangerous tactic from which he may not survive, but it might offer his only hope of survival.

Von Haydn's heart thumped madly as he pushed forward on the stick, feeling at once the blood rushing into his head. He saw the blurred ground rushing by and imagined it scraping his scalp. From his inverted position, he mercifully saw it falling away and he instantly half-rolled to bring the Fokker to normal flight. And then — bullets smashed a wing strut and raced across the Fokker's wing.

The German instinctively kicked on rudder

while throwing the stick over to right before bringing it back into his tummy to tighten the turn, starting the whole stressful procedure over again. Von Haydn could hardly believe the Englishman had followed through the almost impossible danger. Now a tree came rushing into view to fill the Fokker's propeller disc.

Quickly the fighter levelled to miss the tree and the great fighter ace knew his time had come as his aircraft presented itself for the kill. Even now the SE's gun-sight would be targeted on him and in an instant British bullets would rip into his body and send him to eternity. Strangely, he was suddenly calm.

Von Haydn heard the guns, yet his body remained whole and the Fokker flew on. He turned to see the gunfire from the ground and the Britisher's plane jinxing about, belching dense smoke.

By incredibly good fortune, von Haydn had unknowingly led the aircraft over a machine gun-nest presenting the soldiers with a point-blank target. With commendable skill, his enemy crash-landed his plane, and circling above, the German watched him run from the burning wreck. He saw him stand, look up, and salute. In reply, the German ace flew past rocking his wings.

The Englishman had come down well east

of the lines and would be taken by the soldiers while the drained fighter ace coached the battered Fokker to base.

★ ★ ★

'Are you all right, father?' Gunther enquired.

'Of course. Why do you ask?'

'Because you seemed strange. In some way, distant.'

'It's nothing, son. I think it was because of what you were saying about the horrors of this war. It took me back to that other war on the Western Front and the fighting of those days. By comparison it was gentlemanly, but nonetheless brutal. There was little hate between us and the enemy, but we fought to the death, make no mistake about that. After the fear and excitement had receded, many pilots felt pity for their victims. I'm sure it was the same with our adversaries — that's what they seemed to be, adversaries rather than enemies, Gunther.'

'It's not that way, this time father, I can assure you.'

The following day after taking a quick shower, Gunther made a visit to the library and came face to face with Anna whom he hadn't seen for years. He found he was still attracted towards her though much had taken place since their last meeting.

Anna was happy to meet Gunther again but he sensed a kind of strangeness in her that he hadn't previously known, but he was delighted with her response to his suggestion to meet in the evening. He also felt acute disappointment at his leave being almost over.

4

Harry White was feeling mellow as he fumbled with the latchkey of his front door. Earlier in the day Hester had said she would visit her sister Win, who was rather poorly and, since she lived on her own, his wife said she would stay with her overnight.

Harry had therefore decided to phone an old colleague from the force, who was, like himself, long since retired. They'd kept in touch with Christmas greetings and other celebrations, meeting now and then. As Hester was to be away tonight could be such an occasion and his old colleague had kindly invited him to be a guest at his club where he had met a number of Raymond's friends.

The next day, over breakfast, Harry was alerted by his telephone and assumed it would be Hester phoning from her sister's as he wasn't expecting a call.

'Hello,' he said.

'Harry, it's Bob.'

'Who?'

'Bob — Bob Reeves.'

'Oh, Bob. How are you? This is a surprise.'

'I'm not bad, considering.'

'Your grandson, you mean; that was a terrible business.'

'Actually Harry, that's why I'm phoning. Indirectly anyway.'

'How do you mean?'

'An unpleasant event's occurred which was very upsetting to Jenny and me. I phoned you last night but you must have been out somewhere. Anyway, yesterday afternoon Jenny went to the cemetery to put flowers on Norman's grave and she found a small transparent bag taped to his tombstone containing a card. What do you think was written on it?'

'Go on,' Harry said.

'It said, 'SIX, a number not to be forgotten.''

'My God, this is too much of a coincidence! It seems my suspicion of a threat was correct. Do you remember the card Skipper found on his bed during the reunion? It had the same wording, apart from the number. On Peter's card it said SEVEN, on yours it's SIX.'

'That's why I phoned you, Harry. We all disregarded it as some prank at the reunion — except you I think. I noticed your expression at the time, but thought: that's just old Harry's policeman's bit raising its head.'

'You've still got the card, I hope?'

'Yes, I've got it right here.'

'Look Bob, would you mind sending it to me? It's obvious the two cards must be connected but nevertheless I'd like to compare them.'

★ ★ ★

Tom Williams woke up with a thumping bad head. He had just come out of a dream in which a cannon-shell had smashed through the bomber's navigating table at which he had been sitting. He felt cold and clammy and his vision was blurred, though it was slowly clearing. It took some time for everything to come into perspective but when it did, he was mystified to find it was night and he was alone in his car parked on the road outside his own house.

On entering the house, he felt sick and wanted nothing more than to get to his bed, which he did. In the morning he awoke with a clear head and eager for breakfast; he felt he hadn't eaten for days. Having switched on the radio he only half listened as he ate, waiting for the morning news. This was his usual routine.

It was only while he was eating that he realised he was unable to recall the previous day, though he vaguely remembered having been alone in the car when he awoke; Tom was suddenly mystified. Had he been driving on autopilot without knowing it? Or perhaps he'd had a mild stroke while at the wheel, with the subconscious taking over the driving — drawing on the experience of a lifetime behind the wheel. People did have strokes at his age, in fact were inclined towards them, but he felt steady enough now. It couldn't have been a stroke, he decided.

The BBC announcer stated the day and date before reading the news. Tom's knife slipped from his hand to clatter on the plate. Somehow he was missing three days.

Although he didn't like making a fuss, he felt he should inform his doctor about the missing days. He'd be a fool not to, a short explanation over the phone secured an immediate appointment.

The doctor gave his patient a thorough examination, paying particular attention to his eyes and blood pressure but was unable to come up with an explanation. Instead, he assured Tom that he was in fine condition apart from the depressions he suffered, adding that he was fortunate, since depressions weren't a handicap to good health.

Thanking the doctor, he went home to get on with his life.

Tom's little mystery was soon blotted from

the doctor's mind as he dealt with the rest of his day's patients. Then he heard news of a man's body having been found on wasteland at the edge of town. The body had been identified as that of a Mr Lewis whose address, the doctor noticed, was not very far from Tom's. He worried, for Tom had been his patient for many years and although they were not personal friends, he had come to like and respect Tom and wished dearly that he could cure the man's depressions.

Now the doctor really was concerned. In fact, Doctor North was in something of a quandary. Tom, a depressive, had lost three days during which time a neighbour had been murdered. Was his duty to inform the police? Probably only initial enquiries would be required to establish his patient's innocence but, how did the ruling stand on doctor/patient confidentiality in a case like this? He must find the answer.

Tom was horrified when he read about the murder of Jim Lewis and the way he had been discovered by children playing on wasteland. Jim lived only a few hundred yards down the road from him and had moved in about ten years ago after retiring from teaching at a school in Ludlow. Tom remembered when he first met Jim in the pub on the corner. He had been on his own as usual and somehow began talking to him. Jim told Tom, 'When I retired I decided to return to my roots. I had been happy enough at Ludlow but a couple of years before I finished work my wife died and since I've two or three relatives here I thought it best to return home.'

Since that first conversation, the two men occasionally went out together. Tom considered Jim wasn't a bad type, but he found a little of his company was enough. The trouble was, they always finished up arguing politics. Jim didn't seem able to keep off the subject and Tom wasn't all that interested.

It was only about ten days since he last saw Jim, and that was after a six-month break. Tom hadn't enjoyed the last evening at all. Jim had become really abusive in his opinionated way, causing Tom to tell him he hadn't gone out to be lectured and that he might not see him again if he didn't moderate his tone. Now the poor bugger was dead. What a way to go, to be dumped on wasteland!

It was Thursday morning when the police called. Tom was in the bathroom shaving, and on responding to the doorbell he found them there, both with their identity cards — a Chief Inspector Hays and Sergeant Jones.

At the station they questioned him, and

Tom was enraged. He felt like giving them his name, rank and number in answer to every question they asked. That's what he would have done in the war if he had been captured. But that was different as he'd have finished up in a prisoner-of-war camp, no matter what he had said, but by not answering he would have remained loyal.

Detective Inspector Hays had cautioned Tom and now he was questioning him about Jim Lewis' death.

'It's a fact you knew Mr Lewis, isn't it?' the inspector insisted, 'and you saw Mr Lewis ten days ago, on Friday the fourth.'

Tom said, 'I knew Jim Lewis, so what? So did hundreds of other people, I expect.'

'Did you meet Mr Lewis on the evening of Friday the fourth?'

'Yes I did. We spent a couple of hours together at The Blue Boar. Does that make me a murderer, inspector?'

'No, in itself it doesn't, but by the time you left the Blue Boar the pair of you were hardly on the best of terms. The barman said the atmosphere was very cold when you left the bar. He said Lewis had been arguing with you for much of the evening.'

'So what? He was usually argumentative. Why have I been picked out? Not because we argued, you didn't know that until after the barman had told you, when you were already asking about me, so why, Inspector?'

'Because for three days no one knew where you were, not your neighbour, not your newsagent down the road where you routinely pick up a morning paper, nor anyone else we questioned. During those three days Mr Lewis, the man with whom you were having a serious argument was killed. That's why you are here, Mr Williams. Now, it will help our enquiries if you'll enlighten me about those three missing days.'

'I can't, because I don't know anything about them myself,' Tom said.

The inspector sighed, saying, 'That attitude will get you nowhere, Mr Williams. If you want to help yourself, you are going to have to help me.'

'Look inspector, I know it must seem irresponsible, but I really don't know anything about those three days. I awoke in my car late at night not knowing what day it was. If you want confirmation, you must get onto my doctor — Doctor North.'

'Oh, I've already talked to Doctor North; he informed me he had given you a thorough examination and was unable to find anything the matter with you, Mr Williams.'

'Why should I go to the doctor if I thought there was nothing wrong, for God's sake?'

'It couldn't be to build an alibi by any chance?'

'Inspector, don't you think this is rather absurd? Is a man of my age and good reputation likely to start murdering people? What possible motive could I have? Certainly not one caused by a bit of a political controversy. Anyway, I'm not a political animal.'

'Why is your hand bandaged, Mr Williams?'

'I have a nasty cut at the base of my thumb.'

'What happened, how did you cut it?'

'I don't know, Inspector. When I awoke in the car that night it was there.'

'I see, and you have no idea how you received the wound I suppose!'

'None at all.'

'And you remember nothing about your three missing days?'

'From going to my car in the supermarket's car-park to waking up in it three nights later, I remember not a thing, believe me.'

'You say the last thing you recalled was being at the supermarket. Why didn't you mention that before?'

'I've had no cause to.'

'Did anyone speak to you there?'

'No, only the check-out girl. Why?'

'Can you remember anything which didn't seem quite normal while you were there — anything at all?'

'No, nothing — Well . . . '

'Well what, Mr Williams?'

'It's nothing really, seems a bit silly mentioning it, but just after checking out I had quite a fit of sneezing which isn't like me at all.'

'Can you think why you might have been sneezing so much?'

'No, I just started to sneeze. At least a dozen times I sneezed.'

'You say you remember going to the car-park, can you also recall actually climbing into your car?'

'No, I don't think I can. Ah, there is something I can recollect now; as I was getting the car keys I went faint.'

'You went faint. Did you actually pass out, become unconscious?'

'Well I must have done, because I knew nothing until I came to three days later in my car.'

'Very well, Mr Williams, you may leave, but I must advise you not to leave the town without informing me.'

'You mean you still think I'm a murderer!'

'Let's say you may still be able to help me with my enquiries, shall we?'

After Tom had gone, Sergeant Jones who had been sitting in with the inspector said, 'What do you think, sir?'

'I think it's a load of rubbish, Bill. I don't believe a man can become unconscious and, furthermore, remain that way for three days without a doctor finding at least some slight abnormality. As yet though, there's no evidence to enable an arrest.'

'What now, sir?'

'I want to know more about that damaged hand, Bill,' said the inspector firmly. 'Go to the scene of the crime, or at least where the body was found, and search the area thoroughly for traces of blood. Take two uniformed with you.'

Arriving home from the police station, Tom entered his house feeling wretched. He had walked back from his confrontation with the police inspector in a state of confusion. What the hell was going on? Three missing days and now virtually being accused of murder — what was it all about? He was so lonely in his empty home. How often had he felt this way? If only he had a loved one with whom to talk, it would have eased him a little. Eased him to ventilate this dreadful puzzle — just to share.

★ ★ ★

Harry White put down his cup on hearing the front door's letter flap snap back on its spring. The act of bending to retrieve the mail from the floor induced a sharp pain. His back had bothered him for much of the night and disturbed his sleep. Strange how it varied, he thought. Sometimes it hardly troubled him at all for weeks on end.

Perusing the letters, he found the usual circular — that would go straight into the bin — there was a bill, well he could have done without that, and there was an envelope addressed in long hand. What could that be, he pondered? He didn't know the hand, though it seemed slightly familiar. Of course, it was from Bob, he had asked him to let him have that card.

Harry removed the card and read Bob's note. He went to the sideboard and took from a drawer the card he had placed there after the reunion. On comparing the two he found them to be identical, apart from the small change in the wording — 'SEVEN, a number not to be forgotten.' And — 'Six a number not to be forgotten.' The cards were beautifully printed and at first glance seemed to have been done by a printing machine, but a closer scrutiny showed them to be hand printed. 'The hand which had written these cards must be that of an artist or maybe an architect,' Harry thought.

'So you're back, sergeant. Have you anything to tell me?'

'Yes sir, I have,' the sergeant said, placing a plastic bag containing glass on the inspector's desk.

Studying the bag, the detective said, 'Mm, part of a broken bottle, eh?'

'Yes sir. See the mud? The glass has been kicked or scraped some way over the ground, and sir, you can see traces of dried blood in the soil where it's discoloured. Also there's a little directly on the glass itself,' pointed out the sergeant.

'Where exactly was this glass found, Bill?'

'Close to where the body lay, about ten yards away.

'But the ground's fairly dry where the body lay, it certainly wasn't muddy,' the inspector said.

'That's true sir, but the body wasn't far into the wasteland and if you remember, it was fairly wet near the entrance. It looked to me as if kids on mountain bikes had been fooling around,' the sergeant volunteered.

'When we removed the body there were no tyre marks from a motor vehicle, only impressions made by footwear that were smeared as though an attempt had been made to prevent footprints being left behind Sergeant,' Inspector Hays said thoughtfully.

'Or, by the body having been dragged over the ground and over the prints. There was mud on the back of the victim's shoes, if you recall, that would accord with being dragged. If the victim had been pulled by his wrist whilst lying on his back, his body would have naturally dragged over any prints made by the person doing the pulling. At the same time the weight of the victim would cause the smearing of any prints which were, by definition, sir, soft at the time of impression.'

'Yes, Sergeant,' the inspector said, eyebrow raised.

'I wonder why the victim was dragged into the grounds. It would normally be easier to carry him there, not being far from the track to where the body had been left. It must have been a frail man, or possibly a woman.'

'Or an old man! Come on Bill, we'll make another visit to Mr William's home, I think.'

Tom frowned on opening the door to find the police there again. 'Good afternoon Mr Williams, may we come in?' The inspector and sergeant were in the hall almost before Tom had time to reply.

'I don't like this; you're entering my home as though I am a common criminal,' complained Tom. Sergeant Jones thought he was not looking well at all.

'There wouldn't be any difficulties in obtaining a warrant, I assure you, but why make things hard for yourself? You'd avail nothing,' he said. Tom felt the inspector was curter than before.

'I don't understand why you are harassing me. Connecting me with Jim Lewis' death is incomprehensible. I have always been honest and respectable. Why don't you just back off?'

'I hope for your sake I will be able to, Mr Williams, but the time isn't now. Where do you keep your shoes? I see you're wearing your slippers at the moment.'

'Of course, I usually do when I'm at home.'

'Yes. But your shoes please.'

'They're kept under the wardrobe, in the bedroom.'

'Fetch them, Sergeant,' the detective ordered.

'Three pairs sir,' Jones said on his return, placing the shoes on the floor.

Turning to Tom the policeman asked, 'Which pair did you wear during your three missing days and nights?'

Tom indicated the shoes in the centre and the inspector reached to pick them up. 'These shoes are very clean, Mr Williams. Removing the evidence, were you?'

'I cleaned them last night, before going to

bed. I'm not a slob, I shall be using them today,' Tom said contemptuously.

'Not a trace, Sergeant. They could have just left the shop. Now go to Mr William's car and check the foot-wells for traces of soil which I can hand on to forensic.'

'Inspector Hays,' Tom said, 'when this business is over, and you are unable to lay any charge against me, you will not have heard the last of the matter.'

'Before we leave, Mr Williams, I would like to remove the bandage from your hand. My sergeant will help you to replace it with a fresh one. Or, if you prefer, you can come with me to the station to give a blood sample.'

The following day Tom was taken to the station in a police car. Inspector Hays advised Tom to call his solicitor or, if he wished, the police would provide one. He was then cautioned and charged with murdering Jim Lewis at sometime between Friday the eleventh and Monday night the fourteenth of September 1998.

Soil had been discovered in the driver's foot-well of Tom's car, which was consistent with the earth of the wasteland where the body of Jim Lewis had been located. Inspector Hays said that finding the soil wasn't conclusive in itself as similar soil was to be found over a fairly large area. However, with other leads, the soil was at least good circumstantial evidence.

Other evidence being:

1) There were numerous witnesses who had heard Williams and Lewis arguing heatedly in the Blue Boar during the evening of Friday the fourth of September 1998 which could have been a motive for the murder.

2) There was indisputable forensic evidence of the blood taken from a broken bottle found at the scene of the crime, the DNA of which matched that of the accused. The cut at the base of the accused's thumb had been plainly caused by a jagged object.

The jury was out for only fifty minutes before delivering a guilty verdict on Tom Williams. The evidence presented by the prosecution had been overwhelming, with the DNA alone being beyond dispute.

The judge recognised Tom's unblemished character until he had committed this crime, which was by normal standards unprovoked. It was also evident that the murder was premeditated. The law demanded therefore a life sentence. He would, though, taking his advanced age into consideration, recommend a review for conditional release after nine years.

Tom was in no way a weak man. As a young airman, he had been a steadfast member of his bomber crew, sometimes in the most arduous circumstances. His ability and loyalty were never questioned. The feeling of the family atmosphere generated by the seven comrades was most comforting for him. He had himself been one of a family of five, had enjoyed a happy and loving relationship in his childhood years, but on reaching adulthood the family had quickly dispersed far and wide, except for his eldest brother John, who had gone down at sea during the war.

With his two sisters marrying during their teens and his remaining brother living in New Zealand, Tom had virtually been alone since demobilisation from the RAF and he hated it. He would have given anything to have been the head of his own family, but he didn't seem to know how to get on with the fair sex. There had been girls, quite a few in fact and most seemed to have liked him, but somehow none had wanted to marry him.

Because Tom by nature wasn't a loner he felt his life hadn't been at all natural and on balance he had definitely been more unhappy than not. He was a respectable man, always had been and was careful not to inflict his misfortune on others. When Tom was badly depressed there was no way he could hide it, so at those times he kept himself to himself.

Now, through no fault of his own, he found himself in prison where he was to remain for nine years if he were to live that long, which he doubted. He found himself with the scum of society with whom he had nothing in common. Often, when Tom had been depressed he had wished to die, and in a place like this he might consider helping death along.

A couple of weeks after being sentenced Tom's solicitor was granted leave to visit his client. He was alarmed at the change that had come over Tom. The old man's face was pale and drawn, his eyes were sunken and dulled, almost glazed. The solicitor's heart went out to his client, for in his heart he was sure justice had not been done. For years now he had been dealing with criminals one way or another and had developed an instinctive insight into a man's character. This man in front of him was no murderer, not even a petty criminal.

'Good morning, Mr Williams. I won't ask how you are, I can see for myself. I sincerely hope matters will improve for you when you have had time to adapt a little. However, Tom

— I would like to call you Tom please — with our office mail this morning was a letter addressed to me and marked personal. On opening the envelope I found another enclosed which I have here and it is also marked personal. It is addressed to Mr Tom Williams. Being your solicitor I was tempted to open it, but perhaps that would have been too 'personal',' smiled the solicitor.

Tom was surprised; he didn't often receive letters, certainly not marked 'personal'. He tore the envelope open to remove a white card of high quality on which the only words were: 'FIVE, a number not to be forgotten'.

'What is it?' asked the solicitor.

Tom showed the card, saying, 'I've no idea.'

The solicitor remarked, 'Well it's from someone who knew how to reach you through me. It's got to mean something, Tom, but I can't imagine what.'

Tom said, 'At our reunion a few months ago — it's our old bomber crew from the war, we have annual reunions you know — anyway, at the last reunion, a card exactly like this one was discovered on Peter's bed. Peter Newell was the pilot, the skipper of the crew. No one knew why it had been placed there and we just dismissed it as tomfoolery and forgot about it. But Harry wasn't so trite, he always was a suspicious one.'

'Who's Harry?' asked the solicitor.

'He was the wireless operator in the crew; after the war he joined the police and became a detective.'

'You say the two cards are the same? With the same message?'

'Yes, exactly. No, not exactly. The number was different. The one at the reunion said 'seven' but this is 'five'. I wonder why that should be?'

'I can't imagine,' the solicitor said.

'Look,' Tom said, 'do you think you can arrange with the screws for me to make a phone call?'

The solicitor laughed before saying, 'Excuse me Tom, I had to laugh; you're talking like an old lag already, using the term 'screws'.'

Tom managed a faint smile, saying, 'Well, all right; but could you arrange for me to make a call?'

'Yes, an odd one, now and then. Who do you wish to contact?'

'Well it's this number business. You see, there were seven men in a Lancaster bomber, the same number as on that first card, but the number is five on this one. Recently the rear gunner, Bob Greeves, had his heart broken when he lost his grandson, killed in a skiing accident they said. I'd like a word with Bob.'

'What could that have to do with

anything?' asked the solicitor.

'Can't you see? There have been two tragedies in the crew. Bob's and mine. The card I've received says number five. I want to know if he received a card and if so, was it the same only with the number six printed? If so . . . someone is after the whole crew!'

The solicitor looked grim, before saying, 'I'd better arrange for two calls. One to that detective of yours.'

★   ★   ★

When next Tom Williams was led into the visitors' room, it was to find Harry White waiting for him. He sprang to his feet and shook him warmly by the hand. 'My God, Tom, what are you doing in this place? When I got yours and Bob's call informing me what had happened to you, I thought his own misfortune had pushed him over the top. We've got to get you out of here, Tom, the whole situation is absurd.'

'Absurd may be, but I've been put in here by a judge and jury, Harry. What can anyone do about that? It's a miscarriage of justice, certainly, but if I'd been on that jury I would have voted guilty. The evidence was damning and yet it was all a pack of lies. Nothing can be done, Harry. I'm here to stay — until I decide to end it myself.'

'We'll have less of that talk,' Harry said, almost sternly, then, 'Now Tom, I want you to fill me in about the whole of this sorry business. Start at the beginning; miss nothing, no matter how trivial it may seem to you. I want to know everything. Almost how many times you blinked your eyes.'

As Harry walked from the prison he felt it was almost like old times. He was determined to get to the bottom of this botched affair and would strive to clear Tom's name, knowing his poor friend could never survive his full term.

5

'There's one for you and two for me,' Hillary smiled, when she handed Peter his letter. Her husband was still wearing his dressing gown, not even having shaved, but the postman did deliver letters early to their house.

'It's the Chesterfield postmark, must be from Harry White. Now I wonder what he wants?' Peter slit the envelope to extract the letter. 'Funny, this. It's from Harry and he wants us all to meet — the crew I mean. He doesn't say why, but says it's vital regardless of any inconvenience it may cause. He's contacting the others and he'll ask them to phone him confirming that we agree. He'll let us know then which hotel he booked for us. It'll be for one night. Harry says we all should receive his letter on Wednesday but in case the odd one takes an extra day he'll book the rooms for Friday night, making the hotel as central as possible.'

'Why on earth should Harry write you all such a letter?' Hillary sounded slightly alarmed.

'I don't know dear, I'm baffled. His letter must be taken seriously though, he's not a fool. He wouldn't rush into anything without having given it a lot of thought,' Norman asserted.

★ ★ ★

A small anteroom had been reserved for their conference. Harry had told his friends he wanted their discussion to be private. 'It may not matter to be overheard but I'd rather we weren't,' he said.

The anteroom was adequately furnished with comfortable leather chairs. When the waiter, who had brought in drinks, closed the door, Harry said, 'Right chaps, now I'll tell you why we're all here. I will start with what Bob already knows but I asked him to keep to himself; it's a bombshell. I needed an attention-getter and believe me, this is it. Our dear old friend Tom is in prison for murder.'

'No,' Peter gasped, then, 'I wondered why he was missing.'

'Come on, Harry. Tom a murderer? That's ridiculous.' This was Arthur who for once wasn't sounding jovial.

'I didn't say he is a murderer, Arthur. I said he was in prison for murder.'

'But why, for God's sake?'

'Because he has been got at, that's why.

Someone wants to hurt him.'

Peter said, 'Who the hell would want to hurt Tom? There isn't a more inoffensive person alive.'

'That's true, and it's a reason for asking you all here. Now cast your minds back to the reunion. Remember the card, the white one you found on your pillow, Peter?'

'The card on my pillow? — Oh yes, I remember, it was thrown in the waste basket. What about it?'

'Remember what was written on it, do you?'

'No ... Wasn't it about remembering something or other?' Peter said.

Looking grim, Harry said, 'It was indeed but what a good thing I retrieved it. What it said was — SEVEN a number not to be forgotten.' Reaching into his breast pocket, he extracted a white card. 'Now, look what Bob's wife found sealed to their grandson's grave. A similar card but this one says SIX a number not to be forgotten — '

'It looks exactly the same as the other one,' Arthur remarked.

'It is the same, apart from the figure.'

'Any idea who put it there?' asked Jeffrey.

'No, but I intend to find out,' Harry said firmly.

'What's the point? I reckon some imbecile

of a lout is fooling about. Probably on drugs likely as not.'

'I don't think so, Jeff. What lout will bother to move from Newark to Dundee just to fool about with a couple of cards. Look at the quality of these cards. Not the kind of thing a lout is likely to have in his pocket.

'Now, what I'm going to tell you will remove all doubt as to whether we should take this business seriously or not. As far as I'm concerned he was definitely fitted up. Once Tom was found guilty of murder and behind bars, this was handed to him by his solicitor.'

Harry produced the third card. Holding it up, he said, 'Read what is printed on this one, if you please.'

For a moment the group was completely silent as Harry looked from one to the other. Then, Peter whispered: 'We're targeted. Someone is out to get the whole crew.'

'You're damn right. That's why you are here,' Harry told them.

James asked, 'Who the devil would want to kill us? Let's face it, we're a bunch of old men. We are past harming anyone, for God's sake.'

'That's the point. Because we are old men, they, he, whoever, doesn't want to kill us. That would be too easy because we have lived most of our lives. Such punishment would be diminutive. In my view what this madman wants is for us to suffer.'

'Have you any idea at all who is behind this?' It was James who asked, and his face seemed even more highly coloured than usual.

'Not at all. There isn't a lead, other than the cards and they've told me nothing up to now.'

'Have you checked them for prints — fingerprints?' Jeff asked.

'I've done that. Most of us handled the first card at the reunion. It was covered with our prints and badly smudged, anyway, the other two were clean, so I'm sure the first one will have been. It's obvious the Perpetrator was careful to avoid contamination.'

'What do you think we should do, Harry? This really does look a serious business.'

'It certainly is serious. Tom and Bob have already been hurt and I'm convinced neither was accidental. There is no point putting the matter in the hands of the police and asking for some kind of protection. They have been told officially by the Austrian authorities that Bob's grandson's death was an accident, and their own evidence against Tom was readily accepted by a judge and jury. So, we'll have to look after ourselves as best we can.'

'How do we do that, Harry?' Peter pressed.

'Vigilance. There's not much more I can say. We will all need to change our normal outlook on life by constantly remembering there is someone wanting to hurt us. I suggest each one of us think hard what would really cause him grief. It could be more than one thing. In Bob's case it was his grandson. I'm certain the scoundrel had been informed what would really hurt Bob. With Tom, the wretch attacked the poor man's depressions by getting him incarcerated and removing his respectability. Again, the villain is informed as to what would hurt him the most.

'We all should think where our vulnerability may lie, then guard it diligently. In a word, be suspicious, but don't become paranoid. Such action won't be foolproof, I know, but at least we'll be on our guard.

'Now chaps,' Harry continued, 'I want to throw the field wide open by asking you to think hard. Try to come up with suggestions which I may find helpful in tracking this bastard down.'

An uneasy shuffling followed, otherwise there was total silence before Peter said, 'I wonder how the man is so well informed? Not just of what will hurt, but the fact we are a group — a crew. I mean we're all so spread about the country.'

'What about the use of a good private detective? He needn't know to what use his information is to be put,' suggested Arthur.

'It would be costly,' Bob considered.

'I have a feeling money is not a problem,' Harry suggested.

Bob said, 'Assuming this guy is out to get at all of us, how can he know we are 'connected', so to speak?'

'Easy,' Harry said. 'RAF records, they are open to anyone, even today.' He paused; 'Maybe that's where I should start. I might find who has been making enquires recently.'

'Do you think you'll be able to do anything about getting Tom out of prison?' Arthur asked.

'I will certainly do my best. I do have one or two ideas so I think I can handle it.'

'I hope to Christ you can,' Peter said with feeling.

Jeff said, 'If there is a private investigator feeding back information, do you think you could possibly track him down, Harry? If it turned out he didn't know to what use the information was put, he'd most likely be horrified to learn the truth. Under those circumstances he may well tell you who his client is.'

'I agree, Jeff. I have already thought of that possibility.

'Are there any more suggestions?' Harry asked, passing his eye about the group. But no more proposals were forthcoming, until Arthur said, 'I reckon you may well find yourself running up a bulky bill Harry . . . What with travel and hotel costs, etc. and you won't be getting to the bottom of this problem overnight. So I propose we all contribute, share the expenses. What do you say?' He gave a quizzical look at his colleagues.

Their approval was unanimous.

James struggling out of his chair said, 'Shall we repair to the bar if there isn't anything more we can do just now?'

★ ★ ★

Harry White, leaving his hotel on Castle Street, turned to enter the High Street. He was in Cardiff, the capital city of Wales and the home ground of his old comrade, Tom Williams. Harry's mind was as active as it had always been when on an investigation. It really felt like the 'old' days, or it would have if the same ardent spring had remained in his step. Harry's gait was now more of a stroll than the brisk walk of days gone by.

He turned left on to Wharton Street, walked the short distance before crossing to

St David's shopping centre with the RC church of the same name at the far side. Harry knew he would be in need of some good luck if he was able to make a successful start into his investigations here at the supermarket but at the moment he couldn't think of another straw at which to grasp.

It was the checkout girls he had come to see and on stepping into the store he counted fifteen busy at work. 'Might as well start at the first check-out and work my way up,' he decided. Having explained who he was to the first girl's satisfaction, Harry asked, 'Do you work regularly on the check-out?'

'Yes, but I do other duties as well, we all do,' she said.

Harry asked, 'I want you to take your mind back to Friday morning, the eleventh of September. I know it's some time back but please try, it's very important. Were you on the check-outs then?'

'Well yes, I would be. I'm always on on Fridays, in the mornings that is.'

'Good. Can you remember an elderly man checking out? He would have been alone and the same age as me, only not so big as I am. He would have been smartly dressed in a style that might have seemed a bit old-fashioned to you?'

'No, but I get quite a few old men passing

here, though most aren't really dressed in the way you describe.'

'This old man had a bad bout of sneezing just after paying for his shopping. Does that jog your memory?'

'I'm sorry, I recall nothing like that,' the young girl said as she slid a packet over the magic eye.

'OK, dear, I'll let you get on with your work now. Thanks a lot.'

It was at checkout number 8 where Harry's hopes were raised. The girl hadn't served the old gentleman, but she remembered she thought he was going to bust a gut if he didn't stop his sneezing.

'Was anybody else sneezing apart from the old man?' Harry asked.

'No, why should they?'

'Did you smell anything unusual?'

'Nothing at all.'

'You say it was the next cash desk where he paid?'

'Yes, I said so, but Shirley's left the job now.'

'Did she seem to have a sort of irritation to her nose or eyes?' Harry pressed.

'None that I noticed, but then we don't have time to look around, not on a Friday, anyway.

'If the old man was as distressed as you say,

didn't anyone show concern?' he persisted.

'Mrs Morgan put her hand on him. She would, she's a busybody, but she is kind.'

'You mean you know this Mrs Morgan?'

'We all know Mrs Morgan on check-out. She talks too much, slowing us down and upsetting the folk waiting behind her who want to pay for their goods. I think she's a bit dim, myself.'

'Do you know where this Mrs Morgan lives by any chance?'

'No, but Hazel will know, because we were talking about her one day during our break and she said, ''Mrs Morgan lives near me.'''

'Where's Hazel now?'

'She's there, look, third till along. The girl with the black hair.'

Harry found Mrs Morgan at her home in Tudor Street and was agreeably surprised how this 'talkative lady' was on her guard before allowing a stranger into her house. However, once he had convinced her, it was as the girl at the checkout said.

'Oh yes, I recall the old gentleman very well. The way he was sneezing, I thought he might bust a blood vessel. He was so embarrassed. Quite the gentleman he was.'

'Mrs Morgan, after this man finally finished his sneezing, did you see anything more of him? If you did, I'd like to hear every detail please.'

'Well yes, I followed him out of the store — but just let me make us a cup tea before we talk, I'm sure you'd enjoy one. Or, perhaps you'd prefer a coffee, Mr White?'

'Tea will be fine, thank you, Mrs Morgan.'

While his host was out of the room, Harry saw the photograph of the soldier and, looking closer, he recognised Mrs Morgan on his arm. He reckoned she was ten years younger and he wondered about the picture. To his trained eye the house suggested Mrs Morgan lived alone. He was replacing the photo as Mrs Morgan brought in the tea. 'Ah, that's me and my husband, Hugh. He was a smart man, don't you think, my Hugh?'

'Yes indeed. You no longer have him?'

'I'm afraid not. Lost he was, in the Falklands. He was with the Welsh Guards. The poor dear was on the *Galahad*, when she was hit. It was very hard at the time, Mr White, but I'm over it now. Or at least as much as I ever will be.'

Not for the first time Harry thought how lucky he had been. In his war, so many went down whilst he survived and in Mr Morgan's little war, with few losses overall, she had lost her husband.

'Sugar your own cup, if you take it,' said Mrs Morgan, placing the cup and saucer near him.

Harry, smiling, stirred in two spoons, and said, 'Shall we see if we can get any nearer to solving my problem? So after the sneezing, tell me exactly what you saw.'

'Like I said, the sneezing bout was awful but when his face had returned to its normal colour the poor man looked really ill. I saw that he trembled. I followed him out to make sure he'd be all right. He made for the car park and reaching his vehicle he put his shopping bag on the ground while he found the key, I think.

'As the driving door opened he fell sideways but was caught by a man who had been standing by the car next to his, and while holding him, this man opened the rear door. I rushed over to help.'

'What happened then, Mrs Morgan?'

'Well, this fellow said, 'Thanks, but I can manage. I know Tom, he has diabetes, I think he must have forgotten to take his medication.' I offered to go back to the store and call the ambulance but this fellow said no, it would be quicker to take him to the hospital in the car. He got the poor old man in the back seat and then bent to pick up the shopping.'

'Then, I suppose he drove off?' Harry said.

'Yes, but as the car pulled away, I noticed a bank card lying on the ground. I shouted after the car but he can't have heard me so I decided to take the card to Barclays' in the city and told the lady there how I came across it,' Mrs Morgan said rather seriously.

'You did the right thing. What did the man look like? The one who drove the car I mean.'

'He'd be about my age, around forty. He was well made and wore trainer shoes. He was clean-looking but not very smart, or so it seemed to me. You become used to a man looking smart if you're married to a soldier,' she said, with a touch of pride.

'When this man spoke those few words to you, did you pick up any accent?'

'Yes, now I think of it he sounded like he was from London somewhere. Not a posh voice, a bit Cockney-like, though it wasn't strong.'

'Did he wear a hat?'

'Yes he did, it was a brown trilby. Rather old-fashioned for these days and it didn't fit in at all with his trainers.'

'Thank you Madam, you've been quite observant, there's nothing more I suppose?'

'Not really, though I did think he was quite handsome,' she smiled.

Harry said, 'Thank you for receiving me like this, Mrs Morgan, you have been very helpful. I enjoyed the tea — both cups,' he smiled.

He crossed the river from Tudor Street onto Wood Street, passing the bus station. He decided he would look in at the general hospital to check if Tom had been booked in on the fourteenth. He'd be a fool not to, but he'd bet a pound for a penny they'd never heard of a Tom Williams.

Leaving the hospital with his doubts confirmed, Harry made his way to Barclays Bank where a member of staff promptly backed up Mrs Morgan's statement about the bank card being handed in, though the assistant refused to tell Harry the holder's name. It was only after he had convinced Mr Grey, the manager, of his authenticity that the ex-detective-inspector received full cooperation.

Mr Grey said the card which had been handed in on the fourteenth, belonged to the Richmond-upon-Thames branch and the holder's name was Mr K Reid. Harry asked, 'Can I have his address, please?'

'Er, I don't have it here,' the manager replied.

'Come on now! Surely you can get it through your computer system?'

'Well, wait a minute then. Yes, it's here — 102 Upper Richmond Road West, East Sheen.'

'Thanks Mr Grey. What is Mr Reid's account number please?'

The manager looked at Harry over his glasses and frowned until Harry said, 'Come, Mr Grey, every cheque drawn by any account holder shows its number.'

The manager read out 19902668. It was true that Harry didn't have any use for Mr Reid's account number just then, but it was information which could be stored for possible use later. He thanked Mr Grey for his time, but before taking his leave made a final request. 'Mr Grey, can you please give me a description of Mr Reid, I need to know more about the appearance of the man I'm looking for.'

'No, we are a long way from his home branch, I've never seen the man.'

'It was a pointless question really, Mr Grey. Anyway, thank you very much for your help. I'll wish you good day.'

Harry felt he should stay another night in Cardiff. Tomorrow he'd travel to London. Now, though, he was tired. The old man had had enough for one day. As he lay in his bed he felt satisfied with his day. He knew his visit to the supermarket had given him a lucky break — a break which would give him a start which otherwise might have been hard to find. With good detective work one thing would lead to another and he was sure he would get his old friend away from his present unhappy surroundings.

★ ★ ★

At Barclays' Richmond branch, Harry White obtained an interview with the manager by the use of his old police rank. But the manager, rising from his seat to shake his visitor's hand, made no attempt to hide his surprise at their meeting.

Reading the manager's mind, Harry said, 'I retired from the force twenty years ago.' And after the preliminaries, he asked, 'Has Mr Reid had any sums of money paid into his account in recent times which you would think are larger than is customary?'

'There have been two large amounts but I don't wish to mention the sum.'

'That's not necessary as long as you can assure me the amounts are really substantial,' Harry said.

'They are, sir!'

So, Reid has been contracted to do the dirty work. He will be told his targets and how to hurt each one. In Harry's mind, only an investigator could gain that knowledge — a good one at that, he decided.

He asked the manager, 'Has Mr Reid, in your view, drawn any cheques for unusual payments?'

The manager perusing Reid's account, said, 'Yes, if you consider payments made to a detective agency unusual.'

'I would consider it to be unusual,' Harry said with a satisfied smile. 'May I have the agency's name please? I'd also like a description of Mr Reid. I wonder if you can give me that?'

'I cannot,' the manager said, then smiling he asked, 'What do you think of this?' He handed Harry a picture-frame from his desk. It held a drawing of an attractive lady in her mid-thirties.

'Very nice. She is beautiful,' Harry commented, wondering what it had to do with his question.

'Very nice? — It's marvellous! That is a drawing of my wife and if you knew her, inspector, you would see the likeness is correct in every detail. One of the staff was the artist. I had caught her sketching one of the girls and glancing at her effort I recognised the likeness at once. She had only spent minutes on the drawing but the detail was remarkable.

'I called the 'artist' — her name is Mary — into my office.' The manager smiled when he said, 'Mary knew I had seen her drawing instead of working and I think she thought she was in trouble. However, I told her I was impressed and asked if she'd be prepared to draw my wife. I said I'd frame it for my desk if she would come to my home for a sitting. You know what, Inspector? — The girl blushed and said, 'I won't need to go to your house, I can do it as soon as I've got paper.' 'You'll need her to sit, won't you?' I persisted. 'I won't,' she answered. 'I saw your wife last Tuesday when she came to your office.' And this, believe it or not, is the result of Mary having seen my wife once. It is absolutely remarkable.'

'I can't argue with you, that's for sure. You reckon Mary could do the same with Mr Reid?'

'I know she could, if she can recall who Reid is. I'll call her inspector.'

When Mary entered the office she first looked at her manager and then at Harry, before saying, 'Yes, Mr Stone?'

The manager said, 'Mary, I would like you to do a drawing for this gentleman, Mr White.'

'Hello Mary,' Harry said, affably.

'Certainly, Mr White. Just let me have one good look at you, sir.'

Laughing, Harry said, 'No, not of me Mary, I want you to do a drawing for me of one of your customers, a Mr Reid. I wa . . .'

Before Harry could continue, Mary said, 'Oh, Mr Reid. I already have a picture of Mr Reid. I did it for myself. I have it at home.

He's such a handsome man,' the young lady was showing excitement.

'I hope you're not spending all your time at the bank drawing our customers? That isn't what we are paying you for Mary,' the manager said firmly.

'Oh no, Mr Stone, I've only done Mr Reid. He's sort of special you see.'

'I see. Well, we'll find a sheet of paper. You can sit at my desk while you do the drawing.'

Harry was astounded at the speed with which Mary worked without loss of detail. In only five minutes it was completed. There was no way he could judge the picture against the real Reid, but he believed Mary's own confirmation when he recalled how the manager praised her work on his wife. Mr Stone though hadn't personally met Reid.

'Thank you Mary, that looks excellent,' Harry told her, 'but I'm surprised you have put such detail on the tie?'

'Yes I know, but it was such a beautiful tie. I couldn't help but notice the unusual pattern.'

'Do you recall the colour?'

'Yes. It was a dark green and maroon, but predominantly maroon.'

After thanking the manager and slipping Mary ten pounds — telling her to regard the drawing as a commission — he left the bank.

He wasn't exactly surprised when he found 102 Upper Richmond Road West was an empty house. The dirty windows showed it had been so for some time, leaving him wondering about bank correspondence arriving, and how it was collected.

The door of number 104 opened to display a smartly-dressed elderly lady. Harry introduced himself before enquiring how long the house next door had been closed up.

'Too long,' the lady said. 'I wish to goodness someone respectable would come and live there. Just look at it, bringing down standards and it's right next door to me.'

'How long is it since it was lived in?' Harry insisted.

'Oh, a year or more, but it's not even up for sale. Can't imagine what's going on,' the lady said, indignantly.

Harry showed her the drawing of Reid asking, 'Did this man live here?'

'No, he didn't, but he had a key and I have seen him once or twice entering the house but he never stays long. Once, I caught him and I asked what was going on but he walked off ignoring me.'

'Thank you, madam, I'm sorry you've been troubled.'

It seems Mr Reid is going to be elusive, Harry thought.

He had his likeness, if that's who he is, but having his fingerprints could easily prove to be very useful later on. The problem was how would he obtain them and know the prints actually belonged to Reid?

★　★　★

The 'Private Detective Agency' was housed at Barking in a dignified side street and occupied the first floor of a respectable building. Harry sensed an atmosphere of calm. He heard soft music drifting from some hidden source and his shoes sank into a lush carpet. In a corner, by a window-seat, stood an elegantly glazed pot, containing a lush dark green philodendron. Two walls presented pictures showing the West End by night. He thought he hadn't seen anything less like a detective agency. The service provided must be good. It wouldn't come cheap.

Harry gave his credentials to the receptionist saying he needed to speak to the senior agent and, after a few minutes' delay, was shown into a well-ordered office.

Mr Birch, the smartness of his attire matching the surroundings, rose to his feet. 'Good afternoon Inspector White. I am honoured by your visit, how can I help you?'

'Thank you for seeing me at such short notice, Mr Birch. I won't waste your valuable time. I'll get to the point of my visit.'

'Thank you, I am rather busy.'

'You have as a client a Mr K Reid, I believe?'

'I'm sure a man of your profession can't really expect me to divulge my clients, sir,' the man behind the desk said, surprised.

'Under normal circumstances no, I wouldn't. But after 'I've offered an explanation I feel you will have a change of heart, Mr Birch. It is evident that you run a respectable detective agency. Careful, I am sure, not to become involved in any kind of skulduggery,' said Harry, holding the man's eye.

'Certainly, Inspector, we endeavour to maintain a high standard. I think we can be proud of our record.'

'I am aware, Mr Birch, that to date this agency has obtained information — which has been passed to your client, Mr Reid — on the two following gentlemen: Mr Robert Green and Mr Tom Williams. Furthermore, I strongly suspect that at this time your man is in the process of uncovering information on a third person on behalf of your client, the said Mr Reid.'

The head of the agency revealed an expression of incredulity, before asking,

'Where did you gain this knowledge, this inside information of our agency? There must be disloyalty within our organisation. It will be flushed out. I assure you.'

'There is no need for that, Mr Birch, there has been no disloyalty. I was a rather successful detective you know.' Harry unashamedly felt a touch of pride.

'You will not know that Mr Green lost his grandson after your investigation?'

'I'm sorry to hear that, but how does that affect the agency?'

'The grandson was murdered!'

'Murdered? That is terrible, but again, how does it affect us, Inspector?'

Harry continued, 'Mr Tom Williams is now a guest of Her Majesty, serving nine years for murder.'

'I don't understand,' Mr Birch said, bemused.

'I am correct in thinking that the instruction given to this agency was to gain as much information as possible on the targets? Physical, mental, psychological, likes, dislikes, loves, prejudice etc.'

'Yes, it had to be like a market survey, a very penetrating one. We had our best 'man' on the job.'

'Did you not ask the purpose for such information, Mr Birch?'

'Oh indeed we did.'

'And you were told?'

'The information was to be used by an international company who are interested in targeting elderly people with a view to developing and marketing products which would bring satisfaction in their old age. Regardless of personality type.

'The company concerned knew it would be difficult, if not impossible, to survey these people openly, as much of the knowledge required, was extremely personal. The result however, would be much to old people's advantage because it would enrich their lives.'

'You won't know the name of the company?'

'No. The opposition has to be kept ignorant of the development.'

'Mr Birch, can you see now that the company and the project were a cover. A cover to enable your client to gain knowledge on how best to hurt his targets. The 'survey' brought to light Mr Green's strongest passion was his love for his grandson. So, to give the most hurt to Mr Green — dispose of his grandson.

'Then we have Mr Williams. It was discovered that his curse was depression and loneliness, but his priority is respectability. By being framed for murder, which he most certainly has been, he is now in a place where depression will occur more often and will be deeper and where respectability is removed absolutely. Both men have been sent to hell, Mr Birch.'

'But who is behind this, for God's sake?'

'I don't know, but it's not Reid, even though your payments come through him. He's just the hit man.'

Then the agent said, 'You are here of course to ask that we stop working for Mr Reid which we will do at once, Inspector.'

'That, and to ask if you have had any personal contact with the man, but I'll be very surprised if you have.'

'A contact was made once only to set up the business, but he didn't call himself Reid.'

Harry showed Mr Birch the picture of Reid. 'Is this the man?'

'No, I've not seen him before.'

'I expect you haven't, Mr Birch. What I need now are Reid's fingerprints. At this time the only place I can hope to find them is on a cheque he's written out to this agency. I suppose though, they will have already been negotiated?'

'The first two were passed long ago, but a third came yesterday. Reid always pays in advance — you were correct about the third man, Inspector. It's a Mr Beaumont, Jeffrey Beaumont — '

'I'll be grateful if you'll accept a receipt and permit me to borrow the cheque for his prints.'

'Under the circumstances it's the least I can do, inspector,' Mr Birch retorted.

When Harry returned the cheque, not only did he have Reid's prints, but also a copy of his handwriting. With those, together with the man's picture, he felt at last he had some 'tools' with which to do his work.

6

Harry White returned to Cardiff, to find himself in the same hotel room he had vacated after breakfast the previous day. It had been a long day and he was thankful the train from London had made good time. The decision was right to leave his car and to use the train and taxis instead of driving in London, which was an unnecessary task for an old man.

His watch showed nine thirty, not too late to phone Bob. But first, he'd take a whisky from the mini-bar.

Responding to the call Bob said, 'Hello, Greeves.'

'It's Harry. Not too late I hope? I'm phoning from Cardiff.'

'Hello Harry. Nice to hear from you. What are you doing in Cardiff?'

'I'm about the ghastly business of Tom's imprisonment,' Harry told him.

'You didn't waste much time in getting started,' Bob said.

'The thing is, I'm quite pleased with progress so far but I won't be ringing around the whole crew. Instead, I propose to send each of you a periodic progress report. However, I felt I'd like to let you know quickly how things are going, because you were the first victim. My report will inform you of progress made, though I think it will be a bit of a slog before I uncover sufficient evidence to free Tom.'

'Do you really think you will get him out of prison, Harry?' asked Bob.

'Oh, I'll get him out all right. The man is innocent and I mean to prove it, it's just a question of how long it will take. Anyway, like I said, Bob, I thought I would put you in the picture before I turn in, I feel whacked. Remember me to Jenny. She is OK, I hope?'

'Yes, she's fine. She just called, says I've to give you her love. Anyway, I'll let you get your head down. Thanks for calling. And look after yourself, Harry.'

The detective replaced the phone, massaged his eyes and undressed. In the past, he thought, a day like today would have been taken in his stride but now his bed beckoned and when he lay down he briefly saw Reid's face swimming before his eyes, then Detective Inspector Harry White was sleeping like a child.

★ ★ ★

The next morning Harry wanted to take a look at Tom's car. He knew the police hadn't been interested in handing over the vehicle to forensic, because they were satisfied with having found a sample of soil from the car's foot-well. That, together with Tom's unexplained missing three days, his DNA match with the blood found at the scene where the body had lain and the motive — perhaps the weakest link in the chain — convinced Inspector Hays he'd all the evidence that was required to achieve a conviction. He had been proved right.

Harry found Tom's solicitor in his office at Number 3 Sun Street. Mr Jones was keeping Tom's house keys under safeguard but he readily handed them to Tom's friend after discovering Harry's business.

'If that man's a murderer, Inspector White, then my name's not Gareth Jones. Tom Williams told me you were on Lancasters with him in the war and later, you joined the police. He said you had a fine record as a detective. I hope you will be able to come up with something to get your friend free. Although, I have to agree that the evidence against Tom seems conclusive.'

'Tom has been set up, Mr Jones, I haven't the slightest doubt about that. If I don't get him out of prison, it certainly will not be due to lack of effort. In fact I am looking forward to handing you new evidence to enable you to start things moving for his release.'

Accompanying Harry to the door, the solicitor said, 'That will be a happy day, Inspector. I wish you well in your quest.'

After paying off the taxi which had brought him to Tom's home at Number 17 Cathedral Road, Harry went at once to the garage at the head of the driveway. He unlocked the doors and opened them wide to let in as much light as possible. Then, for good measure, he put on the electric light. Harry began his detailed search with the interior of the car as he was keen to get that part of the work over with. It was going to entail a lot of bending and twisting of his body in a confined space which wouldn't be easy, for he was a big man and his bulk had lost much of its former agility. The way his back had been playing up recently wouldn't help either.

An hour later, with aches making themselves felt in parts of his body he didn't previously know about, the detective had nothing to show for his discomfort. He moved to inspect door hinges and window-frames but found not a thing which might have given a lead. A close check of the windscreen wiper revealed nothing of interest. Then, reaching for the side mirror, he pulled it back on its spring and Harry's mouth curled into a satisfied smile.

* * *

Harry sat at the wrought-iron table enjoying a coffee and a cream pastry in the airy tea-room of the garden-centre. An old man with grey whiskers gave a nod to Harry as he passed by. The detective smiled at the old gentleman, saying, 'Good afternoon.'

Pausing, the man asked, 'Looking for something for the garden? Your hobby, is it? In your retirement?'

'The gardening is mostly done by my wife. It doesn't affect her back like it does mine,' Harry said, still smiling.

'Why man, I've gardened all my life and I haven't so much as a twinge. It's Mother Earth you know, she keeps aches and pains away.'

'Care to join me? There's coffee left, I'll fetch a clean cup,' Harry liked the looks of the old fellow, and was sure he would enjoy his company a while.

The man was delighted to stay. Maybe he had been short of conversation recently. Harry experienced this at times. People weren't as ready to chat much, when you were getting older. 'There, help yourself to the sugar. So! You do a lot of gardening, eh? Have a big one, do you?'

The old man laughed. 'You could say that, I dare say. I've had this centre for longer than I care to remember.'

'You own the garden-centre?'

'Indeed I do,' the old man said, giving another laugh.

'Well,' Harry said, 'you are just the man I wanted to meet.'

'How's that then? And my name is Davis,' the old man volunteered.

'White; pleased to meet you, Mr Davis,' Harry took his wallet from his pocket and removed a tiny packet. Opening the packet he extracted a petal. 'This is why,' he said, passing the petal to Mr Davis. 'Can you identify that?' he asked.

The old man, with half closed eyes, studied the petal, then looking over his glasses at his companion, said, 'Where did you find this? It is rare in this country. It's an African plant called euphorbia. Actually, this variety, because it's spiky, is used out there as a barrier against animals.'

'And not common, here about?' Harry questioned.

'No it is not, not this variety. In fact, if it hadn't been of interest to an old customer of my father, who had the centre before me, I doubt if I would have ever actually seen the real plant. Photographs yes, but not the living plant. Where did it come from, Mr White?'

'That's what I'd like to know. I found the petal trapped into a car's side mirror.'

'I don't understand,' Mr Davis said, 'why has a small petal aroused such interest when you didn't even know it was rare? From what we have here, you wouldn't have an inkling of how the plant would look in its complete form.'

'To be honest, Mr Davis, it's not in the interest of horticulture. As a matter of fact, I was a police detective before retiring and now, for reasons I'd rather not go into, I find myself mixed up in some very unpleasant business. I am here because I really do need to know where this petal got caught up by the car. If I knew that, it could be of great importance.'

Mr Davis replied, 'I think because you chose my garden-centre this is your lucky day. I am probably the only man who knows where you will find the plant.

'My father started this business as a young man in his twenties after returning from France during the First World War. You know, Mr White, the war that was to end all wars! My father started in a small way and it was soon evident that he had an aptitude for business. His 'green fingers' were a great help there. At that time, an elderly army major became friendly with my father, largely because of their shared interest in horticulture.

'At the time I arrived to brighten up my parents' life, the major had established his family on a large property near Hensol Forrest, though he and his wife only had one child, a son. My father and the major became good friends and sometimes, when I was small, I'd stay a few days at the major's place as a companion to his son.'

'That's when you first came across this euphorbia, I suppose!'

'I expect so, though I didn't know what it was; I was just a small boy. It grew like a hedge at the bottom of the garden and by the gate. We children quickly learnt not to rub against it because the barbs, or thorns, were dangerous.'

'It was a funny plant to have, wasn't it? Hardly the fashion,' Harry commented.

'Well, it was just one of those things, you know what people are like! It takes all sorts to make a world. You see, the major had retired. He had spent the last years of his service-life in South Africa and had learned to like that country. Since he had come to admire the land so much, its beauty and its ruggedness, he desired something which would later remind him of his happy days there — a memento, if you like.

'To the major, euphorbia fitted the bill. The plant's tough impenetrability and the beauty of its small flower seemed to pay the right sort of homage to the land he had left behind.'

'An interesting story, Mr Davis. But the major will have died long since. Isn't it surprising the plant still remains? There must have been numerous changes since the major's day. I mean, not only to the garden but such as the property changing hands a time or two.'

'Of course you are correct, Mr White. The major passed on in the early fifties; his wife had shortly preceded him. To the last, he had been proud of his home, not least the rough old hedge at the bottom of the garden.

'Now the place is in ruins. After the death of his parents, their son Albert hit the bottle even harder and managed to drink himself to death within five years. Albert had been a great disappointment to the father. During the child's formative years, the military duties of his father prevented him from paying as much attention to the boy as he would have liked. Albert had been mollycoddled by his mother who thought the boy could do no wrong.

'There had been no other children. Besides, the major and his wife were their parents' only offspring. So, the line is now dead and their fine old property is left derelict.'

'Well, Mr Davis, it's been a real pleasure meeting you,' Harry said, as he rose to shake hands with him. 'And I'm sure the information you have given will be most valuable.'

'Pop in any time, Mr White, then we can have another chat,' and with that, the men made their farewells.

The ex-detective was feeling very content with his progress, realising how providential it had been to stumble on the one person who knew about the unusual type of euphorbia in the major's garden. He would require his car from his hotel car park to make the journey to the house, which, he decided, he would do tomorrow. Now time was getting on, so he'd spend an hour or so in the shops to find a present to take home for Hester before freshening up for dinner.

* * *

The major's old home sat in half an acre of land, three hundred yards from the northern edge of Hensol Forrest. Harry drove slowly through the gap that once had been filled by a gate, but that was now submitting to the intrusion of the euphorbia hedge, so that it was no longer possible to drive the car through without brushing it. What had been a well-tended garden was now fully overgrown.

The house had not been vandalised though Harry was able to enter through a side-door, previously forced. The interior was covered in dust and had been cleared of furniture, but there were signs that water had run into the kitchen sink fairly recently because the dust was mostly gone. An inspection of each room showed only the kitchen had been entered, as there was much disturbance of dust leading from the side-door to the kitchen. Elsewhere the dust was virgin and could be ignored. The kitchen was without pots or cutlery of any sort — a fact that made Harry wonder why water had been used. He tried the tap but found it dry, as he had expected. The water would be turned off at the main cock. The liquid which had been poured into the sink must have been brought to the house by someone.

Looking across the kitchen, Harry saw lying on the floor what he had hoped to find — pieces of broken glass. He studied the glass closely, handling only the edge of the pieces. He would take them to be checked for fingerprints, but now he was looking for signs of blood. There were none. Separating a single piece of the glass from the rest, the detective smiled.

Harry dusted the kitchen for prints but got the same negative result, as he did with the pieces of broken glass. He stood there, contemplating. The kitchen was just an empty room except for the glass and a small piece of threadbare carpet remaining in a corner. He was sure Reid had been here with Tom but he had been cautious. Getting Reid's prints though would add a lot of weight to Harry's elbow.

An old-fashioned flowery wallpaper, stained in places, still clung to the wall but it was a poor surface from which to lift a print even if it had been touched by Reid . . . 'What is this?' . . . Harry took a step to the wall on his right. He made out four lines in the form of a rectangle where it seemed the paper hadn't quite butted together. Because of the paper's irregular coloured pattern the lines were not easily seen.

He tapped the wall at each side of the rectangle, finding it to be solid. But there came a hollow tone when he struck within the rectangle. From the centre a screw protruded. He had noticed the screw as he entered the room but had assumed it had held a picture frame at some time. Now he realised the screw had once retained a small doorknob, opening the door of a cupboard set in the wall. He eased the door open to find three shelves within.

The closed cupboard had kept out most of the dust as there was only a slight covering, but Harry could see the thin layer had been disturbed on the middle shelf where a small framed photograph of a roan cocker spaniel stood. 'A family pet from years past,' Harry supposed.

He removed the photo from the shelf to take a closer look and found a thumb print on the framed glass. 'Someone else had noticed the protruding screw and had forgotten his caution,' assumed the detective with satisfaction. The picture was carefully wrapped before joining the glass in a carrier bag.

Striding to the corner where the carpet lay, Harry lifted it from the floor and his scrutiny revealed a dark patch. He sniffed at the patch several times.

★　★　★

In response to a knock, Inspector Hays looked up from the papers laid on his deck to see his sergeant enter the office. 'Yes, what is it, Sergeant?'

'There is an elderly gentleman out there, sir,' the sergeant said, throwing a glance towards the door. 'He says he wants to talk to you.'

'What does he want?'

'He didn't say, sir. Just that he wants to talk to you. He says he's retired from the police force, sir. Says his name is White. Mr White.'

'All right, show him in, Sergeant.'

'How do you do, Inspector. It's good of you to see me like this,' Harry said as he offered the inspector his hand.

'Please be seated, Mr White. How can I help you? I must tell you I'm a busy man and it isn't usual for me to see people who come in casually like this. However, my sergeant says you were in the force at one time.'

'That's correct, Inspector. I was with the Chesterfield police for many years. An inspector there.'

'Were you indeed? But that must have been some time ago, Mr White — er, Inspector White,' he corrected with a smile.

'It was. Almost twenty years ago I'm afraid.'

'Twenty years ago? Chesterfield? Inspector White! Bells are beginning to ring. It can't be Harry White. Not Inspector Harry White, surely.'

'Yes, that's me.'

'What an honour to meet you sir. A man with such a magnificent reputation. During training, and later at seminars, your cases were frequently held as examples from which to learn. You were renowned countrywide amongst the force,' Inspector Hays said enthusiastically.

'Spare my blushes,' Harry said, smiling.

'I remember, years back, when we were at the seminars — and I hope you won't take offence, Inspector — but we wondered why a detective with a record like yours never climbed to a higher position in the police force. It was a mystery to us, Inspector White.'

'Please, let's drop the formalities. Call me Harry.'

Inspector Hays said, 'I think, really, it should have been Commissioner. However, we'll settle for Harry, but you must call me Colin. But the mystery, insp — er — Harry?'

'There is no mystery. I was often offered promotion but I was not interested. You see, I enjoyed my work, Colin. I loved detective work and knew I was doing society a service. I had no wish to change, only to find my job nothing but additional administration, even though I may have gone far. Nor was I ambitious for the extra money that would have come with promotion. I was satisfied with inspectors' pay because I was fortunate to have private means. No, Colin, I just wanted to get on with trying to do what I was good at.'

'A man with his true vocation,' smiled Colin.

'You might say that,' Harry agreed.

'Well now, the purpose of your visit, Harry?'

'It concerns a case recently investigated by your good self. That of Tom Williams.'

'Tom Williams, yes, he's got nine years for murder. What's your interest in him?'

'Er . . . he's innocent.'

'I beg your pardon, Harry. Williams is as guilty as hell. An open and shut case.'

'I readily agree it looks like that from the evidence before you, but Tom Williams was cleverly set up.' Harry opened his case and took out a piece of glass, protected in a plastic bag. 'This glass was found by me at a deserted house named 'Woodside' which is close to Hensol Forrest. Years ago the house had been the home of a Major Owen. The family has died out. I want you to take this glass, Colin, and match it with the blood-stained piece which was found near Mr Lewis' body.'

'But looking at this glass Harry, it seems clean. I can't see a trace of blood to match.'

But Harry said, 'Look Colin, the glass is clean. I'll bet you a pound to a penny that its broken edge will fit into the piece you have, like two pieces of a jigsaw. Tom Williams didn't cut himself with your glass. Someone else used it to cut him, while Tom was out cold. Your glass was then taken with the body to the wasteland to be found as evidence for a later match with the blood from Mr Williams' cut hand. He, in the meantime, was kept unconscious in the major's old house to deny him an alibi. After three days, when dark, someone, knowing his victim would soon recover, drove Williams in his own car, whilst still unconscious, and parked him in his own driveway. It had to be dark so that Williams wouldn't be seen slumped at the wheel by someone glancing casually at the car. To have been seen unconscious, would of course have given credence to his claim of three lost days, substantiating a probable alibi.' Harry stared firmly at Colin.

'You do seem to have come up with something, Harry — providing the two pieces of glass match. But what was to prevent Williams from using the old house as a hideout? Then dumping the body and dragging it into the wasteland where he cut his hand on glass which was lying there. Hardly unusual in such a place. His hand would bleed heavily since it was a bad cut. He'd realise his blood must be on the glass which cut him, so he'd need to find it to remove evidence. He sees the glass that you have brought to me, but before he could see it was clear, the blood from his wound splashes the glass as he stoops to pick it up. He's sure it's the piece on which he had caught his hand. So he takes it back to his hideout. The real culprit was trodden under foot into the soft earth, to be found later by my sergeant.

'That would explain the two pieces fitting together, Harry. Also, your piece of glass is as clean as a whistle. Why should a man with nothing to hide wipe it clean?'

'He wouldn't of course,' Harry said, and he now took the framed photograph of the cocker spaniel from his bag. 'The glass in this frame, Colin, has a good finger print on it. Will you please record it and see if it matches up with this print I have taken from a cheque. I think you'll find they'll match. The person from whom the print came is the abductor of Tom Williams and probably Jim Lewis' murderer.'

'How can you know that?' Colin inquired.

Harry produced the drawing of Reid. 'The fingerprint on the cheque comes from this man, as does, I'm pretty sure, that on the picture. As you can see from the cheque, his name is Reid.

'A Mrs Morgan of Tudor Street had followed Tom Williams in St David's Shopping Centre to the parking lot. She was concerned, because she had seen Mr Williams sneezing uncontrollably and she thought he looked ill. On reaching his car, Tom passed out and was then supported and put in his car by a man who had been waiting nearby. They drove off in Tom's car. The man had refused Mrs Morgan's offer to call an ambulance, saying he could get to the hospital quicker. When I showed Mrs Morgan this picture she immediately made a positive identification.'

'You are saying Williams actually became unconscious?' Colin asked disbelievingly.

'And remained so, for three whole days! I'm pretty sure barbiturates were used to keep him under. I think powder was brought to the hideout, to be mixed into liquid for a syringe and administered about once a day. I also suspect blood was taken away and held in a syringe. The blood later to be squirted onto 'your piece' of glass and the ground where the body was discovered.

'If you can spare the time now, Colin, I will tell you of all my activities concerning this case. I'll leave a copy of Reid's picture. You may want to see if the Yard can come up with anything. I would appreciate it if you will inform me of any developments regarding Reid. If you pull him in, I would dearly like to sit in during interviews.'

'I shall find the time, Detective Inspector Harry White,' Colin said. 'But first, satisfy my curiosity as to why you are showing such interest in Mr Williams.'

'Well, I know the man is not capable of murdering anyone. Also, Tom and I were in the same bomber-crew during the war.'

'Aaah . . .'

Harry's next port of call was Number 3 Sun Street. There, he briefed the solicitor and informed him of his discussion with Inspector Hays. He asked Mr Jones to start procedures as quickly as possible for Tom's release. Accompanying Harry to the door, the solicitor beamed with pleasure. 'This is a happy day, Inspector.'

Harry had an appointment to visit Tom, and tell him the good news. 'We don't know who is the perpetrator of this rotten business, Tom, and as yet I have no idea. So, to prevent him from striking at you again it is essential that he hears no word of your release. Both the police and your solicitor are aware of this and everything is being done to achieve a news blackout. I'm afraid, Tom, your home must be seen to be up for sale. You wouldn't require a home if you were to be in prison for nine years. Of course, you could let it. But I'm sure our man is fiendishly clever. He might check about the rent and where it finished up. I even suggest, Tom, that you get well away from Cardiff as you are obviously known to him or his agent.'

'Leave Cardiff? The man is causing havoc.'

'He certainly is, but at least you won't be in prison. Until you settle down and find a new home, why not stay with one of the crew? Any one of us will be delighted to have you stay and none live anywhere near Cardiff.'

7

Miraculously, Gunther had survived his U-boat war and, shortly after leaving the navy, had married Anna. He had never really loved any other woman, so he had expected his wedding-day to be the beginning of a wonderful life with the woman he loved.

From the start however things were not as they should have been. Anna was warm and thoughtful and Gunther's advances were not rejected, though they certainly were not encouraged. His wife seemed only to be performing a duty. A few months after their wedding day Anna went to her room alone while her husband lingered over his nightcap. Wearing soft slippers, she didn't hear his approach and when Gunther entered their bedroom he saw Anna had taken thc photo of Hildegard from the table and he noticed an expression of love as she gazed into the eyes of her dead friend. It was an expression he had never seen from Anna. He saw tears flowing freely down her face, and when she turned to see her husband standing there her head drooped as though in shame.

Gunther reached for his wife to hold her

tenderly, saying, 'What is it dear? Why are you so upset?'

With her head remaining lowered Anna answered, 'I loved her. I always will. I'm sorry, Gunther, I cannot help myself. We were lovers and I can never forget. In my heart no one will ever replace her, not even you, dear Gunther. I had hoped marriage to you would change things but now I know it never will.'

★   ★   ★

Kurt Haydn crossed the hall of Falkenstein and entered the drawing room. There, he found Hans in his statue mode. As usual the boy appeared not to be breathing during his monument-like stupor and his eyes, while open, seemed to have been chiselled from stone as they gazed blindly ahead.

Hans, now middle-aged, had showed no sign of growing out of his peculiar condition since returning home from the Nervenkrankenhaus all those years ago. Though he had not really been a trouble to the household, he remained a strange human being. From childhood, the boy had been rather odd, but it was Anna's death which had caused him to really flip and thus have to enter the Nervenkrankenhaus.

Anna's life, such as it was, was wrapped

around her son whom she cosseted and spoiled completely. She knew Hans wasn't a normal child but rather than trying to help his condition she heightened his affliction by sheltering him from reality. In some strange way, her attitude towards her son seemed to help her maintain a fantasy of her dear friend Hildegard. By locking her son away from the realities of the world, it helped to remove these from herself. Hans knew of his mother's friendship with the woman he had never known, who, indeed, had died before his own birth. He also knew when his mother was unhappy it was due in some strange way to the death of her friend. But he didn't understand why.

When his mother died, Hans was filled with misery and grief and was frustrated by not understanding how a heart could break. He knew it was that which had killed his mother because after her funeral he had heard his father say to Uncle Kurt, 'Anna died of a broken heart. The love for Hildegard, which she was no longer able to give, killed my wife.'

The loss of his mother and his mental confusion concerning her death worsened Hans' already unstable mental condition to such an extent that it became necessary for him to be taken to where there was constant supervision. Modern times however, brought about new ideas on treatment, enabling his return to the family.

Leaving the house one morning, not saying a word to anyone, Hans made his way to the cemetery. Why he went there he didn't know but he felt a craving within him driving him on, and amongst the forest of gravestones he found where his mother lay.

He had been there on the day of his mother's funeral but he couldn't recall the event — though on that day he had stood at the graveside racked in grief, with confusion sweeping away all his senses. But now, as the tears flowed, he read on the gravestone of his mother's devotion to her only son. Then Hans caught the name 'Hildegard' chiselled into the stone of the neighbouring grave. It was his mother's friend and he thought how strangely close to each other were the lines of gravestones at this point.

First there was his mother's grave. Then came Hildegard's — she must have been there a long time, for he knew she had died before he was born. Reading the inscription Hans was surprised to see Hildegard had not died as he had thought, but had been killed on the fourteenth October 1944. There were four more stones in the line and walking along them he saw they all had the same date and all had been killed. Then Hans noticed the plaque in their midst on which had been inscribed: 'The team. Together in death as they were in life.'

On his return home Hans asked his uncle the meaning of 'The team' and was told about their friendship and how his mother, feeling ill, had left the party early on the night a Luftwaffe night-fighter had been shot down while defending the Third Reich and how it had crashed onto the pavilion. Later that day Kurt was witness to his nephew's longest stone-like trance ever.

The tragedy of the boy worried Kurt deeply. His mother had gone, as had his father. Kurt's heart had bled for his brother, Gunther, knowing how he had suffered a feeling of guilt, resulting from the memory of that heartless Atlantic war. The love and partnership Gunther had hoped for with Anna had not materialised, and there was his poor son, Hans, who had seemed to rob him of Anna's love — though he knew it was really Hildegard who still held her power over his wife, even in death. Finally, there came that awful holiday that Gunther had taken in the hope of lifting his spirits but resulting instead in killing him in a climbing accident. Poor Gunther, he was surely best out of it.

Unusual though it was, Kurt wasn't really

surprised that his brother had left the bulk of his estate to the International Seafarers' Welfare Fund. Such generosity was typical of Gunther. Besides, he knew he had never forgotten those wretches foundering in the cold sea, trying to wrench the oil from their lungs before submitting to the depths.

The death of old von Haydn had caused his estate to be divided amongst his family which had included money put in trust for Hans, money which could only be reached through an executor.

Of course, Kurt was a wealthy man regardless of the money which came to him from his father's estate and which was substantial. He hadn't reached the heights of the banking world without securing a sound financial income. But Kurt did have a financial concern concerning his nephew Hans. The boy was indeed wealthy in his own right, leaving aside the trust set up by his grandfather, and this caused Kurt to worry as to how his nephew might use this money. The fact was Hans could get his hands on it any time he wished, but with his mental problem, there was no saying how the money might be used. This fortune had come to the boy on the death of his mother, but, to be honest, Kurt believed Hans hadn't yet been foolish with his inheritance.

It was beyond Kurt's comprehension — and everyone else's for that matter — how Anna could have been so asinine in making out her will as she had. She had of course made Hans a world of her own into which she retreated, never to stray beyond, save for her fantasy life with Hildegard. Both her parents were tragically killed when the car in which they were travelling was hit by an oncoming articulated truck that jack-knifed into them on a wet road.

Shortly after his parents funeral Anna's only brother emigrated to the USA to try his hand at gold-mining in Alaska. Few made much of a living during their summer's mining, but Wolfgang hit it rich. Then he himself was struck by cancer. The only remaining relative was his sister Anna to whom his fortune flowed.

* * *

Harry White's comprehensive progress report was delivered on the same day to his five colleagues. They learnt the details of Tom Williams' impending release from custody. In the report, Harry brought home to each of them the necessity for Tom to keep a low profile when he was freed. He stressed that, though it was probably only a matter of time before Reid was pulled in, it didn't necessarily follow the whole rotten business would be over. He was sure that Reid was nothing more than a hit man for some individual, or organisation. But Harry had to admit he didn't understand the motive for harassing the crew. He said he was completely in the dark regarding that.

It came as a shock to Jeffrey Beaumont when he read in the report that he had been the next to be targeted. However, Harry had comforted him with the assurance that, for the moment at least, he was out of danger. The detective agency had been alerted and their work concerning Jeffrey's background had stopped.

Seated in his favourite chair, Harry was watching *The News At Ten*. The picture of Bill Clinton, the president of the United States of America filled the screen. Commentators discussed the likelihood of the president's impeachment resulting from his lying about his affair with Monica Lewinsky.

When Hester entered the room with his nightly drink of hot chocolate, she found her husband gazing into the fire and the television turned off. 'You seem to be deep in thought, dear,' she said, handing him the mug.

'I was thinking how things have changed,'

said Harry. 'What used to be private is now broadcast to the world. If you don't mind, dear, I'll take my drink with me. I'll have an early night and perhaps dream of yesteryear.'

'Oh dear, we are feeling sombre,' Hester said, kissing his cheek.

The next morning on his return from a walk in the park, Hester said, 'There's been a call from Inspector Hays, dear. He wants you to ring him back.'

'Inspector Hays? That sounds interesting. It won't be a social call, I'm sure. Now where did I put his number?'

'He gave it to me, Harry. I've written it on the pad by the phone for you.'

'Colin. Harry White here. You rang. Has Reid been pulled in?'

'You've got it in one, Harry, we have him,' Colin said, enthusiastically.

'Where did you nab him?'

'Outside his bank, thanks to you — your information I mean. The London chaps staked out the place knowing he was likely to call at the bank sooner or later since he hadn't a suspicion we were on to him. The young detective who made the arrest remarked about the drawing we had circu-lated. He said the remarkable likeness made his job easy. But the staff had of course been briefed to give our man the nod if a signature

135

was passed which matched the copy each of them had.

'This is great news. Where is Reid now? In Cardiff?'

'Not yet, but he will be. He's being delivered tomorrow, at noon. If you still want to be in on the interview, get yourself down here as soon as you like.'

★ ★ ★

'Please come this way, sir.' The officer led Harry along the corridor and tapped on Chief Inspector Hays' door.

'Come,' called The Chief Inspector, who continued to study the paper before him as the two men entered his office.

'Inspector White to see you, sir,' said the young policeman.

Chief Inspector Hays sprung to his feet. 'Delighted you were able to come Harry. Er, that will be all, Constable.'

With extended hand, Harry said, 'Good morning Colin. Allow me to congratulate you on the arrest of Reid.'

'Thanks, but it was the London boys who made the arrest,' Colin said, with a modest smile.

'No matter. You've got him where he belongs, behind bars. That's all that matters. I have to say I am more than a little keen to meet the villain, though I'm still of the opinion that we will remain far removed from the real brain behind this 'vendetta' on my crew.'

'Have you still no idea what it's all about? If indeed it is the full crew they are after?' Colin queried.

'No I haven't. I don't know why we are being hit, but there is no doubt that we are. Look at the first card found at the reunion. It had number seven printed on it, 'Seven, a number not to be forgotten'. But the card for Bob Greeves at Dundee was numbered six, and Tom William's number five. No, there can't be any doubt, the full crew is marked.'

'I admit it seems so. Harry, have you eaten yet?'

'No, I didn't know when you'd be having Reid in and I certainly didn't want to miss out on that.'

'Right then, The Blue Bell is the place. They make a nice soup and their pork pies are excellent.'

At three-thirty that afternoon Reid was brought into the interview room. He stared at the two men behind the table. One, the younger, whose face seemed expressionless, was surely a detective. Reid had been questioned before by such men — to him they seemed to be a breed — but they had never got anything on him or tied him down. Nor would they this time. But why had he been picked up? He had been held now for almost twenty-four hours but no charge had been made. When he asked why he was being held, the reply was 'suspicion'. Suspicion of what? They would not say. Reid figured they must think they had something on a job he'd done long ago.

He knew one thing for sure: They couldn't have anything on his latest escapades. He had covered himself far too well for that. And who was that old bugger with the detective? The way the man looked at him made him feel inexplicably uncomfortable. He felt the man could see into his soul. But Reid pulled himself together and quickly regained his confident, if rather truculent, demeanour.

Then came the bombshell . . . 'Of course, you will be charged with the murder of Mr James Lewis.'

Chief Inspector Hays had remained without expression as he spoke. Reid, normally calm, felt the blood drain from his face and for a moment the men before him blurred out of focus. He had not been prepared for this. How could they know? Trying to regain his composure, he said, 'What the hell are you talking about?'

Hays said calmly, 'Before we proceed further I think we should remove the need for play-acting.' With that he took a framed photograph from a case at his feet which he placed on the table, facing Reid. 'Afraid of spaniels are you? You seem to have gone all pale again. Doesn't he, Inspector White?'

Harry did not answer, nor did his eyes stop boring into the scull of the man opposite.

'Why should a photo of a bloody dog be of interest to me, for God's sake?'

'Well, if that's of no interest, how about this? It's a fingerprint taken from the framed glass. Guess whose finger matches with it! Like I said, Mr Reid, there is no need for play-acting. It doesn't really matter if you co-operate or not. Either way you can look forward to a life as the guest of Her Majesty. But the burden may be eased a little if your record showed you'd pleaded guilty and co-operated with the police,' the Chief Inspector remarked indifferently.

'What does a print on framed glass prove?' Reid was desperate, clutching at straws.

'Stop wasting my time,' the detective said. 'It proves you were in the place where this photograph had dwelt for half a century. The place where you kept Mr Williams for three days imprisoned and in a state of uncon- sciousness. A place where traces of his blood

139

were discovered. Blood whose DNA matched what we found at the scene of the crime, and which had been deliberately placed there by yourself. That, Mr Reid, sir, is what a print on framed glass proves. Now, shall we co-operate, or would you prefer to look forward to a full stretch with no easement?'

Reid was baffled. Where had he slipped up? He'd been a fool to leave his print on the photograph he'd found in the cupboard, but how the hell did the police discover Woodside? He'd thought the hide had been foolproof. All right, he had left a bloody print there, but he was sure no one had seen him arriving at or leaving the place. Anyway, he'd only needed to make one visit a day to administer the injection to Williams and he'd been careful not to drive the car into the grounds each time. Even if he had, it would have been unlikely to have created a track, because the old tarmac was still fairly well intact. He was sure there had been no danger from the two times he did drive the car in — once to get Williams in and once to get him out. At the time, he thought he was being unnecessarily cautious as he could see no way in which the hide could be suspected.

'Well! What's it to be, Reid?'

The accused stared across the table. It was Hays who spoke, his face still expressionless.

That bloody old man's stare was getting to him — it was almost physical. He knew he was trapped; they had proof of him having been at Woodside and they had Williams' DNA which showed it was his blood found at the waste-site as well as that at Woodside. The blood was to have provided the evidence to put Williams away for a long time. Now the whole bloody business had all blown up in his face.

'What's the deal?'

'There will be no deal. Just a report on your record which will be left to the appropriate authorities to use as they think fit.' The old man's voice came across the table like a blade cutting away any thought of clever wrangling. Who was this old devil who put the fear of God into him? He had spoken but once and already he felt he was foundering.

'I'll be helpful,' Reid said quietly.

'You were used as a hit man and you did it for money, right?'

'Yes.' The old man's mien was awesome.

'Where did the money and your instructions come from?'

'I don't know. In the beginning I received a phone call at my home, a proposition was made. I was offered a sum of thirty thousand pounds to frame a person for murder. I was

141

to receive fifteen thousand to set the job up and fifteen thousand on completion. I was told a key would be delivered through the post which would fit the lock of 102 Upper Richmond Road West, East Sheen, where I would find the money. There would be no more contacts made at my own address. I tried 1471 but the number had been withheld. I think a cellular phone had been used.

Hays asked, 'When did the money arrive?'

'Two weeks after the phone call.'

'So that was fifteen thousand to get you started. Did you not consider just taking the money and running?' Colin asked.

'It had been made very clear that if I accepted the job and then in any way crossed them I would be made to suffer — prior to my throat being cut. There would be no escape. Their research on me had been very thorough. Do the job, they said, and there would no danger and I'd be paid promptly. Or I could refuse the contract from the start, and I'd hear no more about it.'

With his eyes still boring into Reid, Harry said, 'But you didn't refuse, did you? After all, it was only a matter of murder! Why was Mr Lewis chosen to be the victim?'

'After I'd been informed as to who was to be framed and received the details on him from the detective agency, I observed Williams while structuring my plan. The argument in the pub between Williams and Lewis played into my hands. It had been witnessed by everyone there, so they would provide another nail in Williams' coffin.'

'Later you followed your victim to St David's supermarket and when he left the check-out you sprayed him with a toxic gas. No doubt you used a small spray bottle concealed in your breast pocket. You knew there would be a short delay before the spray took full effect. Of course, you knew where Mr Williams' had parked his car, so you rushed to wait nearby for his arrival. When he finally collapsed, you were ready to help him, then drive him away.'

Reid looked in amazement at Harry. 'How can you know this?'

'Remember the lady who offered to call an ambulance?'

Reid said, 'Well how could you know about Woodside?'

'I don't have to tell you that. But I can say that when you got Mr Williams established at Woodside you kept him in a state of unconsciousness with the help of a barbiturate. Having only a single syringe you mixed powder with water into a solution,' Harry surmised with confidence.

Reid felt bewildered. The old man still held him with that intimidating glare which pierced into him.

'How *can* you know I used powder?' he asked, his voice weak.

'There was no water supply, so you brought your own to the house, water which you didn't need for your own use as there was no sign you had *lived* at the house. The kitchen sink had a dry rivulet where a small spillage had flowed. Also there were traces of powder. You have been fortunate not to have been caught before for earlier misdemeanours you will undoubtedly have committed.

'You really are not a very bright man, Mr Reid,' Harry said, with disdain. Continuing: 'Do you really think that if Mr Williams had committed the murder, he would have been so careless when cleaning his car, to only half-clean the foot-well after making such a thorough job of the rest of his car? That plant you left to be discovered in itself gave rise to suspicion. You had no idea that the man you were trying to frame wouldn't be as stupid as yourself.'

Chief Inspector Hays resumed, 'You found the cash waiting to be collected at the house?'

'The first fifteen thousand, yes.'

'Which you banked?'

'No, only enough to cover payment to the

detective agency. So large a sum in *my* account may have raised eyebrows. I didn't want to make any waves.'

'But the later payment, the er . . . pay-off. That was put directly into your account. With the paying-in slip signed Smith?'

'Yes.'

'And the waters remained calm, it seems!'

'Yes, until you bastards came.'

'Are you quite sure you have no idea of the source of the money, or of the directions you received?'

'Absolutely not. I would tell you, if I thought it would ease things for me,' Reid said with feeling.

'Of course, you didn't only use the syringe for injecting barbiturate,' Harry said, taking over the questioning again.

'Obviously I only used it for the injections. What use would it be for anything else, for God's sake?'

'Be careful if you want to get a helpful report,' Harry warned. 'You cut Mr Williams' hand with broken glass which you then left, blood-stained, close to the body. You knew this would be found by the police and be produced as evidence. Of course, by the time you reached the wasteground the small amount of blood on the glass had dried, but that didn't matter. However, you also wanted

Mr Williams' blood to be found in the soil so the police would know the 'murderer' was cut badly enough for his blood to flow . . . the wound providing more evidence after the man was detained.

'However,' and Harry's voice, cut further into Reid, 'you had the problem of coagulation. The blood must remain fluid enough to enable it to soak in the soil. So, with the help of the syringe you transferred blood from Mr Williams to a container, later to be poured on the ground.'

Reid looked at the old man in wonder, the remains of his pretension draining away. This point at least would baffle the police, he had thought, having had no intention of enlightening them. He would have retained some pride in his cunning, but now this had been ripped away by the devil that faced him across the table.

Harry paused. His eyes remaining fastened on Reid, and Chief Inspector Hays sensing his colleague's mood sat as though transfixed, the more to unsettle Reid. Suddenly, his voice terse, Harry demanded, 'Tell me what you know about the murder of Mr Robert Greeves' grandson which took place in Austria.'

'I don't know what you're talking about.'

'Come on Reid. I think you do.'

'I don't know what you are talking about, I tell you.'

'So you say! Have you received any other instructions, other than those which concerned Mr Williams?'

'No. None.'

'Now that's not true, is it?'

To Reid's surprise, Harry sounded reasonable. Then Reid said, 'Ah, yes. A final note instructed me to draw a cheque in favour of the detective agency with directions for them to research a doctor Beaumont, on behalf of the pensioners' research. After I had done that, the message said, 'their' association with me would be finished.'

'Do you still have the note?' Harry enquired. But Reid replied he had destroyed it. Then, another pause from Harry, before reaching to his breast pocket. He removed a white card, which he placed on the table, and he watched Reid's face closely for signs of recognition, but none was registered. He watched him read 'six, a number not to be forgotten'. 'Did you get that card to Mr Gareth Jones, the solicitor, at No 3 Sun Street, in this city?'

'No. What is the card? I don't understand,' Reid asked, puzzled. Harry rested back in his chair and glanced at Colin who gave a nod, then instructed the constable stationed by the door to remove the accused to his cell.

Harry thanked Colin for his patience and, for the want of a better word, his 'hospitality'. 'We've got Reid all right, but I'm no closer to the real villains behind all this, Colin. It seems as though each member of the old crew will be targeted by a different individual. A personal service,' he said, with a sardonic smile. 'When you think about it, it lessens the chance of the person behind these crimes being discovered should a 'hit-man' be caught. Because *his* crime may appear to be a one-off.'

8

James Daly closed the house door behind him and with a smooth action he removed his hat, allowing it to fly from his hand to land on a peg of the hat stand. Betty, who caught the action as she was leaving the lounge, smiled, saying, 'Don't you ever miss?'

'Not often,' her husband answered, as he took off the heavy winter coat which had made him look even more like a beer barrel.

'Who brought you home this time?' his wife asked.

'Graham. He'd done eighteen holes. He's welcome to them in this temperature. Give me the nineteen any time, with its friendly fire and good beer, and Paddy was there; we always have a good laugh if he's around. He really is excellent company, you know.'

'So you keep telling me, dear, but it would do you a world of good if you played more golf yourself. Just look at you, you're becoming as broad as you're long. I do believe if you were to trip over, you'd roll all the way to town before picking yourself up,' Betty said, jovially.

Laughing, James said, 'Well that would be a

remarkable feat since it's uphill all the way. Anyhow, you can talk. Just look at yourself. You haven't seen your feet for years.'

'That's because of my ample breast. A lot of women would give the earth for a pair like mine,' she said.

'Come off it,' James was still laughing, 'you can't tell where breast finishes and tummy begins.'

'It's a good thing I love you, James Daly,' Betty said firmly.'

'Well, I wouldn't have you any other way, my love. Especially when you can produce an appetising aroma like that drifting from the kitchen. It's obvious you don't want me to fade away.'

Betty asked, 'Have you seen the card from Joan? She says the weather is gorgeous in Tenerife with the sun shining every day. They are expecting us to be at their place as usual for the Christmas period. I really do think she is marvellous to put up all the family every year. You would think she had enough on her hands, without us joining them as well.'

James agreed: 'She's good, to be sure, but you would do as much for your sister if she was without children and it was us with the brood. But I admit though, I would miss the celebrations if they were to stop. Her kids are not children any more, but they have matured into lovely people, haven't they?'

'I don't know, James, Christmas seems to come round quicker each year. Strange how time appears to pass faster when you grow older, I remember my Mum saying that and she was absolutely right. Let me see, it will be on us in about six weeks, won't it? Then before you know it, it'll all be over and we'll be back in our old routine.

'I'll have to be thinking of buying Christmas cards. You know, we seem to send more every year. One starts off with a few sisters and brothers to send cards to, then they have children and those have children and before you know it you're sending a postbag out. Do you know, James, I sent over sixty cards last year? Not all to the family of course, but to friends as well. It's lucky I see to it or it would never get done. Of course, it usually is the wives who see to that sort of thing.'

'I don't know, I send them to my crew,' James said.

'Ho-ho, big deal. So you send out six cards.'

'Changing the subject dear, I've been thinking. You know, I really do enjoy the festivities at Christmas. George does keep a splendid array of drinks which is always acceptable to me, and while Joan perhaps

151

isn't as good a cook as yourself, nevertheless her efforts are certainly not to be sniffed at. Providing the food is good and drink is plentiful, I'm happy anywhere. But, I've been thinking. How would you like a weekend break, just the two of us? It's six weeks before Christmas so we could fit it in nicely. Perhaps we could go . . . well it wouldn't matter where we went so long as it was a decent hotel with good food. What do you say, old dear?'

'I think that's a really good idea. A quiet few days somewhere, just lounging around and being waited on. Yes, I'm all for it James.'

In the evening, after the pots were cleared and washed, they brought out the brochures. They enjoyed considering the different possibilities, but finally decided they'd stay at The Blue Bell. This was a place they had not visited before, but it was highly recommended by a close friend. They were informed it was an old but comfortable place, with excellent food and where the landlord and his wife made everyone welcome. The Blue Bell was situated in Cumbria at the edge of the Southern Lake District which suited James, because the drive from Lichfield wasn't too far. He had always enjoyed his driving but these days a hundred miles or so was far enough. A phone call the next morning resulted in a firm booking for the first weekend in December.

Driving north along the A6, having left the M6 at the Carnforth turn-off, they climbed out of Milnthorpe and on topping the brow Betty said, 'I don't think it will be far now, dear. According to the map it's a little before the turn-off at Levens for Ulverston and the south lakes.' Before she had time to lift her gaze from the map, James said, 'We're here. Look, here's the sign, just down the road on the left.'

As her husband turned the car off the road, Betty said, 'Oh yes. This looks rather nice. It must be lovely in summer when these bushes and plants are in full bloom, but I don't expect we'll be using the sun-lounge at this time of the year.'

She soon discovered it suited them very well. It was warm and comfortable and agreeably furnished. A creaking floorboard here and there added to the character. The en-suite room provided them with an ample bed. The couple had long since stopped sharing a bed after they found either one was quite capable of inflicting crushing damage to the other during an odd restless night, but the king-size bed on offer here would leave plenty of leeway.

As one would expect in early December the dining room had few diners, but the waiter informed Betty the Blue Bell had been fully booked many weeks earlier for the coming Christmas festivities. The chef's soup had James drooling, and his enjoyment of the salmon which followed, almost cut out his conversation with Betty. James found the meal met entirely with his expectation. Their table had been set for two, as had an elderly couple's close by. Early during the dinner a few words had passed between the tables but by the close of the meal a conversation had developed, causing James to invite the pair to join Betty and himself at the bar.

They sat around a low table in chairs suitable for their girth. Betty sitting not quite lady-like — which had nothing whatever to do with breeding, but rather her shape — was happy and content with her sherry. James lounged in leisurely fashion with legs crossed, or almost crossed as he wasn't quite able to make it, so he had to be satisfied with one ankle over the other.

'How far have you travelled?' Neville asked, reaching to retrieve his glass.

'We drove up from Lichfield, having decided to take a short break. It's our first visit here. Do you know the place?' he enquired.

'Oh yes, we often come. We enjoy The Blue Bell and there are lovely runs from here, even in winter if the weather is kind,' Nora said.

'Have you come far?' Betty asked.

'Quite a long way really, we come from Norwich. It's so different here with all the hills and everything. It's very flat where we live, you know.'

While the ladies talked, getting to know each other, James caught the barman's eye. 'Bring us the same please, and have one yourself.' With the used glasses removed, Nora raised her drink: 'Here's to our stay, then.'

'I'll drink to that,' Neville said. Before long James was learning about farming. His companion had farmed since a couple of years after the war, right up to when he retired three years ago.

James commented: 'You stayed on well after retirement age then!'

'That's not at all uncommon amongst farmers. Two of my sons have taken over the farm but I still lend a hand now and then. I don't think the boys are too keen about it but they kind of humour me, you know.'

'Was your father a farmer?'

'No he wasn't. As I said, I started after the war. Dad had been in the merchant navy from boyhood. I was in it myself during the fracas with Hitler. Served right through the war I did. Poor old Dad, he went down in

'42. It was the second ship blown from under him; he was in an open boat for ten days the first time. I don't know if he was drowned or what. Could have gone up with the explosion of course, many did. I suppose it was fate which saw me through the lot, but not poor Dad.'

'Believe in fate, do you?'

'It's hard not to sometimes. I remember an occasion in a large convoy. We were south of Iceland and orders came from the naval escort instructing us to move from an inner lane of ships and change places with one nearer the outer lane. It turned out the one we were to change places with was loaded with high explosive and it was thought it would be safer nearer the centre of the convoy. We'd just nicely completed the manoeuvre when the ship carrying the explosives went up with an almighty blast. One minute it had been sailing sedately along, the next, there was only outraged water which looked as if it were boiling.

'Moments later a massive chunk of the stricken vessel crashed down on the bow of our ship with such force it came out of the bow at the waterline. If it hadn't been for the tragedy of it all, it could have been funny. Each time the bow of our ship dipped into the sea, a great spout of water shot high out of the deck, like a huge whale spouting.

'Was that fate? Had her hand, by moving the two ships obliterated one full crew, while saving ours?'

'And what if the navy hadn't given the order to change, and your ship was hit. Would that have been fate?' James asked, his brow puckered.

'I get the impression you are not a believer, James.'

'Well if I was, I'd have no need to take responsibility for anything, would I? No matter what I decide fate would still do her thing. It would mean the whole human race would be like a rudderless ship.'

'I suppose that may be a way of looking at it,' Neville said, 'but has nothing ever happened in your life which appeared incomprehensible?'

'Yes, things have happened, but I am more inclined to think of it as luck. Good luck or bad luck.'

'And which have you had, James?'

'Good luck of course,' he said, giving a wide smile to his wife, who didn't really catch what he was saying because she was busy chatting with Nora, but she knew it would be something nice.

'Give me an example of your good luck, and I shall consider if I think it was fate.'

'OK, then. I'll think of one or two examples. I can go back to the war as well, when I was a flight engineer on Lancasters with bomber command. The first real luck was the whole crew getting through a full tour without anyone getting so much as a scratch. About twenty out of every hundred managed that. Another bit of luck was when a lump of flack took away the heel of my flying boot without removing my foot. Then one night our navigator Tom Williams, had his small navigator's table smashed by an unexploded shell passing through it after entering the bottom of the fuselage to depart out of the top. That shell missed him by about a foot. Not that it would have mattered how far away it was, had it exploded, because the whole area would have been a tangled mess.'

Neville said, 'I reckon that was fate.'

'How about this then? Bob Greeves, the rear gunner, found himself in his turret in between two streams of tracer shells as they passed down each side of the Lancaster's fuselage. The night-fighter which had fired them was so close, that the shells hadn't had time to converge. Even so, if the German pilot had so much as twitched a foot, Bob would have been turned to mincemeat . . . Or this one: the same Bob Greeves, sitting cramped in his rear turret for hours, stiff and cold without heating, and, because of the cramped conditions and his heavy flying suit, was barely able to move. All the same he did manage to compress his back against the curved doors of the turret and stretch back his head. He held the position for moments only but he discovered on returning to his usual position that a hole in the perspex at each side of his head had appeared. That sir, was luck in the extreme.'

'Or was it fate?' persisted Neville.

The next day James ran Betty to Kendal. She thought she'd like to see the shops. James found the town just that little bit hilly, so he was soon puffing and blowing. But the evening brought another excellent dinner, followed by a repeat performance in the bar with their new friends. The next morning brought the most enjoyable break close to its end. There was an exchange of addresses and Betty told her husband she must remember to put Nora and Neville onto her Christmas card list. James thought it was wise not to comment.

★ ★ ★

'I really enjoyed the few days away dear, but it's always good to come home,' Betty said, plugging in the kettle for tea. 'It's a good thing we remembered to pick up some milk on the way back, though I dare say the milk in the fridge may still be all right.'

'Better safe than sorry. I'll just take the case to the bedroom, before putting the car away,' James said.

Leaving the study, later in the day, he remarked, 'I see you've already bought the stamps for Christmas. I'm surprised you didn't buy the cards while you were at it.'

She said, 'I know it's a little early. Before we left for the break, I popped into the local post office for some tissue handkerchiefs. I always like a few in my bag, and I thought while I was there I might as well pick up a sheet of stamps. It will be a job done for later, but they had a poor selection of cards so I'll buy those in town nearer the time.'

'By the way Betty, I didn't know you've taken up smoking?'

'What do you mean, silly? Me taking up smoking at my age after being a lifelong abstainer.'

'I found cigarette ash on the carpet by the bureau. Smoking is one vice I don't have, the cleaner must have been having a drag.'

'Mrs Lamb doesn't smoke. Anyway, she's not been in while we were away, they were not her days for cleaning.'

'The fact remains, there was cigarette ash

on the carpet,' James insisted.

Back at his home in Chesterfield, Harry White stepped from the shower, rubbed himself vigorously with a large bath towel and proceeded to dress. A few minutes later, he called to Hester, 'I'm about ready for that coffee now dear.' Drinking half straight off, he said, 'My, it's good, I was ready for that. I really enjoyed my walk this morning despite the cold, but it doesn't get to you the same way when there's no wind.'

Hester said she was happy about that, adding more sugar to her cup. Suddenly Harry said, 'I'm sure the steeple of All Saints is developing more of a warp.' And laughing, Hester asked him what had brought that on? 'I don't know,' he said, 'but it certainly seemed to be more pronounced this morning. Maybe it was the way the light struck it. Any more coffee, love? — By the way, I'm going to London tomorrow.'

'You are going to where? When did you decide that?'

'I've been thinking about it for a day or two actually. I think I'd better go in the morning.'

'I don't know, Harry, you do come up with surprises at times. Why couldn't you have told me?' Hester complained.

'I'm sorry dear, I should have done. Old habits die hard I suppose,' he looked a little shamefaced. 'Actually, I'm going to RAF Records at Kew. I'm hoping they can throw some light on this problem with the crew. Someone, somewhere, discovered it was our crew that was assigned to EA-D-dog. D-dog was the aircraft and EA — number 49 squadron.'

'I think I know which squadron you were on dear,' Hester said with humoured mockery.

'Such information could have been discovered from records,' Harry continued. 'Though records would no longer know our individual addresses after all these years. Still, the enquirer may well have learnt what they were in 1944 and then it wouldn't be impossible to track us to the present time. But God only knows why anyone should want to. I must get to the root of this evil, Hester. Why should someone have gone to such extremes? Our danger is far from over.'

Down at the Public Record Office at Kew, a security officer at the swing-door directed Harry to the enquiry desk where he was asked the reason for his visit. He was sure the real reason would be rejected out of hand, so he said he wanted to research the 1914–1918 war's fighter ace, Captain Albert Ball, VC. He intended writing the gentlemen's belated biography.

The officer issued a day-pass saying he should go to the Langdale Room on the next floor, but first he must go to the security desk to sign the book and be given a pass number. Harry found he also had to pass through a strict security search to check he was not taking any documents in. Only then did his swipe-card pass admit him to the upper floor and the Langdale Room which contained all the indexes. Inside were five staff members to advise on the index, but the documents, which were in the vaults, had to be ordered by the staff.

Harry was encouraged to discover that many of the officers at PRO were retired police officers. He learnt that the eldest officer there, a Mr Woods, with whom he discussed days in the force, was also due to retire from his present position. Harry turned on all his charm, explaining that he had not only been in the police, but had been on Lancasters during the last war. Taking the risk, he eventually confided the real purpose of his 'investigation' and explained how he and the old crewmembers were being targeted.

Mr Woods did all he could to help the ex-wireless operator of a Lancaster bomber. The staffer was really interested in his work and, as it turned out, was fascinated by the deeds of bomber-command in World War Two. So much so, that he became almost reverent towards ex-Flight Lieutenant White, who told him that what he really wanted to know was had anyone made enquires about 49 Squadron during the twelve months period leading up to July of this year?

Woods said, 'Even so long after the war there is still a trickle of enquiries. Some made in person, others by post. I can't remember anyone wanting information about 49 squadron. I think I'm correct in saying the squadron was in No 5 Group, as was 617. There used to be more enquiries made about that squadron than any other, no doubt because of their Dam's raid. A colleague who recently retired, but had spent his working life with PRO, told me there were always people wanting information about 617. Usually they wanted info to put into books, though most were never published. According to my colleague the market would have been flooded, if they had been.

'However, getting back to 49. To be honest, I don't remember anything for that squadron, but I'll see what the files have to offer.'

Harry was invited to take a chair and asked to wait.

After a long wait, Mr Woods returned, and said, 'I am sorry, Mr White, but there is nothing regarding 49 squadron for the period you are interested in.'

'Nothing!' The old detective gazed at his shoes, in thought. *What if the villain, not knowing which crew he wanted, also didn't know which was their squadron? What then? How could they be traced?*

Turning from the table, Harry said, 'Forget the squadron Mr Woods. Was there an enquiry made regarding a raid or attack on a particular night during the period we're looking at?'

Mr Woods said, 'I'll be back.'

Leaving the room once more and back in the vaults, he removed a sheet of paper, and muttered, 'Ah, yes. I remember this.'

Sitting by Harry's side at the table in the Langdale Room, Mr Woods waved the paper, saying: 'Someone wanted to know about a raid which took place on the fourteenth of October 1944. The target was Schweinfurt. The writer wanted to know how many bombers had taken part and how many were lost. Also, how many bombers had survived a night-fighter attack and where the attacks had taken place. He wanted a list of those aircraft which had survived a fighter attack.

'The enquirer wanted this information to authenticate details from a Luftwaffe station about which he was writing a history. We complied with his request, sending it to the box number on his letter.'

Harry closed his eyes and in the space of a few seconds he relived the whole of his own history during the night of the fourteenth of October 1944.

★ ★ ★

Bob Greeves was the first up the ladder. He threw his parachute through the main door into the fuselage and followed it in, to store it in its place beside the main door. Bob, the rear gunner, was the only crewmember who didn't keep his chute by his side throughout a flight, because there was no room for himself *and* the parachute in the rear turret.

As he fixed the chute, the others were still performing the 'for luck' ritual of christening the bomber's tail, but Bob had already peed because he had to give himself time to get at his willy. The 'Tailor suit' he wore was thick and heavy. This was partly for warmth because it could get bloody cold in the rear turret. Earlier Lancs had a curved perspex panel in front of the gunner, making it the very last object on the Lancaster, since the gunner was flying backwards. Bob always went 'into battle backwards'. But that perspex was removed, leaving an open space to give

166

the gunner a clearer vision into the night. The space let in a draught which Bob didn't think was funny when the temperature at twenty thousand feet could be less than minus forty degrees in winter.

The other reason his 'Tailor suit' was so thick and bulky, was because he wasn't able to wear a 'Mae West' like everyone else — again, there wasn't room in the turret, so they'd built buoyancy into his suit to give him a chance in case they ditched into the sea. All in all, Bob lived through many very cramped hours on many a night. Also, the final section of the bomber became very narrow as it approached his turret, causing Bob to crouch down to reach the turret.

The problem was he also had to crouch when leaving, making for the main door to reach his parachute, should he need it to bail out. If the aircraft was really out of control when shot down, then that was *it*. The G-force would 'fasten' him in the crouched position. All in all, Bob had a merry life.

Finally the full crew was in position. Within minutes Peter, with the help of engineer James Daly, started the mighty Merlins one by one, causing the engines to breath a form of shuddering life through the Lancaster. Each engine was checked for max revs and magneto drop. For the time being, Bob and

Arthur Brown had nothing to do but sit in their turrets. Navigator Tom Williams was busy with maps and, with the help of his bomb-aimer, Jeff Beaumont, checked the 'G' box. While all this was going on, Harry White twiddled the knobs of the bomber's radio.

Looking down from his turret, Arthur saw one of the ground crew disappear under the right wing with his trousers flapping vigorously in a propeller wash. He would be making his way to remove the starboard wheel chock. Turning his attention back to the turret, Arthur gave it a final sweep and at the same time elevated the twin Browning machine-guns. A moment later the heavy bomber was creeping forward.

Leaving behind its dispersal point, D-dog carefully slotted itself into the line of aircraft that were slowly taxiing along the narrow perimeter track making their way to the main runway. Gazing from his elevated station, Arthur made out a black shape racing down the runway with its exhaust faintly glowing. Just above the horizon at the far end of the aerodrome he thought he could see a dim silhouette. Strange, he thought, to think there were seven young men carried within that shadow . . . With no lights, apart from the few weak glows running along each side of the runway, Arthur felt the whole scene was eerie.

Peter gave a short burst of increased power to the port outboard engine to stop the swing to the left. The pace at which the Lancaster was taxiing rendered the rudders useless. Only with the judicious use of brakes and throttles could he steer the bomber at low speed. Eventually, Bob felt the tail of the Lancaster swing round and he knew they had reached the runway and were lining up.

Over the intercom Bob heard James and Peter making a quick and final check of instruments, then James said, 'There's the aldis lamp Skipper, they've given us a green.' The rear turret shook as the revs of the four Merlins rapidly increased and Bob became aware of a powerful slipstream rushing by the turret.

'Brakes off,' ordered the skipper, and bumps from the rolling tail-wheel joined the vibration in the turret. Already the rear-gunner had swung the turret hard to port which was where it would remain until the Lancaster was airborne. In some way this helped to counter the bomber's yaw during the take-off run. Bob saw the faint runway lights appear to move back from the bomber at an ever-increasing rate. Finally, the engine noise took up a new rhythm after the crew heard through their intercoms the skipper call for full power, and the engineer, whose hand had been following the pilot's on the throttles, pushed them through the quadrant.

The vibration from the ground stopped as the aircraft lifted from the tarmac. Though, for the rear gunner, the vibration had already diminished when, earlier in the 'take-off' run, the tail lifted and removed the rear wheel's contact with the runway. Arthur, from his turret, high on the fuselage, saw the dark blur of the boundary hedge pass beneath, followed by a dim glow coming from a single light in the shippon of Law's farm. He wondered if Mary was working there. Mary had been born at the farm, but now it was not just her home, but also the place where she did her war work as a Land Army girl.

He knew Tom Williams had a passion for Mary right from their first meeting on a mess party night. Tom had confided his feelings to Arthur and Arthur quickly understood that poor Tom hadn't a clue. He was like a fish out of water where girls were concerned. Arthur felt really sorry for him, as he could tell just how frustrated Tom was about her.

EA-D-dog climbed into the night sky with more respectable revs now. The throttles had been brought back to give a setting of twenty-two hundred revs. The likelihood of enemy fighters at this stage was improbable, but the gunners were already searching the night sky for friendly aircraft. The air was full of Lancasters and Halifaxes completely blacked out, displaying no external light whatever.

Crossing the south coast and still climbing, Jeff picked up a pinpoint which was confirmed by Tom, who instructed Peter to alter course five degrees to starboard and increase speed by five mph. Peter was feeling the bomber swinging vaguely and knew Bob was operating his rear turret. Below lay a layer of stratus reaching beyond the horizon and reflecting a dull glow from a half moon. Away from the moon, stars brightly twinkled.

Looking down from his prone position in the nose, the bomb-aimer hoped there would be gaps in the cloud over the target. The gunners hated the thought of their Lancaster being seen from fighters above, silhouetted against the stratus. Even now they were able to pick out numerous bombers below, pressing bravely on.

At a height of eighteen thousand feet they passed over the French coast, still covered with cloud. The cloud wasn't bothering the navigator's G-box, for it had picked up the coastline perfectly.

'There's flack going up at two o'clock, Skipper. I'd say it's ten miles away,' James commented.

'The flight plan routes us round that. Someone's off track,' Peter replied.

'And some poor sod's paid for it. I can make out flames falling. They're about to pass through the cloud now. I think it must have been hit by radar-predicted flack to have gone so quickly.' This was Jeff's observation from the nose of the aircraft. He struggled back to join the navigator. Jeff spent much of the flight with Tom, who was at this moment noting the time and position at which the stricken bomber had gone down. The information was to be given to intelligence during the crews debriefing, on their return to base.

The flight engineer calculated the fuel consumption and was satisfied. He turned and smiled at Peter. The pilot was unable to see the expression through James' rubber oxygen mask, but he could read his eyes. Peter, at twenty-two years, was proud of his crew and was very conscious of his responsibility. He claimed he had the best chaps in the squadron.

The Lancaster thundered on through the clear sky with the stratus remaining thousands of feet below. The moon still gleamed and, had it been day, the visibility would have been limitless. The gunners, highly alert, were eager for the moon to sink below the horizon.

The elements were very much favouring enemy fighters as the bomber pressed deeper into Europe with a silent crew, busy with their work and thoughts.

Back at base the battle order stated this was the sixteenth operation for D-dog's crew — as if they didn't know. Fourteen more to finish their tour, but they were already living on borrowed time. Had the crew taken their turn from statistics they would already have been buried. Peter Newell's boys were becoming veterans.

After twenty minutes of complete silence, save the unbroken roar of the Merlins, the intercom clicked on. 'Navigator to Skipper. Turning point in ten minutes. Alter course two degrees port and we'll be spot on.'

'Moving two degrees port, Nav . . . How are things at the back, rear gunner?'

'A bit cold and stiff, Skipper. Otherwise OK.'

An urgent call suddenly broke in: 'Corkscrew starboard GO. Fighter, fighter starboard quarter high.' Before the mid-upper gunner had finished speaking, the bomber's wings were rolling and the nose dropping as it entered a diving turn with the enemy seeing his target slide under his sight just as he had been about to fix a bead. From his mid-upper, Arthur saw his tracers curl under the fighter's wing tip. The rear gunner raced his guns to starboard high, but before he could line them up, the fighter plunged vertically to make his escape.

'Resume course, Skipper.' This was Bob.

'Did anyone get a hit?' the skipper asked.

'No, I only had a chance for a single burst and I missed,' Arthur answered.

'Good show anyway for seeing the bastard — keep your eyes skimmed, chaps. Nav, enter the action.'

'Of course, Skipper.'

As the Lancaster crossed the border of France with Germany, James said, 'The stratus is breaking Skipper.'

From the tail, Bob answered, 'Thank Christ for that. It'll remove our silhouette.'

'Damn right. I've seen twelve poor sods get the chop so far. It's becoming a bloody rough raid and we haven't reached the fucking target yet,' said the mid-upper.

'OK. Shut up everyone and keep searching,' the skipper ordered.

The gen from the intelligence bod's briefing turned out to be pretty good. The track the bomber force had taken, guided it more or less successfully between the flack black spots, though the bods at home had been able to do little about the fighters. Of course, when bombing, there would be no choice but to fly through the heavy box barrage the Germans would maintain over the target with their 88 mms. But heavy flack probably induced more anxiety than it should. True, it was frightening with its shrapnel causing casualties and damaging the aircraft, but the bomber was often able to fly back home. Of course, a direct hit from a heavy shell was normally curtains, but the bomber had its chances with the flack. A successful fighter attack, on the other hand, left little hope.

'Navigator to Skipper. We'll be over the target in twelve minutes.'

'OK, Nav.'

A few minutes later the skipper reached for the mike and switch on his facepiece. 'Who left his mike on? The heavy breathing sounds as if someone's on 'the job'.'

'Sorry, Skip.' The crew heard it click off.

'It seems the pathfinders are doing their bit, Skip. The target's lit up like a Christmas tree.' The Lanc droned on another couple of minutes before the bomb-aimer, who was up at the sharp end lying on his belly, said, 'The bombs aren't dropping. The front of the stream must be there now.'

D-Dog was now sixty seconds from its bombing run but there were still no target indicators to aim the bombs at. Then the

VHF came to life. 'Sorry for the delay, main force, I'll have it for you in a moment.'

Skipper said, 'The master controller's having trouble. In a few minutes there'll be three hundred plus airplanes crossing the target area, so keep a bloody good look out, chaps.'

'Bomber-aimer to Skipper. There's a red TI. Right. Right. Steady. Steady . . . ' The VHF cut into the headsets of all the men in the bombers: 'Ignore red, ignore red.'

'Damn. He must have cocked it up,' James said.

'Be ready to go round for another bombing run, Skipper. We're too close in,' said Jeff, who was no longer studying his sight.

'Christ. Keep a good look, for God's sake,' Peter's hands were clammy.

The VHF came in again: 'Master controller to number two. Take over. Acknowledge.'

Five seconds with no response.

A voice, full of concern, said, 'Master controller to number two. I'm in flames. Take over. Acknowledge, please acknowledge. Over.'

'Number two acknowledging — acknowledging. Cheerio, number one.'

'Cheerio, mate. OUT.'

Tears filled Jeff's eyes, but he knew that almost before they had time to run down his cheeks, the master controller's Mosquito would be in a thousand pieces in the streets below. Amongst the Mosquito's remains would lay its late pilot and navigator. From the height of a few hundred feet from where they made their attempt to mark the target, there had been no escape.

In the darkness, illuminated only from the two hundred plus search lights, which, in a clear sky, gave no reflection, D-dog made its dangerous flight back for another bombing run. The skipper was turning the Lancaster steeply and Bob in his rear turret was fully aware of the added dangers. First, for much of the repositioning, Peter had the aircraft flying against the coming bomber stream in a near saturated sky. He knew they could be seen from above, the Lanc showing against the mass of flares below. Bob himself could see the outlines of planes below them, and he knew at times some German pilots would brave their own flack to make an otherwise easy kill.

Bob therefore had the turret constantly rotating from beam to beam as he combed the sky. This, with the aircraft banking steeply, caused his turret to rock a little on its mounting which had the effect of giving the gunner a psychological fear that the whole unit would fall off the tail. Bob made an extreme effort to keep the rotations going, trying to make his fear of a fighter attack greater than the imagined dread of rolling into space. It was the first time such fear had struck the rear gunner, and later it came to him he'd had an irrational attack of nerves.

Again the VHF came in. 'Controller to main force. Bomb on Green. Bomb on Green.'

On starting the run again, Jeff resumed his patter: 'Left, left, Skipper. Hold it, Ho — oold it. Steady, steady. Right a bit — steady. Bombs gone!' The crew felt the Lancaster leap up from the release of almost eight tons. Jeff saw the silhouette of numerous bombers, and he fervently hoped his own bomber would not be hit by a falling bomb. Then, just as his eye was on it, he saw the Lancaster to his right, about five hundred feet below, go up in a blinding explosion. In moments, where there had been a mighty bomber, there was nothing to show it had ever existed. It had either been struck in its bomb bay by a shell as it was about to release the load, or a falling 'blockbuster' exploded on it.

Though their bombs had gone, Peter held D-dog on as steady a course as the flack torn air would permit. This was a time the crew hated, short though it was. For the sake of accuracy, Peter hadn't been able to take evasive action during the bombing run, and now, there was to be added another ten seconds of level flying as he waited for their photo-flash to emit its three-quarter of a million candle power flash. That was when the on board camera automatically photographed where D-dog's bombs had actually hit.

When Jeff completed the count of ten, the pilot quickly threw his great bomber away from its sustained track as relief swept through the crew. The intelligence bods would get their picture. Suddenly a dark form of a spinning Lancaster with an engine blazing plunged past them. Another one for Tom to log. The thought shot through Peter's mind; 'Why was it spinning? The pilot must be dead . . . as shortly would be his spin-trapped crew.'

'Give me a course for home, Nav.' The crew detected relief in their skipper's voice.

'335 degrees, Skip.' In the clear sky, the rear gunner saw the fires burning for a long time, though he avoided the temptation of looking at the fires directly. He knew his night vision must be maintained for possible fighter attacks. D-dog, now north-west of Frankfurt, droned smoothly on, the crew quiet with the turmoil of the target passed. The rest of the journey home could remain uneventful unless a poorly held course moved the Lanc over the guns. The clear sky, too, still held a real danger from the night fighters which had been steadily building their score. Now, during the bomber's return, the Germans would try to anticipate one of the home legs, for the bombers rarely flew directly to base.

If a fighter attack were to come from a Ju, both gunners knew it would probably be from their blind spot below. The Ju's bank of upward-raked cannons were deadly — to the crews they were laughingly known as the Chicago piano. It was for this reason that the rear gunner called for a banking search every few minutes. From a steep bank to port, then to starboard, he could make a search below. Bob said it also stopped the skipper nodding off. The more conventional night fighter would normally come in from behind, maybe from one quarter. In any case, on a clear night he would place his fighter in the darker sky below the gunner's horizon.

Bob knew the fighters had all the advantage. First, they placed themselves in the darkest part of the sky which automatically brought the bomber above the fighters' horizon in the lightest part. Secondly, the bombers were bigger which, all other things being equal, made them easier to be seen. Finally, the enemy pilot was fully alert, simply because his control had informed him the bomber was there, whereas the gunners could go for hours without seeing a thing and that made it difficult to be one hundred per cent alert at any one moment . . . The element of surprise was usually with the enemy.

The cannon tracer zipped past each side of the rear turret. 'Go. Go,' shouted Bob. There was no time to say where, and with a reflex movement Peter shoved the yoke forward to the right-hand corner and Bob was momentarily pressed hard into his seat with the sudden rise of the tail. From the mid-upper turret Arthur had seen the source of the tracer shells, and when the Lancaster fell into a diving turn, it brought the fighter above Arthur's horizon. He just had time to give a quick burst of his guns before the Lanc's own fuselage hid the fighter.

A moment later the voice from the rear turret shouted, 'He's hit. You hit the bastard. Christ, you got him.'

'Are you sure?' skipper asked, as he pulled the bomber out of the dive.

'Yes, I think it's a ME110, his port engine's on fire and he's going down fast. I'm sure it's not a controlled escape.'

'Mid-upper to Skipper. I can see flames now. It seems to be dropping fast, Skipper. I may be able to watch him all the way down.'

'Can you see anything, Engineer?' the pilot asked James. Peter now had the Lanc in level flight and James, his head in the perspex blister, looked back and momentarily caught sight of the plunging flame before it was hidden by the Lancaster's wing.

'Can you still see him, Bob?'

'Yes, Skipper I can. He's still . . . he's gone in, Skipper. Hell mid-upper, that was a smart bust.'

'Yes, well done Arthur. A bloody good show. Now quiet down, everyone, and keep a look-out,' said skipper.

Shortly after D-dog recrossed the German-French border they saw the stratus still lying there, reaching into the far distance. 'I'm taking her down, Engineer. That stratus may be a few hundred feet thick, I'd say it's at about eleven thousand. We'll fly through it on instruments all the way back, if it still reaches that far. We'll hide and to hell with the pre-plan. We're not pushing our luck any more.'

D-dog broke cloud over Lincolnshire and let down.

★ ★ ★

'Mr White! Are you all right?' Mr Woods said with concern. Then: 'You are perspiring

182

profusely. Please, can I help you?'

'What?' The surroundings came into focus. 'Oh, no, it's nothing. I'm quite all right, Mr Woods, thank you.' Harry touched his brow with his handkerchief, surprised at the dampness he found.

He turned his attention to the letter Woods had placed on the table. There was something not quite true about the sheet. Harry removed a receipted invoice from his pocket, unfolded it and placed it on the letter carefully matching the left-hand sides and then brought together the top edges. But the top edges didn't come together. Not quite. The top corners of the letter were not perfect right-angles.

'Mr Woods, can I ask you to fetch me a magnifying glass, please?'

On inspection, the glass revealed the top edge was minutely sloped. It had been sheared by a different method from the paper's remaining three sides. The sheet had been cut, most likely to remove a letter heading.

'Before the letter was written, this sheet had not been a plain piece of paper, Mr Woods. There has been a letter heading which has been removed. For a request such as this, it is strange that the return address should be a box number. Also, don't you consider it odd

that it is signed, 'Yours faithfully, Researcher?'
The initiator is desirous of anonymity. Do
you think I can keep the letter, Mr Woods?'

'No, Mr White, I really can't let you take it
away. You must know that.'

'Of course I do. It was wrong of me to ask.
I will take a copy though. And, as one old
policeman to another, do you think you could
look the other way while I cut a strip from the
bottom? I can assure you it is important, Mr
Woods.'

'Well . . . be sure it's well below the
signature,' Woods said, looking over his
shoulder.

9

Arthur, pushing the door open with his foot, carried his new swivel-stool into the studio and placed it at the centre of the floor. The room was large and bright, situated at the front of the house where it caught the best light. With the approval of his wife, Mary, he had removed the carpet to leave bare boards and thrown out most of the furniture. These drastic moves had occurred shortly before his retirement, when a great yearning to paint swept over him. From the moment he felt a brush in his hand, he couldn't think why he'd allowed so much time to pass before trying this great pleasure.

The bonus was that he had an almost unobstructed view of Worcester Cathedral from the windows of his own studio. Before his urge to paint, the cathedral had seemed to be nothing more than a rather pleasant part of the overall scene. But now, Arthur saw the magnificent old fourteenth century cathedral tower through a painter's eyes.

Paintings of the cathedral were scattered about the room. Many to the untrained eye looked quite respectable, but none satisfied the painter, even though he would be the first to agree his own eye was far from trained. All the same, Arthur experienced a great pleasure when he detected any improvement in a later rendering. His joy was not confined to buildings, as he also found much fulfilment in trying to commit a great seascape to canvas. Trouble was, Worcester was not all that close to the ocean.

Mary had been surprised when Arthur, ten years ago, said he thought painting would be an admirable hobby for his retirement. To her, he didn't seem the type at all. Somehow she saw painters as quite small people who had long hair and were normally rather untidy and unorthodox in their dress. Her husband, on the other hand, was meticulous with his dress. Even though the large checks, which he so favoured, tended to hit one in the eye. The brogues he always wore were also top quality, but the range of Arthur's brightly coloured waistcoats could well have been treasured by many an artist.

His love of painting had grown to the extent that he seldom attended the social activities of the local rugby club any more, though he had continued to be a staunch member for many years after his playing days had come to a close. Mary said he'd stopped going to the club because he was growing old.

But Arthur would have none of it, saying painting was more fun.

When his wife entered the studio with a cup of tea, Arthur said, 'Mary, did you read the letter from Harry White? I left it on the dining-room table.'

'No, I've been busy in the kitchen. What did he have to say?'

'It's his latest 'Newsletter'. He says he has been to RAF Records at Kew. He thinks he's getting closer to the Perpetrator of the threat, aimed at the crew. He says he has discovered that someone had made an enquiry about a bombing attack on Schweinfurt during the night of the fourteenth of October 1944. What's more, this guy wanted to know which were the bombers that survived night-fighter attacks on that night and where their attacks took place and at what time. The enquirer says he is writing a history of a German airbase and wants to confirm information he has already been given by the Germans. It sounds a bit fishy to me but it's possible I suppose. Especially with what's been happening to the crew, and bearing in mind we were attacked by a fighter that night. I shot it down, as a matter of fact.'

'It's all far-fetched to me,' Mary said. 'Don't you think you may be reading too much into what has been happening? Those mishaps to Bob and Tom! It's probably coincidental they were in the same crew.'

'No dear, we are not reading too much into it at all. The numbered cards which turned up with each event — anonymously at that — are enough to give credibility. They are intended to worry or frighten us. And what about that detective agency? They didn't even know who they were working for. If a man with Harry White's experience is convinced, then I'll back him all the way. And another thing. The correspondent gave a box number as the postal address, in Brussels of all places. Why a box number for such an enquiry, I ask myself? I'm sure the others do too.'

'Perhaps you are right. It's a funny business though,' she said with a touch of scepticism. 'Anyway, how do you like your new stool? It'll keep the weight off your feet while you are working on your paintings. Might seem a bit strange at first though, since you have always painted while standing.'

'I'm sure it will be an asset. See! I can adjust the height and the swivelling seat is excellent. I'm keen to try it out so I think I will have an hour or two now before I leave for the pool. I mustn't miss my work-out.'

Mary said anxiously, 'You haven't forgotten Martin and Philippa are coming for dinner, have you?'

'Is it this evening? I thought it was tomorrow.'

'You really are getting forgetful. I told you on Sunday, when Philippa was on the phone, they were coming Wednesday evening.'

'You are quite right, dear, so you did. I'm looking forward to seeing little Julia anyway,' Arthur said, enthusiastically.

Over dinner he asked, 'How's business, son? Is there any progress with 'Dream Homes'?'

Smiling, Martin said, 'We have a meeting next Monday, but I'm certain it will be just for dotting the 'i's and crossing the 't's. The contract is as good as in our pocket, Dad.'

'Wonderful. You did well to bring that off, especially against an outfit like Jacksons. They're very keen you know.'

'Don't I know it! Anyway, this time we have come out on top. 'Dream Homes' will be building two hundred and thirty-five very desirable properties. That's certainly not to be sneezed at, eh Dad?'

'National builders like 'Dream Homes' contracting to us all the heating insulation on such a scale, is wonderful business. Makes me almost wish I was still involved,' Arthur said. Then, as he removed a fleck of paint from a fingernail, added, 'Perhaps not.'

'Answer that, Harry, my hands are covered in flour,' Hester called from the kitchen where she was making his favourite cake.

'Chesterfield 35136.'

'Harry, it's James. James Daly.'

Harry thought his old comrade sounded stressed.

'Hello James. How are you today? Why am I honoured with your call? Thanks for the Christmas card — by the way, Hester is quite impressed. She thinks it's the most exquisite card she has seen but said she would lay a pound to a penny it was your wife who made the choice.'

'Hester is right. My dear lady did choose it, she loves that sort of thing. Harry I'm ringing to tell you that Betty is ill. I'm really worried, because the doctor can't figure out what is wrong. She is sweating a great deal and her heart is racing and she's also very weak, can't even stand, but the doctor is mystified.'

'I'm sorry to hear that. I wonder if it could be some new bug they haven't previously come across,' Harry said sympathetically.

'You might think me absurd, but I can't help but wonder if a card with number 4 printed on it will turn up! I mean, with the doctor not knowing what the illness is, I can't help thinking . . . Am I the next target?'

'Well, we know one of the objectives of the swine is to place fear and uncertainty in our minds. He will know full well that if any unpleasant event occurs to any of us, even if he has nothing whatever to do with it, there will be added stress increased by suspicion. It seems to me that this fellow is something of a warped psychologist.'

'You are probably right. I'm getting paranoid.'

'Please, I'm not saying that, you may well be correct in your suspicion. We have seen how devious he can be. I mean, look at the different ways he got at poor Bob and Tom! You can't get much more devious than that. I think I should have a look around your place, James, if you can put me up for a night?'

'I'll be pleased if you'll come but I can't imagine what you could find in my home. I welcome your company all the same.'

'To tell the truth, I have no idea what I'll be looking for, but then one often doesn't when beginning an investigation. Would it suit you if I were to come tomorrow? If your wife is so ill, the sooner the better I think.'

'That is really good of you. It will put my mind at rest a little.' He heard the relief in his voice.

'All part of the job. Keep your pecker up,

old son. See you tomorrow then. Bye.'

As Harry replaced the phone. Hester entered from the kitchen, a towel in her hand, saying: 'Who was that?'

'I'm going to Lichfield tomorrow, I'm going to James Daly's place and will be staying overnight. His wife is very ill.'

'Betty ill? What's the matter with her? And what has it to do with you? Why are you staying? You're doing it again, springing another one on me, Harry.'

'Yes dear, but I didn't know until now. Not until James was on the phone, I must go. James is worried to death. He thinks Betty's illness might have something to do with the maniac who's targeting the crew. He might just be right.'

'Well, yes. I know you are a detective and this is a very disturbing business for us all, but why do you need to stay overnight? Lichfield isn't all that far.'

'Call it experience, dear. You see, when I go there, I won't know what I am looking for. If I did, a short time, an hour or two would serve, but as it is, I need to get a 'feel'. It's hard to explain. Maybe it's a bit like being a 'medium', you know, getting a 'feel' so that things come to you.'

'Now I have heard everything! Hard-nosed Detective Inspector Harry White resorting to the occult. Has this been the secret of your success during your remarkable years on the force?' mocked Hester.

Grinning, Harry answered, 'Watch it, witch, before I spirit you away.'

* * *

Answering the doorbell, James said, 'Come in, Harry. Good to see you. My, it's cold out there, isn't it? Take off your coat and I'll get you a drink. A whisky perhaps, to warm you up,' he moved towards the cabinet.

'No thank-you, it's too early for me, but I won't say no to a cup of coffee, please.'

'It's in the jug on its hot plate, and it is fresh. I was about to pour a cup for myself when you rang the bell.'

Settling down in one of James' big easy chairs, Harry said, 'How are you bearing up, old friend? Or, more to the point, how is Betty? Has there been any change since we talked yesterday?'

'I'm going to the hospital soon. You will have to excuse me, because I'll be going this evening as well. I talked to the ward nurse on the phone earlier. She said Betty had a better night and the doctor thinks she is stabilising, which was a great relief. They had been worried at Betty's continuing decline. They were close to losing her, they said. Now they think there can be hope for recovery, but they are still very watchful, not knowing the cause of her condition.'

'If, and we are by no means certain, but if Betty's illness has been deliberately brought on, I think the object would have been death — murder! If that was the case, I very much doubt the steady deterioration would have been arrested,' Harry contemplated.

'But Betty is never ill and if it was deliberate, why my poor wife for God's sake?'

'Well. If 'our man' is responsible and he is targeting you this time, then Betty would be the ideal victim. You do not have children or grandchildren. In fact there is nobody really close to you in your later years, apart from Betty. Remember, James, we, the crew that is, are not being personally attacked. I'm sure the purpose of these crimes is to make each one of us suffer and we can't suffer if we are dead.'

'The bastard's a madman,' James' face became even more highly coloured than usual.

'There is no question about that,' Harry assured him.

'For the moment we will assume you have already been targeted but as I've said, James, it is by no means certain you have. Have you or Betty noticed anything unusual lately, or maybe a fresh face in the vicinity? Seen anything which you knew was out of routine. Done anything yourself that's different.'

'Nothing, except we had a weekend break at the beginning of the month.'

'Did you get involved with anyone while away?'

'No, apart from spending a couple of convivial evenings in the bar with an elderly farmer and his wife from Lincolnshire. I am sure they were as pure as the driven snow. Betty and his wife got on like a house on fire. She sent them a Christmas card. And there was one from them in the post this morning.'

'They were elderly, you say. How elderly?' Harry asked.

'About our age. He served in the merchant navy during the war. Says he was on the Atlantic convoys, as was his father, who went down. He was genuine, I'm sure of it.'

Harry said sternly: 'Now think James, did either of them get anything from you?'

'How do you mean?' he asked, puzzled.

'Such as a visiting card or a photograph from Betty maybe. Does anything at all come to mind?'

'Nothing, Harry, apart from the ladies exchanging addresses. I'm sure there is nothing sinister about the couple.'

'Probably not, but nothing must be taken for granted old friend. Was all in order when you returned home, in the garage as well as the house?'

'Everything. Of course, I wasn't looking for anything but I'm sure I would have noticed if anything was amiss. But do you mind if I visit Betty now? I'll be away about one and a half hours and we can continue this conversation when I return, if you wish.'

'Sure, off you go. I'll do some thinking while you are away. Remember me to Betty and tell her I wish her well.'

'I'll see she receives your instructions. Help yourself to anything you would like,' he said with a smile.

While James was at the hospital, Harry did a lot of thinking and a fair amount of monitoring. Every cup, plate, tin, food container and pan was closely scrutinised. Nothing in the kitchen escaped his attention. Of course, he was aware that whatever Betty had contracted could be no routine form of poisoning. If it had, the medics would have quickly been onto it. Also, if the source was in the kitchen, it was very likely James would have been affected. Not to have made the check, however would have been sloppy detection work. Something of which he could never be accused.

He searched the remaining ground floor. Then much consideration went on the bathroom with its small medical cabinet. Brushes and toothpaste too. Small bottles containing pills, all were carefully checked.

Harry made coffee, took it to the table to sit and think. So far he had discovered nothing suspicious within the house. Should he range his thoughts away from the house? If food had been the culprit, he could disregard their short break, because Betty had not started to be ill until at least two weeks after the break. In any case, he couldn't really feel food had been the cause of her illness because the medics would surely have discovered it. There was nothing more he could do at the moment, so he would sit back and relax in one of James' commodious lounge chairs. Might even have a nap.

He had no sooner relaxed, when a sharp pain momentarily shot through a lower molar. 'Now when is my dental appointment? Next Wednesday, or the following Wednesday?' He reached into his inside pocket to check the appointment card. An envelope came with the card. 'Damn, I forgot to post the bill when I left the house.' He returned the envelope to his pocket, still needing a stamp. He doubted if the electricity board would go bust for the want of one bill.

He awakened abruptly as James came through the front door. A glance at his watch showed he had slept for twenty minutes. As James entered the lounge, he said, 'Ah, you are back then. How did you find Betty, James?'

'She is stable and the consultant says I can allow myself to be encouraged by this. We almost lost her,' he said. 'They know now that there is a deterioration in the central nervous system but are not sure where it is leading, though Parkinson's Disease can't be ruled out.' James suddenly sobbed as his face fell into his hands.

'Let me make you a cup of tea,' Harry suggested, rising from his chair.

'That is kind of you. I think I'll take a 'wee dram', as Bob Greeves would say.' James forced a weak smile.

Harry thought the whisky seemed to play its part in removing some of the tension from his friend, then heard him say, 'I don't know how I would manage if I should lose Betty. As well as being my wife, she is my best friend. Of course I would cope, but at the moment it is difficult to imagine.'

'Now James, have you forgotten already what they said at the hospital? Betty is stable, remember? She isn't going to die. That danger is past,' Harry reassured him.

'Yes, of course. The fact is, Harry, I was a bit confused just then. To tell the truth, I haven't been too well myself. I felt really ill for a couple of days and kept getting very confused. I'm OK now. By God, though, I did feel rotten at the time.'

'Were you ill at the same time as Betty?' Harry asked.

'No. I started a few days before she became ill. A good job as it turned out, because there was no way I could have left my bed to visit her. Anyway, I'm all right now, but I do seem to become stressed rather easily.'

Harry advised, 'If you feel stress coming on, James, just remember that your wife hasn't passed on, but is still with you and will certainly remain with you for a long time yet. Then make a conscious effort to be thankful.

'Now, about the possibility of you having been targeted! I have not come up with a lead in that direction. Though I haven't finished thinking about its feasibility. Also James, it's a bit odd that you should be unaccountably ill at about the same time as Betty.'

'Oh, I really don't think there is a connection. Anyway, I'm better now. Not so Betty, who looks like finishing up with a permanent illness.'

'We can only hope the doctors have got it wrong about the Parkinson's disease. From what you told me they weren't sure. Not a hundred per cent.'

'I hope you are right,' James said. Then added with passion: 'If some bastard is responsible for her illness, I wish to God you could catch him.'

'Without a lead, I can do nothing. I must have a lead, no matter how limited its potential may seem. So far as I can ascertain, there is nothing in your home that seems to offer hope. I wouldn't attach any importance to that fact if the medical folk were able to state a reason for Betty's illness. But they can't.'

'Good Lord!' James exclaimed.

'What? What is it?' Harry asked.

'I've just remembered something. I don't know what has brought it to mind now, but when Betty and I returned home from our weekend break I did come across something rather curious — in a house where nobody smokes, Harry, I discovered ash from a cigarette.'

'Interesting,' Harry commented. 'Are you sure no one had been in the house while you were both away? You do have a cleaner, don't you, James?' he asked.

'Yes we do. We thought of that at the time, but she doesn't smoke. Anyway, the cleaner hadn't been in while we were away. They were not her days.'

'Did you or Betty check with her? She could have been in with someone who does smoke. Like a daughter maybe.'

'Yes, at the time we really were puzzled and we did mention it to Mrs Lamb but she knew nothing about it. After that we didn't give it another thought.'

'Are you sure about the cleaner? How long has she been coming to the house?'

'Oh Mrs Lamb is absolutely honest. Straight as a die. She has cleaned seven or eight years for us. She is more like a friend than a cleaner.'

'Where did you discover the ash?' Harry asked.

'Over there, on the floor by the desk,' James indicated.

'Show me where exactly,' Harry persisted. They moved to the desk.

'There, by the front leg. The right hand one,' said James, pointing to the spot.

'Did you check if anything had been removed from the desk after noticing the ash?'

'No. I didn't really attach much importance to it. I was just a bit puzzled, that's all. But if anything had been taken, Betty or I would have noticed sooner or later. There is nothing missing, Harry, I'm sure.'

'Strange about the ash, all the same,' Harry

said. Then, 'Have you a stamp I can have? I've a bill to post and I could do with stretching my legs a bit, I can post it at the same time.'

'Help yourself. Tear one off. There are three on the desk.'

The old detective pulled his scarf under his chin against the cold clear night, which was the kind of weather he liked. As he was closing the door he called: 'Is there a post box near by, James?'

'There is a sub-post office just down the road, it's a chemist shop as well. There's a box let into the wall, turn left out of my gate.'

The comrades turned in at ten. James felt drained, and Harry would take advantage of reading in bed, which was a pleasure he rarely allowed himself to enjoy at home, knowing the light disturbed Hester. But, perhaps the old man was rather more tired than he had thought, for his book soon slipped from his hand and he was breathing deeply, the bedside light still glowing.

At one thirty, Harry awakened bathed in perspiration and feeling terrible. He saw his hands had a slight tremor which he was not able to prevent. He spent the next few hours in much discomfort, but by six a.m. he was back to normality, though feeling washed out.

James had the breakfast table laid by the

time his friend came downstairs. 'Ah, there you are,' he said, 'three slices of bacon enough?'

'Just coffee, thanks. I don't want breakfast.'

'Are you all right? You don't look too good.'

'To tell the truth, I'm not at my best. I had an awful night, sweating like a pig and was trembling as if I'd the DTs.'

'Were you also dizzy?' James asked.

'Yes, I was. I felt terrible.'

'Harry, you are describing the symptoms I had, only mine lasted longer.'

'Did you tremble as well?'

'Yes I did. I couldn't control it at all.'

'What was it they said at the hospital about Betty? That her central nervous system was affected?'

'That's what they said,' James confirmed.

'James, we are on to something,' Harry White was as near to excitement as he would get. 'There is a lead here somewhere. It can't be a coincidence that the three of us in the same house have had the same symptoms, though to varying degrees. First there was Betty, then y . . .'

'Correction, Harry,' James interrupted. 'Betty wasn't ill first. I was.'

'Ah yes. So you were. Anyway, you and then Betty and now me. It's something in this house, it has to be. But what? My attack being the least severe might have suggested the potency of the cause is fading if Betty had been the first to become ill. But she was not, you were, yet you were nothing like as ill as your wife. Have you had anyone else in the house during the past few weeks?'

'No one, Harry.'

'What about your cleaner?'

'Oh yes, she has come as usual.'

'She has not complained of illness?'

'No. She's been fine.'

'And yet something in this house has attacked us but not Mrs Lamb, even though she has spent much more time here than myself. It seems the answer may be food after all,' Harry contemplated.

'Why food?' James asked.

'Because it is something we have in common apart from Mrs Lamb'

'But that is not the case,' James said. 'When Mrs Lamb comes here to clean, it is for the full day. She prefers to do two full days instead of four half days, so she always has her lunch with us.'

'Well, that goes someway towards knocking the food on the head. Think, James. Apart from sleeping, what could you and Betty do in the house that your cleaner does not? And of course, myself. What have I done? Why should the three of us do whatever we did but not Mrs Lamb? Bearing in mind that she spends a lot of time here, but I've only been here for a few hours.'

'It's a mystery to me,' James said.

'Nevertheless, the cause of our illness lies in this house. I'm sure of it. Hell, it shouldn't require the brains of a genius for me to recall all I've done since arriving here. My presence is the key James, because you and Betty couldn't possibly recall every single thing you have done over the past weeks. But we do know it's something the three of us have done. So, I shall go over my actions exactly,' Harry determined.

'. . . After that, I left the house for fresh air and to post my letter — post my letter — stamp. It was one of your stamps I put onto the envelope. I tore one stamp off from three. Who bought the stamps James?'

'Betty did, she bought a whole sheet the day before we went away, ready for all the Christmas posting. Betty being big on the Christmas cards.'

'She will have sent a lot then?'

'She used almost the full sheet, there were only those three remaining.'

'How about you? Did you use any? The card Hester and I got from you, who addressed and stamped that envelope? You or Betty?'

'I did, I dealt with all the crew,' James said, with a look of comprehension.

'And of course, you licked the stamps and you sent yours off a few days before Betty posted her sackful?'

'Right.'

'We have it, James, the one thing we three did, was to lick stamps from the same sheet. The one who licked the most, all but died. But myself, licking one, was ill a few hours only.'

'It's odd, I must agree,' James said, 'but how could it be stamps? They were bought at the local sub-office and brought straight home. They had never been out of the house before posting.'

Harry said, 'They hadn't been out of the house, but someone had been in the house. Remember the cigarette ash, where it was found? It's incredible how stupid criminals can be. Here we have a professional. The way he let himself into the house without leaving a sign of entry, shows he was no opportunist, and yet he was stupid enough to smoke. We have a lead, James. It looks problematical, but we have a lead,' Harry said, looking and feeling a lot better. 'I'd like another coffee, if you please.'

'Help yourself. I'll see if there is any post. Bound to be the odd card or two,' James said, making his way to the porch. On his return to the kitchen James was looking grim. Without a word he handed his friend a white card on which were printed the words: 'FOUR, a number not to be forgotten'.

'Well then, there is the confirmation. I'd like to keep the card,' Harry said, as he took it from James and held it by its edges. 'Have you a small plastic bag? I will be surprised if there is a fingerprint on the card other than yours, but you never know.'

Shortly before lunch-time James talked over the phone with the consultant at the hospital and was relieved to be told that his wife's improvement continued. Her central nervous system was recovering from the trauma it had suffered, and there was every likelihood she would make a full recovery.

Replacing the phone, he turned to his friend, saying: 'I don't think the news could be better, Harry.' The transformation had been instant, and Harry felt he was watching a different man standing there.

Harry said, 'I'm sure whoever is behind all this will be thinking Betty has died. Until now the cards have not been delivered to the victim until the deed had been accomplished. Although he's failed to kill your wife — albeit by a hair's breadth — I'm sure he thinks he has done so. It would have been a simple matter to check with the hospital. It's my view the bastard is getting over-confident, James. Nevertheless, it would be wise to keep her low profile when she gets home. I'd also like to have the two remaining stamps from the sheet she bought.'

'Harry, what chance is there of bringing this misbegotten bastard to justice?'

'You are the third victim, James, but we have only just started work on your case. Of the other two, Bob and Tom. Well, we've got one behind bars — fifty per cent so far. Bob's case is still a mystery as there are no leads, since the Austrian authorities insist that his grandson's death was due to an accident. However, James, the man we've put behind bars, and yours when we get him, are only 'employees' of the Perpetrator. And it's the Perpetrator I mean to get.'

'You sound sure you are going to catch my man, Harry!'

'Oh, I will get him. Have no fear of that.'

James had not previously seen such fortitude in his friend. Any doubts he may have held vanished at that moment.

★   ★   ★

Harry entered the sub-post office/chemist shop and paused to study the layout. At the far end was the dispensary where the pharmacist could be seen studying a prescription. To Harry's right was the post office counter with its security grille, behind which stood two assistants. Along the wall to his left were the general goods, found in most chemists.

Assuming the pharmacist to be the proprietor, Harry tapped on the glass of the dispensary. The man raised his gaze in surprise before entering the shop.

'I apologise for the intrusion, but I would appreciate a few moments of your time. My name is White. May I know your name, please?'

'I am Hempseed. The name is shown over the entrance,' the pharmacist inclined his head towards the entrance.

'You are the proprietor then! I noticed the name. Allow me to show my credentials. You will see I am a retired policeman, but I am investigating a serious crime and you may be able to help me with my enquiries, Mr Hempseed.'

'A serious crime, you say? I would have thought a serious crime should be in the hands of a serving policeman.'

Though the proprietor was civil, the old detective sensed suspicion. 'You are right, Mr Hempseed, but the serving men are in fact co-operating. The case is personal to me and because of this and because I was a police detective, they have no objection to me proceeding with this case. As I say, Mr Hempseed, your help could be useful,' Harry urged.

'Very well then. First, I'll take note of your identity and your address. Have you a driving licence? I'd like to see that as well.'

Harry smiled and said, 'We could only wish everyone were as careful. It would make our job easier, and help to perplex the villain.'

'Actually, it is from the ladies there that I may get most information, since I am interested in the time when a sale of a full sheet of postage stamps took place. That was on Friday the twenty-seventh of November — last month. Since this is a sub-office, I am gambling with the hope that your staff will know, by sight at least, a large majority of the customers — so, when a stranger is served, that customer may be recalled to memory.'

'I think you are expecting a lot. We have a mingling of new faces all the time,' Mr Hempseed said doubtfully.

'Perhaps so. However on that date a Mrs Daly bought a full sheet of postage stamps. Because I know that Mrs Daly is a regular user of this office, I am hoping one of the staff will remember the purchase. Perhaps we could ask the ladies?'

'Of course,' the pharmacist agreed.

Harry's first question to them was: 'Do you recognise the name Daly, Mrs Daly, as one of your customers?'

'Oh yes, she has been popping in since I started work here over five years ago. She's always so pleasant.'

'Which one is that?' asked the younger of the two.

'You know. She is a short lady, rather fat and has flushed cheeks. You must know her, she comes in most weeks, very friendly she is.'

'Oh, of course I know her. She's Mrs Daly then! I never remember names, though I can remember faces all right,' she said smiling.

'Can either of you recall her coming to your counter to purchase a full sheet of postage stamps near the end of last month? The fact that she bought a full sheet might jog your memory,' Harry said.

'I remember. It was me who served her,' said the younger lady. 'She said she had come to pick up the blood pressure pills from Mr Hempseed and thought she might as well buy her Christmas stamps while she was here, saying it would be one job less at the time.'

Harry said, 'Good. I'm Mr White. What is your name, young lady?'

'I'm Kathy,' she said, glancing at her companion.

'Very well, Kathy. Now I want you to think hard. Did you notice anyone follow Mrs Daly into the shop? Or was there anyone who seemed to hang back while you were serving her? Anyone who seemed not to be behaving quite normally?'

'No, not really. The only thing that did surprise me a little was that the very next customer also bought a full sheet of postage stamps. Not a lot of people buy full sheets from this office as there are no business offices about here you see, and not many people take full sheets home. That's why I've remembered, I suppose.'

'Yes, Kathy, and you've jolted my memory,' Mr Hempseed said. 'Do you recall that this man, after he got the stamps, asked you to cash a social security retirement pension? You brought it to me because the pension book was made out to a female who lived a long way south of Lichfield.'

'Yes, I do remember that,' Kathy said.

He turned to Harry to explain that a pension can be cashed at a post office other than the one at which it has been registered and from which the cash is normally obtained, providing the usual office had stamped the front of the book. The amount is

212

restricted to two weeks.'

'I appreciate that,' Harry affirmed.

Mr Hempseed continued, 'Also one can act as an agent for a pensioner unable to collect their own money. To do this, the person whose name is on the front of the order book must sign authorisation on the back of the allowance. I was wondering why the allowance was being cashed so far from the pensioner's home by an agent. You see, the convenience of cashing elsewhere is to benefit the pensioner who may be away from home, on holiday. I therefore paid particular attention to the identity of this agent.'

'Once again, your caution is commendable,' Harry said.

'He showed a letter addressed to himself, but I told him that wouldn't be adequate. Perhaps I could see his driving licence, I suggested, and the man produced it for me.'

'Do you still remember his name and address?' Harry asked, having little hope for a positive reply.

'Not the name, Mr White. But I do recollect the address on the pension book, or at least the name of the road. You see, my parents live on a road of the same name in this town — Devonshire Road, that is. The pensioner living at number 2.'

'And the name of the town?'

'No problem there, since it was largely because of its distance from Lichfield that prompted me to question his identity in the first place. The town is Droitwich, Mr White.'

'This is very helpful,' Harry said. 'Is there anything at all which you think could be helpful?' Harry asked, looking at the three in turn.

'I haven't quite finished,' said Mr Hempseed with a smile. 'You see, I followed this man out of the shop. It was not that I was following him. Actually, I had left some papers in the car which I needed for the dispensary and I saw the man climb into his car — a nice BMW — and with admiration I watched it pull away. The number plate-showed it to be an R reg — R111. When I was a boy, I played the game of finding registration numbers in numerical order, starting with number one. I don't advise anyone to start doing it, because it becomes compulsive after a time, a habit hard to stop. I still find I'm glancing at reg plates now and then. But treble one was easy to remember!'

'You don't recall the letters then'? Harry asked.

'Afraid not. They were not part of the game, you see.'

'Finally. Can anyone give a description of this man?' Harry asked.

Kathy said, 'I can't. He was just another customer as far as I was concerned. It's simply the fact that he bought a full sheet after Mrs Daly had taken one. It was unusual, so I've remembered that. After he was handed over to Mr Hempseed, I took no more notice.'

'And you, ma'am?' Harry asked of the other lady.

'Sorry, I can't recall anything about the incident. I must have been doing some paperwork.'

'Of course, Mr Hempseed, you should be able to recollect this man, having dealt with him in the way you did?' Harry affirmed.

'Indeed I can. Height? My height — six feet. Weight? About thirteen stone. He dressed well, wearing a smart pinstripe suit and sporting the fashionable five o'clock beard. There was a tasteful tie, had fair hair — not yet thinning — and blue eyes. Even though it was cold, he didn't wear an overcoat but of course, he had a warm car.'

'Thank you. I won't ask more about his clothes as they could be frequently changed. However, since you say he dressed well one can assume that it will be his normal standard. You might say their quality matched that of his BMW. We will not be searching for a ruffian. Just one more thought, Mr Hempseed. The man's walk! Was it normal?

Nothing out of the ordinary?'

'I wasn't aware of his walk, but if it had been other than normal, I probably would have noticed it,' considered the chemist.

Harry said, 'I'm sure you would have. Thank you all for your co-operation which should be very useful.'

The old detective raised his hat, as was the way of many of his generation, and wished them good day.

'I wonder what all that was about?' Kathy said curiously.

Her colleague answered: 'I don't know. The old boy wasn't for saying, was he?'

★ ★ ★

Harry, settled in his favourite chair, reached for the whisky which Hester had already poured. 'How did things go for my dear old sleuth at Lichfield, then?' she mischievously enquired.

'Could have been a deal worse, but the state of Betty Daly doesn't call for much hilarity,' her husband said, a little sternly.

'It was that serious?' she asked, surprised.

'She was only a hair's breadth off death, Hester,' her husband sounded grim.

'What are you going to do about it?' she asked.

'I intend to phone Superintendent Harrison, to ask if I could speak with him at his office. There are a few favours I'd like, including entry into the NPC.'

'The what?'

'NPC — the National Police Computer. I am sure he will co-operate.'

'I'm sure he will dear. In the meantime though, put the case out of your mind. I know how you are inclined to dwell on injustice, but to have it circling around your mind all the time can't help I'm sure.'

Harry turned, saying, 'I don't feel this is a case on which I need to dwell too much, Hester. While the information I gained at Lichfield wouldn't exactly fill a notebook, I do feel with a little help from the super that I'll bring my man to book in double quick time. You needn't worry, I shan't be losing any sleep tonight, my dear.'

Superintendent Harrison came to head the Chesterfield Police Force some years after Harry White's retirement. It was not long however, before the referral of case after case was brought to the new man's attention so as to apply some aspect from them to expedite a case on hand. Most of the cases brought, the superintendent noticed, had been handled by an Inspector Harry White, now retired.

They first met at a police social function to

which one or two ex-policemen had been invited. Harrison at once took to Harry and despite their age-gap they became friends, occasionally visiting each other's homes for dinner. Harry was then welcomed by the superintendent when he entered his office.

'How are you, old friend?' asked the superintendent, raising his bulk from the chair. 'It's good to see you. How can I help? Your call this morning got me curious, Harry. Surely you're not taking up detective work again after all this time?' he said with a laugh.

'As a matter of fact I am, Derek. This is a serious business, also personal,' Harry said earnestly.

'Sounds grim. Tell me about it.' He invited his visitor to take a chair, then returned to his own.

'It's a strange story,' Harry began, 'weird in fact. I think you know that during the war I was a member of a Lancaster heavy bomber crew? It seems a long time ago now and it's mostly forgotten, though forcefully recalled once a year when, for a weekend, the whole of my crew gather for our reunion. We've done this ever since the war. The reunions are always the same, apart from the crew gradually becoming older. It's always held at the same hotel in Lincolnshire — bomber country.

'However Derek, the last reunion was different. A card with some silly words written on it had been placed on Peter Newell's bed. Peter was the skipper — the pilot of the bomber.

'The card could have been construed as a threat to the crew, but it was so ridiculous, the others passed it off as a silly joke played by one of the hotel's staff. But I felt uneasy.'

'That well-known instinct at work again, eh!'

'I suppose so. Anyway, I was right. Someone has set about mentally torturing each member of the crew. The rear gunner idolised his grandson beyond all else. The grandson is now dead — murdered.'

'What!' Derek exclaimed.

Harry proceeded: 'The navigator was framed for murder and jailed.'

A dwindling whistle left the superintendent's lips, before saying: 'I don't believe it.'

'There is more,' Harry prompted. 'The wife of the flight engineer came within a hair's breadth of dying from poison. I am almost sure the Perpetrator now thinks she's dead.'

'My God, Harry! You say you need my help — you've got it.'

'I knew I could rely on you. Thank you, Derek. Actually, I've put one villain away. The bastard who framed Tom Williams. Not that he was the brains behind this affair, only the 'employee' to commit that particular deed. With your co-operation, I'm confident I'll have the poisoner quickly behind bars as well.'

'What do you need, Harry?'

'Very little really. I want you to authorise Doctor Smith at forensic to carry out a test on a couple of postage stamps. I also need a uniformed officer assigned to me, or at least available at short notice. I might require his authority for cautioning.'

The superintendent reached for his internal phone; a moment later he ordered the desk to send in a constable. Presently there was a tap on the door and Derek called, 'Enter.' Harry handed a small plastic bag containing two stamps to the constable who then was instructed by his superior to take them to Doctor Smith at forensic. When the constable had left his office Derek phoned his instructions to the doctor.

'Now, Derek, can I ask you to contact the NPC to see if they can come up with the owner of a BMW R-reg 111? That is all I know of the licence number, but I think the owner lives in Droitwich.'

The computer quickly found a full registration with the Droitwich letters. The car was owned by a Mr Mark Noble, 16

Westside Road, who had a clean licence.

The two men shook hands, the superintendent saying, 'My regards to Hester, and keep me informed Harry. You certainly have a strange case to solve.'

Harry called at forensic to meet Doctor Smith and convey his wishes to him. The two had not previously met. The doctor was of medium height with a high forehead over a thin pale face. His hair was fair, but thinning. At first, the doctor was rather offhand with the ex-inspector and pointedly turned his back and drew a long drawer from the refrigerated cabinet. It contained the body of a battered young man with a nametag tied to a toe. The sight of the boy lying there caused a wave of sadness to flow through the seasoned old detective as he thought again of young Norman and the sad old man in Dundee, who was his grandfather.

Before leaving his department, Harry had prompted Doctor Smith to have his findings on the stamps completed by midday the next day. From the data he learned that the gum on the backside of the stamps had been sprayed with a deadly solution containing Manganese Sulphate.

Harry stepped into the police car which a few minutes previously had drawn up outside his house. It was driven by a young officer by the name of Charles Hook, but known to his colleagues as Chuck. 'Super does me proud, providing a car,' Harry commented.

'He's not a bad old stick,' he replied.

'Right, lad. Point the car towards Droitwich and drive.' Harry was feeling good. Even much of his stiffness had ebbed away, and as Chuck guided the car onto the roundabout, then off onto the A617 for Heath and junction 29 on the M1, Harry gazed up for the thousandth time at the twisted steeple of All Saints. His fascination of the defect may have been due to his absolute commitment to honesty and the straight path, mentally wanting to twist the steeple straight.

On the unusually quiet motorway, Chuck kept the needle fixed on seventy. The officer's smooth driving impressed his passenger as did the young man's temperament. Though they had only spent a short time together, Harry felt he had already largely evaluated him. They left the M1 at junction 24 to get onto the M42 which would bring them to the M5 at Bromsgrove. They were then quickly brought on to the A38 leading into Droitwich.

The response to the knock on 2 Devonshire Road was made by a bent old lady whose joints were riddled with arthritis, which explained the delay in the door's opening. Seeing before him the semi-cripple, Harry apologised for having disturbed her, before identifying himself and the young officer. She introduced herself as Mrs Ashworth and responded favourably to the policeman's request to enter her home. The two men saw a humble abode which was showing signs of dilapidation, no doubt due to the old lady's affliction.

He said, 'I would like to apologise again for troubling you, Mrs Ashworth, but the matter is serious. However, let me assure you at once, there is nothing at all for you to worry about personally.'

'I don't understand. I mean the police and all!' she said with obvious anxiety.

'Please, Mrs Ashworth, don't worry, but it would be very helpful to me if you could answer a few simple questions.'

'Me, answer questions? What could I possibly know which would be of help to you?' But Harry was pleased to see the old lady was starting to be amused, knowing it would help him if she was relaxed.

'Well, let's start off with this. How long have you lived in this house, Mrs Ashworth?' he asked with a smile.

'Since I married my Bill, two years before William was born. My boy would be forty-nine now, if he were still here.'

'You've lost your son? When did you lose Mr Ashworth?' Harry asked gently.

'Poor Bill passed away six years ago now. It was a blessing. The poor man had suffered terribly. It was cancer. William called it the big 'C'. But he didn't outlive his father long. He was taken in an accident six months after I buried Bill.'

'You've had a difficult time, Mrs Ashworth.' After a pause, he asked: 'What sort of accident was your son in?'

'A shooting accident, Mr White. A terrible accident. They wouldn't let me see my poor boy. Said most of his face had gone. Terrible!'

'How did it happen? I'm sorry to ask, but I need to know.'

'I can't see why, after all this time, but if you must: William had gone to London where he had friends, and was also a member of a shooting club down there. On the occasion they were holding a competition and when it was over, a few went to a small party at a friend's house. The man who gave the party showed his new gun to his friends. I think it was something special, but when it was placed on the table the man's young son picked up the gun. William was right next to the boy and he pointed it at William's head. Someone told the boy to put down the gun, but the man who owned it said, 'It's all right, it's not loaded.' If I remember rightly from the report at the time, he told the boy it was safe to pull the trigger, and the boy did. The owner of the gun, who held the licence, was taken to court and found guilty of some kind of responsibility or other, and was sentenced to six months in prison.'

'That is a sad story.' Harry sounded sympathetic, as indeed he was for Mrs Ashworth. Then, after another suitable pause, he asked, 'Do you know anyone who lives on Westside Road?'

'Westside Road? Why, yes I know Mr Noble who lives there. And a nice gentleman he is, but I can't understand why you want to know things like this. What has Mr Noble to do with anything?'

'Will you tell me how you got to know him, please, Mrs Ashworth?'

'It's funny really. You see, shortly before my boy was killed, he came home one day with a lovely new car, saying it was his. Now that really surprised me because I knew our William couldn't afford such a posh car, and when I asked him how he could manage it, he said it was a gift from a friend he had helped. He wouldn't say how he had helped though, but that was typical of my boy, so modest. Anyway, the friend he had helped turned out to be Mr Noble.'

'How did you discover that?'

'Well, after William's terrible accident, about a month after, Mr Noble called on me and introduced himself. He said how sorry he was that William had gone and asked if there was anything he could do for me. I asked him how he came to know our William, and he just said he had known him only a short time, but long enough to regard him with great affection. This amazed me. You see he was obviously a gentleman who was from a different world. Not that our William wasn't a gentleman. He was what some call, a 'nature's' gentleman. You know what I mean?'

'Indeed I do, Mrs Ashworth,' Harry said, smiling pleasantly. 'And did the gentleman help you?'

'Oh yes, to this day he does little things for me. Knowing I find it painful to get about, he will call to see if there is anything I'm wanting from the corner shop, or pop down to the post office to collect my pension. Little things like that. If I say anything, he just says it's in memory of William. He's a real gent.'

'It must make you happy, knowing he thought so highly of William!'

'Yes, it does, Mr White. I feel he was a boy I can rightly be proud of.'

Harry got to his feet, reached out and gently shook the lady's gnarled hand as he thanked her for being so helpful. She said, 'For the world of me I can't see how, but I am pleased if I have been of use. I must say I have enjoyed our little talk, Mr White. It brought back happy memories as well as sad ones.'

'It will help a little further if you will allow me to borrow your pension book. I will see that it is returned in good time for your next payment,' Harry assured her.

'I don't know about that. I don't think I'm keen on letting the book leave my house, Mr White. If you don't mind.'

'I do understand. You are right to be concerned, but remember, we are the police, Mrs Ashworth, so the book would not come to any harm with us. It would be most beneficial if we could hold it for a day or two. And you'll get a receipt.'

'Yes, of course, you are the police. I'll just fetch it.' On receiving the book, Harry made a quick glance at the counterfoil for the payment made at the end of the previous month. He noted with satisfaction the office frank read 'Fields PO, Lichfield'.

Westside Road was a manifest of wealthy properties of which No 16 appeared the most opulent. 'The villain does himself proud,' Chuck uttered.

'Mr Noble either has a very well-paid job

as well as being a villain, or he is into crime in a big way. Probably the latter, since the criminals being used against us thus far have been of a high standard. The murderer of Bob's grandson is not yet known. And that fellow Reid, put onto Tom William, was no slouch, even though he is in prison, where he belongs. Big fish they may be, but they still don't know the man who is *hiring* them. Though, at thirty thousand a time, they are not likely to be overly concerned.'

'Thirty thou, boss! Is that what they are demanding?'

'They are demanding nothing. First they are chosen because of their skills. They are then approached blind and offered the sum. An opportunity to refuse is given, but it is made clear that if they accept and then back off before the business is achieved, they will die.'

'It sounds grim to me, boss.'

'The hierarchy's well covered, Chuck. Nevertheless, I'll catch 'em.' For a moment the young officer thought he *felt*, rather sensed, the fearful resolution within the old man.

Mrs Noble was attractive and of ladylike appearance, seemingly well bred and educated. Though Chuck was a uniformed officer, she had expressed surprise when the two men had identified themselves after her response to the door bell. The elder man — obviously gentleman — respectfully asked if Mr Noble was at home and may they enter the house. 'I am assuming,' the elder said, 'that you will be Mrs Noble?' The confirmation was indicated by an elegant smile as she stepped aside.

Harry and his young officer, were led across the polished inlaid floor of the hall onto the deep pile carpeted lounge. In a corner a four foot high pedestal stood, carrying the bare figure of a Grecian slave in full flight. His left ankle still carried the clamp which had imprisoned him. Elsewhere, a cabinet displayed fine porcelain. Two of them, Harry saw, were Capo de Monte.

Mrs Noble, who had left the room, returned with her husband. For an instant, Harry considered the pharmacist had described Mr Noble very well.

'Good day gentlemen. My wife says you wish to talk to me?' he asked pleasantly enough. 'Though I cannot imagine why you wish to do so — Darling, will you please ring for coffee? For four.'

Noble's attire matched the opulence of his home. His manners were impressive, though the detective's wealth of encounters prompted him to detect an insincerity. In fact Harry soon appreciated the ruthlessness lying below Noble's veneer. The younger policeman however, had already decided that Mr Noble could not be a crook.

Before Mrs Noble could instruct Alice, Harry said, 'Thank you. I don't feel pleasantries should reach too far, Mrs Noble. I regret, your *welcome* will surely diminish as the interview progresses.'

Noble sat up abruptly. 'Interview, you say? This is a different notation. What grounds do you have for this?' Noble remained courteous, though he had taken on a certain firmness. Harry studied again Noble's wife. He sensed strongly the lady was not aware of her husband's true character, and he felt compassion for the hurt she would surely suffer when he'd been removed from her, maybe forever. The man she loved. And, unless she had personal wealth, her lifestyle.

Noble had been sure no unpleasantness could be laid at his feet. For years he had been highly successful in his 'career'. He had been diligent in the planning of all his criminal enterprises, using a brain which achieved much academic esteem at Oxford. Crime had ensured a good life for little effort, and he saw no reason why it should not continue until he chose to finish his career.

Now though, Noble's mind was racing. His

last enterprise — the only one in which the direction came from others — had resulted in policemen being in his house, and in the presence of his wife. He had broken his golden rule where jobs were concerned — never get involved with others.

All the same, Noble couldn't see how the law had got onto him. Surely there had got to be a reasonable explanation for their intrusion. There were only two or three individuals who had any inkling of his activities and they themselves were very intelligent and private criminals. When Noble had received the invitation to dispatch the woman Daly, together with an offer of thirty thousand pounds, he knew it could only have come from one of them. Any one of these men was inordinately cautious so it was natural that they wouldn't advertise their identity. Had the deposit of fifteen thousand not reached him, Noble would have looked at the invitation as some sick joke. As it was, their promise to him that he would die if he agreed, then backed away, was quite in keeping with his own approach to security. No, he considered, the police couldn't be on to the job he had so recently executed.

Harry said, 'In consideration for Mrs Noble it may be better if our questioning were to take place at a police station. In any case, that is where you will be going eventually, Mr Noble.' The usual caution followed.

'My God! What are you saying? Is my husband in trouble?' Mrs Noble, turning to her husband, asked, 'Have you been involved in some accident, Mark?'

But it was Harry who answered her: 'I'm afraid it's much more serious than that, Mrs Noble. It is a matter of — ' he checked himself, hoping to let her down lightly, before he realised it wasn't possible.

'A matter of what, Mr White?' She had become flushed with rising anger.

'I'm sorry madam, I must say it; *a matter of murder.*'

'Ridiculous!' exclaimed her husband. 'Who do you think you are, Mr White, to come into my house and upset my wife with such a preposterous accusation?'

Pointedly ignoring Noble's attitude, Harry asked, 'What was the purpose of your business in Lichfield a few days ago, Mr Noble?'

'I have no business in Lichfield. I haven't been to that town for ages.'

'And what *is* your business?' Harry asked.

There was a short pause before Noble said, 'I am a dealer in the antique trade.'

'What is your business address, please?' Harry enquired.

'What business is my address to you, may I ask? I think you and the constable had better leave my house. I will not have you upsetting my wife like this.' Mark Noble was playing for time, and Harry White knew it.

'Very well, Mr Noble. You would prefer to accompany us to the police station then?'

'Leave my house at once, or else place a charge,' the pitch of Noble's voice had risen.

'All in good time, sir. Now, your business address if you please.'

The criminal, a highly educated if evil man, saw real danger in his adversary. What he saw was hard to single out, but for the first time ever, Mark Noble felt something akin to panic. 'My business is this address. I work from my home.'

'You will be able to show me the stock-room then,' Harry persisted.

'I do not have a stock-room since I don't hold stock as such. I am what you might call a broker in the antique business, tracking down pieces required by wealthy collectors. It is a profitable business if one is good at it,' but Mark felt an emptiness, knowing his explanation to be feeble.

'Working from home? Of course you must hold records of transactions. Perhaps you will be good enough to let me see them,' Harry said, rising to his feet.

'Certainly not,' Noble's smooth countenance no longer remained as he continued, 'Get out of my house. You don't have the right to make demands. I will remind you that you were courteously invited in, by my over-trusting wife. Now leave at once.'

'What you say is true, sir. I cannot make a search unless armed with a warrant. However, before we leave, tell me what was your relationship with the late William Ashworth?' Harry saw a twitch of Noble's upper lip, before he said, 'I know no such person.'

'Now come on, sir, how can you forget the tragic demise of a friend shot to death with a bullet in his head?'

'How do you conceive such fanciful yarns, Inspector?' For the first time he had addressed White as 'inspector' which made him feel the damn man was reaching into his psychology. Harry removed from his pocket a social security pension book, and, opening it at the last franked counterfoil, said 'I see the last payment for Mrs Ashworth was made at the Fields' post office. Lichfield. A city you have not visited for 'ages', I believe!'

'Nor have I. What are you talking about, man?'

'Mr Noble, it will be an easy matter for the authorities to trace the pension allowance slip, on the back of which will be shown signed authorisation for it to be cashed by Mr M Noble on behalf of the pensioner, A Ashworth — Constable, arrest Mr Noble and fasten him to me with your handcuffs. We will take you to the station at Chesterfield, where you will be cautioned and, no doubt, charged with the attempted murder of Betty Daly.

'Chuck, find the maid and bring her to help Mrs Noble.' Turning to the lady, now sitting bewildered, he said, 'For your sake at least, Mrs Noble, I am truly sorry to have brought this dreadful business crashing down about your head.'

★ ★ ★

During the return drive to Chesterfield, Harry again remarked on Chuck's smooth handling of the car, saying, 'Have you considered moving to the Traffic Division, Constable?'

'Yes, I have. I would very much like to move there, but there aren't any vacancies.'

Superintendent Harrison looked up from his papers to say, 'So you're back, Harry. How did you find things at Droitwich?'

'Much as I had expected. The bastard is in one of your cells now, and I have pleasure in handing you the file I've built on him. You will have no difficulties at all in pressing charges, Derek. The man is cold meat.'

'Excellent, Harry. I have read many of your previous cases with admiration but now I have seen you in action. Or at least come close to it, sitting here,' laughed Chesterfield's chief of police.

'You will find, from Doctor Smith's report which is in my file, that the deed was committed with the application of manganese sulphate. When we brought Noble in, he was wearing a suit into which he had probably earlier placed contaminated stamps. At any rate, Noble placed the stamps into the inside breast pocket at the time of purchase, so I think we can assume he will have used the same pocket after their contamination. Your forensic should find evidence of this, which will of course be damning. Also, there is a DSS pension book which had been carried in the same pocket. That book also could give evidence of the poison.'

The superintendent was looking bewildered. 'I don't understand what you are talking about, Harry?'

'All will become clear after you have read my file, which also indicates that there is a likelihood of £30,000 to be found somewhere in the villain's house. This was not mentioned by me during our *talk* at the house as I felt the crook's wife is a lady who had not had previous knowledge of her husband's guilt, and to whom the accusations came as a great shock. But, if I was wrong in my judgement of her, which I doubt, I had to be sure she didn't lay her hands on the money before we can. You see, I didn't have a search warrant with me.

'By the way, will you please get one of your officers to contact the DSS without delay, and ask them to replace Mrs Ashworth's pension book. We will be keeping her original. Mrs Ashworth is a near-cripple and must not be made to worry. Anyway, I have promised her she will have her book in good time for the next payment due.

'Derek, one final thing! Will you do me a favour? Transfer the officer you lent to me, to the Traffic Division — I must dash, or I'll be in trouble with Hester.

'Oh! One more thing. It's not in my report, but you might like to know that the villain is bisexual.'

As Superintendent Derek Harrison reached for his papers, he said, 'That old man is both devil and saint.'

10

The poison quickly dissipated once Betty was past her crisis, enabling a fast recovery. She wasn't quite up to joining her sister for the Christmas celebrations, but the unexpected New Year's festivities were accomplished in fine style. Joan and George came up trumps by holding a New Year's Eve party at their house, though the remains from the Christmas festivities still lingered. Normally, George and Joan went to friends for the New Year, but they decided after Betty's near-death experience, they'd do something to make amends.

Betty, studying her image in the mirror, tried for the umpteenth time that day to do something with her hair. In the morning she had visited her hairdresser, the one she always used because they did it so nicely. But this time they had made a complete mess of her hair. 'It's no use. I can do nothing with it,' she thought. Replacing the brush on the dressing table, she went downstairs.

'It's my hair,' she complained to James, 'I can't do anything with it. It's not at all like my hairdresser to do such a poor job, she's normally so good.'

'Don't blame your hairdresser, dear, it's that damned poison. Hair won't get rid of it like the body. It will need time to grow out.'

'I hope it won't take long, I can't be walking about like this. I look terrible,' Betty said with consternation. Then the phone rang and because she was looking again at her hair, this time through the mirror above the hall table, she picked up the phone to say, 'This is Betty Daly — oh Harry, it's you! How are you and Hester?'

'We are both very well, thanks Betty, but more to the point, how are you feeling now?'

'Oh, I'm fine. I wasn't up to the Christmas festivities, but we had a lovely time at the New Year. We went to my sister Joan's place. It was so good of her, to lay on a special do because I'd missed out at her usual Christmas party.'

'I'm so pleased. Anyway, all that nasty business is behind you now Betty, so I think you must put it out of your mind completely. Can I have a word with James please, if he's at home?' Harry asked.

'Yes, I'll fetch him. Love to Hester please.'

'Hi. I'm calling to let you know the next newsletter's going out to bring the boys up to date, James. But, since you and your wife were the ones involved this time, I thought I'd have a word.'

'Is the bastard inside? That's all I want to know,' James said with feeling.

'He's inside all right, my friend. He will be locked up for a long time. I assure you, he'll find prison rather different from his beautiful but ill-begotten home.'

'Harry, there's one thing that's been puzzling me: If we became ill from licking those stamps, why were there no traces of poison discovered on the desk? The stamps must have been doctored in the house. I mean, Betty purchased them at the post office and brought them directly home. There was no way that the stamps got away from the house, Harry.'

'Ah well, you see old friend, those stamps we licked, were not the same stamps which your dear wife brought home. Oh no. Noble had bought a similar sheet from the same office right after Betty had made her purchase and it was those which had been sprayed with a mix incorporating manganese sulphate. Of course, Noble knew where the house was, that information had been given to him when he accepted the job. It came out at interrogation — as I expected — that he had received a deposit of fifteen thousand together with a small spray bottle containing the poison. Though Noble had no idea where the instructions came from, he was informed how his victim must die. The money, by the way, was found at Noble's home.

'One of the reasons Noble had been chosen, was because of his long successful 'career' in housebreaking, amongst other skills. He must have thought he'd received a real piece of luck when he saw your wife buying the sheet of stamps, because he had been staking your place for some time, watching both your movements, waiting for an opportunity to make an entry. Having gained access, Noble was going to have to find some suitable material to be sprayed with the poison which would later be digested by his victim. The stamps were a godsend. He realised they would all be used during the busy Christmas season, thereby creating a sufficient intake of the poison. It is generally known that it's the wives who send the cards. Once in the house, all he had to do was find the stamps and switch them with the ones he'd already prepared.'

'It's good to hear Noble as well as that man Reid are banged up. You are doing a good job, Harry. Is it too much to hope you are any closer to finding the enemy who is masterminding all this?' James asked hopefully.

'Not much, James, but I just may be seeing a faint glow at the end of the tunnel,' Harry said.

'Can you tell me about it?' James asked eagerly.

'Sorry, I'm afraid I can't. It's still sort of abstract at the moment. Anyway, James, I must be getting along. Take care old chap.' The line went dead.

Harry went to his study after informing Hester he didn't want to be disturbed. Her husband, she knew, was about to do some thinking which could go on for five minutes or five hours.

He made a mental review of all that had taken place since the reunion but remained completely in the dark regarding the death of Bob Greeves' grandson. The visit to records at Kew had lifted the veil a touch in that he was sure the questions asked of records by 'researcher', was to gain a lead to the whereabouts of D-dog's crew.

'Researcher' whose address was a Belgian box number? The villains were British, evil men doing a job, but it seemed the real enemy might be a foreigner — unless he had set a red herring! And then his request. It had been written on paper with the heading torn off. Why? Why not simply use a normal plain sheet of writing paper?

Harry went to his desk and took the four white cards together with the strip he had taken from the foot of the 'researcher's' letter. He placed a powerful magnifying glass over one of the cards. Looking through it, he noticed that one card had different cuts on the bottom and right-hand edge and another card on its top and left-hand edge.

He concluded the cards had been taken from two different corners of a larger single sheet. The glass had magnified the damaged grain where the cuts had been made by hand. A study of the remaining cards indicated manual cuts on all sides. So, the sheet from which the cards had been taken was larger than the sum of the four pieces. What could he glean from that he wondered?

Putting on his winter overcoat, Harry informed Hester he was off to town to make a call at Goodmans, the printer. The white cards, having previously been checked for fingerprints, were found to be clean. Now Harry hoped a good printing business might be able to say who had manufactured the cards, or rather, the material from which the cards had been cut. Goodmans was established in 1882. The third generation now ran the firm. Their standard of work was high and the firm was capable of handling large contracts.

The present proprietors were John and Luke Goodman. In the past Harry had been friendly with the elder brother Luke, even though Harry was ten years his senior. But with the onset of old age, their friendship had rather faded. In fact, Harry wasn't sure if his old friend was still in harness. He could be retired, Harry thought, then realised how long they had been out of touch.

Opening the shop door, he heard the ring of an old-fashioned bell, suspended on a leaf spring above his head. It seemed anomalous to him, because beyond the door lay a large, modern stationary department, displaying goods in a manner to give strong impact, in the style of any progressive sales outlet.

A member of the staff, a smart lady in her thirties, asked, 'Can I be of help, sir?'

'Good afternoon. Thank you. I would like to see Mr Goodman, please. Mr Luke, that is,' Harry said.

'Mr Luke is usually to be found in the office attached to the printing rooms. He's not too keen on being disturbed these days. Who shall I say wishes to see him?'

'Say Harry White wants a word. I think he will see me,' he said.

Luke returned with the assistant, saying, 'It's been a long time Harry. How are you these days?'

'I'm very well, considering old age and poverty,' Harry smiled. He thought Luke was standing up to the ravages of life very well.

Then he remembered he was ten years his junior. 'But can we have a few words in private, Luke? I am hoping you may help me to unravel some nasty business which has come my way.'

'Sounds ominous. We'll go to my office at the back,' Luke suggested. 'We are bound to be interrupted in the shop's office. Follow me, I'll lead the way.'

When the door had closed, Harry said, 'My, that's better. What a row those machines make. This room must be soundproof.'

'It is,' Luke confirmed. 'Now how can I be of help?'

'I would like to take advantage of your expertise.' Harry took the cards and the strip of paper from his pocket, and placing them on a table, said, 'I would be grateful if you could tell me who is the manufacturer of these.'

Taking one up, Luke said, 'This is top grade material, and so is this paper,' he added, after a further study. 'But, as to who produced them, I can't help you there, Harry. I'm sorry.'

Suddenly, Harry felt thwarted. He knew now he might have hoped for too much from the printer. After all, as far as he could tell, there were no markings at all on the cards, not even a watermark on the strip of paper. How could Luke tell who was the manufacturer?

Seeing the obvious disappointment on Harry's face, Luke said, 'Is it so important for you to know the manufacturer? I can see the material is top quality but I wouldn't have any difficulty in getting hold of a similar grade for you, Harry.'

'Thank you, Luke, but you don't understand and I don't want to give an explanation at the moment. But I am not wanting replacement paper. It's a matter of detection work, Luke. A knowledge of the manufacture of these particular pieces may be of vital importance to me.'

'If it is really *that* far-reaching we may be able to help you. What I said Harry, was that *I* can't help you. But, one of my major direct suppliers probably could. You know we are big in the printing business and that makes us a valued customer. Leave the card and paper with me and I will get on to them without delay. I think we will get the answer.'

'I do hope so, it will be a great relief, but I shall only hand over one card and the strip, if you don't mind. They could turn out to be as valuable as gold-dust.'

★ ★ ★

Jock Campbell received another set of instructions. The form was the same as it had

246

been for his work concerning James Daly. Discover as much as possible about the life history of Arthur Brown. As before, he had been supplied with the man's address. And, as previously, Jock's acceptance of the job was to be absolutely binding; though again he was assured he would hear no more should the job be declined.

There was no way he was going to decline. Not with the money they paid him, whoever *they* were. Fifteen thousand pounds still didn't come all that easy.

His last job, the first from these people, had been simplicity itself. Getting the low-down on James Daly and his wife had presented no problem, then he sent his findings to some box number. But what they did with his information he hadn't a clue. Nor did he care.

Now, he had been given another job to do and he couldn't wait to get started. Still, the way in which he had been contacted was strange, and he hadn't the least idea by whom. They were hard men though, of that he was sure from what had been made clear to him if he accepted the jobs. Still, fifteen thousand pounds deposit for each job, followed by another fifteen thousand on completion of each job would do for him.

Jock Campbell knew that this time his report must contain more information than

Daly's report. *They* had not been too happy with that effort. It was too sparse. They thought there was just enough for them to do their work and get a result, but if they failed because of it? Then it would be exit Jock Campbell — for good! Jock assumed the result had been achieved, for he was still here and with another assignment.

Well, with that kind of money, Jock hoped for more assignments still, so he'd give his best shot even though the threats had disgruntled him. He hadn't been dragged up in the Gorbals without learning a thing or two. All the same, his sense of self-preservation warned Jock that he could very well be out of his league. Far better to earn his payment because of sound work, then maybe more would follow.

Obtaining sensitive information was nothing new for Jock. He was good at it, even though it was mostly gained by coercion. However, when he was given this assignment it had been stressed that he must not make waves. After the report had been received, Arthur Brown or any of his cronies must not suspect anything. All the same, the Scotsman longed to know to what purpose the reports were to be put. But he could live without the knowledge, knowing if he were to discover it, his own demise would swiftly follow.

Research showed that Arthur Brown, who was born the twenty-eighth March 1922 had seen his first light of day in the city in which he still lived. He had done well at grammar school where his academic achievement was above average and he was an excellent all-round sportsman. When playing team games, his enthusiasm was contagious to all around, but never more so than when on the rugby field.

From what Jock could glean, Arthur was popular, and even as a boy he had a fair sense of justice. Though he was as a lion when on the playing field, he was like a lamb off it. This side of Arthur's character showed unashamedly if a weak or less spirited boy was set upon by a school bully. Fortunately, Arthur's school had high standards, not only in its educational work and sport, but also in its moulding of future citizens, which largely curtailed the development of bullies.

But, the school wasn't a hundred per cent bully-free. Jack Crawford was a big boy who had a similar build to Arthur. Jack was not a sportsman, but he was a bully. The victims he enjoyed bullying most were small boys. Arthur recognised that Jack was a sadist and that made Arthur come close to hatred. It was an emotion he had not experienced previously and when he felt it now, he wasn't sure if it was Jack or himself he disliked most.

Arthur's roughness and strength on the playing field was well known, even feared, but there was no malice there whatsoever. Then came the day Arthur stumbled upon a gruesome scene in the woods behind the school. To be more correct, he heard the screams from a distance which led him to the scene. Young Butterworth, a junior who always looked undernourished, was roped to a tree and being whipped by Crawford who, in his frenzy, had not been aware of Arthur's approach. The boy's face was bleeding profusely from the heavy blows which Crawford's fists had previously administered, and now, as Arthur rushed forward, the bully's boot kicked savagely into Butterworth's guts.

Arthur's fourteen stone crashed down onto a wholly surprised Crawford who found himself at the receiving end of unimagined violence and where his cries for mercy went unheard. Finally when Arthur stepped back it was to gaze down at the bully, the gory wreck twitching amongst the leaves. Then, tenderly, he released young Butterworth from his bonds and carried him back to school.

Although Jack Crawford had surely got his deserts, Arthur had become troubled later when he realised to what extent he had awarded his justice. At the time it was as though a mix of pity for the boy and hatred towards the bully had justified his extreme retributions. Now, Arthur knew it had not been right, and he vowed never again to use violence which went beyond that required for adequate self-defence.

Jock Campbell learnt, that day in the woods behind his school, that Arthur was to become the lifelong enemy of Jack Crawford.

After leaving school Arthur was invited to play rugger for his county, where for two seasons he proved to be a great asset in the back row of the scrum, before leaving to do his bit against Hitler with the Royal Air Force. On the other hand, Jack Crawford somehow managed to convince the military that his hearing was way below par. He successfully acquired a safe position on the local council. A few years after the war, he put himself forward for the council and was elected.

On his return to civvy street, Arthur obtained a degree from Birmingham University in civil engineering with the intention of carving out a career with some large company. But after a couple of years with Hardfast Engineering Ltd, he felt his individualism was suppressed, so decided to risk starting on his own with a heating and insulation business.

When Glowarm started, Arthur and one employee worked on small projects, with his technical knowledge augmented by practical guidance from his tradesman, Jo Burns. Arthur quickly learned all facets of the business. However, it was a struggle not to fall too far into debt during the first eighteen months of business. Then came the break when he was contracted to supply the heating system for Doctor March's new school.

For seven years Dr March was the headteacher of Arthur's old school. Now, like Arthur, he had decided to venture forth by opening his own educational enterprise. It was by far Arthur's biggest contract to date.

Shortly after the completion of Dr March's school, the local rugby club, of which Arthur was a leading member, voted for a fine new clubhouse. Arthur got the insulation/heating contract.

Glowarm was rapidly building a reputation for sound workmanship and on-time completion. By taking on more men, the proprietor was able to apply himself wholly to the administration and growth of the company.

Jock Campbell's scrutinising showed that Arthur Brown had courted and married a Miss Mary Blandford and had sired three sons. His wife Mary was a short, slight woman, who like her husband, had served in the RAF during the war. It was said that the Browns had little in common but had still achieved a very happy union. Their youngest son, Martin, had to his father's joy, entered the business and was now chairman. The middle boy, Ben, though well into middle-age, was still a popular tennis coach in Australia. His eldest son, Sam, was to retire shortly from his veterinary business in the Cotswolds.

Jock Campbell's further probing brought the animosity of a certain city elder towards the popular Arthur Brown into focus. Jock saw that hostile council activities had prevented Glowarm from achieving even greater heights. It hadn't been difficult for the investigator to find that the fly in the ointment was a gentleman by the name of Jack Crawford.

Jock also found that, over the years, where planning permission had been necessary for a construction, this had been denied time and again when Glowarm was a subcontractor. The building trade in general eventually became suspicious. They realised that if they were to involve Glowarm then their chances of gaining planning permission were greatly reduced. In many cases this resulted in a near boycott of Glowarm despite the firm's otherwise fine reputation.

Jack Crawford was able to instil fear into his colleagues, despite maintaining a two-faced popularity with the electorate.

Having learnt of the intense hatred Jack Crawford held for Arthur Brown, Jock was surprised to find that Crawford had bought a house built by a firm who had subcontracted to Glowarm. But then he discovered that Crawford was the second occupant of the property and therefore the resale of the house could serve no further benefit to his enemy.

During the building of a small exclusive estate, where Glowarm had won the heating contract, Arthur met with an unfortunate setback. Responding to a trade advertisement, he purchased a new design of heating boiler. The new boilers offered greater heating efficiency while the construction of their outer casing was tidy and pleasing to the eye. Furthermore, the cost of the boilers to Glowarm was appreciably less than the equipment Arthur had used to date.

When work on the estate was almost complete, an urgent communiqué arrived from Whittaker & Co alerting Arthur of a crucial fault in the R223. A major valve in the boiler had a design fault which became critical at a relatively low pressure. This allowed a high pressure of unburnt gas to develop. When ignition for timeset starting took place, there was a real possibility of the pressurised gas igniting. The following explosion could be powerful enough to bring the building down.

Whittaker & Co expressed profound regret for causing inconvenience. They would gladly stand the full cost to replace the R223 boilers with the R224 which would be on line in three weeks. The manufacturers pointed out that the valve built into the new R224 could not replace the valve in the R223. Although the outer appearance of the two boilers was identical and the fitting of the pipes leading into and out of the appliance was the same, major internal design had been changed.

It was difficult for the builder to have much sympathy for Arthur. For it was he, who had to make excuses to the clients for the delay in completion, apologising for the inconvenience caused, which in some cases was significant.

Several years after the building of Green Acres Estate, one of its smart houses was bought by Alderman Jack Crawford.

All this intelligence had been gathered by Jock Campbell and put into his report. Jock felt he had done a sound job, removing any threat that had accompanied his work on Mrs Daly. Why his *employer* wanted such reports, which paid so well, he couldn't imagine. Nor did he care. He sent off the report to a box number. Almost by return he received fifteen thousand pounds. The two jobs had netted him sixty thousand. Not bad. And not taxable!

Two weeks to the day after Jock Campbell sent off his report, Dick Leach answered his telephone. 'Yes, who is it?' He spoke with a deep, gruff voice, so that the caller couldn't be blamed if he thought it had emitted from a rough giant of a man. Actually Dick was rough, but he was short and very stocky. He had a thick neck and black cropped hair. He was dressed badly, and didn't look too intelligent. He was in fact very bright.

'Mr Leach?'

'Yes. Who is this?'

'You don't know me, Mr Leach, but I know a lot about you. We can be of mutual service. I have a proposition for you.' The caller's voice had a smooth and cultivated drawl.

'Who the hell are you?'

'Never mind that. Just listen. I have a job where you can put a few of your many talents to good use. Like I said, I know a great deal about you and not the least that you are a crook. A successful one.'

'I'm not so stupid as to admit anything to a faceless fool, let alone to accept a blind proposal. Now tell me who you are, or bugger off.'

'I think you will accept *this* proposal, Mr Leach. For a surprisingly little work, I am offering you thirty thousand pounds.'

'Don't waste my time. Now come clean, or I'll put the phone down,' Dick had never been anyone's fool. He wasn't going to start now.

'For God's sake just hear me out. There will be no pressure to make you do the job after I've informed you what we want. If you accept, there will be thirty thousand pounds in cash. You will receive fifteen thousand even before you start. The money will reach you through the mail, together with your instructions. If then, you decide not to go ahead, you will be told how to return the cash. You can see, there is nothing to lose, Mr Leach.'

'You are saying that you'll put fifteen thousand up front? Very trusting, aren't we!'

'That's right, we are. However, Mr Leach, I . . .'

'Oh yes. I thought there'd be a however, but or something,' there was strong sarcasm in the coarse voice.

'However, Mr Leach, if after receiving your instructions and the deposit you accept the offer, and then back off for *any* reason, you will have your throat cut. That's a promise.'

'Christ! You are mad.'

'Perhaps. But you have nothing to fear if

you refuse after receiving the instructions, as you won't hear from us again. Likewise, if you accept and the job is completed.'

After hearing the click of the phone, Dick Leach stood for several seconds. Then, replacing his own instrument, he decided to dismiss the whole business until he saw the money on the doormat. He felt sure it would not arrive.

★　★　★

About the same time as Jock Campbell sent off his report, Harry White got a message from the printers. Luke Goodman said that one of his suppliers had been able to trace the source of the cards and paper. They had been produced by a firm in South Germany — Zandeof of Bergisch Gladbach, Koln.

Harry was delighted to receive some solid information about the cards at last. But he had been thinking the manufacturer might have been based in Brussels.

★　★　★

To his amazement, Dick Leach found himself fifteen thousand pounds better off. Though despite his outward appearance, his success in the world of crime had ensured that he was far from being a poor man. Now, sitting behind the wheel of a midnight blue truck, he slowly guided the vehicle through the darkened yard. Shortly before, a crony had 'killed' the security lights, and with the truck lights off, the villain edged his way to the big metal gate of the compound.

Big bolt cutters sheared off three padlocks and a strong jemmy completed the job. The yard of Whittaker & Co was tidy but well stacked with various domestic products. Most of the articles were obsolete, though some had been carefully crated and would be placed in the main inside store as space became available.

With the help of his accomplice, Leach loaded a number of new boilers and general equipment. This was a blind, as he wasn't in the least interested in such equipment. What Dick Leach was really after was one of the old R223 boilers, several of which were dumped in the far corner.

The operation had gone remarkably smoothly. The truck had left the yard twenty-five minutes after its arrival. As he drove with a load of domestic goods, leaving Birmingham behind, Leach smiled to himself. He had come a long way since his days as a plumber's apprentice.

11

The tyres of the large black limousine squelched on the chippings of the Willows driveway. Mr and Mrs Crawford were on their way to the airport from where they would take off for their holiday destination in the West Indies. The fact that Jack Crawford and his wife were being chauffeured by a council driver in a council luxury car, and thereby breaking the rules, bothered him not one jot.

Debbie Crawford cleared her desk at the travel agency, grateful her working day was done. She was feeling drained. Leaving the building, she turned left to go down the busy street and bumped straight into Charles Wainwright. At once Debbie's fatigue lifted.

Debbie had first noticed Charles two months ago just after he began working at Dixson's. She badly wanted to meet the man. But on the occasions they passed in the street he hardly noticed her. She had given him flashy smiles as she passed but the response was minimal. The man must be the shy type. It couldn't be anything else because Debbie knew she was attractive to men, but she really wanted to be screwed by this one more than any of the others. Now that they had collided she wasn't letting him escape.

That same evening they met up in the pub, as she had arranged. At around ten-thirty Charles said, 'Shall we move on to the disco?'

Debbie moved a little in her chair as she hesitated. The action had caused her short skirt to climb higher. She said, 'I have a better idea. Why not go back to my place?'

Charles felt a rush of excitement. Then he caught just a glance of her lace panties. They were black, hardly covering her crutch. In his loins he felt a developing ache. He said, 'I thought you lived with your parents. I'm not sure I could relax, even if they are out.'

Laughing, Debbie said, 'Oh, I don't think you would be relaxed. Not for sometime, anyway. You needn't worry though. It's not my home we shall go to, darling. I'll take you to my grandparents' place. They are on holiday. The house is empty.'

Because it turned her on more, Debbie said, 'Let's do it in the old bugger's bed. I'm sure he's kinky anyway. You should see the way he looks at me sometimes. I am certainly not naïve but it worries me occasionally. I suspect he'd tried it on with Mum at one time. I know she can't stand him, though I can tell she tries not to show it to Dad. After all, he is his father.'

'Come on, Debbie, your granddad must be over seventy years old!'

'I know that, but you don't know the old bugger. Anyway, screw granddad. Er, correction. Screw me.' Debbie's clothes flew far and wide, then she attacked Charles, disrobing him almost as quickly, before throwing herself onto the bed.

She lay on her back with knees bent, legs apart. 'I'm just a simple girl. Nothing fancy. Just give me a good old fashioned fuck.'

★ ★ ★

Holding two brushes to the light, Arthur selected the smaller of the two. His next half-hour would be spent on detailed work near the foot of the canvas. The first stroke was interrupted by the ringing phone. With a mild curse he replaced the brushes on the palate.

'Hello. Arthur Brown,' he said into the phone.

'Dad. It's Martin. Have you heard the news yet?'

'What news?' Arthur enquired.

'Obviously you haven't. But didn't you hear an explosion about six-thirty this morning?' his son asked.

262

'I did hear something in the distance, yes. I wasn't fully awake just then. Why? What was it?'

'Take a breath, Dad. The Willows went up. It's only rubble now. They say there is nothing left standing.'

'Wait a minute. The Willows! Do you mean Jack Crawford's place over on Green Acres Estate?'

'The same.'

'Good lord. How did it happen? What happened to Jack? Is he dead?'

'No. It seems he and his wife are away on holiday. It was on local radio at eight a.m. But they don't know the cause of the explosion, not yet anyway.'

'What a turn up for the books. Old Crawford blown up, eh!' Arthur said, barely suppressing a smile.

Later, when Debbie met Charles out of work she said, 'Have you heard what's happened to my granddad's place? It's bloody blown up.'

'Yes, I know. I was told you are a bombshell. It looks like you climaxed on delayed action.'

★ ★ ★

Dick Leach couldn't resist returning to the scene of the 'big bang'. However, not being a fool, he continued to drive past the spectacle. As he did so, he uttered aloud, 'Good God!'

As per instructions, two days after the job, Leach made his way to the 'drop' where he found the balance of the payment. Having no idea where the instructions or the money had come from, he drove away thirty thousand pounds the richer.

As Leach picked up his money, Arthur Brown too picked up the post from the mat. Amongst his mail he found a white card on which was written 'THREE, a number not to be forgotten'.

On seeing the card, Arthur's pulse increased slightly. He had been targeted. It was his turn now. Then, he felt suddenly puzzled. At once Arthur went to the phone and called Harry White.

'Chesterfield 35136.' Arthur recognised the voice.

'Harry, it's Arthur. It's happened to me. I've got the white card. Just picked it from the doormat now.'

'Oh Lord! What's happened, Arthur?'

'That's the strange thing. Nothing has happened. I don't know why the card has been delivered.' Arthur sounded bewildered.

'What about your family? We don't get attacked directly, you know. The swine means to give us prolonged mental anguish,' Harry reminded.

'Certainly, that has been the form up to now, but I know of nothing in my case.'

'Look, I'd like to come over to your place now,' the firmness of Harry's voice got through to Arthur, who said, 'I'll be waiting at the door.'

Mary had prepared one of the spare bedrooms for Harry. Now, the ex-air gunner and wireless operator, were relaxing in the lounge, having made justice of the dinner prepared by Mary. Their discussion was centred around the Perpetrator and his white cards. 'This is a new slant,' Harry was saying. 'Previously he has sent the cards after he knew the crimes had been successfully executed. Or, in the case of Betty Daly, *believing* it to have been successful. But, and I am sorry to have to say this Arthur, in your case the crime is yet to be committed or completed. The man is, you see, a fiend. I'm sure he is first trying to hit you psychologically. He's creating fear by the use of uncertainty. For some time I have felt the man is a sadist, Arthur. This is just a primary to the real thing.'

Arthur said, 'I can't understand why this is happening at all, but why *our* crew anyway? What did we do that others didn't, Harry?'

'At the moment, that remains a mystery. By the way, I've traced the manufacturer of the cards. It's a firm in Gladbach, Germany.'

'We went to Gladbach one night, didn't we? I remember Bob saying, 'I'll be glad when we are back,'' said Arthur, smiling.

'Yes. Us and two hundred others. As you say, why us? Of course, our Lancaster was one of those attacked by fighters that night. A fact which seemed significant to the person who made the enquiries at RAF records.'

Arthur asked, 'Does it seem the Prepetrator of these crimes is in Southern Germany, then? I mean, the raid was there, as is the paper manufacturer.'

'Yes, but remember, the target that night was not Gladbach. It was Schweinfurt. I considered at one time that the fellow might be a Belgian but now I think the box number there was used to confuse the situation.'

The friends put the subject of the Perpetrator aside and passed the time chatting, as friends do. Strangely, Harry didn't feel he wanted to think more about it at the moment. Tomorrow he would focus his mind. For the time being he intended to enjoy the company and hospitality of his old flying comrade, one of the men with whom he had shared so much danger all those years ago.

'How is Tom Williams and his depressions these days? Have you heard recently from him?' Arthur asked.

'Haven't you heard? I thought the crew knew. Jenny felt so sorry for him when she learnt of the murder conviction and his prison sentence. She knew he was troubled by depressions. Bob said she felt so deeply that such a man had to spend the rest of his days incarcerated. He said she took my recommendation to heart after he was released. About not returning to his home, I mean. So, Tom is with the Greeves' at Dundee now.'

Arthur said, 'This is news to me. Do you know how they are making out?'

'Wonderfully, by all accounts. Bob told me Tom's a new man. Says Tom hasn't felt so content for years. Jenny and he are getting on like a house on fire and Bob says he himself is happy having him about the place. Says he likes his quiet ways and gentle consideration about everything.'

'It must be grand for Tom. It's to be hoped it won't all turn sour eventually,' Arthur said.

Harry said, 'I don't think it will; they're giving it six months and if things are still working out OK, Tom will become a permanent paying guest.'

'Will you have another glass before we turn in?' Arthur offered.

'Go on then, twist my arm, I'm enjoying our chat. We love our wives dearly, but it's good to have a man's company at times.'

The next morning, Arthur and his guest were still at the breakfast table when his son Martin called. Martin was surprised to see Harry and recognised him at once, even though it had been many years since last meeting him. Martin had only been a small boy at the time.

After the pleasantries, Martin told his dad he was on his way to the office but had broken his journey to ask if he had heard anything more concerning the explosion at The Willows. Arthur said that he hadn't and, anyhow, what might he expect to hear?

'Well, I don't know really, but it had to be a gas explosion hadn't it? It's hardly likely someone placed a bomb under the house.'

'What's this about?' Harry asked.

Martin gave a brief explanation, mentioning in passing that Glowarm had worked on the estate during its building. Arthur added that he didn't like to see any building being accidentally destroyed, but if there had to be one from the Green Acres Estate, then the right one had been chosen.

'Why is that?' Harry quizzed.

'Well Jack Crawford is not a very nice individual. He and I were at school together.

He was a dreadful bully. He was one then and he's remained one throughout his life,' Arthur told Harry.

Harry said, 'I can't imagine anyone bullying you. At school or elsewhere.'

'Oh, not me. Not at school anyway. I gave him a severe beating once for badly terrorising a small boy. It stopped his bullying at school. He and I were the same year you see, but I made myself an enemy for life. Crawford is the kind of coward who never forgets, and from his position on the city council he has been able to do me a lot of damage over the years. Many of the councillors are afraid of Jack so they do his bidding. I'll give him one thing — he has somehow been able to persuade the electorate that he is a good guy — little do they know!'

'What kind of damage has this man done to you?' Harry asked.

'Numerous things, but where he has been most successful from his point of view, was by blocking planning permission to any firm that used me as a subcontractor. That tended to make the firms blacklist me, even though they really didn't want to. Of course, we got by, but Crawford did make things difficult at times.'

'And now his place has been blown up?

And, a few days later you received a white card? Interesting!' The old detective's mind was swinging into action.

'Surely, you can't make a connection there, Harry. The destruction of The Willows will give Crawford the pain, not me.'

Harry said, 'If we have learnt anything about our adversary, it is his thoroughness in finding detailed information concerning his targets. To my way of thinking, Arthur, it may not be a coincidence that misfortune has fallen upon your antagonist at the moment you received your white card. Did you say this Crawford fellow is away?'

Martin said, 'Yes! But I've heard he's returned because of what has happened. He can hardly have got his bags unpacked.'

Harry said, 'Had he not done so, it would have appeared that Crawford was himself implicated in the destruction of his own house. However, I think he will have been as surprised by the event as everyone else. It's in the cards that Crawford is unknowingly playing his part in the scheme of things to get at you, Arthur.'

'I don't see how,' Arthur said.

'Nor I,' Harry commented. Then added: 'Yet.'

Martin, who had joined the two for coffee, got up from the table, saying, 'I'll have to get

270

to the office — You know. While the cat's away — !'

Later that morning, Harry made his way to the Green Acres Estate and was as surprised, as others had been, by the utter destruction of The Willows and judging from the houses around, he could see it must have been a fine property. If the house had been of an individual type he wasn't able to tell from what remained, but the drive had been, in fact still was. It was made with small white pebbles.

As he stood viewing, Harry heard the crunch of tyres on the driveway. Turning, he saw the car roll to a halt. A uniformed driver opened a rear door and Harry studied the large, heavy man stepping from the car. He heard the driver say, 'This is terrible, Alderman Crawford.'

Crawford looked at Harry and asked, 'Who the hell are you?'

'Oh, just an inspector,' Harry answered truthfully.

'From the council? I don't know you!'

'Nor I, you,' said Arthur's friend, as he turned to walk away.

Harry had been in Worcester for three days but his deliberation had not yet thrown any light on Arthur's white card. He was sure that some disruption was heading for his friend but in what form he still couldn't tell. The only thing about which Harry felt fairly certain was that Jack Crawford's house would be somehow connected. Though, at this stage Crawford would not knowingly be involved.

Harry White did not believe in coincidence. The house in which Glowarm had taken a part in the building, and which is later lived in by Arthur's foe, blows up. Followed almost at once by a white card landing on Arthur's doorstep, that was too much for Harry to ignore.

It was at three o'clock in the afternoon of his fourth day when Harry heard Arthur's phone ringing. Knowing his friend was busy in his studio, Harry called up, asking if he should take it.

'Hello, is that you, Harry?'

'Yes! It's Martin, isn't it? Your father's in the studio. I will call him. Expect you want to talk to him?'

'Yes I do, please,' Harry thought Martin sounded tense.

'Hello son, what is it?' Arthur asked, running his hand down his smock to remove a little paint.

'Dad, the fire, or rather explosion at The Willows. It's taken a new turn; in our direction. You remember the original boiler fitted in the house? The R223 which turned out to be faulty! If you recall, it was a valve in the 223 which caused the trouble.'

'Yes, I remember it all right, it cost Whittaker & Co a lot of money, one way and another. But what has the R223 got to do with The Willows' explosion? That boiler was replaced by the 224, along with the others on that estate.'

'That's what I understood, Dad, but I wasn't much involved at the time. The point is, the firemen, who inspected the scene, discovered a valve which they handed over to some inspector. He recognised the valve coming from the invalid R223 boiler which, he has pointed out, should never have been fitted in the house. It is established that the explosion was caused by the boiler!'

'That's absolute rot!' exclaimed Arthur. 'I witnessed Jo Burns with my own eyes making the change-over from the R223 to the R224. It is impossible the R223 caused the explosion.'

'Well, Dad. I don't know how we are going to convince these people. If we don't, we are in big trouble. They've made it official, you see. Furthermore, Jack Crawford has learnt that there is no way he can claim insurance. The boiler was illegal and that invalidates his policy. I'm told he is already on to his solicitor to sue Glowarm.'

'This is ridiculous, Martin. I was there during the changeover. Anyway, we will have a record of it in our files,' his dad affirmed.

'I don't think that will account for much in the hands of a smart lawyer. He'd say that they were not genuine, that Glowarm 'set them up'. Trouble is Dad, the real proof has gone. With Jo as witness there would have been no problem, but of course, the poor guy died last year,' Martin lamented.

Arthur felt a wave of heat sweep through his body. His son was going to suffer terribly if this affair was not sorted out. Of course, he himself still had an interest in Glowarm. He held a fair number of shares, but it wouldn't strike him as hard as it would Martin. Now that his mind had focused on the possibilities, Arthur could see it was possible the firm might liquidate and his son become a bankrupt. It frightened him to think what compensation would have to be paid to Jack Crawford. There would be the full value of a very expensive house. All the inconvenience caused, and no doubt Crawford would make a claim for compensation of a supposed nervous illness brought on by stress.

Arthur said, 'Try not to worry too much just yet, son. With your approval, now that you are the head of the firm, we'll fight this tooth and nail if we must.'

When Arthur entered the lounge where Harry was seated, he moved to the window and looked across at the cathedral. Much of the church could still be seen from the ground floor. Harry continued to read for a few minutes before saying, 'You are strangely quiet, old friend. Got something on your mind, have you?'

'It's the reason you are here, Harry. The card and all that. I have just received very disturbing news. God knows what you will be able to do about it.'

Harry said, 'Well, let's start by giving me a brief history of your firm and also of the people who used you as a subcontractor when building Green Acres Estate. Were there any incidents during that period which could have been considered out of the ordinary?'

'There certainly was something out of the ordinary,' Arthur said. Then he went on to tell Harry all that had occurred concerning Whittaker & Co and their boilers. He concluded with the fireman's discovery of the R223 pump after the explosion.

By now it was late afternoon. Harry said, 'You've given me something to think about, Arthur but there is nothing to be done today. But, tomorrow is another day.'

★ ★ ★

That night Harry slept a long peaceful sleep. His mind was quiet. And that sixth sense once more remained faithful to the old detective. In another bed however, the occupant turned and tossed all night.

At ten in the morning, Harry introduced himself to the senior duty fire officer, who granted his request to see the valve that had been found at the scene of the Green Acres Estate incident.

The valve turned out to be bigger than Harry had expected but of course, any weakness the design held wouldn't be shown to the eye.

'Don't you think there is something which is not quite right about this object?' Harry asked, turning the valve in his hand.

'From what I can gather,' the officer said, 'that valve wasn't right at all. In fact it caused the explosion.'

'I'm not referring to the valve's efficiency. What I *am* referring to is the clean metal which doesn't at all appear to have been subjected to the heat of flames. The explosion not only blew the house into thousands of pieces, but also caused an intense fire, did it not?'

The fire officer said, 'I take your point, but the explosion had in fact blown that valve well clear, hence the lack of burn or heat damage.'

'Where exactly was it found?' Harry asked.

'About a hundred yards along the drive-way,' the man replied.

Looking at him, Harry said, 'In that case, for this valve not to have been impeded during its journey of a hundred yards down the driveway, the walls of the house would first have to have been cleared from its path. But we are talking in terms of micro-seconds for this valve to have reached a wall after the explosion. Surely, the walls were still in the process of disintegration?'

'Then how did the valve manage to be a hundred yards from the house? In any case, while there may be no obvious heat marks scorched on it, the valve is clearly bent and twisted,' observed the officer.

'I am of the opinion that this valve was deliberately placed where it was sure to be found. First it had been distorted by some heavy blow, or perhaps with the use of a vice. It was meant to be found. In fact, it was imperative that it should be,' Harry asserted.

The fire officer looked at the visitor in amazement. 'Are you suggesting the house was deliberately destroyed?' he asked.

'Exactly! Do I have your permission to retain this damaged valve?'

'I'm sorry, sir. It cannot be released just now.'

'Then I hope to have it later. In the meantime, please be sure it is kept safely. I will need it for the police.' He thanked the officer for his help, then made his way back to the street. The young officer, somewhat bemused, watched the old man leave the station.

Harry made himself known to the local police. Inspector Wilson listened to what the ex-inspector had to say. Inspector Wilson was a young man and the name 'Harry White' meant nothing to him. However, since the old man had once been in the force and, like himself, an inspector, he'd pay polite attention. He would give the old man five minutes of his time, he decided.

After half an hour's talk, Inspector Wilson called for coffee and biscuits. Initially he had felt dismissive of Harry's opinions concerning the destruction of The Willows. But as the talk continued, he learnt that Harry was staying with Mr Arthur Brown. That was of some small interest. He recalled how his father would reminisce on Arthur's skill with a rugger ball.

Inspector Wilson asked, 'As you are staying with Mr Brown, you must know him well. How did you meet him? Via the rugger fields, perhaps!'

'I met Arthur during the war in bomber

command. We were part of a crew in a Lancaster.' Harry decided to tell the young inspector the full story of the crew being targeted, and finished by saying, 'Now the Perpetrator is paying attention to the mid upper gunner, Arthur Brown.'

Inspector Wilson said, 'I have never come across anything like this. The man must be mad.'

'Precisely!'

'How is he attacking Mr Brown?' Eagerly the younger man moved a little forward in his chair.

Harry told of Arthur's former connection with Green Acres Estate, the work his firm had done there. He explained of his own suspicion of The Willows' explosion and how the valve of an old R223 was found a hundred yards along the driveway. In fact he told Inspector Wilson all he had discovered to date and of his remaining suspicions. Then he thanked the young man, saying he would keep him fully informed and hoped finally to place enough evidence on his desk to enable him to press charges against a villain or two. With that he returned to Arthur and Mary, in time for tea.

After the table was cleared and the two were settled in their lounge chairs, Harry said, 'Now, we'll discuss your problem,

Arthur, and with the result from my investigations today, I hope I can put your mind a little at ease. I'm firmly coming to the opinion that the explosion at The Willows was deliberately caused by the installing of the R223.

'Impossible! I told you. I was there when the changeover to the R224 was made by Jo Burns. Anyhow! What do you mean, deliberately? I wouldn't do such a thing. Not even to Jack Crawford. In any case, he didn't move into the house until years later.' Arthur looked hurt. He was disappointed that his old friend could think such a thing of him.

'Steady down, Arthur. Of course you couldn't do such a thing. I mean you, of all people. Never! You have missed the point I'm making, which is — while Crawford left the house empty, someone entered, changed the boiler over, then left. Knowing what would happen after setting it to reach maximum temperature.'

'I'm sorry Harry. I can't buy that. Someone would have to lay their hands on an old R223. Fix it, then, after it exploded, it would not be distinguishable from a 224.'

'I'm afraid you are not giving credit to our foe, Arthur. He is thorough, and his intelligence work is always of a high standard. To enable him to plan this attack on you, he will have learnt all about the history of your business. And that, my friend, will include a lot about Whittaker & Co because of their involvement with you.

'Do you remember I told you the firemen found an R223 valve on the driveway away from the house? Well, it will have been put there to be sure it was found. Already you know the result from Martin. He thinks he has you stitched up. By he, I mean the Perpetrator. 'He' knows full well that Crawford will sue Glowarm. He'll know about the value of the house with its invalid insurance, of Crawford's hatred for you and how Crawford will take you for all he can get through your son. And above all, Arthur, at least as far as the Perpetrator is concerned, he knows your good name will be in tatters — the man who knowingly installed faulty boilers. As always, he is after mental anguish.'

Arthur said, 'To me it is incredible that someone would break into a house, change the boiler and then blow the place up. There must have been a considerable risk of being discovered.'

'Money, my friend. If the stakes are high enough, some people will do anything. It's clear that our adversary is swimming in the stuff and doesn't mind at all about dishing it out. If it will achieve his ends,' sighed Harry.

Arthur, looking sickly, replied, 'You mentioned earlier that you hoped you could set my mind at rest, a little. To be honest, I don't think you have, Harry. I haven't learnt anything that could put my mind at ease.'

'Arthur, Arthur! Your worrying is clouding your thinking process. At the start of the day we knew nothing other than the probability that Crawford was going to knock you for six by suing. Now however, we are almost certain the explosion was no accident. But, and this is an important but, Arthur. It was made to look like one. Crawford believed — as he was meant to — that his home was destroyed by your dishonesty in knowingly allowing an inferior boiler to remain in the heating system. The field was left open for him.

'Even the Perpetrator was so sure his plan would succeed, he actually got the white card to you as soon as he knew the explosion had occurred and the faulty valve was found.'

'Do you really think the man who is targeting the crew is actually doing the full planning? Isn't it likely he will be paying others to see that we suffer?'

'No, I am sure detailed instructions initiate from one source. I would say there will be a 'general manager', who is probably based in London, that correlates the business of each villain.

'What should put your mind at ease a little, Arthur, is that we now know that a villain is responsible for The Willows.'

'And that Harry White is a detective!' Arthur said, smiling.

'Exactly!' Harry exclaimed. 'What's the chance of a cup of tea? I'd like an early night. Tomorrow I shall be away for the day — giving you both a break.' Harry grinned.

Mary at once exclaimed, 'Oh, Harry. There's no need for that. You're no trouble at all. Arthur and I love having you here!'

'That is nice to know,' he said. 'Actually, I am going to Birmingham, Arthur. Will you ring your office in the morning and get hold of Whittaker & Co's address in Birmingham? I must talk to those people.'

* * *

Harry said, to the well-dressed gentleman who occupied the general manager's chair at Whittaker & Co, 'It's kind of you, Mr Fulton, to receive me at such short notice.'

Mr Fulton replied by saying, 'You were very persuasive on the phone. What can I do for you, Mr White?'

'Can you tell me if you have had a break-in recently; a robbery?'

'There was a break-in, not long ago. But

you surprise me that you know of it. What can you tell me?' the chairman asked.

'It's more of what you can tell me, Mr Fulton. I will be grateful if you will let me have all the details of the break-in as far as you know them. How quickly was the robbery discovered?'

'It took place during the night. It was discovered the next morning, when the men who work in the yard found the big entrance gates had been forced. Looking into it further, it was discovered the overhead security lights had been tampered with, also the alarms. Whoever it was that broke in knew exactly what they were doing. After displaying such expertise, I would have expected them to have been after a more valuable haul than was stolen.

'I can't for the life of me understand why they didn't break into the main storage department within the building proper. They would have found a goldmine of goods in there. The yard is used mainly as a loading area, but sometimes it is used to take an overflow when sales are not keeping up with production,' Mr Fulton said.

'What's the position in the yard now?' Harry asked. 'Was there much stock there at the time of the break-in?'

'There was stock, but not much. Mostly

crated domestics for businesses and the building trade.'

'You'll have a list of what was taken, of course?'

The general manager reached into a drawer. 'I have the list here.'

'May I see it, please?' Harry asked, reaching for the sheet. He made a quick glance, and said, 'I see. They took only seven articles.'

'No! They stole only five articles,' the general manager asserted. 'They are identified — two refrigerators, one humidifier, one heating boiler and one dishwasher. All of which were crated.'

'Do you hold any old stock in the yard, to have it out of your way?' Harry pressed.

'We don't often have old stock. If we did, it would show poor production planning. When a product becomes obsolete, as it must eventually, we may have a few left on our hands. In that case they are sold off at a knockdown price.'

Harry surprised the chairman once more, when he asked: How about the boiler, R223? I believe that became obsolete. Were they also sold off at a knockdown price?'

'Good God! What do you know about the R223? *They* certainly were not sold off. The R223 is not only obsolete. It was a disaster,'

Fulton said indignantly.

'So what happened to them, I wonder?' The detective's brow lifted.

'As I recall, most were destroyed, though work on them was interrupted due to a rush order being placed by an important consumer. Come to think of it, I can't remember the demolition work restarting on the R223s. There could be a few left,' the chairman surmised.

'Perhaps out of your way, in the yard?' Harry suggested.

'Yes, probably. Put away in a disused corner somewhere. But why are you so interested in the R223? How can that boiler be of interest?' The chairman sounded a little annoyed. He had forgotten about the R223 and he could well do without being reminded about it. The R223 had caused him a lot of grief in the past.

So as to placate the chairman, Harry said, 'Of course, your stores department will still hold records of the remaining R223s. It's obvious that you run an efficient outfit, Mr Fulton.'

'I am sure there will be records remaining. But, I ask again, why are you interested in the R223? I've told you, it is unsafe.'

'I am interested because very recently an R223 boiler was installed in a house to blow it to smithereens.'

'Impossible! There are none in circulation.' A touch of aggression showed in the chairman's eyes.

Harry said, 'Please, Mr Fulton, be assured there are no insinuations directed at your good self. You will remember I mentioned that seven, not five articles had been taken from your yard. If we check through your stores I am sure we will find an R223 missing. An inspection of those remaining will also show one is minus the main valve.'

'What the hell is the good of a main valve without its boiler? That particular valve won't fit any other boiler.'

'The thief had his reason, I can assure you Mr Fulton,' Arthur declared.

'Very well, I will help you to get to the bottom of this. We'll visit the stores and then the yard together.'

The investigation by the two men served to confirm Harry's suspicions. One R223 and an extra valve had gone. Mr Fulton asked, 'If, as you assert, the villain wanted only the R223 with an extra valve, why then, did he take another five crates of domestics?'

'As a cover for the break-in. The thief will have reasoned that the boiler and valve, being cast away stock, wouldn't be missed unless a tight inventory was made. So he made it easy for the five articles to be seen as stolen.'

After a pause, Mr Fulton remarked, 'I'm not sure why you have bothered coming to the factory, Mr White. It seems to me that you had nothing to learn from the visit as you already knew what had taken place. You knew the R223 and a valve was stolen. Something even we hadn't noticed.'

'It was logic which created strong suspicions. But, I had to have confirmation, Mr Fulton. That I now have.'

Harry thanked Mr Fulton for his support and wished him good day. When clear of Birmingham, he pulled into a wayside cafe, bought a coffee and used the pay phone to confirm with Mary he would be home for dinner.

At the dinner table he told them what had been proven during his visit to Whittaker & Co. Arthur asked what had prompted Harry to go to Birmingham?

'Because,' Harry told him, 'we were fairly sure that the resident boiler at The Willows had somehow been replaced with an R223. The reason for the 223 valve having been placed on the driveway, was to make sure an investigation would give the impression you had never changed over to the R224 at the time of installing the heating system. Furthermore, you had told me the year the Green Acres Estate was built, was also the time when production was halted on the faulty boilers. I concluded that, after all this time, if there were any old boilers of that model remaining, then they would have been dumped somewhere by Whittaker & Co.

'The fact that there was some old stock wasting away would have been discovered by an agent acting on the instruction of his unknown *employer*, the Perpetrator. From his early reports, he would have reasoned much the same as myself. Confirmation from the agent of the R223's existence then enabled the Perpetrator to complete his plan for targeting you. Sending out his orders to the villain.'

Laying down his napkin, Arthur said, 'Sounds feasible and your insight truly amazes me, Harry. All the same, while useful ground has undoubtedly been covered, I will still look as guilty as hell to Crawford's insurance company, enabling him to sue Glowarm to the hilt.'

'I can't disagree with you on that, old friend. But I haven't concluded my investigations yet, so bear with me a little longer. You will see all is not lost.'

Later during the evening, Mary, Arthur and Harry joined Richard Attenborough's excursion through Central America on TV. Arthur's mind was soon focused away from his problems as they wondered at the ways of life in the wild.

Harry looked a second time at the bedside clock. Could that really be the time? He stretched. Ten-fifteen. Even at this hour he felt he'd like to have a longer lie-in. He'd be glad when this crazy business with the crew was over. But he knew he must not allow himself to become lax concerning the problem. The unexpected could come at you at any time from the madman, and the Perpetrator was certainly that. Up to now, the man was simply moving on from one crew-member to another. If only he could find the brains behind the whole dirty business! He wanted the 'organ grinder'. Not just his monkeys.

'Ah, here you are Harry!' Mary exclaimed as her guest entered her kitchen. 'Help yourself to the coffee. It's on its hot plate.'

'I apologise, for coming down at this time. I simply slept in.'

'I know, but don't bother about it. I took you a cup of tea when you weren't down as usual, but you were so sound asleep I hadn't the heart to disturb you.'

After breakfast was finished, Harry addressed Arthur: 'Well, we know how The Willows went up and how you have been framed. What I propose to do today is to try to discover how we can prove your innocence.'

'I can't see how you are going to be able to do that,' Arthur said. 'I wouldn't know where to start.'

'It's a matter of thinking it through and trying to figure out how you would do the job if you were the villain. We already know that an R223 was taken from Whittaker & Co. The rarity of that boiler, together with the dates of the robbery and the explosion being so close, makes it almost certain that the two events were related.

'If what I have said is correct, then the villain required a vehicle to transport the boiler to The Willows. Furthermore, he also needed to transport the R224 away *from* the house. The vehicle had to be a large van or a lorry, probably the former. Remember, the villain removed six fairly large objects from the factory yard, so he needed at least a van to do the job. I must try to trace that van or lorry. And the boiler which was removed from the house. The boiler is the crux of the matter, of course. Find that, and you will be cleared. So if you'll excuse me I will go about my business.' Harry put on his coat and left the house.

Although the old detective knew exactly where he was going he hadn't mentioned it to his friend. Even now, as though he was still a boy, he liked to maintain a little mystery. If he were to succeed, then his actions would quickly become known. But, if by not being secretive, it could help to ease his friend's anxiety, he would then of course deny himself the pleasure.

Harry knew for the villain to succeed there must be no way that the removed R224 boiler could be found. A possible place would be to lose it on a large rubbish tip. But the Perpetrator would know full well that should suspicions be aroused, any tip would be thoroughly combed. Of course, Harry was already convinced that the man had to be a psycho, and as such, he would think he could make no mistakes. There was no doubt that he was clever. Certainly clever enough to have figured that the best way of 'losing' the boiler would be by handing it to an auto-crusher.

The robber, whoever he was, would need to lose the remaining articles stolen from Whittaker's yard. They certainly could not be taken to the crusher's yard because questions would be asked why newly-crated goods should be destroyed. But, if those particular goods were found abandoned they might cause some bewilderment. But, since the robber assumed that the old boiler was not going to be missed from Whittaker's yard, the abandoned goods would simply remain a mystery.

All these thoughts which ran through Harry's mind turned out to be close to the mark. Dick Leach, when returning with his haul from Birmingham to Worcester, temporarily left the major roads to find a quiet spot where he was unlikely to be observed. There, in the darkness, he dumped the crated goods. Happy in the knowledge they wouldn't be traced back to him.

For the whole of the next day the van still containing the boiler was locked away in his garage. At 12.14 a.m. Leach drove the boiler to The Willows. He hid the vehicle in Jack Crawford's garage and moved the boiler to the house, using a commercial hand trolley.

He found the details in his *employer's* instruction were correct. The lining up of the pipes, both to enter and leave the boiler, was the same for both models. The job was, as his instructions suggested, straightforward, enabling the crook to complete the fitting within an hour. All that remained was to turn on the main gas supply, light the burner and set the valve to maximum heat. Leach did not fit the gauge which would have cut off the gas to the burners when the temperature got too high.

The same trolley which had carried the

R223 to the house brought the R224 to the van. As Leach drove away, he stopped about a hundred yards along the drive, got out of the van and placed a valve from an R223 boiler on the ground. The villain was not in the least worried about the slight indentations his wheels had put into the drive. He knew there was no possibility of tyre prints being lifted from small loose stones.

Dick Leach locked the van in his garage and decided he would grab a few hours' sleep before he executed the next stage of his instructions. He had already informed the friend who'd accompanied him to Birmingham that he would need his help again. The instructions were to damage the R224 boiler beyond repair, so that it could be taken to be destroyed without arousing suspicion.

As always, the instructions were explicit. Leach must leave Worcester and drive the van south for ten miles, travelling parallel to the river Severn. He then had to find a tall deserted red brick building. The building was four stories high and the upper floor, because of its dryness, was at one time used for storage. In those days heavy bags containing produce were hoisted from ground level up to an entrance built into the outer wall of the fourth floor. The hoist, above the entrance door, allowed the suspended sacks to be swung through the opening on to the top level.

Leach found the old rusty hoist. He saw that with a little effort it could be made to work. After freeing the hoist's movements they placed the boiler on the concrete ground directly beneath. Rope, leading down from the hoist, lay on the floor by the wooden door and Leach kicked it over the edge to watch it snake down towards his friend and the boiler. Having secured the rope to the boiler the man joined Leach on the top floor.

Together, they pulled on the rope and saw the boiler slowly lifting from the ground until it was level with their feet. Then, on the count of three they let the rope go and the boiler rushed back towards the concrete, hitting it hard. The damage was not repairable.

★ ★ ★

Harry, working his way through the industrial estate, found what he was looking for.

KEN ALLAN
AUTO WRECKER AND CRUSHER

A workman, whose overalls looked as though oil and grease had been thrown at them, pointed his boss out to Harry. Mr Allan had just finished removing a half-shaft from a written-off Ford Escort.

'Can you give me a few minutes of your time?' Harry asked.

'Yes, what is it you want?' Mr Allan looked about forty-five. There was brown curly hair escaping from the back of his woolly hat, and the overalls he wore were covering a belly that looked capable of holding a pint or two. The proprietor's grimy hands indicated he was not only an office-based boss.

'Shall we go into the office?' Harry suggested.

Asking to be called Ken, he threw a cover over a chair saying, 'You can sit there. Now what can I do for you?'

Harry began by showing his identity card and explained he was a retired policeman. From his breast pocket he produced an official letter which had been signed by the local chief constable. The letter stated that retired Inspector Harry White had his approval to question any willing citizen of Worcester. 'I think you may be able to help me, Mr Allen. If you can, I would appreciate your co-operation.'

'I will be pleased to help if I can, Inspector. It will not be the first time I and my staff have helped the police by any means.'

Thanking him, Harry asked, 'Can you recall a boiler having been brought here to be fed into your crusher sometime during the past week?'

'I certainly can, though I wasn't here when it arrived. Of course, Inspector, you will know that a crusher at a place like this is normally used for crushing car engines. So, when a boiler comes along I am not likely to forget it. In fact, I don't recall ever having a boiler in the crusher before! However, there is another reason why the boiler sticks in my memory.

'The bloke handling the crusher was an inexperienced 'Job experience' lad, sent from the employment exchange. The youngster shouldn't really have been left on his own. Anyway, he directed the boiler into the crusher. Trouble was, a part of the boiler was made of cast-iron and the lad didn't know that cast-iron wouldn't crush like the alloy of engines. It just cracked, shattering into small pieces, of course,' Ken said laughing, as though he had told a joke.

'Do you think you could still find the shattered cast-iron pieces?' Harry asked.

'Difficult, but not impossible. We would need to find exactly where we dumped that batch, then sort of sieve through it, like. But that iron might be in hundreds of pieces. It will be no use to you at all,' the auto-breaker affirmed.

'Mr Allan! What I am interested in is the serial number that will have been imprinted into the boiler during manufacturing. I think it will be out of the question to obtain the number if it was imprinted into the metal. That will be a fraction of the original size. But, if the imprint is in the cast iron, we may be able to find it, don't you think?'

And find it they did. Ken set a couple of his men raking at the spot where the boiler was dumped.

They worked for half an hour before they were satisfied no more iron pieces remained. Then they took their sack to the office and handed it to the boss. He tipped the contents onto the floor.

The slivers of iron came in sizes measuring from a few inches down to a pinhead.

Harry and Ken, on their knees, sifted the fragments until they had three pieces which, when fitted like a jigsaw, contained the R224's serial number — WB/R/2746.

Harry thanked Ken Allan for his help, saying, 'You have contributed more than you realise towards justice being done.' But before leaving the yard, and with the three pieces of iron safely in his pocket, he asked, 'That security camera standing high in the yard. Is it always activated?'

'Always at night, when the floodlights come on. But if the day becomes very dull they activate.'

'Could the lights have been on the day that boiler was brought in?'

'I don't know but they could have been. I wasn't here then, if you remember!'

'Well if they were,' Harry pressed, 'will you still have the film? It was recent.'

'Yes, we'll have it. I always keep them for a while just in case, you know,' Ken said to the inspector, feeling quite efficient.

'Good,' Harry said. 'Can I ask you to assist me a little further? With the help of your work-experience youth — the lad you said took receipt of the boiler — will you go through the film taken that day and ask the lad if he can recognise the vehicle that brought in the boiler? If he does make an identification, see if you can read the reg number. Also see if there is a business name painted on the vehicle. The camera might even have picked up a mug shot of the driver. If you do find anything, hang onto the film until I or the local police pick it up.'

'I'll arrange that for you,' Ken said.

'Thanks a lot. If it turns out to be time-consuming, please submit your bill to me.' Harry handed Mr Allan his card.

He found Arthur in his studio busy working on a new canvas. Already the image of a Lancaster shrouded in fog, showed up. The big bomber stood deserted in the dampness. It was viewed from the front, slightly from one side. As the eye passed down the body of the aircraft the tail showed only ghostly in the fog.

'I'm impressed,' Harry said, as he studied the canvas. 'I didn't know you did these sort of paintings.'

'I never have before, but I found myself thinking of the old days. I just wanted to get it down. All kinds of memories returned as I worked on it. It's weird really, the brush seems to have a mind of its own. You see, I'm not concentrating in the normal way, Harry. Just remembering! But I feel you have broken the spell, my friend.'

'I'm really very sorry if I have. I hope it will return. To me, you seem to have been inspired. I daresay some would call that surrealism.'

'Don't feel you have disturbed me. It's time I finished, I've been at it since just after you left. Anyhow, what kind of a day have you had?'

'Good, I think. Take off your smock, come to the lounge and I will tell you about it.'

Mary brought coffee for the two men. It

was still an hour from dinner and she could see the cold winter air had freshened Harry's face. 'This is good coffee, Mary.' Then turning to Arthur, he asked, 'Will Martin still be at the office?'

'I'm sure he is. He never leaves before six o'clock.'

Harry said, 'I expect the office will have records of past work and books, showing details of materials used, etc.'

'Of course. We are fortunate with our office manager who's been with us for years and is very efficient. But why do you ask?'

'I'd like you to give them a ring, Arthur. To see if they can come up with the serial number of the R224 boiler which was fitted into The Willows. Do you think they will have it?'

'Yes, it should be in the files.' He phoned the office and asked to speak to Martin. The manager said, 'You have just beaten him to it Mr Brown. Martin was about to ring you. He's here now.'

'Dad! I was about to ring you. I've got a letter from Crawford's solicitor saying they're suing for damage, neglect and mental distress to their client. It's very serious Dad. They could destroy Glowarm, and there've already been nasty articles in the local press about the firm and its directors. And even though you are retired from the firm, dad, they are besmirching your good name. Of course, we all know that Jack Crawford's behind that. All the same, we're starting to get some pretty nasty mail. Most of it anonymous.'

'I know, son. I've had some posted to me here. Three letters in fact. One was most abusive and personal. Of course the writers are scumbags. None had the guts to sign their names. They're typical of Crawford and his cronies. Anyway, please look in the files for me. Harry wants to know the serial number of Whittaker & Co's R224 that we fitted at The Willows. Shall I hold on, or will you ring me back?'

'I'll have it in a few minutes, but I might as well call you back, Dad. Cheers for now.' The phone went dead.

'It looks like you will get your serial number, Harry. I don't know if you got the gist of that, but things are turning bad with Glowarm. Martin is as worried as hell, I can tell. But he is trying not to let me see it.'

'And you, old friend, it's getting to you as well. Isn't it? The Perpetrator's working on your mind through your son's misfortune. We all know that is his way — not to hurt the crew physically, but to torment our minds.'

'But for Christ's sake, my son has nothing to do with this. The Perpetrator's mad of course, but that bastard Crawford is ruining Martin just to get at me,' Arthur said, close to despair.

'It's true what you say,' Harry said, 'but it will be exactly as the Perpetrator planned it, madman or not.' Then the phone rang and Harry saw his friend's hand was shaking slightly.

'Hello, Martin?'

'Yes, I've got the number for you. You had better write it down.' As he completed the number, Harry looked at the serial number he had taken from the breaker's yard and put it next to it. WB/R/2746. They matched. He couldn't help but laugh at the expression of surprise that came to Arthur's face. 'You had the number all the time, Harry. What are you doing?'

'I just wanted confirmation, me old son. You can inform Martin his troubles are over. More to the point, so are yours. I have proof which will stand up in any court that a R224 boiler was removed from The Willows, to be surreptitiously replaced by a R223.'

Arthur sat slumped in his chair, as though exhausted. But his smiling face showed he was completely relaxed now. 'Mary,' he said, 'oh, Mary!' She bent forward and kissed his lips. Then, Harry saw this slight female figure almost lost from sight as she was hugged into the bulk of the huge and loveable man.

As for Harry? Well, he felt he had been rewarded for his efforts. But if only his aches would ease a little. Kneeling and bending amongst the cast-iron hadn't helped his back at all.

★   ★   ★

Inspector Wilson shook Harry's hand. He wished him a safe journey back to Chesterfield. He was sure that, with the evidence Harry had offered, arrests would follow. He would do his utmost to track down the villain who had taken the boiler. Later that day he would check to see if anything had showed up on Ken Allan's film. He and Harry would keep in touch.

Hester heard the car drive into the garage and she was in there before her husband was out of the car. 'Welcome home! It seemed a long time. I have been lonely without you.' Her husband winced as he climbed from behind the steering wheel. 'Your back playing up, dear?' she asked. 'Yes, just a bit,' Harry said.

After asking about Arthur and Mary, Hester was keen to learn all that had occurred in Worcester. After all the years, it still fascinated her how Harry managed to

304

ferret his way to the crux of the cases he investigated. Even to this day his skill remains, she thought.

Harry talked with Inspector Wilson a number of times during the following days. He also had a couple of conversations with Arthur and decided it was time to get out the next progress report for the crew.

★ ★ ★

Jeffrey went to check the letterbox and found his mail had arrived — not all of which were bills, he marvelled. One envelope had been written by Harry White. He recognised the handwriting at once and wondered what his friend had to tell him this time? He would read it with Zoe, because his wife also needed to be kept abreast with the danger.

Zoe said, 'Honestly Jeffrey, it's all really frightening. I mean Harry, bless him, he keeps knocking them down, then another devil pops up.'

'Well,' Harry went on to say, 'Arthur then told me that this fellow, Jack Crawford has really caught a cold. You see, the insurance company, like the police, are satisfied that the R224 was illegally replaced by the R223. The boiler and extra valve stolen from Whittaker & Co and the date of the theft was no

305

coincidence. Also, because the R223 was condemned as a hazard long ago, and the proof of a switch having taken place, the insurance company has rightly invalidated its policy for the house and its contents. Jack Crawford will have to cover the full cost himself, if he can.

'Eventually all this will become public knowledge and it will be Crawford who will be disgraced, while the good name of Glowarm and of Arthur will be re-established.'

'Thank God for that,' Zoe said. 'It must have been a frightful worry for the whole family.'

'There is more to come,' Jeffrey told her. 'Harry says that the police at Worcester received a call from a woman using a mobile phone. Her voice had sounded in shock, but eventually she made sense. A car and ambulance rushed to the scene down a country lane a few miles from town. Arriving there the police found a van, beside which lay a man face down in a pool of blood. A paramedic turned the man onto his back to find his throat had been cut. The man's name was Dick Leach and, on further investigation by Inspector Wilson, a white card of high quality was found pushed down the neck of Leach's shirt. On the card were written three words: 'YOU FAILED ME'.

'My God!' Jeffrey said. Then after a pause, he continued to read: ''A close inspection of the van brought to evidence a small white stone embedded between the treads of the front inside wheel. The stone had come from a distant quarry with which the city council had placed a large order for stones of a similar size. It had been a one-off order, to be used in connection with a municipality development of a leisure area. The point was,' Harry continued, 'the place has no access for vehicles.

' 'However, the stone taken from Dick Leach's van also matched those stones which made up The Willows' driveway. This discovery raised the question of how it had come to pass, that the type of stones used for Crawford's drive were the same as those ordered for the leisure area?

' 'A check of orders, invoices, etc. revealed no purchase of the stones from the council by Alderman Crawford. Enquiries are to continue. It is very probable charges will be brought against Crawford.' Then Harry made the comment, 'His disgrace will be assured.' '

Jeffrey said, 'Harry signed the report, but then added: 'PS The fact that Dick Leach was killed for his failure, supports my suspicion that the madman believes Tom Williams is rotting in a jail and Betty Daly was successfully poisoned.

' 'From my interrogation of Reid, when I was in Cardiff I learnt that once the contract was accepted, to back off or to fail, would result in the throat being cut. None of the villains know where those instructions came from, or by whom they had been issued. Read and Mark Noble can thank their lucky stars they are in jail, should their failure be discovered.' '

12

'I have to pack my bags again, Hester. I must get to grips with the Perpetrator one way or another. He is still the cause of much anguish, short-lived as it may be, except for Bob and his grandson.

'I am having success in tracking down his subordinates, but if I fail to find the head man, I'm sure that those members of the crew who have not yet been targeted soon will be. Also, if he should ever discover that Tom's and James' misery was so short-lived, I am sure he will hit them again. Somehow, I must find this man, or we will continue to suffer. That's why I'm going to the paper factory in Germany.'

Hester, looking concerned, said, 'Deep down I know you are right. But I can't help feeling you are getting rather old for this sort of thing, Harry. You never have a minute to yourself these days, and now you say you are going to the continent.'

'You might be right. I admit I do feel my age at times, but what else can I do when it's so serious? Even with my best efforts the swine has still caused a great deal of worry.

Fortunately, I've been able to see that much of it was short-lived: Betty is well again and Tom is out of prison. Glowarm is still in business and Arthur has returned to being a happy man. Furthermore, one villain is dead and two have been jailed. But we can't claim success for Bob Greeves and his grandson, can we? I am sorry, Hester, I can't stop now. Anyway, we could be the next to be targeted. This madman won't stop until he thinks we all have been hit.'

'What do you expect to achieve in Germany?' Hester asked.

'I must admit that my feeling is rather vague regarding the visit. I have so little to go on. But I do know who manufactured the cards used by the Perpetrator. It's not much, but it's all I've got. Anyway Harry White does not like being led by the nose, which is how it has felt to me — always chasing after the events that have occurred, instead of preventing them from happening.'

★　★　★

Herr Staab welcomed his British visitor with a warmth that almost embarrassed Harry. There was none of the Teutonic stiffness which he had half-expected from a man holding the high position of sales director in a

310

large manufacturing company. The man had an easy, almost casual manner, which exposed much charm. How different was the secretary who led him to Herr Staab's office. She was stylish, but very offhand with her curt mannerisms. Even though her English was very good, her words were clipped when addressing her charge. Harry wondered if it was attitude, or simply the age gap between them. He doubted this as he considered all the experience her position must have given her.

As for Herr Staab, he had expected a younger man from the Island. There had not been a lot of correspondence to bring about this meeting, but it had been neat and to the point, expressing an earnestness that should be attended to. Now the correspondent was before him and in minutes only, Herr Staab had accessed the inner strength of the man — a strength, he felt, that had not diminished with his advancing years.

The old detective did not confide in Herr Staab the whole story behind his visit. But he did successfully convey the fundamental need for his requested information and assured the German that his help would contribute greatly towards justice being done. Herr Staab, conscious of the Britisher's background, had no quarrel with this. Harry produced the cards together with the strip cut from the 'enquiries' letter. At once Herr Staab recognised the premium product of his company. He stated that though numerous customers did make purchases, the amounts ordered were small. The types of people who would buy this product were those who wished to convey to others the eliteness of their firm. The card, sold in sheets of various sizes, might be placed behind glass in impressive reception halls, probably displaying some proud achievement of the company. He told Harry that when light was played onto a sheet, it would appear to shimmer, and so catch the eye.

In response to Harry's wish, Herr Staab asked his secretary to bring the names of all clients who had ordered the special card over the past five years. As Herr Staab explained, even the customers who did take the cards only ordered infrequently because of their specialised use.

★　★　★

They pulled the car in from the road, and left it at the edge of the park, glad to be out of the London traffic. As they walked in the park it was easy to tell the men were looking for someone. The pair were smartly dressed, in a slightly common way. One removed a cigarette from his lips. The movement of his hand caused a diamond ring to flash as it caught the sun. A moment later the man stood and said, 'That's him, there.'

'Where?'

'By the lake, feeding the ducks.'

'Mr Big actually feeds ducks?'

'Almost every day. He likes ducks. Anyway, get a good look at him so that you'll know him next time.'

'Are you sure you want me to do this? You've known him a long time, Dave.'

'I'm sure, stitch the bastard up. I'll see you are all right.'

Dave and Rod Shaw had known each other for nearly forty years. They had gone to the same school, when they weren't nicking off. They'd lived in the East End during the bad old days on the same street, three doors apart. The kids were streetwise by the age of ten and Rod headed a gang of older boys by the time he was twelve. From Rod's suggestion the gang began to rob as a team and became much more efficient. By the time Rod was fifteen he had real discipline in the gang. Then, at seventeen he left.

Rod was no longer to be found in his old haunts, and no one knew what had brought about the change in him, apart from Dave.

Rod didn't miss the gang, because he didn't give a fuck about anyone, though he did miss the power he had wielded over the boys. There was only Dave for whom he had any feeling, and that was pretty feeble. He had no real sense of loyalty towards his so-called friend, but felt he had to have someone to talk to at times.

What Dave knew was that Rod had decided to get himself an education. His petty robbing and muggings were leading nowhere. It was all right for the other kids who were only interested in getting a fix, a can of lager and a rape when the opportunity came along. It had been OK until now, and Rod certainly had not missed out on any of these. But now he had grander ideas for his future, aimed at a swell flat in the West End, a shiny limo and classy women.

He knew he would have to wise up; learn about a few scams — how, and who best to blackmail without getting caught; maybe get a good protection racket operating somewhere. Even do a bit of illegal importing. Then when he'd got some real money together, he'd find a way of fixing the odds. Of course, by then he'd have his henchmen: Thickies, who'd do as they were told for a few pounds and who enjoyed violence, just so long as they were the ones dishing it out. In the meantime though, he'd put in more time toughening himself up and picking more fights, choosing those who he was sure he could smash. He planned to be thought of as a hard man. Not too difficult, he thought, so long as he made sure he never crossed a real hardie.

Before he could achieve all this, Rod knew he'd need to serve an apprenticeship with a master crook. He was sure he would be able to work his way into the crooks' world when it was seen he would do anything. Once in, he'd see that time proved his loyalty. There were ways he might get to be a favourite. He knew he was a good-looking young man!

Twenty years had past since the start of Rod's apprenticeship and his guardian's assets were now under his control. The guardian himself long since began to putrefy, while cosily wrapped in a weighted sack, lying on the bed of the Thames. During the climb up the criminal ladder Rod had kept a faith, of sorts, with his old streetwise mate, Dave.

There were times when he felt that Dave was the only one with whom he could talk. He hadn't been the brightest boy on the block but he knew how to keep his mouth shut when it was necessary. Rod never fully confided in anyone, but he'd reveal more to Dave than to most. He looked after him, seeing he went short of nothing. What really pleased Rod about the man was the way he carried his dress and how poshly he had learned to speak. He had become quite the gent, and having him about the place did Rod's ego no harm at all. He had to admit that his old mate was an asset, a property worth possessing.

One would be hard-pressed to find a man who had the ability to use people as efficiently as Rod. As Mr Big, he had ways of inducing people to comply with his wishes. He had learnt early in his career that intelligence of the criminal class gave him power. Over the years, he regularly sent his agents — small time crooks with a degree of intelligence — to towns around the country, collecting what information they could on the local villains. With all expenses paid and a wad of notes for their wallets, it was a welcome job during the 'quiet times'. All knew, however, that they would pay dear, if they brought back misinformation. The intelligence they gathered had more than once proved useful when Rod required 'assistance' in their area.

Had they known of their existence, the police would have moved the earth to get hold of the Rod Shaw's files. As it was, they knew precious little about Mr Big himself. They knew of his existence, but only as a shadowy figure. Many of his rackets were known to the police and charges were made from time to time, but it was only the minnows who found themselves up before the beak.

Rod's ideas about crime were clandestine — at least where he himself was concerned. His methods were to set up a scam or crooked enterprise through others. He'd funnel money and instructions, then pay them off when the job was done. These people had no idea who was providing the goodies, but this was not a worry because for any expenses occurring — such as the purchase of a property — the cash always reached them ahead of the bills.

By the time the new enterprise was ready to open its doors, the deeds, or rent agreement, were signed over to the 'proprietor' who had a good deal, paying little or nothing at all. If the business was straight everything was in his name. If it was not straight, well he took his chances like any other crook. However, straight or not, much of the profit from the business found its way to the ominous Mr Big.

Rod had a home on Canary Wharf, ran a big BMW and had a villa in Marbella. Women came and went like the tide, often to weather the storm badly. Since first placing his foot on the ladder to crime, Rod Shaw had just gone one way: upwards.

During the big man's progress, Dave had simply tagged along, always there if wanted but contributing nothing more than his presence. It suited him and it suited Rod, since he never felt overshadowed by the lifelong companion. Domestically though, their lives were poles apart. Rod's womanising was unceasing, though it was never allowed to get in the way of business. On the other hand, Dave was, and had been for years, besotted with one woman.

Alice's father was the landlord of The Open Well, a popular drinking-hole near the East End. Dave, because of Rod's growing success, had moved away from the area long ago. This evening he had taken a shower, put on his favourite silk tie, patted aftershave lotion onto his skin and admired himself in the mirror. He thought he was looking pretty smooth and was satisfied that he had done the right thing when deciding to wear the light grey suit. The trouble was, he had no plan for his night's entertainment. He felt like a change, but didn't know what.

Sitting on a corner of his bed, he glanced through the local advertiser for ideas. On a centre page a number of pub logos were displayed. The Open Well was not one of

318

them but it did come to Dave's mind and he thought it might be interesting to pay a visit. It seemed a long time since he'd been down there, and he thought he may even meet one or two of the old gang. He'd feel good when they saw how he had gone up in the world.

However, Dave didn't see any of the old gang, but he did see Alice. At first he didn't recognise the girl who was helping behind the bar, then the penny suddenly dropped. Alice had grown into an attractive young woman. She had full lips and high check-bones with a swathe of auburn hair falling across one side of her face. When she smiled she showed even white teeth and her eyes joined in the merriment. Dave thought he had never seen any woman so pleasing and was completely captivated long before his evening was through.

It was Dave's good fortune that Alice had registered him from the moment he walked up to the bar. At first she gave him a cheery 'good evening' as she would to any customer, but she found her eye constantly roving in his direction. From his appearance and the way he talked, it seemed to her the man was a 'gent'. And what wouldn't she give to have a female version of that flashy diamond ring? Before the night was out, Alice decided to set about trapping her man. Two months later the happy bride stepped from the church into a roller.

Since then Dave and Alice had been happy together, living in a lovely house in a classy district. If his neighbours at times wondered about the source of his opulence, none suspected it was from the criminal activities of Mr Big.

It was in response to Rod's phone call that Dave and Alice joined him at their West End Club. Dave had been happy about the invitation. He enjoyed clubbing and Alice was always game for a night out. This was one of the better places in town, but it wasn't generally known that Rod Shaw was the proprietor.

The club had a reputation for good food, fine wine and a desirable clientele. Rod thought of it as his jewel. The evening passed pleasantly, and it was evident that Rod's partner, whom he had introduced as Clare, was having a wonderful time and Rod seemed so attentive. Then, around midnight an old acquaintance came to their table to pay his respect to Rod. He also reminded Dave of the times they had spent together at the snooker tables and Dave said they had been happy times, and he enjoyed their games together but it seemed a long time since they'd played. At that, Rod suggested the two of them should go to the snooker table, saying to Dave he would see Alice got safely home. Dave gave a questioning look to his wife, who responded by saying he should go and have a few games if he wished.

On the journey from the club, Clare was furious when Rod stopped the car and told her to get out, telling her there were taxis over the road. The fact that it was raining heavily and she was not dressed for such weather mattered not at all to him. Alice was amazed at Rod's change of attitude, and the cunning grin which came to his face frightened her. She asked him why he had ditched Clare like that, but the grin simply widened.

Dave returned home in the early hours, looking forward to his bed. He had thoroughly enjoyed his night and was pleased he had been persuaded to round it off in the snooker room. On entering the bedroom he had expected to find his wife asleep, but she was pacing the floor and Dave saw the stubs of half a dozen partly-smoked cigarettes. This in itself was unusual since Alice objected to smoking in the bedroom. Suddenly his wife held him tightly and he felt the trembles passing through her. He became alarmed, never having seen his wife like this. She had always been fit and strong, but now he saw how dreadful she was looking.

He asked Alice what had happened, but she was almost incoherent, only answering, 'Rod, it was Rod.' Suddenly Dave realised his wife had been raped.

13

'Are you saying your visit to the paper factory has been a waste of time?' Hester asked.

'Not exactly. Perhaps I had been hoping for too much though Herr Staab couldn't have been kinder. Fortunately, firms which use the card are limited, but the trouble is, they are spread all over Germany. Even if I were to call at each of the firms how could I find out which one had been the source of 'our cards'?'

'I don't recall you ever being so despondent as you are now Harry. What are you going to do?'

'It's not so much feeling despondent as being tired. I propose to take it really easy for a few days, then I'll come up with something. Just you see, my dear!'

★ ★ ★

Len Willson read the letter a second time after checking the postmark informing him it had been posted in the London area. It did not show the sender's address, nor was it signed.

Dear Mr Willson,

I'll start by assuring you that my letter is not a hoax. Nevertheless you will be wasting your time if you should consider attempting to trace the sender. Such action, I might add, would be a highly dangerous move on your part.

I know a great deal about you: your way of life and your ability to invent, which I also know is usually put to criminal use. You are known to the police, but to date they haven't been able to pin anything on you.

It is because you are smart that I shall make an offer which will make you £30,000 the richer if you accept, and furthermore, I will never make contact again.

To learn details of what is required of you, and to receive a deposit of £15,000 in cash, go next Tuesday, between 4 and 4:30 p.m. to the village of Askham Richard which you will know, it being only a few miles from your home in York.

Near the duck pond, which is opposite the village pub, is the entrance gate to HM's prison for women. Walk twelve paces alongside the wall at the right of the gate to find a dead letter box. It is behind the loose stone at ground level. If, by 4:45 p.m. after studying the instructions you decide not to carry them out, then replace them together with the cash and you will hear no more about the matter.

Take this warning seriously, Mr Willson: Should you:

A   Abscond with the cash.
B   Take on the job and later back off.
C   Take on the job but fail to complete it, your throat will be cut.

If you decide to do the job, you will be informed after the completion when to return to the dead letter box to pick up the balance of your payment. That will be the last you will hear of the matter.

For a few seconds Len Willson remained staring at the letter, not knowing what to make of it. But suddenly it became obvious; someone was pulling his leg. That someone though had to be close, knowing him to be a crook. If it was a joke Len wasn't laughing. What though if it was straight? Thirty thousand quid is a lot of money. There was a way of finding out, but he'd have to wait until four a.m. next Tuesday.

On Tuesday evening Len locked himself in his home with fifteen thousand pounds in cash lying in a drawer. He had a lot of thinking to do — not if he should take on the job, but how to carry it out; the instructions said they were confident he could use his own initiative.

★   ★   ★

Louise stood looking through the window, gazing across the garden and the river Kent towards the hills of Tebay. Peter Newell, lowering his book, looked across at his daughter, smiled and said to himself, 'She'll be studying the clouds again.' Already the morning sun shining from a blue sky was warming the valley air, sending it on an anabatic journey up the hillsides. Soon it would form into gaseous wisps as the rising air gave up its water vapour. It would not be long before cumulus, the type of clouds beloved by glider pilots the world over, would be floating across the open sky.

As a young man Peter had enjoyed flying, and he certainly had been proud of his crew during the days of the mighty Lancaster. He said his was the best bomber crew, but there were doubtless plenty of other skippers who would have challenged that assertion. Yes, Peter had enjoyed his flying, providing his plane had an engine of course, and the flight was away from enemy territory.

He knew he could never be at home in a glider. He needed to feel the reassurance of powerful engines at his fingertips. Not so his daughter, she maintained that engines provided brute force and removed much of the skill of *real* flying. Louise is forty-two years old now, he thought, but her interest in gliding showed no signs of fading. If anything she was even more enthusiastic, and the girl was good, there was no questioning that, not with two international diamond certificates to her credit, and only needing one more to complete the set.

Such a slightly built little thing she was. Neither himself or Hillary were big people, but his Louise was really petite. He also knew that his daughter was not only beautiful, but kind and with more than a fair share of charm. It seemed strange that her interest lay in the world of flying. He thought she would not look out of place in a ballet.

'Are you thinking of going to the club?' her father asked.

'I'd love to, but I can't make it today. I've

too much to do at the shop and it's Ann's day off, but I hope to go tomorrow. High pressure is building, so we should have good cumulus with a nice high cloud base for a few days before an inversion drops down to spoil it all.'

'If you go, will you be staying overnight at the airfield?'

'Yes, I'll stay in the caravan and leave the Cirrus rigged after the first day's flying, ready for flying the next. I must get off to the shop now, Daddy. I've to keep earning a few pennies you know!'

The following day her drive across the Pennines from Kendal was, as ever, beautiful. The early hour had the sun climbing up the clear eastern sky and Louise was glad she was wearing her sunglasses as she drove onward. On such a day, which held so much promise of good soaring, she still got the old excited tingle. At this hour the road was still quiet enough to allow swift progress and soon Settle was behind her, then Skipton. The flat top of Ingleborough was lost below the western horizon.

A few miles short of Harrogate she pulled over, bringing the car to a stop alongside a converted caravan which served as a roadside snack-bar, feeling a coffee would go down well. There were a couple of drivers enjoying a huge English breakfast, their lorries parked nearby. The smell of the fried bacon on the morning air was really mouth-watering. The men's plates were piled with bacon, eggs, tomatoes, mushrooms, black pudding and fried bread. The cook did wonders with his little snack-bar.

Over to her left the sun was lighting up the giant white 'golf balls' of the American Intelligence gathering station, and Louise glancing towards the west, saw the first cumulus forming over the hills, but she knew it would be sometime before that meteorological phenomenon would develop over her aerodrome at Rufforth.

Refreshed by the coffee, she continued to make good time and was soon through Harrogate on the road to York. Short of that city she turned the car from Rufforth village to travel a further mile to reach the entrance of Rufforth aerodrome. After leaving the road, she glanced in her rear mirror and noticed dust rising behind the car from the track, then remembered the fifteen miles per hour limit to lessen the damage. 'When will they get it tarmacked?' she asked herself.

'Hi Lou! It should be good,' Mike said, glancing up at the sky. He was walking from the clubhouse as Louise parked the car. She guessed he'd be going to the hangar to bring out the motor glider. Mike did a lot of instructing on motor gliders these days. 'Well good luck to him, I'm a purist,' she said to herself.

'Is there anyone in the clubroom, Mike?' she called after him.

'Half a dozen in there,' he said, 'I guess you will be wanting help to get your glider rigged!'

'You've got it in one,' she said, laughing.

'Don't worry, someone will give you a hand to get it out of its box,' he said, continuing towards the hangar.

Twenty minutes from opening the trailer's door, the Cirrus was ready to fly, but the sky over the airfield was still blue. Nonetheless, Louise hitched the towing gear to her car and pulled the glider to the launch-point at the end of the runway, ready for take-off when the sky 'bubbled'. She unhitched the machine to park it safely, then stood back to admire the graceful lines of the Cirrus, which never failed to please her.

She would return to the clubhouse to wait, maybe have another coffee while keeping an eye on the sky. It wouldn't be long before the thermals got going, so she'd take her parachute from the car and put it in the cockpit; then have the coffee.

As she was about to close the glider's canopy, Louise noticed the roll of white masking tape protruding from the cockpit's pocket, and remembered she hadn't sealed the gap at the top of the stern post by the rudder. The gap allowed a lever to be inserted so that the tailplane could be locked safely when rigging the glider. Not to tape over the hole didn't really matter, but it tended to make things look a bit tidier. A moment later the chore was done.

Later that evening, as she lay in bed before sinking into sleep, Louise thought of the joy of the day. The promised thermals had not let her down. They had lifted high as she covered a large area of Yorkshire. After three and a half hours of idyllic flying she decided to return to base to take the rest of the day at her ease. She had started out from home early that morning and she had planned to go with several club members to the Spotted Cow at Tockwith for her evening meal. Furthermore she knew from experience that tomorrow would be an even stronger day. After tomorrow, conditions would weaken and the excellent visibility would deteriorate as the inversion lowered. A strong inversion, Louise knew, acted like a lid which prevented the warm rising air to climb through it. With the inversion strengthening, the lid lowered, and with more and more smoke and dust being taken up, the rising air becoming trapped in an ever-lowering band.

What Louise also knew, was that the low inversion would set up lovely sunsets, as the slanting rays from the setting sun became refracted by the impure atmosphere. None the less, lovely as it was, it wasn't any good for gliding. Still, that would not occur tomorrow. No, tomorrow should be a peak gliding day she thought, as she drifted into a peaceful sleep.

The next morning was much as she expected, with a slight dampness on the grass. During the night stars had shone from a clear sky. But since the dew was slight, the cloud base would be high when the day's cumulus formed. Though the first wisps would be rather low, they would heighten with a strengthening sun and drying ground.

She walked to the glider to remove the cover that had been placed over the nose and canopy. Dew would have formed on the wings but at least the canopy would be dry. She'd wiped the glider down, then towed it to the end of the runway, ready to climb into when the thermals got going.

Later, as she made her way to her glider, she noticed a man strolling around it. He stopped at the tail as if to study the whole flying tailplane which was rather unusual on gliders. The man, whom she did not recognise, stepped away, paused again to take another glance before walking off in the direction of the car park. Louise smiled; he was probably admiring it, she thought. She could understand that because she couldn't stop admiring the Cirrus herself when it stood nearby.

At 11.20 a.m. the towrope was attached and the batman signalled the tug to roll slowly forward until the rope became taught. She heard, through the open clear-vision panel in her canopy, the increase in the roar of the tug's engine as they started off down the runway. Quickly, her wing-tip holder could no longer keep pace, but Louise just had control as the ailerons began to bite into the airflow. The coarse movement of the joystick would soon tighten as the flow of air increased with the gathering speed.

At two thousand feet she pulled the tow release, watched for a moment for the rope to fall away before making a climbing turn to her left. Over her shoulder she noted the tug diving steeply down to the right until it was lost to view as it flew into her blind spot below.

The car, driven by the man Louise had seen at the launch point, stopped on the road just after leaving the track, the dust still hanging in the air. He stepped out to look skywards from where the faint sound of the tug seemed to come. Then he saw the diving machine. He caught the sun as it flashed off the turning Cirrus, the glider looking small and alone in the huge sky. Climbing back into the car the man grinned as he drove off.

Though the wind was light, Louise flew a little way upwind of a forming cumulus floating high above. She reasoned the source of hot air feeding the cloud, came from a rubbish tip in which a fire burned. Suddenly the glider flew out of smooth air into turbulence but the pilot held course for two seconds before throwing the Cirrus into a sharp fifty-degree bank to the right. She had found the centre of the thermal at the first attempt. Together they climbed away gaining height at six knots.

From take-off Louise had not really been comfortable, and now, at two o'clock, her back was aching a lot. Of course it was the club's parachute she was wearing which caused the trouble. She was lucky to have it really and when she first put it on it had felt fine. Derek was naturally clumsy, but to trip with a bucket of water so that it spilt all over her own parachute, was something else. What was the man doing with the water anyhow? Then she thought, be fair, Derek is a hard-working member. Probably he'd intended to wash an aircraft down, or something. Anyhow, she shouldn't have left the chute on the ground when she returned to the car to fetch the fruit gums she liked to have when flying.

It was no good. She'd have to turn back. She had been making such good progress too, but there was no way she could continue the Diamond distance attempt with her back becoming more and more painful. She still had a long way to go to complete the required five hundred kilometres and without an engine it wasn't as if she could just keep on heading for the turning points. No, she must continue to find thermals in which to regain the height lost by each glide out. But the search often took her off track.

Reluctantly Louise turned for base. She thought sadly, you don't have better days than this, and not many as good during the year. Suddenly her disappointment changed to alarm. The rising sound of the airflow caused Louise to instinctively apply pressure to ease back on the stick but it remained where it was. There was no movement at all.

She saw the nose drop as the horizon climbed up the canopy and, like her heartbeat, the noise of the airflow increased. The Cirrus, normally so sensitive with its all-flying tailplane, would not respond. With desperation she tried readjusting the trimmer, hoping it would bring the glider to a flatter glide angle but the speed kept increasing as the nose continued to pitch down.

Now the faster airflow passing over the Cirrus' wings was creating much more lift, and Louise saw the green earth replaced by blue sky after the nose passed through the horizon, this time in a climb. She'd felt the 'G' force pressing her down when the glider had pulled out of its dive. With the nose pointing steeply upwards, the sound of the airflow faded completely and the Cirrus fell into a deep stall. She felt as if her tummy would reach her mouth. And at that moment when all the controls should have been 'sloppy' the stick stayed solid.

The next manoeuvre was even steeper. Due to a sharper dive producing still more lift, the glider pointed vertically up, and as the sound faded completely, Louise braced herself for a vicious hammerhead stall. She knew the same manoeuvre couldn't continue much longer because, sooner or later, the wings would lose their parallel line to the horizon and take on bank to one side or the other. Then, the Cirrus would no longer be diving clean as it went spiralling earthwards. The speed would still increase, as would the lift, but instead of being pulled up into a climb, the ever-increasing lift would act to pull the banked glider inwards and so tighten the spiral. 'G' force would increase to make the pilot and machine heavier. Eventually Louise would become unconscious as the blood was forced down from her brain. She wouldn't be aware when the glider broke up as a result of structural failure.

All this flashed through Louise's mind and she was even momentarily glad that she had been made to take the British Gliding Association's Bronze exam, all those years ago. It was time to get out!

With seat-straps already undone, she waited for the Cirrus to lift out of its dive before jettisoning the canopy. She would try to get out as the aircraft slowed. The blast of cold air hit her face, and a lot of effort was required to stand on her feet. This had to be achieved by pressing hard down on the rim of the cockpit on which the canopy fitted. She needed to reach a crouched standing position as the glider stalled and she would have been hard put to have remained in the cockpit as its nose fell away.

She toppled as she fell and was alarmed when the air, rushing past at a hundred and twenty miles an hour, flung her arm away when she tried to reach the handle which would open the chute. Aware now of the pressure, her second effort succeeded and she pulled the handle across her chest until her arm was reaching straight out at the side of her body. She heard the slap of the opening canopy, felt a jerk, then found herself descending in a silent world.

Louise alighted gently in a field sixty miles south of Rufforth. During the descent she had seen the Cirrus crash over to the east and was bewildered when her thoughts momentarily settled on the fruit gums lying in the cockpit's pocket. She felt calm as she walked to a nearby farm, though she noticed her hands were shaking. Using the farmer's phone, she rang the club where, after learning of her adventure, they promised someone would be sent to bring her back.

Peter Newell reached for the phone and recited his number and heard a lady's voice say, 'Daddy, it's Louise. My glider has crashed but I'm OK.'

Peter, interrupting, said, 'You've been shot down?' then realised what he had said. 'Crashed! How? What happened?'

* * *

'I'll answer that,' Harry told his wife as she was about to get out of her chair.

'Hello, Harry White speaking,' he answered.

338

'Hi, it's Peter Newell, how are you, Harry?'

'Fine, thanks. It's nice to hear from you. Are you OK?'

'Yes I am, but I've had a bit of a shock, though probably not as much as Louise, the poor girl.'

'Why? What's happened now, Peter?'

'She's crashed her beloved glider, but you'll never guess how — she had to bail out! Though she's all right, thank God.'

'Bail out? What on earth happened?'

'That's the point, no one knows, but they haven't had a chance to inspect the wreckage yet. Louise said she lost all elevator control, the stick was jammed solid. No one has heard of such a thing happening before with a Cirrus and there are plenty of that type about. That is why I'm calling you, Harry. I thought you should know. I mean, so much has been happening to the crew these past months. I can't help but wonder if my turn is here, and I am to be made to suffer through Louise?'

'Well, it is easy to become suspicious about almost anything these days, Peter. But Louise is all right, isn't she? None the worse for her experience?'

'That's true. She now says she might have enjoyed the experience if it were not for the loss of her Cirrus.'

'There may be some grounds for your fear, Peter. As I said, one can't be sure of anything these days. So it might be a good idea for me to take a look at Rufforth. I can get as far as Wetherby up the M1 from Chesterfield, then it's only a few miles along the A224. Actually I think I should have a word with your daughter.'

'When are you thinking of going?'

'Oh, first thing in the morning. One must strike while the iron is hot.'

'Well, Lou said she'd be staying a couple of days. Said she couldn't see any reason for not doing so while she has the opportunity to fly a club glider.'

'Seems to be a glutton for punishment,' Harry commented.

'I think you are right,' Peter said.

At eleven the next morning the dust trailed behind the detective's car as he headed for the clubhouse. He recognised the old RAF hangar, and remembered that Rufforth had been a wartime station. It brought to mind Roger who had lived near him. He landed here from a raid, minus a leg, or rather was after the medics removed it. He had left a lot of blood in the rear turret.

Harry had never met Louise, but on entering the clubhouse he recognised her at once. The photograph her father had shown the crew during a reunion, proved to have been a good likeness. Peter was so proud of his girl. If the Perpetrator was behind this, then the swine knew what he was doing.

Stepping towards her, he said, 'Louise?'

'Yes, I'm Louise. I am very pleased to meet you, Mr White.' He was impressed by her great charm, which was in no way helped by her flying attire.

'How did you know me?' Harry asked, surprised.

'I spoke to Daddy again last night. He told me you were coming.'

Smiling, Harry said, 'I hear you have been having fun and games recently.'

'You might say that,' she laughed.

'Let's take a stroll,' he suggested, wanting to talk to her away from the others.

When in the open, he said, 'That must have been quite an experience you had yesterday, Louise.'

'It certainly was, but you know if it wasn't for losing the Cirrus, I wouldn't have missed it for the world. I won't say I wasn't frightened, because I was. I mean, it was *really* scary, just sitting there while the glider seemed to have a mind of its own and not being able to do anything about it. But, you know Mr White, once that parachute opened, you will never know how much I felt the joy

341

of living. It was wonderful.'

'Well, I am glad you are safe. Have they recovered the crashed glider yet?'

'Yes, it's still in its trailer, over at Bob McLean's place. You will have passed his workshop as you drove along the dirt track.'

'I think we should see Mr McLean. Perhaps you will introduce me to him.'

On entering the workshop Harry saw a young man in white overalls at work on an upturned fuselage. He was repairing the wheel box, damaged by a heavy landing. 'There is Bob, over there,' Louise said, pointing at a slim chap wearing a face mask. 'Looks like he's been using the spray gun.'

'Bob, this is Mr White, a friend of my father. As a matter of fact they flew together in Lancasters in the war.'

Removing the mask, he said, 'That was a little before my time. I'm pleased to meet you.' He offered Harry his hand. Then, looking at Louise he asked, 'What do you think of this young lady's recent activities then? I think she was very lucky.'

'I was wondering if you could throw any light on the cause of the accident, Bob?'

'Well, I haven't looked at the wreckage, it only arrived early this morning but from what Louise has said, it sounds like there was trouble with the whole flying tailplane, or the connections leading to it from the cockpit . . . Jim,' he called, 'leave that job, and help us to get the Cirrus out of its trailer.'

'The tailplane has been ripped off. Probably from the impact when the glider hit the ground. Can you slide the sternpost further out, Jim? I'll take a closer look at it.' Bob looked through the gap at the top of the post.

'Good God!' he exclaimed. 'What on earth is this?'

'What?' Louise reached forward to peer through the gap.

'Look,' Bob said. 'There's a load of gunge in there, all over the fittings for the tailplane. It is rock hard. No wonder your stick was locked. But how was that possible?'

'Did you remove the masking tape from the gap?' Louise asked.

'There was no masking tape,' Bob replied.

'But there was, I remember putting it there. I always do.'

'It couldn't have torn off during the crash, it sticks too firmly and it's far too flat,' Bob said.

'Well I know I put it on,' Louise affirmed.

Harry, who had been keeping his counsel, said, 'It is obvious the tailplane's fittings have been tampered with, but they must have been clean when you rigged it. You would have

343

noticed if it wasn't. Was the glider left alone at any time afterwards?'

'It had been parked out in the field all night, then in the morning I towed it to the launch-point at the end of the runway. I didn't return until I was ready to fly.'

'And everything seemed normal to you?' Harry asked.

'Yes, everything was normal . . . except.'

'Except what?' the detective urged.

'Well, when I returned there was a stranger admiring my Cirrus. Or, at least, I thought he was admiring it.'

'Can you give his description, Louise?'

'Not really, but he was wearing a light grey cap — you know, with a peak. I would say he was in his thirties and of medium height. I remember, because he watched for a moment as I took the parachute from the car to put it in the cockpit. Then I remembered I hadn't worn that chute before, so it was necessary to adjust its straps before placing it in the cockpit. With my own chute, I normally just pull the straps over me and fasten them while sitting in the glider. Of course, with my own chute the straps are adjusted to fit me and they stay that way.'

'Why weren't you wearing your own chute?' Harry asked.

'I would have if some idiot hadn't poured

water all over it. To think that I had been cursing the club chute because it made my back ache. Then it saved my life.'

'When did that happen? The water spill, I mean.'

'Shortly before I went to the launch point for take-off.'

'But for that water spill, you would have been using your own chute, and everyone would know that?'

'That's right, Mr White.'

'Tell me, where do you store your chute when you are not flying?'

'In the club's parachute store, where it is warm and dry.'

'Is it easy to identify it as belonging to you?'

'Yes of course, it's kept in its bag which has my name painted across it.'

Harry remained silent for a moment. He was remembering his own chute during the war. Then he asked, 'Where is your chute now? Can I see it, please?'

Louise answered, 'Yes. At the moment it's in the store, but it will have to be sent away to be dried and repacked.'

'I recall one can open a cover flap to check if a piece of red thread is intact. If it is not, it shows that the chute's release has been accidentally pulled, so breaking the thread.

Do you check the thread before flying?'

With a guilty smile, Louise admitted she didn't, adding, 'Hardly anyone does.'

'Right, then. Let's go and check it now,' Harry said.

When the inspection flap sprang open, she exclaimed; 'My God!' They saw the release pin attached to the handle to open the chute, had been severed and was only being held in place with adhesive tape to stop the handle from falling away.

'I can't believe my eyes,' Louise said, having gone pale.

Bob McLean said, 'There's some sod trying to murder you, Louise.'

Harry suggested Louise should pay the club subscription for the *idiot* who spilled the water. And Bob said that someone, probably the bloke wearing the cap, had squeezed a substance on to the moving attachment to the tailplane. He was very curious as to what could lie inert for a given time, and then set as hard as a rock in a second.

* * *

Les Willson opened the envelope which had been franked by a London post office. Its contents instructed him to arrive at the dead letter box on the coming Friday at 2.30 p.m.

'The day after tomorrow,' he said to himself, with satisfaction.

At 2.25 he was half a mile short of Askham Richard, with the duck pond coming into view, when he was overtaken by a powerful motor bike, its rider dressed in full cycling gear. Les was shocked to see the bike go into a skid, then lie flat to slide along the road. He had to brake hard to avoid running into it. The rider was skilled, and had known exactly what he was doing. Even the limp, as he walked to the car was an act. He lowered his window to ask if the rider was all right, but the man, still helmeted, leaned forward.

The last thing Les Willson saw in this life, was sunlight glint off Sheffield steel. Though he had been slashed from ear to ear there was not a drop of blood on the hand which held the knife.

Harry White heard of the slaying from a news report and knew that Louise's would-be murderer had paid the price of failure. A failure which the villain had not even been aware of, but which was indicated from the printing on the quality white card discovered in his pocket.

14

From behind his chair Hester rested her hand on Harry's shoulder, saying, 'It's lovely having you at home like this, dear, not having you running off every five minutes. It's been more than a month since that swine sabotaged Louise Newell's glider and parachute. Maybe who ever is behind all this sick activity will give up further attempts.'

Harry said, 'I very much doubt that. He knows he has had two failures, Arthur Brown and now Peter Newell. Fortunately he is not aware that his plans for Tom Williams and James Daly also failed, but I am sure he will think up something fresh for the other two. Then there is Jeffery Beaumont and myself. It is quite obvious from the numbering of the cards that he is after every one of us.'

'It is awful,' Hester said, with feeling.

'What is awful,' Harry said, 'is I can only act after the deed is done, or at least well on its way to being done. That is so frustrating. It makes me feel I am having to dance to the perpetrator's tune.'

'I'm sure you are exaggerating, dear. Don't forget you have put two men in prison.'

'Yes, and we also have four men dead, even though two of them were villains. In the meantime here I am waiting for something to happen. I am not really in control, Hester, that is the truth of the matter. If only I had come away from Germany with a firmer lead, something to get my teeth into. God! I'll be glad when we have got this whole rotten business behind us.'

Hester said, 'What you need, my dear, is a lucky break. Just one lucky break, and I'm sure you'd never look back.'

'There are not any fairy godmothers in this life. Only hard investigating and a deal of assumptions to follow up. There is no other way, Hester. Believe me.'

'And what about that famous Harry White's sixth sense?' his wife asked, with a smile.

'That has nothing to do with luck. It is something within me — part of myself — a gift, if you like.'

Just then the phone rang and, making for it, Hester mused, 'Now who can that be, I wonder?' Returning from the hall she said, 'It's for you Harry.'

'Who is it?'

'Didn't say, but it's a man,' she said.

'Hello.'

'Mr White?'

'Speaking. Who is this?'

'Please excuse me, but I wish to withhold my name. However, I do have information which I am sure will be of interest to you since it concerns the problem you and your associates are having these days. I'm sure you know what I mean, Mr White. Or should I say Detective Inspector White?'

'What do you know about the crew, or my associates?'

'Not a great deal, inspector, but I know a man who does. In fact this man would like to talk with you, but before he will, he wants me to receive a promise from you.'

'A promise? What sort of promise? Who are you?' Harry asked again, sounding forbidding.

'I told you, I will not give my name, so please don't ask. However, I will try to explain as regards the promise. I am acting for a gentlemen who also does not wish his name made known to you, not for the time being at least. But this man does want to meet you. As I am his confidant, I can assure you what he has to say should at least help with the problem we know you are facing. The promise which is required as a result of any information he gives is that he will not be implicated in anyway.'

'You say you are acting for this person. Are you his solicitor?'

'No, not his solicitor, I am a close friend.'

'It sounds to me,' Harry said, 'that this so-called gentleman is nothing more than a common informer from the criminal community. No doubt he will want payment for his service!'

'He is not a common informer and he certainly does not require payment beyond a promise that he won't be involved and that you will keep the source of information received strictly to yourself. Now, Inspector, do you want help or would you rather have the situation stay as it is?'

The line went quiet, causing the caller to ask, 'Are you there, Inspector?'

'Yes, I'm here,' Harry said. 'I want to meet this man, I therefore give my promise. However, if I am misinformed or deceived in any way, or if I discover your man has committed acts of violence or worse, then I will consider the promise to be annulled. Is that clear?'

'We can live with that. You will be contacted again. Soon!' Harry heard the click from the instrument being replaced.

On relating the conversation to his wife, Hester's brow lifted as she said, 'And you say there are no fairy godmothers?'

Three days later, Harry had no difficulty in identifying his man from the description he had been given. He was smartly dressed, but in some way failed to give the appearance of a gentleman. Years ago Harry might have suggested the man's attire leaned towards being 'spivvy'. The time was 2.30 p.m. The rendezvous; the entrance foyer of a large Birmingham Hotel.

Noting Harry's age, his brown trilby and *The Times* newspaper he'd agreed to carry, the man called, 'Inspector White, I think!'

'That's right. And your name?' Harry asked.

'Call me Dave for the time being, Inspector. Shall we talk over a drink?'

'Providing it is coffee, or even tea,' Harry said. Then, in the hotel's coffee shop, he continued, 'Now, tell me how you know about my troubles and those of my friends?'

Dave said, 'After you have confirmed to me your promise not to involve me in any actions you may see fit to take.'

'With the conditions I gave to your friend, I give you my word, but I assume you are in fact a crook,' Harry said.

'You assume wrong, Inspector. Apart from stealing on the streets when I was a kid I have committed no crime.'

'May I ask the source of your income?'

'Let's just say a benefactor,' he said, looking directly at Harry.

'Very well. Now tell me what you know and why you are prepared to tell me. But let me guess. If it's not for money it will be for revenge.'

'You are a shrewd man,' Dave said, hiding his surprise before asking, 'Have you heard of Rod Shaw? Known to London's underworld as 'Mr Big'.'

'The name means nothing to me. I have been retired from the force for many years, as I am sure you know. I feel you will enlighten me, however.'

'That's right, I will. I already have your promise not to involve me, but I also want your trust, and indeed, a degree of understanding.'

'I think you mean you want help to remove any guilty feeling you may have,' Harry said, his voice carrying a touch of scorn. There followed a moment's pause during which time, he decided, he should not antagonise the man. Instead he must gradually appear to befriend him for their mutual benefit, certainly until he could discover if the man had anything to tell that was worth listening to. 'Tell me what lies behind your desire for revenge, so that I may understand your motive better and thereby judge your credibility.'

Following the detective's request, the pause

now came from Dave before he began, 'Inspector, I don't know a great deal about you, but the little I do suggests you are a hard man but straight. And you don't give your word unless you intend to keep it. Because I believe this, I will not prevaricate in any way. Rod Shaw and I grew up in the East End, in fact we lived in the same street and were in the same gang. You might say we were tearaways. We robbed, fought and generally terrorised the district.

'On reaching his late teens, Rob's ambitions grew. He knew the life he was leading would lead nowhere. He wanted to chisel his way into the big time. He was, is, clever, hard and diverse. He'd stop at nothing to get ahead. A big boy quickly recognised this and Rob convinced the man of his loyalty towards him, even to the extent of becoming his lover. It did not matter that Rob was no homosexual, not if it helped him gain his aspirations, which it did, eventually becoming the boss's lieutenant and confidant. But, with his life ebbing away from his body, weighted down on the bed of the Thames, the boss realised his mistake.

'That was long ago, when Rob took over all his dead boss's interests — a foundation from which he built a criminal empire. Oh yes, Rob Shaw has come a long way since his days on the streets. He is not known as 'Mr Big' for nothing.'

Harry asked, 'What part have you played in all this villainy?'

'Since leaving the streets, none at all,' Dave answered.

'From your upbringing on the streets you can hardly have gained much in the way of qualifications, Mr — what is your name? I don't feel ready to address you as Dave.'

'I am Mr Parker. I have nothing to hide from you, Inspector.'

'As I was saying, Mr Parker, I doubt if you have qualifications but you appear to be affluent. If I am any judge, that is not a costume ring you are wearing and I see you wear bespoke attire. So, what is the source of your opulence, may I ask?'

'Rob Shaw,' Dave answered, smiling with disdain.

'But you say you have taken no part in his activities since boyhood, Mr Parker.'

'That's right. I haven't.'

'Perhaps you will explain?'

'I have lived on Rob by simply exploiting his weakness. Because of his way of life, and of course his character. He is a man who cannot give anything more than superficial friendship. Even though he lives the high life and is a womaniser, part of 'Mr Big' is lonely.

There is no one with whom his ego will allow him to confide during his low or lonely moments. Rob is not capable of giving true friendship. He is far too self-centred for that.

'Since childhood I am the only one from whom he can derive comfort during a low period. He also knows that domination is nothing to me. All I want is a quiet and comfortable existence, and he knows it. Although I'm sure he doesn't think it, he buys my understanding; not to say sympathy. Knowing I am not ambitious for power or influence, he trusts me completely. He sees to it I go short of nothing.

'But do not be misled by this, Inspector. It is not friendship, or even generosity on his part. No, it is an emotional insurance, knowing I'm always there. My ways are in fact the reverse to his. While Rob is an ardent womaniser and crooked adventurer, I am a one-woman man. My wife and I are devoted and have been from the early days of our relationship.'

Harry, shifting in his chair to ease his aching back, said, 'To me it seems Rob Shaw is your insurance. Without him, where else would you get the luxury life you seem to have? What's caused you to change your attitude towards him?'

Dave Parker's expression stiffened before

saying, 'The heartless bastard raped my dear wife. That is why, Inspector!'

Harry, now clear in his own mind about the deep feelings and motive of Dave Parker, felt he could rely on his informant. The man didn't even want money. 'That's all very well,' he said, 'but what has all this to do with me and my troubles?'

'I don't pretend to know many details about you and your colleagues, but I do know that all of you are being targeted to be made to suffer. I also know that 'Mr Big' is involved!'

The old man felt his heartbeat increasing, a rush of excitement. 'In what way involved, Mr Parker?'

'I have known for some time that Rob holds confidential files on successful criminals in the provinces. His files are unknown to those men, and none have ever had a police charge brought against them. Now, some time ago, Rob was contacted by an unidentified person from the continent. The call came from Belgium and Rob was astonished at the caller's knowledge of his criminal activities and his awareness that there were no depths to which Rob was not prepared to stoop, if the price was right.

'The mysterious caller gave a vague outline of his requirements, but Rob told him to get lost and do his own dirty work. However, his interest developed when he learned of the amount of money which would be involved. Rob himself would finish up better off by a sum reaching well into six figures. Of course, he asked why he should believe the payment would be honoured. 'Because, if you agree to act as my 'manager' you will receive half a million pounds before you even lift a finger,' said the caller.

Harry asked, 'Am I to take it that Rob Shaw was to organise the hits, so long as he stayed close to the caller's plan?'

'I think that was the idea,' Dave said, 'but Rob never really discusses his business with me. Though I could see he was excited, perhaps saying more than usual.'

'And he was offered a large sum up-front to prove good faith? That fits. That's the Perpetrator's way.'

Dave said, 'The who?'

'That is what we call him, no one knowing who he is,' Harry answered.

'Anyway, after a long discussion with the caller, Rob took on the assignment, though he was taken aback when told that if he backed off after accepting the deposit, or if a failure came about which was directly due to Rob, he would have his throat cut. No one had previously dared to threaten 'Mr Big'.'

Any doubts Harry may have harboured about the caller being the Perpetrator had been removed and he asked, 'Did Shaw get access to large sums for financing the operation?'

'Yes, he did. He was also instructed what the payments must be, with conditions the same as his own in the event of failure. The difference was, it became Rob's responsibility for arranging any throat-cutting which might become necessary. Whereas if his own demise be required, well, that had already been taken care of.'

'What you have told me, Dave, is very interesting. Perhaps taking me one link closer in the chain to the Perpetrator, but he still dwells in a mist. If you want to help, you must try to discover his lair. How does Rob Shaw raise contact with the man when it is necessary?'

'He doesn't. It is always Rob who is contacted and then only if a plan has failed in some way. The man seems able to keep tabs, but we don't know how. I know it worries Rob as it demonstrates proof of the danger to himself, should he cock things up. That, and the knowledge that there is no way out now he is involved. Still, Rob doesn't make mistakes, otherwise he'd have been inside long ago. Or at least he didn't until the bastard raped my wife. I expect you to bang him up for a long, long time, Inspector.'

'That I will do, Dave, after I have discovered the Perpetrator. In the meantime you must be on a constant lookout for any hint which might help me in that direction. Now that I know of Shaw's existence I am sure I already have sufficient evidence to put before the police to put Mr Shaw away for life.'

'How can I help? I've told you Rob doesn't discuss his business with me.'

'Maybe not, Dave. But after all your years together you cannot be considered a threat. If you were around when he received a call from the Perpetrator, it may give you a chance to trace the call,' Harry suggested.

'Come on,' Dave said, 'I've told you he only makes contact if things in some way have not gone to plan. They might not go wrong any more and even if they did, how would I know?'

'You will if you make it go wrong.'

'Christ! How can I do that?' Dave said, alarmed.

'Simply by finding which of my colleagues is the next target and the type of attack we can expect. We will make sure the villain with the contract will fail. The Perpetrator, with his usual quickness, will be on the phone to Shaw. You make sure you are there.'

'I think it could be done,' Dave was looking grave. 'I don't think an alarm would ring if I just seemed to be showing idle curiosity. Anyway, one of your friends is a doctor, I think. I know he is already targeted, the next to be hit.'

Alarmed, Harry said, 'Jeffrey Beaumont! What's the plan for him?'

'I've no idea. But I heard Rob laughing, he thought it a great scenario. I should think it is something quite complicated to amuse him like that.'

'For God's sake, find out,' Harry urged.

Dave said he would do his best, but if the plan was involved he was sure Rob would not go into details. He dared not press to the point of raising suspicion. Then Harry asked how many failures there had been? He of course could only know of the successes. And Dave said there had been two failures — one in Worcester and another at Lichfield. That made Harry feel better, for he knew now that the Perpetrator was not aware that Tom William's place in the Cardiff prison had been taken by the villain Reid for the murder of the retired schoolteacher, Jim Lewis. Nor did he know that Betty Daly's would-be murderer had failed and was also in prison. James, his wife Betty and Tom remained safe — at least for the time being.

As soon as he arrived home, Harry phoned Jeffrey Beaumont. He had called from Birmingham but nobody had been at home. This time there were only three rings before Jeff picked up the phone. 'Doctor Beaumont.'

Harry recognised the voice at once.

'Hello Jeff, it's Harry White. I'm glad I've caught you at home. I rang earlier, you must have been out. How is Zoe? Well, I hope. And yourself, of course.'

'Yes, we're fine thanks. Hope you and Hester are too. You say you rang earlier, it's not trouble, I trust?'

'Well, I hope not. At first I considered not telling you, so as to prevent you and Zoe from getting worried, but I quickly realised that would have been irresponsible.'

Before he could continue, Jeff cut in to say, 'It sounds serious, Harry!'

'Well, the thing is you are being targeted. It seems to be your turn, old chap.' Jeff felt his heartbeat increase, but his thoughts went out to Zoe as he remembered the Perpetrator always went for the family — except for Tom who was alone. 'Have you any details?' he asked.

'Sorry, unfortunately I am completely in the dark. But I had to tell you, so that you will be even more on guard, Jeff.'

'You're right, of course. Obviously you will keep me informed if you discover more?'

'Naturally. Be comforted from the knowledge that we have had our successes. I will do my best, I promise you.'

'I know you will. We are all grateful for your wonderful support, Harry. We'll keep in touch, old chap.'

Two days after his warning to Jeff, Harry was on the phone again. This time in response to a call from Dave Parker, who said, 'I have news, Inspector. Instructions have come through to Rob telling him to set up the plan for dealing with yourself.'

'At last! What is to be my fate?'

'I don't know, but I do know that the villain who Rob will choose in Chesterfield will present himself at your home, identified as an electricity board official. That's as much as I know, but you should find that to be useful, Inspector.'

'I certainly should. I'm sure I'll get an opportunity to cause the man's failure. If I succeed, the Perpetrator should soon be on the phone to Shaw so be sure to be around when he does. Starting from tomorrow, I want you to ring me every morning so that I can inform you of the time of the villain's failure. This will remove the need for you to hang around Shaw before it's necessary. That could arouse his suspicion, since I assume it's not your routine. Immediately after the Perpetrator has called Shaw, you pick up the phone and dial 1471, then memorise the number given. I want it!'

Five days after Dave Parker's first call to Harry, the doorbell rang at the Whites' household. The time was 10.30 a.m. The lady of the house, on opening the door, was confronted by a pleasant young man who identified himself as an employee of the Electricity Board, saying, 'Good morning, madam. The Electricity Board is in the area making a check on appliances. My work should only take about twenty minutes, so if I may come in, please?' The man made a step forward.

Hester raised her hand to stop the man and said, 'I'm so sorry, but you've come at a bad time. I am on my way out and can't delay, but I'm surprised the Board didn't make arrangements with us. Could you return tomorrow afternoon? I am sure to be in then. I really am very sorry, but they should have made an appointment, Mr Cooke,' she said, glancing at his identity card.

'Yes, I'll be able to fit it in tomorrow afternoon, and I apologise for our people having been so lax,' the man said with a friendly smile. Then turning away, he added, 'Until tomorrow, then.'

When the door was closed, Harry said, 'Now Hester, put on your coat and go out. The man will be on his guard so we mustn't arouse his suspicions.'

When the man from the Board arrived the next day, Hester said, 'This is Mr Cooke, dear, he has come to check our electrical appliances.'

Mr Cooke said hello and Harry said he thought it unusual, as he couldn't recall having them checked before like this. But Mr Cooke told him it was a new policy the Board had introduced due to a rise in the number of household accidents. Now they were to make random checks. Harry said that perhaps it was a good thing.

Harry then excused himself, saying he had work to do. As arranged, Hester busied herself with chores while remaining in the presence of the electrician. When she brought out the Hoover the man said he would like to check the carpet-cleaner's plug before she put it into the socket. However, his inspection deemed the plug to be satisfactory.

While Hester remained occupied, the man continued his checking, finally commenting it was as well he had called. He had found a wire coming loose on the dehumidifier and sooner or later it would have caused a short. Then, closing his work-case, he enquired if they had electric fires in the house. But Hester said they hadn't because the place was centrally heated, though the immersion heater in the bathroom could be unplugged. 'I must check it,' the man said.

Hester led Mr Cooke to the bathroom and as they passed by the lounge she heard men talking within. On their return from the bathroom Harry stepped from the lounge saying, 'Ah, there you are. Have you been able to find anything wrong?'

'Only a minor thing here and there. Nothing serious,' the man said.

'That's good. Show me,' Harry moved towards the kitchen.

'Well I've had a look at all the plugs and renewed a little wiring on your dehumidifier. Otherwise everything is fine,' he said.

Hester said, 'And he put a new plug on the cord of the electric iron.'

'What was wrong with it?' Harry enquired.

'It was becoming burnt and needed renewing.'

'I would like to have the old one,' Harry said.

The man said, 'It will be no good to you because it's kaput. I'll throw it in the rubbish when I get back.'

'I see. Wait, I'll be back.' A moment later Harry re-entered the kitchen, this time with two young men, one of whom was wearing a policeman's uniform. Hester saw the colour drain from Mr Cooke's face as he heard her husband say, 'This is Detective Sergeant Forrest and this officer is Constable Young. Surprisingly, Constable Young served his time as an electrician before joining the police. Be so good as to remove the plug from the iron, constable!'

Cooke eased himself towards the back door, but the detective sergeant smartly blocked his way. The constable quickly had the plug opened and, turning to his colleague, said, 'What have we got here then?'

The sergeant pursed his lips and replied, 'Umm, explosive. Semtex, I'd say.'

Constable Young, wearing a twisted smile, turned to his sergeant to say, 'Shall I, or will you?'

'Go ahead, Constable,' the sergeant said.

'You do not have to say anything that may harm your defence if you do not mention it, or question anything that you may later rely on in court. But anything you do say may be given in evidence against you.'

Harry accompanied the group to the station and after safely locking the villain in a cell, he asked to borrow Cooke's house key. It had been taken from him with the remainder of his personal effects, one of which identified the villain as Max Harewood.

As the old detective was about to leave the station, Constable Young approached him. 'Sir, would you mind telling me how you knew it was the iron plug which had the explosive? After all, there were other plugs Harewood had checked, no doubt to give the impression he was there for the reason he gave. But you knew which plug to go for. How did you know, sir?'

'Because my wife told me he had cut it free and replaced it with a new plug. You will remember I asked him why, and he said it was becoming burnt so he changed it. That was a mistake. The iron plug was one of the sealed rubber type, not easy to open, and, had it been burnt, my wife would have smelled it at the time, Constable.'

'I see! Sir — they were saying in there that the explosive would easily have blown Mrs White's hand off if she had put the plug into its socket.'

'Yes Constable, it would,' Harry said, grimly.

While making his way to Harewood's house, Harry noticed an elderly couple walking towards him on the pavement. The gentleman was wearing extremely dark glasses and walked with the help of a white stick. The lady with him held the leash of a black Labrador guide dog.

Suddenly the lady fell, her foot tripping on the gentlemen's stick. She went down heavily on the pavement. Harry rushed to offer assistance and managed to get her on her feet again but he could see she was badly shaken. As he continued towards Harewood's house, his thoughts went to Mr 'Big' and his type, who lived in the lap of luxury from their ill-gotten gains, while the two old people, so grievously afflicted, struggled on with their lives.

Reaching Harewood's house he let himself in with the latchkey, knowing there would be no danger from within as he had learnt the villain lived alone. His wife had left him three years previously. It was in a chest of drawers, the middle drawer containing a number of pullovers and jumpers, his search finished. Under the garments laid neat wads of notes.

Miss Gregson, a prim spinster of forty-five let herself into her office. It was ten o'clock on a Monday morning. She bent to pick up the mail and noticed amongst the letters a post office form to collect a parcel at the local office. There had been no one to accept it from the postman when he'd called. She went at once, before taking off her coat.

On returning to her office with the parcel, Miss Gregson, the secretary for the 'Help of the Blind' sat looking down at fifteen thousand pounds. She was speechless after reading the enclosed unsigned note which said the money was a donation to the Society.

15

Neil Davenport moved the flag away from the hole to allow the golf ball a clean drop. The colonel remained bent over the putter as the ball rolled a full twenty-five yards over the short turf of the eighteenth green. When it dropped, a broad smile spread over his heavy jowelled face.

'One of these days I'll beat you,' Neil said, handing the colonel his ball.

'Perhaps you will but I think it'll take a year or two before you do that. You need a lot more practice, my boy. I'll see you in the mixed lounge after we have showered,' he said, as he made to replace the putter into his golf bag.

In the lounge, Neil commented, 'The place is almost deserted,' handing the colonel his beer.

'They will be out on the course. Remember, we teed off early. We'll see them coming in shortly. There is a foursome on the eighteenth now,' the colonel said, glancing through the window. 'Doctor Beaumont is out there with them. Did you see what the local paper had to say? They have certainly done the old boy proud. I don't begrudge a word, mind; Jeffrey is a damn fine fellow.'

'Which one? I don't know the man, I only recently moved to Stroud you know.'

'Yes, of course. He's the tall, elegant-looking chap with the flowing moustache. Wouldn't have been out of place in the regiment during its early days, though he was airforce actually. Lucky to have survived, I'm told.'

'What has the paper had to say then?' Neil asked.

'Well, the doctor has lived and practised all his life in this town. Even after retirement he continued good works, sitting on a number of committees, using his influence to the benefit of local charities. For years he served as a magistrate; was also Chairman of the Local Medical Committee and a member of the BMA Council. I think he was also the Chairman of its Ethics Committee. We can say that the good doctor is a pillar of the community. I for one have not heard a bad word spoken against him. Why, he was the captain of this club some years ago.

'You may think, Neil, that he had his finger in every pie, a real committee man. You know what I mean! We've all known the type who just wants to push himself forward, feeling he is important. But Jeffrey is not like that, as a matter of fact he's very unassuming, though he still manages to assert much influence.'

'What decided the paper to highlight him just now?' Neil asked.

'Recently Jeffrey Beaumont said he was withdrawing from most of his social works. He had decided to take his wife Zoe on a world cruise before it was too late. In any case he felt it was time to relieve the pressure. To relax more. He said the stress was starting to tell. The town council in recognition of the esteem in which the doctor has been held for so long, had arranged an evening to be held in his honour. Hence the story in the paper. I doubt if you could find a single taxpayer objecting.'

★ ★ ★

'The Local Medical Committee broke up their meeting in a happy frame of mind. Final arrangements were completed with Doctor Beaumont's son, the extremely competent surgeon working at Cheadle in the nationally recognised cardiac unit, directly under the senior consultant there, specialising in heart valve replacement. Mr Paul Beaumont will leave Cheadle to be consultant at the satellite Centre of Excellence being commissioned by The Stroud NHS Trust. There he will be

Director of Surgery responsible for overseeing techniques used and for authorising suitable suppliers of equipment.'

The chief accountant of Stroud's NHS Trust said to the interviewee, 'I am happy with your references, Mr Hogg. What makes you want to move here from Basingstoke, when you seem to be well-established there?'

'The truth of the matter sir, it's my wife. Mrs Hogg has never really settled in Basingstoke. She is from Stroud you see and all her close family are here. She misses them a lot, but I don't mind the move if it makes her happy, just so long as I can get a post.'

'You realise we are only offering a temporary position until Mr James is fit to take up the reins again?'

'Oh yes, I understand that but even a temporary post will be useful, especially with the expense of moving.'

'Very well then. From my point of view you are ideal since you are familiar with the workings of the NHS,' the chief accountant said.

★   ★   ★

Lounging on the sundeck Jeffrey said, 'It's only the third day since the ship reached the warmer weather and I'm already feeling ten years younger and you, my dear, are becoming beautifully tanned. Don't overdo it, you know how dangerous we have learnt the sun can be.'

'Don't worry, I've put factor twelve sun block on, so I should be all right,' Zoe said. And for several minutes the couple was silent as they laid back enjoying the warmth. Then she said, 'I'm so proud of our son, and delighted he's returned to live in Stroud. I did miss him when he was away, you know.'

'I do know dear, so did I. Paul has achieved the high hopes I held for him. His success gives me such a good feeling.'

* * *

Paul Beaumont was pleased with the new cardiac surgical unit whose standard of equipment was every bit as high as that at Cheadle. The Mitral Valves used by the department were produced by ABC Biotechnique, the same company which supplied the unit at Cheadle. The valves were excellent and he knew their price was right.

Mr Hogg was also satisfied with his new position in the accounts department of The Stroud Hospitals NHS Trust. Much more than his colleagues might imagine. After all, the fifteen thousand-pound deposit which indirectly came with the position was already safely tucked away at home. From his new position it was straightforward to intercept accounts coming in from ABC Biotechnique. It seemed, for sometime at least, that the orders for the Mitral Valves would remain at about twenty per month at £2,400 each: invoicing at £48,000 by ABC Biotechnique.

Hogg had no difficulty in setting up the new company of CBA Biotechnique, registered in the Isle of Man with nominee directors there. It was easy to intercept ABC Biotechnique issues and replace them for £2,800 each — total £56,000.

The trust pays CBA £56,000 pounds per month for six months. Then CBA pays ABC £48,000 per month for six months, establishing a pattern and a gain of £48,000.

For the next three months CBA Biotechnique continued to receive payments from the Trust but made no payments to ABC Biotechnique. Hogg knew that the terms of supply for ABC Biotechnique would cause them to seek legal redress after three months of non-payment.

Ten months after Mr Hogg had been employed by the Trust the chief accountant was astonished to discover amongst his mail a letter from the law firm Hargreaves, Warwick & Co who were acting on behalf of ABC

Biotechnique. The letter warned that legal action was to be taken against the Trust for the recovery of three months payment, totalling £144,000.

A wave of heat passed through the accountant as he read the solicitor's letter again. However, he was sure that payments had always been made as he himself signed each cheque. A check of the bank statement confirmed the cheques had been passed. Clearly, there was a mistake which must lie in the system used by the biotechnique company.

Further demands reaching the Trust from ABC Biotechnique quickly showed the amount requested differed from their records. This enabled the Trust to discover that CBA Biotechnique existed and received payments. Investigation into the company, found it to be registered in the Isle of Man, which also brought to light that the money had been redirected to a private account set up in the Isle of Man.

It was learnt from the manager of the bank that the account holder, a Mr P Beaumont, when opening the account, had produced his water bill as proof of his address.

What Mr 'Beaumont' seemed to have overlooked when he cleverly forged the change of name and address on the bill, was the customer reference number. The bank had kept a photocopy of the bill and when the Trust's investigators approached the Water company with the reference number, the true name and address turned out to be that of Mr Paul Beaumont, the consultant head of the Cardiac Surgical Unit of Stroud Hospital NHS Trust.

Jeffrey and Zoe Beaumont came ashore at Portsmouth, both bronzed and fit, having enjoyed their holiday of a lifetime. Although they had loved every minute of the experience, they were happy to be back, and were looking forward to seeing their son to learn how he had settled in Stroud. Of course, they were keen to tell him all about the wonderful times they had enjoyed.

As the couple was passing a news stall in the arrival hall the doctor stopped dead in his tracks. His eye had caught the headlines in one of the tabloid newspapers.

EMINENT STROUD SURGEON
HAD FINGER IN THE TILL

Another paper blazed:

CARDIAC CONSULTANT ON THE FIDDLE
NHS loses thousands

Jeffrey gathered up both papers. With trembling hands, he read to his wife:

'Mr Paul Beaumont, a consultant in the Cardiac Unit of The Stroud Hospitals NHS Trust has been charged with deception, and is accused of misappropriating thousands of pounds.

Although the full amount of money stolen by Beaumont is known to the Trust, they will not reveal the sum at this time. But it is said the amount may run to over a hundred thousand pounds.

Staff at the Trust were bewildered by the discovery. The consultant's competence is held in high esteem by his colleagues. The Centre of Excellence was commissioned by Stroud Hospitals NHS Trust barely a year ago, Mr Beaumont being the first head of the centre, which was already winning national acclaim.

Doctor Jeffery Beaumont, the father of the accused, was for many years a practising general practitioner in the town. He enjoyed an excellent reputation amongst the townsfolk not only as a skilled GP, but also for his service to the town.

The doctor continued, long after his retirement, to give valuable service on many of the town's committees. He was for many years a magistrate and a governor of a local school, Chairman of the local Medical Committee and a member of the BMA Council and Chairman of its Ethics Committee. Worthy local charities could always rely on the doctor's organising ability to help raise funds.

Doctor Beaumont Senior has for many years been a true pillar of the community. It is sad such a man should have to bear the shame of his son. The son is already suspended by the Trust and is to be referred to the General Medical Services Committee.

Mr Burns, a lifelong friend of the doctor, commented, 'I am not sure that a man of such integrity can stand up to the disgrace brought into his family.'

Zoe said, 'I don't believe what I'm hearing. Paul could never act in such a way. He is too much like his father. There has to be a mistake!'

'Of course there has, dear.' Jeffrey said,

slipping a comforting arm about his wife.

Back at their home in Stroud the Beaumont's answerphone had recorded messages of sympathy from all the crew and some of their wives. Harry White had asked Jeffrey to call him back as soon as was convenient.

After listening, Zoe remarked, 'You have good friends in the crew, dear.'

'The best,' Jeffery agreed. 'I'll get on to Harry straightaway.'

In Chesterfield, a moment later Hester heard her husband say, 'Yes, Harry speaking. Is that you Jeffrey?

'Yes, it is. Thank you for your kind message. Zoe and I have just got back from our holiday and what a homecoming it is. Zoe is absolutely devastated, even though we both agree there cannot be any truth whatsoever in the allegations.'

'Of course not, old chap, but it is a dreadful business, covered as it is on a national basis by the media. It must hit you all very hard. What we have to do now is prove Paul's innocence by finding the true culprit.'

'You think there is a culprit Harry, and it's not a genuine mistake?'

'Tell me, Jeff, have you received the white card? It is usually received almost immediately after the target has been successfully hit.

Or at least if it is thought to have been successfully hit.'

'I found it on the doormat when we arrived back.

'What was the message?'

'It said, '0+3 A NUMBER NOT TO BE FORGOTTEN'. That's odd, isn't it?'

'It seems obvious that the Perpetrator is to have another go at Arthur Brown and Peter Newell whose would-be executioners were themselves executed. Then of course he failed with me. But, the fact that +3 was stated and not +5, confirms the Perpetrator is ignorant of his failure with Tom Williams and James Daly, thank God. Of course it's not a mistake, your card proves that, and don't you remember I told you that you were being targeted months ago? A scam like this required time. The Perpetrator was out to destroy your son's reputation and so get at you. He is a clever swine, we have known that for some time. I think I'd better get myself down to Stroud without delay. I'd like to stay at your place, if that's OK with you both?'

'Of course it's OK, any time, you know that. Can you manage to be here by tomorrow?'

'I can. The sooner the better, I'll be with you by early afternoon.'

Harry was welcomed by the Beaumonts

with both affection and appreciation. He had expected to find his friends distressed, but perhaps not to the extent they were. He had thought, when talking to Jeffrey the previous day, he had given rise to confidence. But the couple was hit very hard by the nation-wide witch-hunt conducted by a branch of the media.

By way of encouragement, Harry told them the news — of which he had already made a draft for his next newsletter to the crew — of how he had successfully frustrated the Perpetrator by forestalling the planned attack on Hester. This had resulted in Harry's own agent partially tracing a phone call made by the Perpetrator on learning of the failure. The call had been made from a public box in the Taunus region of Germany. This was still something of a needle in a haystack, but at least only a bale where all but the last bale had been removed. As mentioned in the last newsletter, he had learnt from Herr Staab that his only customer in that area who ordered the 'White Card Sheets' was a bank in Frankfurt.

In Stroud, as with earlier investigations, Harry introduced himself to the local police who, on learning of his credentials, readily informed him of any progress they had made. Then he called on the Stroud Hospitals NHS

Trust before finding his way to the chief accountant.

When the accountant found that Mr White was working with the knowledge of the Stroud police he became fully co-operative, fetching all the invoices and bills concerned. Harry learnt of the bogus company which had been set up in the Isle of Man, and of the so-called P Beaumont bank account there, and how the water bill had been produced as proof of name and address.

After some thought, Harry turned to the accountant saying, 'Mr Paul Beaumont has been stitched up.'

With a wry smile, the accountant said, 'From the evidence, I think Mr Beaumont has stitched himself up.'

'Has there been any movement among your staff within the last year? Harry asked.

'No. We are a contented department, people don't leave once they have settled in.'

'How long is it since the most recent member joined your staff?'

'It must be three years now, apart from Mr Hogg, a temporary, filling-in for Mr James who has a prolonged medical problem. However, we are expecting Mr James to return very soon.

'Who is Mr Hogg and when did he start with you?'

'He is the clerk sitting at the desk by the window in the next room. When Mr James was taken ill about a year ago, he was temporarily replaced by Mr Hogg,' the accountant said.

'Has he given you cause for concern since he has been with you?'

'None at all, he gets on well with his colleagues and his work is quite satisfactory. Surely, you can't suspect him?'

'In this case I can suspect anyone, sir.'

After further talk about the staff in general, the accountant escorted his visitor to the exit. This took them past Mr Hogg's desk where the detective paused as he took his pen out of his pocket. Turning to Mr Hogg he casually asked if he might have a plain piece of paper? Mr Hogg obliged by handing him a sheet.

On his return to the house and finding his friend in the garden, Harry asked, 'Do you have keys for your son's house, Jeffrey?'

'Yes, we have a set, just as Paul has one of ours. Why? Are you wanting to go there?'

'I would like to have a look around, if you have no objections. Do you by any chance know where Paul keeps his bills?'

'I don't, but he does have a small office, I imagine they will be there.'

An hour later, Harry locked Paul's house behind him, and was soon informing Jeffrey he had taken Paul's water bill. The next day he called in to see the inspector who was investigating the NHS theft. 'I have here,' Harry told him, 'Mr Paul Beaumont's water bill, together with this sheet of paper handed to me by a Mr Hogg. I would like you to check if a fingerprint from each match up.'

'Why do you want the prints?' the inspector asked. 'We have already arrested Beaumont for the NHS crime.'

Smiling, Harry said, 'Nevertheless, it would be a favour if you could grant my request.'

Two matching prints were discovered at which point Harry informed the inspector of his visit to the accounts office of the Stroud Hospitals NHS Trust. An order was made to block Mr P Beaumont's account held in an Isle of Man bank.

Harry then made his way to the house of Mr Hogg, the address of which he had obtained from the chief accountant, accompanied by a constable and a warrant. His search of the premises revealed a sum of £27,670. The £15,000 balance had obviously been paid out to Hogg, while £2,330 pounds must have been used from the £15,000 deposit paid twelve months ago. Harry secured the money in his pockets.

The evidence Harry had collected was handed to the local police inspector, resulting in the arrest of Hogg. This was followed by his confession a few days later.

When the inspector enquired from Harry how he had discovered Hogg so quickly, the old man simply smiled, saying, 'One thing leads to another.'

After the story of Paul Beaumont's disgrace and his father's despair had faded from the papers, it was the end of the matter as far as the media were concerned, or so they thought. But the trial of the true culprit brought the whole matter to life once more.

As a result of a concerted PR programme, presented by the Stroud Hospitals NHS Trust and the town's council on behalf of Doctor Jeffrey Beaumont, much of the media renewed the story. They threw a favourable light on both the doctor and his son. One leading Sunday paper wrote an impressive potted history of Jeffrey Beaumont, starting with his hazardous days on the Lancasters in World War II.

After Harry White had sent the anonymous £15,000 to the Institute of the Blind, he had felt so happy that some good had come out of all evil — although that action had not entered into his newsletter. Indeed, he hadn't even informed Hester of the gift. Now he found he had over £27,000 which certainly should not be returned to its source. Nor was it needed for evidence, there was plenty of that regardless of the money.

The crew, all having received a copy of the same letter, were surprised at its contents. The letter, signed by Harry, explained how a large sum of money had come into his possession, the source of which they all knew. 'I would like to make a proposal,' the letter went on, 'that the money be handed anonymously to a worthy charity. The cash certainly should not be returned to source and, so far as I know, cannot be justly claimed by any authority. Gentlemen, if you agree with the suggestion, I further suggest that each of you choose a list of charities then send that list to me.

'From your lists, I will write a master list without mentioning names. The master list will then be sent to you to enable you to place a tick against one charity only. Return each master list to me and, if all agree with the scheme, I will forward the money anonymously to the charity which has the majority of ticks.'

Later, the official of the RAF Benevolent Fund was astonished, when he finally succeeded in opening a heavily sealed parcel, to see thousands of bank notes spill over his desk.

16

'You are going to Germany again! Will it never end? You are more like a roaming gypsy than an elderly retired gent.'

'Believe me, Hester, I shall be as pleased as you when I can put my feet up,' Harry said, 'but if we are ever to sleep peacefully in our beds I have to follow every lead which might take me to the Perpetrator.'

'Yes I know, but, honestly, Harry, what can you expect to gain from the knowledge that Rod Shaw received a phone call from a public box somewhere in the Taunus? It's probably a large region and you don't even know from which box the call was made.'

'That's right my dear, I don't, and while it might help if I did know, it does at least eliminate a vast area of Germany. More importantly though, we know from Herr Staab that there is only one customer in that part of the country who ordered the specific type of card which we received. That customer is the von Haydn, Merck & Co in Frankfurt. A director of the bank, Herr Schiller, has agreed to meet me in his office as a result of our correspondence.'

'Well, I hope something will come from your meeting or it would be a long journey for nothing,' Hester commented.

Everything about Herr Schiller's office was big: the wide windows with curtains almost reaching the floor; the high ceiling with its plaster carvings by tradesmen long since dead; the comfortable chairs for visitors, and the huge desk. In fact, the only thing which was not of splendid proportions was Herr Schiller himself.

The banker had little hair and heavy glasses, which seemed to make his eyes almost disappear. He was of short stature, slimly built. Tight lips gave an air of firmness, and despite his small frame, Harry quickly got the impression that Herr Schiller was not a man to trifle with. He had met such men before, hard men who knew exactly what they wanted and usually got it.

Schiller came from behind the desk to proffer Harry a bony hand which looked as if it had never lifted anything heavier than a pen. With a tight smile he said, 'So you are the Englishman who writes such persuasive letters!'

Harry, towering over the banker, replied, 'And the Englishman who thanks you for your indulgence.'

'From our correspondence, Mr White, I

believe in your working days you were a detective with the English police. May I ask that you produce some evidence to that effect?'

Harry was not surprised by the banker's request, but was happy with Schiller's caution. He produced an envelope containing a number of papers. After a few moments' study, Herr Schiller enquired, 'Do I address you as inspector, Mr White?'

Smiling, Harry answered, 'Since I am not addressing you as director, Mr White will do.'

The banker's eyes narrowed. He returned to his chair and Harry was aware that he was being closely scrutinised before the banker said, 'What is the reason for your visit to Germany beyond those stated in your letters, which did not state a great deal beyond their persuasiveness?'

'Herr Schiller, I have spent much of my life using interrogation techniques. It is not difficult therefore to recognise if they are used on myself.' The old detective knew that if he was to get anywhere with the banker he would have to bring about a change of attitude. He said, 'I would like to relate a story to you which concerned Winston Churchill and Franklin D Roosevelt — During a visit by Churchill to the White House, Roosevelt accidentally saw Churchill leaving the bathroom after taking a shower. His guest was in the nude. Roosevelt at once apologised, but Churchill, raising a hand said, 'The Prime Minister of Great Britain has nothing to hide from The President of The United States of America'.'

Herr Schiller smiled and his lips were not as tight. 'And I have nothing to hide from you, sir,' Harry said. He felt he had the measure of the banker's psychology and so decided to tell the full story of how the crew was being hounded by a madman whom he believed lived close by. Harry was sure that if Herr Schiller was made to feel involved, the man's ego would receive a boost and so encourage his help.

On the completion of the tale, the banker was at once amazed and fascinated. 'And so, Herr Schiller,' Harry continued, 'you will see how the white cards have become so important. They are the Perpetrator's weakness, his only weakness. Without them he would never have been traced, but now, and with your help, I believe he will be brought to justice.'

'If caught, where will this man be held and tried?' Herr Schiller's quick mind thought it had noticed a brief pause before Harry answered, but decided it must be his visitor's slower thinking capacity.

'When the villain is brought to book he will of course be handed to the German police, together with all the evidence. Your courts are sure to see justice is done.'

'I see. Please bear with me a moment.' The banker reached to press a button before speaking. He ordered that a Herr Block report to his office.

'Herr Block, I want you to meet Mr White from England, which is the reason I am talking to you in English. Please show the card to Herr Block, Mr White. I want to know if the bank has had a use for the card, which to me seems to be unusual?' Herr Block accepted the card and took it closer to the light. He then angled it, causing the light to strike the card from different points. The strange reflecting effect showed at once. 'Yes, Herr Schiller, we have used this card in the public relations department. The cards are delivered in large sheets, this piece has been cut from one.'

'I have noted the unusual reflection. What do we use the cards for?' Herr Schiller asked.

'We use it within the banking profession itself, when we wish to impress. It does not normally come before the public because of the high cost.'

'Excuse me.' It was Harry who spoke. 'Do you know if this type of card has ever left

393

your department other than for the reason it was intended?'

'No, even the bank does not use it often, therefore we carry only a small stock.'

'Could a member of staff have taken a card for personal use?'

'Your question has jogged my memory, Mr White. I now recall a senior partner of the bank, Herr von Haydn, who retired about a year ago. He asked for a few sheets of the special card. He said he intended spending some time painting and thought watercolours on the card could be most effective. I think he would be proved correct.'

'Herr von Haydn taken up painting? That will be a new venture for him, but I'm sure he will achieve success as he has with everything else. Herr von Haydn is a fine and able man!' Schiller exclaimed.

'Was he with the bank for long?' Harry asked.

'Almost the whole of his working life. One might say he was 'the bank'. It wasn't the significant financial house it is now when he joined it, shortly after the war. But like the rest of Germany, it was built to its present splendour and it was Herr von Haydn who provided the main thrust.'

'Did he serve in the war?' Harry enquired.

'He did not. He wasn't fit for service. I

think his eyes were below standard. I feel that at the time Herr von Haydn didn't agree with the war but I am sure he would have served the Führer well.' Harry saw Herr Block glance at the banker and Schiller coloured slightly, before saying, 'But his brother Gunther was a U-boat captain and was presented with the Iron Cross by the Führer. Furthermore, the old man's father, Baron von Haydn, was the famous fighter ace from the 1914–18 war. He was honoured by the whole of Germany. Of course the title of 'Baron' is no longer used, more's the pity.'

'Did Herr von Haydn have children?'

'No, but his brother, the Captain, had a son. From what I have heard, he was a disappointment.'

'Why a disappointment?' Harry pressed.

'I don't know much about him but I believe he spent time in a mental hospital.'

Harry knew everything was leading to the Perpetrator and asked, 'May I have Herr von Haydn's address?' But Herr Schiller said it wasn't known, and again Harry saw exchanged looks between the two men. 'But the bank must have his address,' Harry insisted.

'If it has, the permission must come from a full board meeting. Three members of which are on the bank's business in America and will not be in Germany for the next ten days.'

Harry knew Schiller was lying and he saw too the surprised expression that came momentarily from Herr Block. Herr Schiller dismissed Herr Block and then, proffering his hand to Harry, brought the interview to an abrupt end, saying, 'I wish you well with your mission Mr White,' while showing him the door.

On reaching the entrance hall Harry went to the desk behind which sat a commissioner and asked if he understood English.

'A little,' the commissioner replied.

'Will you please phone through to the Public Relations Department to inform Herr Block that Mr White would like to talk with him. He knows who I am!'

'You say he knows you?' The commissioner said, curiously.

'Yes, it's all right. He will see me.'

After a short conversation in his mother tongue, the commissioner handed the phone to Harry. 'Herr Block,' he said.

'Ah, Herr Block, will you be so kind as to give me a few minutes of your time? I will come to your office, if I may.'

'Certainly, Mr White. The commissioner will direct you.'

'It is good of you to see me, Herr Block. I am hoping you will help me to obtain Herr von Haydn's address. We both know it is known to the bank. In any case he will probably have an account with you.'

'Of course we have the address. I apologise for Herr Schiller, he is a difficult man, I'm afraid. Please be seated. Since you have a bona fide reason for asking I am sure they will give it to me. However, you will understand, that I first have to talk to Herr von Haydn before handing you the information. I trust I'll find him at home.'

A few miles after passing through Konigstein, where on the outskirts of the town Harry noticed a number of women playing tennis at their local club, he parked the hired car in the grounds of *Haus Falkenstein*, an old and impressive property with well-tended gardens. The whoosh of the car's automatic lock was followed by the sound of footsteps on a gravel path and, turning, Harry saw an elderly gentlemen walking towards him from the garage. The open doors showed that three or more cars could be given shelter there.

'Good afternoon. You will be Mr White, I think!' The man spoke in perfect English. 'I have been expecting your arrival after a call from the bank. I am Kurt von Haydn. How do you do?' The man extended a hand in greeting.

Normally, on meeting someone for the first

time, Harry would make an immediate but superficial assessment of a person. It would take some time before he would place them in an appropriate slot. However, with Kurt von Haydn he felt at once an empathy, even warmth towards him. Harry was surprised by his own feelings, as he was initially cautious. But the old detective was wise enough to be extra careful, as his liking for the man could cloud his judgement. It would not have surprised Harry had he been told that the feeling was mutual.

Settled in the house, Harry was offered a drink by his host — for that was how he already saw the German — but he said it was too early in the day for him; however he would appreciate a coffee.

A coffee quickly appeared and Herr von Haydn said, 'Now Mr White, tell me why have you come all the way from England to visit me?'

He was surprised to hear himself say, 'Harry, please call me Harry.'

''Harry', it will be, and for me, Kurt, if you please.' The two men smiled.

Harry suddenly felt uncomfortable as he remembered the true reason for his visit, but he also remembered the awful stress his crew and their loved ones had been through. 'It is going to be difficult to explain my reasons,

Kurt. But it must be done. The trouble is, I will probably have to implicate your family in a very unpleasant business which I fear will alienate you.'

'You sound serious, please explain.'

'We are about the same age, we both remember the war. At that time I was in the Royal Air Force, a wireless operator on Lancaster bombers. We know what Bomber Command did to Germany, though in all honesty, I cannot feel guilty for something we felt had to be done.'

Kurt said, 'I also know what the Luftwaffe did to Warsaw, some Balkan cities and to the Dutch city of Rotterdam. None of those countries had declared war on my country. Nor had Russia declared war but none the less, Germany razed much of it to the ground. But why do we bring up such unhappy times? I hoped all that was behind us!'

'I shall explain. You might know the Lancaster was manned by a seven-man crew. My colleagues and I were fortunate in surviving the ordeal, and our luck has continued to this day in that we all are still fit and well. Each year the crew holds a reunion over a weekend, but we rarely talk of the war. As you might imagine, the wartime experience was responsible for creating a deep friendship amongst the crew which still lasts to this day.

'At our last reunion, Peter Newell, the pilot, discovered a card lying on his bed with the message 'SEVEN a number not to be forgotten'. At first we were puzzled, but the others quickly decided it must have been placed there by one of the hotel staff, playing the fool. We were known at the hotel. You see we had held the reunions there for years.

'However, Kurt, I could not readily dismiss the incident. Perhaps because I had been a policeman in the CID. Also, I could not imagine a young prankster taking such trouble with the high quality printing, and the card itself seemed rather special.'

Harry then produced the original card and handed it to Kurt.

Kurt exchanged his spectacles for closer study before moving to the light where he angled the card. Looking at Harry, he said, 'I am surprised at what you have given me! I know this material which to the best of my knowledge is produced by a single manufacturer. I wouldn't have thought it was available in Britain. I have a few sheets myself which I got from the bank. I like to use the cards when painting with watercolours, it gives a wonderful effect — Makes me seem a better painter than I really am,' Kurt added, grinning like a schoolboy.

'Do you have many of the cards?' Harry asked.

'About a dozen sheets, I imagine. They are quite large.'

'This small card, together with others I have, was manually cut from a sheet. Have any of your sheets been cut?'

'No, I haven't noticed damage to any.'

'Can you remember how many of the sheets you brought from the bank?'

'Yes, I brought fifteen home.'

'Do you know how many have been used, Kurt?'

'Three to date. The paintings are still in my studio.'

'Where you also keep the unused sheets, I expect. Can we check the stock, please?'

In the studio, Kurt took Harry by the arm, saying, 'There are eleven sheets, not twelve. Let us return to the living room where you can tell me more of this strange business.'

From their seats they saw a man reclining in a garden chair, reading at the far side of a lawn, which prompted Harry to comment on the perfect day.

'That is my nephew Hans out there, he spends a lot of time in the garden,' Kurt said.

Harry handed a slip of paper to Kurt, saying, 'Are you able to tell if this could have been cut from writing paper which you may have?'

'Yes, it could be, but that is not uncommon as it is used for personal correspondence by the bank. I do have some in my study, here at Falkenstein. Where did you get it?'

'It was cut from the foot of a letter in England.'

'I see.' Kurt realised his visitor was volunteering limited information. Then Hans stepped into the room from the garden and said, 'I saw the car parked, uncle, I wondered who had called.'

Harry rose to his feet and Kurt told him, 'This is my nephew. Hans, this is Mr White, from England.'

Hans at once appeared bewildered and almost stumbled as he uttered 'Harry White'.

Harry saw Kurt's eyes widen as he exclaimed, 'You know Mr White's first name!'

'No, no, I must have heard you talking, uncle. I don't know this gentleman. But I think grandfather met his father.' It was now Kurt who looked bewildered as he stared hard at Harry, saying, 'I don't know what the boy is talking about, but he worshipped his grandfather, von Haydn. He was of course . . . ' he stopped and continued staring at his guest, then said, 'Harry White! — Your name is Harry White and you were in the

RAF. Was your father a flyer in RFC during the first war? Was he also named Harry? Did he fly SE5s and hold the rank of captain? Was he taken prisoner of war?'

'The answer is yes to all your questions. My father went down, hit by a machine gun nest while dog-fighting behind your lines.'

'This is astonishing. Captain White, your father was in combat with my father. It was a struggle about which von Haydn, the hero of Germany, never tired of telling, though about the rest he had little to say. I think it was not only because it was the most difficult and skilled fight he had experienced, but also because they both survived.'

'How did von Haydn know it was my father?' Harry asked.

'Because the combat made such an impression, he felt he must meet the pilot. My father knew exactly where his adversary had landed and went at once to the army unit which had taken him. However, they had already handed the airman over to other authorities. But of course, father was able to learn from the unit the name of the airman who had been their prisoner.

Harry gripped Kurt by the hand and said, 'My friend, if one of those brave men had won that fight, then one of us would not have been here.'

Then Hans, whom Harry thought was turning the colour of stone, shouted, 'If my grandfather had killed the Englishman, my mother would still be with me.'

Kurt, feeling awkward, said, 'Don't be foolish, boy, von Haydn was your mother's father-in-law, not a blood relation.' Turning to Harry he said, 'Please forgive the outburst, the boy was very mother-orientated, you understand. Though Anna died some years ago, Hans still badly misses her.'

'You don't understand. If my grandfather had killed that Englishman, this man could not have killed my mother.' Hans seemed to stare right through Harry.

Any doubt which may have remained in the old detective's mind had been swept away. Here, before him, stood the Perpetrator. With some embarrassment Harry faced his host saying, 'I know this must distress you, Kurt, as indeed it does me. Especially as I am so aware of your kind attitude. But, I need to see your nephew's room and I would like you to remain with me.'

Kurt hesitated, glancing at Hans. 'You think this is necessary?' he asked Harry.

'I'm afraid so. I really do apologise for the intrusion. Please accompany us, Hans.'

When in his room, Harry asked Hans if he would bring what remained of the card sheet he had removed from his uncle's studio.

'A card? I do not have a card.' Hans said.

'Hans, you mustn't lie. I can see it from here, on the top of your wardrobe.' Kurt reached up to retrieve it.

One side of the sheet was jagged, cut in steps. Harry asked Kurt to lay it flat.

The detective took several white cards from his pocket and placed them on the sheet like an easy jigsaw puzzle. They fitted perfectly.

Incredulously, Kurt asked, 'From where did you get those pieces?'

'It hurts me to tell you that they came from your nephew's would-be victims.'

'In Britain, you mean? Hans has never been to your island.'

'But you have been to Belgium, haven't you, Hans? You used a post office box there when corresponding with RAF records in London.'

Kurt was bewildered again, but much more than earlier. He said, 'I am lost. I don't understand this at all.'

'Again, I am so sorry, Kurt. You will understand, but for the moment it might be best if you just listen. However, the strip of paper which I showed you earlier, came from the foot of a sheet of your personal writing paper. That sheet, which also had its header removed, is lying in a file at RAF records,

London. It had been posted from and the reply was sent to Belgium. The letter enquired about a bombing raid which took place on Schweinfurt on a night in October in 1944. The pretext of the letter was to help the enquirer write the history of a German night fighter unit, based in this region at the time, and which was in action that night against the bombers. One action took place in this area against a bomber which was manned by my crew.'

Kurt told Harry he remembered the night of the raid on Schweinfurt very well, because the local tennis club's pavilion was destroyed that night.

'It was your bomb that destroyed it,' Hans said, bitterly. 'The same bomb which killed Hildegard, my mother's dear friend, the friend she could not live without.'

'You are mistaken Hans, all our bombs were dropped on the target at Schweinfurt. The Lancaster had been unloaded by the time of the fighter attack'

Kurt said, 'It was not a bomb which destroyed the pavilion, Hans. It was a night fighter which crashed onto it after being shot down.'

Harry said, 'Records show we were the only aircraft attacked in this area. Our mid-upper gunner shot the fighter down.'

'Herr Arthur Brown of Worcester,' said Hans to the astonishment of his uncle, who commented, 'I have lived with you all these years, Hans, yet I do not know you! How is it possible that you know the names of the men who manned that bomber?'

'Records gave Hans the identification of each aircraft that came under fighter attack that night and where the attacks took place. Or rather, of those which survived the attacks. He could then get the names together with their present addresses from the squadron's association,' Harry explained.

'But why bother communicating from Belgium?'

Harry said, 'Hans was trying to safeguard his identity. I'm sure he didn't expect questions to be asked at the records office, but just in case, he threw in a red herring to create confusion. Hans wasn't known to anyone in Britain, he was not even known to the crook that carried out his instructions. But a lot of moncy was involved. IIow is it your nephew has access to such large amounts?'

'It didn't come from his father, Gunther.'

'His father is dead? On my visit to the bank I was informed your brother survived the war. A U-boat captain, I believe. But then of course, he must have survived. Since it was after the hostilities when he married.'

'Yes, Gunther came successfully through the war but was later killed in a climbing accident. It was a terrible tragedy, my brother was a fine man. Certainly he had shared much of father's estate, but he left the whole of that to an International Seamen's Benevolent Fund. He never forgot the suffering which took place at sea during the war. He left nothing to his son, knowing he had been well provided for from his grandfather's estate. He could not have known however, that Hans was to come into money in his own right, far exceeding the whole of von Haydn's assets.

'Hans had no surviving grandparents from his mother's side of the family. Anna, his mother, had just one brother who, before dying of cancer, had struck gold in Alaska. He became immensely rich, and he left the whole of his wealth to Anna.

'Anna, who was never able to recover from the loss of her friend Hildegard, died of a broken heart, even though she married my brother. Regardless of her grief for Hildegard, Anna idolised her son to such an extent that she couldn't appreciate Hans had a problem. The whole of her fortune and the mine itself were willed to Hans, though of course it is taken care of by executives. My nephew is an extremely wealthy man, Harry. There is nothing to prevent his access to any amount of money.'

Harry said, 'There is much sadness in what you have told me, though it does explain how cost was no obstacle for Hans to carry out his plans.' Then the detective turned to Hans saying, 'You have come to the end of the road now, you are discovered. You have caused much misery, as was your intention, but you did not mean it to be so short-lived. Of course, a number of lives have been taken due to your activities, but with one exception they were the wrong people. You have failed in your evil task.'

'Liar, I did not fail! I had a setback on two of you murderers, but I am taking care of that. They won't escape again,' the madman screamed.

Kurt, leaning against a table for support, seemed to have put on years. Staring intently at his nephew he said, 'How could you do such a thing? Your grandfather would have disowned you.'

'No he wouldn't, because I haven't failed,' Hans screamed.

'You fool. Von Haydn would disown you because of your wicked intentions. Not because of failure. You have disgraced his family.' Kurt showed a contempt not normally to be found in his character.

In a calm voice, Harry asked, 'How did you murder Norman?'

'Bob Greeves' beloved grandson. You can't say that your rear gunner hasn't suffered mental anguish.' Then, to his uncle, he said with triumph: 'See, I didn't fail.'

'How did you bring about his death?' Harry pressed.

'It was the simplest to plan but it would be the hardest to detect. I gave a German crook instructions with what was to him, a lot of money. Though like everyone else, he didn't know its source. I learnt from my people in Britain about the holiday, where the grandson was going and when. I knew a great deal about all you murdering swine.

'My agent took up a position amongst a crop of rocks which were strewn to one side and well down the slope. He laid almost buried in the snow, looking through binoculars. It was easy for him to recognise Norman in his yellow woolly hat. In any case, the agent had identified him the previous night in the hotel. When he was sure the next skier racing down the hill was his target, he sat up, waving his arms as though in distress. The skier came to his aid and my agent cried out, 'It's my leg, I've broken it. The pain is killing me. Please try to straighten it.' When the young man bent forward, my man killed him. Striking him hard on the head with a piece of rock.

'Earlier, my agent had found a nearby rock, the edge of which was similar to the piece he used as a weapon, so any wound or indentation made on the head would seem to have come from that. Especially since the agent smeared the rock with Norman's blood. He did this immediately after the kill and before the arrival of the next skier and then rushed away down the rest of the slope carrying the bloodstained rock in his bag.

'He knew,' Hans continued, 'the skis of the curious holiday makers would have left their marks in the snow long before investigators arrived. The impressions left by his own skis would be well criss-crossed by others, even those which led the short way to the slope, making his escape. Back at the hotel the agent washed the rock he had used as a weapon, before discarding it.'

'How did you learn about your contact in London?'

'You mean Rob Shaw?'

'Of course! I know all your decisions were managed by that man. How did you know of him?'

Harry saw an astute smile cross Hans' face, when he sneered, 'From your own English newspapers.' And the old detective knew he would learn everything as the Perpetrator's ego took control.

'I read about the bent prison officer. They are known as 'screws' are they not? An officer, who himself served a prison sentence for taking bribes to smuggle drugs to prisoners. It was easy to have him tracked down and he willingly accepted a few thousand pounds to tell who the prisoners considered to be the smartest crook in the London underworld.

'I was very careful in the way I made contact with Shaw. At first, for some reason, he said he thought I was crazy.' Harry saw the pained look on Kurt's face. 'But when I told him the amount of money that would come his way, he seemed to show interest, though he wanted me to prove my good will by providing a suitable deposit. After he had accepted my first half million, I got first-class co-operation. Though he never knew with whom he was dealing.

'I told him of my plans for each of you and Rob saw to it that they were executed. I made one exception, that was for Louise Newell. This was because Rob told me that Les Willson, the man he had chosen for her execution, had a fertile imagination and had successfully committed big crimes in inge-nious ways. I ordered Rob to let him have a free hand as I would be most interested to see what he came up with. The man failed and so his throat was cut, as per instructions.'

Kurt drew in a short gasp.

'Of course,' continued the Perpetrator, 'Louise and yourself will be dealt with again, but the difference where Louise is concerned, is that it will be my plan this time.'

'Hans, don't you understand? You have had six failures from seven attempts.'

'No. No. I failed only twice and that is going to be corrected,' he screamed.

'Listen to me — Reid is serving life for the murder of Jim Lewis. Your intended victim Tom Williams is a free man, living a happy life.' Hans' body stiffened, knowing he was hearing the truth. How else could this English detective know about Reid?

'Betty Daly still enjoys her food, sharing it with her happy husband, James. Of course Mark Noble is imprisoned, having lost all. I am sure you will know that Doctor Beaumont and his son have had their reputations fully restored. And of course there was the Arthur Brown fiasco — well you have had Dick Leach's throat cut, so you know all about that.

'You have had only one success — Bob Greeves' grandson. One success out of seven. I say you are a failure, Hans von Haydn, the disgraced grandson of the great von Haydn whom Germany rightly honoured.'

Harry stood in stupefied surprise as he witnessed Hans stiffen like a board, his eyes unreal. But suddenly, all stiffness left the body as it collapsed onto the carpet to take up the foetal position, knees bent, fingers in the mouth. Kurt caught the last word to be uttered by his nephew — 'Mother'. The figure was as stone.

★　★　★

The prosecution council made good use of the evidence which they received from the Metropolitan Police and other forces around the country — most of whom had received their evidence via Inspector Harry White, retired.

On the last day of the trial, when the jury gave its verdict, Dave Parker occupied the same seat he had occupied throughout the proceedings. On the occasions that the accused had glanced his way, Dave revealed distress and concern. Now came the word 'guilty' on all counts — even for the murder of his mentor, whose bones were removed from the weights at the bottom of the Thames. The bones were not identified, but the circumstantial evidence was overwhelming.

The judge spoke with disdain of the prisoner's involvement with throat-cutting, bribery, forgery, prostitution and terror. The total sentence would exceed his remaining life span. The judge's final words were, 'Take him down!'

As Rob Shaw, who delighted in the name of 'Mr Big', was led away, he threw a final stare at his lifelong friend. He saw the pity written on his face but, as Dave turned away to leave the court, Mr Big was not able to witness the change to another expression — of utter contempt.

Epilogue

The old man, proprietor of the Saracen's Head for many years before he handed it over to his grandson, had passed away. The grandson had never been happy running the pub but had not had the heart to do anything about it while the old man was alive. His grandfather, many years ago, had taken over from his father and the Saracen's Head had remained his home to the end.

With his grandfather dead, the grandson was no longer troubled by conscience so he sold the hotel which provided him with the money to achieve his ambition of starting a new life in New Zealand.

The new proprietor said to his barman, 'Those old fellows over there are such a happy lot, I wonder who they are?'

The new barman replied, 'I don't know, but I think all seven are booked in for the weekend.'

TWO HOURS TO DARKNESS

Antony Trew

For most of her crew the Retaliate's Baltic cruise is a routine one, and her sixteen nuclear missiles no more than a silent threat to the Russians. But the submarine's captain, Commander Shadde, is obsessed with the communist menace and haunted by the memory of his one act of cowardice. As the submarine approaches the end of her voyage, a letter from his wife threatening divorce pushes Shadde to the brink of madness — in a vessel where nuclear war is just a touch of the button away . . .

OUT OF ORDER

Charles Benoit

Jason Talley lives in Corning, New York. His friends are Sriram Sundaram and his wife, Vidya. But after Sriram confides he's planning to return to India, the next evening the couple are dead — the cops call it murder-suicide. Jason decides to fulfil Sriram's quest and books himself a trip to India. Travelling, he meets Rachel, and together, they embark on a journey into danger . . . Sriram was a computer genius who had sold out his colleagues, and Jason has sent details of his trip to Sriram's e-mail list, hoping to meet up with Sriram's past. But when he does . . .

DARTMOUTH CONSPIRACY

James Stevenson

September 1942: Luftwaffe pilot Karl Deichman must bomb the Royal Naval College in Dartmouth, despite knowing his cousin and childhood friend is resident there. Yet his orders give him no choice — the attack must proceed . . . After the war, Karl returns to England, haunted by the thought: *Did I kill Andrew?* His quest leads him to a former secret agent, a wartime spy, and an ex-RAF Spitfire pilot; but as he uncovers the secret of the Dartmouth Conspiracy, he is drawn into a lethal trap. And it will be more than sixty years before the final jigsaw-piece falls into place . . .